# A HAPPY NEW WAR

## THE UNSTOPPABLE WARPATH OF THE UNKILLABLE JACK CHURCHILL

*Volume IV of the fictional biography*

# BENJAMIN BLACKIE

Page/Turner

***A Happy New War:***
The Unstoppable Warpath of the Unkillable Jack Churchill

Copyright © Benjamin Blackie 2024
Cover art & image designs © Benjamin Blackie 2024
- Paperback Edition -

Typeset: 20, 12, 11.5 pt Baskerville Old Face
11.5 pt Rainydays by *bruag*
11.5 pt Arial Narrow
10 pt Times New Roman


FIC014050

1. Historical - Fiction. 2. World War, 1939-1945 - Fiction.

I. Title.

A823.3

ISBN: 978-0-6486321-9-1

Published by Kindle Direct Publishing
2024

*A word from the Author.*

*The idea of this war story was originally planned to be a nonfictional, unauthorized memoir - historically referenced, explicated accurate true tale that Jack Churchill is perhaps best deserving. It was intended to be served in its fullest and most autobiographical form. In many ways, it is still very much incorporated into the final product, albeit with a dash more flamboyancy for flavouring.*

*I delved deep into the historic abyss of significant and trivial detail alike, researching anything and everything remotely related to Jack Churchill primarily during the Second World War. During this process, I had a spellbinding epiphany that would drastically divert the direction of my manuscript. I flexed my artistic licence and remodelled the adjective, fact-based documentation, striving to still deliver the details amongst the type of entertainment that would now be categorized as fictional action/adventure. What better way is there nowadays for being informative than through the artform of storytelling? The revelation came whilst exhuming those buried accounts, hearing those firsthand versions and unsung war stories documented in soldier diaries, video documentaries, and recorded cassettes made by the families in their elder's twilight years. I peeled back layers of history, uncovering for me what I believed to be the quintessence of the man himself, especially the eccentric archetype. He was built different … why not tell his tale differently? It became evident that Mad Jack Churchill was anything but as colourless as the black and whites depicted him to be in old photographs, not that that was ever thought to be the case. Consequently so, I supposed him to be deserving of something more stimulating and amusing than another run-of-the-mill nonfiction publication. He was more than just history, he was legend. After all, what is believable about a commando charging onto a beach during the Second World War with a sword and longbow? Any form of chronicle would be deemed doubtful by any audience and branded* fabricated and untrue … so I took it that step further from the beginning and just ran with it.

Thus, my intention became to make this book (and any subsequent books) just as action-packed, saucy, and humorous as they were hard-hitting, historically accurate, and to pay heartfelt respects to what transpired all those years ago. I aspired to tick all the boxes, pull out all the stops, and leave no stone unturned whilst retelling the true story.

As a result, born out of a playful and fictitious gambit, the final draft of the novel based on this man's extraordinary life shaped up as more of an action-packed and extravagant fictional biography rather than a stale history lesson. An entertaining bedtime story instead of a monotonous research article. And why not have fun with it? If you are a staid history buff, allow for the mere prologue of this novel to act as your assessment of what is to come and how to receive it. If your nose turns at this notice, don't bother turning any more pages … because yes, I allowed myself to have a blast telling this story, as I believe Mad Jack himself would. Not as a form of gloat, but for the entertaining factor that one could not doubt coursed through his veins along with pure heroism.

Although a work of fiction, <u>The Unstoppable Warpath of the Unkillable Jack Churchill</u> is built on a solid foundation of true historical fact, down to names, quotes, dates, and locations. This has been done intentionally to recreate as accurate a retelling as possible and to help respectfully keep the memories alive of those long since gone from this world. A vast amount of research went into the development of the setting for the saga. Irrespective to the improvisation in this fictitious retelling, pages drenched with additional palates of detail constructed by the author's overactive imagination, Churchill's story was born from a thorough understanding of the legend through the method of true accounts dated and written by those closest to him at the time.

*So here it is - a glass raised to the man.*

*This literature, however fictitious as it may harmlessly digress, is a celebration of a gentleman born from the stuff legends are made of.*

*A fête of his fate, a bit of fun, action, romance, and war - in its dubitable inexplicitness - lays a sincerity paralleled with the eccentric essence of Mad Jack Churchill. I hope this is conveyed entertainingly and with all due respect.*

*<u>You have now been cautioned of the fictitious recounting that threatens to entertain as well as enlighten. Enjoy.</u>*

**O.K., go.**

# PROLOGUE
## *Merry Christmas, and ...*

The sterling stare of *Jack Churchill* twinkled open.

Head resting on a goose-down pillow in the bleak darkness of a quiet bedroom, he had become prematurely awoken from a barely tranquil slumber in the middle of the night.

Unlike the haunts of most military men, it hadn't been from the horrific stress and recurring memories of warfare that had caused him to stir, rather a certain craving of purpose; a call to arms. It dwelled within the forefront of his mind like an itch needing to be scratched, and he couldn't rest soundly until a task were completed.

*Finally, he was returning to war ...*

Lying in bed, a genuine grin formed beneath his pencil moustache.

One of sincere happiness.

Unable to return to sleep, Churchill whisked the blankets off and slinked out of bed, bracing the cold. He did this with a gracious deadening, mindful not to disturb his love as she slumbered deeply in the double bed beside him.

Over his shoulder as he sat lethargically on the edge of the bed, Jack cast *Rosamund Churchill* a glance. Her dark hair tousled, she rested peacefully, tucked beneath the covers and facing away, completely unaware of her husband's rousing.

After the considerate pause, Jack hoisted himself into the night air.

Quietly, Churchill donned his hanging robe and headed downstairs in their recently purchased two-bedroom cottage in *Dumbarton, Scotland*. The cottage wasn't much, but was affordable, and located just around the corner from Dumbarton Hospital, where Rosamund worked as a nurse. The two had aspirations to eventually move into a larger residence nearer Jack's hometown of *Deddington*—conditional on Jack's service status and, of course, the forecast of the current world war.

Down the set of creaky stairs, Churchill obtained a sense of time. Judging by the light bleeding through the edges of the drawn curtains of the dining room and the faint chirping of birdsong, it was dawn.

With every sweep of the swinging pendulum within the grandfather clock, the clicking cogs would echo within the quiet surroundings of the landing. The ticking was all that could be heard within the silent environment.

Once down, he rounded the polished timber balustrade of the staircase. Upon doing so, he bypassed a bookshelf loaded with vertical spines of displayed literature of various fiction and nonfiction authors. Many of the consistent designs that always caught his eye were that of Rosamund's prized *Land of Oz* collection, which included the first edition of *The Emerald City of Oz;* a title which Jack had painstakingly obtained as a gift for his then-girlfriend a year ago.

It felt like yesterday.

*How time flies.*

In passing, he cast the book spine a sentimental gleam.

In the open, rug-laid living room and connected kitchenette, Churchill surveyed the tranquil space. He was surprised to see that the fireplace still glowed with embers. The night prior had been a romantic one for him and the missus—a farewell, of sorts. An *adieu.* Following a magnificent roast, they had retired upstairs to spend time, resulting in neither one of them venturing back down to properly stoke or maintain the fire and, as a result, it had burned out messily onto the hearth tiles.

He stepped over, tightening the cloth knot on his warm garment before getting down low and using a fire-poker to push some of the charcoal off the sandstone mantel, tidying the masonry fireplace. Upon rising to his feet, Jack's eyeline inadvertently sought out the displayed Christmas cards issued to them via the post by the family. T'was the season. His youngest brother and his wife, *Buster* and *Olive Churchill,* had their five-year-old son *Marky* write the message this year. Their card stood beside another from middle brother *Thomas Churchill* and his wife *Gwendoline,* and their daughter *Rosemary.*

This could have been the first year Jack Churchill let himself fully engage the Christmas spirit; embracing family and tradition, seen not through the eyes belonging to a bachelor or a soldier of war ... but as a patriarch of a household; a husband and a family man, full of wholesome entwine.

But alas, it would not last. Not this year.

Both unfortunately—and fortunately, for Jack—war was calling.

Churchill turned to face the kitchen. A peculiar sound had just caught his attention, and he focused through the darkness to the plates stacked on the benchtop. Their new kitten, a male moggy by the name of *Toto,* had long since found the scraps from their supper and was helping himself.

"*Toto!*" Churchill growled in a disciplinary tone. The feline was young and still learning not to jump on benchtops, however Jack understood why the kitten gave into temptation. Despite the obvious intentions of an alley cat, that special budget roast that Ros had cooked last night was delicious.

And besides, even though Jack wasn't exclusively a cat person, lil' Toto was simply too adorable to be mad at.

"*Geddown!*" he hissed after he saw the beast recognize his tone and still remain disobedient whilst his tiny pink tongue more quickly polished the plate. He was fast to dismount once he distinguished his owner's stride forth, and was even quicker to disperse to the shadows.

Every moment since finishing that shared dinner, his pending departure had weighed heavily on Churchill's mind. He wasn't anxious about his next mission to the north—of that, he was eager. In fact, the thought of the danger energized and excited him. His apprehensive unrest could be chalked up to his subconscious constantly reminding him that this was the first time he would be embarking on a crusade and leaving something behind; love. His wife, his family. There was a weight on his shoulders with this ship-out, and it was a bloody nuisance of a thing to be carrying along with his customary longbow, his arrows, his bagpipes, and sword.

It may have been the right time of year for mistletoe and jolly big fat men, but a very out of place experience to be felt by a man as complex as Mad Jack Churchill. Could it have been that the years of haunting visits by his imaginary Scottish friend offering posthumous life advice and warfare ideologies had finally rubbed off on his psyche ...?

Compromised his conscious mind ...?

Worn him down ...?

It had been a while since the undead ghoulish geezer had paid him a visit—*he had probably just jinxed it.*

An off-putting sound at Churchill's six caused the fearless British Commando to almost ruin his pyjamas as the modest wooden Christmas tree in the crook of the lounge room violently rattled, dropping decorations as though it contained a *Looney Tunes* cartoon character.

Caught in the reverie, the unguarded Churchill gasped and spun.

His reflexes were on-point, however the sound he made was questionable and could almost certainly be perceived as unbecoming of a green beret.

It *was* December. Christmas was a couple of weeks away, perhaps Father Christmas had decided to visit Dumbarton early this year?

That, or his prior mental cursing of *Lieutenant-Colonel Sloan MacLeòid* had summoned him forth from the shadows, and he was about to gain a visit from *the Angry Scotsman* in true foreboding fashion.

The ornamental Christmas tree that Rosamund had delightfully decorated shook some more before toppling over completely in front of Churchill's socks on the rug, crashing down with a dozen tinkles of garlands and hanging tinsel wrapped between dismal wooden limbs.

"Bloody hell," Churchill muttered, jumping frantically again as the same small cat, Toto, came tearing-ass out from within the toppled tree. The kitten's little claws gained ample traction in the dense wove of the Persian rug before he took off up the stairs, letting loose a wild yet playful meow as he ran.

The pet was undoubtedly glad his human was awake during his witching hour, and it was now time to play.

"Lunatic!" Churchill uttered after the kitten whilst lurching forwards to collect the fallen-over Christmas tree, standing it back up with a shake and a jingle.

After he did so, Churchill froze stiff.

The sudden instinctual suspicion of a figure standing directly behind him, breathing over him, caught his cognizance and, just like many times before in his life, he prepared to welcome his unexpected guest from the underworld ...

"Hullo, sir," Jack confidently remarked a moment before turning around, fully expecting to see the visiting ghost of Sloan MacLeòid standing behind him. Frankly, he was surprised MacLeòid hadn't performed his usual trickery, appearing behind him in a bathroom reflection during a washdown or whispering over his shoulder whilst he was taking a piss.

Churchill added as he turned away from the tree, wearing a coy and unsurprised regard upon his mug. "Long time no ..."

... his expression fell flat.

*There was nobody there.*

He searched left to right in the cobalt hue of the early morning, entirely expectant of his visitor's lurking presence, trying to pull a quick one on him.

Churchill stood, dumbfounded. "... see."

It was like something had gone wrong here.

*Where could he be hiding?*

Curiously, the only thing wrong was his expectation.

After an extended moment, Churchill caught his face in his hands. Perhaps he was more tired than he had anticipated prior to getting out of bed, causing lapses in his picture-perfect prediction and aerating his intuition.

While his raised heartrate subsided from the scare that Toto had given him, Churchill rubbed his sleepy eyes in the lonely quiet of the cold morning air in the downstairs space ... and that was when he heard it:

... a strange shuffle.

His attention slowly blinked over to the fireplace at his flank, searching the source of the falling grains of dirt and ash from within the chimney stack. In the silence and with a composed brow, he observed the disturbed debris as it rained down within the chute. He wasn't largely worried at first. After all, it was not entirely abnormal that a wind current or perhaps even the weight of thawing snow had caused a minute avalanche within the walls of the chimney. However, with each fleeting moment, the rummaging above grew exponentially more cumbersome.

Churchill's nonplussed ogling focused into a trained stare of concern as the overhead shuffling grew, sending more soot and chunks of baked charcoal dropping below.

*Something was in his chimney.*

Almost preordaining any reaction the soldier could have issued given this advance, ruling out the obvious that it could have been a bird or a rodent, the black leather boot of someone's foot suddenly appeared amidst the cloud of floating ash.

The sight caused Churchill to startle; caused a man monikered *Mad* Jack to question his sanity. Querying his consciousness, he probed his brain, making sure this was not a dream state.

Another boot descended, stabilizing whoever was within the crawlspace, and it was then Churchill noticed the white fluffy hemming of the intruder's *Coca-Cola* red pants.

Churchill reared up another step as the figure quickly hooked beneath the mouth of the fireplace, fully presenting the obese figure of none other than *Saint Nicolas* himself.

*Fucking Santa Claus ...*

His back was turned at first as he stepped out from the fireplace entrance, slinging over his shoulder a hefty sack bearing the outlines of various shaped packages: Christmas presents.

Oddly, it wasn't so much the actual existence of the childhood mythos Father Christmas that weirded Jack Churchill out the most, nor even the logistics of how the jolly fat fellow fit down his smokestack—the passage would have been twelve inches at most. Rather, it had been that that he was visiting Dumbarton two weeks early.

*Was the magic true?*

Churchill's stare intensified as the figure manifested before him, facing the fireplace from where he had just originated.

"*Ho ho ho ...*" the *Kris Kringle* catchphrase rumbled as he eventually turned to face his audience of one, presenting his white fluffy beard and slouching red cap.

He didn't fully catch it at first, however it seemed that Santa must have hailed from the United Kingdom considering his *Glasgow* patter—the abrasive dialect of a *Glaswegian,* and an accent all too familiar.

Finally, Santa unveiled his face.

*It was Sloan MacLeòid.*

"Sir?" Churchill gasped, realizing the depth of this deception. He'd gone all out for this one. For the very first time Jack was witnessing his invisible friend wearing something other than his *Queen's Own Cameron Highlander* formal service dress and kilt. His expectations had been well and truly subverted given his timing and his entrance.

"*Yoo expectin' someone else, laddie?*" spoke MacLeòid, heaving the Santa sack onto the rug like he was dropping anchor.

"I was expecting *Saint Nicolas,* not *Saint Ridiculous.*"

With an earnest grin ballooning between each cheek, MacLeòid humoured Churchill's early morning jest. He was quite the *Johnny on the spot* with the one-liner considering the hour.

"*Well, hardy ha-ha. Yoo be gettin' nuttin' bar a lump'o coal in yoor sack dis yeer.*"

"I'd expect nothing less. The ladies do say that I am a naughty boy," Churchill retorted just as wittingly.

"*Wawl, thay used to et least, eh? Befoor yoo wen'en tied tha knot.*"

"Touché ..." deciding to take the moment of digression to realign the course of their conversation. "I haven't seen you for quite some time, sir. You here to sing me *Jingle Balls?*"

"*Aye. I've nawt seen ye at war fur quite sum tyme, Jackie.*"

"I was implying more to the outfit. New gig in the afterlife?" Jack remarked in reference to his costume. "*Satan Claus* got you delivering goodies for the kiddies?"

"*Wha? Yoo mean ta sey er man can't jus' vessut 'es mate befoor he schips owt ta fecht er war?*"

Churchill pursed his lips, resigned to the visit.

"Been a while, old boy."

"*Aye, been er while since yoo ponied up an' set owt to slog a Hun en tha noggin, too, my lad. It be only tradition that I send ye owf wit a earful of insight an' various platitudes, would et not?*"

"Touché, once again, sir."

Taking a step with his war-minded wisdom and judiciousness, and a further offering of obligatory clichés, MacLeòid strode forth to address Mad Jack straightforwardly.

"*Nay, Jackie, I knoe yoo'll do me proud en tha fecht. Thus tyme, I've come merely to wish yoo a Merry Christmas ...*"

In the verbal hiatus, Churchill's gaze floated through the air, resting upon the spirit Scotsman's sermon as his enlightening words illuminated the darkness before a drawing dawn.

There was always a second part to this festive stock phrase, and Jack expected the denouement like the flow of lyrics to a song, only this time, the words were ... *wrong?*

"*... und a Happy New War.*"

# A HAPPY NEW WAR

*The Unstoppable Warpath of the Unkillable Jack Churchill*

*'When you have to kill a man, it costs nothing to be polite.'*
*– Winston Churchill*

The brisk air of the chilly morning may not have been as cold as the day prior, but due to the sleet that had formed, the environmental trade-off was a mud puddle-littered minefield that was impossible to navigate cleanly. Due to the numbers of their funnelling drive from the barracks to the open, fenced yard, it was typically too late to react before the inmates had dunked their feet into a brown slick.

"Oh, fuck meee..." American journalist *Felix Hardy* groaned with a heightened displeasure, marching amongst the crowd of herded prisoners. He took a moment to lift his sopping-wet, tattered boot out of the puddle. His limb was soaked through to the sock.

Unconcerned, the other POWs flocked around him as he idled.

Tired and dirty men, each in matching mismatched, frayed, and equally as tattered winter military coats droningly paraded around him like a liquid current around a snag. They resembled a mob of the undead, zombified and prematurely aged, mindlessly numb.

There would have been almost a thousand inmates in the *Sachsenhausen Concentration Camp* in *Oranienburg,* but almost everybody knew everybody. Even with rations scarce and warmth sometimes even scarcer, these multinational Allied men were all on the same side of the playing field: they weren't *German.* Although the ranks of the *British Commonwealth* seemed to dominate within the prison camp, every soul was united within the same barbed wire-insulated fences.

"*Bad luck, chap,*" an English POW remarked from the throng of the many as they spilled around the inmate with the drowned appendage.

"Thanks, Bill," Hardy replied after the man, right as another prisoner danced closely around his sudden halt in their formation.

"*Oi, there's a wet patch there, chap.*"

"*Puddle there, mate.*"

Hardy eyed the other guys, mildly aggravated. "Yeah! Thanks!"

Those within the Sachsenhausen-Oranienburg were designated a little differently to most generalized camps. The occupants interred were designated as primarily *'prominenten'*; high-profile or political prisoners of war—the highest valued offenders to the European oppressors of *Nazi Germany.*

Numerous pilots, freedom fighters and resistance members, civilian teachers, poets, artists, and various other men of various other vocal and social, political statuses who Hitler's heroes deemed too important to execute for fear of loss of intelligence at a later date were all now permanent residents inside the concentration camp.

The gaggle of POWs were layered in overcoats scavenged from battlefield corpses by the aspiring *Grim Reaper* workers of Nazi Germany. The tattered, soiled and stained, ill-fitting winterwear bulked their weary and malnourished frames, giving them a cattle-like appearance and acted as an oppressive weight that sank them into the muddied fields, giving them a flock-like gait and shuffle.

Each day after first light, like clockwork, these condemned many were permitted their 'freedom' and 'exercise' and were marched out from within the confines of their centralized wooden barracks—strictly under the observation of their armed captors in the circumferent guard towers, of course. The men were given the opportunity to gulp whatever fresh air that they could through their noses as they pressed their gloomy and expressionless faces against the rusty wire mesh of the perimeter enclosures.

Although allowed to roam free within the fences, not a second would pass where the convicts weren't under the constant patrolling guard of the derogatory soldiers of the *Schutzstaffel.* Each guard was armed with either one of the newer semiautomatic Gewehr rifles or the high-powered Karabiner bolt-action rifle.

As the horde of prisoners flowed from the barrack blocks and out into the yard where they started to disperse across the containment field, the wet-socked Hardy happened to catch a glimpse of his good buddy Jack Churchill as the British officer conversed with some other prisoners whom Hardy had not yet had the pleasure of meeting.

Hands within the pockets of his overcoat, Churchill dispersed from the group, checking his flanks as he sauntered clear of their gathering. He effectively made a beeline to Hardy, and the two of them conversed by a nearby patch of fence that overlooked the wet woods to the east.

"Who's that?" Hardy asked, looking back.

Churchill kept his stare noticeably afar. "Don't look at them."

Due to the abrupt nature of Churchill's remark, Hardy tore his view clear, unsure where else to point his peepers. He scanned the yard elsewhere, the fence, the mud, and then lost focus. "Why? Who are they?"

"Prisoners of war."

"Ha-ha, Jack."

Churchill replied sternly, trading a casual glance to his wing and then back again as though this was nothing but a thing. "Don't concern yourself, Felix."

Knowing when he was shut out, Hardy's brow elevated. "Uh, O.K."

After standing idle in the mud of the yard for an extended moment, Churchill deliberated a cause, pulling Hardy in tow. "Come this way."

He obliged, stepping on with the ever-enigmatic captain across the yard. Whilst they strode, Hardy's attention diverged as he pulled out his crumpled notepad and snub-nosed pencil. "So, then. Where were we? What shall take place next during the unstoppable warpath of the unkillable Jack Churchill?"

Churchill frowned, repulsed by that title. "The *what?*"

Hardy shrugged. "It's a *working title.*"

"It's god-awful, long, and too wordy. Nobody's going to want to read that rubbish," leaning on the wire of the fence, again testing the boundaries of the German guard, Churchill faced Hardy with his hands still in his pockets.

"We'll work on it."

With tolerance, Churchill bowed his head.

"O.K., so ...?"

Churchill finally obliged, taking a big breath in. "Christmas, 1941 ... this is the one you've been waiting for, lad. The big one ..."

Hardy hissed: " *Yesss.*"

And Churchill confirmed: " *Operation Archery.*"

For this retelling, Hardy was excited. Notwithstanding, he was unfamiliar with many of the details from where Jack had last left him in this biography: between the wedding and Archery. "What of the *commando castle?* Yours and Ros' honeymoon following the wedding— thanks again for the invitation, by the way," he jeered having just completed the chapter regarding the marriage of Jack and Rosamund— now officially *Mister and Missus Churchill.* "Get lost in the post, uh?"

"My lad, at that point in time, other than our escapades during *the Battle of Dunkirk* and the odd *Q-and-A* for your chip-wrapper of a newspaper, we barely knew one another ..." Churchill defended with a playful but stern undertone.

"I know, I know," the American journalist joked lightheartedly. Jack had a point, though since the time in question—across the operations, the battles, the wars, and everything in between—the two had formed a strong bond; one that unfortunately found them as cellmates facing an uncertain fate.

"The time *between* the operations?"

"The time between *Claymore* and *Archery* ..." Churchill recalled, sinking deep between the pages of his own mental recollection. This era brought warmth to his heart and a smile to his face. "The unit's honeymoon period."

"And, *your* honeymoon?"

"Unfortunately not. After the wedding, Ros and I had scheduling conflicts with our wartime commitments."

"Oh," Hardy remarked, surprised yet understanding the times of rations and social sacrifice. He jotted the detail down in his pad, illustrating the beginnings of another chapter in the saga of Mad Jack Churchill.

"I meant honeymoon for Commando," Churchill necessitated, putting them back on track and dictating while his biographer documented. "A rather large difference of Commando was that after the stay at *Inveraray*, the troops did not live in an army barracks, per se. Instead, accommodation was what each soldier found for himself in the area of the base, paid for by his daily allowance."

Hardy bobbed his head. "Neat."

"Oh, it was a win-win. The arrangement encouraged the men to use initiative, set an alarm, organize travel time, et cetera. It gave them more privacy, spared them the usual mundane maintenance and cleaning duties, and let the unit move at short notice. And to that, in 1941, our lodging was at *Kelburn Castle.*"

"*A castle?*"

Churchill pursed his lips and nodded. "For a time, following Claymore, No.3 was undeniably bulletproof. The planning and execution of *the Lofoten Raid* was seen by Whitehall as a great success in its entirety. However, they soon wanted more from it and from Commando. There was a lot happening in the *War Office* that saw regime and budgetary deviations put any sort of follow-up mission on hiatus. Now a battle-hardened unit, Commando had proved itself prosperous, and we knew that it was time to expand and conquer while the iron was hot. We did this from our new lodgings at Kelburn Castle on the outskirts of the new training facility in *Largs*—once known as the *Hollywood Hotel*, requisitioned by the Royal Navy in 1939. The grounds were huge, and there was plenty of quarters for the troops by the base if they couldn't find rent in the town. These big Commando developments were inclusive of *Laycock* finally getting approval for his *LayForce*, albeit not the vision he had originally dreamed of. Nevertheless, his *lovechild* spawned from the British Army, acting as a sort-of sister company to Commando, and received orders to begin carrying out raids on the communication lines of the *Afrika Korps* along the North African coast in April. This was a conquest that would drive LayForce through *Bardia, Crete, Syria,* and *Tobruk* by July. They were giving the Huns bloody noses in the Middle East around the same time that we were gearing up to give 'em *what-for* in Northern Europe in 1941 ..."

"Hence, *Archery?*" Hardy concluded, familiar with what came next at the end of that year. He knew it well as he was personally involved in the triumphant event in *Norway*.

Jack nodded. "We were planning to wish the Huns a *Merry Christmas,* and *a Happy New War* ..."

# 1

## *Commando Castle*

There was a whirlwind of positive change blowing a political gale at *Whitehall,* greasing the gears of the British war machine as it did so.

The men of the now infamous *No.3 Commando* graduated from the *Inveraray CTC (Combined Training Centre)* and relocated to the upgraded premises in *Largs,* located in *Ayrshire,* along Scotland's west coast and the *Firth of Clyde.*

The area was tranquil, and popular with tourists local to *Glasgow.*

One of the peculiarities of the commando unit was that the troops did not dwell in standardized barracks in designated camps like they had in Inveraray. Instead, they lived in accommodations that each soldier procured for himself and paid for from their service allowance. This arrangement encouraged the initiatives of civilian living and spared the men the usual monotonous maintenance duties of an otherwise G.I. army barracks. Ultimately, the notion was well received and even started a trend.

Naturally, seaside resorts like *Weymouth, Hastings,* and *Paignton* became favoured choices as lodgings by Commanding Officers since they had plentiful supplies of local bed-and-breakfasts and guesthouses. The vast majority of troops found supplied accommodation in the repurposed Hollywood Hotel, located directly on the new base grounds, and the closest thing to an army barracks—and a far cry at that.

The administrative arrangements in Largs for Commando were crude to say the least, with the main offices housed in a repurposed local ice-cream parlour called *Nardini's,* while the troops established their headquarters in converted offices at a gasworks, a coal yard, and a cigarette kiosk. It was functional but not pretty.

As for the current roster for Jack Churchill's latest *Merry Men,* it was a case of *'mi casa, su casa'* at *Kelburn Castle* and the surrounding grounds ... *aka: Commando Castle.*

Regarded by most as the godfather to No.3 Commando and justifiably so, *Lieutenant-Colonel John Durnford-Slater* had managed to accommodate many of the founding members since the Inveraray recruitment and subsequent rebirth of Commando in the many rooms of infamous Kelburn Castle through the connection of one of their members; *Lieutenant Peter Young.* Young knew the Lord's son *David* who was currently serving in the Royal Navy, and the whole thing made for an extremely fortunate arrangement resulting in the founding members of No.3, living like kings during their stint in Largs.

Kelburn Castle was a thirteenth-century estate.

*A castle in every sense of the word.*

Away from the town, the grounds were located south of Largs, between a rise of steep hills which hid the moorland blocks above, with an overlooking view of the *Kel Burn River.*

Officers of Durnford-Slater's choice were able to fill the accommodations consisting of ten guest bedrooms, that could be shared by use of multiple bunkbeds like in a regular barracks, as well as two more rooms converted to contain even more bunks. What they had created during this time was just like standardized army garrison quarters, only, *with style.*

Along with Durnford-Slater and his regulation lampshade moustache at the castle, were a string of what could be considered now as *commando veterans:*

The recently promoted captain, a baby-faced man whose age belied his rank, *Peter 'Young' Young.* Young Young was ambitious, perhaps frustratingly so, though showed great promise of a prosperous career within Commando to come. He had proved himself during Claymore.

The dimpled cheeks of pretty boy *Arthur Komrower,* who prior to his personal No.3 Commando recruitment by Churchill, was a soldier rather lacking on paper and service history accolades. Mad Jack knew Komrower well from their *undisclosed* and *redacted* tour of duty in Switzerland in late 1939, and their history went further back than either man cared to recognize. He had also proved himself during the Lofoten Raid.

Another occupant at Kelburn was the ex-heavyweight boxer magnificence of *Captain John Frederick Giles (JFG).* JFG was a man whose experience in the ring was well evident upon his face. The once ruggedly handsome gent bore slit scarring due to years of competitive boxing. He wore a slightly swollen jawline and had a permanent cauliflower ear within both imbues of cartilage, and was also present during Claymore.

Existing recruits *Dennis O'Flaherty, Hank Peace,* and *R.L. Wills* were present, of which, the latter still remained the only British

Commando to date to have taunted *Adolf Hitler* directly via radio communiqué. *Corporal 'Dildo' Dillon* was a younger ex-Highland infantryman with heavily blemished skin who had fast become a star player with a sniper rifle having taken great part in their infamous operation.

Of *Second Manchester Regiment* alumni, the troopers present within the ranks of Commando were longtime religious exemplar *Padre Jos Nicholl,* the valiant and reliable chewing gum addict *Corporal Ernest 'Knocker' White,* and the fiery eyepatch-wearing, carrot-topped Scotsman *Sergeant George 'MacWilly' MacWilliam.*

Of these original ratpack, there was only one absentee ...

*The man himself.*

Their most notorious and eccentric commando ...

And arguably *the* most renowned member ...

The recently promoted, founding member and veteran warfighter, reaffirmed second-in-command of No.3 Commando, the one and only *Major John Malcolm Thorpe Fleming Churchill.*

A man of few words and strangely shy of the public image, Mad Jack Churchill had reluctantly become both a show pony and a poster boy for the British Commando. On workdays, on Sundays, *on war days*, he would forever don the formal headgear of the commando: the green beret.

Cleanshaven, dabbed generously with cologne, and always in a pressed battledress with polished silver buttons, Churchill dressed, walked, and acted as though he knew he was the main character in his story. Exclusively sporting a sculpted, pencil-thin moustache above his upper lip, owing to his handsome façade and overall reputation, and accompanied by a confidence-exhuming aura, Jack was often described by his physical resemblance; as *Errol Flynn with a dimple chin*—and quite fittingly so. A lateral scar indentation marked his left cheek, giving him a ruggedly handsome look.

Since his promotion, Churchill was also becoming known as the *Mad Major* by the underlings of No.3, as well as other Commando brigades. These included the new expansions within Commando such as *No.4 (still at the Inveraray CTC, Scotland)*, *No.1 (Dartmouth Garrison, Devon)*, *No.2*, formed under the command of *Lieutenant-Colonel Newman* from a new batch of volunteers after the formation of the *11th SAS Battalion, No.5 (Bridlington, UK)*, and *No.6 (Scarborough, Yorkshire)* under the command by *Lieutenant-Colonel Fetherstonhaugh,* a battle-hardened territorial officer previously holding the substantive rank of captain from the *Queen's Royals.* On the topic of additional Commando manpower, there was also an all-Scottish unit known as *No.11 Commando.*

Although this castle housing arrangement may have been alluded to being a case of favouritism by other groups in Largs, these indictments were promptly debunked once it became understood that the reasoning behind the point-unit's positive discrimination at Kelburn was so that they could undergo further extensive training on the castle grounds at strange hours. No.3 was still an experimental unit, and thus was a regular guinea pig for the King's army, constantly forging new instruments to be housed within the Swiss army knife of tools—and weapons. Once rumour of the unit's extensive extra training circulated to dilute the gossips of special treatment, other soldiers within Commando were either glad to be outside of the focus or more keen to join; which only made them train harder to gain the attention of Durnford-Slater. That being said, this was mostly the former, as the scheduled Commando training was already comprised of the most rigorous of daily physicality and isometric exercises, as well as ever-changing operation-specific training on every other day. This unit was still re-writing the very SOP basic training issued upon enlistment. They were pathing the way, brick-by-brick.

Ever since No.3's victory with the Lofoten Raid, many of the greener commandos, such as Wills, O'Flaherty, Peace, and Dillon—who may have seemed wet-behind-the-ears in comparison to men like Churchill, Durnford-Slater, White, MacWilly, and even Komrower—were now seen as of a *veteran tier*, like their respective mentors before them.

To any of the new recruits, these men were legends ...

Celebrities ...

Gods ...


During this quiet time between operations, and while the Commando numbers quadrupled, an exceptionally busy Jack Churchill split his sleeping arrangements.

Throughout the workweek he would retire to the castle with his Merry Men, bunked in a room at the castle with his secretive-past-shared friend, Arty Komrower. On weekends, he would return home to his wife, Rosamund Churchill. Home being an hour drive north to their recently purchased two-bedroom cottage in Dumbarton.

These hospitable weeks soon rolled into months.

At Largs, the men of Commando trained harder than ever, evolving from the unstoppable influence that they already were, to an even tougher assemblage and a true force to be reckoned with. Their CO, Durnford-Slater, spent most of his time between his new office in the castle and visiting Whitehall, drawing up battleplans and proposing further raid missions in the north, submitting them to his superiors within the

*Combined Operations Headquarters (COHQ).* To Durnford-Slater's constant frustration in dealing with a War Office that continuously preferred to play it safe with Britain's re-entry into the war, his plans were—at least for the time being—constantly shot down by officiaries; specifically *Admiral of the Fleet Roger Keyes,* director of the COHQ. The man was nearing retirement. He wanted not for his final command to yield failure. For a sting, Commando was a gamble he was not willing to wage.

In July and August of 1941, No.3 saw some administrative and personnel changes due to an influx of fresh recruits. During this period of exponential growth to the battalion, they sadly surrendered Padre Nicholl due to the chaplain's ulterior calling to Christianity, of which he was very much a member of evangelical tradition. Nicholl had spoken to Churchill—even since their early days in the Second Chesters—about how he hoped to one day become ordained and serve as a curate elsewhere; somewhere his endless bounds of guidance and ability to spread belief could be used to its fullest potential. They all understood that if he had left Commando, it could only have been to take another step towards becoming a reverend, and it was hard to hate him for pursuing that path, especially between the battles of war and in a time where the people sought faith the most.

As such, No.3 lost, but also gained new capital members:

The first to join the ranks of Commando, as well as the family at Kelburn Castle after the June recruitments, was an old friend of Durnford-Slater, a highly renowned and unconventionally tall (six-foot-six) signals officer by the name of *Lieutenant Charley Head.* A veterinarian during peacetime, Head quickly earned the nickname of *Head job* due to his given surname in combination with his initiation into a group of gutter-humour lads, and the fact that he was always overly-eager to please others as a new arrival to an already established unit. Head volunteered to perform any and all tasks—even the shitty ones, of which eventually the men remarked upon hearing a pending task as *'it seemed like a Head job'.* He both loved and hated the vulgarism, but all the same could not deny it brought a grin to his face as it did the others and it never got old. Since his energetic arrival, he had become a sour and cynical gent, whose tendency for laziness now that he was sitting comfy, even his old friend had come to notice.

Joining No.3 at the end of the June recruitments was a highly recommended team leader *Captain Herbert William Louis 'Algy' Forrester* and his legendary facial brush. A newspaperman by trade, Forrester had military training as an artilleryman in the Royal Artillery.

An affable fellow, he was renowned by his absolute *womb broom* of a moustache that he tamed daily. The thing was comical and certainly beyond army regulation, but it was because of that candour that he was somehow allowed to maintain it while drafted, with the official response to any complaints being if someone were to grow a moustache as big and as proud as Forrester, then that someone should be allowed to wear it anywhere—even into battle.

A new unit doctor joined from the stellar medical corps, a winsome Irish corps captain by the name of *Sam 'Sorry' Corry*. Corry was fast remembered by his long hair on top, always soaked in grease and needing to be pushed back. Bangs often appeared to block his vision whenever his face was down, and Churchill had remarked that the fellow should clip them lest he accidently sew them into a wound in the heat of battle.

*Sergeant Joe Mills* was a last-minute entry. Perhaps with a harrowing past, the man may have seemed a tad introverted, but apparently came alive once a war was initiated inside of him. A solid recommendation from somebody reputed, alone, was probably enough to get Jack Churchill to sign him on. The man seemed normal enough, though his arched brows made it seem as if he was always frowning; like he got pissed off one day and then the wind changed on him.

Lastly, No.3 welcomed a talented quartermaster by the name of *J.E. 'Slinger' Martin* for the administrative position, as the unit was fast becoming home to a manifold of battalions inside the Special Service Brigade, thus warranted such a specialist role. For a new recruit, the age of Martin was easily becoming the talk of the military town. At fifty, Slinger was by far the oldest recruit—actually, the oldest commando. A veteran of the *First World War*, he had served in the *9th Queen's Royal Lancers*, where he climbed to the rank of *Quartermaster (QM)* from conscription. By all army guidelines, he should have been too old to serve with Commando, but Martin did not allow a problem like age prevent his duties, proving himself time and again in physical evaluations to Colonel Durnford-Slater. He joined in their pre-dawn jogs and even had a go at the obstacle courses. He may have not been coming first, but then again, it was not a race. The way Churchill saw it, Slinger Martin was more fit than any one man currently keeping a leather cushioned seat warm at Whitehall, so who were they to judge?—and he expressed this view openly during an instance of his selection becoming questioned. There was no retort from those upon mount high. Martin had been declared by medical authorities as officially *'too old to serve abroad',* but apparently some of this paperwork went missing from Durnford-Slater's desk and could therefore not be verified when the time came for operational clearances, and his name was usually just added to the list. He immediately fit in with the men of No.3 with his gallant charm and charisma. Along with a daily anecdote of wisdom and advice from his years of service, even just as a QM, Slinger fast became an invaluable member of No.3 Commando.

Churchill recalled at the first instance of meeting the man, Slinger Martin had taken his hand a second time after the formalities to express how he had heard the stories of Mad Jack and asked if they were true. To which Churchill replied: "*Only the good ones.*"

Slinger, the new quartermaster for No.3 Commando, then went on to express how highly he thought of Churchill's persistence of medieval armament and choice of weaponry. He mentioned that he *knew a thing or two about kickin' arse,* and that once he was established as QM, he could look into *assisting in Mad Jack's saunter against the Hun.*

Eventually the names of hero soldiers who would undoubtedly go down in history joined up. Men such as *Eric de la Torre* and *George Peel* joined the regular ranks of No.3 Commando. Even *A.J. Cork*, recently demoted and fresh from the brig after weeks of enquiry following the debrief of events during Operation Claymore surrounding purported tergiversation, requested to rejoin a Commando battalion. Strangely listed as a referee by Cork, Churchill was solicited about his re-recruitment application and about the possibility of him re-enlisting. Jack stated that he was a man of forgiveness, that he didn't mind if Cork was given a second chance and rejoined Commando, furthermore, that he was glad, because he was one hell of a fighter—provided, however subjectively, that it wasn't in *their* section of No.3. Cleared of much serious wrongdoing and stripped of rank, Cork remained a Commando and rejoined with the new recruits starting at the bottom of the food chain—albeit, far away from No.3 at Largs. He joined a demolitions detail in No.6 Commando, in Yorkshire, where he began climbing the ladder.

Churchill heard about his selection months later, and that Cork had managed to scale the ranks of non-commissioned officers, from private to corporal, eventually a sergeant. Jack actually relished this news upon it befalling his ears, and he couldn't help but issue pouted lips and a nod of astonished admiration.

*1941, September*
*Kelburn Castle*
*Largs, Scotland*

On a beautiful Autumn Sunday morning, the exterior garden greens glowed lushly, alit by rays of golden sunshine streaming through the shade of the tree canopies.

Within the castle, the most minute of sounds reverberated down the long and connecting rug-lined stone halls of the ornament-littered interior. The air seemed forever stale, and the temperature always cold within the olden premises. The chime of the pendulum tick from the antique floor-standing grandfather clock in the main foyer was distinct and audible, even in linking rooms due to the echoic passageways.

This Sunday morning, the lodging commando troops were relaxing on their day off. Either snoozing, taking their time grooming themselves, or even just lounging about with a good book or morning paper. Some were absent from the grounds, having returned to their family homes to visit relatives over the weekend.

On his return from a morning jog, dressed in his mismatched baggy threads, a sweaty Durnford-Slater bumped into castle owner *Lord Glasgow* at the front of the castle. He and his official entourage of liaisons and clerks were preparing his luggage in one of the cold and dark halls of the lower level and by the large double doors of the front entrance; a space constantly manned by a young Jewish butler named *Jean-Ralphio*— the new generation serving the role of castle aide after his father's recent retirement as the Kelburn Castle doorman after 59 years of service.

Durnford-Slater was still clammy from his cockcrow tread across the bridge and into the *Kelburn Country Centre*, where he went to people-watch and pick up a newspaper from the kiosk, and thus wasn't desiring a chit-chat with their glorified landlord. Glasgow was fine, but in an extremely small doses sense.

"Ah, Colonel," Glasgow's aristocratic tenor announced while one of his assistants abetted him in putting on his heavy overcoat; a *Tielocken* Burberrys weave he picked up in *Haymarket* for a hefty quid. Quite luxurious and expensive. Though fashionable and practical, it talked business.

From within the echoic foyer, Durnford-Slater had no choice now but to approach. His eagerness to avoid him was almost too overpowering to accommodate conversation this morning with the socialite. In most cases, a respectable nod or a greeting would suffice, as most of the time it would seem Lord Glasgow wanted little to do with or to get to know any of the army men he had staying at his castle. The fact Glasgow was due to attend a business venture in London first thing tomorrow and that he would be gone for a couple of days was the only real reason Durnford-Slater felt the need to discourse with him: to hastily aid in seeing him off.

"How do you do, sir?" Durnford-Slater regarded as he came near, folding the newspaper beneath his elbow in order to offer him a handshake.

Whilst being dressed by his help, Glasgow eyed the effects of brisk exercise on the man. It was likely a stench he never acquired recreationally.

At that same moment, a noisy motorcycle arrived at the estate, encircling the driveway loop that passed the front foyer doors and traced the circumference of a garden pond housing a water fountain and a period piece statue replica of *Leonardo DaVinci's 'David'*. The harsh sound of the bike's motor broke the men's attentions momentarily. It was familiar, and sounded like it was Jack Churchill's bike, only it couldn't have been, Durnford-Slater thought; he was at home with his wife this weekend, unless he was misremembering. Churchill would normally return to Largs for training on Monday morning, usually meeting them at the grounds. Never before had he returned on the Sunday prior—perhaps there was trouble in paradise.

"Even the Lord himself took rest on Sunday, Colonel," Glasgow kindly stated referring to Durnford-Slater and his current state and appearance.

"Eh, well yes. Use it or lose it, they say, in regard to physique ..." Durnford-Slater felt awkward bringing up fitness with an obviously pampered, and lazy patrician. "Besides, got to go the extra mile to keep up with some of these new recruits."

"Speaking of ..." Glasgow segued—he had a talent for somehow managing to transition a conversation topic, even when there was no actual relative segue, and especially if the topical matter concerned him. "The stump?"

*Point in case.*

Durnford-Slater's brows raised. "*The stump?*"

He was perplexed for a moment before remembering an ongoing request by Glasgow that had genuinely skipped the colonel's busy mind.

"Oh, yes, *the stump!*"

"Yes. Any updates?" Glasgow enquired as his assistant helped flatten his overcoat collars. He then whispered in his Lord's ear a reminder of their departure schedule to arrive at their commitments in London on time—per chance attending a sycophantic elbow-rubbing meeting with fellow lords and ladies whilst in the capital.

Durnford-Slater had honestly forgotten about the stump.

The deal was that in return for the nobleman's never-ending hospitality for his men at his home, which included some extra liberties, the colonel had offered to have his troops safely attempt to use ordinance to blow up a pesky old tree stump located on the grounds. The stump had been giving the groundskeeper of the manor much grief the past decade and had somehow defeated all conventional means of its removal. Durnford-Slater had assured Lord Glasgow that No.3 could eliminate the troublesome, wretched stump by *unconventional* means, without harming a nearby plantation of saplings. The estate grounds had a collection of unusual and exotic trees and expensive gardens, and together, the plant collection was of high horticultural value—award-winning, even.

All out of options, Glasgow approved of the explosive idea.

Prior and in confidence to Durnford-Slater, Glasgow even referred to some of the plants and trees around the premises to be both older and more valuable than the ideals of Commando. This had been the first instance of which any of the men of No.3 saw Glasgow for a bureaucratical bigot; a possible clue to something veiled beneath his generosity towards the British Army potentially having a hidden agenda—probably even a political one, aimed at Parliament, or more likely in this time of profitability, the War Office at Whitehall.

"Eh ..." Durnford-Slater uttered as his vision retracted out of focus as he raked his mind for a response that didn't make him seem incompetent.

"*A plan is in action!*" a confident British voice stated as he entered through the same doubled-door entrance currently held open by Glasgow's aides. It was none other than Major Churchill, relieving his lieutenant-colonel in the nick of time before too much social awkwardness set in.

Off the back of his introductory sentence regarding the stump plan, Churchill added to the well-respected doorman with a short but sweet handshake, who in-kind returned the welcoming beam. "Jean-Ralphio."

"Major," Jean-Ralphio whispered sheepishly with a respectful nodded gesture, not desiring to interject their conversation in any way. The help at Kelburn Castle were like all those in the position; seen but not heard.

Churchill was always one to befriend the most seemingly insignificant of characters during his walks of life. He respected all men performing their respective jobs, whether they were the boss or the janitor.

"Jack," surprised at his arrival, Durnford-Slater's regard held a trace of delight in his tone. And regarding the plan for the stump, he bobbed his head, a little unsure. "It is?"

"It is," Churchill nodded, his confidence further saving his CO as he interjected himself into their conversation in the foyer.

"Major Churchill," Glasgow welcomed kindly. He eyed the items in Jack's possession as he casually entered the premises dressed in his military commons, with his green beret aslant.

"Sirs," having approached the group, Churchill regarded with a respectful nod and a glance between both Lord Glasgow and his military superior, Colonel Durnford-Slater.

"Well, gentlemen, I must be going," stated the heavyset Glasgow.

In a stride, Churchill positioned himself alongside his commando brethren and the two attempted to hide the fact they were gleeful about his impending absence. They always preferred it when Glasgow wasn't lurking about their military business, as he had a habit of doing so.

"Safe travels, sir," Churchill remarked as he and Durnford-Slater sauntered the entourage out and to the shaded drive bay. The aides loaded his luggage into the trunk of a parked *1933 SJ Duesenberg;* there were only four seats in his vehicle, so the other two assistants of Glasgow's party would be riding in a separate car, a dark *Rolls Royce*, that was currently chaperoned behind the Duesenberg forming a stopgap convoy.

After a few moments, everybody climbed in, and the doors were closed firm for travel. Glasgow wound down the window of his soft-top Duesenberg and slung his arm out to add about the tree stump. "Get rid of that bastard, would you?!"

"Will do, sir!" Durnford-Slater gestured.

Churchill held up his arm in farewell.

"Fine-o-fine, sir! We have a plan!"

Together they watched the Lord and his convoy leave the Kelburn estate before returning back into the castle. Jean-Ralphio closed the door behind them and disappeared to return to his household duties.

In that instant, Durnford-Slater had so many questions, such as *why was he here* and *not still at home with his new wife*, but only one seemed to rise to the surface.

"So, what *is* the plan, Jack?"

Churchill turned to him, projecting a sense of uncertainty considering how confidently he had just spoken about the plan. "I have no idea ..."

Durnford-Slater opened his mouth with inhale. "Ah."

He was not surprised.

The two stood awkwardly for a moment before Churchill suggested the one thing presently on his mind—and it wasn't how to resolve the tree stump debacle—but not before dropping some of his trademark wit.

"Rather *stumped,* actually."

Durnford-Slater did not humour him. He nodded, expressionless, even though Churchill baited an easy laugh.

"So, then. Tea?"

Durnford-Slater bowed. "Sure."

They moved on.

Retreating to the sunroom and lounging out upon Glasgow's cushioned armchairs, the two sipped tea and spoke about Jack's weekend; about how Churchill was originally supposed to be away in Dumbarton with his wife for the whole weekend.

He informed Durnford-Slater about how Rosamund's sister was seven months pregnant to her husband in a town north of Helenslee, and that she was planning to visit her along with their mother. She was planning on staying at the family house in Helenslee this night, therefore leaving him alone in Dumbarton—hence why he was free to return early.

With that understood, their next point of inquiry was the issue of the pesky tree stump. Glasgow had been on Durnford-Slater's case about the favour since the boys of the No.3 had moved in back in April. Time was getting on, and it was a fair reminder by the man of the manor.

"It's settled, then," Churchill remarked, calling for the butler of the house—a man who was in no way a servant to the army men currently lodging at the Kelburn Castle, but he attended to their side in the sunroom all the same. "We get some TNT from Slinger. He'll sign it out, no questions asked. Head can pick it up on his way for the barbeque."

"What barbeque?" Durnford-Slater questioned as the butler joined them in the sunroom.

"*This* barbeque."

*... Durnford-Slater sensed an all too familiar hint of mischievousness underlining Churchill's tone ...*

"*Sirs?*" Jean-Ralphio beckoned upon his arrival.

"Take a seat, Jean," Churchill insisted—a treat while his boss was away on business. "Go on, I won't tell anyone. Put your feet up and enjoy a cuppa, my lad."

Jean-Ralphio gleamed down to the tray he had earlier prepared for the gents. It consisted of cups, a pot of tea, and what few sugar rations they had on hand. "Oh, I, eh... I shouldn't, sirs ..."

From beneath the skirting, Churchill's leg pushed the chair out at their table and after an ounce of further consideration, the servant took the seat. A second after that he took the pot.

"The barbeque we're having in the courtyard by the tree stump we're about to blow up," Churchill instigated now that Jean-Ralphio was present. He was a key factor. "All the lads are back here usually by about two o'clock on a Sunday, yes? With Glasgow checked-out, we can even have some of the reservists over here until late and make a day out of it."

Durnford-Slater remained silent.

Churchill insisted. "Sir, we must enjoy this calm before the storm."

"Jack, I don't know ..."

"Come on, I've already organized most of it. The lads have pooled their ration tickets, got us some bangers, some loaves of bread, and I've called in some favours with the boys at the brewery to get some crates of beer."

The butler nodded along. It sounded good—mostly, because he knew that he would be invited to the said barbeque and not just serve at it. He quite enjoyed the company of the military men when Kelburn was minus Lord Glasgow.

"Jack, I ..." Durnford-Slater murmured distastefully. He didn't like the sound of this. They were like kids throwing a house party while the parents were not home.

"Sir," Churchill insured, even cracking his winning smile that somehow won over every argument. "What could *possibly* go wrong?"

Lunchtime inevitably came about. Throughout the day, the troops of No.3 Commando periodically received their word-of-mouth invite, and arrived on the Kelburn Castle grounds right on time for a late lunch. The lawn became a regular parking lot of vehicles and bicycles, much resembling a market fair or a picnic park. It was a grand day for outdoor festivities and the castle grounds were full of luscious and flourishing greenery for as far as the eye could see.

A focal point in the distance before a wide tree trunk was a white canvas pinned to a block of hay: Churchill's archery target, set up currently at sixty meters. He hadn't practised in a while, but the range was still set up from the last time he had loosed a few downrange.

There were almost fifteen guests in total.

Not a bad turnout considering it was a last-minute shindig.

Along with help Jean-Ralphio by the entrance, Churchill welcomed them, offering them a glass of warm lager upon their arrival—served in some of Glasgow's finer pilsner glasses. What a treat, indeed.

Due to their residency within the castle, No.3 regulars *Young Young,* Peace, the ever-comedic R.L. Wills, and *Dildo* Dillon attended. Soon after, the brute JFG showed up in a borrowed base truck. He brought his younger brother, fellow commando *Bruce Giles,* for the lunch. Pirate-impersonator extraordinaire MacWilly showed up along with forever chewing gum-munching Knocker White. The two of them were slightly loose already coming via the local pub in Largs, having received the invite for the last-minute BBQ after committing to a few rounds of darts at the local. They scored a lift with the Giles'.

O'Flaherty and Komrower seemed the only regulars of the guild who were absent, but in their wake, others from No.3 arrived via invitation, such as newcomers *Sorry* Corry, George Peel, and Eric de la Torre. These men were still rather shy in the midst of the No.3 band, and this was all the more reason Churchill saw social outings like this as great for team-building.

"*At least the doc's here in case someone gets blown up,*" a voice called as the guests wandered through and to the rear outdoor alfresco and grass area. Without much context, this seemed to worry Sorry Corry and his perfect head of hair for an instant. He exchanged a glance with de la Torre as they took up chairs on the lawn around a set-up trestle table, issuing pleasant smiles between sips of their frothy beverages.

Forwarding a glance to his new friend, Peel, and perhaps feeling at home in No.3 for the first time more than ever, de la Torre had distractingly smooth skin on his face and neck that glistened outdoors—smoother than a baby's bottom. So much so, the men questioned whether it was due to a shaving and skin nourishing routine, or if the lad in his mid-twenties was just yet to grow a single facial hair.

The narrow face of George Peel received the expression from his fellow newcomer, equally as unknowing of how to perceive the humour. Conversational caution remained constantly to the wind. The men simply held onto their respective smirks, nodded, and played along with the crew. The drinks would help cure any awkwardness as the bonds were forged.

The men enjoyed each other's company for an hour or so before Durnford-Slater arrived with his friend Charley Head. They were late due to having to organize with Slinger Martin to come in and open the Hollywood Hotel armoury and for them to sign out some deemed 'perished' explosives for unscheduled disposal.

Also accepting the invitation, Slinger himself arrived just after, once he had accomplished some other duties at the household of which he lodged accommodation. He showed up after lunch, just in time for the prearranged demolition.

When Durnford-Slater and Head arrived, a few noticed that Head was carrying something in a protective satchel which they all recognized was for typically transporting explosive charges when they were in a combat zone.

"Oi, sir?" the one-eyed Scotsman pirate, Sergeant MacWilly, opened his boisterous mouth over a lager. It was a throwaway. Casual. "What yoor boy got in dat there baggy, eh? Dynamite er somethin'?"

From behind their beers, the others laughed in their slouched at-ease positions.

Colonel Durnford-Slater held up. "Yes, actually."

The group went silent for an awkward moment and exchanged a glance. *Was he serious just now?*

Jean-Ralphio cooked the sausages, sliced the bread loaves, and brought them from the kitchen and out to the dressed table outdoors. Sausages made during wartime included a higher concentration of filler material to make the limited meat content go further, mostly done with an abundance of potato. Unlike traditional sausages, the potato content when heated would expand and produce loud popping noises, earning them the nicknames *bangers*. This itself inspired the boys to make many demolition-related jokes whenever they would hear them go off from the kitchen, and much at the expense of the men setting up the explosives.

Laughter and banter were at an all-time high.

On more than one occasion that gleeful afternoon, Churchill recalled taking in the sight of his men—his Merry Men—enjoying each other's company; forging the very brotherhood bond created by those serving in the armed forces. The power of alcohol and socializing.

There were jokes about Charley's amazing head jobs, Young Young's age belying his face, and how his girlfriend—a lass by the surname of *Duckworth*—must have been a cradle snatcher because he looked to be in his teens, and appreciation of newcomer Algy Forrester's soup catcher of a moustache. The thing was majestic.

Camaraderie circulated amongst the men the only way Brits knew how: through repartee and sketches forced upon or about one another. Each man equally took the piss.

Once the feast was done in the early afternoon, it was time for the impromptu main attraction. With a beer in hand and spreading his neatly shaped pencil moustache with his fingertips, Churchill stood focal and announced to them all what target they had planned to take out—with Lord Glasgow's permission—the large tree stump ... and that this was due to be accomplished with some live ordinance.

After the good meal and some even better beverages, most of the men made comment on the topic of stump removal—all of a sudden, they traded their green berets for green thumbs and were experts on gardening and horticulture, like most men were after a couple of pints and a feed. The varying suggestions were all things Glasgow had reportedly tried to rid of the stump, such as poisoning the roots, chopping the core, and so on. Churchill admitted that *yes*, TNT sounded extreme, but it was the last straw.

Although some had their reservations, most of the men thought it was a hilarious approach and couldn't wait to sit back (at a safe distance) and watch this tree stump get blown to smithereens.

When it was time, beer in hand, Durnford-Slater supervised his friend, Charley Head, as he packed the explosive in a dug trench that ran beneath the stump. He questioned the packing, to which Head regarded was '*just the right amount*' and '*to relax*', that this, confidently, '*wasn't his first rodeo*'.

Honestly, *what could go wrong?* It was just a bunch of mildly intoxicated soldiers playing with explosives at a barbeque.

Needless to say, Charley Head was not the expert on demolition that he so fervently convinced others he was. They were yet to realize, but he had overdone the explosive charge by a factor of ten.

Once the warning gestures ran, the men all picked up and moved their lawn chairs back an extra twenty paces. Most of the men remained standing, cradling their lagers, rather than resuming their seats, watching as the final touches to the bomb were planted and the detonation cord ran. Head and Durnford-Slater strolled away carefully, feeding the fuse wire out from a coil as they walked.

"That's the quickest head job I've ever seen!" one of the commando jokers heckled as they all watched on with their drinks in a group chortle.

With his spare hand that was not carrying the detonation plunger, Head issued the crowd of onlooking larrikins the V-sign. Durnford-Slater smirked as they halted a safe distance from the tree stump—what they deemed to be a safe distance, anyhow.

After a moment, they prepared the wire of the detonation cord and Durnford-Slater nodded to Mad Jack, who in-turn faced the crowd of partially concerned and anxious, entertained spectators. He gave them a signal to block their ears and close their eyes—which, he also did, partly with his glass of gold in his other hand.

Head put his hand on the plunger and eyed his CO one last time.

Durnford-Slater nodded ...

*He plunged the lever.*

*squeak—BOOM!*

In the tranquillity of the calm Kelburn Castle grounds and surrounding estate, the behemoth detonation echoed like a crack of ground-level thunder, disturbing the quiet setting usually bathed in constant serenity. In all probability, the blast shook the tectonic plate beneath the layers of earth.

The circumferent tree lines shook leaves as an innumerable amount of birds scattered to the skies in a panic.

Ducks and other calm wildlife along the embankment of the Kel Burn to the south also dispersed in an array of frightful motion, flapping their wings and squawking erratically in the deafened aftershock.

Serviettes and peripherals were blown a gust. The picnic tables and chairs placed about the lawn clacked together as did several empty glass bottles, some even toppling over from the shockwave.

As the ringing in their ears subsided, the shrouding men could be heard laughing hysterically and gasping for air following what they had witnessed.

And the aftermath ...

*A rather unforeseen and unfortunate result.*

The force of the shockwave thrashed against the closest outer wall of the castle, assaulting the solid stone surfaces and blasting them with dust, but also fracturing every glass window along the southern face of the building façade. Glass shards from broken windowpanes speckled down into the surrounding hedges and gardens, tinkling in a constant orchestra of sound following the detonation of the TNT beneath the old tree stump like a windchime in a gust.

Due to the location of the lower placement, the massive tree stump uprooted from the blast, rising vertically into the air, showering every surface for fifty yards in a sprinkle of cold black dirt. Resembling an out of ocean octopus with severed tree roots as tentacles, the stubborn stump elevated approximately fifteen-feet in the air before the unbeatable force of gravity brought it slamming straight back down. The intact heavy stump landed several paces to the side of its original habitat, coming down over the precious neighbouring gardens that Lord Glasgow had been seeking to protect.

With an earth-trampling *thud* the stump crash landed into the cultivation display, destroying an array of beautifully coloured plants and flowers, and crumbled the stylized rock retaining wall that housed the garden bed. It landed so heavily that it formed a crater in the fertile earth of the botanical garden. Its severed roots were now protruding upwards like the legs of *Wicked Witch of the East.*

When the attentions of the men of No.3 were restored, they wiped their faces and shook their hair from the unexpected spray of earthly grains. Recovering, the men united and gravitated closer, coughing through their hysterics as the cloud of grey smoke overcame them. Nobody was harmed.

"Blood-y-hell!" Durnford-Slater grumbled, fishing dirt from out of his ear cartilage.

Churchill sat up on his rear. The explosion had shoved him onto his buttocks on the cold grass. He still held his glass, though now it was mostly empty of alcohol, having inadvertently tipped it over his shoulder, like the ancient custom of throwing salt.

"Holy bollocks," he remarked, glancing about and finding his beret that had been knocked off his noggin. He placed down his beverage on a nearby table and quickly jogged in close to Durnford-Slater and Head, who were retreating from the smoke cloud with their heads down and eyelids closed from the fogginess. The two of them had just eaten a mouthful of dirt and their ears were probably slightly concussed.

"You gents alright?" Churchill asked.

"Right as rain!" Durnford-Slater shouted with his finger in his ear, scraping out black grime. His face was black.

"Fuckin' hell!" Charley Head remarked, wiping his eyes clean. He had dirt in his gritted teeth, spitting profusely. "Yep! Might've overdone that one!"

"You don't say, lad!" Churchill exclaimed with a grin.

Nobody present had been expecting that unforeseen display.

A veil of eerie silence followed, where the men of No.3 regrouped further and cast a view at the repercussions of the TNT in the garden. They each watched as the three closest men returned to sight from the grey haze.

The silence lasted about the same amount of time that the cloud of smoke did before the open air blew it away and restored visibility. All that remained other than Durnford-Slater, Head, Churchill, and the smouldering empty pocket where the troublesome tree stump had once been rooted, was now an unattractive pocketed crater filled with residual smoke.

There was a further moment of pause amongst the men ...

... *then they erupted in cheer and applause.*

Some idiot in the crowd even bellowed the brigade's mantra:

"*Let's go, No.3!*"

The only man not completely overcome by celebration was Colonel Durnford-Slater. During the Merry Men's merrymaking, his focus scaled the wall of the multilevel castle, assessing the damage to the brickwork and the countless cracked or shattered glass windows.

*Regrets were mounting.*

While the alcohol-buzzed men of No.3 pranced around and hooted, he quietly brought his hand upon his dirt-peppered face as if to ask *what have I just done?* After all, the responsibility of these actions and the possible repercussions all fell on him.

The revelling group hadn't paid much attention to the MP jeep in the distance as it cruised in. The car crept along the Kelburn Castle driveway and disappeared behind the angle of the castle walls. The occupants would have certainly heard the explosion.

Shortly after, two messengers in military suits rounded the estate, easily finding the location of the barbeque bash—as if the massive resounding explosion hadn't triangulated their location like a beacon.

"Excuse me, Colonel?" the voice from one of the uniformed runners queried, requesting the attention of the group's commanding officer. They were both equally confused by the attraction this day, as well as eager to vacate; to disregard their corroboration regarding what they had just been in the vicinity of.

"Eh, yes," Durnford-Slater remarked, shaking away his wish to curl up into a ball and weep.

One of the messengers handed him a bound manila folder and then they both poised a salute. With a weighted conscience, Durnford-Slater returned the gesture, and the two men withdrew to their car and left just as quickly as they had arrived.

Within the noisy foray, in his distinct peripheral vision, Churchill's attentiveness detected the notion. He took leave from the raucous crowd of off-duty commandos in the interest of attending his CO, sensing something was the matter. This unexpected, escorted delivery must have carried some importance if it was transported on a Sunday and via MP messenger rather than ordinary telegram. It could have had something to do with the colonel's operational propositions composed by the COHQ.

Jack cued supportingly. "Sir?"

After an extended pause of consideration, Durnford-Slater quickly unwound the twine seal and took a peek at the contents of the memorandum. The header was branded with an imperative that the contents of the documents were for *his eyes only*.

Durnford-Slater's brown eyes scanned the pages with much anticipation. His concentration then blinked and fluttered away from the sight of printed letters and found a focus upon something in the near distance as he handed the classified documents to his trusted second-in-charge for a peek. This was a clear representation of his level of respect and trust towards his second-in-command, a man who had, on multiple occasions, assisted him in drawing up many of the potential battleplans for targets in the north.

Churchill handled the memo.

"It's from Whitehall ..." Durnford-Slater's stare glazed over slightly.

His view went from the greenery to—for the first time—noticing the colours of the white, black, blue, red, and yellow circles on the canvas of one of Jack's archery target boards in the near distance, of which there were many holes over and around the bullseye.

Whether or not anybody had bothered to listen to Durnford-Slater's ideas or read his planning, No.3 officers had long since been intercepting rumours of an up-coming combined operation that would be taking place one day soon ... could this day have possibly come?

Churchill's focus expanded as he took in the information that the pages withheld.

"The operation is a go ..." in a breath, Durnford-Slater added whilst he stared out into the pastures. He seemed astounded by the news he had been desiring to hear for months. Finally, he turned and faced Churchill. "*My operation.*"

Finishing inspecting the papers, Churchill's stare lifted onto Durnford-Slater.

"At long last, Jack, we will learn if our training has made us the fighting force we intended to be."

"What will you call it?" Churchill quizzed as a divergence. This upcoming Combined Operations mission was born of some of his own ideas, birthed as John Durnford-Slater's theoretical brainchild.

Beneath the bristles of his lampshade moustache, a smug smile developed over the colonel's lips as the arbitrary codename came to his mind through an observation; a random interpretation inspired by a present visual.

*Mad Jack's target in the distance.*

"*Archery.* Operation *Archery.*"

'In the weeks to follow, a letter arrived in the post from Glasgow's legal team requesting reimbursement by the British Army. The letter catalogued all of the collateral damage that had been caused by the TNT blast, including the breaking of every window in the castle. The Lord added as a post-script that 'when one of the maids had pulled a chain in the downstairs servants' lavatory, the cistern had come off the wall'. Durnford-Slater stated he felt that was perhaps stretching it a bit.'

# 2
## Operation Archery

1941, November
Combined Operations Headquarters
Whitehall, London

"Good morning ..."

Through the situational awkwardness they fashioned, the pleasant voice of Jack Churchill greeted the seated secretary behind the desk as he and John Durnford-Slater struggled to carry a large board of wood into the Combined Operations Headquarters in Whitehall. The entire building had been as quiet as a library until these two had entered, shuffling through the front doors and carpeted halls, carrying a two-by-one metre flat board causing the upmost kerfuffle, most inelegantly and askew. Compiled of softwood and folded paper, the entire thing probably only weighed ten kilograms, however due to the length of their commute this morning and their trounced hardships, it seemed as though it weighed a metric tonne.

The cherry-lipped, lash-twinkling brunette secretary to the admiral held onto her hospitable pearly white beam as she cocked her eyebrow at the sight of the two uniformed gentlemen and their dramatic entrance via the long hall. She said not a word in retort to the men in formal officer's suits beneath slanted green berets as they struggled a pivot through the open doorway to the admiral's office wing. She withheld any formal reception or greeting until they finished transporting the large *thing*.

"... explain to me again ..." Churchill commented with a cynical tone to his CO and friend, Durnford-Slater. This morning had truly become an impromptu test of their alliance, for the two had struggled to carry the board which housed a highly detailed model of an island in the *Vågsøy* municipality in the *Sogn og Fjordane* county, Norway. Their crude scale replica was concealed beneath a modest veil of secrecy; a light canvas sheet which had, by now, all but fallen off. The three-dimensional map focused in great detail on the southern half of the islands, surrounding the central town of South Vågsøy. All details were made as accurate as possible due to the thanks of recent aerial photography and geographical intelligence. The three-dimensional model had been constructed on a block of plywood filled with folded paper houses and clag-pasted figurines, grafted all over by lead pencil markings, tacks, and strings of twine. The goal was to accurately represent the Commando and Navy units for the up-coming presentation and briefing of his mission.

On the way in, many of the toy figurines that Durnford-Slater had borrowed from his children's playsets and glued onto the board to represent the Troop movements had fallen off and been discarded somewhere on the streets of London.

"... why didn't you just build it here and leave it ...?" Churchill questioned after they placed the model down carefully on the carpeted floor and he took a walk back down the hall of the office collecting several toy army men that had fallen off. He tossed them back to his stressed colonel who was clearly a tad anxious about their pending confidential meeting. Durnford-Slater had constructed the entire detailed model during an off-site weekend at his family home to help with planning for Operation Archery, and had asked Churchill to help him carry it in this morning for the meeting with the War Office. They had been reluctant to attempt fitting it into an automobile, so the two highly decorated military officers took an end of the board each, wrapped the thing in a drop sheet, and hopped on a train in the early hours of the morning. The result was two highly frazzled adult men bickering like children; the age of whom, should have been the ones playing with the toys mounted upon the plank.

"I didn't think of it until last weekend!" Durnford-Slater defended, fixing some of the mould. He barely caught the toy army men Churchill tossed to him—*at* him, more like—throwing them much harder than what was necessary.

"Why not? If you did, we wouldn't have had to carry the darn thing all the way in here. And you wouldn't have lost your boy's two snipers and half a dozen riflemen down the gaps of the twopenny tube ..."

The men of MIA statuses to which he was referring were the toy soldiers mounted on the end of the scale model that were not glued on properly and had been bumped off. They had disappeared into the abyss of legs belonging to the busy commuters with whom they had shared the public transport this morning during rush hour, hence the appropriate *Missing In Action* category.

"You're the reason we lost those men!" Durnford-Slater responded, in-kind. Their conversation appeared to be a reflective contrast to losing *real* men. His voice lowered as he cast a glimpse to the secretary at the desk, reminded of her proximity. A sudden wave of embarrassment overcame him, and he quietened his tone an ounce.

"Pardon?" Churchill retaliated, pacing out his frustrations. "How is it my fault? You're the one who didn't stick 'em on properly! Should ask your kids for arts and craft lessons next time, *sir* ..."

Durnford-Slater shook his head as he immediately began to apply fresh paste to the board in order to reconstruct the model for the briefing. Needless to say, the lieutenant-colonel had gone all-out for this morning's briefing with the chiefs at the War Office.

Churchill attended to the secretary, brightening the case with his winning smile—his attention was immediately drawn to two things. First, that the secretary to the admiral's office was no longer Roger Keyes' granddaughter, *Annabelle Keyes,* and second, that she had been replaced by another specimen of female grace. In typical Jack Churchill fashion, attention was focused upon her effervesced irises—a dark bronze with a hazel allure that truly sparkled—framed by luscious dark lashes that were accentuated by cosmetics.

The change in staffing likely had something to do with the recent changes in office, the largest of which was the removal of *Admiral Roger Keyes* and the appointment of a new Chief for the COHQ, *Commodore Louis Mountbatten.*

Churchill announced so that the secretary could check her appointment notes. "Ma'am, how do you do? Colonel Durnford-Slater and Major Churchill to see the commodore for this morning's briefing. Apologies for our lateness."

"Please take a seat, sir. I shall inform the commodore of your arrival. It shan't be long," she addressed and returned a smile that challenged Churchill's own winning grin. There was the added flutter of her lashes upon his good looks that Churchill failed to avoid and instinctually engrossed upon the surface.

Churchill returned to the waiting chairs, near Durnford-Slater and his plywood model which he now, exhaustedly, pivoted on a diagonal angle to stow it against a wall.

They sat in silence, catching a breath from their morning journey.

Neither one of them knew Mountbatten well. Churchill had never met the man, and Durnford-Slater only during official business hallway passings. His promotion to Commodore and Chief of the Combined Operations had been sudden, though the man's reputation preceded him. Considering his history of combat and heroism with a fantastic naval career off the back of the first war, Louis Mountbatten had been a favourite candidate of *Prime Minister Winston Churchill* to head his star

COHQ from the start—it had just been a case of availability, with Mountbatten unwilling to leave his tour prematurely, insisting to stay with his crew aboard the *HMS Illustrious.*

Prior to the Illustrious, Mountbatten was captain of the *HMS Kelly,* which was sunk by German dive bombers in May during *the Battle of Crete.* Mountbatten was mentioned in dispatches in August 1940 and again in March 1941, when he was awarded the Distinguished Service Order.

The months following the success of Operation Claymore had been politically troublesome for Whitehall and the COHQ, as it appeared the sudden supremacy at Keyes' fingertips had become too organizationally overpowering. Admiral Keyes' fall from office and his ill-treatment of LayForce had exposed the rigidities between those responsible for the day-to-day comportment of the war and those with longer-term objectives. Over time, Prime Minister Churchill had reluctantly agreed that Keyes was not the man to accomplish that task, but he was just as aware that he could not permit such a fundamental ambition to be relegated.

Thus, from this new beginning, the Mountbatten remit was more extensive than that of his predecessor. Prior to his promotion, Mountbatten had served as an adviser to Keyes and the Combined Operations, and from an outside perspective, his experience seemed scarcer, and therefore more inadequate than what Keyes had ever been in office. Yet, in these few weeks at the helm, Mountbatten had already made better use of the tools at his disposal and appreciated that organizing small-scale raids was to be only the first step in a campaign of combined operations that would eventually bring him greater authority to help win the war.

Although still only in the first verse of a new chapter, Mountbatten's tale had been one of lionheartedness. When he had taken over office a month ago, after the months of bureaucratic powerplays and arguments in Parliament that had caused many staffers to request transfers into other roles or offices, he struggled to carry out even his most basic errands. The Combined Operations Headquarters was only left with a total personnel of two dozen workers, including admin typists and messengers that were borrowed from other offices inside Whitehall. The COHQ had no regular RAF or Royal Navy officers (only non-commissioned officers/reservists) and no signals specialists—Mountbatten's field of expertise serving as a commander of the *5th Destroyer Flotilla* aboard the Kelly prior to his advisory role at Whitehall.

Undoubtedly, Mountbatten's new upbeat fife benefited greatly from America's entry into the war three weeks after he took up his post. The military and industrial strength of the United States made it easier to contemplate a second front in the European Theatre. It went without saying that a COHQ side mission was to trek to Washington and ask President Roosevelt for a fat loan.

In short, Mountbatten's disposition abetted his fast success.

He was cousin to the king, and a flamboyant Royal Navy officer of audacious intelligence and boundless vigour. His obvious ambition and a fundamental desire to vindicate his father, *Prince Louis of Battenberg* (who had retirement forced upon him once the First World War began, when anti-German sentiment was running high), repelled some with whom he had connections. Thus far, at his young age of forty, his energy and enthusiasm for scientific knowledge made him seem modern and helped to draw the best out of the interservice staff he recruited into his new COHQ. This was only solidified to men like Colonel Durnford-Slater more by Mountbatten listening to both high- and low-ranking officers who proposed detailed operation ideas. Plans of action; specifically, <u>attack</u>—like Durnford-Slater and his Operation Archery.

And here we are, today.

The six-foot slender man with rectangular-shaped features, a Greek nose, and dark hair that was Commodore Mountbatten pushed open the leather-padded soundproof double doors that led to the main briefing war room.

He announced enthusiastically: "Gentlemen!"

Behind him and inside the room, the lights were mostly dimmed, and those already present within appeared to be viewing slides through a bulb projector on a drawn canvas screen.

Mountbatten's lanky arm outstretched towards Durnford-Slater as he stood and straightened his suit, shaking the man's hand. There was a courteous remark about the charming three-dimensional model brought for the briefing, and Durnford-Slater unveiled it for a peek.

*Mountbatten couldn't help but grin like a child.*

His eyes glistened about it, soaking the intricate detail. He was keen to see more, however tore his attention from it in order to properly salute and then warmly shake the hand of Churchill.

"Major Churchill."

"Commodore," Churchill responded with a dip.

"Congratulations on your promotion. You deserve it."

"And to you, sir."

With a squinted stare through the darkness beyond Mountbatten's shoulder, Churchill noted that those already inside the war room were the other crucial members involved in Archery, such as men from the navy, air force, and various liaisons from other effective services, including the *Norwegian Independent Company 1 (NOR.I.C.1)*.

"Sorry we're late, sir," Churchill added respectfully, and, as a throwaway with which to best test their new boss' sense of humour: "The Colonel insisted he bring his toys to play with whilst us men go over the brief."

Mountbatten chuckled as a partially discomposed Durnford-Slater cast Churchill a sideways glance that withheld the wish to deck him one. He should have been embarrassed, but much to his chagrin, the colonel had gotten used to Churchill's societal ways by now—even at his expense; the man always knew how to break any form of ice with a joke, and in the British Army, higher-ups rather relished a good jibe rather than the atypical stale anecdote.

They were both surprised when Mountbatten, himself, leant in to assist collecting the model off the floor and help bring it in for the briefing. He took an end along with Durnford-Slater and stepped backwards as Churchill leaned in to further prop the door for added clearance. They carted the board into the war room and received strange looks from the other half dozen men of form and rank already seated around the table smoking cigarettes and drinking tea—some even swirling a brandy. In that regard, it appeared Mountbatten was just as accommodating as Keyes when it came to generous hospitality. He had learned this quality well from his predecessor and planned to maintain it.

The attractive brunette secretary with a gratuitous waddling backside wrapped in a tight black skirt upped from her desk and assisted in pushing over the thick doors after they had all entered, fastening their privacy.

Notably, the acoustics within the sanctum reverberated differently once the doors were sealed.

The layout of the office-like war room was very much how Churchill had imagined it to be six months ago, in the build-up to Operation Claymore. This time, he was permitted *inside* for the briefing and faraway from the libidinousness and the danger of flirtatious temptation by any secretaries.

Located somewhere deep within the recesses of the momentous London building, probably somewhere off the blueprint, this was the type of soundproof, clandestine meeting chamber one would expect to read about in a *Dick Tracy* comic.

Once the model piece was positioned on the table occupied by the half-dozen military-suited silhouettes illuminated by the residual light cast by the projector, Churchill backed up several inches and caught a glimpse of the wall art with his peripherals. The office décor was predominantly themed oil paintings of famous battles of the *First World War, Waterloo, Trafalgar,* and *Agincourt,* nondivergent in their artistic style. There were also paintings of several heads of states, such as Prime Minister Winston Churchill and King George VI. The portions of wall not decorated were littered in detailed world maps with pinned notes, diagrams, black and white photographs and aerial reconnaissance snaps, much alike the type of intelligence work his brother *Thomas Churchill* obtained for Great Britain.

Currently, the war room housed an ensemble of bigwig military and bureaucratically attired English gentlemen. Like the brief prior to the Lofoten Raid, each member present was there to represent a combined cooperation from a various front within His Majesty's Military and War Office, respectively.

Through the hovering haze of tobacco smoke brightly lit by the illumination of the bulb projector, *Brigadier J.C. Haydon* was the only man Churchill recognized. On his desktop was a saucer to house his teacup of steaming *Earl Grey.* Haydon was a high-ranking commander in the Royal Navy and was a part of Archery to command the ships involved in the raid, basically inhabiting what *Rear Admiral L.H.K. Hamilton*'s role was during Claymore. He even had a trope of his own: a fixation for Earl Grey tea. Much alike Hamilton's tobacco pipe obsession, where he would be chugging like a chimney to conquer operational stress, Haydon would be constantly sipping on a breakfast beverage.

In the near dark, Durnford-Slater shook hands with or respectfully nodded across the table to all those present, greeting them thusly while Churchill finished taking in the surroundings of the office like a bewildered child at an amusement park.

"... and this is *Major Jack Churchill,*" Durnford-Slater announced once around the front of the room and in the light of the projector, recalling his man's attention. "He is my Executive Officer for Archery, and therefore privileged to the information that will be divulged today."

Churchill's focus centred.

"*Gentlemen,*" Churchill bowed, still obtaining profiles of the seated men in the lack of light just as Mountbatten switched on the lamp nearest them, restoring luminosity. Almost simultaneously, the bulb projector film seemed to reel out and automatically switch off, eliminating the ominous theme within the war room and replacing it with that of nothing more than a formal meeting.

"Major," one of the men greeted vocally while others simply nodded from behind their clouds of smoke, planted in their comfortable chairs.

"*Juck?*" a tiny voice called, and Churchill recognized it instantly. Eyes adjusting to the new light, the familiar Norwegian liaison stood. Not only did he fast approach Churchill with a welcoming handshake, but he issued him a shoulder-to-shoulder embrace which exhibited their previous operational history. He looked the same: clean-shaven, with set dark hair, but perhaps his eyes read that new heights of confidence had been reached since their last meet—not that the former actor was ever shy of poise.

*It was Martin Linge.*

"*Marty?!*" Churchill retorted joyously. It had been some time. "Great to see you, old boy! How do you do?"

"Well, thank you," Linge replied utilizing his improved English language standards. He was clearly here to represent the NOR.I.C.1. portion of the operation, who would be accompanying Commando in the landing teams.

"How was your wedding?" he next asked in an extension to the formalities. Their display of camaraderie out before the other important men was a telltale sign of Churchill's relevance to the operation, piquing the interest of anybody who didn't know the man beyond the mythos of *Mad Jack.*

"Good—great, actually!" Churchill remarked, glad to see him and honestly rather surprised that he remembered the events of his personal life.

Mountbatten intervened, "I see that you two have met."

"Yes, sir."

"Yus."

With an introductory furthermore, Mountbatten waved an open hand around the room. Jack nodded respectfully to each man in-turn. "Major Churchill—from the navy, this is *Rear Admiral Harold Burrough* for oversight, Brigadier Haydon who will be aboard the point-ship, and from the *SOE, Commodore Charles Hambro.*"

Churchill acknowledged them all, somewhat recalling Haydon from his involvement with Claymore. Haydon undoubtedly remembered Churchill's name all too well due to his unwarranted presence aboard the *HMS Princess Beatrix,* where he had effectively *snuck aboard* unauthorized.

"Major," Haydon remarked rhetorically, enjoying his steaming tea. "You have the authority to be here this time?"

"That I do, sir," Churchill grinned. He made eye contact with Hambro, recognizing that he had met him somewhere before. He was overcome with a sudden sensation of familiarity.

"Eh, yes, Jack Churchill," Hambro recalled standing from his chair and taking a stride in close to request Churchill's hand for a firm grip. "We've met once before, haven't we?"

"I believe so, sir. Right outside these very doors, six months ago."

"Yes, yes ..." Hambro recollected, quickly returning to his seat. He hinted at Haydon's last glib remark. "Invitation to Claymore or not, if I recall correctly, my reports stated that I have *you* and *Lucky Laycock* to thank for obtaining the rotor wheels from the sinking *Krebs?*"

Churchill nodded modestly.

"Jolly good job, old boy. They were invaluable."

"It was, eh, mostly Lucky's luck, sir," Churchill said self-effacingly, still upstanding while Durnford-Slater found a seat.

"Luck *may* have had something to do with it. It takes more than *luck* to storm a sinking enemy vessel ..." Hambro regarded, shuffling his pack of cigarettes so that one cycled out and he prepared to light it. "Unless you really are *mad.*"

"Madness gets you aboard the sinking Krebs, sir. Luck gets you home the rotor wheels to an Enigma cypher machine ..." Churchill explained vaguely; the hidden connotations behind his sentiment seemed yet to be surmised by the SOE agent, and Hambro simply nodded as he resumed his seated position eyeing the major.

"Don't be modest, Jack," Mountbatten announced over the accord of praise, gesturing a hand at a chair for him to sit beside his CO. "You're a hero. We all know it. Your men all know it. You should be as proud of yourself as your country is of you. Take a seat."

"Many thanks, sir," Churchill pronounced with a warm glow.

"Can I get you a drink, gentlemen?" Mountbatten generously offered prior to seating himself. "Coffee? Tea? ... Brandy?"

"Eh, a Brandy sounds wonderful, thank you," Durnford-Slater replied instantly—he noticed it was what most of the other men, including the commodore, were drinking—and after the morning he had had, he felt as though he could use a nip of something. When Keyes was in office, it was nothing but Whitehead 199 Fine Scotch Whiskey, though it seemed Mountbatten was new-age: this man had a whole selection shelf. The man had gotten carpenters in to install an open bar in the war room, able to accommodate anything to anybody.

"Sure. Major, a drink?"

"Eh, any whiskey, sir?"

Mountbatten's lips puckered as he nodded respectfully at the man's brash choice of morning beverage—and obliged.

Rear Admiral Burrough regarded directly towards Mad Jack. "You *do* realize that it's only just after nine in the morning, Major?"

Churchill responded with wit and a humble nod. "It's five o'clock somewhere, sir."

Mountbatten scoffed jokingly.

Following Jack's throwaway, Rear Admiral Burrough snorted singly and after an extended pause of silence, spoke as he swirled the rich brandy in his snifter glass. "Major *Churchill.* Any relation to the PM?"

Churchill tucked in his chair further and flattened the front of his suit. "That's a negative, sir. I am, however, related to a *Robert* Churchill, aboard the *HMS Exeter.* You may know him as *Buster?*"

Burrough took a moment to swirl and then sip his brandy in a snifter, squinting through the haze of hovering smoke from his cigarette.

During the awkward absence of sound, Churchill added to break any left-over ice, as well as further the description with a tad of humour. "He looks like me, only, less handsome ... balding at the edges ... he can't grow a groom to save his life."

Burrough didn't exactly burst out with laughter, but he did perform an acknowledging nod after Jack's follow-up.

"Yes, *Buster Churchill.* I believe I do know the man. He has recently requested a transfer into the *Fleet Air Arm,* has he not?"

"I believe he has, sir."

"Is he as mad as you?" Burrough questioned with a challenging tenor in his voice. Through the cloud of tobacco mist that hazed beneath the dim poker light in the room and the silence of the observing audience, he judged Churchill's reaction from across the boardroom table.

Churchill bit his tongue before retorting. This question was shaped and delivered with a tone that warranted a challenge, but it could also have been a playful jab if the admiral had read Felix Hardy's publications following the events of *Dunkirk* and their daring escape. Men who read that periodical either wanted a piece of Mad Jack or asked for his autograph, there was no in-between.

He felt the stare of his CO draw across his focus.

Churchill was always a hothead when placed under scrutiny by higher ranking superiors—something both he and Durnford-Slater had never been short of since fighting and winning the Commando/LayForce tug-of-war.

In that instance, he attempted to read the admiral for a tell.

An Oxford-educated first war veteran, Burrough had a reputation built upon concrete-solid respect, and he was just as hard. Even if he had once been a LayForce supporter, which was unlikely due to his role in the navy, surely, he wouldn't hold any ongoing resentment towards Commando—or to a Dunkirk hero.

Churchill instead deflected, choosing not to risk offending his operational superior. He made direct eye contact with Burrough through the tobacco cloud, attempting to gauge the man's intentions like they were each sporting a hand in poker.

His reply was simply put and with a spirited undertone.

"He's even *madder,* sir."

Burrough again snorted a chuff as he tapped his cigarette on the edge of an ash tray. If he was testing the rumoured *Mad Jack*, then Churchill had possibly just passed. He spoke with a genuine manner before bringing the smoke back up to his lips. "I'll be sure to put in a good word."

"I would appreciate that. Thank you, admiral."

Mountbatten asserted his voice once the pleasantries were exchanged and handed Churchill his amber-filled crystal, to which he wordlessly gestured thanks. "Gentleman, we're here today for the preliminary operation briefing for the Måløy Raid, of which there is but one paramount objective from our Prime Minister ... *to give Hitler a black eye.*"

All men in the room watched as the commodore returned to his seat, standing behind it to address them all more focally.

"Colonel, if you may ..."

"Thank you, Commodore," Durnford-Slater stood as Mountbatten sat, and Churchill watched with esteem as his CO took centre stage above his homemade model in the briefing for Commando's next war.

"Gentlemen, I present to you: Operation Archery ..."

'Their destination would be the Nazi-occupied village on Vagsøy Island, Norway. At the risk of history repeating itself in wake of Operation Claymore, this raid was on yet another important fishing town approximately 100 miles north of Bergen. The raid would again take aim at economic targets under the thumb of Nazi Germany, such as shipping and processing plants, however, this time the men of No. 3 Commando would also deliberately seek a fight with a German garrison.

'It was time to see what they were made of—and, this time, with an audience ... the whole nation. Operation Archery was to be one of the first British operations captured on film and faithfully reported back to the people of the United Kingdom via on-site war correspondents and reporters in the field ...'

'Jack could think to recommend none-other than yours truly. Me: Felix Hardy, signing on.'

*1944, September*
*Sachsenhausen Concentration Camp*
*Oranienburg, Germany*

"... I remember the day a representative from the War Office contacted me regarding the available positions for war correspondents," out in the glum natural light of their muddy yard at the Sachsenhausen, Felix Hardy momentarily took the talking stick and expounded due relevance, taking the mantel from Churchill and recalling the history both their past's shared.

Mad Jack was now leaning against one of the boundary fences and oversaw the muddy yard of many raggedy trench coat-wearing, baggy-eyed, pale and sickly POWs at the Sachsenhausen.

Not as brazen towards the temperament of their German hosts and the itchiness of their trigger fingers, Hardy stood a good four feet from the perimeter fence with his notepad.

"In contrast to some of the greens at *Reuters* and *Pathé,* I was a veteran at reporting in the field. Only, prior to then, I had done it of my own accord. I had cut my teeth in France. They sold it hard. I remember your government was overly keen on selling the positives of the war effort ..."

Hands in pockets, Churchill craned his neck as he pondered.

It would not have been abnormal for Whitehall diplomats to want to try and sell positive war activity—especially after the Dunkirk retreat. "Well, it's one thing to tell a soldier he's going overseas to fight a war, let alone get reporters to sign up to go tandem. Usually you lot jumped at the opportunity to report from the front, but this was different. This was an incursion led *by* us *against* the Huns. Not a defensive posture behind a frontline in Europe somewhere; with that typically accompanied some luxuries. This was different. This was *all-in* and *balls-out.*"

"And more money."

"*And more money,*" Churchill agreed. The British war effort was desperate for funds. Gaining the interest of the more prosperous inclined and positive affiliations with the affluent only sold more war bonds. And however disproportionate to the truth they may be within newspapers such as what gets reported in *the Battlefront Gazette,* the stories like what Hardy published about *Dunkirk Jack* did just that and then some.

The two shared a snigger at the ugly truth.

"Yeah, well," Churchill couldn't help but rationalize with a soldier's stance at politics throughout the convolution and arguable discrepancy of the British war machine and her well-oiled parts. This part was particularly black and white. "After all, bullets cost quid, lad. And we needed a lot of them."

Hardy couldn't disagree.

After their short digression, he persisted justified sincerity:

"Well, I signed my ass up, didn't I? Had to be at *Scapa Flow* at dawn on Christmas-fuckin'-Eve. Pack for a cold reception, they said. Thanks again for the colourful reference," the reporter jousted with a black satirical, reminded just how far his humour had strayed since being within the company of Jack Churchill's *Merry Men* of Commando. Palms open towards their present paradise, he pondered. "This job has brought me all I ever wanted in life."

Churchill smirked as Hardy raised his palms, denoting their present status as captured prisoners of war in Germany.

"Oh, well, you're quite welcome, good sir. We at the Sachsenhausen are glad to hear you are enjoying your stay," Jack sold their circumstances sarcastically and with a rather out-of-place enthusiasm. Upstanding within the slink of his vertical barbed-wire hammock, he waved his pocketed palms about the yard and spoke in his best sales pitch. "We have luxury suites and facilities, and many activities to keep you entertained during your stay. The yard for leisure during the sunlight hours, with optional barbed-wire obstacle courses where you may taste test our fine selection of tetanus and fungal infections, relaxing mud-slick facials beneath the murky clouds, or perhaps even a gentle massage from some of the armed guards if you stray too close to the beautiful fence lines. I hear the minefields of an evening are just gorgeous before a sunset scape."

"Do the masseurs give happy endings?" Hardy played.

"Oh, they finish you off, lad, don't you worry," Jack joked, and jeered further. "Haven't heard a single complaint from satisfied customers."

Hardy shook his head to dissipate his grin as Churchill continued. The fact that they still found comedy in what could have been regarded as the worst place in the world was remarkable.

Jack added, "I hear the ones along the eastern guardhouse have the grip of a silverback gorilla. They'll get you stiff as a board one way or another."

Hardy's peepers watered as they pinched closed. The hilarity was all the more sincere given the hurt of their circumstances, and the laughter exhausted him in his malnourished state. Their sense of humour here was as dry as it was dark, and their situation was so fucked up that you had to laugh or cry. They had come to realize this reality.

"Scapa Flow ..." Churchill's mind hung on Hardy's callback. That part of Scotland had been where Commando and all those who were a part of Operation Archery had prepared for the raid, running practice passes and dry runs on the cold shores from the landing crafts. The naval ships all berthed out on the coast, one by one, preparing for transit.

*Preparing for war.*

Churchill's memory realigned where they were up to in his retelling to Hardy, and he reinserted himself back into the timeline.

"About two nights out, it got real. For everyone. I returned home to visit Ros one last time before the mission. It was after a row of busy days practising with the lads ... preparing for our voyage, from which we brave few may never return ... and many didn't ..."

Hardy concurred, bobbing with respect.

*He knew what was coming next.*

'Jack went on to tell me about the last night before Archery, where he returned home to the Dumbarton cottage he shared with his newly wed wife, Rosamund. They enjoyed a romantic dinner. Afterwards, they slow danced to their records, ultimately whisking themselves upstairs early as lovers.

'One of the most important things to remember about the chronicle entailing this Happy New War is that it doesn't just orbit solely around Mad Jack Churchill this time. The camaraderie of Commando is crucial to retain. His Merry Men, the courageous champion commandos of No.3, were not just along for the ride with our titular character for Archery. Outside of the detail regarding his own forays, Jack reiterates that those men were the real heroes present on the shores of Måløy and Vågsøy that fateful day after Boxing Day raid. Alike the many battles to come for Commando, the bravery, valour, and fortitude of these men shan't ever be forgotten, furthermore those who *made the ultimate sacrifice for their country, and sadly never returned. May their battle cries echo for eternity …'*


*1941, December*
*Durnford-Slater Residence*
*Devon, England*


Visiting his hometown *Devon,* John Durnford-Slater had received a warm welcome from his beautiful wife *Gladys,* nicknamed *Dar,* holding their five-year old girl, *Jennifer.*

The man bearing the status of *lieutenant-colonel,* the *fearless first commando* of No.3, was absent in this picturesque evening setting. Here resided a loving father and husband, shown differently in this setting afternoon light as he scooped up his happy, smiling daughter as she was let loose out the front door.

John held her in his arms, cuddling her gently as she playfully removed his green beret and wore it proudly. He climbed the front step, further embracing his beautiful wife of seven years with a kiss as she welcomed him home for the night—this, his final night before the embarkation of another great commando crusade, on which he risked his life for the land along with a great many other brave men.

Tonight would be a special night with his loves, for it could be the last time Durnford-Slater would lay his eyes on his family …


*Drouthy Neebors*
*Largs, Scotland*


On their final night, John Frederick Giles and his younger brother Bruce could be found at a local splash known as *Drouthy Neebors,* soaking a stress-free outing in the nightlife of Main Street.

The two blokes held extensive histories playing rough sports.

JFG was a man of only average height, but what he lacked in height he made up for in physical mass. He was a passionate weightlifter in his spare time, often showing up the No.3 boys in weight but always a source of encouragement for their exercises.

The brothers had both played rugby almost their entire lives, and for JFG, more recently semi-professionally earlier on for the *Clifton Rugby Football Club.* He had quite the reputation of easily flattening any man who stood in his way like a charging juggernaut and, judging by his size, it would not be hard to appreciate just how bloody easily he would manage this.

JFG had received his first commission into the *Gloucestershire Regiment* and had also won the heavyweight boxing championship of the *Army Southern Command*. His experience in the ring was forever etched upon his face in the way of bald patches within both of his eyebrows from slit scarring. He also wore a slightly elongated jawline thanks to multiple degrees of fracturing.

Bruce Giles had taken up boxing after his monstrous brother's legacy run, albeit as a lightweight. As a result, the two now each proudly wore cauliflower ears, scar tissue that would mark their looks for life.

Tonight, these two brothers bonded over a pint, enjoying a quiet laugh before becoming joined by some of the other soldiers who had less significant others or did not have local family. Such commandos by the names of Arthur Komrower and Knocker White. The gents spent time, sung loudly and enjoyed each other's company, in many ways, forming their own family ties ...

Rumour had it, that Komrower had even gotten a handy out back by a sloppy lass from there with a wonky eye named *Sheryl*. He would never live this down amongst the lads.

### Outskirts of the Haylie Reservoir
### Largs, Scotland

That same prolific evening, Dennis O'Flaherty could be found quietly relaxing beneath the stars as they shined in the night sky. A handsome young man, with protruding ears and gleaming hair, forever cemented in place with a tube of pomade.

Naturally a bit of an introvert, he would be spending his final night in solitude, reflecting, drinking. Comfortable.

Wrapped in his many layers, he parked in a discreet location by the outskirts of *The Haylie Reservoir*, located just southeast of Largs, and mounted the hood of his mint *Ford Anglia*.

It may have been cold out, but this zone of seclusion was a favourite pastime of O'Flaherty's. It was a memorable experience shared long ago with his father, since passed of a heart attack, where they would relax and gaze at the stars for hours. Although never divorced, O'Flaherty's father had not had the best relationship with his mother. Although Dennis did not know it back then, he gathered now this was just his dad's way of getting out of the house and away from the missus. Their time spent had left a lasting impression, and it was now a welcome isolation that calmed this soldier's nerves before an engagement.

Probably also like his father had shown him, he enjoyed a carton of smokes and few nips from a bottle of Macallan to himself before eventually making his way back to the lodge and catching up with some of the other lads who had stayed in for the night.

A moment transpired in the tranquillity of reflection, where he wondered if he would be seeing his father again sooner than expected ...

*Dumbarton*
*Dumbarton, Scotland*

The one-eyed Scotsman and veteran *Merry Man* to Mad Jack, George MacWilliam, looked a treat in his service uniform. It was rare the ogre pressed his greens and donned his service ribbons, but tonight he was taking a special lady with whom he had recently rekindled a fizzled prior romance out on the town.

It was humorous to see the brute so nervous ...

After a deep breath and a knock on the door of her Dumbarton billet, a young, curly haired brunette bearing a spectacles patch of her own, evidence of a medical condition resulting in blindness, opened the door. She must have been almost ten years his minor, but the fiery-haired Scot had never felt more in love. And clearly, neither had she.

Their passion was unique and cycloptic.

Between the two of them... they had a pair of eyes.

*A match made in heaven?*

She lurched out, happy to see her man, and embraced him with her skinny twig arms and reeling him near without so much of a word expressed. Their lips locked and the bouquet of flowers MacWilly had bought on the way over landed on the doorstep.

She towed him inside of her small nurse's residence, slamming the door shut. What she apparently hungered for right now wasn't on any menu.

They kissed and fornicated, expressing young love as though it could have been their last chance to feel it. MacWilly had refrained from explaining the details of his trip with the army tomorrow ... the reality was, tonight could have been the last night they would be together ...

*Peel Residence*
*Lanark, Scotland*

An only child, George Peel spent his last night before the mission with his religious family, Scottish mother and Welsh father, at their home in *Lanark*. Funnily, it became revealed that the narrow-nosed commando shared the same facial trait with his dad.

A household of animal lovers, the spoiled family dogs were ecstatic to see him home after many weeks: *Boris* the Beagle and *Dorothy* the Dachshund. Recent newspapers printed cautionary tales of pet owners during the heavily rationed period being fined for giving their pets food intended for human consumption, however that did not stop good egg Peel from procuring some chicken necks at the local butcher who had recently restocked on his way home. The pets loved him for it.

After saying Grace before dinner, helping his mother with the washing up, he assisted with putting his crippling father to bed, who suffered with early onset Parkinson's disease. In a feign tone, George Peel muttered the Lord's Prayer alongside his mother before bidding a farewell and heading back to Largs late at night in preparation for their early morning adventure and march to war.

A perceptive woman, she knew that her son did not share the same religious values as their family did, but Peel's mother implored that he took with him a fob keyring she had picked up at the donation shelter where she volunteered. It featured *Saint Christopher*, the patron saint of travellers, and was a token offering for his safe return from the foray.

Peel accepted the keyring, receiving her many prayers for his safe homecoming from the Nordlys as she watched him leave with stinging eyes and an aching heart—one that both parts yearned for his safe return, as well as overflowed with love for her son, and pride for his duty in the British Army. She could not be prouder.

Peel was a religious man—perhaps by credence of a strict upbringing.

However, something in his adult years had caused him to second-guess that faith. Such was evident later, when sitting on his bed at the Largs base, by the young trooper's apparent aversion to the Holy Bible he held within his fingers, disposing of it into an agape drawer.

He pulled the Saint Christopher keyring from his pocket, placing it atop the book before closing the drawer with resentment.

*Hyde Park Picture House*
*Leeds, England*

After dinner with their parents, R.L. Wills decided to head out and see a late-night film screening with his younger, stunted brother by the name of *Wally,* who rarely got out.

*That Hamilton Woman* was the movie.

It was a romantic flick, and they copped many sideways glances from other patrons upon buying the tickets to the screening at the Hyde Park theatre, with most of the target audience being couples.

Because of his physical hindrance, the extent of his brother's outings was to the local cinema. He saw most film screenings, regardless of the genre. And, to be honest, Wills kind of had a thing for *Vivian Leigh* at the moment anyhow, so there was no disputing the session ... though, it wasn't about the entertainment. It was about the moment.

On what felt like his last night on earth, Wills mostly enjoyed the simple things; watching his sheltered brother laugh and be amused.


*Dalry Town Hall*
*Galloway, Scotland*

Overlooking the calm swells of the *Water of Ken* from their prime position of the *Dalry Town Hall* carpark in their *Crossley Motors* hardtop, Peter Young wore an ear-to-ear smirk as he enfolded into his new love, *Joan Duckworth,* a local Gallovidian.

Joan had been spending the early days of the festive season with her family in Galloway, and so he had travelled to see her. Young's visit was a surprise, where the young commando had informed her of his mission embarkation the following day, and that he could be gone for some time, perhaps even into the new year.

This impulsive romance and resulting seclusion would be the first night the two would overindulge in each other's presence, spending the night in the laid-back seats of that comfortable old Crossley.

*The Sanctuary House Hotel*
*Westminster, London*

Put up at one of the finest hotels in London prior to his departure with the rest of the Combined Operations, Martin Linge was keen to retire to his lodgings following a dinner downstairs in the elegant bistro.

His motives tonight were twofold.

A foreigner in these western lands, Linge was of late more reclusive of enduring the nightlife with the other Norwegian soldiers accompanying him in England. He knew few people, with the majority of his army friends meeting them en route to their objective in Norway.

Additionally, he had a letter to reply to.

The addressee was his son, *Jan.*

At nineteen, he was pursuing an interest in engineering.

Barely stripped out of his uniform attire from the day, Linge wore a grand smile on his mug as he rested on his bed. He had Jan's letter laid out above his own pen and paper, being sure to not miss a single reply to his beloved son, of whom he was exceptionally proud.

He would now take the time to be sure that his son knew this before he potentially lost the chance to ever reply ...

*Hollywood Hotel (Largs Base)*
*Largs, Scotland*

Flying solo like he did most nights was the enigmatic Joe Mills.

Seemingly, this Sergeant had not much going for his social life, although some would come to speculate that he came off the back of a harsh mid-year divorce with a girl in London.

He wanted to get as far away from that old life as possible, hence his ambition to obtain recruitment into one of the most dangerous and exciting special forces known to the Western world: Commando.

Laying in his bunk all alone, Mills tipped back some flask booze, enjoying his own comfort and solitude whilst happily listening to second-hand music from a source in a connecting room.

Also, at home at the Largs base, Algy Forrester spent his night taking a long shower, using up all the hot water whilst mostly everybody was away for the night.

Wearing nothing but a towel, the solid figure now stood before his own reflection in the mirror, tailoring his beautiful moustache with a grooming kit and special beard oil he had procured whilst visiting America. Rumour had it, *Wyatt Earp* had once endorsed the product.

*It suddenly became clear whom Forrester's role model was.*


*Kelburn Castle*
*Largs, Scotland*


Hank Peace was a quiet man.

From his billeting at the Largs base, he ventured downstairs after plucking his furrowing eyebrows in the mirror, finding fellow Kelburn Castle lodgers Eric de la Torre, Owen Dildo Dillon, and old man Slinger Martin in the common space and connecting spaces. George Peel heard their commotion later in the night and joined also.

They shot some solicitated snooker in Lord Glasgow's sports-decorated game room, had many beers, and told some war stories; spoke about current affairs; about women.

Durnford-Slater's personal old friend and newcomer to No.3, Charley Head may have been a bit of a snob regarding fraternizing with the subordinates, however, he too was on his own tonight at the castle. After a few noisy hours, Head joined them in the games room, eventually accepting a warm lager and a sit-down, and conclusively, a laugh with the lads.

Bonds formed.

Head opened up the most since they had known the bloke, and they all got to better know one of the fine leaders they would be following into battle tomorrow, and the coming months ...


*Churchill Residence*
*Dumbarton, Scotland*


In the middle of the night, head resting deep within the cushion of a goose-down pillow, the sterling stare of Jack Churchill opened from slumber.

Unlike the haunts of most military men, it was not the horrific stress and memories of war which caused him to awaken, but rather a certain craving of purpose; a call to arms. The impending sensation dwelled within the forefront of his mind, and he couldn't rest soundly until a certain task had been completed.

*He was finally going back to war ...*

A genuine grin formed beneath his pencil moustache.

One of sincere happiness.

Unable to return to sleep, Churchill whisked the blankets off and slinked out of bed, careful not to disturb his wife as she slept deeply in the double bed beside him. He quietly headed downstairs in their two-bedroom cottage in Dumbarton, judging by the light bleeding through the edges of the drawn curtains and the faint chirping of birdsong, it was dawn.

Once down, he rounded the polished timber balustrade of the staircase, into the open living room and connected kitchenette, Churchill surveyed the tranquil space. The fireplace still glowed with embers from the night prior, a romantic farewell for he and his lady.

His attention homed, blinking about the fireplace and searching for the source of what appeared to be falling grains of dirt and ash from within the chimney stack. Almost preordaining any reaction the soldier could have issued given this advance, a black leather of someone's boot suddenly materialized amidst the cloud of floating ash.

The sight caused Churchill to startle.

Another boot descended, stabilizing whoever was within the crawlspace, and it was then Churchill noticed the white fluffy hemming of the intruder's *Coca-Cola* red pants.

Churchill reared up another step as the figure quickly hooked beneath the mouth of the fireplace, fully presenting the obese figure of none other than *Saint Nicolas* himself.

*It wasn't Santa Claus ...*

*It was Sloan MacLeòid!*

"Sir?" Churchill gasped.

"*Yoo expectin' someone else, laddie?*" spoke MacLeòid in his *Glasgow* patter, heaving the Santa sack on the rug like he was dropping anchor. He had gone all out for this deception on his haunt. "*Thus tyme, I've come merely to wish yoo a Merry Christmas ... und a Happy New War.*"

# 3

# *A Happy New War*

*1941, December*
*17th Destroyer Flotilla*
*Norwegian Sea*

Beneath a stormy afternoon sky, powerful waves thrashed loudly against the bow of the cluster of travelling Royal Navy warships as they thrust across the winter tides of the Norwegian Sea.

A newfangled titanic fleet, the seven warships of the *17th Destroyer Flotilla* enlisted by the admiralty were currently en route to the Nordic destination, pending the valiant Commando operation.

From the bridges to the bows of the ships, visibility was nil to zero.

The dark grey metal of the ships was layered in hoarfrost and rime, designed to bare constant weathering assault by the vapour of salt spray from the ocean.

The weather and temperature in this location of the globe given the time of year was practically the embodiment of hell on earth, freezing over. In conjunction with the battering equilibrium of the tide causing the 3,000-tonne warship traveling at 24-knots to rock almost forty degrees off her horizontal axis, it was nature's reminder that no mortal man was supposed to survive these far northern tides.

For this operation, the landing force would consist of over 500 commandos, with nearly the entirety of No.3 Commando supported by two Troop units from their brother brigade, No.2 Commando, as well as a detachment of Norwegians from the NOR.I.C.1 led by Kaptein Linge—most of whom had been involved with the previous Lofoten Islands raid last March, so they were only too familiar with the type of raid Britain had in store.

Prior to boarding their LC *(Landing Crafts: the new abbreviation for the USA-loaned Higgins boats)* vessels for the raid, the ground troops were spread across the two carrier ships: the *HMS Prince Charles* and the *HMS Prince Leopold.* These two ships were presently accompanied across the seas by a formidable flotilla of warships consisting of three O-class destroyers: the *HMS Oribi,* the *HMS Onslow,* and the *HMS Offa,* all carrying four 4-inch armaments for sea-to-land artillery support for the operation, as well as various anti-air cannons for deterrence and protection against the enemy in the skies.

The flotilla was led by Hunt-class destroyers the *HMS Chiddingfold* and the *HMS Kenya:* a 31-knot, 6-inch gun cruiser, that would also serve as the headquarters vessel during the operation. Under the command of Brigadier Haydon, the Kenya was currently on-point in their arrow-head formation across the ocean, upon their four-day voyage which had disembarked on Christmas Eve from Scapa Flow with a brief stopover in *Sullom Voe* in the *Shetland Islands.* Delay had ensued as a force-8 gale bared bleakly on the dark northern horizon ahead. As a result, they were forced to stay a day off Sullom Voe until the storm diminished, and all hands were called on deck to pump more than 100 tons of seawater out of the vitals of the Prince Charles.

With clearing skies, the flotilla finally left port at Sullom Voe, traversing northerly before arcing on a downward approach towards Norway from the Arctic Ocean. This was a similar route to which they had taken for Claymore to further avoid detection by the enemy. They risked a less acute angle of travel in the interest of making lost time.

Flanked and transported with the arduous naval escort and maritime support for Commando's big raid, the COHQ and Durnford-Slater's operational planning also made provision for coordinated air cover. Perhaps for the first time, with sea, land, and air support, Archery would truly be a *combined operation.*

The official objective: *to give Hitler a black eye.*

A militaristic interpretation: the key targets were enemy strongholds and munition stows located on the lower half of the *Island of Vågsøy,* currently ensnared by Nazi occupation and ascendancy dictated by the arm of the *181st Infantry Division, Wehrmacht,* under the command of *Lieutenant-General Kurt Woytasch.*

These once civilian-owned and -operated processing establishments were contributing vitally to the German war machine across occupied Europe, now more so than ever since the loss of the facilities along the Lofoten Islands earlier in the year. With the enemy depending on this port of manufacturing, Operation Archery had inadvertently become a linchpin against Nazi Germany.

In conclusion, other than merely liberating the Norwegian people in Nazi-occupied areas, the overall objectives were to destroy the factories entirely, rendering them useless and, by extension, freeing the lands of any possible regression. The facilities processing the manufacture of kerosene and coal oil across the island were inadvertently responsible for the production of glycerine used for explosives and munitions manufacturing, easily transported via ship to the enemy fronts, specifically the Arctic Russian front.

Subsequently, there existed a high-tech telephone exchange in *Måløy* which also required detonating by Commando, as well as various military installations spread throughout in need of vanquishing—particularly in the town of the main commune, *South Vågsøy*. This was inclusive of a barracks located in a neighbouring village to Måløy called *Holvik*.

In addition, due to intelligence offered to the War Office by their friends in the SOE, there was also rumoured to be an updated Enigma codebook somewhere on the island, used to communicate with assorted HQs across Germany and through to Berlin. Exclusively via Commodore Hambro, Durnford-Slater and Churchill had become privy to this information during their briefing at Whitehall, but it was not information fed down the pipeline for obvious secrecy reasons. Obtaining such enemy intelligence was therefore to be considered entirely a secondary objective, and only to be pursued on a tangent if evidence supported its definitive existence on the day.

The officers in charge reminded their men of the events of the Lofoten Raid, and how their utilization of a surprise attack encountered little to no resistance. Lieutenant-Colonel Durnford-Slater personally advised Commando that the Germans were fast learners; that they were to expect a fight this time around. The *HMS Tuna*, a navy submarine performing reconnaissance, reported in to apprise them of this, having spotted high numbers of armed infantry, machine gun sentries, and anti-air nests across the island. They even believed to have spotted an armoured tank patrolling on the island—however, this was unlikely, as the Germans would have struggled bringing something as cumbersome as a tank this far north. The rumours of such an armoured beast lurking the island were quickly dismissed. There were two enemy-occupied airfields within range at *Herdla* and *Stavanger* that could respond to an attack with air support within minutes—hence their need for RAF support for this mission.

An important en route mission brief was conducted aboard the Kenya one day prior to the action—Boxing Day—which the higher-ranking officers and Troop leaders attended. It was then that some of these men first learned of their destination, operation time, and their objectives for Operation Archery, already on their way to their destiny. Prior to this, officers beneath Durnford-Slater and Churchill knew only of their operational motive, although some of the men could deduce it would be somewhere beneath where the Nordlys radiate.

As of even Boxing Day, non-commissioned officers and the troops of Commando beneath Troop leaders were still yet to be advised of their duties for the raid. Final individual mission briefings were planned to be attained later in the day, prior to their arrival and landings at 0700-hours the subsequent day, December 27—their *day of days.*

Needless to say, Commando were going to decimate the 181st Infantry Division and burn their positions at Vågsøy and Måløy to the ground. They would capture or eliminate any and all hostile forces they encountered with extreme prejudice, whether that be *armed boche, quisling cunt,* or if he stood in their way, jolly ol' Saint Nic himself on his return flight to the North Pole.

Give Hitler a black eye?

*He's gonna get two!*

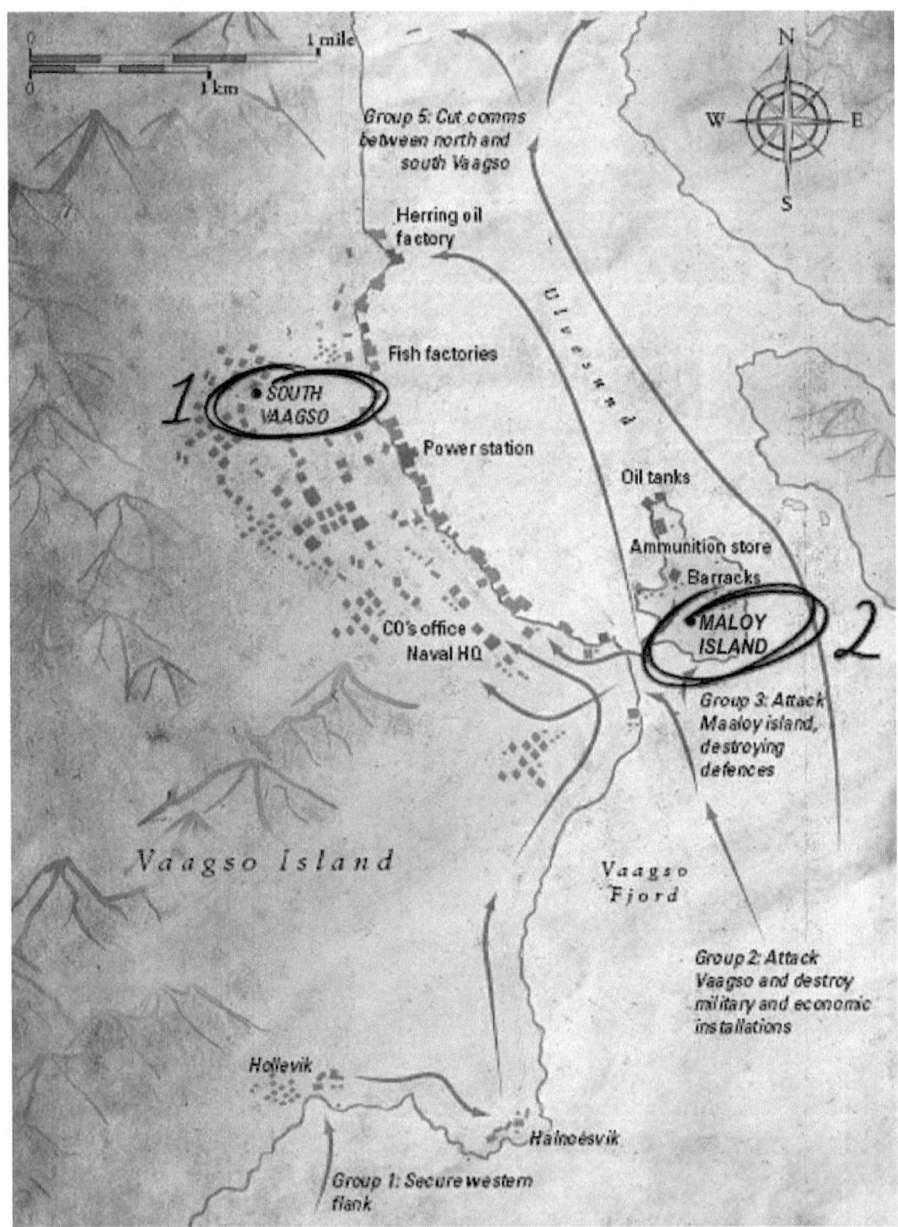

**'OPERATION ARCHERY'**
Commando Raid, Vågsøy and Måløy Islands, 1941

For the raid, there were *five vital objectives* over *two main towns*.

The combined landing forces had therefore been segmented into five units, to be commanded by five leaders from No.3 and No.2 Commando, respectively.

*1) The South Vågsøy groups (Durnford-Slater command):*

*Group 2* consisted of the largest portion of ground troops, commanded by Lieutenant-Colonel Durnford-Slater personally. This was approximately 200 Commandos across four units, known as *'Troops'*. *One Troop* (led by Captain Bradley, compiled mostly of *'distant relative'* No.2 Commando members), *Two Troop* (Lieutenant Komrower), *Three Troop* (Captain JFG) and *Four Troop* (Captain Forrester; with Kaptein Martin Linge attached, leading the Norwegian section), would assault various designated targets throughout the town of South Vågsøy. Disembarking from the Prince Charles, Group 2 would land at two locations; a southern and northern point, where they would each converge into the middle of the town. The Troops would push onto the shores in their LCs, utilizing a timed deployment of RAF smokescreen for concealment, charging the icy beaches.

Their amphibious landing and subsequent ground assault would undoubtedly result in dangerous street fighting in the urban and close-quarters environments of the occupied Norwegian town. There was rumoured to be an enemy headquarters in a centralized, multistorey guesthouse known as the *Ulvesund Hotel;* one of the tallest structures on the island, located in the thick of it and likely heavily defended. The ground assault objectives were the annihilation or capture of the remaining enemy forces present in town, all-encompassing the hotel and warehouse district. Demolition objectives along the way were *i)* the power station located along the harbour, *ii)* the fish factories, and *iii)* the kerosene and coal oil manufacturing factories located by the docks.

*Group 5* would be headed by *Captain Birney.* Once the initial assault was well underway and, principally, after the FlaK-88 cannons were destroyed on Måløy Island (a Group 3 objective) to ensure their safe approach, this smaller unit would pass by the coastal villages on the destroyer Oribi, sailing north along the *Ulvesund Fyr* passage. They would land ashore, gain access to, and block the main and only road that connected South Vågsøy from the neighbouring townships in the municipality of the rest of Vågsøy island to the north, denying entry by any potential enemy reinforcements that could be stationed at *Rødberg* or further beyond. They would also contain or eliminate any attempted exodus from the South Vågsøy action.

*2) The Måløy Island groups (Churchill command):*

*Group 3* would be led by Second-in-Command Major Churchill himself. After severe shelling by the navy on hostile island targets had been conducted, they would mop up any of the German garrison remaining on the remote and isolated Måløy Island (a small, connected island just off the coast of *South Vågsøy*). Churchill would command over 100 men, comprising of *Five Troop* (commanded by Lieutenant Peace), and *Six Troop* (Captain Young) in LC landing parties berthed from the carrier Prince Leopold. The two Troops would spearhead what enemy remained on Måløy, instructed to take prisoner of, if not shoot to kill, all who posed a threat. Concurrently, they would accomplish their demolition objectives of *i)* the tall wireless tower the enemy used for all communications off Vågsøy Island, *ii)* the ammunition storage bunker, *iii)* the oil storage on the rear of the island, and *iv)* the numerous FlaK-88 cannon turrets facing the fjord, of which intelligence provided by the Tuna suggested a total of four. Once these tasks were complete, Group 3 would remain on Måløy Island as a reserve for Group 2 on the main island.

*Group 1,* led by *Lieutenant Clement,* had the mission to take the enemy barracks at the small village of Holvik, located along the south coast from South Vågsøy and Måløy Island respectively. They would then hold and form a reserve while Groups 2 and 3 performed their ground objectives upland.

*The reserve group (Haydon primary command):*

*Group 4,* led by *Captain Hooper* and the well-respected Canadian-born veteran warfighter, and the new spear of the even newer No.2 Commando, *Lieutenant Graeme Black.* They would endure the raid as a floating reserve aboard the Kenya and remain geared and prepared to be set to purpose by any means *(back-up, support, ammunition running, prisoner escort).* He and his 100 men would remain at an organized and vigilant post, able to be deployed at a moment's notice.

*1941, December 26*
*HMS Prince Leopold*
*Norwegian Sea*

After what felt like an eternity in thrashing waves and ill-tempered sea storms, the weather transformed into something hospitable the following day. If it maintained, it would give those aboard the flotilla a day's rest before the day of days.

Under the clear skies and the brisk sea air on Boxing Day morning, Scottish folk music from the bagpipes purred and skirled loudly aboard the lower open deck of sailing transport ship the Prince Leopold whilst she cruised across the Norwegian Sea, still in the aloof passage formation of the traversing 17th Destroyer Flotilla. Those awake and present for the better weather festivities aboard the outer deck happily clapped along in rhythm and even danced about, linking arms and slapping their palms in a small pit that formed out before a man blowing on the pipes—a splendid sea air show for all those watching.

Major Jack Churchill was undoubtedly the man responsible for the bellow of the bagpipes. Jack's set were a 1931 *Robertson of Edinburgh*, contained in a green and black crisscross-striped tartan bag, and then housed within a khaki haversack. They were of a custom constructed comprised of African blackwood, engraved and hallmarked full silver. The set was arguably too heavy to take to war ... but that hadn't stopped Mad Jack so far.

Churchill was putting on a demonstration for the press reporter and his cameraman present from *Associated British-Pathé*, as part of the British Military war correspondence initiative, which consisted of a handful of daring reporters from several mainstream media firms permitted aboard for the operation, risking their lives to record footage to document for all prosperity.

From Pathé was popular press reporter *William Mericle,* a high-profile, well-respected connoisseur columnist dubbed on film and radio as *the Miracle Man.* His presence onboard their operation to the north had gotten a lot of the gents all rather starstruck. Whatever footage he and his cameraman recorded would be sent home and edited by *Eugene W. Castle*, primarily of *Castle Films*, and later broadcast across the country. The captured footage would be instilled in the archives of history forevermore.

And today, the men aboard finally had their chance to not only be interviewed or be captured on film by Mericle's crew but get the chance to meet the pretentious Miracle Man, himself. Thankfully, the weather was holding out for them to gain some great material aboard the deck as their flotilla voyaged in the open air.

Emerging from around a deck corner, more rugged up than most of the commandos singing and dancing along to the medley tune, was small-time American journalist, Felix Hardy. He was also present for Archery, representing his British-based paper *the Battlefront Gazette*. He was five-five with dark features and a defined jawline, and still pale in the face from almost two whole days of below-deck misery due to severe sea sickness. The bags under his eyes hinted that last night's rest had been as bad as the previous. If he didn't shape up soon, this foreign correspondent would be covering the raid distantly and from the sick bay.

Intending to get some fresh air, he had surfaced for the first time in a long time—and just in time to be blasted by Scottish folk music.

Too sick to show his envious stare upon the Pathé pressman at this moment, he silently lent against a pole nearby some soldiers as they bared big smiles and starry eyes of enjoyment befalling Churchill's pipes. Most of the men of the navy and army had long since gotten their sea legs and, although seasickness wasn't unheard of by the men of Commando, the turbulence of the sea no longer bothered the majority.

The pitch of the Scottish instrument finished up and Churchill communicated with the gentleman reporter. Beneath his green beret and below his freshly trimmed pencil moustache, he was all smiles and handshakes with Mericle before he left the spotlight along with his doodlesack. Mericle had all but promised to feature Churchill in his footage of the voyage, referring to him as many of the younger Commandos did as *'The Mad Major'*.

When a swarm of young soldiers in search for their fifteen minutes of fame enclosed around Mericle and his cameraman for some further publicity shots, Churchill concentrated on the man in the background, fading from the glow of that spotlight. He approached his friend Felix Hardy.

"How are you feeling?" Churchill asked over the volume of cheering and laughter as he holstered the blowstick of his hanging bagpipes.

"Next question ..." Hardy articulated flatly. The poor chap never drifted too far from the railing along the edge of the boat, just in case he felt the need to heave once again.

"I went to find you yesterday to wish you a Merry Christmas, but I was told you were remaining in your bunk with a bucket?"

The ghost-faced Hardy shook his head with a hesitant smile. "I don't know how you lot do it. I've been a nonstop tap ever since I got onboard this god-damned ship."

"Blast, I had gotten you a present and everything ..."

Hardy smirked at Churchill as though it were a likely tease.

"Yeah, right."

After a second, Churchill leant over the rail along with his American friend, who had his face down over the edge. It wasn't that he needed to spew at the minute, but he now lived in a forever cautionary state due to the wicked nausea. Like many other commandos, Churchill had followed a home remedy of seasickness: a combination of beer, cheese, and pickled onions. Although the cure seemed to work, most men found it more distasteful than the illness itself.

Jack planted a soft pat across his shoulder and nodded respectfully to a lad as he passed behind them, headed for the ruckus at the front end of the boat with the reporters and the cameras.

"And then there is this," Hardy mumbled, casting a gleam towards the crowd of excited troops on the bow. There was such a big turnout since word had gotten around that the Pathé team were doing interview scoops that men were seated along the upper deck with their legs dangling over the edges, even just to get a glimpse of the media gathering.

Churchill's eyeline pursued Hardy's enviousness.

"The British Army has entrusted me with a duty. I am the first official foreign war correspondent to be employed, and I can't even do my job properly. Not in this state."

"Nonsense," Churchill regarded in attempt to cheer up his friend. "I've seen you do your job under worse circumstances than these. I'd like to see those bellends perform while they're being shot at on the back of a motorcycle blitzing our way out of enemy lines in France."

Hardy scoffed, recalling their escapades in Dunkirk.

"The Miracle Man is great, sure, but there's a reason I recommended for *you* to report Archery."

"Well, between this asshole and the other asshole onboard the other ship from Reuters, the story thus far has pretty much all been covered. And I got diddly-squat for my paper."

Churchill paused for a moment, allowing for Hardy to feel even more sorry for himself. It was understandable, and he could tell his friend was as blue about the situation as he was green around the gills.

"*The story* has barely even begun, lad. We haven't even started the mission yet—"

"Jack, I can't even afford a gun-cam like what they got! They're using equipment that costs what I currently make in a year! They're recording both picture and sound, *simultaneously,* and *live.* The *Reuters Newspapers Agency* guys over on the other boat have *two* cameras for Christ's sake!"

Hardy dipped in a frustrating gesture, referring to their equipment: portable film cameras, shaped on a pistol-like mount for grip and portability. They captured pristine black and white video as well as mono audio while Hardy had a still-image camera dangling on a strap around his neck and portable office stationery folded in his breast pocket.

"And then there's little old me: I've got this old piece of garbage and my trusty pencil and notepad."

"It's not all about the tools, lad," Churchill remarked—Hardy may not have caught the reference to its fullest extent, but it was an allusion to Jack's own choice of weaponry heading into a war, which would undoubtedly be his bow and arrows and sword. "It's about the results."

"Yeah, well, I think they will have me beat in this battlefield. All the content is gonna be soaked up by those cameras before I can even finish a paragraph."

Churchill bobbled his head along with his thoughts.

"What?" Hardy questioned, noticing his throwaway gesture.

"What if I gave you something Pathé and Reuters won't get ...?" he enticed.

With his interest suddenly perked, Hardy revolved.

"Oh? Do go on."

Churchill winked. "You might want to write this down ..."

Jack had intended to give his writer the truth on the chinwag mystery of No.12 Commando's involvement in all of this, considering they weren't on the guest list to the Archery party, but all soldiers involved in their raid saw them preparing to leave port around the same time in Scapa Flow. In fact, No.12 and their own naval armada had mounted a secret raid code named *Operation Anklet* which would take place in the Lofoten Islands approximately an hour or so before Archery. It was to be a diversionary raid, predestined to draw away any German naval and air forces to further guarantee the success of Operation Archery.

"Eh," Hardy retrieved his notepad from one of the many inner pockets of his overcoat with his fingerless gloves and struggled to find his pencil nub. While Churchill waited, Hardy nervously found the lead pencil and noticed it was blunt, and so he made him wait longer whilst he searched through his pockets again for his tiny portable pencil sharpener. "Sorry... just a second..."

Churchill's face drained flat while he waited.

This enormous mouthful of hot gossip he had reserved exclusively for Hardy's paper just waited behind a pair of closed lips.

Hardy found his trusty metal pencil sharpener and leant over the edge to let fall the shavings. The air was cold. So cold, his fingers struggled to manoeuvre his pencil into the sharpening slot and the twisting finesse required seemed almost jittery.

He manually *twisted, twisted,* and *twisted.*

The shavings dropped off and sailed into the salty overboard air. One of the shavings even travelled downwind and got caught upon Churchill's attire. He flicked it clear with an awkward *don't-mention-it* demeanour.

Hardy pocketed his sharpener, organizing his pencil in favour of taking down these important notes, only, as he touched tip to paper, the fresh lead tip broke.

Under Churchill's unimpressed eyes, Hardy anxiously searched again for his pencil sharpener, eventually fumbling it and dropping the metal piece to the deck wood at their feet.

He snickered nervously and squatted down to collect it, almost bumping his rearend into a passing soldier in doing so, who in his already worsened state, almost toppled over before retrieving the possession under Churchill's patient gaze and returning to standing height.

Once up, he sharpened the pencil again quickly.

Again, he manually *twisted, twisted,* and *twisted.*

Finally done, he stowed the sharpener in his pocket before bringing his writing hand back around to his notepad, ready to—

*He fumbled the pencil.*

The two men watched as it dropped and sailed overboard, casting a hollow ligneous *ding* against the outer railing of the ship before it faded from view overboard, disappearing into the wind current and passing blue ocean far below the travelling ship. Gone forever.

Without words, Hardy looked up. Faced Churchill.

Blankly, Churchill stared back.

Hardy blinked.

*The silence was deafening.*

"I'll ... just, um ... go and get another one from—"

"Felix."

"—my bags."

"Felix!"

Hardy paused in his defeated state.

His eyeline lowered onto what Churchill was holding extended in his possession. It was a small parcel gift, enfolded in Christmas-themed tawny wrapping paper and bound with a ribbon.

"Merry Christmas," Churchill added warmly, making good on his previous comment about having bought Hardy a gift.

Hardy's eyes widened and his brow lifted.

He hadn't actually thought Churchill had gotten him a present as he had said earlier, genuinely considering Jack to be up to his usual prankster self.

After an elongated moment, Hardy took the gift and unwrapped it, unveiling a rectangular box with a closed sliding lid. He opened it to reveal a fancy ink pen. Personally, he preferred not to rely on the new-age ink pens, as they were prone to leaking when stored in pockets, but for this he'd make an exception—plus, it had some sort of a twist-cap fitted.

"It's a pen knife," Churchill informed as Hardy removed it from the box, tucking it and the wrapper under his arm in order to remove the pen's cap.

There was a hint of confusion as beneath the lid that Hardy removed was an actual pen tip, used for writing in ink. Black liquid ink was visible on the tip.

"... that is *also* a pen," Churchill added with a grin.

Hardy quickly discovered that hidden under the opposite end of the pen, under a twist-cap that opened in a counterclockwise fashion, was a two-inch double-edged compact blade.

"*Whoa* ..." he remarked under his breath, checking it out.

"Thought it might come in handy one day, given your knack for danger and imperilment," Jack insinuated, given their adventurous past and perils, thus perhaps one day needing a hidden knife to escape endangerment.

"Like, right now?" Hardy smiled—a real smile, the first since he had left port in Scotland and come down with the sickness.

Arranging himself and his notepad, Hardy reasserted the cap and fidgeted the pen around so that he could use its non-business end.

Lastly, he declared to Churchill, salivating for the story: "O.K. go."

*1941, December 26*
*HMS Prince Charles*
*Norwegian Sea, Norway*

The armada of ships travelling towards Norway continued on their way through the clear night sky, venturing beneath the emerald green glow of the cosmic northern lights.

At present, their voyage was on track for their scheduled deadline in reaching the *Vågsfjorden:* the crystal-clear bay surrounding the Vågsøy and Måløy Islands and the operational position for the naval vessels during Operation Archery.

Aboard the interior of the Prince Charles carrier ship, the men predominantly under Colonel Durnford-Slater's portion of command for the operation convened in a meeting before their evening dinner in the large below-deck mess hall. Although this was mostly Group 2 men, Group 5 were also aboard prior to their exchange onto the Oribi.

The assembly was formal and well-ordered with their proceedings.

Respectful silence was observed while their CO finished addressing them all at their seats and tables from the rear of the metal-walled room by the ship's kitchenette.

Lieutenants Charley Head and Dennis O'Flaherty stood by Durnford-Slater's side, with Head acting as second-in-command of Group 2 and the overall South Vågsøy portion of the raid.

Beneath their command, they had such leaders as Captains JFG and Algy Forrester (and his enormous moustache), and Lieutenant Arthur Komrower. Also found present was the eyepatch-wearing Scotsman Sergeant MacWilly, who would later be parting for the Oribi as a part of Group 5 to act upon their tangent objective tomorrow.

Present from Durnford-Slater's Group 2 north assault team of the raid, One Troop, was Captain Bill Bradley and his second-in-command, *Sergeant Ramsey,* both good additions from No.2 Commando. They would be escorting the demolition party members from No.6 Commando—which included the particular crooked nose of a familiar face to those veterans of No.3, one Sergeant A.J. Cork.

Until now, the former LayForce loyalist, Lister-right-wing, and ex-No.3 Commando, had flown under the radar to any recurrent members of Commando. Due to his questionable off-beat actions in the past during Operation Claymore, the man had basically become black-listed from ever being involved with No.3 again—his assignment for Archery as a part of No.6 demo had clearly been an unexpected oversight. His expulsion had slipped through the cracks.

Although Jack Churchill had not gone into detail about what exactly had happened between him and Cork six months ago causing his sudden ejection—probably to save the man a court marshal and jail time, and therefore ruining his life—the Merry Men of No.3 had since all become aware of his disloyalty and treachery through whispers and scuttlebutt. Narrowly surviving the court marshal and possible imprisonment for his disloyal actions in the Lofoten Islands, Cork had been demoted, docked pay, and even sent to another section within the outskirts of Commando—a demolitions party, which had just so happened to be rostered to accompany No.3 for Operation Archery.

In the crowd of assembling commandos, MacWilly stood out.

The one-eyed Commando carried the enormous Mk.II Lewis machine gun single-handed up by his shoulder. The machine gun had a 97-round disc magazine mounted upon the top of the receiver which made the design unique and distinguishable. The machine gun wasn't typically used by Commando, due to its size, weight, and cumbersomeness. It had a thick and long tubular cooling shroud that extended twenty-seven inches and four-point-five bore—not to mention it was heavy as fuck. However, not for this Scotsman, who was built like a brick shithouse and could muscle the weight for the superior firepower.

In true enigmatic-form, MacWilly had named the gun: *Louise.*

The pouch carrier for the weapon's circular pan mags were housed at the front, worn in a belt over the neck like a saddlebag. Arguably, they resembled a pair of titties.

The kitted-out MacWilly recognized Cork's stupid gonzo nose in the crowd and approached the distinguishable presence through the commando gathering with an expression beholding much bewilderment. His remaining eye shot barbs through Cork's sinister-shaped brows.

"*Oi! What tha fuck are yoo doin' 'ere, eh?!*" he questioned antagonistically as he approached, cutting a beeline through the crowd. Another man from No.6 who was clearly unaware of Cork's past dealings with No.3 by the name of *Johnnie Dowling* strafed briskly to support their newcomer demo comrade.

From One Troop, Sergeant Ramsey pushed his way into the crowd of soldiers, placing a hand upon the fiery MacWilly in the interest of preventing a sudden blue in the sea of green fatigues and charged testosterone.

He remarked calmly. "Sergeant, what's the beef?"

Cork eyed MacWilly coquettishly, noticeably a little tense in the target zone of the big red haired, one-eyed Scotsman. He knew him from his time spent in No.3 as well as that he was a good friend of Jack Churchill and undoubtedly had his back no matter what.

Coming to his rescue, Cork's bald friend with an underbite aided supportingly, "Oi, what you mean?"

"I said, what the *fuck* are yoo doin' 'ere? In that uniform?!" MacWilly aggressively grilled, allowing for Ramsey and another man from No.2 to hold him back for now—but this flame-haired Scot was renowned for his sweltering brashness, and he had his sights clearly set on Cork for some reason unbeknownst to those of No.2 and No.6 Commando.

"Sod off, Sergeant! I'm authorized to be here!" almost on the backfoot, Cork ultimately argued.

"*Authorized?* Yoo should be in a farken pit, ye dumb dog!"

"Oi!" Dowling guarded, becoming defensive, pressing a hand briefly against MacWilly's staunch and, in turn, touching one of the two hanging drum pouches on his chest. He recoiled like he'd accidentally touched a broad's boob and glanced down. "What the fuck are these anyhow, mate. Proper pair of over-the-shoulder-boulder-holders, eh?"

Dowling cheekily pinched the brass button of the closed eyelet, pinching it like a nipple.

"Aye?!" MacWilly boiled—his cycloptic eye locking onto Dowling for an instance, and he confronted him to a buff.

This escalation also needed defusing.

"Come on, lad!" Ramsey remarked, patting MacWilly on his shoulder and trying to steer him back into the crowd, facing forwards and towards Colonel Durnford-Slater who was centre stage. And he was right. No matter their quarrel, they were all here for the same reason today— regardless of past transgressions, whatever they should be.

Dowling disarmed further, "Yeah, let's keep some of the fight for the enemy, eh?"

MacWilly seemed to allow the peace—at least for now, and he allowed for his blokes to fend him off the topic. He raised a fist and pointed at Cork. "You just stay the fuck away from me and my boys, yoo hear? Yoo an yoor lil' boyfriend, aye?"

Ramsey calmed again. "Come on."

"And yoo, Sergeant," MacWilly explosively remarked at Ramsey—a man in cahoots with the accused. "I'd watch yoor back if I were yoo! Yoo might find a wee knife in it!"

"That's enough, Sergeant! Come on!"

No.3 regulars that were visible in the crowd and also overhearing the ruckus were Corporal Knocker White, expert marksman Dildo Dillon, newcomer troopers Peel, radioman de la Torre, as well as unit doctor Sorry Corry. The men all recognized Sergeant Cork's uninvited resurgence, noticing that he was with them aboard the Prince Charles and headed for Vågsøy. Those who knew wondered if Mad Jack knew that the man who betrayed him out in the field was onboard. His presence could cause waves bigger than those felt over the last few days in the Norwegian Sea.

To the left, the freshly shaven Kaptein Martin Linge and his dozen trained soldiers of the NOR.I.C.1 were also present for the audible dispute. The confrontation in the below deck hall had provoked quite the scene.

Right before their colonel could address the men in the hold, Komrower noticed Linge and his Norwegian soldiers.

"Pfft," he huffed laying his eyes upon them. "Thank God the cavalry is here, eh?" Komrower muttered with a disrespectful undertone to a soldier by his flank. His ongoing contemptuousness towards the Norwegians had been prevalent ever since their last operation together, when the fallout from a social situation had caused him to see their nationality in another light. He had voiced his opinion about Linge being a show pony unable to back his horse—then again, perhaps it was an instinctual animosity existent between the two prettiest boys of the operation. Ever since Komrower had learned that Linge used to star in popular films before the war, adding to his glowing social aura amongst the men, he disliked him even worse.

Just then, Linge's eye caught Komrower's.

He offered him a genuine show of respect, bowing his head.

Expressionless, Komrower just looked away.

*The assembly commenced ...*

Colonel Durnford-Slater announced to them all:

"... *Gentlemen*, the time for fun and games whilst we've been en route to our mission, is over. We reach our destination during the night, with an oh-four-hundred reveille for a top-secret, predawn raid on the Island of Vågsøy. As your COs have undoubtedly stressed, our previous raids in the north were seen as cake walks compared to this. That is why I want to put upon you an operational mandate for this mission, and that is *no unnecessary risks.* Now that's a directive that comes from *Commodore Mountbatten,* himself. We have the numbers. We have the firepower superiority. The enemy will have strengthened their defences, and we are expecting a fight—the fight, that you all have been looking for!"

The men cheered.

"Training for!"

They praised again, bashing on cutlery and clapping their hands.

Durnford-Slater allowed for the men to settle before he continued. "... a fight, I have no doubt, that we will win, as Commando does not know how to fail. Once we're done with tea, I expect lights to be out by twenty-two-hundred-hours for some decent rest to be procured. It is going to be a long day tomorrow ... I assume Major Churchill's team aboard the Prince Leopold are conducting the same formalities ..."

*HMS Prince Leopold*
*Norwegian Sea*

The mess hall of the Prince Leopold was practically a rowdy pub.

The atmosphere was lively and with music blaring. Soldiers were laughing, shouting, chanting rhymes, and singing loudly, enjoying their meals and breaking bread with one another under the most uplifting celebratory standards. They bashed together their mugs of juice and cared little for the overspill.

The career ambitious and recently promoted Captain Peter *Young Young* was amidst the crowd, wielding a smile as he sternly made certain his men did not stray too far out of line. He very much did not adore the ideals of Jack Churchill's unfettered pre-celebratory festivities, among other things. To say he had nothing but respect for his major would be propaganda at best, and like a couple of others within the No.3 ranks, he believed that the need for an advertising show pony promoting Commando was long passed. It was time for resolve now. With a similar military career and operational history as Mad Jack, even to himself, Young sometimes remembered not to confuse any admiration with jealousy.

In short, he may not have preferred Churchill's management style ... but, all the same, he would not hesitate to take a bullet for his brother.

Amongst the crowds of officers and NCOs alike, were Lieutenants Hank Peace, Wills, and JFG's younger brother, Bruce Giles, all enjoying the same chaotic merriment.

Major Jack Churchill wandered through the crowds of his Måløy raid Group and Troop units, an enduring smile upon his maw beneath his sculpted pencil moustache whilst he observed the atmosphere and camaraderie.

His hands were wrapped behind his back, and his customized sword sheathed proudly at his hip; a lethal and bareknuckle-looking Scottish broadsword with a customized hilt incorporating the iconic design of the menacing US M1918 trench knife knuckleduster-style eyelet handle. The design had been purposefully adapted onto the body of a 38-inch, single-handed claybeg sword.

Possession of the claybeg sword was a permanent surplus to Churchill, kept tenure for the sake of personal attachment. The overkill weapon had become a specialist tool without an exclusive objective. An overstatement beyond rationale.

Anyone who had seen the claybeg unsheathed and up close would have observed the blade's unique, traditional finishing, which caused miniscule meandering variations in silver tone, hinting that a thirteenth-century-style *Damascus steel* had been employed during the forging. Damascus steel was a blend of two dissimilar alloys of metal. Depending on which metals were chosen by the forger and how they were treated, the rigidity and durability of the material varied with the ultimate goal being performance and longevity; in this case, a blend of austenitic stainless-steel and high carbon steel had been selected, obtaining an overall hardness akin to *C47 Rockwell.*

The double-edged sword was considerably lightweight and adaptable, and the special metal of the blade was rumoured to be nigh indestructible.

There was said to be no alcohol aboard any of the ships, therefore the risk of the men partying *too hard* was inconceivable. However, these be Englishmen, after all. It would be out of line if there wasn't alcohol.

It wasn't long before Churchill was issued his doodlesack between the echoic metal walls of the below deck hall and was urged to play them an upbeat song or two whilst they sipped teas and 'various beverages' after tea. He did, graciously, as Captain Young moved through the crowds with his temperament dropping as did the hour. He shouted to remind his men of the time and of the *lights-out* call by 2200.

He was heard by some.

*Ignored by many.*

From an outside perspective of the neighbouring carrier ships in their voyage, it was clear which one was commanded by Durnford-Slater and which by Churchill.

Even though there were less men aboard the HMS Prince Leopold, it made twice as much racket as any other ship as the flotilla voyaged across the reflective open sea.

Beneath the colourful glow and rhythmic radiance of the aurora borealis gases known locally as the Nordlys, one of the boats expelled volume across the distance: the iconic *purr* and *skirl* of Jack Churchill.

It soon subsided.

At this ungodly hour, the Prince Leopold was a ghost of the night, sailing silently across the tranquil waters beneath a twinkling night. The revelry had recently ceased, and the only noise to be heard was the ambient lapping that was the void of an inky nighttime sea.

Out on the deck beneath the stars and the otherworldly colours of the northern lights as they elegantly drifted above the reflective ocean, Felix Hardy stood wrapped in a blanket and scarf over his numerous civilian layers. Unlike the commandos, this correspondent was unbound by a curfew. The night was cold and icy, but this lightshow was unmissable. The air smelt of salt tides.

In the invisibility of night at sea, the flotilla of royal navy ships silently cruised towards a snowy and rocky landmass to the south-east. In keeping with their deadline to reach the objective, they were making perfect time.

Giant icebergs were visible as they passed, even shoved clear out the way by the enormous bows of the warships with barely audible creaks and groans.

Right at that moment, Hardy's ears pricked at the wail of an odd pitch. His searching view brought his gaze over the railing and down into the inky black water in time to see something large and smooth breach the surface of the ocean.

Before his brain could process the outlandish sight of the slithery, alien mammal, a blowhole atop of what must have been a whale exhaled like a spout.

The wilderness spectacle made Hardy beam life as the creature swum higher, exposing more of its slickly dark body, even gyrating as it moved. Hardy was then able to make out the whale's head and eye as it coasted beside the boat.

"Thought I'd find you out here," the serene voice of Jack Churchill filled the air, and Hardy twisted at the neck, startled.

He let shut the lid of the hatch which led inside the middle deck, suppressing a sliver of red *'stealth light'* from within; a secretive mode of which all ships had engaged upon preparation for disembarkation and operational *go* within hours. The time was now after three o'clock in the morning, and all ships aside from their naval crews working the night-shift were about to be rudely awoken—if they weren't already awake in anticipation.

"Jack! Quick! Look!" Hardy exclaimed. Instantly, his view returned overboard, and he searched for the whale once again, but it seemed to have gone.

Jack approached and asked as a follow-up: "Can't sleep?"

Hardy's shoulders seemed to sink.

He bothered not to inform the speculative Jack Churchill of what he had seen—or thought to have seen. He shook his head, then noticing that Churchill was already attired in his khaki battledress. Overlapping leather belts were wrapped over him, like an external pad stitch. His pants tucked into his tall combat boots and seemed baggy, probably because he wore some long-johns beneath. In addition for the cold reception, he also wore gloves, and a camouflage scarf tucked into his collar. Naturally, his knuckle-duster hilted claybeg sword was sheathed at his hip and, of course, his green beret was upon his dome.

Churchill's buttons were shined and sparkly on his collars and cuffs, possibly even a decorative silver—something definitely not general issue.

"You're ... looking the part," Hardy remarked after an extended gaze up and down Jack's attire, in disbelief that they were that close to go-time. The only thing the Commando was missing was his ranged weaponry. "What is it you say? *Properly dressed?*"

"*Any officer who goes into action without his sword is improperly dressed,*" Churchill regarded, placing a palm upon his sheathed sword. "That of which, I am not."

Hardy's head bobbed as he took in the view over the ocean scape one last time. "I can't tell if you're going to war or to a ceremonial dinner."

Churchill raised his arms and assessed his cufflinks.

He had obtained them years ago whilst in France with his best friend *Rex King-Clark*, who had also served with him in the Second Manchester Regiment. He had decided to sew them onto his uniform for what he believed was proper practice.

"And *no,* by the way. I can't sleep," Hardy finally answered Churchill's question. "I was, eh, whale watching, actually."

"*Whale watching,* eh?" now sharing the railing, Churchill scanned the dark and abyssal view of the sea at night.

"Yeah, I saw one out here earlier, swimming alongside our boat."

"Oh?" Churchill remarked, seemingly unconvinced. "Be sure it's not an enemy submarine."

*Hardy's view dropped as he second-guessed what it was that he saw.* He even panned his view back down to the water, trying again to spot motion.

"I'm kidding, Felix. There would be nothing out here but icebergs and sea mammals ..." Churchill noticed Hardy's relief. "Besides, if it really was a U-Boat, it'd be far too late already."

"Uh-huh," he gnawed at Jack's stupid anecdote continuation. "Shouldn't you be getting some rest?"

"I can't sleep before a war," Churchill remarked, leaning on the railing and gazing into the seascape view along with Hardy. To their aft side was the Prince Charles. Churchill imagined if it wasn't so dark and foggy across the distance, he would be able to see Durnford-Slater doing the exact same thing over that ship's railing, undoubtedly just as sleepless ahead of the raid.

Churchill eyed Hardy, helping his friend keep focus.

"Ready for some FISH and CHIPS, lad?"

The very thought of food caused the American to wince, referring to his seasickness from earlier. "Oh, I don't think I could stomach a thing with my gut like this ..."

Jack chuckled, "No, Felix. It's an acronym. Military slang. It means *Fighting In Someone's Home* and *Causing Havoc In People's Streets.* This operation is on occupied civilian land. There's likely to be a great many Weegies just getting about with their daily lives—granted, under jackboot heels of the Gerrys—but nonetheless, I dare say the British Army will have need of your people skills to a certain degree. I need you in your best form ... like you were in France."

Hardy couldn't help but feel humoured by Mad Jack, and played it down, "And which form was that? A puddle of cowardly piss, or frozen solid hunk of useless shit?"

Churchill was taken back, and once again squared up with Hardy.

"Don't be so hard on yourself, lad. I've seen experienced soldiers fare worse than you did in the thick of it. We each bring something different to the war ... and you, you bring your humanity, sarcasm, and complaints, too."

"O.K., alright. I get it," the journalist dismissed at a scoff, waving him down with his hand.

"But truly, Felix. Some of these boys are chomping at the bit for a fight. I fear they may devolve into animals. You, in that instance, could be the voice of reason to make them apply logic and rationale, rather than aimed anger and frustration. You may save lives, in your own way." Churchill delivered this with sincerity. He had hoped that it wouldn't be lost in their banter, and that the American would see the gravity of the situation; after all, Jack felt responsible for him, and wouldn't always be around to keep him safe when called away on the battlefield.

"*Sir,*" a tiny British voice quietly remarked behind them. "*We're approaching the fjord.*"

"Thank you," Churchill replied and the Prince Leopold sailor dismissed. To remain in synchronization with the plans for the raid arrival time, they could just about feel the deceleration in the flotilla's motion across the sea.

Jack eyed Felix. "You may want to get ready. Reveille is at 0400."

"*Reveille?*"

"Yes, you know: *the wake-up call,*" Churchill explained. "Breakfast at 0500, weapons check after that, and then we board the LCs and wait for H-hour."

Hardy seemed to hold an unsure or possibly uneasy stare.

"Then ...?"

"Then, *we go to war,*" Churchill insisted more plainly.

Reality sunk in around Hardy.

Bobbing his head, he appeared ready for what was required from him this day. He stood up straight, committed. "I'll see you in there."

Once Hardy promptly returned to his quarters to get ready for the operation, Churchill lingered a moment longer to take in the amazing colours in the Norwegian skies at the predawn hour. The green and blue gases of the auroras borealis were just as vivid as any of the other times he had seen them, however their hypnotic dreamscape spectacle was always captivating. Now that the night was revolving towards the brightening of day upon the distant bluing horizon, they were beginning to desaturate.

"*Beaut'ful, en-et?*" the husky Scottish voice commented from off-side.

Churchill didn't startle or scare. He knew who it was.

His eyeline lowered and a smug smirk formed in the corner of his mouth. After all, *he was alone—so who else could it be?*

"Indeed, it is," he retorted simply as the deceased incarnation of Colonel MacLeòid stepped into view, raising his sleeves over the same railing to lean beside Churchill. He took a fast glimpse over his shoulder, ensuring they were alone for this tête-à-tête. "Visiting me again so quickly? I was starting to think that I'd gone *sane.*"

"*Yoo're standin' on tha top of the world beneath a green sky, watchin' owt fur either Loch Ness or Moby Dick frolickin' en an icy ocean, Jackie,"* MacLeòid turned to face him. "*Yoo tell me, en this moment, what es sane?"*

"I'll tell you what it's *not ...*" he eyed MacLeòid before he finished. "... *you* telling *me* I'm about to encounter *Friedrich Feind* on this operation, huh?"

MacLeòid grunted and turned away his view. It was his usual modus operandi to fuel Churchill's madness whilst in the fray.

*Jack knew him too well.*

"Eh?" Churchill pressed, knowing he was right. "Try and convince me to *get mad* and kill every enemy I encounter? Try and make me see his face out there through the fog of war."

"*Aye, Jackie, I git et. I'm nit gon' do dat no more, eh? Yoo've owt-grown me games.*"

"Yes, I know you won't. Because he's not *my* enemy. Not anymore. That strategy of yours is what's been *out-grown*, sir."

"*Tea an' bickies, den?"* MacLeòid stated as he stepped away, referencing the supposed moment of clarity Churchill had earlier in the year, when he had written and invited his old enemy such, attempting to make a new friend out of an old enemy. "*I hope he got yoor wee love letter, laddie. Maybe ef he dud un yoo ain't lookin' fur him, he won't pull tha trigger when he sees yoo first owt en da fog o' war while yoo owt dere tryin' ta give Hitler a brown eye.*"

Churchill didn't bother to turn or acknowledge his parting words. He was not falling prey to his silver-tongued bollocks this time.

He merely corrected his invisible friend. "A *black* eye, sir. We are here to give Hitler a *black eye,*" he eyed MacLeòid at his flank on the railing. "Nothing less, nothing m—"

Cutting their usual expositional chit-chat short, the tiny British voice of a sailor probed from close by and behind Churchill: "*Eh, sir?*

Churchill's stare defocused. Went vacant.

The shy sailor huffed. "*W... who are you talking to, sir?"*

After an extended moment, Churchill spun and passed a random ship sailor who was observing the lone army major speaking aloud with a dumbfounded expression. Churchill threw an implication over the railing as he disappeared inside the deck around a corner, off to perform his role in prelude to the operation.

"Moby Dick, cadet. Moby Dick."

A second later, the unconvinced, hovering sailor timidly approached the edge of the railing.

His view grew wide as he took in the scape of the dark and still ocean surface ... and then, slight silky movement caused him to make out what appeared to be a figure standing out of the water.

*It was the breaching tail of a whale.*

The raised Y-shaped tail then slashed down hard against the surface of the water, scaring the living shit out of the sailor, who audibly shrieked before quickly hustling back towards the hatch and retreating inside from the horrors of the night.

When Jack Churchill stepped one foot through an open hatchway that led into the greasy-scented hull from the outer deck, his peripheral peeked the edging that ran along the starboard side of the ship—what he saw was eye-catching.

Given the big day ahead, there was extraordinarily little activity about the Prince Leopold at this hour. Other than various deckhands and navy seamen performing their duties, not a commando was stirring.

In spite of this, the lone dark figure beneath the moonlight glow through the green borealis hue captured his attention on the outer deck. Draped in thick inky shadows, the silhouette contrasted by the emerald radiance of the radiating northern lights in the hemisphere.

Churchill's doubletake revealed more detail.

The glow of a lit cigar's inhale.

The man had seen him first. Identified him. It was almost like he had been waiting for Jack to saunter along this precise side deck ...

"Still seeing ghosts, Jack?" the voice of the man spoke, catching Churchill in his lingering moment midway through the hatchway.

Churchill stepped out from the red glow of the passage, allowing for the cadet to pass back inside and close over the door, giving the two men an ounce of solitude.

Walking closer, Jack put his hands in his coat pockets.

His sterling stare intensified over the shadowy figure as he slowly strolled closer. The voice was familiar, but one belonging to a man he had not seen or heard from in years.

As he moved closer, distinguishing details crept in as the overcoated character pushed off the cold wall of the ship's keel and planted his elbows on the railing, casually leaning over the edge of the ship.

It was then Jack saw who it was—and understood his insight into Churchill's own private contexts about *seeing ghosts.*

He finally retorted. "I am seeing one right now ..."

Tilting in the light was the aslant face, cap-clad head belonging to one of the renowned veteran warfighters recently recruited into No.3's brother battalion, No.2 Commando. This ghost from Churchill's past was a fair-haired fellow, with the bulk of his golden dome compressed beneath his green beret. He bore a bushy blonde imperial moustache that illuminated when he puffed smoke from his thick cigar.

"Mad-*bloody*-Jack," the man stated with a nod of recognition. "How the heck are ya?"

Churchill huffed out his nose, truly realizing who it was.

He shook his head, never thinking he would see this guy again.

Rather than answer the rhetorical question, Jack simply acknowledged with a nod. The relative query was asked by a man named *Graeme Delamere Black*, a lieutenant from No.2 beneath Captain Hooper who was in command of Group 4 and the floating reserve who would remain stationed upon the Kenya for the duration of Archery.

"*Grae.*"

"I was starting to wonder if I would run into you at all for this op," Black remarked, relaxing his view across the passing ocean scape. "Or if maybe I'd save my entrance for when I'll be saving your arse in the heat of battle. *Yet again.*"

Churchill scoffed at the remark. "I don't remember reading your name amongst the list of new recruits?"

"That's because I didn't apply for No.3."

"No.2, then?"

Black jiggled his head, staring out to sea.

The *tip of the spear* of No.2 Commando, Graeme Black was a notorious daredevil formally of the *South Lancashire Regiment*, and before that the *Queen's York Rangers*. Prior to soldiering, a history of employment that only a few men know, Black used to make women's handbags for famous fashion designer *Norman Hartnell*. In between his range of various gigs however, in 1939, Black became a member of the fanatical and clandestine *Orde Wingate* group, the *Auxiliary-Ops*. It was here he met and trained with a green Mad Jack Churchill, as well as a motley band of other randoms deemed *combat elitists* by the British Army Intelligence, in the *Swiss Pennine Alps* until their experimental *black-op* was disbanded—and deleted from history. He and Jack, alike, were each sworn to secrecy and issued an immediate *RTU (Return To Unit)* within their respective army entities. None of the men had really heard from or seen each other since with the exception of Komrower.

Although, arguably as close as brethren as comradery would entail for two men sharing a trench in war, the two had not exactly *got along* during that extraordinary time, hence Churchill never offering him for recruitment into No.3 back when Durnford-Slater had rebooted Commando fifteen months ago.

"Well, I heard about Commando when you lot were traipsing around in the Nordlys for the Lofoten Raid back in March. Thought I'd come see what all the fuss was about," Black eyed Jack. "Cheers for the letter of recommendation by the way ..."

Churchill permitted the jab.

He had refrained from extending an invitation to Black when Durnford-Slater was hungry for experienced recruits to fill the ranks within No.3.

"Must have gotten lost in the post?" Churchill replied sarcastically. These two had history. There was no sense in pussyfooting around the fact that Black already knew that Churchill had purposely not invited him to his war party. There was a tinge of bad blood between the men, but not enough to justify the onset of fisticuffs ...

*Just passive-aggressive tones of voice!*

"I heard *Calvert* was offered a spot. *Ruffell*, too. And I see Arty definitely got an offer," Black dismissed, taking another big chug of his cigar. Not getting an invitation like had fellow ex-aux-ops compatriot Arthur Komrower, Black was clearly affronted and potentially offended.

Personally, Churchill had skipped Black's offer due to his haphazardness and hotheadedness. He was too much of a daredevil and, although some would argue that was just the thing a ferocious unit like No.3 needed, Jack knew first-hand what it was like trying to tame this particular beast.

"What do you want me to say, Grae?" Churchill bartered.

"You needed recruits?—"

"We needed recruits that would follow orders, not charge into battle half-cocked and half-witted!"

"*Mike,* though?" Black uppercut. His argument was valid, and it was true. That very sentiment went against what Jack was saying about his alleged fallibility. *Mad Mike Calvert* had been invited, and he was just as crazy as Grae. He knew it and Jack knew it, and it therefore countermanded his argument somewhat, boiling it down to an obvious pure distastefulness.

Churchill accepted the rout, and he pondered a moment.

Fact was, back in the day, Calvert had taken a chance with him by inviting him to join the aux-ops. Albeit, the madman Wingate was basing his recruitment process on the craziness of the warfighter, not his dutiful stature as an abiding soldier. Their exercised tactics certainly befitted the term they monikered for themselves by the end of the short-lived term: *the Berzerkers.*

"I owed Mike."

"You didn't owe Mike a lamb's bollocks."

All divergences and disagreements aside, it was splendid seeing Graeme Black alive and well again. Even more so now that Jack was seeing him donning the green beret of the Commando. Perhaps he was wrong in cutting him from the list.

Churchill appealed as he strode closer, holding out a hand as a formal gesture of compromise. "Agree to disagree, then?"

The blonde-furred maw of Graeme Black eyed the open-palm offer. He was unyielding for an extended moment before swapping hold with his cigar, freeing up a hand in order to clamp Churchill's with a tenacious, testosterone-fuelled grip ...

Their hands clapped airtight as they tensed. Like *that:* the clap of their macho embrace, a bridge was built overflowing water.

The two firmly locked eyes.

"King's oath, cunt," Black stated with the harshest of profanity, sure as a rifle sight on Hitler's toothbrush moustache that he would pull the trigger with his friend, Mad Jack.

"When do you leave for the Kenya?" Jack then asked, speaking operationally. Their role in Group 4 was to stay aboard the point ship, the HMS Kenya. If and when Haydon gave the order, their reserve would storm Vågsøy and help the ground units. They were essentially backup— one that hopefully they would not need.

Churchill took a welcoming pose on the railing beside his old teammate, and the two shot the shit for a moment over the Norwegian Sea.

"0700-hours."

Jack nodded, acknowledging. "You sleeping?"

"Are you?"

Churchill snorted and smirked.

*They both knew the answers to those questions.*

After a moment, Churchill upped from his leaning posture and they wished each other luck for the mission. He set off backwards towards the hatchway that led inside the ship, leaving Black to remain in the shadows.

"Jack," Black called one last time before he could vanish. "Don't disdain your ghosts. They're often more right than you'd think."

# 4

# The March of the Cameron Men

*1941, December 27 – the day of days.*
*South Vågsøy*
*Vågsøy, Norway*

*0700-hours ...*
    The winter sun did not rise in Norway until nine o'clock.

    Still saturated in the darkness of dawn, the island of Vågsøy went quietly about her routines as the enemy-occupied civilian establishments began to operate for the day. This day was possibly the first day of business for several ventures following their permitted Christmas holiday break, as it was the 27th of December.

    Areas like the fishing dock and the pier seemed to buzz with activity.

    Vague yellow lights brightened the dark dawn hue with several small vessels visibly moving along the icicle coast. Similar composure flowed further inland, within the village of South Vågsøy. Facilities and warehouses were active with dim powered lights and the presence of steam from their many stacks.

    The area's inhabitants were oblivious of what was to come ...

    *War.*

    Due to the occupation, there was an array of German army establishments and countless coastal defence emplacements, such as sniper outposts, machine gun nests, and anti-air cannons manned by the soldiers of the 181st Infantry Division. The 150-some German infantrymen were under the command of the tarnished Nazi officer, Lieutenant-General Woytasch.

    Apparent by the oversaturation of red, white, and black Nazi propaganda in the form of banners and swastikas hanging from any applicable expanse, their operational headquarters had been instituted throughout the floors of the Ulvesund Hotel, located in the centre of South Vågsøy. Battle-post positions had been erected by the front and rear entrances behind layers of impenetrable sandbag barricades. The balcony above the front entrance that lead into the defendable foyer had also been lined with fortifications, seated with belt-fed, two-man operated MG34 nests that bore eagle-eyed views of the entire front area. Shooters crawled upon her icy roof, patrolling near an operating searchlight.

As the dawn hours slowly began to brighten from the eastern horizon, the enormous aerial searchlight mounted upon the fourth-storey roof of the Ulvesund powered down with an audible *fuzz* by the rugged-up stahlhelm soldiers manning the position. Finished with its use for the night, the operators covered the light up with a weatherproofed canvas sheet.

Throughout the town, the soldiers about to be coming off the gruelling nightshift guard duty following what would have been two days of heavy eating and celebratory drinking had their eyes glossing over, daydreaming, and yawning whilst leaning across their mounted machine guns. The morning guards who would undoubtedly be equally as tired, nursing hangovers and still wiping the sleep from their eyes, would be currently preparing for their incoming shifts as the daylight rose. This was the most advantageous time an enemy advance could have struck Vågsøy Island, as awareness was low, and guards were sloppy. Luckily for Germany, it was nigh implausible that any force would do so the day after Boxing Day. Surely.

Hush and eerie stillness draped the dark streets of the village town of South Vågsøy, which was across the bridge from the heavily German-occupied Måløy Island in the bay/fjord—more accurately: the *Vågsfjorden (Nordfjord)*. The Vågsfjorden was surrounded by several other low-population Norwegian towns and inlets within the Vågsøy municipality Sogn og Fjordane.

Still half a world away, the light from the rising sun began to ascend over the icy and jiggered rocky mountain slopes behind South Vågsøy, cascading a growing luminosity as the snow-white caps of the hills captured and refracted the distant ultraviolet rays. The whole area seemed to glow vibrantly with a neon hue, almost as if the faded auroras borealis from the previous night had charged the landscape with a sense of surreal psychedelic ether.

The geographical sunrise wasn't until nine a.m. This provided a silhouette profile from an ocean view of the land, and as each minute passed, the intensification of brightness seemed to tiptoe into dawn, leaving the morning sky clear and spotted with distant stars and galaxies seemingly visible for light years.

The western entrance to the icy fjord waters—the same entrance that would be used by any invading forces and could berth an entire flotilla of warships—was located between fishing towns *Hovden* on the isle of *Husvågøya* and *Vombaneset*, further east the town of Holvik. The town of South Vågsøy was located just south of that. From there, the Ulvesundet Fyr passage travelled north, beyond South Vågsøy, towards ice towns *Sildegapet* on the south side and *Husevåg* to the further north.

All in all, the winter scenery was as serene as it was silent.

*All that was about to change...*


*HMS Kenya*
*Vågsfjorden, Norway*


*0701-hours ...*

From the observation platform in the front of the bridge of the Kenya—the point-ship and mobile HQ for Archery—Brigadier Haydon lowered his binoculars, eyeing the focal point in the distance.

Flanked by two naval captains whom he held with high esteem, he informed what it was he could see protruding the ocean's surface: *the conning tower of the British submarine.*

The HMS Tuna submarine beaconed right where she was supposed to, according to their asdic device *(pre-sonar)*.

"It's her," he confirmed. "Time?"

"Right on clock, sir," one of the men checked a handheld precision pocket watch. "Maybe a minute behind."

"One whole minute?" Haydon regarded as he handed his man his binoculars. "I'll take it. Report?"

A radioman sitting along the console in the bridge wearing a bulky pair of headphones that covered one ear sat askew, facing his CO. He nodded and held a thumbs-up gesture.

"As planned, sir," a captain relayed, and Haydon received.

The Tuna was running reconnaissance for the operation. If she had nothing new to report, then it meant their initial intelligence projections—information also captured by the same submarine days prior—was still current, and their expectations of the enemy capabilities remained the same.

"Very well," he remarked, twisting and facing away from the faintly lit windshield of the bridge. "Inform the Commandos to prepare boarding the landing crafts. Signal the air force to commence their patterns. Gentlemen ... *we are a go.*"

"*Aye, sir!*"

"*Aye!*"

There was suddenly a flurry of activity within the bridge of the Kenya as seamen and sailors prepared for the commencement of Operation Archery.

*It was happening.*

This was the point of no return.

*0729-hours ...*

An outside view showed a calm and tranquil water surface upon the wide mouth of the Vågsfjorden, with a motionless, inky current and slip tide headed inwards.

The barely visible conning tower of a submarine submerged just below the surface. She began to dive as she withdrew, peeling westerly, shrinking into the icy abyss just as, passing in the opposite direction and heading east and into the bay, the giant bodies of seven silent warships covertly cruised by beneath the cover of darkness and absolute silence. They were like apex predators, procuring a position of which best to pounce an unaware prey.

The Kenya led, trailed by destroyers Onslow, Oribi, Offa, and Chiddingfold, then followed the big and heavier troop carriers Prince Charles and Prince Leopold bringing up the rear with their ground troop payloads.

The ships kept their interval by means of an ancient device known as a *towing spar*. This was a white-painted flotation device, like a small buoy, towed behind each warship. The floats left visible wakes behind them, and each of the following vessels had only to keep a visual on the buoy to stay on position during their infiltration into the enemy waters of the Vågsfjord ...

### HMS Prince Charles
### Vågsfjorden, Norway

*0757-hours...*

Aboard the Prince Charles were the men of Durnford-Slater's landing parties; Groups 2 (G2) and Group 5 (G5). The masses of men were currently congregating within the cold steel halls of the winding and twisting stairwells within the carrier ship.

Those that could stomach it before the deadly mission had eaten, and every man had prepared themselves in warm clothes and sweaters, leather-strapped with ordinance and gear, and donning either a steel brodie helmet or a warm woollen beanie for a cold reception—and packed an assortment of deadly arms for an even colder reception by the residing Germans.

The Norwegian soldiers were present in their clique. Although sharing the British brodie helmet, they were uniformed slightly differently, favouring the hide jerkins across their torsos, and were typically armed with varying weaponry which they had brought along, such as Automatgevär and Husqvarna rifles.

The ground forces aligned in various formations, all pointing towards the upper deck access points, ready to pour out at a moment's notice. When word sounded, they would march into the dispatchable LCs, be lowered to the icy pond of the Vågsfjorden, and voyage inland for the ground assault once the air force bombs and navy shells had found their mark on all enemy outposts visible from the fjord.

The G2 objective was the town of South Vågsøy, headed by Durnford-Slater on-point. The men of G5 were led up by Captain Birney and would join the ranks of the destroyer Oribi via their LCs, rather than heading coastal like G2. Their primary objective was much further upstream, along the Ulvesund Fyr, where they would beach somewhere along the road heading north and cut off any potential reinforcements.

In the echoic metal halls of the ship, the forty-some geared-up soldiers in chin-strapped tin hats under Birney's command carried an assortment of weaponry. Ithaca 37 pump-action 16-gauge shotguns, trusty Lee-Enfield bolt-action rifles with the ability of deadly bayonets to be fixed at a moment's notice for close-quarters combat, or Thompson submachine guns; some with compact 20-shot stick magazines, others with extended drum magazines. The commandos prepared grenades, at least one for each man, either fragmentation *Mills Bombs* or smoke. Some even took both, and multiple of.

Among the hustle of preparing soldiers, the voice of a journalist animated for his coverage as his cameraman filmed footage of the Commandos strapping weapons to their persons, stacking spare ammunition, sharpening their BC-41 trench knives:

"... *down below, the toughest men in the British Army head for their destination in much the same manner as the warriors of old. In their dimly lit quarters ... men prime their grenades ... gripping their daggers like a Captain Kidd or Long John Silver ...*"

The G5 men passed G2 within the tight confines of the stairwells and corridors within the warship, headed above deck: their call had come to mount LCs and dock with the Oribi, which would travel the Ulvesund Fyr passage after the other assault teams had landed. Amidst the passing crowds, men nodded and dipped their helmets with respectful gesticulations, wishing each other good luck. They patted each other across the shoulders or backs in a sportsmanlike fashion.

At the end of the queue, Birney met Durnford-Slater, and they exchanged whispers.

"*Good luck, Captain.*"

"*And to you, Colonel.*"

The geared men shook hands and then from behind Birney, the eyepatch wearing Sergeant MacWilly MacWilliam emerged, carrying his massive Lewis machine gun up by his shoulder.

He paused for an extended moment where his sole eye made eye contact with Durnford-Slater. There was a hint of both readiness and hesitation.

Durnford-Slater amped his man up, for MacWilly was the long-term one-eyed friend of Jack Churchill's who had served with him in France in the Second Manchester Regiment, where he had lost his eye in combat. Durnford-Slater knew this character more than most within the Commando ranks. "Ready to get 'em, trooper!"

"*Aye, sir!*" in a tone befitting the pirate-like feature of his eyepatch, MacWilly called before charging upstairs behind his G5 CO.

Durnford-Slater watched them trudge up the final flight of stairs within the echoic steel staircase and he turned away from the dawn light brimming the edge of the access hatch and faced his men—notably Head, JFG, and O'Flaherty—who were directly stacked behind him with their brodie helmets donned.

O'Flaherty seemed to be struggling to get his strap on tight enough and Giles was supporting him like a big brother.

"You've gotta have it on tight!" JFG instructed, "Otherwise you're asking to get shot in the head!"

"*I know!*"

"Here," JFG further assisted, but it seemed that the luck of the draw had issued O'Flaherty with a defective helmet chinstrap. They got it as tight as possible and left it at that, but it was bound to come undone during the action of the raid.

Behind the men in the stairwell was a chain of anxious and enthusiastic peeking faces, all draped in khaki and geared in leather and steel, some even donning dark streaks of war paint across their nose and cheeks for extra camouflage during the pending skirmish.

Not all of them may have looked it at this moment ... but these Commandos were ready for a fight. Durnford-Slater knew it deep down.

The Reuters Newspapers Agency reporter could be heard around the corner of their formation column as he and one of his cameramen pointed a gun-cam across the queue of zealous Commandos as they anchored in their positions, showing professionalism, discipline, and tact as they waited for the green light to march on.

"... *In the dark hours of the morning, even the tick of a watch sounds loud as the deathly silence precedes zero hour ...*"

*HMS Prince Leopold*
*Vågsfjorden, Norway*

*0801-hours...*
On the other troop carrier—the Prince Leopold—which cruised into the peaceful dawn Vågsfjorden behind the arrow formation of their destroyer entourage, the atmosphere surrounding the soldiers pre-boarding the Higgins boats was much the same for Group 3 and Group 1 (G3 and G1).

Stacking the tin can corridors that headed towards the upper decks and their LCs lined a single formation column of geared commandos, literally armed to the teeth. In the connecting mess hall, men prepared their loaded weaponry with a hundred metallic *click-clacks* and *chit-chits*, all the while pinching their BC-41 commando knives between their fangs like deathly privateers, keen for encounter.

The green-beret-clad Major Jack Churchill eyed his men as they moved from the wide-open belly of the Prince Leopold mess hall, which now doubled as their armoury prep stage, and then as they jogged on, upping the halls towards the upper deck entrance. The tables of the mess cafeteria once filled with trays of oats, eggs, teas, and coffees, were now wall to wall with an array of arsenal sorts. Their lead quartermaster, Slinger Martin, was onboard and had arranged the assorted equipment for the lads while they were preparing for battle.

The men collected their submachine guns, shotguns, or ranged rifle preferences, even doubling up with the available semi-automatic sidearms for back-up. Some men even took two handguns, stashing them in any available pocket; tucked under any available belt space. Extra grenades were favoured by all and, thus, stowed. As these men were anything but *G.I. Joes:* they were permitted to kit up with whatever they felt they needed to complete the task at hand.

Sauntering through the armoury scene of their call to arms, Churchill dipped his beret-covered head as he observed them equip, loading firearms, lining their belt caches with spare magazines, filled to the absolute brims.

The audio of the serenity was a cacophony of men cycling the bolts of their rifles, chambering rounds in metallic breaches. Pumping the foregrips of their shotguns and feeding shells into the cylindrical tube. Clutching the pins of their machine guns, preparing to set their fire-modes to automatic, accompanied by the shuffling of combat boots.

The men were only ready once their guns were in condition zero.

They racked the metal slides of their pistols, collapsing the cocked hammers before holstering them at their hips or beneath their armpit strap holsters in an assortment of customized layouts.

"Gear-up! Safeties on—*for now!*" Churchill reminded as he waved them on. His hands rested upon his many hip holsters as he observed the rally; one hand in particular over the custom knuckleduster hilt of his claybeg sword. Jack had always been inseparable from the trademark sidearm, and they had all expected to see him eventually take it into battle once again.

"*Sir!*" "*Yes-sir!*" the helmeted-strapped war-faced men abided as they passed, forming formation up the stairs and taking a knee behind the queue to the deck.

Present in the mess-turned-armoury was Lieutenant Clement, who was in command of G1. His smaller detachment of fifty troops were arming up to take two Higgins boats westerly of their approach and capture the enemy barracks at the small village of Holvik. They would be departing the Prince Leopold moments before Churchill's G3—an event to be coordinated with the same time that G5 left G2 over on the Prince Charles.

Churchill shouted across the commotion within the mess as the remainder of the Commandos finished their armament preparation. "Lieutenant Clement?"

"Major Churchill!" Clement replied, holding a hand up beside his ear so that he could hear over the volume of trudging combat boots on grated floor and a dozen weapons being loaded at any one time.

"Are your men ready for departure?"

"Yes, sir. Waiting for the order."

Churchill bowed in retort.

Conceding to the likelihood of probably requiring a firearm for this incursion, rather than relying on his mere bow and arrows, Churchill prepared a heavy circular magazine for the M1928 Thompson at his disposal. This variant had a wooden forward pistol grip for added recoil compensation, and the gun was loaded with the fifty-round drum of .45 ACP ammunition, weighing an extra five pounds.

Captain Young weaved in out of the lines to appear beside his CO while he stood at one of the many armoury tables. In charge of Six Troop, Young was also Churchill's second-in-command of G3 and tackling Måløy Island.

Churchill acknowledged him upon his sidle. "Captain."

"Sir." Young Young muttered, eyeing the weaponry. He had already acquired his kit-out. It was a rare sight seeing Mad Jack armed with a weapon made this side of the Elizabethan era—and thus, he joshed, "They fire bullets, Jack ... are you ill?"

Churchill couldn't help but beam playfully at the quip, adding the submachine gun around his neck via its khaki strap along with all the other hanging paraphernalia, such as his P-37 braces to hold his pack, respective leather straps; one to his binoculars case and the other to his trusty shoulder archery quiver, slanted with protruding feathery arrow ordinance—which caused Churchill to stand out like a goose quill amongst lead pencils—and lastly, of course, his bagpipes bag. Jack also carried what appeared to be a laterally shaped canvas bag used by gunners to carry spare Bren gun parts—predominantly the length of a machine gun barrel.

JFG's younger brother Bruce Giles passed by and collected a gun from the tabletops, as did several other familiar faces such as Peace and Wills. They were all together in Five Troop, under Giles' command. As a part of G3, they would all be assaulting Måløy Island together.

Churchill halted Wills' pace, surrounded by men.

During Claymore, this joker had used the captured enemy radio communication devices to, rather comedically, send a transcript directly to Adolf Hitler, himself, taunting the Führer of Nazi Germany. The event had gone down in Commando history, and Churchill recalled that occurrence now with a relevant throwaway.

"Wills, if you manage to speak with your mate Hitler again during this raid, can you kindly ask him why he is yet to appoint *General Franz Halder* as the holder of France? Seems like a wasted opportunity to me."

Wills and the surrounding men grinned and smirked.

"Yes, sir."

"Good lad," Churchill bobbed, letting them move on.

After they joined formation of the stacks in the halls, Churchill scanned to his right, spotting Hardy, who was dressed in a walnut barnstormer coat, topped with a fedora hat. The American reporter wore it over his layers for the cold that the army had supplied for him. He wore the same baggy combat pants over similar leggings and big boots as the commando troops, and even strapped himself with a handgun from the armoury at his right hip in a khaki Pattern 37 holster that caught the eye against his mostly civilian attire. He stowed his notepad and his pen in another easily accessible pouch bag slung around his neck. He carried a tin hat that he would eventually intend to mount upon his combed and styled dark hair.

A smile curled on Churchill's face as he laid eyes upon him.

"Felix," he jerked his jaw, containing his sneer at the sight of the out-of-place journalist. In fact, what made him laugh wasn't out of absurdity of Hardy's appearance—quite the contrary. Felix Hardy truly looked the part, but there was no way he could let him know that. Churchill jeered with a nod, "Be sure your helmet doesn't slide off your head from all that brylcreem, lad."

Hardy simpered sarcastically and popped the brimmed steel army helmet upon his gelled hair, not bothering with the leather strap. He held his arms out by his side. "How do I look?"

Walking in close, Churchill shuddered a look at his holstered weapon; an American M1911A1 .45 calibre pistol.

What they were doing today was dangerous—for soldiers and news crews alike. It was doubtful that an armourer would have issued him the firearm, for there were always the lingering objections to having an untrained man wondering about with a gun, but no commando was about to confiscate the weapon from him.

"Is she loaded?"

"Uh, yeah ..." Hardy remarked, unsure. When he had taken it off one of the first tables, he had inserted one of the corresponding clips in the bottom of it. He removed it from the holster, presenting it. The hammer was back and the safety was on, which suggested that the journalist at least had basic knowledge on the weapon's functionality.

This scenario suddenly felt reminiscent of France, just prior to the Dunkirk Evacuation, when Jack had to instruct him on weapon handling once before.

Not intent on embarrassing the yank, Churchill discreetly elicited hold of the handgun, safely press-checking the chamber on his behalf. If it were primed and in what was known as condition zero, brass from the charged bullet would be visible and the weapon ready to fire. The pipe was empty, and so Jack racked the metal slide for him, *click-clack*, then flipped up the safety latch. He did not collapse the hammer, as the M1911A1 had been designed in such a way that it could safely be stowed while cocked.

Winking discreetly, Churchill handed it back to Hardy.

"Now she's loaded."

Hardy saw the user operation and learned thusly, nodding in understanding. "Thanks, Jack," he remarked genuinely, thrusting it gently in his holster. Hopefully he wouldn't need it this day.

"That's your secondary here today," Churchill stated, then pointed to his other pouch that housed his notepad and pencil. "*That* is your primary weapon, understood?"

Hardy nodded. "Understood."

"*Jack!*" Captain Young called and stepped through the busy crowd of commandos, offering Churchill a three-cell magazine pouch for his weapon. He had noticed that his CO had no spare ammunition for today and this shouldn't be something forgotten and discovered once they were in the heat of battle. "Thought you might want some spare ammo, sir ...?"

"That won't be necessary," Jack remarked, jerking his head towards soldiers in the line. "Give the extra bullets to the men."

Young probed with a frown, "But sir ... what if you run out of ammo for your primary weapon?"

"*Primary weapon?*" Churchill patted the submachine gun, casting it a mere gleam. "My lad, this is a back-up weapon ..."

Young stood puzzled for an extended moment. Then again, *Mad Jack Churchill* had no protective helmet—instead, he favoured his green beret. He had a sword at his hip—instead of a simple knife or dagger, and now, seemed to want to even reject the use of a real-world weapon in exchange for ... *what?* For the first real time since Young had known the man, he was beginning to understand the mythos surrounding the far-fetched and walking anecdote prior to Commando recruitment.

*He had honestly thought that was all a joke.*

*... but now he had to follow the man into battle.*

Young couldn't hold back his reaction this time. His face panned away with a blank expression whilst he scratched his forehead beneath the brim of his brodie helmet. "Okay, I'll bite: primary weapon to what ...?"

Just then, as if on cue, the No.3 quartermaster Slinger Martin appeared with a long and flat armament carton not too dissimilar to a rifle crate. The contents seemed lightweight compared to what was usually transported in such a case. "Sorry I'm late Major Churchill," through the noise of the kit deck, the older QM informed.

"Eh, *yes!*" Churchill remarked excitedly. Discarding logic, he shoved his hanging submachine gun aside in order to address the delivery with open hands as Slinger placed the carton upon the nearest armoury table, and all those present gravitated towards its unveiling.

In the background, Young's unenthused blank stare somehow fell upon the focus of Felix Hardy who was still nearby, and who cocked his head at the whole scenario as he leaned in close. It was odd to him too, but for some reason the foreign journalist wasn't surprised by any of Mad Jack's antics. It was as if he had been seated at this obscure and incomprehensible juncture before.

Out of earshot and with a playful smile in the curl of his mouth, Hardy simply quizzed Captain Young. "First time going to war with Mad Jack, eh?"

*Young didn't accept the query by giving a retort.*

Martin remarked before leaving. "Like we discussed, sir, don't lose count this time ..."

While Slinger Martin and Churchill shared a good snigger ...

... Hardy and Young exchanged an awkward glance.

*What would that have possibly meant ...?*

"Good luck to you, chaps."

"Thank you, Slinger," Churchill took the man's hand in wayward part, and Martin filed off to assist elsewhere during the armaments.

Young moved in even closer to witness what it was Mad Jack Churchill had acquired for their mission. It must have been something cutting edge, perhaps experimental. Something arduous and deadly, and certainly not standard issue to the army or navy.

Churchill's fingers wriggled into the box edges and removed the lid, revealing the *medieval* contents: *a wooden takedown longbow* and *mysterious arrows.* The bow was his newest edition after destroying his original piece during the Battle of Dunkirk. This piece was slightly more modernized, more compact. The device was to be assembled from two halves, screwed together in the middle handle piece. Once compiled, the constructed unit was just as strong as any archer's armament.

"Seriously?" after a pause, Young remarked with a raised brow. Until now, he had hoped that the arrows already housed in Churchill's shoulder quiver were for decoration only.

Churchill reached in and equipped the bow, examining it with the narrowed eyes of a genuine toxophilite. He had ordered a tweaking to the upper and lower limbs, where the bowstring loops nocked. Slinger knew a man skilled enough to mend the changes, and had it shipped through the brigade armoury. Care of Martin, it had arrived back just in time before they departed Scotland.

And it was in that moment, Peter Young truly witnessed Jack Churchill in his fullest form ...

*Sword on hip; customized brass eyelet knuckleduster hilt.*

*Bagpipes beneath his arm in case of musical occasion.*

*Dressage of standard issue commando fatigues; battledress pressed neat and with reissued silver buttons, bound in a winter scarf.*

*Leather arrow quiver distinct upon his right shoulder.*

*Green beret framing his pale features and blonde hair.*

*Neatly trimmed pencil-thin moustache above a dimple chin.*

He was like a storybook caricature come to life.

"What did Slinger mean by *don't lose count?*" Young finally enquired as he gazed about the other contents: more arrows. These ones had different coloured feather fletching compared to his standard white.

Churchill already had arrows prepared in his quiver—two dozen bodkin-tipped war arrows to be specific. They were housed in a special leather cylindrical quiver; the same custom piece with a magnetic bookend sewn into the bottom to moor his arrows; the ambiguous designation *'MD-1, 1939'* grafted into the pelt. The magnet held the metal heads in place whilst he potentially ran, jumped, and manoeuvred in the fray of combat. It had served him well in the past.

In the mix now were several other types of strange arrows.

Instead of wooden shafts, they had grey metal, slightly less aerodynamic bodies, likely made of lightweight aluminium. The custom projectiles were differentiated by their coloured fletching.

*Missiles that mimicked arrows.*

Of this experimental type, there were two yellow and two red.

The lot of customized arrows were stowed in wrap, one apparently custom made completely of some type of leather hide cushioning and insulation. They became unravelled in the carton latched into a coil with their assorted fletches. The pile resembled a thin bouquet of flowers.

The yellow arrows were complete with a series of highlighted indication lines painted horizontally on the body. They had simple sharpened pike tips on their business ends. The red arrows had no painted lines along their shafts, but their tips were swollen with some sort of supplement and seemed very forward-heavy. The heads were also smoothed into a nub rather than shrill and were painted with a copper-bronze tint. There was also a small, dangling safety pin where the tip met the aluminium shaft that resembled a hand grenade primer.

To further Slinger Martin's creative accuracy to meeting the British Ordinance Committee's guidelines, three red *X*s along each rear of the arrows indicated that they met the waterproofing standards—the same indicators as the No.36M Mills Bombs. Also like the Mills Bombs hand grenades, the arrows were each marked with a green band, signifying they were packed with *Baratol:* a type of HE (high explosive).

Churchill took the arrows by the feathered ends and raised them one by one over his shoulder, added them to his existing shoulder quiver stash. Next, he took the two pieces of his new takedown longbow and inserted them into a reserved canvas bag he had amongst his others. The bag was made to carry a spare Bren machine gun barrel, which just so happened to be the perfect size for the longbow pieces. In the pouch of the bag, he tucked the few coiled bowstrings—one linen and hemp, one rawhide (which he preferred)—for assembly in the field when needed.

He finally eyed Young to reply to his relevant question about losing count. "Can you count to ten?"

Young blinked. He gave a delayed response. "Yes."

"Good. Then we'll be fine."

His gear clanking with every step, Churchill left the Commando captain and the American journalist to remain perplexed a moment longer before pursuing his wake.

"You know why they refer to you lot as his *Merry Men,* right?" Hardy asked before moving on. Young didn't respond promptly, intended to be left processing the bit of irrelevant information Hardy no doubt would issue as a punchline.

Deadpan, Young answered unenthusiastically and as if he hadn't heard this one about Mad Jack before. "Let me guess, it's because we're following into battle *Robin Hood?*"

Hardy tilted upright, sarcastically aghast. "No!" he then smiled brightly, just as satirically, "Robin Hood was at least sane ..."

*Vågsfjorden*
*Vågsøy, Norway*

*0834-hours ...*

In the covert dark of dawn, the floating armada stealthily entered the Vågsfjord, unobserved and undetected by any enemy lookouts or outposts, as planned. It seemed possible that the belvedere at Hovden, which was their biggest threat of detection upon entry, was currently unmanned due to the holidays. If so, a grave mistake by the enemy.

On-point of the formation, the Kenya destroyer moved towards to the southern side of the fjord gape, allowing for the Chiddingfold to lead the carriers Prince Charles and Prince Leopold into the bay south of Holvik. From there, their prearranged multitude of mounted Higgins landing crafts began loading with commandos, and were then hoisted onto the water's surface.

Meanwhile, the destroyer Onslow closed on the static Kenya's starboard quarter as did the Offa on her stern flank. All cannons of the destroyers were locked, loaded, and manned by His Majesty's finest Royal Navy seamen dressed in gloved and helmeted battle armaments. Spotters with binoculars watched the horizons, scanning their vectors for any movement that suggested any enemy awareness, and also, for the targets of which to pre-emptively destroy when the signal was given.

The destroyer Oribi drifted in last and remained near the entrance of the fjord, with her guns aligned west to protect the flotilla from any rear assaults.

*0842-hours ...*

Within the many landing crafts located on the water were the three landing assault forces: Groups 1, 2, and 3, each compiled of two to four Troops, with numbers totalling approximately 350 of the 575 Commandos enlisted for the raid of Operation Archery.

Driven by trained operators from the navy known as coxswains, over two dozen identical diesel-powered box-shaped Higgins assault landing crafts zoomed from the position of the two tall warships as they loomed in the fjord, flanked by the destroyers.

The trailing current streams behind the LCs resembled torpedoes from the tubes, aiming for the snow-clad islands across the fjord.

Other than rushing air and the hum of the motorized Higgins boats as they travelled in an arrowhead formation, skimming across the icy open waters, the sound of distant birdsong was all that was to be heard as the stiff cold dawn began to thaw into lukewarm daylight.

About to crash the gates now, their surprise attack was *still* completely undetected by the oblivious German enemy in Vågsøy.

*How close could they possibly get before the enemy realized?*

The alarms would raise any second now ...

*... so why not sound it for them?*

It was time to go loud.

*0847-hours ...*

A sudden illumination caused all the brodie helmet-wearing Commandos standing within the two dozen Higgins landing crafts to gaze into the starry dawn sky above.

Behind them all, the Kenya had fired her gun, breaking the silence. This was not a cannon shell, however ... but a flare.

A single, highly visible golden phosphorous burst known as a *star shell* soared between the distance of the flat Vågsfjord and the Vågsøy Island landmass. The object seemed to slow as the pitch of the trajectory peaked, arcing downwards and now dropping above Vågsøy in a slow descent. The powerfully bright twinkle of the golden flare irradiated the snowy and rocky island, exposing the hidden infrastructure beneath the layers of dawn shadow, dangling like a lit chandelier.

The entire island and the sporadic enemy outposts located around were now a visible turkey shoot for the out-of-sight Royal Navy armada in the bay.

Amidst the hundreds of helmeted domes of rubber-necking troopers, one man still in his formal green beret twisted about. Where most men gawked bearing anxious frowns or wide eyes of anxiousness, Jack Churchill wore a comfortable grin slyly beneath his moustache.

*It was going to be a nice day for a war.*

*0848-hours ...*

*BHOOM!*

*B-BHOOM!*

*BO-BO-BO-BHOOM!*

Somewhere in amongst the onset chaos, the Reuters reporter shouted for their news coverage of the operation while his loyal cameraman filmed the event presently brightening the skies.

*"... with the firepower of almost fifty shells a minute, every gun on our ships opened up in a furious broadside. All hell is let loose as the coastal batteries are smashed into pulps ..."*

As predicted following this morning's infiltration, the German reactions were slow to the bombardment. Completely caught off-guard, they were alerted to the attack only when shells from the Kenya's twelve powerful 6-inch guns began to fall on the German barracks area on the afar Måløy Island.

Nazi infrastructure detonated, exploding into shards of wood and pegging in fiery eruptions of unprecedented, brutal force, showering the surrounding areas with flaming debris.

Sandbag barricades covering machine gun nests were annihilated, popping like cooked corn from the array of direct hits over specific targets, alit by the aerial star shell fizzle as it crackled like static lightning.

There existed a series of dark Opel Blitz trucks parked near stacked fuel barrels beneath a camouflage tarp. In a chain reaction, the whole entity went up in a great ball of a glistening orange and golden fire, thrown outwards by exploding force. The power from the shockwaves even lifted one of the large trucks, tossing it onto its side in a crumpled, burning wreck. One particular truck, parked closest to the cusp of the island, flipped over the edge, tumbling almost two whole circuits before it splashed down into the basin, covered by the splashes of raining debris.

Once Måløy Island at the fore had been sufficiently shelled, the Offa and Onslow's 4-inch cannons joined in on other marked targets about the larger island at the rear. German troops along the coastal defences were quick to disperse, diving and sliding into their muddy trenches and bunkers as the snow-clad shores ignited like early New Year's Eve fireworks. Caught napping after the holidays, they could do nothing but cop the brunt of the unrelenting onslaught. Seeking shelter from the surprise salvo, they held onto their helmets and blocked their ears as the deafening barrage thundered and quaked.

In the total proceedings of this quick naval bombardment, some 400 shells were fired into ground fortifications in less than ten minutes.

The result: utter annihilation of the enemy's coastal defences.

Beneath a cold dawn sky of hot whistling shells, the Commandos in the two and half dozen Higgins landing crafts currently journeying towards the shores across the icy surface of the Vågsfjorden watched as the navy peppered their upcoming island defences with their cannons, absolutely pummelling the opposing vanguard. The decimation of German emplacements was unyielding and uncompromising. They literally paved the way for their assault landings, leaving nothing but craters, ashes, and spot fires amidst the rocky, snowy shoreline.

Retaliatory fire from any functional German battlements was minimal.

The stridency of the ear-splitting pitches of the shells passing above their heads was only then outdone by the diaphragm-jolting blasts as the screaming ordinance discharged into the smoky coast up ahead.

The commando troops within the humming boats couldn't even hear themselves shout over the torrent of unremitting cannon fire. Not even inner monologues could be heard. All sound was momentarily supplanted by that of the devastation.

From the water's still edge, they watched as multiple enemy targets were destroyed in fiery and tremor-inducing eruptions across Måløy Island, then continually on the mainland. The town across the bridge was dotted by cannon fire, as were several targets throughout South Vågsøy, such as obvious machine gun nests and artillery cannons capable of damaging the royal fleet parked in the fjord.

Further north-west, the small village of Holvik was also hit by fire, specifically from the Oribi. They shelled the village which housed the enemy barracks ahead of Group 1's aloof, vital objective.

The barracks building itself was hit by several shells before the wooden structure exploded outwards in an immensely fiery display in the distance.

The warships softened all land targets so that the Commandos' assault could push through defences with ease.

And with that, came the next step in this advance.

In the rear of the front travelling Higgins boat of the group assault, Colonel Durnford-Slater assessed the array of goodies laid out before him on the console. At the helm, his boat was leading the five other boats of the southern-most assault on South Vågsøy. Presently floating parallel to them in the Vågsfjorden, Bradley's One Troop would charge forth for a more northerly landing and strike the herring oil factories up the coast with the assistance of No.6 demo, thereafter, working their way back down on land and meeting the assault in the middle of Vågsøy.

The signal from the landing force to the navy to cease fire was to be the sight of *ten* vertical flares arising from the LCs on their ascent. To save valuable time, Durnford-Slater had not only organized to have the flares prepped and ready at his disposal in the lead boat, but also to have ten flare *guns* at the ready.

Durnford-Slater grabbed a loaded gun off the console and with his thumb cocked the large claw hammer of the Very pistol.

He hoisted his wrist into the air above his head.

*Pufffff...*

Burning bright red, the flare thundered into the sky above their travelling Higgins boat. It was quickly followed by another at a slightly curved angle, then another, recurrently ...

In travelling formation across the water, the view from a closely neighbouring Higgins LC saw Durnford-Slater's point boat launching the flares. The bright red sparkles caused the immediate area around them to glow with a pinkish haze as the calm reflection of the Vågsfjorden mimicked everything like a mirror.

Major Jack Churchill's beret-wearing head brought his view into a low tuck. From the astonishing sight of the climbing flares in the smoky skies above the fjord, he panned left and to two LCs at their flank.

He could see clearly beneath the glow that these LCs were manned by the men of G1, led by Lieutenant Clement. As planned by the deployment of the signal flares, these boats now peeled off on a westerly tangent, headed towards their target at Holvik, where there was a supposed enemy barracks positioned within the fishing village. It had just been well-shelled by the Oribi, and it was up to Clement to intercept any remaining German forces lurking behind in the smoky aftermath and silence them before they could attempt to reinforce the defences near the town of South Vågsøy from G2's assault.

From his position slightly higher on the console step of his LC, Churchill witnessed their coxswain bank at the wheel and lean into the turn, taking them on an acute westward approach. Beneath the brim of his beret, he saluted them for what it was worth, to wish them luck.

Following that moment, the sense of hearing slowly returned to all Commandos within the assault ships, as the broadside from the navy seemed to diminish—even before Durnford-Slater's ten flares had finished signalling. Even though Brigadier Haydon aboard the Kenya had gotten the message early and ceased fire, their colonel followed through, juggling gun after gun, aimlessly firing shot after shot into the sky like a knuckle-headed cowboy in a saloon.

"Are we slowing down?" a trooper questioned from behind the overly kitted standout, Mad Jack. Their assault ships were making good time voyaging across the fjord from the warships, but another step was yet to happen before they could beach the icy shores and storm the island.

"We are," Churchill announced behind his men, turning to face the navy coxswain and stoker from the Prince Leopold. The two navy men operated the often-temperamental mechanics of the diesel engines and expertly steered the flat-faced vessel.

The coxswain nodded. The drivers had orders to wait for the smoke before getting too close on their approaches. Churchill's bonnet-clad head scanned the skies, and he read the schedule. Searching west in the sky, he remarked, "We're to hold."

"Hold for what?" Felix Hardy shouted attentively past the soldiers.

There was an underlying tone reverberating in the air.

Audio filled the void left by the ear-splitting pitch and hum from the clamorous cannon blasts which had just subsided. While the seconds ticked and the distance closed of the crafts emitting the pending reverberations in the sky, it suddenly became clear to all the men what was coming.

*The RAF.*

*"For that!"*


*0858-hours ...*

Pervading the airspace above Sogn og Fjordane and sweeping in a low-slung westerly approach across the Norwegian Sea, a squadron of Royal Air Force bombers and fighters came roaring into existence. From their view up high, they had been chasing the rising sun upon the distant horizon.

Their dawn target location was an easy mark thanks to the bright and luminous floating star shell. From up in the sky above the Vågsfjord, they could see everything as clear as day.

The ten *Handley Page Hampdens* and nineteen *Bristol Blenheims* were flanked by two squads of nimble *Beaufighters.*

Hampdens were twin-engine bombers. They were long and skinny, with a tube-like fuselage, and were among the most unusual looking airplanes, but on this day, they trundled in to fulfil their mission alongside their Bristol cohorts from the RAF.

Half their mission was to dump smoke bombs on the landing sites, concealing the amphibious Commando landing. The other half was to drop bombs on indicated targets further inland or obscured from the naval cannons. Targets like the sighted enemy strongholds and gun emplacements along the coastal embankments, which a handful of Blenheims flanked by Beaufighters appeared to be doing along the opposite side of the Vågsfjorden. They prepared to deploy bombs along the southern and easterly coasts that outlined the fjord, such as the enemy cannons in *Rugsundøy* to the east, opposite the coast to Måløy Island.

From the naval assault moments ago, the hovering haze of smoke which resembled settling cloud was alit by the strobing flares and spot fires below, softly illuminating all ground targets. The bombers cut through the fog, able to see the snowy white earth below clearly in order to accurately drop their payloads.

The Hampdens were in first, deploying phosphorous shells which detonated a calculated fifty yards above the shoreline in a line of big white clouds of hot scorching debris. The only objective of this was to block visibility from the shore to the boats, which it did, providing perfect concealment behind a thick, impenetrable, sizzling smokescreen.

Utilizing the planned subterfuge to its advantage, the LCs briskly throttled forwards, heading towards the coast and into the thickening smoke shield as it dropped, deploying before the sight of the island like a curtain masking their approach like clockwork.

*0859-hours ...*

The view of the operation from the bridge of the Kenya was panoramic. Aboard the point ship located the furthest in the fjord and closest to the action, they saw everything as it excitingly unfolded.

Brigadier Haydon had just authorized the RAF bombers, who had previously been in a holding pattern out of range, to enter the fight and dash in low to drop the smokescreens for the landing forc—

*... boom—BOOM!*

The entire destroyer suddenly quaked and rumbled as they were fired upon by a hostile originating east—from the enemy lookout at Rugsundøy. Hitherto, the enemy position seemed to have been sleeping.

"What the devil was that?" Haydon remarked after feeling the impact quake. One of his sea captains stood confused, and a sailor in a headset quickly reported loudly after the aftershock shaking of the vessel.

"*Sir, stern-side has been hit by cannon fire.*"

"Damage?"

"*Nil, sir,*" the sailor shook his head and removed his communications headset an inch off his ear to report. He was slightly baffled by the reports he was hearing from below deck. "*It's coming from the other side of the fjord. Small guns, sir. four-point-seven-inchers.*"

"Felt more like five-point-ones," Haydon corrected after listening and feeling the reverberations. His far superior knowledge about naval warfare was often stellar. "A bloody nuisance, nonetheless," he added, stepping over to the stern side of the bridge and raising his binoculars to better see the distant German anti-air emplacement there. In the dark shadows of dawn, he could see their distant muzzle flashes along the coast of Rugsundøy as they fired again. Almost a full second after, the impacts were audible.

Unlike Hovden, the outpost seemed manned but barely capable of inflicting much damage from this far or to ships of this magnitude.

"*Sir, return fire?*"

Haydon removed his eyeglasses and shook his head modestly. "Negative. Hold fire. They're about to meet their maker ..."

They watched from the Kenya's bridge as Rugsundøy became bombed by the squadron of sailing Blenheims. Their payloads were of full-charge and right on target, quaking the snow-clad hillside emplacements with so much force that the tremble caused an avalanche to slide down over the enemy outpost. The icicle landslide buried the manned emplacements in a haze of snow, powder, and rock.

Men who witnessed it cheered, however their celebrations were cut short as an attentive observer amidst the bridge spotted more enemy activity in the distance.

"*Sir, enemy trawler in the bay! Two-o'clock!*" a British sailor shouted and suddenly all heads turned, and all hands were back on deck. A general alarm bell sounded at a wail.

"*Aye, enemy two-o'clock!*"

"*Aye, enemy ship passing seventy-degrees northeast! Mark?*"

"*Mark! Seventy-degrees northeast!*"

Haydon hastily stepped into position, scanning east towards the breaking dawn along the horizon with his colleagues; sharply pursuing their mark.

Out in the flat seas of the dawn Vågsfjorden, emerging from somewhere beyond South Vågsøy where there must have been port access along the Ulvesund Fyr north passage, was a German armed trawler tearing ass across the flat surface.

The ship was small in comparison to the British destroyers, but her AA-guns could still do some major damage—predominantly to the bombers in the skies.

Haydon laid eyes on the armed trawler, spying it like a snake in the grass. The German ship was known as the *Foehn*, and he immediately saw her bow turrets firing flak diagonally and towards the RAF squadron over South Vågsøy. She was pushing out into the Vågsfjord to get the right angle of attack and swat as many of the bombers out of the sky as possible.

"*Sir, do we engage or leave her for the Onslow?*"

"You bet your left bollock we engage, lad," Haydon shouted. "Get us in range!"

*Vågsfjorden*
*Vågsøy, Norway*

*0900-hours ...*

An elongated finger of smoke bombs had been dropped along the coast approximately 200 yards in front of the commando-packed assault

LCs. The array of speeding crafts rapidly closed on the beach. Fortunately for the operation, there was practically no wind this morning, which gave the smokescreen an ideal amount of density. Visibility contracted to less than twenty-yards due to the vapour concealment.

Beneath a sky of buzzing RAF aircraft formations, the two-dozen Higgins boats came thrashing onto the icy shores. When they entered the thick and ominous veil of smoke, the men started to cough and wheeze. The potent aftermath of the incendiary phosphorous product responsible for such an impenetrable smokescreen seemed to slowly dissipate as the men also acclimatized through squinting eyes, leaving only the white cloud which resembled fog along the morning coast.

Explosions detonated in the distance over South Vågsøy as the bombers dropped their payloads, cremating anything still breathing after the navy salvo.

The abrupt blasts of more naval guns sounded-off behind them in the Vågsfjord, seemingly firing at offensive targets, as well as more cannon fire to the north and across the fjord in the east, near Rugsundøy. The environment was a cacophony of battle noise.

Above them on the coast were discharges in the smoky airspace above the island, as German AA positions lit up the sky with bright volleys of trailing white flak against the RAF planes.

Needless to say, *it was all bloody happening.*

In the eastern-most section of assault boats, a signal was given by the navy coxswains carting the G3 members of Churchill's command. His troops occupied eight of the Higgins LCs of the formation, while Durnford-Slater's men occupied the majority to the west.

A voice shouted from a neighbouring boat which housed Five and Six Troops. Troop leaders Captain Young Young, Lieutenant Hank Peace, and Lieutenant Bruce Giles heard the notice across the water, between loud and echoic blasts.

*"Sixty seconds!"*

These G3 members would be touching the rocks at approximately the same time as G2, just across the water of the fjord between the Vågsøy and Måløy Islands. A second later, the signal was given in their own boat by their own coxswain, and Young felt for the pin on the top of his Thompson's receiver, pinching it back for fire. As well, he flicked his weapon off safety, as did several other troops judging by one of the only audible sounds within their vicinity being that of a dozen tiny *chits* and *clicks.*

God only knew what would be waiting for them once they reached their arrival ...

They were prepared for whatever welcomed them on the other side of this boat ramp when it fell, ready for bloody war.

"*Sixty seconds! Get ready!*" their own coxswain announced loudly over the mayhem.

The men within the boat exchanged nervous looks.

They felt their portion of travelling LCs break away off, banking right and towards Måløy Island. Parting from the masses, they heard their distance audibly grow as the small boats carved through the shallows.

Young was probably the more battle-experienced of the three familiar faces, having been present in a command role during Operation Claymore along with Durnford-Slater and perhaps a few others, and the assertive look upon his warpainted-face said it all. From within the tray of the Higgins LC, the commandos could see nothing of what waited ahead. The protective walls of the steel tray were above their heads, fencing them in.

"Sixty seconds, lads," Churchill remarked after stepping down from the rear console footstep and gently manoeuvring through the crowd of anxiously waiting commandos in the boat tray. He made his way to the front and by the ramp door—where he would be leading them.

The men aligned with him, their fearless leader.

They joined his rhythm, filing in. They were like pumped and amped sprinters waiting at the start line for the gun to go off.

"There's just enough time for something ..." he paused mid-way and eyed a few of his lads within the group. He let his submachine gun dangle from its strap in preference of transitioning to another of his deadly weapons ...

The point-boats belonging to G2 sections Two Troop, Three Troop, and Four Troop, which comprised the commands of Colonel Durnford-Slater, Captain JFG, Captain Forrester, Kaptein Linge, Lieutenant Head, and Lieutenant Komrower were also given a sixty-second countdown indication to their landings.

Feeling their boats veer left and towards the mainland, they prepared their clutched weapons and assumed a bracing stance, for any moment now, their boat would run aground, potentially ferociously. They would beach, their doors would fall open before them, unfolding like a ramp, and the contained men would explode from the vessel onto open land to assert their position and formation for the assault. Theoretically, they could be met with violence and hostility from beyond the nether ... God only knew what awaited their arrival on the shores.

The men across the charging boats prepared themselves mentally.

Knocker White, Dennis O'Flaherty, Dildo Dillon, as well as Mills, Peel, de la Torre, Sorry Corry, and countless other brave soldiers courageous enough to don the Commando flash upon their sleeve.

Although they had selected a less focal position to mount their landing along the grimy and rocky beach, for all they knew, there was possibly an enemy machine gun emplacement just watching them land ashore.

The troops would entrust the low visibility of the smokescreen with their lives, but they were trained to expect the unexpected and prepare for the worst.

*Click-click ... chit ... click.*

Weapons chambered everywhere and were taken off safety.

*Chit-chit!*

The foregrip of a pump-action shotgun in the hands of a trooper racked loudly beside Head's head and it caused him to flinch. The man didn't apologize, just merely nodded respectfully to his leftenant. Head returned the gesture, pulling up his Thompson and checking the drum-magazine was attached correctly before pulling back the pin with a virile noise of his own.

Above the hum of the Higgins boats in the formation ...

Beneath the droning reverberations of the RAF in the sky ...

Piercing the noise of the distant explosions and bombing ...

... the sudden, strange skirl of a bagpipe whistled throughout the proceedings of the pending dawn assault. The underlining *hummmm* from the Scottish instrument filled all the remaining airspace.

It wasn't so much that it got louder as it transpired, but that the many ears of the hundreds of commandos within the LCs became attuned to the Scot sack as it boisterously performed the familiar tune of *The March of the Cameron Men*, and they all seemed to exchange half a glance out of confusion before smiles cracked and the tense atmosphere seemed to lift a little.

Tension dropped. The soldiers exhaled and relaxed.

Men chuckled and hooted.

Became enthralled and calmed.

For an instant, the weight of the war on their shoulders was elevated and they were able to breathe.

*In the moment, they became reminded of their brotherly bonds, their kinfolk and country, and the reason they fought this fight.*

As the melody of Frimley floated across the water to him and their boat, and Durnford-Slater begged the question aloud, utterly confused by the out of place noise.

Pulled out of the zone for an instant, he raised his neck about the crowd, menacing a frown, " *Which bloody fool is that?*"

Beneath the childish grins and lurks, the commandos all knew who it was: Mad Jack, of course. It was his battle chant.

The skirl and hum of the pipes seemed to fade into the distance as Churchill's Måløy Island-orientated G3 LCs began to split formation from Durnford-Slater's G2, headed ashore to advance via foot to South Vågsøy.

After an extended moment of softness beneath the constant chaos of distant warfare and explosions, the unexpected then happened.

Right as the bellies of the assault ships were about to beach themselves upon the granite rock shores of the mainland, breaking the icy boundaries between sea and land, a blasting enemy flak detonated low above the coast.

*Bo-Boof!*

So low, in fact, that it actually damaged one of the passing Hampden bombers in a fiery display of shredded metal and popping debris.

The pilot must have lost control, causing an errant sixty-pound phosphorous bomb intended for further smoke cover farther up the coast to drop early and detonate *directly above* two of the incoming Higgins boats ...

Durnford-Slater occupied one of them.

*The casualties of this mishap would be massive.*

Blinking phosphorous coated the Higgins boat, dowsing all those onboard with blistering flame.

*0902-hours ...*

The view from the trays aboard Churchill's veering G3 landing crafts was one of dread and disquiet.

Aboard his LC compartment, the commandos helplessly observed the nightmare accident unfold beneath the golden glow of aerial flak and smoke haze.

Churchill ceased playing his pipes, peeled his lips from off his blowpipe to watch the ill-fated accident as it unfolded.

He uttered: "*Oh no ...*"

The commandos had all witnessed seconds ago the Hampden bomber becoming struck by flak, causing the screaming aircraft to manoeuvre bizarrely and, somewhere in the chaos, the airplane prematurely released its payload early and above a friendly advance ...

Helpless to intervene, they watched as the phosphorous charge crackled brightly below the winded flightpath, detonating in the low skies above the progressing LCs belonging to G2 as they began their final assault. They each saw the hot white glow of fizzling light blanket above and overtop of at least one boat—the most forward, leading boat—just as it reached the finish line of the shore, showering them in what was glorified Greek fire.

The sizzling white phosphorous showered down upon them like an unstoppable flow beneath a magma waterfall.

The only thing powerful enough to break their stares away from the frightening scene of friendly fire was that of the damaged and crashing Hampden bomber in its failed evasive arc of flight. It came screaming down towards their own Higgins boats in the fjord.

"*Oh, shit!*" someone shouted as every head within the group of landing crafts dipped for cover, and the thing inadvertently dive-bombed their location.

The incoming spiralling RAF plane overshot their position by mere metres, managing to pull up at the last second to avoid a collision with the crafts on the water's surface. It passed by so closely that it ripped up spray from the water's surface in its updraft.

*vvvvvVVVHROOM!*

In an awesome, gut-wrenching display, the crashing bomber roared past in a deafening flyby that quaked their speeding motorboats like sea storm turbulence, making waves in a calm current. The coasting LCs veered in their course, nearly banging into one another due to the force of air, tossing up waves from a current.

The heads of the onboard commandos raised in the seconds that followed in time to see the smoking Hampden crash-land in a skimming glide across the icy Vågsfjorden, finally planting still and throwing a gigantic tidal wave of momentum in the water before she rested afloat. She had touched down in the backdrop of the giant navy destroyers who would undoubtedly quickly attend to rescue any survivors. It had been a soft landing, through the ship would sink in seconds.

*Everything suddenly sizzled in hot, hissing white.*

Brighter than a sunspot, the lead Higgins boat was afire.

*"Get overboard!"* one of the men within Durnford-Slater's vessel shouted in a continual roar as almost everybody reacted at once within the landing craft beneath the flickering, simmering lightning storm of perpetual blinking brightness.

Durnford-Slater's eyes would have grown wider if it wasn't for the vivid glare of the pulsating phosphorous causing him to painfully squint in order to see. He swore, blocking the searing shine with his arm.

*"Blood-y-hell!"* he muttered, almost inaudible.

Scattering and attempting to mount the tall edges of the tray-like death box, the panicking occupants were suddenly now within the confines of a volcanic eruption. Their sudden shift in movements caused the propulsion of the racing Higgins to suffer slightly as it rocked from side to side, losing speed in immediate buoyancy corrections.

What proceeded ... was tragic.

The blistering white phosphorous of the flare shell dropped over the two frontal boats, scalding the side of one of the LCs while completely blanketing the other, turning it into an encapsulated firepit of cascading sparkles that grew as oxygen fuelled it. It burned hot enough to roast nearby men alive, pulling them into an oven.

The water between the two boats and around the point LC sputtered and hissed like lava from a volcano, even spilling into the beach, fizzing as it scalded the water, burning hot enough to glow even once it subsided beneath the shallows, bring the surface temperature to a boil.

"Whoa!" the narrow-nosed Peel articulated within the second boat as the dread and alarm set in about the men like wildfire. He and several other commandos witnessed a squelch of white-hot incendiary lick the edge of their Higgins' tray, instantly causing the metal to turn a hellish red, radiating from extreme heat like a blacksmith's anvil plate.

At the rear of their ship, whilst his wide-eyed stoker held on for dear life, their coxswain drastically spun the steering wheel and cranked levers, turning their boat drastically to the left and away from more of the falling phosphorous dump. Due to the manoeuvre, their boat tipped diagonally, causing the commandos within to topple into one side—thankfully, the side most distant to the errant bomb. The extra height they caused in the gyration assisted in shielding them from further overspill as the flames lapped.

Ultimately, this caused their LC to crash into the neighbouring craft right as they both touched land, banking in hard and tight together, somehow beaching on the rocky shores safely.

In a conjoined collapse, the men all fell forwards, colliding into one another in a kerfuffle. In the seconds that followed, they stumbled to collect themselves, find their feet, their guns, and they halted only to hear the screams from the neighbouring men in the point ship as they sizzled like lobsters in a frying pan over a hotplate. The unnerving sounds struck them all with despair.

*Durnford-Slater's Higgins was an absolute inferno.*

Drifting aberrantly in the shallows, it beached like a crash-landing of molten brazier, spilling boiling hot bitters over its tilting, brimming edges.

Within, men were burned to death by the flares.

The blinding phosphorous was so hot that people literally melted.

The extreme heat of the sticky, searing substance chewed into the confines of the steel boat like acid, hissing like a cornered reptile. Blinding, glowing chunks of pure brimstone danced about their scampering boots in the bottom of the tray in an array of fizzing sparks, setting ablaze to any*thing* and any*one* it touched or came near.

*An errant inferno.*

Within the LCs, commandos were packed like sardines ...

Twenty to thirty troops per boat ...

*There was literally nowhere for these men to run.*

Troops dropped their rifles as they became engulfed in flames. Abruptly possessed by the scalding, they barged into each other like some sort of satanic mosh. Phosphorous had dowsed over men's shoulders from above, leaking off the circular brims of steel helmets, practically melting through them like magma. Due to the heat, the iconic brims folded from the weight of the man-made molten.

Grown soldiers screamed and wailed with utter trepidation. Like insensible zombies, they slammed into the walls of the tray, into one another, like encaged beasts. Steaming like demonic entities, they rolled across the confine walls, the floors, like they were demonically possessed.

It was an impossibility to dowse such a specific flame, even in the icy waters of the Vågsfjorden.

*Weaponized phosphorous was designed to be inextinguishable.*

Even in the water besides the boat, the white-hot remnants of the blinking payload dropped with a splash, causing the icy waters of the shore to bubble and boil while it illuminated beneath the surface, like a sweltering moon pool.

Those fortunate enough to not be directly beneath the smoke bomb in the front half of the LC were able to quickly react, falling back against the rear walls, piling up like a throng. In the pandemonium, some men even mounted the elevated console where the coxswain resided during transit. He and his stoker both upped the open-air wall that was lowest near them to abandon ship as the incident unfolded. A blaze set in their wake, and bulwarks of fire climbed the tray walls like a cauldron.

Amidst the hellish chaos, Durnford-Slater pushed his friend Head backwards, shoving him up the console as allied troopers continued to combust into flames right beside them. One of the men was one of his much-respected lieutenants and long-time friend of Churchill's, Arthur Komrower, who happened to be right at his side as flames from the scorching incendiaries bounced about like a pinball death trap.

The two watched as a burnt trooper dropped to his knees right before them, barely able to breathe through the smoke. The white phosphorous severely melted Komrower's hands and face, and anything exposed was red raw. The steel brim of his brodie helmet dipped beneath the dowsing, reaching melting point within seconds and bowing, collapsing around his face. It had perhaps saved his life.

As he trundled agonizingly away from the inferno presently engulfing the front end of the LC, Komrower's hands drooped from his body as if they were made of wax.

Durnford-Slater instinctually sacrificed hold of his weapon and caught Komrower as he collapsed through the fog of fume, and was immediately regretful of his decision as his arm and uniform threads caught alight from touching the sticky fire scorching Komrower's back.

Emitting a shriek, Komrower bounced off Durnford-Slater, up and spinning as the flammable incendiary glued to his body like tar, and the flames climbed through clothing like an absorbent. He shouted in fret as he immediately tripped and fell into the solid steel wall beside Durnford-Slater, who had no choice but to shove the trooper clear in order to reach forwards and grapple the lever on the console which read *hatch disengage.*

After Durnford-Slater had pushed the squirming Komrower away, his gloved mitts instantly ignited into flames. Luckily, he had been wearing leather gloves that somehow managed to save him contracting anything but mild burns as, fast as lightning, he stripped himself of them immediately, assisted by Head by his flank. Once rid of the burning gloves, the two bashed out the flames on Durnford-Slater's sleeves as they, too, caught alight, even climbing to his neck collars.

The ungodly fire ascended past his elbows within seconds. It was terrifying how quickly the incendiary seared, aiming to consume everything as quickly as oxygen turned to fire.

In the smouldering chaos, these two commandos at the rear of the LC managed to follow many others up the rear console step, rolling away from the licking flames, managing to hoist and free-fall off the edge of the boat and into the knee-high water outside the craft.

Thanks to Durnford-Slater's actions, the ramp at the front of the LC disengaged. It had effectively been trapping the men inside a cooking oven. Out poured what remained of the panicking troops of the LC as soon as they were able, collapsing out into the shallow water of the beached vessel. Some of them tripped on the already deceased, charred bodies that lined the floor of the boat, and therefore could not even make it out.

Vision fell upon a lively commando trooper as he snagged and collapsed, buried at the legs by another burning casualty of the errant incendiary. Screaming in fright, he tried hard to drag himself to the edge of the boat where there was water, tried to pull himself free of the burning remains, only to succumb to death as his body became engulfed in flames from the chest up, searing his throat and chin, broiling him alive. The demonic fire caught him, seeking to reel the survivor back into the fray as his fatigues ignited like raw tinder. The commando bellowed a cry of agony, arms outstretched towards the members of the neighbouring Higgins boat who had ran across the beach to help ...

The shoreline onlookers became overwrought by dread as they witnessed the aftermath, and they paused to witness him and many others be burnt like a log on a fire.

The armed men from the adjacent Higgins vessel ran quickly after their ramp deployed, thrashing through the knee-deep water in attempt to assist their injured comrades—their distress beaconed like a bonfire. None of them were expecting the casualties to be so high, or the sight to be so shocking. It almost robbed all of them of their mental capacities and their mobility in the moment.

Troopers Peel, de la Torre, Knocker White, and even Algy Forrester became unexpectedly paralysed by the sight of nearly twenty of their men in flames, dead or dying. The sense of helplessness and shock overcame them instantly, and they froze stiff.

"*Medic!*" Captain JFG shouted as he ran in from the beholding bunch, heroically throwing his submachine gun onto the dry pebbles of the shoreline in time to dash into the ice-crust shallows and push one of the flaming commandos with all his might backward and into the water—dowsing him for his own good. He got down low, pushing the man into the icy waves with his bare hands, putting out the fire with a blistering thrash of swell in the interest of saving his life.

Other men quickly assisted, doing the same, nearly drowning men to save them.

Norwegian Kaptein Martin Linge and his men of the NOR.I.C.1 were next to arrive on the shore, running from the next LC that landed along the coast with a grating grind on the rocks.

Luckily, none of these G2 landings were met with opposition.

Where his Norwegian brothers refrained inclusion in the bedlam, Linge heroic nature took over. He tossed his weapon and helmet onto the land in the same manner JFG had, sprinting past several bystanding British commandos, more desperate to assist. He grappled with a burning, screaming man as he strutted from the ramp of the smoking LC, wrestling with the flames that were consuming his fatigues. Linge tackled him down into the wet, pushing him under the cold water as an icy wave rushed over them both. His actions resembled murder by drowning, but it was to save a life, not take it. The burned man emerged, gasping for air.

He was starved of oxygen, but glad to no longer be dying from an inferno blaze.

... the man was Lieutenant Komrower.

Komrower's burnt pretty face emerged from the wet, assisted by Linge, sporting full-thickness burns to his arms and around his neck and jawline. His face was pink, and his eye was bloodshot from a subconjunctival haemorrhage; a burst vessel in his eyeball due to extreme heat. Through clenched teeth, the icy water seemed to soothe the charred flesh burns as he had become submerged.

Now drenched and cold, Linge extended a hand to Komrower. He knew just how tough these commandos were and could somehow tell that this was not a towel throw-in for Arty Komrower, and he was right. Even though severely burned and in obvious pain, he was still up for the mission.

In partially numbed agony, Komrower accepted the result, rising to his feet via the hoist of somebody he held mild prejudice against—seeing him completely in a different light. He witnessed his unwavering, non-discriminating heroism. He held the British in the same esteem as his people. The radiance surrounding this man wasn't just a flavour of the week that Komrower solely didn't relish ... he was the real deal.

Linge and another trooper from the shoreline, Knocker White, further assisted him to land where many other men had established a light perimeter while they assessed the casualties.

The commando medics led by Sorry Corry were there within seconds having landed in a LC behind the wall of white smoke, and they assisted where they could. He saw to Komrower, who was alive thanks to Linge.

Veteran tough-guy and renowned Merry Man of Mad Jack's, Knocker White, extended an embrace to Linge in gratitude. He was thankful of the Norwegian's undying devotion to Commando, saving one of his people at the risk of his own life. Linge accepted it and, without words, the two drenched men caught a breath after the immediate chaos, suddenly true allies—friends.

Still breathless from the chaos and now soaked through, Durnford-Slater and Head finally rounded the rear of their roasting Higgins LC. The aground boat resembled a bonfire on the beach.

These two were completely soaked, but alive. They walked in amongst the wounded, assessing the damage. Several fatalities did not even make it out of the LC. Their lives were claimed by the phosphorous. Numerous men were floating face down in the drink; their charred remains would need to be dragged to shore.

"Perimeter up!" Durnford-Slater shouted, staying the course. He shouted so through chattering teeth, shaking from the pain and through the cold that seeped through the service dress beneath his snow smock. Wet from the drink and now absent his primary weapon, he withdrew his handgun out his shoulder holster and cocked the hammer with his spare hand, prepared for action, as should be the remainder of his men as they raced to establish a defensive line before their landed boats. Although this was a tragic event, it was to be treated as nothing but a minor setback to Operation Archery. The show must go on.

Shivering both from the cold and the adrenaline of the event, he dropped to a knee in leagues behind a few other armed commandos as they followed his order. They postured defensively, guns up and facing the island.

"Colonel?" JFG called as he stomped in close to his CO, scooping up his gun from the pebbles and assuming a defensive position with his weapon out front. "You okay?"

"Captain! Report?!" Durnford-Slater shouted, cradling his small weapon with both hands. From what he could sadly see, most of Two Troop had been killed or severely burnt before even making it ashore.

"Perimeter established! Two Troop is down by half!"

"Captain Corry!"

"Sir!" Corry responded, busy, but able.

"Set up a mobile triage near the munitions for the wounded. Ferry them back to the ships ASAP. Two, Three, and Four Troop, on me! We're headed for objective east!" Durnford-Slater boomed, leading the way with minor burns and a handgun.

A multitude of commanding voices affirmed and instructed in Durnford-Slater's rouse. These brave and unstoppable commandos were the tip of the spear, headed straight for the heart of South Vågsøy.

"*Yes, sir!*"

"*Sir!*"

"*Three Troop, on me!*" the booming voice of JFG shouted as he upped from his defensive poise, commanding the forty men within his Troop. He was surrounded by solid fighters: men like Knocker White and a fellow with the nickname of *Drain*—the Troops' radioman. Durnford-Slater's radioman, the smooth-skinned de la Torre and his pal, George Peel, were also amongst those on the coast.

"*Four Troop, let's go!*" beneath his broom moustache, Captain Forrester announced, waving his Thompson above his head to positively charge his men. O'Flaherty and Martin Linge's motley randoms of the NOR.I.C.1 detachment were amidst and in tandem with Four.

"*Two Troop, everything in order?*" Durnford-Slater shouted as he passed Lieutenant Komrower as Corry finished wrapping a dressing around his burnt arm. It was going to take a lot more than a wet bandage to fix this troop, but his overconfidence got the better of him.

"*Fuckin' oath, jolly good, sir!*" Komrower announced as he drew his Browning sidearm from his right hip holster with his nondominant left hand, resting his burnt and now bandaged limb to be wrapped. The man was literally half-baked, but still in it for the fight.

Durnford-Slater nodded assuredly, respectfully, before rotating about on the spot as he and his right-hand man, Lieutenant Head, led the charge along the shore.

"*Let's go, No.3!*" he bellowed as they all ran in full force along the beach.

The mandates were well received.

As one, the army of almost 200 commandos from more than a dozen landed LCs moved as a whole, weapons up and at the ready. They ran parallel to the line of white smoke that ranged along the coast before they finally emerged from it.

Before them was a clearing that bordered the now war-torn fishing town of South Vågsøy. It was time for the assault.

# 5

## *Vågsøy and Måløy*

*Måløy Island*
*Vågsøy, Norway*

*0905-hours ...*

The five Higgins landing crafts assigned to Churchill's assault group hastily short-stopped the shores of the small enemy-occupied landmass: Måløy Island.

Daylight rose, brightening the dawn around them, glowing clearer by the minute as morning welcomed their charge with energy and vigour.

Steel underbellies scraping the rocky land, the LCs stopped fast against the sharp, icy rocks, tactically beaching. In an instant, the ramps collapsed as their momentums ceased, and the landing parties dismounted, energetically leaping ashore with their guns up and safeties off, sweeping the foreign landmass across the barrels of their weapons' iron-sights.

Churchill was first out of the middle ship, Thompson in hand.

In the low morning light, he strafed aside with the wooden buttstock of the machine gun firmly against his shoulder. Across the gun's aim, he scanned for hostiles within his tight vector, allowing for his men to exit the landing craft at his flanks. Performing horizontal and vertical sweeping patterns of their own, they quickly fell into formation along the edge of the rocky island shore; the sound of the waves crashing against their feet.

They had purposely selected to strand their LCs on the lower end, below an elevated side of the island, where Måløy clambered into a fleeting overhang. The rockface provided adequate cover for their landing and would not take much effort for the men to scale.

Måløy Island had been shelled hard by the Kenya.

From their low sea-level position along the edge of the fjord, looking up the rocks of the petite precipice, smokestacks rose amid the island like place-markers for destruction. There appeared to be no hostile reception awaiting their disembarkment.

Downrange from their location, the remnants of an overwatching coastal enemy machine gun nest was visible. The sandbag barricades of the housing had been split, and the contents had collapsed halfway down the dubious rock formation, as had what was left of its German gunners; deceased and still steaming from the hot engagement.

"Let's move!" Churchill commanded now that his men had dismounted the LCs—last out from the metal tin can crept the out-of-place American journalist Felix Hardy and his notepad. He looked about the location, completely out of place but entirely enthralled.

Churchill took Six Troop north and towards the section of the island, where, above, a thin, single-lane bridge connected Måløy Island to South Vågsøy. Stowing his gun, he began to mount the rocks with almost two-dozen other men. They would engage Måløy from a westerly origin.

Meanwhile, Lieutenant Peace took another thirty around the southern external of the island. There, they would scale the rocks and take a southerly approach onto the island. The rest of the men would guard the rear and hold their parked LCs as a hind reserve. Only once— *if*—there was gunfire, would they advance as backup.

"Let's go No.3!" Peace called their brigade motto as he bolted with strident energy around the cusp of the island and followed it south. Once he and his men of Five Troop found a suitable incline that they could safely climb, they would escalate to the island peak to perform their sweep. Their origin into Måløy Island would put them right near a set of anti-air guns thirsting for complete detonation—if the earlier naval barrage hadn't already done it for them.

Around the rocky southern nib, Churchill struggled to mount some of the terrain leading up beneath the cemented lumber bridge supports, even with the assist of the beams. It wasn't long before Captain Young found Churchill from his position amidst his Troop and called for Bruce Giles to come forth with his grappling hook and rope line.

In an over-shoulder hike, they tossed the line up onto the land and then pulled, fishing for a snag. Once the metal end caught on the rocks above the overhang, they used the aid to trek up the tall surfaces before reaching topside.

"On me!" Churchill regarded, taking to the rope first.

"Sir?" Young halted their major at the risk of embarrassment in front of the other nearby men. His brow inverted, he added, "Don't you think one of us should go first?"

Churchill paused for a moment.

Young Young was a great officer for a command role and top bloke. The colonel honestly could not have selected a better distinguished commando to lead Six Troop, but like Churchill had encountered many times in the past from direct subordinates, Young's desire to lead in accord to that becoming of precise military stature often clouded his willingness to proceed without question—especially if Mad Jack was at the helm. It was odd how his preference to lead from the front was considered unorthodox.

"Relax, Young," Churchill uttered between them while he clamped the rope and prepared to ascend it. He added with a flare of grin, "If I die, *then* you'll get to be in charge, eh? What faster way to a promotion is there than letting me do my thing?"

"What happened to *no unnecessary risks?*" the baby-faced Young Young voiced aloud as Churchill scaled the rope above them. This was the directive for Archery, as dictated from Durnford-Slater; from Mountbatten, himself.

Against the hierarchy pretence concerning his CO status for these two Troops, Churchill was up the rocks first and into the spotlight of war, weapon up and remaining low. At present, he was currently the *only* Ally on this Axis land.

The up top was a whole other arena ...

The flat area of the island showed mostly only remains of what was once an enemy stronghold, compiled of partially flattened camouflage tents and infrastructure, as well as collapsed concrete structures still emitting pillars of thick smoke from the naval artillery strikes. The entire area was visible only through a constant veil of black smoulder, alit by a backdrop of random spot fires due to the explosive barrage.

Unmoving uniformed bodies of the enemy were strewn about the grounds, resting amongst twisted, burning metal corpses of destroyed trucks and caved-in buildings. The place was a warzone aftermath.

Machine gun nests were vacant, the sentry gun facing the sky.

It was eerily silent. Vacant. A ghost outpost.

So far, there seemed to be no movement at all. The Kenya had shelled the absolute nutsack off the Måløy Island enemy establishments, neutering guard towers and decimating garrison buildings, denying almost all of the fight from the boche on the ground. Only a few of the German FlaK-88s remained visually operational, erect for them to destroy. The rest was already ruins.

Through the war fog, Jack spotted an objective:

Central and standing tall amidst a clearing was the enemy wireless tower. The skeletal metal structure was grounded by sturdy anchor point cables that branched outwards, bolted into the island.

Churchill had planned to mount his attack from the south, cutting down any remaining enemy forces near this fortification first, taking down the tower before any German broadcasts could reach out for help. Then, he and his group would be onto the other objectives. However, judging by all the rising smoke about Måløy, most of these targets may have already been destroyed by the barrage, doing half their job for them—not to mention eliminating the enemy supposedly occupying this outpost. They had been annihilated by the naval salvo, barely leaving scraps for the commandos.

While Churchill scanned the area from his position low by the snowy rocks by the bridge access road, some of his men amassed in the background, stacking up just out of sight on the slope after mountaineering the short rockface.

Once more than half of them were ready to move, he gave the order via a hand gesture, which was relayed by Young to the rest of the Six Troop troopers.

"*Move!*" Jack ordered, stirring first with a firm hold on his weapon and tracing his direction over his poised gun barrel whilst he moved. Commandos followed him, scanning the vacant environment.

He commanded as they shuffled in advance. "*Space out!*"

In the spooky silence of an absent enemy, he and several others scattered in a spread formation out in the open, cutting through the haze. The lot were quickly surprised as, all of a sudden, an active enemy truck could be heard approaching from the mainland via the bridge at their flank. The dark-tan, six-wheel Opel Blitz open-tray troop carrier chugged along the passage, revealing itself to them through a cloud of lingering smoke. It headed straight towards the exposed and astray commandos as they crossed the opening.

"Come on, lads," Young relayed, following their intrepid major. "Keep your spacing!—"

"*Watch out!*" someone warned from behind near the bridge, spying the inbound vehicle with a sudden urgency.

"*Oi! Incoming!*"

"Major!" Young called, breaking formation and suddenly halting.

Both he and Churchill were on-point, and therefore on the roadway, directly in front of the inbound vehicle as it approached along the misty bridge.

The two commando officers spun and raised their submachine guns in tandem at the rumble of the rapidly approaching, shaky truck. At the same time the driver seemed to notice *and* recognize them as hostile. With no other options, he *sped up.*

*The engine throttled monstrously.*

The commando troopers presently unexposed to immediate danger simply lowered their stances, simply stepping away near the local cover of the slope to take a knee, all the while Young and especially Mad Jack Churchill remained imperilled ...

From their unbridled positions in the middle of the road crossing, they opened fire with their automatics, fearlessly holding their ground against the advancing truck.

Breaking the silence of their covert landing, their Thompsons thumped away wildly, resembling chattering typewriters, pelting the metal bonnet and glass windshield of the incoming vehicle with a dozen sparks and sparkling pops. The glass turned into a spiderweb of frosted dots, and the bonnet hissed smoke from countless perforations.

After an extended burst of gunfire directly at the enduring truck, Young upped from his kneel and strafed widely aside, urging Churchill to do the same over the lurid shooting as more of the commandos by the bridge aided, opening fire from their off-side positions at the bridge target.

The truck got peppered to shit.

The side of the open-tray truck's cabin was a pinwheel of bright sparks and chipping paint. The front tyre burst loudly as it travelled, throttling less aggressively now that the exposed driver had undeniably departed life due to all the onslaught; evidence of his slaying abounded as a spectacle of red gore expelled from within the cabin, painting the breaking glass from the inside—both the windshield and driver's side window, that shattered outwards.

The truck ... was dead.

It slowed in its advance, cruising.

After the fusillade brunt of gunfire against the incoming truck seemed to expire, Churchill fired an extra line of bullets across the fractured windshield and into the lifeless vehicle as it rolled dead-stick past him in a crescent path, just to be sure of its incapacitation.

Twirling back around and on guard towards Måløy, Churchill swept his arms down low as he rotated to face the potential island threats now that the truck had been eliminated. The area became again draped in an eerie silence, even following that loud circumstance with the surprise truck attack.

The men watched with obvious signs of concern as Churchill's movements remained tactical and calm. He barely strode out of the way in time to dodge the decelerating, stalling vehicle as it rolled past, dead-stick. It didn't seem to faze their fearless leader as he kept guard, onto the next target, nonetheless enclosing on Måløy from behind his smoking Thompson as though that takedown was nothing but a thing.

"*Move! Move!*" he barked, keeping an eye on the ominously vacant island positions.

Amidst their advance, the smoking and whistling truck gradually lost speed. An incessant hiss from its hood, the truck trundled past their formation, finally lumbering to a halt as it bumped into the remnants of a partially destroyed building a little further onto the island.

The commandos of Six Troop upped and fanned out about the mouth of the island town, taking up defensive positions on the corners of buildings and anything else they could use for protective cover whilst their teammates pushed up around them, and they judiciously enveloped the Måløy Island stronghold.

Everybody was on edge, but on-point.

The men of Commando utilized their training well, visible through the constant transfer of attentive posture and poise during transitional movement, efficiency, and precision of awareness. Their guns were forward, but they had each other's backs throughout. The firm stares of the men beaded across the iron-sights of the weaponry clenched tight in their grasp, pinched close in their shoulders.

With the forward grip of his Thompson out before him, Churchill slowly approached a centralized medium-sized structure with a blown-out wall near a double-doorway. There were the remains of a small machine gun nest out the front of it, apparent now by a series of toppled barricades, leaking sandbags, and spilled belts of brass chains. This told Jack that whatever this building housed, it was military and high profile due to the defences and fortifications.

From the hole in the wall—thanks to the navy—black smoke exuded from what must have been another direct hit upon the roof above, caving it in and exploding it outwards. Multiple spot fires still burned inside, blazing hot flames from within, raining flakes of ash like snowflakes.

Nothing appeared to be alive within.

What had once been an enemy operations centre for the island, likely for communications and relay, given the location of the signal tower, now only projected a sense of death and thawed decay. Churchill deduced as much by the singed communiqué papers blowing about the wreckage, and the damaged radio board that sat aslant the side wall and the arranged desk furniture amongst the ruins. Through the piling smoke, he observed deceased soldiers in grey uniforms spread about the collapsed debris; their pale and bloodied hands protruding the rocks and rubble. Among the dead were clerks and radiomen, very few with weapons other than the odd sidearm in a belt holster. Perhaps lowly communications officers caught in the midst.

Churchill pressed open what was left of the destroyed wooden door with the barrel of his submachine gun. He spied in the connecting hall more departed and buried soldiers, most likely the men belonging to the machine gun nest out the front, who had sought refuge from the naval barrage inside—but had instead found death from above by the direct hit by a bomber.

The insignia of the deceased soldiers read that of the Wehrmacht 181st Infantry Division. These were all men under the command of Lieutenant-General Woytasch: their big bad boss-man of Vågsøy, and a high-value target on their radar for capture.

Jack's sterling stare twinkled, scanning across the bodies in the muck.

Although it was possible that a high-ranking officer such as Woytasch could have been deceased within this mess, they had no time to identify those specifically killed in action. It would have been highly unlikely that the generalleutnant himself would have been present at the Måløy stronghold at such an early hour—however, as Churchill took a step away from the rubble, a differing element of attire did catch his attention and caused him to doubletake.

A dead man amidst the remains seemed to don a differing uniform than the men of the 181st. He was no guard, nor clerk, nor radioman. Not an officer—of that division, anyhow.

Churchill's stare intensified upon the white insignia on the man's black arm patch ... it seemed to resemble a *flower* or a *star—*

Interrupting his thoughts, a contained, abrupt explosion out on the street caused Mad Jack to spin and watch the origin directly across the road as Bruce Giles ordered one of the troops to disable one of the close 88s with some explosive. They had promptly accomplished the task, and now a demolitions trooper jogged over to the next cannon in order to do the same thing with an internal *pop* blast, decommissioning the enemy guns as per their objective.

*Gunshots ensued.*

There was some action up the street.

Churchill quickly moved out of the wreckage and took a corner by the edge of the exterior. His view focused in time to see that it was commando gunfire; men searching the ruins of a German hideout must have encountered trouble within, and were decisively giving them what-for.

Holding, he watched from outside the conflict zone as the gents persisted tactfully for a moment before firing some more shots blindly through a vacant doorway. All the while, another man prepped and tossed a Mills Bomb impact-detonating grenade in an under-arm throw inside the premises.

The men recoiled and tensed a second before the bomb exploded.

*Boof!*

In a pocket of discharging air, the impact grenade detonated within the structure, blowing thick black soot and stone debris past the stacked men cowering at the doorway. Whoever the charred individual was inside was certainly toast now.

Quickly, they then moved in as a team, signifying the confidence of commando success. They pressed inside, clearing the sector before re-emerging.

Upstanding now, Churchill examined G3 as the sections within Six Troop swept through each pocket of the Måløy Island stronghold with ease. The atmosphere emitted a sense of accomplishment; that all grounds of this small island had been taken from the enemy.

Like his very thought had jinxed it, the voice of a commando shouted and fast after, a few men ran to assist. Churchill hurried after them with his weapon raised, however, he lowered it upon witnessing a mass surrender of enemy troops around the bend.

Welcoming him around the corner of the street, he saw that from some of the large enemy barracks buildings at the end of the road, partially uniformed and unarmed German soldiers were emerging into the open with their hands above their heads ...

*They were surrendering.*

Commandos enclosed around them; weapons trained.

They rounded them up in the open street like herded cattle.

Wearing his winning grin at this victory, Churchill took some casual strides forth to approach these prisoners of war. It seemed whoever had survived the navy shelling and the RAF bombing were, for the most part, dazed and demoralized by the bombardment. This lot had completely given up.

Up ahead, just beyond the clearing where the radio tower was situated by another pair of 88s, Churchill could see Peace bringing Five Troop onto Måløy via the northern incursion. They had mounted the island with no real resistance, and a flank of his men were quick to stack upon and enter a partially destroyed enemy barracks, performing a pincer movement on the few enemy men who remained on the island. They withdrew with a handful of surrendered survivors at gunpoint, adding them to the cattle.

Churchill watched as Peace signalled one of his men to disable the German gun establishment, and he did so promptly by improvisation. The soldier collected from the abundance of stick grenades in the many pockets and caches of nearby Germans, then crammed four or five down each mouth of the FlaK cannon barrels before tugging on the fuse of the final entrant—*then ran like his arse was on fire.*

With seemingly anticlimactic detonations contained within the steeled barrels, the cannons exploded, becoming disabled, left as smoking, flowering wrecks.

In the distance, Churchill signalled at Peace who nodded back that all the German guns had been taken.

*Had they really just taken Måløy Island so easily ...?*

In the kerfuffle of jogging commandos rounding up German prisoners, all of whom surrendered without a fight, and securing the immediate area, Major Churchill focused his view ahead and he tipped upwards. He took in the sight of the tall wire frame radio tower: their prime objective on Måløy.

He turned his head. "Let's get a sapper up here!"

"*Demo!*" another troop at the end of the street relayed.

In the time it took to get a demolitions man brought forth from the ranks, Churchill signalled Peace to take his Troop and seek the entrenched bunker entrance, located further along the north and towards the oil tank reserve on the top of the island.

Peace gestured affirmatively, and he and his men in the distance upped from their defensive stances and headed towards the next objective.

"*Sir?*" a young sapper remarked as he jogged in near with a large haversack full of goodies that went *boom.* He wasn't carrying a rifle like any of the other commandos. His kit layout was decked out differently so that he could carry more of a variety of devices and charges, such as *Composition-C* plastique explosives and an assortment of fuses and primers to ignite them, from shoelace burners to detonating cord, blasting caps to timing pencils. He was skirted by a man with a pump shotgun who doubled as an assistant, and Felix Hardy who was tagging along with the rear group.

Churchill nodded towards the antenna structure up ahead. "You know what to do, trooper! Bring that god-ugly thing down!"

"*Yes, sir!*"

Churchill eyed Hardy as he anchored, taking a position by some nearby ruins and surveying details for his newspaper back home. "You having fun?"

Hardy's focus snapped to Churchill. His borrowed British helmet was so loose it made his head wobble like a drunk on a jog. "Uh, yeah, sure!"

"Good," Churchill comfortably cradled his weapon, observing the operation.

"Jack, I don't mean to sound pessimistic, but ... is this ... is this really it?" Hardy remarked half-heartedly. So far, Archery was turning out a lot like how Claymore had been described by those who took ground ... it was simply *fizzling out.* The enemy had gone limp before the fun had even started.

Churchill cast a look to him and then about the area, possibly plotting his wild imagination. Through all the excitement and resonance of victory, something here wasn't right.

It was in the air.

*Jack could feel it.*

Hardy watched him, waiting for a response.

In that extended moment of silence, he could see that Churchill was wondering the exact same thing ...

*Then Mad Jack smiled.*

Fondling the forward grip of his Thompson submachine gun, he turned to face Hardy without a direct response before shaking his head and looking away. His finger itched the trigger pull, hungry for more war.

"I sure hope not, lad."

*Halnoesvik*
*Vågsøy, Norway*

*0909-hours ...*

Concurrent to the north-westerly raid action, Two LCs occupied by Lieutenant Clement and the forty troops of G1 pulled in close to a rock formation below the slopes of the small corner town of Halnoesvik on their way to their objective in Holvik.

This neighbouring civilian town had not been shelled like Holvik.

That nearby destruction was visible as plumes of dark smoke over the nearing horizon as daybreak brightened the starry velvet sky, causing all landmasses and obstacles to silhouette.

The rush of their assault landing pumped adrenaline through the veins of the commandos as their LCs beached, and they promptly formed a group on the edge of Halnoesvik. They next progressed into the seemingly abandoned narrow town that hugged the outskirts of a road between the Holvik fishing village and South Vågsøy—the source of many deep-toned explosions and echoic machine gun clapping in the distance.

With a hand-gestured order, Clement's men moved in and secured the town, filing in two directions and keeping their spacing.

There were Norwegian civilians about the vicinity.

For the most part, the inhabitants seemed scared, sheltering within their residences, however the commandos knew that there was always the possibility of quislings lurking about: those locals loyal to their fascist land occupiers.

As the troops of G1 moved along the morning streets, scanning in-between and down the shaded sides of houses, they noticed curtains being pulled over, draping the dull light of candles within the many premises. They monitored this situation with caution.

From the houses as they passed, they could hear a baby crying ...

Perceived the hushed, anxious conversations of men and women ...

Soft footsteps shuffling within the hollow wooden structures ...

With every faint sound, the advancing commandos trained their weapons, sweeping from perspective angles, prepared to react to any aggressive action, to any potential ambush or counterattack.

While G1 progressed, they happened upon an exposed elderly man in a doorway, wrapped in a frayed hickory coat and a bluestone cap. He seemed harmless, observing their incursion on the land seemingly without a care in the world.

Clement was amongst the front of his cautioning troopers as they came near his house by a curvature in the road, and he halted to maintain eye contact with the old gent. Peacefully, he lowered his weapon and showed a friendly, gloved palm.

The old man stared blankly at first ...

... then subtly signalled across the street at a double-deck building.

*Perhaps a silent caveat?*

Clement followed his gesture and marked the suspicious house.

It was particularly dark and quiet, and ominous.

"*Boys!*" Clement called at a whisper, gently gaining the attention of those soldiers around the area. He hissed. "*Psst!*"

Three or four of the nearby commandos heard their lieutenant's call for attention and they ceased their exploring to focus, grouping in a defensive formation near the corner of a building in the—

*Bam!*

A thunderclap rang out from one of the dark orifices of the building.

It was a single shot—a pot shot by what must have been a slow bolt-action rifle and fired in a cramped position held by an enemy in the top floor of the building.

The bullet chomped at the grime between two soldiers positioned in the vacant street, causing them to curse and break apart.

"*Shit!*" one of the men swore as he upped and darted away, finding cover behind the edge of a nearby house. The other simply dropped to a knee and trained his sights on the wooden window embrasure where he believed the gunshot had originated from, sighting the blackness that lurked beyond.

"*Watch out!*"

"*Contact close!*" voices shouted as the commandos around the area homed in on the sudden action, taking up various firing positions.

Another shot boomed within, and this time the men saw the muzzle flash from the sinister window space. They promptly returned fire tenfold with their automatic submachine guns, lighting up whoever dared engage them. Their weapons gnawed the vantage to splinters and penetrated the wooden walls like they were made of mere thatch.

Due to the obsessive amount of retaliatory gunfire, they didn't hear anybody collapse inside.

*But it mattered not, for they were taking zero chances today.*

After an extended moment of extended bursts within the premises, the gunman within dared fire again, blindly letting loose another round out from the same window within which he apparently had ample cover.

"*Grenade out!*" a commando declared as he looped his rifle onto his shoulder and dashed several paces forth with a primed hand grenade explosive, pegging it with precision through the same window gap with nothin' but net.

He dove in strafe, ducking behind cover as a couple of seconds later they heard a German within fumble and shout in pani—*BOOM!*

*The top level exploded outwards.*

He dead.

HMS *Kenya*
*Vågsfjorden, Norway*

*0912-hours ...*
*BOOM! Miss ...*
*BOOM! BOOM!*
*Miss ... Miss ...*

For several minutes now, the Kenya had been engaged in intense naval warfare whilst manoeuvring its enormity in the open fjord. The warship was simultaneously targeting enemy fighters in the skies above Vågsøy Island whilst also engaging the armed trawler known as the Foehn, attacking from the north-east in the same Vågsfjord.

Upon noticing the flotilla of navy warships positioned within the bay, the Foehn had opted to cease fire upon the RAF bombers, rather attempting to cover its own ass in retreat. *The little kraut ship that could* showed some real ballbags taking on the British destroyer and her compatriots positioned by her flanks, trying to hold her own whilst she clearly panicked and devised a rushed backpedal up the Ulvesund Fyr.

The Foehn became peppered by shells from the accurate long-range cannons aboard the Kenya, and after she had taken a few hits across her starboard-side, seemingly out of ammunition, it appeared as though her kriegsmarine operators desired to run her aground on the mainland in favour of abandoning ship.

"One more hit and she's for Davy Jones! C'mon, lads!" Haydon bellowed as he paced within the busy bridge of the Kenya, overwatching the sea battle.

Her cannons fired again at the travelling trawler as she sped parallel to the island, throttling like a bat out of hell and away from this unwinnable confrontation.

*BOOM! BOOM!*

*Miss ... Miss ...*

The calm surface of the fjord beyond the Foehn erupted in giant geysers of water, spouting upwards thirty feet and mere inches from her roving bow and bathing the trawler with seawater.

The Kenya fired again, unrelentingly.

*BOOM! BOOM!*

*Miss ... Hit!*

The aft end of the German ship suddenly ignited in a gigantic ball of hot orange flames, bright and radiant in the blue dawn light. The direct hit upon her end immediately sunk the vessel's rear, slowing her movements just as the trawler reached a vacant section of land in the middle of the coast. She coasted in, incapacitated and taking on water like a discarded tin can.

Sailors aboard the Kenya cheered at the distant sight.

Haydon lowered his binoculars and simply nodded in utter contentment. The destruction of that enemy vessel was just another notch on his belt for all he was concerned.

"Merry-bloody-Christmas, Gerald," he quipped, raising his teacup for the first time since the battle had begun and taking a sip from the surface with a tiny *slurp.*

*South Vågsøy*
*Vågsøy, Norway*

*0915-hours ...*

In a monotonal manner of speech, press reporter from Pathé, William *the Miracle Man* Mericle, orated for the archive footage as a cameraman captured the action in the distance from the shoreline behind the marching commandos.

"*... The main landing is at the little town of South Vågsøy. In the face of stiff opposition from a German garrison, the Commandos, still watched over by the RAF, gain the rocky slopes and set about the defenders ...*"

Simultaneous to the unfolding events of the capture of Holvik by G1 to the south and the destruction of Måløy Island by G3 to the east, Colonel Durnford-Slater's G2 arrived at their access point along the shoreline of South Vågsøy. Any moment now, and Clement would take the barracks, and Churchill would destroy the wireless tower.

After trekking from their LCs embankment further south, Durnford-Slater led the charge of nearly 200 British No.3 and No.2 Commandos to the seaside adjacent to the urban area.

In a combined jog, the soldiers proceeded along the pebble and slate rock shore, leaping planks of driftwood and trudging pillars of ice. In the coastal backdrop of their progression, the impenetrable wall of hovering smokescreen that blocked sight of the Vågsfjorden began to thin.

The dissipating haze faded into the Ulvesund Fyr channel to the north, where they witnessed their secondary section, One Troop, cruise north in the dim obscurance of the morning light. They would progress in their LC towards their entrance point alongside some wooden docks located before the herring oil factory: their demolition target.

Light was glowing beyond the east horizon, about to break the velvet skies. Sunrise in Norway was late this time of year.

Following Durnford-Slater's charge, the men of Two, Three, and Four Troop acknowledged their CO's gesture to advance upon them reaching their incursion zone by some modest timber huts. He waved his pistol above his head, signalling them onwards; to get into position.

The mass of Commando swarmed the lip of the shore, awaiting behind ample concealment for the attack.

Captain JFG of Three Troop took point alongside Durnford-Slater as did his adjutants and communications officer (radioman), and they crept lowly to peek towards the shoreline crest to observe the enemy-occupied village. This point-squad was comprised of Lieutenant Charley Head and marksmen Corporal Dildo Dillon, with his scoped Lee-Enfield sniper rifle, as well as de la Torre and his fifty-eight-pound radio backpack which currently crushed him as he laid down on his chest.

The group pushed out beyond the dissipating smoke cloud tracing the coastal embankment and either took a knee or a prone posture, pausing a moment to lay eyes upon the cold coastal fishing village. The town of South Vågsøy stretched out about three miles between the shoreline of the icy fjord and the snowy cliffs of the mountainous range behind.

They narrowed their stares to locate the domiciles beyond the phosphorous haze which obscured the view of their infiltration from German soldier or quisling eye, searching any enemy positions that may have remained in this skinny settlement.

The Norwegian inhabitants who had been up and about their day's business had long since retracted into the woodwork, playing it safe. It was mostly elderly and families with children left behind. Most of the younger men that could fight had fled to England to join the forces of Free Norway some time ago.

Those who had remained behind longed for the day when the detested invaders were driven out—and *today* may be that day. Upon a closer look, in the form of symbolic graffiti and hidden icons on building walls throughout the mainland of Vågsøy, there stood evidence of existing patriotic protest against their Nazi aggressors. The Norwegians had never given up hope. Good thing, because their prayers had been answered ...

*Commando was here!*

Well-weathered wooden slat buildings and tin sheds comprised the urban streets of the icicle town. Whatever paint had been used to colour the structures had long since faded, worn by the freezing chill of the arctic air and the harnessed reflection of the sun from the calm, clear fjords and surrounding snow-covered mountains.

Dim warm lighting blushed from within many of the single-storey homes of the populous belonging to the occupied village. Smokestacks from several active chimneys were confirmation of liveliness within, and these commandos needed to remember that there were many civilian inhabitants present. Due to the nature of such, the village housings had been spared from any naval barrages to limit the collateral damage of innocent folk and would need to be individually cleared of any enemy presence by the men. This meant gruelling house-to-house fighting, for which they were well trained and prepared.

"What do you reckon?" the boxing-scarred eyebrow of JFG raised as he quietly queried to his colonel's ear. He had just concluded a fast headcount of the troopers within his unit as they piled up low along the shore just out of sight, awaiting orders. They were eager to storm the beaches.

Behind them, tracing along the water's icy edge, Captain Forrester commanded the men of his unit forth where there rested a lumber pier providing ample concealment leading into the village. They were conscientious not to break visual contact with Group 2, but also not to allow an established angle of fire by any potential enemy in the village.

The remaining men of Four Troop that included O'Flaherty and a rifleman by the name of *Sherington*, as well as Linge and his Norwegians, all advanced into town on a rightward flank. Once into the streets, they would hone towards the warehouse district that contained the Power Station; another of their main demolition objectives.

Durnford-Slater slipped a coy gleam to his cover neighbour.

"I think we kick the bastards while they're still down."

JFG concurred. "Fucking oath, sir."

"*Let's go, No.3!*" Durnford-Slater hollered after pausing for a breath. His foot soldiers were in an inseparable tandem, and their formation tight, staying with him as he initiated the charge into the battleground, raising up tall and waving his pistol.

Captain Giles shared his exhortation with his nearby men.

Men released energetic battle cries.

With a mighty charge beneath a warfront biodome of zooming fighters and their chattering machine guns, the echoic thunder of bass from cannon fire and detonations in the distance, the commandos surged into town with charged stamina.

Amid shouts of vigour, the Brits spaced their advances and moved in sporadic columns, splitting into twos or fours in order to divide targets as gunfire rained down from the enemy in the peaceful village.

*They hadn't seen the enemy as of yet ... but they had packed expecting a cold reception.*

From boarded window ledges ...

From top-storey barn windows in storehouses ...

From multiple dug-in enemy emplacements, enemy gunfire barked deafeningly over the shouting relays of commandos as sporadic intervals opened-up into their wide advancing line.

The blaring electric bursts from a tongue-tied heavy machine gun nest covered by stacked barrels and sandbags barricades could be felt juddering the diaphragm like a drummer playing a high tempo beat on their chest.

The stocky JFG led the boldest charge out into the open space between the south beach and the first of the village buildings, followed by the more cunning men of his Troop. Bullets *whizzed* and *snapped* about their frames as they carted their rifles, sprinting towards interval finish lines.

Knocker White roared with might as he charged in with volume, both from his war cry and the barrel of his shotgun as he slowed only to fire the pump-action repeatedly towards the distant enemy emplacements, peppering them with buckshot that flinted sparks like blacksmith hammer beat forge against an anvil.

New recruits; a radioman known as Drain and rifleman George Peel were preparing to march behind them. These two tin hat-wearing troopers were tasked with keeping the fifty-eight-pound wireless strapped to Drain's back within reach of their Troop commander on the frontline.

They courageously upped from concealment, and began their charge into the action as enemy gunfire rained down hail around them, kicking up pebbles and crunching snow. They exchanged a partial glance after bounding into one another during the pandemonium, each man equally as scared and excited to be a part of this action as the other; proud to follow heroic, renowned men into live combat. Beneath the brims of their strapped helmets, they both dropped open their jaws and bellowed out a whoop before charging in at full pace, sidestepping salvo and dodging death like they had bought a ticket.

Invisible *hisses* and *cracks* filled the air as hot German projectiles rained about their heads, even nibbling the vicinities beside their pacing arms as they breathlessly ran forth, gaining distance. Bullets tugged at their sleeves in their respective passages of motion.

Golden tracers from hot machine gun bursts sizzled like molten steel as the commandos miraculously darted in the open, all men fast to slide low behind new cover once clearing the deadly expanse.

Back at the beach, Durnford-Slater was yet to advance with his entourage. Exposed in the fray and gesturing commands, encouraging his men to press on, waving his gun above his head to draft them forwards.

The injured and obviously weakened Lieutenant Komrower of Two Troop took a second to catch a lungful before charging with his unit into the fray. He was limping and writhing in pain from his many strapped burns, yet stubbornly willing to push forwards at all costs. He had even conceded to using a large stick of driftwood he had found along the coast as a cane for his movement, and his most loyal men were at his flanks and matching his pace.

"*Let's go! Let's go!*" Komrower shouted, waving his team forwards in his lieu, just like Durnford-Slater was.

"Captain!" Durnford-Slater shouted across the fighting at Komrower as a wave of brave souls pushed on around them, mounting the cusp of the shoreline cover and hurtling into the skirmish. "I want you and some of your men to remain! Lockdown the beach and establish the FOB. Assist Corry with the wounded and oversee the intake of POWs!"

Komrower recognized forlornly the message that lurked within his tone. It was only logical that he should not be on the frontline or on-point for the advance into the town. He was now a liability due to his injuries.

"Sir!" Komrower acknowledged with a nod and, although disheartened, without hesitation. He tossed his cane away with an ounce of visible displeasure from becoming subtracted from the good fight just as it begun. With a deep breath of acceptance, easily tolerating his colonel's logical choice, he returned his view to whoever was left within his Troop still on the decline of the shore. The medical attachment was in tandem, as was a radioman and several other free hands who had brought up extra ammo upon stretchers.

It was not as though Durnford-Slater was benching him.

Rationality was a sensible resolve to any assault, and a mobile headquarters and signal post needed to be established somewhere accessible but just out of harm's way, and someplace men could send runners for more ammunition or grenades, as well as a place to cart the wounded for treatment by men like Sorry Corry, who was the lead corpsman for Archery.

Komrower pulled back behind the slope of the shoreline and to where the Commando FOB *(Forward Operating Base)* would become established, just behind the concealment of a rocky recess. There were men unloading carry carts of ammunitions and various other frontline commodities. It was also where press reporter Mericle and his cameraman lingered beside cover, just short of the frontline.

"I've got eyes on that MG," Dildo Dillon calmly remarked from his position next to Head and Durnford-Slater. Pockmarked skin hidden behind the edge of the telescope, he spied with one eye open through the lens mounted upon his brown Lee-Enfield bolt-action. He had just slithered to the brim of the entrenchment, overlooking the battlefield beyond, and could make out the pesky enemy machine gun nest that seemed to be the biggest defensive threat to the commandos.

Durnford-Slater spun low to address his report, spying what it was that his marksman had observed and took a moment to consider a tactical deliberation.

"I've got an aspirin ready for the headache you're about to give him!" Head ordered with certainty—but Dildo hesitated, refraining for Durnford-Slater to affirm an order. "Come on, mate, end the wanker!"

"Colonel? Do I break cover?" the young commando queried. Understandably, their current position low along the shoreline was yet to be fully noticed by any enemy infantrymen in the village currently firing upon the breadth of advancing commandos as they progressed from the coastal fog.

Shooting from here *could* potentially draw attention to their location overseeing the assault advance ...

Through a gust of sweeping air that cleared the dissipating smokescreen for a trice, they could see the house with the small outdoor sitting area where the machine gun nest had been established beneath the overhanging cover of sheet metal. The gunner was pivoting a bipod-mounted MG34 on a sideways angle, spraying at movement as the commandos scurried between cover whilst they invaded the urban streets of South Vågsøy.

"We shoot now, and we give away our position ..." Dillon stated. His finger was on the trigger and the crosshair of his scope rested upon the zoomed image of the oblivious lone German gunner in the nest. Beneath the distinguishable German design of the stahlhelm helmet, the man's entire body jerked with every burst of recoil from the heavy machine gun. He was barely visible through the metal embrasure that the Germans had improvised for cover, but Dillon had a line of sight thanks to the aid of his sniper rifle scope at a groundward-angle.

"Take him out," Durnford-Slater ordered sternly. "We'll soon need to displace."

Charley Head's attention bounded from Durnford-Slater and upwards into the skyline. Audible prior to becoming visible was the unmistakable pitch of an incoming enemy aerial swoop assault.

A second later and Durnford-Slater's brow tightened before his expression dropped flat. His head swivelled, pointing at the velvet skies over the village.

Commandos everywhere along the shoreline saw and heard the pitch of the German Me-109s as they came sweeping in low, tracing the smoky south-east shoreline. They had obviously noticed all the small-arms fire at ground level, alerting them to an invasion from within the smoke-screen.

"I think that *soon* might be a *now!*" Head remarked as he pushed up and to his knees, keen to vanish from the open area. Nearest him, de la Torre did the same, squatting beneath the weight of his wireless pack as his face scanned the skies for incoming fighters. Men who were lying low for protection from the village all simultaneously had the same urge to run the gauntlet, upping from the terrain and charging forwards and into the fracas of open battle to dodge death from exposure.

*The incoming wails grew louder ...*

Amidst the late movers running for cover, Mericle and his cameraman decided to risk it all and push forwards. They did so successfully and out of sheer luck, just so happening to dodge several ricochets from pot-shots aimed their way.

"*Let's move!*" Head shouted, anxious to go.

"Wait!" Durnford-Slater called, clutching his lieutenant's snow smock in a balled fist so firmly to prevent him running out in the open from their position—not while that machine gun was functional.

The enemy gunner pivoted around, spraying suppressive fire at several desperate commandos who had just now upped the shoreline and made a dash for cover. Several of them did not make it, becoming some of the first regrettable casualties in South Vågsøy this day.

"Not yet!" Durnford-Slater remarked in a shout as a laser of tracers from the machine gun's overshoot beamed hot golden lines above their heads, causing Head to drop back down.

*If they ran now, they were dead men.*

*That machine gunner had to go first!*

*... wwwwhhhirrr ...*

*The incoming strafing run grew louder by the tense second ...*

"Oh ... *shit!*" Head cursed. His eyes grew wide looking towards the incoming squad of Me-109s and their raking paths of destruction as they traced a strafe along the coastline, targeting humans. Shattering rocks and pockmarking the beach, the aerial firing squad drew a line towards their position ...

*It was coming straight for them.*

"Not yet!" Durnford-Slater repeated, sensing his friend's yearning to move once more—and rightfully so.

If they stayed put, they would die.

If they moved out *right now,* they would also die.

They needed a window of opportunity ...

"Dillon, now's the time! Take the shot!" Durnford-Slater requested calmly as not to overstress his marksman. Hiding his anxiousness well, he then focused back around and at the incoming blitz from the German fighters.

*His rate of breathing intensified ...*

*His heartrate quickened ...*

"Dillon!"

Defying equal pressure in that tense moment was the marksman, himself.

"Hol'on! Just a tick, sir ..."

As the two yellow-nosed fighters came screaming along the coast, spewing desecration from their large calibre cannons and hammering the rocks with lines of sparks and brimstone, Dildo Dillon remained calm and still. He had since lost line on a kill-shot of the German machine gunner and was exercising patience in order to gain anoth—

*A clear shot aligned.*

He took it.

*Bam!*

Dillon fired ...

*... the machine gun ceased.*

The coastal battlefield exhumed an eerie and sudden quiet—a noiseless chasm, replaced by the increasing howl of the incoming squadron of German fighters, spraying their machine guns along the coastline like streams of urine carving a name in the snow.

*wwwWWHIR ...*

"He's down! I got him! Go! Go!" Dillon bellowed, not even cycling his bolt-action before leading their advance into the onslaught.

Due to the lack of the MG34 resonance, the volume of the firefight momentarily decreased, reduced to only trading potshots from rifles, and the odd retaliatory or cover fire from a commando's submachine gun as the troops moved up into the town—all men racing the fighter's zoom along the coastal shoreline.

*... vvvVVROOOM!*

Blowing downward gusts of air, the Me-109s disbursed the lingering haze of the smokescreen with its powerful updrafts.

It was a couple of days early for New Year's Eve pyrotechnics, but the rocky beach behind Durnford-Slater, de la Torre, Head, and Dillon crackled like arrays of supercharged fireworks as they miraculously moved from the line of fire just in time to keep their lives.

Conjoined in their charge, the commandos fired their guns blindly at the many ground-level enemy positions as they stormed the contour towards shelter, covering their own advance as best they could as the Germans fired down upon them from the many residences, storehouses, and fishing huts.

They made it to the safety of concealment as a hailstorm of gunfire assaulted the wooden structure, exploding it to splinters as the soldiers dove out of sight, avoiding death by the skin of their teeth.

*Måløy Island*
*Vågsøy, Norway*

*0918-hours ...*
   *Blam!*
   A secured padlock on an armoured door got shot off.
   Once removed from the latch, the entrance to what was believed to be a munitions cache was kicked open by a tough, six-foot-tall commando with a Tommy gun. He boldly strut inside the dark confines of the suspected enemy hold, flanked on either side through the doorway by other men of No.3, comprising of Troop leader Lieutenant Peace with his Colt handgun up by his ear.
   The area within was musky and still.
   The dust from their explosive entrance hovered in a haze in the tight storage boundaries, lingering while their pupils adjusted in the darkness within. They traced the vicinity walls, scanning for movement or questionable profiles silhouetting in the dark recesses.
   There appeared to be none.
   "*Clear!*" a trooper reported as he lowered his weapon, examining the contents they had discovered within.
   A portable flashlight blinked on from Peace's free hand, and he shone it through the dust. The warm beam exposed entire wall racks of German rifles and stacked boxes of ammunition. One box had its lid pried open, exposing large shell ammo used in the FlaK-88s on the island.
   "Blow it," after nodding his head, Peace stated with precise intent before receding out the door into the morning light. He was followed by the recoiling men with the Thompsons as two demolition troops moved in with their bag of tricks.

Shortly after, Five Troop got clear of the concrete dugout entrance.
   They backed up and turned to observe the bunker be blasted by a well-placed brick of plastique explosive, which in turn ignited the bombs and bullet accumulations within the ammo cache with an epic chain-reaction that shook Måløy Island like an earthquake.

*South Vågsøy*
*Vågsøy, Norway*

*0918-hours ...*

Whatever retaliatory defences the Germans lacked during Operation Claymore six months ago, they were making up for during Operation Archery.

Under substantial enemy fire, the British Commandos spaced out in their advance through the tight village streets, wrapping corners of the snow-white South Vågsøy with their wits about them. They manoeuvred with militaristic finesse and calculated progressions, sweeping each corner with their weapon sights, communicating, and covering each progressive advance.

Men were largely shot at as they dashed across intervals of exposure, however there appeared to be minimal immediate casualties—the commandos were nimble, agile, and deadly in their combined resolve. They acted as a team, covering, flanking, assisting. These elite commandos did not even have to remember their training; it was ingrained within them. They were conditioned killers. Strategic awareness and tactical thinking now came naturally, and their expertise was paying off.

They began ploughing through the urban winter land, kicking in doors, going house to house, sweeping every avenue as they progressed with the raid. The dawn advance through the dissolving coastal smoke-screen was the commencement of a treacherous skirmish between brodie and stahlhelm helmet-clad warriors.

Khaki versus grey toy soldiers in a fight where all bets were upon the west, nevertheless, the German resistance proved a determined foe. The arm-wrestle was underway throughout South Vågsøy.

In the anarchy of the loud chaos, geared commando troops drove their boots through the boarded-up wooden doors to the many homes, checking house by house for enemy combatants—more often than not met with an empty establishment or by a cowering Norwegian family. Regretfully, they trudged their muddy combat boots across the soft rugs and knocked over the furniture.

Ofttimes, the trespassing soldiers were met with an empty domestic home, still warm from a civilian family's recent occupation and now seeking shelter in a rear bedroom, or attempting to board themselves up in a cellar, teary-eyed and scared out of their wits. Children had been lamentably forced from the slumber of their cribs during the raid, now to be stowed away beneath beds, guarded by their equally as frightful non-English-speaking parents in nooks or behind bookcases. Upon their wide-eyed faces, the looks of genuine fear with the expectation of certain death or world's end were ones the commandos would never forget upon their many intrusions.

Their intruding conduct was that of a necessary evil.

Many of the families awoken by the naval barrage and bombing of enemy positions around their village, if not staying quietly at home and cowered in a back room, had flocked as one towards the local church—a safe haven that surely not even the Germans would encroach.

The commandos did their best to be courteous with their invasive inquests. Naturally, the British were born of a certain gentlemanly quality. Chivalry was in their blood. After intruding a home, they lowered their weapons and comforted the families as best they could before moving onto the next house, apologizing for the disturbance with the upmost good manners.

The local population may not have initially appreciated their enforced liberation from Nazi Germany, but once the conflict subsided, stability could be restored. Once the drapes of swastikas were torn down to the ground and burned in the streets, they would come to realize their freedom from their invisible shackles.

A Reuters reporter commentated the footage as they witnessed the commandos in action:

'... *Many Germans were roasted to death in homes they made strongpoints and from which they doggedly refused to emerge, even when grenades or a fusillade of shots had set the rooms about them on fire ... Norwegian men, women, and children, anxious to go to England, were running back to our barges, some in tears, some laughing, all rather scared ... Heavy gunfire reverberated down the fjord to add to the clamour of explosions and the heat of battle ...*'

After narrowly evading death from above and then again from in front of their advance, Durnford-Slater followed his lieutenant into the booted-in back door of a nearby civilian residence. The vacant home provided shelter from the bullet storm.

It was much warmer indoors than it was in the street, however, the wooden walls and winter-proof insulation of the home did little for overall noise restriction. The battle of South Vågsøy was still exceptionally loud from inside.

"Clear!" Head remarked with a low voice now that they were indoors, safely holding up his submachine gun muzzle so that his colonel could enter the house behind him. They had entered what appeared to be a conjoined laundry, shower, and kitchenette with a timber table in the centre.

There was no sign of the inhabitants, however the stove was still hot, and a fresh boiled pot was on the counter. Dillon moved inside past the officers, kinked at the knees and low. Due to the enclosed manoeuvrability, his rifle slouched in hold and his M1911A1 sidearm became outstretched, tracing each corner of the connecting accommodations. The rooms appeared empty, but when he finally tried the last bedroom door, it did not budge.

"Sir, locked door!" he reported barely above a whisper.

Durnford-Slater, Head, and de la Torre became attentive. The radioman slipped off the heavy wireless from his shoulder and planted it down upon the set dining table, shoving the stacked cutlery and plates with a clatter. Dillon quietly set down his long wooden rifle against the doorframe, drawing his BC-41 trench-knife in his free hand with his fingers through the brass eyelets. He crossed his arms, with his pistol and looked back to his superiors.

"Breach?"

Head and Durnford-Slater moved forwards with their guards partially up. The hallway confines were tight.

"Hold," Durnford-Slater raised a hand as he saw Dillon prepare to kick it in so that they could search it for enemy, ready to absolutely punch, stab, or shoot the shit out of anybody that lingered inside. There was something about this house—this *home*—that was non-threatening to the colonel's instinct. "If there are any Huns here, I doubt they would be hiding ..."

"Are you sure about that?" Dillon responded with a frown, keen to break the door in with his finger on the trigger.

"Would they not have shot at us in the back door on our way from the coast," Durnford-Slater explained logically, insinuating that from the doorway they had entered, any enemy present within would have had a prime firing position when the fighting had started.

Head and Dildo Dillon both watched with reserved confusion as their CO pressed down the hall, lowered his weapon, and raised his knuckle to tap lightly on the wooden door like a kindly visitor.

"Hello in there?"

During the silence that followed, Dillon and Head exchanged a glance in the hall. The two of them were ready for action, while respectfully adhering to their colonel's wishes at this diplomatic extension.

Outside at this present juncture, the gunfight was vociferous.

Between flamboyant gunshots, men shouting, and the odd explosion via a tossed hand grenade or shell from the ongoing distant naval or aerial battles boomed loudly, bringing in dust from the ceiling rafters and rattling stored glassware, the circumstance was anything but calm.

However, a voice finally responded.

It was barely audible; a murmur by a weeping adult, possibly hiding with a family, spoken from within the confines. There was a rasp that underlined the tiny, scared voice, which only communicated to the commandos more of the speaker's noncombatant demeanour.

It was then that the trigger-happy killer commandos stood down.

Hearing that frightened Norwegian voice from within, they fully realized that there was no threat behind the door. Dillon and Head both envisioned a scared family; two loving adults attempting to stuff their children beneath a bed or in a closet, and the reality suddenly hit them as their tense shoulders began to lower. If anything, *they* were the threat here.

Durnford-Slater eyed Dillon, giving him the accepting nod.

Dillon humbly reacted, flicking the safety by the hammer of his pistol, simultaneously holstering it whilst sheathing away his deadly trench dagger.

The three commandos returned to the kitchen, where the radioman was attempting to reach the Kenya to give an update and find out where Clement and Churchill were at presently with their concurrent Måløy and Holvik objectives.

Flag raised at this location and deeming it their signal post for this portion of the raid, Colonel Durnford-Slater mandated the capability to communicate with the rest of his own Group and further coordinate his four Troops in accomplishing their objectives in South Vågsøy.

"Corporal where are we at with the communications?" he questioned his radioman after storming back into the kitchen. de la Torre was still attempting to gain anything but a static hash over his radio. The stress was causing his perfectly smooth skin to blush.

With genuine displeasure, his posture dropped as his CO entered the room. "Sir, still nothing ..."

"*Nothing?*" Durnford-Slater's brow inverted.

"Oi, what do you mean, *nothing?*" Lieutenant Head exclaimed, cutting sick as the adrenaline of war turned his tone a little bit condescending.

"I mean, there is too much going on ..." de la Torre stressed. "Between the geometry of the hills around Vågsøy, the enemy wireless tower on Måløy, and probably a second relay somewhere in this locale, I ... I just can't get a signal out."

"That's not to mention the geography of where we are," Dillon input. "What? You're telling me that green shit that was in the sky doesn't affect radios?"

Ignoring Dildo, Head probed de la Torre. "What do you mean *probably a second relay?*"

de la Torre shrugged, uncertain with his hypothesis. "I'm not positive, but usually this sort of static strain happens when there is something constantly transmitting—something big. Something targeted."

"Like the antenna on Måløy?" Durnford-Slater logically proposed while Head wiped his receding hairline of stress sweat.

"Like that, yes."

"Jack will bring that down in no time, I'm sure."

"Look, I'm just guessing, sirs. All I can tell you is that our equipment is fine, so it's not a problem on our end. I guess that there is too much interference, and it's blocking signals. As it is, I can barely even reach our neighbouring Troops' wireless units—and some of them are within shouting distance outside!" de la Torre accentuated. "It's as if someone is sitting out there on a great big radio, holding down the transmit button ... we can't broadcast until they let go and clear the airwaves."

Durnford-Slater paid grave attention to the predicament. He was understanding of their communications hindrance and understood fully that it was not his soldier's fault.

With Captain Bradley's One Troop the only unit clear on their independent demolition objective along their northerly approach into South Vågsøy (the kerosene and coal oil manufacturing factories located by the docks), Durnford-Slater had to find a way to remain in relay with JFG's Three Troop and Forrester's Four Troop (also commanding what remained of Komrower's Two Troop) in order to delegate and coordinate accomplishment of the remaining tasks—not to mention ... *the other thing.*

*John Durnford-Slater cast Charley Head a hidden glance ...*

*... sweat beading from his brow, his adjutant returned it.*

Durnford-Slater checked his wristwatch with angst.

The notion was as if time was against them, and there was a hidden deadline approaching that only the commanding officers knew of ...

It was now 0920-hours.

"We've got forty minutes, gentlemen ..." Durnford-Slater muttered at Head, shaking his sleeve. The heat was on.

Right now, all the Commando Troops knew to do was fight the enemy out of the village. Lieutenant Head understood the necessity that was radio communiqué during such a grand-scale and combined operation. The lack of communication during such a mission could be of a disastrous totality, if not result in complete and utter failure.

Head asked, concerned, "John, what are we going to do if we can't get comms back up? Without radio, the timeline of objective completion could get mislaid ... Targets could get confused ... How are we going to signal the navy and the air force when we need to?"

Durnford-Slater seemed well composed given the current circumstances. He had absolute faith in his men and knew that, even with a momentary loss of direction that they would improvise, achieve, and overcome. He was confident that his troopers knew their roles and their jobs.

He eyed his lieutenant. "The men are *Commandos,* Charley. They don't know how to fail."

Head jerked his chin and added under his breath.

"They don't know what to expect when the hour strikes oh-ten-hundred either, do they ..."

Not privy to the information about the 1000-hour deadline, the overhearing de la Torre and Dillon swapped a discreet, concerned glance.

Durnford-Slater eyeballed Head for an extended pause, and then ponied them all back up. Truth was, if they had known about the deadline ... they probably never would have come along for Operation Archery ...

*Holvik*
*Vågsøy, Norway*

*0920-hours ...*

After swiftly liberating Halnoesvik, Clement and the commandos of G1 headed north-east along the connecting rocky road. They marched towards the revitalizing light of the coming day, trailing the view of the climbing smokestacks that would take them to the outskirt fishing village of Holvik.

When the troops arrived at the post-bombarded scene, they spotted what remained of the enemy barracks behind the village.

They were welcomed by only a handful of aggressors from the reserve garrison who had survived the naval salvo and aerial bombing. They seemed muddled and disorganized, barely able to orchestrate a durable defence against the British invaders.

A mounted machine gun awoke to their presence in Holvik as the British trotted into town, causing them to drop down low and on either side of the run-off ditches that lined the raised rocky road. The troopers drew on their advanced training regimes as they commando-crawled with their weapons cradled before them, shuffling beneath live-fire as the constant sweeping stream warped sound over their heads.

This resulted in a pair of casualties when two commandos barely made it into the trench line in time, becoming injured by raking shots across their legs and hip respectively—neither was fatal.

Another trooper became injured attempting to drain their fire by valiantly breaking cover multiple times and engaging the emplacement blindly. His hand and wrist got shredded by the ferocity of the German machine gun, resulting in him losing a finger along with his weapon as it sprang from his grip with a spark and an aggressive snag.

The heavy machine gun in the nest was operated by two Germans: a gunner and a loader. Both men were shellshocked and panicking, and their desperation became obvious due to their overzealous defensive behaviour. This was the same trigger-happiness that required them to hastily reload, resulting in their ultimate downfall.

When the machine gun's blaring buzz ceased, several commandos who had slithered like serpents close to the position upped on their knee and unloaded vengeful fire upon the nest, popping the helmet from the head of one of the German soldiers and then tacking the other down with lead as he ran and became exposed, striking him with multiple hits across his back.

Bullet-riddled, he collapsed face down into a sleet puddle before the fiery barracks ruins, where there seemed to be further movement by surviving enemy rallies with rifles.

With the big gun down, Clement ordered his Troop to move up and secure the area, which they did with strategic ability, remaining low as they fanned out upon the flanks and gained sustainable concealment behind obstacles.

The men trained their weapons on the housing of the barracks, where between the remnants of the shelter and the spot fires that illuminated the scene in the background, several German infantrymen could be seen squatting behind cover bearing small-arms.

After a short-lived stand-off with what little enemy was left in Holvik, Clement was surprised to see many of the soldiers raising their hands from behind cover with a desire to surrender. This was delayed by a handful of German soldiers who Clement discovered later to be of a different unit, engaging while others were waving white flags.

These men in the dark-collared grey uniforms were fighters.

With small automatics and pistols, they put up ample contest—more so than the local garrison members who tossed in the towel practically at first sight.

Before the resisting group of dark-collared German collaborators were finally put down and killed in action, G1 suffered two more casualties from their stubborn reluctance to join the surrender.

*South Vågsøy*
*Vågsøy, Norway*

*0921-hours ...*

This snowy, serene fishing village had become a battleground.

Captain Algy Forrester and his men were pinned across limited cover, with aggressive gunshots sounding loudly within their surrounding area. He had managed to bring the forty men of Four Troop, the two dozen stragglers from Komrower's incapacitated Two Troop, as well as Kaptein Linge's tagalong Norwegian troops, to a hold-point just up the icy pebble shore, in the north-west vicinity of where they had last seen Durnford-Slater establish a FOB and signals post. The men were scattered in precarious positions amongst a series of wooden sheds, huts, and low walls, trading fire with enemy locations in defilade.

Even though they were now infinitely in the thick of it, every soldier was within concealment whilst they held and awaited orders. Men kicked in the doors to some of the vacant family houses, turning over furniture and even smashing out the glass windows in order to gain advantageous positioning on enemy locations further in the town.

The fiery fight in the ice was heating up from the initial simmer, now bubbling to a blistering boiling point. Casualties were starting to multiply on both sides. Not including the horrific LC incident sustained during their arrival, so far on the Commando side, only light flesh wounds and grazes had been verified. Notably, quite a few of the enemy had been gunned down in the urban snowy streets as they scattered to find ample cover in which to mount a defensive posture.

Above all the surrounding gunfire throughout the dimly lit village, Forrester announced aloud from the circular hole beneath his broom moustache. "The hard part is done, gentlemen! We have made it ashore!"

Listening through the sound of warfare, the men closest to him paid great attention while he cradled his smoking Tommy gun. The weapon was positively cooking after having been returning some hefty gunfire at the enemy from his position.

"Isn't the hard part going to be the fight, sir?" nearby, Dennis O'Flaherty questioned as he ducked his head from a close ricochet against a sheet metal panel above them. There were several enemy shooters slightly up-slope from their position, firing down from multiple enclosed locations hidden in either wooden houses or sheds, or even ducking the corners of the buildings outside like jack rabbits.

"*The fight?*" Forrester frowned as he rotated around behind concealment, preparing to inch out and once again shoot at the enemy positions. "The fight is where the fun begins, Lieutenant."

O'Flaherty and Sherington swapped a nervous glance while their moustachioed captain unleashed several more extended bursts at a few distant targets in confined positions, causing the distant German shooters to hastily recoil. Forrester then returned low behind cover after showering his squad mates in brass shell casings, just in time to dodge a hailstorm of returning enemy fire.

The sentiment made him chuckle because they all missed.

He had a rather abnormal laugh, like he was garrotting on his moustache.

"Sir, I can't get a signal on the radio," the voice of Sherington shouted through the mayhem, realizing again that their communications were scrambled and otherwise down. Unbeknownst to them at this juncture, this problem was spreading through the Commando forces like wildfire. "What should we do?"

Without even looking, Forrester remarked, "Swap that walkie-talkie for a rifle, trooper."

"Yes, sir!" Sherington responded, doing so.

O'Flaherty helped the radioman clip the walkie-talkie piece on his communications backpack. He questioned seriously, "Orders, sir?"

Forrester shrugged. "Keep giving them the business."

"Roger that," O'Flaherty replied with an unsure nod beneath his wobbly tin hat. The chinstrap was undone causing a lot of loose movement upon his dome. He was clearly inferring that they should make a move to an objective, such as the larger warehouse buildings and power station located along the coast to the north—towards Bradley's One Troop demolition objectives.

"Do you concur, Kaptein?" Forrester shouted over at Martin Linge, who was behind the cover of a snowcapped firewood log cache along with a few of his NOR.I.C.1 men, also busy engaging the enemy.

Linge heard the Brit and simply raised a *thumbs-up* gesture.

Forrester chuckled some more from behind his womb broom bristles before rotating around in the tight space, preparing to fight the good fight some more. "My man!"

Sherington and O'Flaherty swapped an unsure exchange and mirrored sentiment, this being their first real gunfight.

*War was madness.*

*0922-hours ...*

While the battle in the streets of South Vågsøy raged on along the coast, the two dozen men of Bill Bradley's One Troop aboard the lone LC arrived at their destination unhindered and uncontested.

The coastal wharf area had been bombed by the RAF and shelled by the navy, as had the rest of South Vågsøy, albeit to a far less extent as there appeared to be fewer enemy fortifications throughout the converted civilian location. Other than noted machine gun barricades and a presumed presence within the weathered real estate situated at the dock land entrance, the place was cold and bare.

Heat resonated and smoke rose from a destroyed rifle emplacement, hit directly by naval artillery during the initial barrage. There were a cluster of dead soldiers lying in the snow and sleet, with torn, seared uniforms. Scattered Karabiner-98k rifles and toppled stahlhelms were strewn about the place.

In the shallows of the docks were two bombed shipping vessels.

They had sunk into the icy water, protruding from the shoals now as recent wreckages. Remnants of splinted, smouldering deck wood, collapsed masts, and floating debris littered the edge of the embankment.

One Troop's Higgins boat pulled in fast to the northerly docks, bashing into the lumber pier with the brunt of their steel assault landing craft.

The onboard commandos sprung to action, leaping from the vessel, guns up and sweeping their sectors as they progressed.

Twenty pairs of heavy combat boots chuffed the wooden planks beneath the miasma scape of the pending war blaze both in the air and on the ground below.

In the brightening morning sky, fighters of the RAF still battled hard against squadrons of Luftwaffe. In the radiant fog of the aerial arena, mounted machine gun weapons chomped away as the airplanes danced and wove like feathered ornithurine pursuing insects in the mist. Lines of glowing dots discharged as tracers from their guns chattered, chasing one another to fiery deaths and cataclysm.

Deep detonations resonated in the distance.

Dozens of grenades boomed and hundreds of gunshots exchanged while Durnford-Slater's commandos clashed with the kraut at full-throttle pace in South Vågsøy ... however, there was an eerie silence up the northern coast.

With sentinel eyes, Bradley's men tactically entered the wrecked docks, leading the way from behind their weapon sights. In standard two-by-two formations, the troops took positions, covering each other's progress as they cautiously advanced in-land—their militaristic movements were like reading from one of the textbooks they had written back in the Inveraray CTC, where they cut their teeth.

By Captain Bradley's side as they sought concealment by some stacked shipping crates covered by a blue weather canvas, second-in-command Sergeant Ramsey took the men of his charge forwards and to the office structures further ahead. Inside, a light betrayed those within the dark room, casting their shadows to dance across the walls.

*Gerry was stirring.*

Bradley gave the order to *hold* by flexing his closed fist up by his shoulder. Behind him, men such as Cork and Dowling amidst the demolitions party of No.6 stood-by, waiting for these boys from No.2 to clear the path ahead.

There were tense moments of silence while Ramsey's section progressed to more advantageous fire positions to better take down the enemy forces that remained within the housing at the north docks.

"*Pssst,*" Johnnie Dowling whispered through his underbite. He shared the same cover behind a tall stack of damp pallets and rusty metal barrels as Cork. "Oi, Cork!"

Sergeant A.J. Cork turned his head past his weapon, humouring the trooper with some chinwag whilst they waited for the order to proceed. The docks, after all, were primarily a No.2 Commando objective, with No.6 demo only needed after they had moved in and taken the fish oil factories, and they required demolishing.

"You still haven't told me why that Scottish wanker from No.3 wanted to bash your head in earlier?" Dowling asked in confidence. Cork had been befriended into No.6 and the two were respectively mates, regardless of any shady pasts. "What did he mean by all that nonsense he was dribbling?"

"It's a long story," Cork shook his head dismissively. Dowling watched as his brow as it seemed to invert, and Cork's eyes lost focus for an instant. "... one I am not overly proud of."

Cork's shoulders and chin raised, and his posture changed.

He clearly wanted to change topic and focus on the mission—

Suddenly, there was a loud outburst of crackling gunfire, and all heads peeked forwards in time to see Ramsey's forward section of commandos assault the enemy's pillbox outpost at the land entrance to the docks. There was little retaliatory fire from the Germans held-up within, and the position was taken swiftly and with ease, laying waste to those inside with extreme prejudice.

Bradley gave the order to move the rest of One Troop forwards, which included the handful of No.6 demo members in tow. They advanced between the northerly docks and the partially engulfed thirty-foot-tall storage tankers of the fish and herring factory and warehouses, gravitating them geographically towards the direction of the raging battle in South Vågsøy—where they heard the explosion and witnessed the fall of the giant wireless tower over on Måløy Island—undoubtedly Major Jack Churchill's doing.

"There she goes, gents!" Ramsey commented, spinning on the spot as the Troop made tracks between the dismal cover of small shacks and huts on the snowy slope a stone throw from the fjord. They were making use of what little dawn shadow still remained as the rising light beyond the eastern horizon began to illuminate the white surroundings of Norway.

Ramsey informed Bradley as he peered out from refuge after they all heard the delayed bass of the collapse from afar.

"Sir! Enemy communications tower destroyed!"

"Mad Jack strikes again!" Bradley remarked in awe and infamy, holding his advance for a moment of reflection. He was, like his men of action at this stage of the Archery excursion, full of smiles and grins.

With G3 bringing the wireless tower down, it basically meant that Måløy Island was now in the hands of the British, and all that remained was Vågsøy Island, itself.

The men of One Troop carried on low in the cockcrow hour, advancing like hunting predators towards timorous prey, targeting their next objective: the neighbouring fish and herring factories along the fiery coastal strip.

The large tankers at the factory were already alight, burning an elegant and glowing stout of hungry orange fire, due to the bombing runs by the RAF. It was now time to finish the job.

There was still much to discharge to ensure that the German supplies were completely devastated ...

*They progressed onwards.*

*Måløy Island*
*Vågsøy, Norway*

*0924-hours ...*

"Inform Brigadier Haydon that the guns on Måløy Island are ours," Churchill declared to Lieutenant Wills, after the trooper made his way into Måløy with his clunky radio backpack.

The G3 radioman responded, "Yes, sir!" and immediately lowered to a squat to access his gear, moving his walkie-talkie to his face and cupping his mouth around the microphone.

Churchill revolved around in time to watch the dutiful sapper and one of his mates come trotting hastily away from the wireless tower, having just set the timers of the explosives. This range was what could be called a 'safe distance' only by the daredevil gents of No.3 Commando.

If they squinted hard enough, they could see the fuses burning at either ground-level anchor point of the tower. As the smoking string line reeled closer into the applied plastique explosives, there were two concurrent detonations of a small yield.

*Ba-Bang!*
*Wh-Whiz...*

Straight after the blasts, they heard the sharp whips of high tensile steel cables elasticize as a sudden slack reverted. The lines from the anchor points disappeared from sight in the blink of an eye, and the tall skeletal tower began to creak and minutely sway in the cold breeze ...

There was one last cable attached at the hind.

There was a designated putty charge on it, like the others, but it was yet to blow, and was hopefully not about to dud.

"*Come on, now ... there she blows ...*" the overconfident sapper remarked in a hiss after a few seconds and from his position over Churchill's shoulder. He and the rest of Six Troop prepared to observe the gradient tower come crashing down.

The anticipation in the time spent waiting was deafening.

The sapper urged again, beneath his breath:

"*Come on ... come on ...*"

... but there was no third and final explosion.

"Trooper?!" Young Young finally queried from his safe spot across the street, where he and a few others in his Troop sought cover from the detonations. "Correct me if I'm wrong ... but is that not meant to blow up and fall over about now?!"

The sapper sighed, disappointed. "... yes, sir."

Young raised his arms in a shrug, gesturing question of *well, why had it not?*

Churchill gazed upon the sapper and noted his discontent.

"Apologies Captain, Major ..." the sapper committed with a salute from his brow, upping to pass Churchill and the others, and attempt to restart the volatile device. He stopped his demo partner with a hand gesture. "No, you stay. I'll go an—"

"Wait a tick," Churchill ordered abruptly, placing his arm out to halt the courageous commando from returning to that malfunctioning brick of plastique explosive by the tower. "Is it just that the fuse went out?"

"Probably, sir. But if not that, it could be the explosive, itself, has duded," the sapper conjectured, showing that his expertise in explosives belied his young age. "It's just too bloody cold out here for the Comp-C to detonate efficiently, even when the fuse burns into the putty. I'll go and massage the block and then try lightin' a fresh fuse."

Churchill's knowledge on explosives was apparently inadept, as that execution sounded risky to him. "Is that safe?"

"Sure," the sapper's brodie bobbed. Truth was, it wasn't safe in the slightest—but as far as explosive-tinkering went, it was somewhat of a SOP. "We should have better luck after I give her a rub, but I think we'll need to switch to det. cord after this."

He upped to leave again, and Churchill stopped him.

"Hold, trooper. Don't go near it," he shook his head, eyeing the primed plastique bricks at the base of the radio tower across the distance. That shit was set to go off at a whim. "Do you lads remember Commodore Mountbatten's mandate for this op?"

Churchill's interrogation refreshed sense into their minds.

"... '*No unnecessary risks*'..."

In the background, Young Young rolled his eyes at Churchill's *do as I say, not do as I do* attitude thus far on the operation—and likely beyond. He liked to lead from the front, but not lead by example. To an aspiring group of loyal commandos who idolized him, it was rather contradictory, and was unreasonable to expect them to decide the right path on their own accords.

"It could still go off," Churchill added with sound logic, to which, although it was general practice and the sapper had the upmost confidence that an accidental discharge right now was not the case, who was he to argue with his commanding officer. He took a backseat.

"Sir, a rifle grenade, then?" a commando showed initiative and questioned aloud from off-side of their major. Although a rifle grenade could have definitely done the trick, and a direct hit anywhere near the prepped charge should have been enough to set off the primed explosive, Churchill had something else in mind ...

Something more meticulous.

*More stylish.*

"Negative. Save that for the enemy, lad."

"Can't one of you just *shoot it?*" Hardy probed from his official spectator's seat for the operation. Surrounding commandos tossed him a curve ball gleam. In one second, the American received half a dozen scowls and frowns by many of the surrounding British commandos who knew better. As they all knew through training, plastique couldn't detonate from bullets or gunfire, not that any of them had tested it personally. It was what made the putty device so safe to carry as a substitute from its TNT dynamite predecessor that would sweat in hot conditions and just about detonate if someone farted around it.

Churchill took a second to retort at the journalist. "Felix, your ability to question our tactics is fast making you a *backseat commando.*"

"At least I'm not a *backdoor commando ...*" Hardy remarked under his breath at Jack. Thankfully for him, the taunt was received by all those within eavesdrop as a playful joust and not an actual insult—the British were anything if not welcoming of explicitly crude humour, something most Americans did not get.

Even Churchill grinned, although he tried to conceal it behind both his stagnant pencil moustache upon his maintained stiff upper lip for the sake of his role today as fearless leader.

"Hold this ..." a call to action, Churchill dropped his unslung submachine gun into the sapper's arms. They then all watched as the Mad Major drew two three-foot sticks from his hip bag, and put them together at one end where they inserted. His wrists quickly twisted, screwing them together to make a bow—his longbow.

A few of the commandos exchanged a glance.

For some, this was a divine moment: watching Mad Jack Churchill stringing his longbow in the field; in war. There was excitement amass the looks of contentment; some of confusion.

Once assembled, Churchill looped a drawstring end on the bottom limb nock. Quite adept, having done so hundreds of times in the past, he then posed a strange stance, using his body weight to manipulate the taut wood. He stuck his leg between the lower-end of the bow, leaning the curvature of the bend against his thigh in order to reach his arm over the top-end, pulling it in with a flex of the core. Once the limbs concaved, he latched the flemish twist loop, carefully allowing the wood of the yew bow to release and strain with an anchored power and lethal intention.

With a wordless conviction, Churchill began to walk out in front of the men. His saunter into the exposed Måløy street was not unlike he was taking position at an archery contest, lining up a downrange target board for a bullseye.

He had a clear line of the sight at the radio antenna from here.

"Major Churchill?" Young questioned with a frown.

Everybody was watching.

Once in a satisfactory spot, Churchill drew one of the thicker grey arrows with the yellow cock feathers from the other thinner shoulder quiver. He nocked against the bowstring, pinching the shaft with his index finger at the bow hilt to pin it in place whilst, with his other hand, he withdrew a pair of compact wire crimpers from a pouch pocket.

This extra deed to drawing and dismissing an arrow seemed unusual.

It turned heads. Commandos gawked.

Troopers even repositioned to get a better look.

Along the rear of the aluminium arrow body were lines etched in paint. The notches were increments representing time in seconds. They represented a countdown clock for the pencil detonator's fuse that was housed within the length of the customized arrow, devised by No.3 Commando quartermaster, Slinger Martin.

For this type of explosive arrow, Slinger had given Churchill the option to crimp fuse, igniting the internal timer selectively, anywhere between two seconds and two minutes, serrated in perpendicular lines along the elongated body. Once the crease was crimpled along the housing, the timer began corroding the wire holding back the coiled spring behind the striker. Once released, the restrained striker would push the internal pinhead into the primer, igniting the percussion cap and miniature rod of plastique explosive which lined the hollow body of the arrow shaft—and then *explode!*

The whole device was like a mini Bangalore torpedo, only, delivered via longbow.

*Dubbing it a Bangalarrow should catch on.*

"Twenty seconds should do her ..." Churchill muttered under his breath as he crimped the aluminium body of the devised timed explosive arrow at the specified red marker. He tucked away the clippers and assumed the position, all the while remembering to count down in his head.

He raised the longbow and drew the draw to anchor point, aligning the barely visible explosive target in the seeming nonchalance of the instance. He calculated distance, range and windspeed before—

"Sorry, Major," Wills interrupted at a shout, extending his walkie-talkie radio piece towards Churchill. "It's a rubbish signal, but I've got the Kenya on the wire. Brigadier Haydon requests a sit-rep. I think he wants to know why the tower is still standing ..."

Countdown ticking and drawstring straining, Churchill still found the time to pause in this position; bow drawn and ready to fire. There were mere seconds remaining before the explosive device would explode in his midst, but the commando was as cool as a cucumber.

Churchill announced over his shoulder to the radioman:

"Relay this: *Måløy battery and island captured. Casualties slight,*" Mad Jack faced forward. The seconds were counting down, and his target was ahead of him. "*Demolitions in progress. Churchill out.*"

*He loosed the draw.*

*Sch-TOFF ...*

The lightweight projectile launched from the bowman.

Although slightly heavier than a normal arrow, the aluminium projectile traversed like a bolt of lightning, barely visible to the respective naked eye.

In a slink, the dark horizontal tracer made a beeline from the archer's stance of the beret-clad Jack Churchill and to the base of the wireless tower, where the prick of the metal arrow penetrated the remaining middle brick of plastique explosive to the concrete base, staking it as if it were a hunk of malleable clay.

*... 3*

*... 2*

*... 1*

*BOOM!*

The primer within the arrow popped, causing the main charge to detonate at the centre of the wire frame tower in a powerful blast that lifted the layers of fallen snow two inches from the ground and from every surface in a gust of fury.

The blast wave tremored the whole island.

The explosion caused a collapse under the tremendous weight of the tall antenna structure, triggering an instant instability that welcomingly teetered on the edge of ruin.

The wireless tower let out an awful metallic groan as its supports subsequently gave in, reeling in a disintegrative breakdown of twisting metal and folding brass across the open space, kicking up a large amount of dust and powdered snow from the impact on the ground before the British Commandos.

*Objective completed.*

*Holvik*
*Vågsøy, Norway*

After rounding up the prisoners from the Holvik barracks, Clement was urgently called upon by one of his troopers to inspect one of the fallen enemy fighters in the dark-collared uniforms.

He had just radioed aboard the Kenya and informed Haydon of G1's mission completion at Holvik.

These departed troopers were clothed in grey uniforms, much the same as their Wehrmacht hosts who were stationed in Vågsøy, but they were certainly not part of the 181st Infantry Division. Their uniforms appeared to carry more visible merit than standard Wehrmacht, as well as differing insignia that included a unique *Siegrune* icon upon the black collars, not unlike what was worn by members of the intimidating Schutzstaffel.

"... what the devil?" Clement remarked, finding it odd—but it got deeper. His trooper tilted the dead man's chin, exposing the uniform insignia fully so that his CO could see more clearly.

The trooper remarked conspicuously, "See what I mean, Lieutenant?"

He had noticed the inconsistency with the deceased German soldiers' uniforms upon performing a perimeter sweep after G1 had successfully taken Holvik. There was something amiss here—something not in line with their intelligence on their encounterable advisories.

The boggled Lieutenant Clement observed as he positioned upright, panning his view about the debris-collapsed area. There were a couple of these men strewn across here, all deceased in distinctive blazes of glory. "These blokes appear to be *SS*. No wonder they put up such a fight!"

"Yes, sir."

"SS?" A nearby trooper remarked. "What in the bleedin' hell are they doing in Vågsøy?"

Clement's scan resumed over the bullet-riddled corpse.

Another outstanding emblem on their special service uniforms was that of what appeared to be some kind of white flower against a black arm band. It was a symbol of some sort of illustrious special unit that seemingly nobody present had ever heard of ...

This troop had been shot dead along with the others while they had attempted to shout and rally the other surviving soldiers of the barracks to collect arms and fight their British aggressors and to defend Holvik. It was as though the regular German infantrymen wanted to surrender, but these SS men preferred martyrdom, attempting to entice the Wehrmacht boys into more combat against the invading commandos.

"We count four of them, sir," the trooper reported after a brief cataloguing of the deceased. "They were fighting amongst the surviving soldiers, maybe even taking charge of the regular Huns."

Clement shook his head, still a little confused.

"Whoever they were, they put up a better fight than the regular Gerrys ..." he wondered as he gazed upon the golden haze that hovered above the dawn horizon. Beneath it, like an erratic heartbeat, were flashes of erupting explosions and volleys of anti-air tracers spraying into the starry morning sky. The constant percussion of explosions and rattling gunfire transpiring in the distance was the sound of the ongoing warfare as Operation Archery raged on in other towns along Vågsøy Island.

*God only knew what fate had in store for the commandos ...*

"Get me Brigadier Haydon back on the wire," Clement ordered decisively, distrustful of the unnerving turn this incursion may have just taken. "We must warn the others what they're in for ..."

# 6
## *Deadline*

*0930-hours ...*

Daybreak illuminated South Vågsøy.

The vivid ultraviolet rays broke the crest of the icicle islands, purging the dawn hue entirely as it cast its own lateral curtain.

The escalation of brightness from dawn into day unveiled some gruesome detail resulting from the bloodshed and destruction of war. Crimson squirts and even pools of red blood were a stark contrast against the predominate white palette of the wintery scape, and the visibility of thick dark smokestacks from all the burning property and infrastructure about the island was more evident. The morning sunlight failed to shine through the pluming veils, and they in turn cast shadows, proving the wake of destruction so far caused by the raid on Vågsøy and Måløy.

At the rate Commando were pushing on the Wehrmacht defences, where they were located now was perhaps no longer considered the frontline. They had punched through it.

Gunshots emitted all around the fishing village as the assault raged on in urban warfare and close quarters combat. Men fought from house to house, window to window, even engaging in mêlée-belligerence in some extreme cases, clashing with fists, buttstocks, and bayonet blades.

Stern German rifle fire valiantly versed the advance of the aggressive British, and the continuous thunderous inundation of their submachine guns.

Fuse-lit grenades were thrown in skyward arcs overhead, back and forth, landing between wooden shacks and on the top of thatch roof tops, blowing smouldering debris all over the place.

In what was deemed their signals post, located along the front row of small village huts along the icy coast overlooking the Vestfjorden, Durnford-Slater grew fervently more concerned by the minute. He probed to his young radioman as he trod into the kitchen of their occupied Norwegian home.

"Still nothing?"

Radio operator de la Torre raised his hands in wonder at Durnford-Slater's question of an update regarding their sudden deficiency in communications once they reached Vågsøy island. de la Torre had been painstakingly fiddling with his portable wireless unit on the kitchen table, still wondering why the transmissions were received fuzzily and garbled at best.

In the time it took him to check his wrist-mounted timepiece again—the tenth time in ten minutes—Durnford-Slater witnessed his trooper resume eating what appeared to be smoked kippers on brown toast from the table in the middle of the room. There were several breakfasts arranged. Whoever had prepared them had been rudely interrupted by this raid right as they were about to sit down for the most important meal of the day.

The colonel frowned, shaking his sleeve back down over his wristwatch. "Trooper, are you right, there?"

With disappointment upon his brow and his mouth full of sustenance, de la Torre placed the bitten bread back down onto the plate and scooted it aside, shaking his head abashedly whist mumbling his penitence. Like many of the commandos who had suffered from sea sickness on the way over, they had barely eaten this entire time only to be presented with a banquet of arranged foods at their fingertips throughout these Norwegian homes.

"I'm sorry! I'm sorry!" de la Torre better pronounced a few seconds later after he had managed to chew some of his food. He looked longingly at his CO. "I'm a stress eater!"

Durnford-Slater cocked his brow dismissingly.

"John, anything?" Charley Head questioned as he breezed into the room after strolling the hall. He immediately noticed de la Torre had helped himself to the nourishment arrangement on the table, and thus strafed in casually to take a biscuit for himself with his spare hand, Tommy gun in the other. As he did, de la Torre snuck another fast nibble in, suddenly overwrought with guilt.

"Lads, seriously?" his calm unnerved, Durnford-Slater remarked with an acute tone. "We're in the middle of a battle, here! We're on duty! And this isn't our food!"

de la Torre expressed regret, "Apologies, sir."

Head finished the biscuit and brushed the crumbs from his fingers before cradling his weapon in both hands. With his mouth still full he said the same thing whilst Durnford-Slater shook his head in lighthearted disbelief.

Two men from outside were heard approaching their house, and it caused concern and caution.

Head and Durnford-Slater both tightened their stances on the unlikely chance that it could have been an enemy rush during this skirmish, however, it was just a corporal by the surname of *Pattinson* running in from both the cold of the chill and the heat of the battle. He was nursing a gunshot to the left hand which he had wrapped in a rag and torn a split to tie it off tightly as a makeshift tourniquet.

"*Sirs!*" he saluted with his bloody hand and a grimace to follow when it hurt to perform the signal. Trailing behind him through the same backdoor of the residence was another pair of familiar troopers, Peel and Drain. The latter was supposed to be Three Troop's radioman.

"Corporal," Head responded, noticed the others and squinting through a waft of smoke. "Drain, is that you?"

"Sir."

"Flaming Nora!" Head turned to Durnford-Slater, who stared perplexed at these new arrivals who appeared to be misplaced in battle.

Peel and Drain peered inside the warmth of the interior.

The lieutenant-colonel denoted a hint of chafe as he questioned them through the open doorway. "Men, are you lost? Where's the rest of your Troop? Captain Giles moved along the left flank once we got off the beach!"

"Yes, sir! Sorry, sir!" Drain announced.

"Blood-y-hell!" Durnford-Slater exclaimed, growing more distraught at this operation's chaos by the minute. Unable to communicate with the other Troops, the stress was beginning to eat him alive.

"We've been separated, Colonel!" Peel excused. "Then we noticed that communications were down. Thought we'd come in and let you know, sir."

"We are aware!" Durnford-Slater stated bluntly, circling the table for a moment to peek out of a tall window port. He exchanged a look with de la Torre and Head around the cliquey kitchen. Albeit moot, this info provided intel in and of itself, for it confirmed that it wasn't just *their* portable that was having problems. All bandwidth was flooded. Their communications were compromised. This could have been very, *very* bad, and the *deadline* was soon upon them ...

"Sir, Group 3 has just brought down the wireless antenna on Måløy," Drain further remarked as he took a step into the doorframe, now talking in a lower tone while Peel positioned himself defensively just outside, keeping an eye out for hostiles.

"How do you know?"

"We saw it," Drain confirmed, and Head and Durnford-Slater exchanged a confused glance, one of which confirmed an earlier theory of de le Torre's.

de le Torre accentuated, "The tower is down, and yet we are *still unable* to raise any comms with our Troops *or* the navy ..."

"The power station?" Head threw in.

Durnford-Slater shook his head after a brief consideration. "No, negative. The power station could be blamed for some interference, but what we're encountering is purposely blocking everything out-going from land. If Jack took out that antenna and we're still without any undisrupted communiqué with our people, then there *must* be a secondary enemy communications headquarters somewhere here—somewhere within *this* village."

"Would it not have to be something with an erected antenna to disrupt our signal?" Head frowned. They had no intel on a structure matching that description—the initial recon performed by the HMS Tuna would have marked it during their surveys.

Knowledgeable in such things, de la Torre affirmed with a nod.

Head assisted their chain of thought. "Early intel *did* suggest that there was a mobile antenna in South Vågsøy, but it was disproven once they considered Måløy Island the only communications station."

"I knew it ..." de la Torre contested. He had not been privileged to the operational information prior to Archery but was proud to know that his skills and knowledge about radio waves and communications had brought him to the correct conclusion earlier.

The officers stared him down, and he felt obliged to explain.

"If you rig a high-rate outbound wireless console with the right array of frequencies, you effectively have yourself a CB radio jammer, sir. It wouldn't be hard. Some lowly Hun operator would have nothing to do but tinker around these parts. They could have been cooking one up in their spare time."

"Our channels are encrypted, though."

"It's not about cracking encryptions," de la Torre explained in layman's terms. "It's about who has the loudest white noise."

"*White noise?*"

"Yes, sir. Static. Over in occupied France, the Nazis have been jamming our local broadcasts from the BBC for months by emitting an ungodly hash over our signal. It jams it."

"Sods," Head growled, unknowing of that fact. "I love the BBC."

"We all do, sir."

Durnford-Slater bobbed his head while the others chatted, pulling out his silk map of Vågsøy and other papers of mission intelligence issued to him prior to Operation Archery. The information had mostly been gathered by the Tuna, which had performed vigorous reconnaissance in the weeks building up to the now. During the in-depth brief, it had been initially suggested that the enemy had established an alternate relay in the lower village, perhaps a fall back for Måløy Island.

"... the source of their findings regarding a secondary antenna in the village had been solely based on the fact they had witnessed *'men carrying what appeared to be radio transmission equipment and cables'* into the urban extremities ..." Durnford-Slater read aloud from the detailed intelligence.

"You brought the whole brief with you?" Head asked, stepping around the table and helping him source the material in the many paperclipped pages.

"I did."

"Why?"

Durnford-Slater paused for a second, delivering his monotonal response offering an inch of sarcasm. "In case the plan changes and we need to assess whether or not the enemy might have a second headquarters with a radio antenna capable of jamming our outgoing transmissions and we can't contact the ships?"

At an immediate loss of words, Head blinked about himself.

"Point taken."

Durnford-Slater and his adjutant assessed the many pages on the kitchen table. de la Torre broke protocol and allowed himself a glimpse of the top-secret works, leaning in from the side. Trustingly, he was permitted as such by Durnford-Slater as this was a dire case and he was the closest thing they possessed to an expert.

"During the briefing, I made note of where they had thought to have seen the men carrying the equipment and cables ..." the colonel dropped his finger on the splayed map and determined sternly. "*There.* That's got to be it."

He had found on the map the original proposed location of the enemy relay and potential source of their outbound communications. His view raised, seeking Drain and Peel from outside and waving them in.

"*Troopers.*"

"It looks like, well, *a dwelling*," Head commented, regarding the proposed mark on the map amongst a bunch of housing. "It doesn't look any bigger than the house we're standing in."

Peel and Drain entered the kitchen, treading in snow and mud.

"*Sir?*"

"*Yes, sir?*"

"I need you to get word to Captain Giles on the left flank. There is an enemy relay with a secondary antenna located in South Vågsøy. It must be eliminated ASAP. This needs to happen for us to establish comms to the remainder of the raid with both our Troops and the navy, and ... troopers, it is *imperative* that this objective be completed before our scheduled check-in at ten-hundred-hours. *Ten-hundred-hours:* this is paramount, understand?"

Peel and Drain swapped a gleam in their stance.

They nodded.

Possibly, their colonel's stress level from his growing concern for communications had wavered his mindset or memory, but the two shared the same confusion regarding the request.

"But, sir ..." Peel spoke in a cautious tone. "... the *communications are down,* how are we—"

"Find Giles in person. Tell him. Show him."

Durnford-Slater marked the map with a pencil, then scrunched and folded the page hurriedly. He bestowed the importance to George Peel— entrusting this young commando trooper with what could potentially be the linchpin to the enemy's defence of Operation Archery.

He then directed to Drain, "Stand by the wireless once their relay falters. I predict once it is gone, we will have full bandwidth of the radio waves in Vågsøy."

"Yes, sir," both Peel and Drain obeyed before heading out.

"Remember! Get it done before ten-hundred-hours!"

Head followed the two troopers out, even partially covering their departure into the fray of noise and combat before stepping back inside the Norwegian home/signals post to approach Durnford-Slater. The tense colonel was hunched over the dining table, still deep in thought and trying his best to maintain a leader's mindset with the shitty hand of cards he had thus far been dealt.

"You want me to go with them?" Head asked, inferring that that was a significant task to have handed just Peel and Drain with. He appeared to have an absence of confidence regarding the commission.

"No, negative," Durnford-Slater shook his head, staring off into space for an instance before his eyes locked onto his friend, Charley

Head. "Because we're going *out there* to take out that power station and the hotel; complete the whole bloody mission, by hand if we have to."

Head frowned, and de la Torre beheld a bemused gaze.

He was surprised that the lieutenant-colonel and commanding officer for the entire operation was even considering stepping foot onto the battlefield frontline—onto the front row of a chessboard along with the rest of the pawns. It was preposterous. "*You are* going to go *out there? Into* the *battle?*"

Head watched as Durnford-Slater pinched a few slices of shaved ham and dropped it onto a slice of the porous brown bread, folding it over and scoffing it down. This was hypocritical, having just told him and de la Torre off for doing it whilst on duty.

Head simply huffed under his breath as de la Torre watched with his mouth agape in astonished incredulity.

Durnford-Slater responded with his mouth full:

"I'm a stress eater, too."

*0936-hours ...*

Slipping on some ice, Trooper Peel led the quest to find their Troop captain amidst the snowscape skirmish and unfolding urban battlefield in South Vågsøy.

Right now, the time-sensitive task of seeking JFG in amongst all the chaos was more important than advancing on the enemy.

They got shot at by random Germans from random houses, but rarely shot back unless it was to cover each other's exposed angles or daring movements between concealment as they progressed along the hazardous left flank in their minor expedition.

Skirting the rear of the disorganized frontline, the venturing Peel and Drain bumped into captured uniformed German soldiers and plain-clothed Norwegian quislings being escorted at gunpoint by commandos. Herds of panicking civilian refugees seeking cover went along with the masses, headed away from danger. In typical clumsy fashion, Peel slid and skated on some ice out before them, causing the pace of the marching line to momentarily falter, observing his inelegance.

"*Cack!*" Peel murmured before pressing himself up from a knee.

Wordlessly, Drain assisted. One more slip-over by the trooper, and he would be requesting an inspection of Peel's boot treads to make sure somebody hadn't grinded them bare.

"My goodness, you slip over a lot."

Peel bobbed his head.

He changed the subject, recalling that he barely knew this chap from Adam. "Why do they call you *Drain?*"

"It's my name."

"What's your real name, though?"

Drain refused with a satirical huff. "Don't worry about it."

After a stretch, they next came across other commandos from Three Troop sporadically laid out behind firing positions, engaging enemy positions ahead.

The real war hit them suddenly when they came around the next corner and discovered a group of four commandos who had been caught in an enfilade flank by the enemy, resulting in two casualties. Both of the deceased men were lying lifeless in red-spattered snow near their compromised cover. The two surviving men weren't overly better off. They were pinned and stuck in place, unable to adequately return fire for fear of being hit.

"'Scuse us, gents, but have either one o' you lads seen Captain Giles?" leaning out of their refuge, Peel queried from behind the two in the predicament. Adding to their angst of having just seen their mates slain moments ago, this line of off-beat questioning was understandably received a little callously.

The two troopers were both too scared to move a muscle. They twisted from behind their pinch, shouting in explosive retort.

"*Watch out!*"

"*Oi! Get back!*"

*Th-th-th-th-thwack!*

The timber panel above Peel's head suddenly detonated with automatic gunfire and he recoiled behind safety, barely outrunning the onslaught. The same shooters who had killed the two commandos and now held a line on this lot had a line of sight on his rear position. It wasn't just typical rifle fire, either. These cunning krauts had fully automatic Schmeissers, adding to the suppression factor.

"Buggery! That was close, eh?!" Drain remarked after the extended bursts from the enemy position ceased and he shuffled in front of Peel whilst he caught a lost breath.

Drain then moved an inch at a time and took a glimpse at the wayward enemy. He could see the loft window of a wooden house across the road and along the next incline. It was an advantageous position indeed, and covered all angles of these poor trapped sods' escape avenues from their interval of cover.

"Oi!" Drain hollered to the two men in the hardship with his face barely peeking the corner. Their objective here was more important than their stand-off. "You two seen JFG or nah?"

"*Negative!*"

"*Not since the beach!*" the other added.

"Poo," Peel cursed. This job was proving rather fruitless.

Drain shared his look of displeasure at the result.

"*Oi, what's ya names?*" one of the voices called.

"Peel."

"Drain."

"*I'm Curry and this is Holt. You lads from No.2?*"

Peel and Drain exchanged a look. They had never heard of either one of these guys. "Nah, No.3. You?"

"*Yeah, No.3.*"

"Truly?" Peel said softly and looked to Drain, bewildered. Neither of them recognized either one of these two troopers, but then again, No.3 Commando—Commando in general—had really stacked up its numbers in the past six months. There were a lot of new faces, and it was reaching the point where not everybody knew one another.

"*Yeah. October batch.*"

Peel pouted as he and Drain now comprehend why. "Yeah, we're from July."

"*Ah...*" the other two realized the same thing. The blasé tone in their conversation during this battle was almost humorous it was so indecorously out of place.

"Well ... g-good luck, eh?!"

"Yeah, good luck, lads!"

"*Oi, hol'up! We're bloody pinned here, boys!*"

"*Yeah, how's about givin' us a hand, eh?!*"

The dutiful duo were getting ready to try another route along the left flank when Peel and Drain heard the second bit, and genuine repentance drew them back. Although of course, Peel and Drain wanted to help assist these blokes out of trouble, they couldn't take the risk of not completing their main objective if they got hit or worse, not to mention the delay from the time it would take to complete this side quest.

Before they had a chance to even discuss what could or could not be done for these two commando comrades, suddenly, Peel acted without hesitation, inching to the edge of cover and bringing about his readied Thompson with his finger across the trigger guard. Without speaking a word, Drain did the same, in utter solidarity with helping their brothers out.

"Yeah, alright! We're gonna cover you! Run back to us!" Peel shouted before exposing any inch of his body.

"*Okay!*"

"Ready?"

"*Yep!*"

"Covering fire!" Peel and Drain both bellowed before they stepped out, both high and low from their shared cover and let loose sustained automatic gunfire at the enemy-occupied house before the shooters could get a shot off. They hosed their fire across the façade of the building, specifically around the windows, concentrating their fire as much as they could as well as being sure to suppress the enemy within.

Their American machine guns carved up the occupied house, chomping the timber window frame to splinters and even bringing down the edge of the roof in a snowy collapse.

All-in-all, the act was a success, and the two new commandos quickly darted from their pinned positions and slid in low behind new cover with their rescuers, leaving the enemy for nothing.

"Cheers, lads!"

"Thanks!"

The lot took a moment to shake hands and exchange pleasantries the British and gentlemanly way.

"You boys want to tag along?" Peel asked, reloading a stick-mag from his smoking Thompson. "We're out to find the captain and get a plan in action to take down a secret enemy relay in town—direct orders from Colonel Durnford-Slater."

Holt and Curry swapped a look of eagerness.

"*My word, yes!*"

"*Lead on, chaps!*" the men remarked, reloading and catching a breath before becoming additions to Peel's conquest.

They set off at once, and unsurprisingly, Peel slipped in the snow first hoof off the mark, becoming propped up by his cohorts. "Cack!" he whimpered, shaking it off, somehow yet to become exhausted by his unending ungainliness.


Bobbing and weaving between haphazard shelter and remaining low and out of sight of the enemy wherever possible, this motley band of troopers moved on with their cause.

Following the clumsy George Peel as he danced in the snow, unable to progress more than ten steps before throwing his arms out in shock from a near-miss collapse in the snow, radioman Drain and the two other members of JFG's Three Troop progressed in a file. They passed behind a few more friendly positionings of commandos presently engaging the enemy, raining hell down on defence positions in Vågsøy.

Their search for JFG had begun, good and proper.

They came up behind some upbeat fighting and the trading of gunshots, creeping up and addressing friendlies from behind concealment.

"*Oi, you lot seen the captain?*"

Nope.

They found another group. Asked the same question.

Nope.

"*You seen Captain Giles?*" the men questioned as they appeared behind more friendly shooters a little further along, distracting them from the fight for an instance in the hopes to obtain a location on JFG. In a partially destroyed village house, one of the commandos in action finally responded with some intelligence, informing the group that Corporal White had passed their position not long ago, headed into South Vågsøy.

This was good news and the first proper lead they had discovered on locating JFG since they began this mission.

Knocker White had a reputation within No.3 Commando, and he would probably be fighting alongside JFG, if not be aware of his exact location and where to find him.

"Knocker White passed you lot?" Peel queried, stepping inside their house ruins, over a lot of collapsed debris, trying not to fall on slanted sheets. Drain followed while the other two tagalongs waited outside.

"Yeah!" one of them answered.

"How long ago?"

"About ten minutes ago. He pushed up *thataway.*"

"... further *in* the village ... in there?" Drain's brows inverted from worry. This meant their path took them further into the heat of battle and deeper into the skirmish.

"Yeah, *thataway,*" the commando added. "Him and that crazy new Mills kid from the June recruits. They're kicking in doors and tossin' in bombs! Blowin' every bloody thing up!"

Right at that moment, enemy fire came smashing through the partition and hole in the wall, shattering more glass from the window ledge and breaking scattered ornaments within the house they occupied. All of the men crouched down lower, taking cover for an instance before one of the angry commandos returned blind fire with his Tommy gun, spraying barely over the windowsill in their general direction.

"*Cheers! Good luck!*" Peel shouted over the gunfight and opting this to be a great time to vacate. With Drain in pursuit, he hastily headed back outside to regroup with the others. They safely flanked around the next few houses in hopes to catch up to Knocker White's onwards assault.

"They went this way!" Peel informed as he led.

Bullets swept the angle of the stilted house as Peel was about to break cover, and he recoiled in the nick of time not to be cleaned up.

As the ricochets pelted the wooden side of the residence and pockmarked the snow on the ground, the men stacked up on his mark and remained behind concealment. Their route had well and truly been cut off at this juncture, so they reared up and found another, quieter way.

The group dropped back a row of houses, moving from house to house, checking each corner wisely before someone would dart across.

The battle raged on further in the village, the action becoming more diluted now that they had diverted south, and it wasn't too much to say that the sensation was somewhat eerie in the stillne—

*They suddenly came face to face at a corner with two armed soldiers!*
A stand-off—they stopped lifeless in their tracks, held dead to rights.
*Weapons raised.*
*Hammers cocked.*
*Fingers tightened on the triggers.*
*Chit-chit!*
*Clic-click!*
One of the men tensed a shotgun at the bridge of Peel's nose.
*They were absolutely point-blank.*

There was another shorter man in a black beanie with the shotgunner, holding an M1911A1 handgun outstretched in either hand, and he strafed out with a line on multiple targets in the street. These two soldiers seemed fearless and confident in their stances.

Drain and the other two troopers were slow to react peeling out from behind Peel, but they did so sternly, boldly, with their weapons up and at shoulder level—and fortunately ... *nobody fired.*

*It was Knocker White and Joe Mills.*

"Jesus Christ! You lot ..." Knocker White remarked, bending at the elbow in order to direct his Ithaca pump-action towards the sky. He took a moment to loudly gnaw repeatedly on the chewing gum within his orifice whilst breathing through his nostrils.

Thankfully, dawn had brightened enough that the Commandos could quickly identify each other in the morning light.

"Bugger me!" Drain sighed, lowering his guard and hunching over the snow. His heart was pelting a million miles an hour, stowing his body's adrenaline reaction to the combat situation.

"You lot almost got lit the fuck up, lads," the overconfident Sergeant Mills stated, perching both his hammer-cocked handguns by each side of his rosy cheeks. The man was the type who seemed comfortable in hell, forever frowning. He was at home in this chaos.

"What are you lot doing out this way?" White asked.

"We're looking for Captain Giles. I've got orders from the colonel, sir," Peel responded, wiping the sweat from his forehead. "We were cut off from moving ahead back *thataway,* so we decided to whip around back and see if we could catch up to anyone."

"Yeah, well, that's going to have to wait. We need your help first," Knocker White situated sternly. "We were chasing down a group of Gerrys that we saw leg-it down this way with what looked like a signalling kit."

Curry frowned. "What's a *signalling kit?*"

"Flare guns. Probably to light up marks on the ground for their fighters to target," Mills expanded plausibly. It was a creditable supposition.

Knocker White expanded, "We're worried they're going to slip past our front and flank our boys. If they find our FOB on the beach, they could shoot flares at it and mark it for an aerial strike. So, we've decided to break the line and hunt them down."

"... and did you find where they went?" Drain queried, sharing concern.

Before it registered, they heard the barely audible but unmistakable sound of a weapon being chambered from a position overlooking theirs.

*Bam! Bam! Bam!*

*Baaaaaaaang!*

Gunshots from an overabundance of weaponry trained their way erupted from a dwelling on their enfilade; a cunning defensive manoeuvre by the enemy. They had likely seen, watched, and waited until the six stray commandos became fully exposed before engaging.

*Lucky for Commando, they were a shit shot.*

Bullets erupted against the sparkling snow and earth about their combined footing, shredding the lumber shack behind their stances. The barrage caused the row of commandos to react instantly, inadvertently dancing and falling low to dodge. They dove, slid, and rolled down a sloped embankment of which they had been standing parallel, miraculously not receiving a single casualty.

Knocker White grazed his knees, and Curry lost his rifle in the immediate kerfuffle as they tumbled down the snow-covered gradient. The helmet got shot on George Peel's dome, causing it to ricochet, kickstarting his reactive impulse. This time, he was happy to stumble— down the same hill.

In a mini-avalanche of sorts, the lot collapsed down the decline.

Foliage was buried beneath the loose snow on the slope, and they kicked up petrified twig and cold leaves, coating them in umber brown.

Peel and Drain were first down the hill, using their travelling momentum to swiftly steady themselves and leap a shonky knee-high fence before bursting in through the side of a thatch-roofed home—chased by a hailstorm of pursuing bullets. Peel shoulder-barged in through the closed door, slamming so hard he knocked it from its mounted hinges in a waft of disturbed dust while Drain dove in head-first through an old window shutter, smashing the timber panels and glass, tumbling inside the building in a fit of loud destruction as bullets raked the wall beside his passage.

There rested a nanosecond of tranquillity after the two entered the humble, wholesome Norwegian home at the bottom of the gradient slope. They could not help but pause to notice the incongruity of the interior: the whole place was wonderfully decorated for the festive period, with a thick Christmas tree wrapped in coloured paper tinsel, lined with box-shaped presents enveloped in colourful wrapping paper.

Family heirloom ornaments were proudly displayed throughout, and the stone fireplace against the wall was on and roaring, having warmed up the inside of the home. In the centre, the dining table had been set for what appeared to be a family of six—or at least six guests ...

*And then here they came.*

Curry and Holt followed the linear trail behind Drain and Peel.

The pair of evading soldiers fired over their shoulders, offering return fire towards their aggressors up the slope as they sprung up from their hip-slides and reels down the embankment. Covered in snow and twigs like they had just gone twelve rounds with Frosty the Snowman, they quickly escaped inside the same undisturbed Norwegian abode.

Holt scuffled inside after barely sticking the landing, while Curry courageously remained outdoors a few seconds later to attempt further retaliatory fire upon the enemy up the hill. He had his weapon shot from his hands in a bright flash and metallic *whip!* whilst becoming strafed across the shins by gunfire.

With a roar of might, the troop collapsed to the sleet and muck just shy of the doorway, becoming buried in splinters from the enemy's continual overshooting in their wake.

Incoming next was Mills, sliding down the slope sideways and in better control of his decline than those before him. He fired his two handguns aimlessly in retort at the German ambushers in their elevated positions, whilst Knocker White skied shoulder-first down the snowy embankment of frozen brush behind him, cradling his shotgun.

In the cloud of tossed snowy dust and blind bullet whizzes from the enemy, White suddenly snagged on buried foliage below the snowfall layer, causing him to revolve into a thrashing snowball of debris and twirling commando fatigues, crushing brittle hibernating plant life in his whacky whirl. Out of control, he was sent cannon-balling through a picket and wire garden fence lining the property from this short hilly reserve, tumbling wildly.

Once down the bottom, he managed to control his somersaults and rolled to his feet. Unable to stop his decline, he leapt over the wounded commando in the doorway at the last second, where he crashed into Peel who was holding in the doorway. The two collapsed inside as more bullets pulverized the walls of the residence above and around their beings.

Overshoot rounds punctured the wooden walls and blindly shot everything to shit inside, ruining the furnishings.

"*Come on!*" Peel shouted whilst collecting himself, but Knocker was already back up and there to assist in rescuing the wounded Curry. He tossed his shotgun into the floor with an iron clatter and pirouetted on his heel, launching out into the doorway and back into the fray like a trapdoor spider.

He and Peel reached down and latched onto the screaming commando's epaulettes and webbing, briskly dragging him to safety right as more deadly gunfire traced their movements by inches, loudly assaulting their senses.

Indoors, the continuous assault tore through the wooden walls above their heads, detonating furniture and ornaments within the household in a ballistics display of blind anarchy. While they recoiled within the dust and debris cloud, the lard that was Mills finally came crashing in through the other window, located further along from where Drain had entered.

Like Drain had done, Mills threw himself through a latched timber shutter and a glass window to escape the firing squad up the hill. It must have been the same group of cunning Germans they had been pursuing moments earlier. They had dubiously doubled-back after picking up on their commando tail, luring in their pursuers masterfully.

The six trapped commandos got down as low as they could on the rug-lined floorboards of the home as, from above, fragments of thatch and splinters from erupting wooden frames snowed down upon them.

During the bedlam, it was too loud to communicate.

Peel squirmed about and saw Knocker White who, even in the core of the chaos, tended to their wounded man, acting fast to tie off the man's leg wounds as all hell broke loose around them, burying them in splinters of timber and dust.

Peel's view panned around the floor where he spotted Holt and Drain, each taking turns to reach up and grab at some of the bowled fruit and sliced cake that had been arranged by the family prior to their abandoning South Vågsøy approximately an hour ago. They were like scavengers.

Mills was alive, too, pressing his back up against a wall between two windows and shielding his head with his two empty handguns whilst bawling at the top of his lungs for the onslaught to finish.

More intermittent gunfire kicked off again from up the hill.

The Germans were trigger happy, their suppressing fire was relentless and their ammo seemingly unending. Bullets minced the walls of the home and shredded all curtains and fixtures within. Hot lead ruined anything the men attempted using for cover, shattering ceramic pottery and objects from the many shelves, causing padded furniture to erupt into balls of stuffed cotton or quills that floated around the room like an aroma.

Peel's eyes blinked as a juicy red apple rolled off the table above his head and dropped onto the rug right in front of him like an offering from the gods. At least it wasn't a grenade.

Once he realized it was food, he inched forwards on his stomach, crawling with his gun in both hands and his dented brodie on tight. Like a snake, he slithered, following the rolling apple as it headed across the room like a sentient entity, luring him towards a pile of fallen and broken fragments from the topside of a sideboard ... and where, amidst the random debris, rested a relic which thunderstruck him to the core: *a small silver box,* about the size of a box of matches. There was a cross engraved neatly within the scroll art of the silverwork, and it spoke to Peel's soul more so than the fruit did.

Time seemed to slow.

Volume of the chaos lessened, became echoic.

*Wide eyed with reverence, Peel's hand crept forwards, slinking in a snake-like motion beyond the apple, eventually attaining the silver trinket.*

He took the time to examine the treasure. The unit entranced him. Found him while he was lost in the pandemonium. Comforted him in the chaos.

Inside the tiny box were miniature pieces of tissue paper. It took a moment for the young commando to compute, as it was in Norwegian, but it was then that Peel realized that they were parts of the *New Testament* of the *Holy Bible.* There was an odd moment of clarity that overcame George Peel, and without dwelling more on the context surrounding his existing religious boundaries, rather than discard it, he stowed it into his chest pocket. His mother had offered him a token for safe travel, and he had discarded it ... he wouldn't ignore this devout signal so blatantly. The universe was clearly telling him something.

For the rest of his days, Peel knew not why he had collected the tiny silver casket. Perhaps it was that he felt he needed God on his side that day and that with it, the man in the clouds would look out for him just that little bit more.

Audio returned to normal.

It was still loud as hell.

"We can't stay here!" Knocker White shouted after scooping out the old chewy from his gob and tossing it. He somehow kept it together as plentiful enemy fire pelted in through the walls and windows all around them. "Oi! Drain, Peel ... *the other chap I don't know the name of,* on me!"

The constant enemy gunfire had even sawed the legs on one end of the dining table in half, causing it to tip and envelop Peel and Drain like a bunker shield. Thankfully, the bullets could not penetrate both the walls and the thick timber of the dining furniture, and the table stopped a lot of the incoming projectiles with chiselling thumps whilst they obeyed the attentiveness of their ranking soldier, Knocker White.

"Everybody present?! We've got to get out of here, and we've got to work together!" he deliberated over the noise of the pandemonium. They may have found cover from the ambush, but this house was fast becoming a kill-box, and they were sitting ducks.

The men looked to White for leadership, and he achieved it in that moment. He dragged the maimed commando onto the fallen wooden door that Peel had knocked off its hinges on the way in, and the other troopers shuffled over to assist him in carrying their wounded mate upon it like a stretcher.

"Mills!" Knocker called, about to ask the man to give them covering fire, but the bloke already knew.

"Got it!" Mills nodded, using the side releases of both his freshly loaded pistols to close both the racked metal slides simultaneously. He revolved around in his low space and poked an arm out each window port, unloading shot after shot towards simultaneous German positions up the hill, causing them to shut the fuck up for a moment.

With tensed forearms, he roared with might as he fired the entirety of his pistols up the hill at the enemy as behind him, the rest of the men bugged out of the frail and war-torn Norwegian household, carting Curry on the makeshift door stretcher.

Once clicking dry, Mills followed suit and escaped out of the same side door of the home, somehow eluding their German aggressors and evacuating the shootout in six solid pieces.

The audio from the gunfight faded in volume behind their wake ...

*At least, for now.*

After the shortest of moments to collect themselves, the motley group of Knocker's heroes moved out.

From behind the barrel of a shotgun, Knocker White led their barge through a closed-over door to another neighbouring Norwegian home. Peel and Holt trailed with Curry on a stretcher, followed by Drain and eventually Mills, puffing and wheezing, striving to reload both his slide-locked handguns at the same time; with both guns piled in the one hand by the handles, sorting two fresh 7-shot magazines from his near-endless stash and inserting them into the slots underneath of the pistols. Once each gun was fed, he held one in each grasp and pressed the slide releases with his thumb and index finger respectively, charging each weapon for more combat.

Once inside the shade of the residence, Mills closed back over the door. Their guards remained partial, scanning about the shadows within this new quiet interior. Over their own heartbeats from the adrenaline and sprinting and as their hearing returned, they were reminded of the ongoing and overarching battle currently taking place in the north-westerly direction of South Vågsøy.

They could still the sound of more gunfire from the old position.

The Germans must have still been under the impression that the British were still trapped inside of the timber house, as they were yet to let up the constant fusillade, hellbent on chewing through it like termites.

"Hold up here," Knocker instructed, taking the time to tug a splinter of wood from his grazed cheek and pad the bleeding. He had sustained it on their journey, whilst tumbling head-first through the fence.

Very important, he next took the time to unravel a fresh piece of gum on which to munch. He was like an addict with a nervous twitch when he was without chewing gum during a stressful situation. Once in his gob, he huffed through his nose, calming himself, alleviating his heartrate.

Drain and Holt carefully let down Curry's stretcher.

"Someone's going have to run him back to the medics," Peel stated, imposing that it was not going to be him.

"Aye," Mills agreed rather flippantly, pointing at Peel and Drain dismissively. "You two, go."

"Beg pardon?" Drain frowned, equally as rowdy. "What's your fuckin' problem, then?"

"Yeah, you lot, off ya's go," Mills pronounced his statement further as he marched towards the two with an ounce of aggression in his strut. "Knocker, if it wasn't for this lot, we'd have caught them Gerrys up there and taken 'em out. But because of you, we missed the opportunity, and it nearly got us fuckin' smoked. Now look at us getting pushed further and further from the front. We've gotta get back up there, and back onto the line!"

Drain argued. "Well, too bad. We've got a job to do!"

Mills had nothing of the sort. "Yeah, well *so do we!*"

"Oi, settle," White stated, interjected himself into this discussion and pulling rank. The hothead Joe Mills cooled his engines and withdrew, shaking his head.

"We'll flip for it, okay? One of us, one of you."

Peel and Drain exchanged a look.

"It's only fair," Knocker added in the stalemate.

From across the room, Mills concurred.

He was not happy about risking his opportunity to get back into the action and kill some Germans and complete their respective objectives, but as White said, it *was* fair.

They flipped a coin between Mills and Knocker and then Peel and Drain. Mills and Peel both lost out and would be escorting the wounded Trooper Curry back to the beach FOB.

There was silence for a full ten seconds while Knocker White put away the penny that had just sealed their fates for the remainder of Archery.

*Mills was fuming.*

It was like he had just been benched from the game.

Peel, too, having to pass on their quest solely to his counterpart Drain.

Knocker White spoke up. "If you hurry, you can get back to the front before it's all over, gentlemen. Drain, *new bloke*, on me."

"Holt, sir," Holt introduced.

"*Holt*, okay. Stay on my arse, Holt. Do what I do!"

"Yes, sir. I'll need a weapon."

"What?" White frowned in Holt's face. It would appear that the corporal may have been a tad more hearing impaired than the others, as he was yet to use his indoor voice like them.

"I, eh," Holt restated nervously, "I don't have a weapon, sir."

"Where the fuck's your gun, trooper?"

"I, eh, I dropped it ... back on the hill ..."

After an awkward stance, Knocker White stepped forth and drew a spare pistol from his belt punching it into the trooper's middle with reiteration of his orders. "Stay on my arse! Do what I do!"

"Yes, sir," Holt cradled the gun low and with both hands.

"What's the plan?" Drain asked, adjusting the strap for his wireless on his shoulder. They had to get Knocker White's objective over and done with so they could move on to finding JFG and subsequently tackling that next objective.

They all watched as Knocker White cautiously peeked from the concealment of their building, attempting to see up the hill and at their nuisance German shooters. All the while, down in his hands, he fumbled with a packet of confectionery, removing another new piece of gum and inserted it into his eager mouth. He was doubling up for this one.

"We flank 'em," he stated, chewing hungrily whilst loading a few more 16-gauge shells into his pump-action. "Hit 'em from behind," he eyed the fellas, "Gerry seems to like that, eh?"

"Yes, sir," while Holt revelled in the bawdiness, Drain offered Peel a look of uncertainty. It was up to him to carry the mantle now, maintaining Durnford-Slater's orders.

"Good luck," Peel offered, along with the folded chart their CO had issued him to pass onto JFG. The scrunched map of South Vågsøy was marked in pencil with the proposed location of the enemy relay and potential source of their outbound communications: their 1000-hours deadline objective.

Entrusted, Drain accepted the map like a form of deputization.

He gave Peel a confident nod, accepting the passed torch.


*0939-hours ...*

"John," Head questioned Durnford-Slater whilst they waited unwearyingly for their push out of the signals post and into the battlefield. "What are we going to do if Peel and Drain cannot find JFG in time? Or what if they do, and they fail to find and destroy this supposed enemy relay that is blocking our transmissions?"

Still in the kitchen, de la Torre's ears seemed to prick to the missing context of his officer's conversation ...

Head added, forebodingly, "... before the deadline?"

de la Torre grudgingly inserted himself into their privileged conversation. "Pardon me, sirs, but ... what *deadline?*"

Durnford-Slater elaborated after pausing for a second and reconsidering the value of the pre-existing confidentiality. de la Torre may have not been privy to the finer *plan-B* or *fall-back* details concerning the mission, but this was becoming increasingly more prudent to their current situation. Soon, the secrecy may not matter at all.

Durnford-Slater felt Head's stare befall him as he gave up classified information to a trooper.

"Ten-hundred-hours. That's the deadline."

de la Torre's focus bounded from his colonel to the lieutenant.

"What happens at ten?"

"If we have not yet established an update with Brigadier Haydon aboard the Kenya by ten-hundred, then the Royal Navy and the Royal Air Force will consider pulling back under the assumption that the land assault has failed. That *Commando* has failed."

"But Commando doesn't know how to fail?"

Durnford-Slater chortled at that smugness. "It is *the navy* about which we are speaking. Asking for the benefit of the doubt is *optimistic* to say the least ..."

Head expanded further. "They'll pull our air support and sea cover. We would become stranded."

de la Torre gulped. "They're going to ... leave us here?"

"They'll cut their losses," Head justified where Durnford-Slater's words fell absent of reassuring resolve to his man. "You've got to look at this from a bureaucratic point-of-view ... Whitehall can't afford another botched Commando operation."

"It's a combined operation ..." Durnford-Slater supplemented. "Communication is key. Without it, it all goes *tits-up* as one might say. We have overcome calamity after mishap, delay after impedance ... but if we encounter just *one more* hindrance whilst this operation continues to circle the sink, Archery could go the way of Commando's previous failed exploits."

The info hit de la Torre like a tonne of bricks.

The lad almost wanted to cry at the reality of the existence of bureaucracy behind this war effort.

Present in the connecting room, Dildo Dillon peeled his sentry guard away from his post at the northward-facing window to pay attention to the hot and controversial topic currently being discussed. He now knew the odds at stake.

"But ... Commando doesn't know how to fail?" de la Torre questioned with a low tone. He still held his colonel in the highest of esteems, but the realization of this certain reality brought him down a peg and shone a whole new light on him and the British Army.

Durnford-Slater said not a word to defend it. So far, even with all the great publicity Commando had received up until now in the press, Operation Claymore had been the only real successful operation—and to an extent, that was a bare-naked fluke. They had caught the enemy literally with their pants down, resulting in an easy victory.

But he knew the ugly truth. Always had.

Head scoffed in Durnford-Slater's wordless wake. "Look behind us, lad. All Commando has *ever* done is fail ..."

"So, what's the bottom line, here?" de la Torre inquired genuinely.

Head fulsomely muttered. "That we're shagged."

Durnford-Slater shook his head, unable to shine any illumination on their present situation. "Not yet. But one more big snag here ... and I fear it will pull at a thread to unravel our entire outfit."

Head shrugged. "And *then* we're shagged."

On the faraway tundra rocky cliffs that overlooked the action in South Vågsøy, a different group of special soldiers observed the exchanges of gunfire across the distance. They did so via their blinking muzzle flashes, witnessing the sporadic explosions of thrown hand grenades as they crept towards the panoramic scape in formation ...

*Who were they ...?*

These silent, deadly hunters were dressed in saddle-brown leather strappings over snow camouflage coveralls, complete with white balaclavas to hide their faces. These faceless, unknown, portentous soldiers seemed almost a third-party belligerent in addition to the British Commandos versus the German Wehrmacht currently clashing in the warzone.

... one thing of certainty: their allegiance was to *the Führer.*

As well as dressed for the stealthy occasion, these menacing, mysterious adversaries were also geared for such, packing an assortment of long-range Karabiner rifles with mounted telescopic sniper sights.

Invisible predators across the cusp of the rocky caps, they crawled into tactful locations, lying prone or inching up over the cover of certain rock obstructions.

Creeping like spiders.

Slithering like snakes.

With every inch, they gained advantageous positions that were the best from which to inflict venomous strikes upon the invading Western enemy down below in South Vågsøy.

*This was about to become an astronomically big snag ...*

*... pulling a vital thread.*

It was time to thwart the raid of these westerners.

*Let the shagging of Operation Archery commence.*

# 7

## Kingdom Come

*Måløy Island*
*Vågsøy, Norway*

The remnants of the collapsed wireless antenna on the island resembled the exposed steel rib-cage of a mammal carcass now that the smoke was dissipating.

On their way to the final objective on the north end of Måløy Island, unexpected crackles of small-arms fire rocked the seemingly subdued scene.

Green beret-clad Major Jack Churchill, along with several other dutiful commandos in steel helmets and woollen beanies, converged on the source located on the back end of the small landmass.

With their main objectives on Måløy near complete, it was now time to secure the prisoners for transport, mount-up, and prepare to aid G2 in South Vågsøy—an unlikely scenario, considering Durnford-Slater had taken the largest portion of the most lethal commandos ashore with him to make short work of the disorientated, decimated enemy forces, likely accomplishing his tasks with ease.

*They'd be home in time for tea at this rate.*

The view from the back end of the island was of the icy Ulvesund Fyr passage, which bled out to the north between South Vågsøy and Sildegapet. The final traces of dawn hue were being eradicated by the rising of the tepid sun, vanquishing the night and bathing Norway with pure daylight.

After hearing the gunshots, Churchill and the other commandos ran to the corner of the block where there seemed to be another small enemy garrison building tucked away next to a large, double-storey wooden warehouse with a chained door. Out the back of this shed and progressing off the island down into the water, was an industrial ramp which resembled a *slippery dip* slide, similar to what one would find at a children's playground.

The conveyor belt travelled the entire way down into the fjord. Linking at the bottom was a small pier and vacant dock besides several large labelled industrial tankers of stored oil: coincidently, the destruction of this was their final demolition objective on Måløy.

The two-storey garrison block seemed as though it had received an artillery shell through its ceiling, bringing down a substantial portion of the rear end and right side next to the shed. This prior damage reduced more than half of the building to crumbled concrete, wood beams, and dusty rubble.

Currently herded like cattle were approximately a dozen captured Wehrmacht soldiers, standing out the front at the gunpoint of several armed commando troopers. The prisoners had their hands mounted upon their heads, and those who were attired in uniform and strapped with leather holsters had been stripped of all weaponry and munitions. Every pocket had been thoroughly searched, turned out for intelligence.

This crowd of prisoners included one possessing the rank of a kommandant *(commander)* and was likely one of the officers in charge of the entire Måløy Island stronghold. His self-righteous and arrogant expression confirmed his command when compared to the sea of angst and worried inverted frowns around him.

There were two Norwegian women included among those arrested from the block—civilians from the mainland; and most likely quislings loyal to the occupying Germans. They would have expected to catch a few of them on the mainland of South Vågsøy, but not the strictly German stronghold on Måløy. They were each clothed in oversized borrowed army jackets and scarves and wore seemingly nothing much beneath those. They were probably ladies of the night—prostitutes—ferried in by the soldiers for the previous evening's celebrations.

Still seemingly intoxicated, both of the women staggered in amongst the POW round-up, with messy heads of hair, lazy eyes, blotched eyeshadow, and smeared lipstick. One of the quisling darlings even had a bottle of champagne still glued to her paw and a tit out of her lingerie which failed to be concealed beneath the borrowed undone jacket. Seemingly unintentionally, the sleeves and collars of the borrowed jacket were up, worn like some sort of party animal.

Led by a now bloody-nosed Captain Young, the British troopers had them all encircled and at gunpoint, but there must have been some resistance still from within the garrison building in the background. There was the sound of commotion and men were on alert.

"What's going on, Captain?" Churchill questioned as he jogged with his Tommy gun in his hands and his longbow now strewn across his back.

He instinctively checked the flanks for danger as he approached and took a situation along the outside of the building, now beside Young and some other grouped troopers who were taking cover from a possible threat within.

American journalist Felix Hardy was a few steps behind Churchill's group, and he slotted neatly between the stacked British soldiers. He was trying to keep up as well as keep a low profile, all the while not get in the way.

"There's still a couple of Gerrys holed-up inside, Major," one of the other troopers reported while Young Young painstakingly wiped the bloodstream leaking from his nose. He hissed under his breath with ache and frustration. "We took these ones with ease. A dozen soldiers and two Norwegian hussies, eh ... *'comfort women'.*"

"*Comfort women?*" Jack uttered, glancing over the two broads.

"*Ey, I is not Norwegian! I is Belgian!*" one of the panda-eyed ladies objected from the throng. She was tripping over her own collapsing high heels and slurring her English words. She was the one in the borrowed officer's jacket and with her nipple caught on the edge of her underwear exposing most of her right breast.

"*I not. I Nor-norweegn,*" the other garbled in a softer voice, equally as offended and just as likely to vomit at any moment. She practically burped bubbles.

"*Oi! Back in line!*" a trooper with a gun remarked. He waved the weapon in their direction and jostled the women back into the group of POWs. Quislings got treated with the same minute level of respect as the German soldiers, if not even less.

The reporting commando continued to Churchill. "They were all walking out, surrendering, when at the last minute two of them tried to fight Captain Young for his weapon."

Young's watery eyes scanned across the scene with much underlining dissatisfaction.

Jack's brow raised. "Hence the bloody nose?"

"Yes, sir."

Churchill was genuinely confounded. German soldiers were nothing if not disciplined. Resistance after surrendering to the enemy was a heinous gesture and could often result in the entirety of the conceding group becoming slaughtered. Defiance was usually unfathomable—of course, unless prior commanded by their superior. In actuality, being a hero at that point, no matter what army one was loyal to, typically only accomplished getting everybody else killed.

"They didn't follow their kommandant's orders to surrender?"

"No, sir. They won't come out, either."

Churchill's eyes rested upon the kommandant in the crowd of POWs.

*The kommandant stared back inanely ...*

It was as if he withheld an odious admission.

The fact that there existed operatives within these enemy numbers who would disobey the orders of a kommandant meant that they were either contravening their superiors—improbable for the loyal G.I. Gerrys of the 181st—that they were quislings, and therefore not bound by any *Geneva Convention* rationale regarding surrender to the enemy, or lastly and most unlikely of all, the kommandant was not the superior officer to these particular German soldiers ...

Churchill dipped his stare at Young, noting his blood-smeared maw.

"Are you alright, Young?"

The disgruntled CO of Six Troop bobbed his head. He was watery eyed and clearly pissed off as he gave his mopey explanation. "Bastard bloody slapped me when I wasn't lookin', mate. I'll be right."

Mad Jack nodded, sure.

Young still had possession of his weapon, and his life—something that the German aggressor who attacked him no longer did. The partially clothed and deceased soldier who had attempted to disarm Young was now laying on his back in the doorway with three bullet holes to his chest.

The corpse wore no military paraphernalia, just dressed in dark pants and a white undershirt that was now stained crimson from bloody fatal gunshot wounds. As such, the man may have been a local who was collaborating with the occupying enemy force, hence why they refused to obey the kommandant's orders to follow their surrender.

Churchill conjectured after thinking it through, "The bloke was likely a quisling, same with the other one still inside. It's why they aren't submitting to the kommandant's orders to surrender. That could be the real reason why he isn't listening to *old mate* over here."

"We thought that, too," the trooper reported, tilting his head towards the body and bringing Major Churchill over for a closer inspection. "Then we noticed his pants and shoes: German officer attire, don't you think."

Churchill focused on the fact while his brain scrambled to make sense of the scenario. He was beginning to suspect an ominous underscore to this ongoing orchestra of war. There was something lurking in the shadows, missed by reconnaissance ... something unknown even to the thoroughly vetted issued intelligence.

*German soldiers posing as quislings ...?*

*But why?*

"*Sir!*" a voice called his attention away from the suspicious circumstances lying in the muck, and Churchill's view raised to the incoming trooper who had just come from the opposite side of the neighbouring storage building. He had just brute-forced the door with some other commandos and secured the contents within the shed. "It's full of mines."

"*Mines?*"

"Yes, sir. Sea mines, sir. It gets worse: the whole building is fractured inside. All the rows of shelving holding the mines have toppled over and are incredibly unstable. Suggest we gain safe distance before the whole thing blows sky high on its own?"

"What's the likelihood of that?"

"Demo guys say it's almost a certainty."

Churchill's brow loosened and he nodded.

The commandos near the storage building had been given the urgent order to move away from the structures and they did so without hesitation once learning it was imminently about to blow up. They assisted in guiding the prisoners, shepherding them like proficient heavy bollock sheepdogs to dopey bullocks.

Mad Jack lingered a moment, approaching the dangerous edge of the cliff and observing the rocky slopes on the rear of Måløy Island. It was roughly a sixty-foot rocky decline down to the fjord, maybe less. He studied the slippery dip-like ramp that connected the shed down to the water by the oil tankers. It all made perfect sense now: it was a conveyor belt to the water top that the Germans had established to convey the sea mines down safely and efficiently. Luckily for their operation here today, the Germans had apparently set aside this task for the new year, as the Vågsfjorden had been cleared by the submarine's reconnoitre.

The trooper bravely remained with their major within the vicinity of this highly volatile building full of mines. "We can detonate it to be safe but cannot destroy it without taking out this entire connected building. That means cremating whoever is left inside."

"Fine-o-fine. They've had their chance to surrender," Churchill accepted, responding to the commandos responsible for transporting the POWs. "Rig it to blow on my mark. Let us get this lot out of here, gentleman. Move everybody back."

Now that he had fixed his nose and collected himself, Young aggressively interviewed those in the know within the crowd marching up on the group of prisoners. He seemed kind of pissed that this lot had got the drop on him, possibly permanently disfigured his looks. "Oi, *you*, that bloke inside there giving us grief, is he a friend of yours?"

At Young, the German prisoners retained their dumbfoundedness.

Granted, most of them probably couldn't speak English, either.

Young especially implied the two prostitutes in his haphazard interrogation, drawing focus upon them specifically. "He was dressed like he was havin' a party. You lot sort him out last night or what?" Young levelled his voice at the two women—right as one of them stumbled onto her rear-end on the mud and the other hunched over, seemingly about to hurl—and she did, causing everybody, German prisoners and British commandos alike, to wince in disgust.

"Captain Young," Churchill announced formally, verbally restraining his man from potentially mistreating the prisoners of war. It was understandable that Young Young was angry about being dog-shot by one of the Germans (or possibly a quisling), maybe even a little embarrassed, but there was a procedure to handling the interviewing of POWs that Churchill had to abide at all costs. "Come on, chap, let's get back in formation."

"Jack, they know who's in there!"

"And they'll be heavily interrogated once they're ferried onto the *Kenya*, believe me," Churchill put a hand on his young subordinate's shoulder, whisking him away. "Whoever is inside there is about to be blown to kingdom come for their impertinence. Don't stress, lad."

Young slowly bobbed his compliance, smoothing his nose and sniffling blood and mucous with tense pain. It still hurt like a bastard.

While Churchill escorted him from the situation, he felt the peepers of the older and more experience-lying kommandant trace upon them. He was watching them ... studying them ... possibly even *understanding* them, for all they knew.

It was at that instant in their departure that Young, too, noticed the kommandant's lingering gawk upon them. The eye contact upon both he and Churchill was one of an obvious withholding of information. The lips of the German leader seemed to curl at one corner, as if something were mildly humorous.

"You what, mate?" Young exclaimed in a rowdy joust, indicating the kommandant's attention towards them.

Churchill stopped, anchoring Young's aggressive charge.

"Eh? You havin' a good time this mornin', eh? Cockhead?" Young pestered at the German from the side. His blood was still up. "How many of your fuckheaded friends are holed-up in there, eh?" he questioned in a more serious tone amongst the POWs. He took a few steps, breaking out of Churchill's guided embrace, perceiving wholeheartedly that this commander of the garrison on Måløy Island would know the answer. He singled the man out, directing his submachine gun between them at his hip to show he meant business. It unsettled a few of the POWs.

After a second passed and he was sure of the German commander's concealment of intelligence regarding the situation, Churchill sided with Young's principle. He arced his voice to the crosswise.

"Get a translator here on the double!"

"*Sir!*"

The entire herd of prisoners halted due to this.

They were at what could be perceived a partial safe distance from the building of question.

In the tense seconds that followed, Churchill took the mantle from his man and sidled in between Young and the kommandant, addressing him from behind his sterling stare of piercing blue eyes.

"You understand me, don't you ...?"

The Hun said not a word, lest it incriminate him further ... though he didn't hide the fact he was found guilty as charged.

"How many of your men are left in there?"

"Only zee one ..." the kommandant finally replied in a surprising fashion, both with his compliance and the fact he understood and spoke exceptionally good English. With his hands still on his head, he responded to this British major without a sense of fear.

"... but he iz not one of mine."

Churchill scowled. "What do you mean?"

The commander grinned and snorted a laugh.

There was a certain hint of disobedience and defiance in his eyes, and he seemed to appease his own yearning by knowing something they didn't. However, Churchill read him like an open book.

"You are the highest-ranking officer at this outpost ... Why don't you save that man's life and order him again to give up? I do not want to have to kill him. I will accept his surrender," Churchill responded with a degree of stalwart sincerity.

From behind Churchill, Young racked the pin on the top of his Thompson, showing him that they meant business. The brute gesture became waved clear by Churchill's hand as he once again took it upon himself to interrogate this Nazi prisoner. He could control his well-being that way.

A few edgy seconds passed, but no more words were exchanged.

The two officers simply stared each other down in the silence.

"Trooper!" with haste and aggression, Churchill shouted whilst still death-staring the kommandant and his smug look.

"*Sir?*"

"Get these prisoners out of here!"

"*Sir!*"

Inclusive of the kommandant, the dozen German prisoners and two comfort women marched away for lock-up and interrogation, but most of all, also held at a safe distance from this soon to become detonated explosive situation. It was rumoured to blow big.

Churchill regarded the following as a passive threat for the kommandant as those around him began to trudge on. "You may not tell me anything, but you will sure as shit tell them onboard our ships. They will be much more persuasive than I ... and much less well-mannered."

As the line-up of POWs began to move in formation, the kommandant whispered something between just Jack and himself.

"*Viel glück.*"

Following his transposition, Churchill's blue stare squinted.

He heard the words muttered by the smug German and distinguished the translation as carrying some relevance. Of what little German he understood, he knew generalized expressions such as *good luck*.

In the seconds to follow, Jack decided to not let it fly.

"*Oi!*"

Demanding to know, Churchill advanced on the kommandant in the line-up, pacing beside him in the driving line of POWs. This informal interrogation did not halt the dispensation of the commandos marching the prisoners off for processing, however it did slow it a tad.

Jack growled. "What do you mean? Who is in there?"

Not gaining a response, Churchill's progression ceased alongside the POW's miserable procession, and he held back, watching the prisoners slog on, under arrest. That would be all he was going to get from this loyal German Commander, but the kommandant had clearly hinted that this ally of Germany was not one of Woytasch's 181st Infantry Division at Vågsøy—perhaps not even of the German Wehrmacht.

*But if not Wehrmacht ... then who were they?*

Churchill shook his cuff and checked the time on his wristwatch.

In operational pretence, every second counted, and they were beginning to run slightly behind schedule. He wanted to waste little time in accomplishing his tasks here on Måløy Island, of which just one remained.

"Major?!" Young exclaimed with a newfound fury. He had repositioned himself along cover lengthways the exterior of the garrison block entrance. Young jerked his head at the doorway beside them. "Permission to blast this bugger into the next world, sir?"

"Fine-o-fine," Churchill remarked with the tip of the head, onboard with the idea of an assault. "Hold," Churchill held Young and the men of Six Troop's assault, and he moved out and into a position where he was not in the line of fire of the hostile within the doorway, but so that the said hostile could unquestionably hear his words clearly, no matter how fortified they had made themselves within. It was obvious Churchill desired attempting to negotiate with the holed-up Hun one last time, rather than blow him up with the sea mines and fuel reserve.

Alongside the building, Churchill shouted. "Oi, you hear me in there? *Hullo?!*"

His voice echoed throughout the vacant and dark barracks.

Whoever was inside certainly heard his tenor.

"This is your last chance to surrender before we blow you to kingdom come ... do you hear?!"

From inside, they all heard the distinctive and purposeful metallic sound of a weapon being primed. It was likely done out of expressive showmanship. Whoever the hostile within was, he meant business, and he was holding his ground.

"Is that your *final* answer?"

From within, a barrage of gunfire expelled at the entryway.

It was not specifically aimed at Churchill.

Churchill inched aside as bullets slammed into the mud across the floor. It was a definitive declaration that he in fact did *not* wish to surrender.

Young asked afterwards. "Satisfied?"

Churchill cocked his head. His work was done here.

Per se, he gave Young the kill order and walked away.

"All yours, Captain."

"Stack on me, lads! Let's blitz this cocksucker," Young ordered as he clenched the wooden forwards grip of his fully automatic M1928A1 and prepared for a forced entry. Almost instantly, his immediate detachment of Six Troop commandos had formed on either side of the entrance way, queuing for a breach entry on Young's command.

"It's *one* on about *twenty*," Hardy declared quietly to Churchill as Jack strolled near him at a safe distance of the action He counted their numbers as the commandos prepared to assault the lone remaining German soldier who was barricaded inside.

"Hardly seems fair, eh?" Churchill remarked simply ... and then something tweaked to him—his face dropped. It was a twinge in his sixth sense or alluring foresight of the potential outcome. "Young, wait!"

Their assault breach halted at the last second and they hesitated, waiting for their major's orders.

"*Sir?!*" Young grinded his jaw. His finger was tensely wrapped around the trigger. There was a fire ablaze within this commando, intent on bloody revenge.

Peter Young was thirsty for vengeance against this lone German soldier, and Jack knew where he was coming from, but ... he was hung-up on something. The expression of that German kommandant was burned into his brain, and it left behind an eerie afterglow, resonating the caution that he would normally throw to the wind.

Even to himself, Churchill could not describe it.

He had a bad feeling about whatever it was that lurked beyond that door and within that barracks. It felt like a deathtrap.

"... let's just blow it," Churchill decided, opting to do with the collateral alternative.

"*What! Why?*" Young loosened his stance, as did the others who were stacked behind him, prepared to enthusiastically follow the fully automatic assault. It was clear that Young wanted nothing more than to spill a kraut's blood by his own hand, and not just detonate him to *kingdom come* like Mad Jack had said.

"It's safer."

Young argued. "Oh, what, come on ..."

"Sir ..." a trooper caught Churchill's attention as the entire group began to march away so that they could blow it all sky high. He handed Churchill the det. cord coil, offering it to him in order to be the man responsible for lighting the fuse, so to speak.

"Cheers," Churchill remarked as he accepted it personally, allowing for everybody else present to go the way of the POWs and towards the centre of Måløy Island and of a safe distance. Churchill, Young, and Hardy, lastly followed behind, unravelling the rest of the coil towards their safe distance, with Young bringing up the rear guard with his submachine gun. There were no nibbles, though. Whoever was holed-up within, remained, about to become entombed in a deafening inferno.

Once everybody had left earshot—except Hardy, who didn't necessarily count—Young felt the need to challenge Churchill—as a friend, not as a subordinate army officer. "You know, I never expected to see you scared ..."

"Pardon?" Churchill's brow rose. He ceased unspooling the last of the line for a moment to address his subordinate and commando chum.

"Mister *no-unnecessary-risks ...*"

Churchill had not ever seen Young use such an insubordinate tone of voice, but he received it from the man he knew beneath the uniform, not the rank. Churchill was a stern superior, but in sight of what had transpired here today, he fully understood where Young was coming from. He decided to hear only the playful jeer of the tone, and not the defiant manner that may or may not have co-existed.

"That's *Major* no-unnecessary-risks to *you*, lad."

Young scoffed, but his dispute remained invalidated.

"Did that whack to your beak dislodge a part of your brain or something, Captain?"

Young held his ground. This conduct was unlike him, and extremely unbecoming of a military officer, however, he believed resolutely in his rationale until now. He wanted blood, and felt it justified.

Churchill eventually elaborated. "Look, I have been where you are now ... I know you want to *mount-up, giddy-up,* and charge in there *half-cocked* and blow this Gerry's guts all over the wall. But let me tell you something, *Young* Young, do you really think I lived through everything I've been through ... the *Burmese Rebellions*, the skirmishes along the *Maginot Line*, the ambush at *L'Épinette, the Battle of Dunkirk, the Lofoten Raid ...* all by running in *half-cocked* like a half-wit?"

Young blinked, barely even thinking about it.

"Yes—"

"*Yes!*"

Young's response was amplified by the voice of the eavesdropping Felix Hardy, who answered the same question with the same word at the same time, same definite tone, and the same esteem regarding the lesson.

Jack eyed him in a *fuck off* manner, and Hardy made himself scarce.

"Well ... I ..." Churchill, unable to think of a retort, fleetingly stuttered before fast finding his feet. Now that it was ready and they were at a safe distance (by commando standards), Churchill offered the coil and the plunger to Young. "... here."

Young accepted the plunger, honestly expecting to hear some profound wisdom from Major Churchill. He would have been accepting of it.

Jack furthered in the seconds that followed. "It's not all about dick-swinging, *Captain Young Young.* I learned, and I'm alive. But that is not without forming a thick skin towards impulses and acting rash. You'll learn to pick your battles."

Young nodded, accepting the advice for what it was worth.

"How's about you do the honours?"

Although still disgruntled, Young obeyed, having accepted the detonator device. Technically, he was still getting even with the one who wronged him and busted his nose.

With next to no hesitation, he pushed the extended plunger into the device emitting a tiny mouse squeak before—*Bhoom!*

*HMS Kenya*
*Vågsfjorden, Norway*

*0940-hours ...*

Now that the wall of covering smoke along the coast had dissipated and daylight was fully upon Vågsøy and Måløy, the view of the active raid from the bridge of the Kenya as she hovered out in the bay was a sight to behold.

Encapsulated by the snow-clad hills skirting the rear of the scape, the thousand perpetual booming echoes of heavy fire from the guns of warships reverberated across the Vågsfjorden. The force of the rumbling sound was enough to crack ice.

Other than the fiery detonations of explosives upon objectives, there was the hammering of the powerful AA cannons, the roar of automatic machine guns, bolt-action rifles, and the blasts of grenades located sporadically throughout Vågsøy itself.

This far back in the Vågsfjorden, the small-arms gunfire from the house-to-house skirmishing in-land was barely audible across the distance, discernible only as faraway crackling. Hand grenades and other detonations could be heard as muffled thuds.

Above the landmass hovered a veil of translucent fog.

This was a haze comprised from a culmination of the rising smoke of the raging battle below, natural thawing temperature, and the remnants of Luftwaffe and RAF aircraft battling as they still dogfought above, stirring the mixture in a waft. Every so often, the anti-aircraft guns aboard the Kenya or the neighbouring destroyers floating in the bay—the Oribi or Onslow—would sound-off with their anti-air automatics at a nimble enemy fighter who had drawn within proximity. The resting sea beasts swatted at them like insects, assisting their flyboys in the aerial skirmish.

The partially sunken remains of the German armed trawler, the Foehn, which had attempted to run aground in a last-ditch effort to elude their attackers in the Vågsfjord, was now visible. The ship was a wreck, still burning from the inflicted damage.

From the east coast, Durnford-Slater's G2 had embarked upon the greatest impetus, thrusting forwards and taking ground from the enemy, resulting now in time-consuming and casualty-enduring urban warfare in the streets. Meanwhile, a portion of his Group, One Troop, led by Captain Bradley, had landed up north, and had taken the docks and set the fish and herring factories ablaze. The giant tanks ignited like giant furnaces.

The Troops would eventually all converge in the middle of South Vågsøy, taking the power station along the coast and the tall hotel building at the back of the strip; a known enemy stronghold, and likely the head of the snake.

Brigadier Haydon momentarily placed down his saucer and teacup.

With the aid of the spectacles, he observed dozens of units of Commando jogging along the beach, joining the fray. They were escorting what appeared to be captured German soldiers and local quislings to holding stations along the shore, prepared for transport vessels which would soon be en route.

He let out a murmur, lowering the binoculars to pinch the tiny eyelet of his teacup with his fingers and take a sip. It was as if the more he supped the Earl Grey, the harder he concentrated. It invigorated him.

He could see that the men of Churchill's G3 had secured Måløy Island, and even witnessed their destruction of the colossal wireless antenna tower that was situated there for enemy communications. Along with G1 Lieutenant Clement's small detachment of men who had branched east and taken the Holvik barracks, Churchill was the only other Group to report to the Kenya that their objectives had been a success. They had heard diddlysquat from anyone on the mainland.

"Still no word from anybody within Group 2, sir," a sailor remarked as he took a step nearer to Haydon against the large and bright bridge windows. He was holding a pair of binoculars of his own and had been assisting the brigadier with keeping an overwatch of the raid.

Haydon frowned.

This lack of communication was unlike the boy scout Colonel Durnford-Slater. Even a simple situation report to inform the navy that tasks were ongoing was yet to be received.

"Our operators are confirming some sort of interference coming from the island. Once Churchill's men secured the tower at Måløy, the signal strengthened on our end, but we still cannot reach any of our Troops on the main island. They're being cut off by something ..."

Finishing his cup, Haydon must have copped a bitter residue in the bottom of his tea. His yellowing teeth clenched as he swallowed, and

Haydon checked his wristwatch whilst one of his assistants stepped in and refilled the cup from a freshly brewed pot. Haydon appreciatively observed the catering while the voices of others aboard the bridge filled the air with relevant reports.

"Twenty minutes until deadline, sir," a sea captain informed.

"Lieutenant Clement reported something else interesting from his findings in Holvik ..." a radio operator reported. He passed along to Haydon a typed transcript of the G1 commander's report which had come through over wireless in the last few minutes.

Haydon read the sentence.

His cup was now filled with fresh steamy liquid, and he instinctively reached to the side in order to obtain the beverage, bringing it cautiously to his lips while his eyes scanned the page.

As the flavour of the blend hit his tongue, his concentration intensif—

"*SS?*" he prematurely removed the teacup from his maw to poise the rhetorical question to the operator after. "Are we sure that this transcript is accurate?"

"Yes, sir, that's what he said."

"Intelligence stated nothing about an *SS* presence on the island ... only *Wehrmacht.*"

"Yes, sir. Group 1 encountered enemy soldiers from an outside unit present at the Holvik barracks. Upon further examination of the fallen, Lieutenant Clement specified that they wore an unidentifiable unit badge. The only certainty of their insignia was that they were a branch of the SS ... should we inform Colonel Durnford-Slater?"

Coolly, Haydon passed the transcript to his sea captain as he slowly raised his tea back before his face, ready to sip again while his mind evolved into deep consideration and thought, however the lucidity of their present communications dilemma prevented such. "I would love to, sailor ... but unfortunately, we believe that the radiomen of Durnford-Slater's Group are unable to receive our communications."

Cradling his warm drink, Haydon paced closer to the wide bridge window, casting a deep stare out over the raid.

The sailor made a suggestion. "Perhaps they can hear us but not send any outgoing messages?"

"At this point in time, I'd rather not blast the radio waves with sensitive information on the off chance that he can hear us. They're on their own for now..."

"Aye, sir," the radioman took his leave, leaving Haydon momentarily alone with his thoughts to ponder the potential added risk to the operation if elite members from the Schutzstaffel were in the enemy's midst ...

Beside the brigadier, the sea captain pondered regarding the latest intel. The sailor theorized further: "Could just be a lone SS officer? Someone shown up at Vågsøy to inspect the outpost? Wrong place, wrong time sort of deal ... Could be *nothing*, sir."

"Could be *everything* ..." Haydon acknowledged with a degree of uneven optimism drawn upon by experience. "Could be a worst-case scenario slowly unfolding before our eyes. Could be that an entire first-class army of killers checked into the island hotel for the holidays for all we know, Captain."

The sea captain visibly conceded.

"Commando may have just inadvertently pissed on a hornet's nest."

"What would you have us do, sir?"

Haydon shook his head, subtly parking the matter for the time being. "Nothing we can do. Not until we hear back from our ground troops."

A minute later, entering the bridge from the rear hatchway was Captain Hooper and his second-in-charge with a golden blonde imperial moustache, the fiery loose cannon Lieutenant Graeme Black.

Both men were of No.2 Commando. They reticently entered the Kenya's operations deck from their staging ground with the rest of the G4 floating reserve down below.

Although not exactly an intrusion, their presence was unorthodox.

Hooper hailed politely as he moved through the hive of activity of the operations deck sailors and radiomen and addressed the navy brigadier. "Sir, permission to enter?"

Haydon twisted to catch sight of him, pulling his view away from the panoramic view that oversaw the distant raid. "Granted. Should you not be below deck, Captain? Awaiting orders?"

Haydon could only assume that the commandos assigned to Group 4 were, at this stage, becoming restless from inaction. For the past two hours, they had heavily geared and armed up, and were left blue-balled and itching for combat. They were just waiting—*praying*—for that radio communiqué from the ground troops requesting immediate reinforcements.

Hooper spoke on behalf of Black and himself. "It has been over an hour since launch. We were hoping for an update, sir? How is the raid progressing?"

Regulations denied access to any members of the army aboard the command deck during a live operation, let alone be apprised of every detail, however Haydon was nothing if not a reasonable commander. Therefore, he accepted Hooper's request for knowledge regarding Operation Archery thus far.

"Groups 1 and 3 were successful," he turned, placing his binoculars down upon a desk and approached the audacious No.2 Commandos. "Group 5 has embarked towards their objective to the north, skirted by the Onslow. So far, all is going to plan, except we do not know the landing Group progress."

Hooper frowned. "Sir?"

"Yes, Group 2, they're ... yet to report in. However, all things seem operationally sound from afar; the docks have been secured along the coast, the factories were destroyed soon after by your friends in One Troop. Although we're not blind, for some strange reason we are mute as to how the fight is going against the enemy in the city ... we aren't assuming the worst, but there is a non-negotiable deadline fast approaching—a deadline that the navy will be adhering to."

Hooper nodded, aware of the deadline.

He straightened his posture.

The news, although lacking, was still good.

"Thank you for the update, sir ..."

Teacup and saucer in hand, Haydon waggled whilst Hooper prepared to return to his post. He could tell that it was not the news Group 4 wanted to hear. They were longing for a reason to enter the fight. It was visible just below the surface.

Hooper offered as he vacated: "The floating reserve will be standing by for when *you* or Durnford-Slater need us ..."

Haydon dismissed and Hooper walked away, collecting the eavesdropping Black on his way out and into the metal corridor and stairs which took them back into the bowels of the ship and to where G4 was located.

"What *deadline?*" Lieutenant Black questioned now that they were in a confined and surreptitious area without listening ears. "What's Haydon talking about?"

Hooper halted, finally facing his man out of a thousand-yard stare that lasted but a moment. This information was restricted to anybody not a part of the operations brief for Operation Archery, for obvious reasons.

Black was no rookie trooper. The Canadian-born, Norwegian Independent Company-served and trained, South Lancashire Regiment officer graduate, who had volunteered for the Commandos and been enlisted in the No.2 outfit in July had quickly distinguished himself. Yes, he was a hothead, alike a great many men who signed up before him, but just the right type that Commando aspired to embrace within its ranks.

Black purposely overstepped with his perception. "Because, if that means what I think it means, there is no way I am leaving my boys out there to rot!"

Black's statement was a lit fuse.

"You drop me off before you leave, you hear?"

"Relax, Lieutenant," Hooper reassured. "Commando has the full support of the Royal Navy."

Hooper then led their passage to regroup with G4 and await instructions.

Stern beneath his blonde moustache, Black's maw asked.

"When's the deadline?"

Hooper paused midway down the echoic metal staircase and turned back and see his trooper. "Ten-hundred-hours."

"That's in twenty minutes?"

"Less. Let us hope the ground troops need us before then, lest we miss all of the action."

Hooper craned his neck as he turned to march on, leaving Graeme Black to clench his jaw with fury—a fury he hoped to soon release upon the enemy the best way he knew how.

*South Vågsøy Village*
*Vågsøy, Norway*

*0942-hours ...*

Still inside of the Norwegian house/signals post, radioman de la Torre queried Durnford-Slater as the apprehensive lieutenant-colonel trod into the darker living area. This was the same room where commando marksman Dildo Dillon was kneeling on a chair by a front window. From the position, he could survey a sector of the fishing village as well as the tall, rocky slopes behind South Vågsøy which advanced up into the snow-capped mountain range. The drapes had been drawn, which helped to minimize visibility from any remaining enemy positions beyond the locale, which by now, had been pushed away by the assaulting commando forces. In a hemispherical impel, the entire battle had been pushed away from the coast, although there was still the thunderclap of sporadic gunshots, proving hostility was within proximity of their location; their (so far) ineffective signals post, due to a lack of radio waves.

His face behind the scope of his sniper rifle, Dillon asked: "If you don't mind me asking, what's next, sir?"

Pacing back into the kitchen and spying out of the drawn window above the sink that faced east, Durnford-Slater methodically paced. "We may need to try and move to higher ground ..."

Durnford-Slater peeped beneath the frilly curtain outside, noting the start of the rocky slopes on their left flank were located behind where JFG had taken his men of Three Troop. He eyed an area where the rise of the rocky elevation was accessible. From above, they may have better luck overcoming the enemy's jamming capabilities in the village.

"Higher ground *could* work," at an educated guess, de la Torre affirmed.

Durnford-Slater spoke with his focus out the sliver of light coming in through the curtain-draped windowpane. "All we must do for now is get a signal out to the Kenya. Surely, they can see from afar that we're in the process of completing our demolition objectives. A simple sit-rep will buy us the time we need to ..."

*Durnford-Slater's attention drifted ...*

Out the window, his stare squinted afar ...

Frowning, his eyes fixated on the rocky ridge that semi-encircled most of South Vågsøy, trapping the village in like a border fence.

Across the distance, he spied movement upon it ...

*A curious development.*

There appeared to be many men along the elevated range, dispersing lowly and in a motion fitting of militaristic formation and execution. They were holding place, possibly even *assuming* a position above South Vågsøy—an advantageous position to possess.

He could not immediately recognize this reconnoitre as an existing part of their roster, for JFG's Troop was not that far out of the village, and Clement's Group 1 would still be a lot farther west and likely still at their objective at Holvik.

*They were an unknown entity ...*

A few exasperated seconds passed.

*Who were these guys?*

"Charley ..." Durnford-Slater tilted his view aslant a moment before turning his face to lay eyes on his lieutenant. His tone was one of question. "... did we have men up on the ridg—"

*Smash!*

The glass behind the curtain fold Durnford-Slater had raised with his fingers unexpectedly shattered inwards, flaking in razor-sharp shards. A high-velocity projectile punctured a plate mounted on a shelf in the kitchen space, missing him by inches.

The bullet had been fired from a sniper rifle, long-range.

Although it took a second for him to put two-and-two together, it had obviously originated from the source of movement in the distance upon the rocky cliffs above the village.

*Whizz—splat!*

Following the tinkling of the initial fracture of glass, another incoming bullet fired through their position. This one grazed the side of Durnford-Slater's sideburn as he reeled, just before striking the centre-left side of Corporal Pattinson's chest as he stood idle in the kitchenette.

The poor trooper was killed instantly.

*Shot straight through the heart!*

"*Down!*" Head shouted as he reacted, as did Durnford-Slater, applying pressure to his new wound as warm blood flowed on the side of his face.

The two hit the wooden floorboards of the kitchenette at the same time as the knees of Pattinson. Departing life, the young commando had been robbed of his existence without so much as an elucidation of comprehension to the fact. The grip around Pattinson's Lee-Enfield released an instant before the trooper plummeted face-first in a heavy *whump!* staring emptily across the floor level. He emitted a singular cough before blood quickly pooled out from beneath his collapse.

Almost two full seconds after that, de la Torre found himself still standing in the middle of the subjected kitchen, stunned by the sudden onset of chaos. Blinking profusely about himself, confused and confounded by the strange, silent onslaught unfolding around him, Durnford-Slater reached up and grappled onto the radioman's uniform, tugging him down and out of sight of any windows—and just in time, too. A split-second later, another long-ranged bullet drafted through the same window port, barely missing the trooper and embedding into the inner timber wall in the absence of his targeted bodily contact with a loud *whizz-chunk!*

Additional shots cracked more of the glass of the window.

Bullets slammed against inanimate objects or interior walls within the residence.

The shots were unsettlingly accurate for the extent of which they travelled from the distant ridge. The shooters were so far away that their gunshots were barely audible at such a long range.

It fast became apparent that there were at least a dozen sharpshooters upon the overseeing ridgeline, and they were all loosing round after round from their precision rifles through any gap they could, knowing with a seeming certainty of the men's presence within, which exuded intelligence.

*These huntsmen had stalked their prey.*

They must have deduced that the few invaders hanging back, not unlike those in this very house, were high-profile targets. SOP dictated that those positioned at the rear of the frontline assault were of command value. Moreover, a meticulous and logical approach of engagement would suggest that eliminating marks in a rear-to-front sweeping pattern meant less attention to the kill. Soldiers were less likely to notice their comrades fall if they were behind them, rather than in front ... and *South Vågsøy would have been a sniper's delight from the ridgeline.*

*"Get down! Get down!"* Head repeated in a shout as debris popped and smashed around them like the work of silent, spasming poltergeists.

Behind them in the living room, Corporal Dildo Dillon was fast to shove himself away from the windowsill as the glass before his face shattered into a thousand shards and slivers, covering him in shrill sparkle.

After a few seconds to collect himself, Durnford-Slater crawled in nearer to the others. They had congregated against the archway joining the rooms with their heads down low and out of direct sight of any of the surrounding mountain ridges.

In the absence of their presence, it had fallen silent.

However, the distant shots continued—the snipers likely moving on to the next exposed target, lighting them up like a turkey shoot.

Dillon questioned, noticing he was bloodied.

"You all right, sirs?"

"Fine."

"Snipers! I'm guessin' from up on the north-east ridge!"

"They're on the ridge, alright! I saw them!" Durnford-Slater insisted, assessing the severity of his face wound. His ear had been clipped, judging by the amount of blood and burning sensation. It was not fatal, but it was a nuisance.

"Listen to those shots! There's gotta be many!" Head conjectured, judging by the sheer amount of shots and rate of fire for such ranged weapons. They would have had to be using precision rifles, typically bolt-action, and unquestionably combined with some sort of mounted telescopes in order to acquire such accuracy.

Another sporadic shot flung in through the window port, slamming another inanimate ornament located across the room. It shattered, raining down. Durnford-Slater clenched his eyelids closed as debris rained upon his head from above.

This was exactly the kind of *one last delay* he was worried about ... *and it got worse.*

"Oh, there's definitely more than one ..." he regarded, recalling spotting the movement of what appeared to be an entire enemy faction a fraction of a second before the shooting had started. He had noticed a few still getting into position amongst the rocky slopes.

It was a whole other hostile army ...

*A sniper army.*

He eyed the others precariously. "A lot more."


*0944-hours ...*

With the sun rising over South Vågsøy, increasing visibility tenfold since the raid had begun an hour ago, daylight brightened everything through the dreary and storm-threatening clouds hovering over Norway.

Although all shooting and activity had ceased down at the Norwegian houses at the bottom of a short slope, the acquainted group of four cunning German soldiers who had roamed to the rear of the British advance with a signalling kit in attempt to inflict some damage, remained in position within the top-storey of their hideout. The house had a perfect firing position on the lower section of the village, including some of the shoreline—an angle just shy of where they believed the commandos had established their Forward Operating Base; what they wanted to target, attracting aerial assistance.

Quietly mincing chewing gum between his tensed jaws, the clammy-browed Knocker White led his motley crew's stealthy crusade to exact retaliation on these cunning attackers. The ambuscade of which they had inadvertently triggered seemingly cut them off from reaching the forward operating base on the beach by becoming prey.

With his pump-action clamped tight in a sweaty-palmed grip, he, Drain, and Holt had sneakily flanked their position and approached from a blindside to their location. The knackwurst occupants had only recently ceased their intermittent fire down on the house of which they had last seen the Englishmen flee, and it was extremely likely these krauts had no idea they were being outplayed. It had taken time for these commandos to successfully outmanoeuvre the enemy's vantage point, but they were now directly outside and below the location, ready for action.

Further south and below the frontline, between the village houses and coming from the shoreline, Peel and Mills were on their way *back* into the battle. The two had just jogged to the edge of the island to drop off the wounded Trooper Curry at medic Sorry Corry's mobile triage station.

They had vacated immediately to return to the fray, only, they had hit a hiccup ...

"We're lost!" Peel stated as the two breathless commandos held for a moment, peering out from behind a timber hut in a quiet area, seemingly adjacent to the echoes of the raid battle. They appeared to be too far west.

"We're not lost!" Mills exclaimed with haste and with a pistol glued to each extremity, peeking out and spotting the adjacent rocky slopes. They seemed to be the same rock formation located behind the double-storey house they had been shot at, above the slope that they had all rolled down moments ago. This had merely been an alternate route. He gestured, "See!"

Calmly, Peel peeped out from cover, scanning the familiar entity that Mills observed. Admittedly, the rising daylight seemed to make the entire area seem different.

"*There's* the slope ... and *there's* the house..." Mills commented as both their gawps now laid upon the house where Curry had been wounded. The once quaint residence resembled a block of Swiss Cheese after the Germans had put a thousand holes through its walls. Mills' view escalated up the slope and to the houses that surveyed the area.

"That means that we were getting shot at from up th—"

There was a singular gunshot. It was close by.

Another loud shot followed, trailed by the incessant rattle of a small-calibre submachine gun ...

The two troopers inched out to try and spot the source of the close action, where they located the double-storey house the exact same moment a random German soldier was shot out of the top-storey window like something out of a *Charlie Chaplain* skit.

"Watch out!" Mills barked, pulling back with Peel.

Collapsing alongside a hundred shards of broken glass and wooden debris, the soldier's limbs flailed as he let out a screech that increased in volume as he dropped lower and closer to them.

Launched from the second-storey window of a house that resided over a hill slope, the fall resulted in what equated to over a four-or-more-storey drop.

The freefalling soldier vanished from their sight as he passed them midway up the incline. The sound of his body slamming into the earth was audible even to them at this distance.

*Thwump.*

They desired to rendezvous with Knocker White, Drain, and Holt before too much activity expired. This wasn't so that they didn't miss out on the fight, per se, more so they could do their part.

The clinking of glass shards rained down on top of the deceased German after he fell to his death and after being shot in the chest and flung out a high-up window and, after an interval of perception, Peel and Mills halted in their tracks to glance up the slope and at the source of that evacuation.

From the hovel in the building where the German had been forcefully evicted, they spotted the known wielder of a gun powerful enough to launch a human being like a stuntman from a cannon, Corporal Knocker White. After performing the fascist extermination, he leant from the attic space with his Ithaca 37 pump-action, gleaming out of the window space.

*The counterattack action had begun!*

Mills and Peel began to sprint from cover, playing catch-up.

Through the chaos, he spotted them down below in the urban environment and nodded as Peel and Mills picked up the pace, double-time, charging uphill in favour of joining him in the war.

After that little bit of action, Knocker White stepped back into a dimly lit upstairs attic space inside of the double-storey stronghold. He pumped the bole-brown foregrip of his shotgun, once again leading with it through the urban skirmish.

He saw beyond Holt and Drain as they checked the other two dead bodies that they had just despatched within the vacant Weegie residency after breaching the front door. The enemy within were caught off-guard on the lower level and were thus first in-line to receive the barrel of the slapping shotgun when all three commandos breached the entry behind them like a gust of savage gale force wind.

White had announced their presence a nanosecond prior by voicing loudly his catchphrase *knock-knock!* before driving his boot into the door, charging in guns blazing.

"Clear!" White finally stated, commending the textbook breach and sweep with a pleased affirmation glancing back at their carnage. He took a second to straighten the gas lantern that had been knocked over during all the fuss—and luckily not smashed, setting the entire house aflame.

Drain and Holt had been fast to cry havoc! but before they could even target an enemy within, Knocker White had blown a round of buckshot through each of their chests, one after the other, then rushed the final man up the steps and shot him out the same window he had camped them from. The termination job appeared relatively easy for such a trained killer.

In the aftermath of action, Drain knelt over a body cradling his Thompson. He and Holt had not even shot their weapons to assist with the attack. Knocker White was far too aggressive and quick on the trigger, and the enemy had practically lined up for him and his shotgun, which included the last Hun, who had posed rather elegantly before the upstairs window prior to being promptly shot out of by the power of the gun's blast.

The commandos quickly checked over the bodies.

From the shredded Wehrmacht corpse, Drain cleared a side-mounted magazine-fed MP35 *maschinenpistole.* It was one of two that had been used to rain down hell upon their prior lower position, judging by the abundance of spent brass and empty magazines scattered across the wooden floor of the residence. This particular submachine gun had

had its buttstock blasted to splinters when Knocker White had discharged its Gerry owner into the next world.

"These were definitely the culprits, sir," Drain confirmed.

White began trotting back down the rungs of steps leading from the attic, treading on and crunching the rattling rolling shells that dropped with metallic tinkles to the floor. He took the time after sorting ammunition to spit his used chewy out onto one of the downed bodies, reloading another piece of gum into his salivating orifice like he did some 16-gauge shells into his hungry, racked shotgun tube.

"Bloody good job, boys," he uttered.

Holt remarked with a scoff. "It was all you, sir!"

Drain added a big beam. "Yeah! We didn't even do anything!"

Holt chuckled, stepping in front of the doorway of which they had just breached. He added, riding the high. "I didn't even get a shot o—"

*Thwick!*

His eye socket became absent his eyeball ...

The thing popped like a pinched boil.

The off-sight sound of a *ping* against the back wall emitted like a telltale sign of an exit wound. He had been shot through the back of the head, and the bullet had travelled out his eye socket, taking the peeper with it.

Somehow still alive but severely confounded and deteriorating more by the passing second, Holt continued to speak in stutters from his position in the exposed doorway, slipping quickly into incoherency.

"... s-shot ... the a ... a gun-nggh ..."

Inside, both Knocker White and Drain's triumphant expressions dropped flat. They were confused for a full second as to what the actual fuck had just happened midway through their mate's narrative, interrupting his story as if he had an impediment.

Victory smiles and the winning grins worn by their combat success suddenly erased from existence as they heard the distant echo of a deviant rifle's crack, originating somewhere up the rocky cliffs behind South Vågsøy. The shooter would have had a perfect angle on this location and on Holt.

*Holt's eye had burst!*

*Popped!*

In an abrupt and ghastly display of gore, the trooper's head had only flinched minutely from the puncture through his skull, the penetration value had been so course. The exit wound met little resistance as the bullet travelled out his soft tissue, dislodging his eyeball. The injury to his mental capacity and cognitive abilities caused the soldier to become momentarily entranced in an instance of numb perplexity before he impulsively collapsed, overcome by shock.

He had to search hard to find the words that were just on the tip of his tongue seconds ago, somehow unable to finish his sentence. The inebriation was frustrating and confusing ... and then it hit him, like he was being drained of life.

"... a shot off ..." Holt eerily finished his sentence before his left eye blinked in an uncomfortable spasm. Trickles of red blood began to pump from his empty eye socket as he concaved his legs, dropping onto his side in the open doorway to the building. Still awake, and yet somehow unable to feel any pain or suffering from a sudden onset loss of motor function, Holt suffered a sudden onset of confusion more than anything.

The deterioration was mercifully instantaneous.

"*Fuck!*" Knocker White cursed as he reacted. At the same second Holt's wearisome body planted upon the floor, he leapt from the stairs and out of view of their ambitious sniper. He accidentally swallowed the fresh gum he had in his mouth, resulting in a splutter and expression of displeasure after he assumed cover.

Drain was much slower to react from the shock of the scene, and it was not until White reached out and shoved aside the radioman that he responded, curling up tight in the corner of the room beside the entrance. His eyes were fixed on Holt for an extended moment, utterly shocked at the display he had just witnessed.

From this angle, he could see Holt's expression finally nullify.

From this angle, White saw the entry wound on the back of Holt's head; a torn hole through his woollen beanie.

Another rebound *pinged* inside of the room as a subsequent shot was fired in their direction, possibly at Drain the instant before he was pushed out of sight. A rung of timber stairs behind them in the room detonated into splinters, popping magically.

"*Stay back!*" White hissed as the two hugged in tight.

They were pinned—*yet again.*

*How would they get out of this one?!*

"*What the hell was that?!*" Drain shouted.

Knocker White quickly evaluated the situation, making the appraisal in livid recoil. "*Snipers!*"

# 8
## Death From Above

Indoors of the disastrous signals post, Durnford-Slater, Head, de la Torre, and Dildo Dillon were forced to remain low and out of sight of their new faraway foes whilst more bullets from the sniper sights targeted within. Any inanimate object within the rooms they were pinned inside of that may have resembled a mark was blown to smithereens.

*... wwhiz—THWUCK!*

Upon a quick glimpse above a windowsill, the lumber of the weather-stripped ledge loudly fragmented into splinters, causing Charley Head's head to drastically withdraw. His heart skipped a beat.

The last thing he had seen with his reconnoitre was the twinkle of a half-dozen lens flares upon the rock formations bearing down on South Vågsøy. As the morning sun rose, it caused the reflective glass optics of their sniper scopes to mirror specks of light across the distance, visible in beaconing glistens across the distance.

*"Fuck! Fuck! Fuck!"* Head panted, crawling down low and to the others who lined the debris-littered floorboards in the fog of ash and dust.

"Feel better now?" Durnford-Slater casually queried having just watched him gander the window, nearly costing him his life. Head had desired to try and catch a glimpse of the rocky ridge snipers of which Durnford-Slater had already surveyed with his own eyes, acting against the wise advice to refrain.

Still panting, Head bobbed, a little clammy. He deliberated a statement whilst catching his breath. "I saw 'em up there! You can catch their helmets silhouetting over some of the rocks and see the flares of their optics. John ... there's a great sodding lot of 'em up there!"

"I gather approximately twenty additional hostiles," Durnford-Slater recalled from his visual memory—a mental photograph he had taken the instant before they had become sniper fodder.

Tucked in low, Head elbowed the wall beside him with frustration. This unforeseen hassle was another rather large spanner in the works, for it would not only be them being fired upon by these slithering sharpshooters upon the rise. Many commandos down in the skirmishing streets would be blindsided by them in an absolute annihilation. They could not even get on the radios to coordinate a counterstrike against the attack or even issue a warning. The snipers could simply eliminate targets from afar, and then effortlessly move onto the next continuously.

"What are we going to do? We're trapped in here!"

Before Durnford-Slater could concoct a plan, they all watched Commando marksman Dildo Dillon scramble to his knees in the confines, remaining hunched low and cautious of any portals of exposure. He carefully shuffled his way towards a position by the large curtain-covered windows at the front of the house.

"Corporal, what are you doing?" Durnford-Slater asked sternly.

"Just want to take a look, sir."

"Corporal, they have every viewpoint locked-in with scopes. You will barely get your head up before it's blown off your shoulders! Stand down."

Head intervened, having just tried to make an inspection out into the fray and nearly losing his noggin. He was speaking first-hand. "Dildo, the Colonel is right. These guys have got some serious talent, mate."

"Talent? They ain't ever seen talent like this, sirs ..."

Everybody watched as the ardent marksman ducked down, contorting like a vampire to avoid the exposure of daylight via the window space that Durnford-Slater and Head had both been targeted through. The enemy snipers would undoubtedly still be watching in the interim; waiting for the kill.

Dillon crawled back into the living area, approaching a different viewpoint. Redeploying slowly to remain unseen and out of peripheral range of any of the rocky slopes or the mountains.

"Corporal?!" Durnford-Slater sneered in a *what did I just say?* manner.

"Sir, trust me," Dillon defended respectfully as he got into position on the opposite side of the room, just beneath the windowsill of an intact glass windowpane that was a decorative feature; from floor to head height. They watched as he removed his brodie helmet, mounting it like a puppet piece upon his BC-41 blade and begin to crane it on an angle, leaning like an enticing sniper lure. "... it's the only way to draw these types of buggers out. I need to gauge his range, his distance, even his response time and accuracy."

"I'd say he's pretty darn accurate, Corporal," Durnford-Slater offered whilst still padding his head wound. His ear throbbed unendingly.

Head deliberated to Durnford-Slater in the meanwhile. "Honestly, John, we need to come up with a different plan. One that doesn't include doing the most obvious act of retaliatory stature one can think of ..."

"I concur. Corporal, we don't really have time for this stunt."

Dillon stayed the course, concentrating. "Sniper warfare is a patient man's game, sirs."

He then slowly raised it into view of the window ...

*The worm on the hook.*

The others in the silent room watched on in suspense.

Any second now, that helmet was about to be mistaken for a British soldier's head and be shot off by any number of snipers, giving a more accurate reading of their enemy's hand for an adequate riposte ...

... only, much to their surprise, it was not.

*The bait was not taken.*

Dillon's arm got tired in the hoisted position after a stretch of time and so he reeled his arm back, twisting to face the others with a temperament of confusion upon his face. The others seemed equally as bemused by this and how their anticipation had built-up but led nowhere.

Head tilted closer to Durnford-Slater by his side, and he spoke in a low tone, offering up a suggestion to the outcome. "Perhaps the snipers got bored? And displaced?"

Durnford-Slater had considered that ... but something just was not right about this. Sure, it was a convincing enough ploy, especially to the snipers at long range, but it was in that expectation that the conclusion belied the result.

*Could they be all clear ...?*

*Were these snipers smart enough to displace after firing ...?*

*... or were they too smart—and this was a deadly gamble.*

"We should move now," Head recommended, basing his advice on that evidence. "While it's quiet. While we can."

Attention suddenly came back upon Corporal Dillon as he began to make range adjustments to the telescope mounted on his Lee-Enfield rifle. He next prepared his hold on his ranged weapon, tactfully winding his elbow and forearm through the leather strap for better posture and taut grip. Exercising physical discipline, he allowed for himself to slowly roll from his flat position, prone by the windowpane.

As he deliberately inched in a slow revolve, telescoped rifle sight first, he gained a view of the distant mountains ... of the rocky slopes ... *of the existing snipers, lying in wait—*

*...w-whiz—THW-T-THWACK!*

The men cowering in the kitchen all flinched with kneejerk reactions from the cluster of loud, sudden impacts. They happened all within a half-second of each other.

Bullets struck their peering man, visible by the resonating cloud of crimson mist that puffed like hissing gas, lingering behind Dillon's head following an exit path of multiple projectiles. The scope mounted upon his rifle had also exploded with a metallic *crunch* and *pop* of the telescopic lenses within, shattering along with the glass from the window as it showered down through the torn curtain drape.

Instantly a dull doll, Dillon's body slumped over onto his back, sprawled out limp and lifeless. The departed commando's empty face gawked outdoors, now without either one of his eyes in his sockets and blood spouting torrentially from his agape mouth. It was an unnervingly hollow stare.

*He had been sniped multiple times in the head!*

The enemy snipers had this place locked down airtight.

All at once, the stares of Durnford-Slater, Charley Head, and de la Torre all became expressionless before a sudden rush of adrenaline surged through their bodies.

de la Torre wrapped his palm tight around his mouth and closed his lids from the ghastly sight, trying hard to wipe it from his mind. His mouth withered, wanting to say something, but he was robbed of his lungs.

"*Jesus-fucking-Christ!*" Head exclaimed. His stare was wide as the bare and empty red sockets that remained allowing for a front-row view of Dillon's minced brain and fractured skull.

*His pale face literally cried blood.*

Durnford-Slater quickly lurched forward, latching onto Dillon's bootstraps and dragging him inside, causing streaks of thick scarlet blood to coat the floor like the initial pallet of an artist's alla prima. Once their friend was clear of collecting any more damage, Durnford-Slater tossed one of the many fallen curtain veils upon his demise.

His view lastly sealed, filled with remorse in the miserable moment.

He hadn't wanted Dillon to try and peek that angle ... but they had to fight this somehow, and it—he—had been their best shot.

"Who the *bloody hell* are these sods?!" Head frustratingly exclaimed, crawling over onto his rear now that he was in a deeper part of the kitchen, further away from the living room and away from the deceased commando.

Durnford-Slater's dim stare slowly unveiled and he shook his head.

"Whoever they are, they're no ordinary German infantry."

Had Commando bit off more than they could chew?

*This elite force may have just met their match ...*

*0945-hours...*

At that same moment on the westerly vector of the same fishing village, Knocker White and his assorted commando clique had become cast from the frying pan and into the same fire. The savage snipers had them pinioned.

"Right'o, who the *fuck* are these cunts, then?!" White bellowed from his distorted position in the corner confines of a small Norwegian house. To their knowledge, the Wehrmacht they were supposed to encounter had no long-range capabilities—at least not to this extent.

At present, the shotgun-wielding corporal was contorted in a nook by the doorway opposite a mentally shaken Drain, who was just as stuck as he was and left with the resonating mental image of watching Holt just punch his ticket in the doorway.

The open entranceway between them was the only way in or out of the premises, and there appeared to now be an array of overattentive sniper scopes hovering across it like invisible lethal search lights.

"Cocksuckers!" Drain remarked distastefully, his emotions running high. They had just successfully liberated this enemy stronghold, only to become stuck here by their distant cousins on the ridgeline. He denoted a scary revelation, "Whoever they are ... I'm pretty sure they just used their own soldiers as bait to get us to stand still."

Knocker White eyed him. That was a scary sentiment, indeed.

"*Knocker!*" a familiar voice shouted outside the building. It was Mills, originating from the eastern-side, and hopefully out of the scopes of these snipers. "*What's goin on in there?!*"

"Mills?!" White recognized the man's voice and was immediately concerned for his friend's well-being. "Mills! Stay out of sight! Enemy snipers on the north-east ridge!"

"They got Holt!" Drain added sorrowfully.

An idea suddenly sprung to mind and White's brow loosened as his stare intensified. From his cover behind the door, he scanned the debris and dead body-littered floor, wall to wall searching for something that would have been discarded by Gerry.

His concentration was so strong that he ceased his fumbling over sorting a new stick of gum from his pocket packet. The gears in his brain clicked into place, eyes focused, and Knocker White placed the fresh piece of bubble-gum on his molars and began chewing fiercely.

"What is it ...?" Drain asked, noticing White's attentiveness.

He spoke between chomps. "How fast can you run?"

Drain cocked an eyebrow, preparing to be honest.

He implied his fifty-pound wireless pack. "With *this* on, not very fuckin' fast, sir. Why?"

Knocker White jerked his head at an object on the floor.

It was an item in the freshly deceased Germans' possession, and what had initially caused them to give pursuit.

A case ... a kit ... *a way out!*

*It was the signalling kit.*

Only problem: it was out in the open, exposed to the heat of observing sniper scopes of trigger-happy sharpshooters seemingly capable of picking the fleas off a dog's bollocks at 500-feet.

Outside in the shadow of the same structure, and out of sight of the snipers along the ridgeline, Joe Mills and George Peel both sought refuge for a moment in wait.

"Hell's bells," Peel moaned, shaking his head at this new hindrance of shooters lining the ridgeline overlooking most of South Vågsøy. "We haven't got time for this ..."

The complaint from the newer No.3 Commando recruit was noticed by the veteran commando, and it sat badly with Mills.

Mills interrogated with a scowl. "You got somewhere to be, trooper?"

"No, no, I jus—"

"Because we got men in trouble here! Whatever muck you're shovelling is just going to have to wait until we rid of these mountain-range, piles-ridden, sodomites, understood?"

"What's the time?" Peel asked.

Mills frowned upon him. "What the bloody hell for?"

"Just ... humour me. Please."

Mills checked his wristwatch. "It's almost ten, *why?*"

Peel shook his head, distraught.

So far, they were failing their colonel's orders having not located Captain JFG or taken down the enemy relay. It was beginning to weigh heavily on this private's mind.

Peel retorted with an ounce of sincerity within his tone that caused even Joe Mills to sit up and pay attention. "Because if we can't get that enemy relay down and a signal out to our navy to stay, then we're *all* going to have *somewhere else to be* ... we'll be running for the boats."

Thinking quick, with his BC-41 combat knife tied with a shoestring through the brass eyelet, Knocker White threw his makeshift grapple at the kobicha-brown case housing the signalling kit across the room. It was an item of importance vital to the objective of these recently deceased

German roamers; and their whole reason for valiantly breaking their enemy's frontline and attempting to find the FOB along the coast.

Inside the kit was a flare pistol and various ammunition capable of highlighting targets for the fighters still lurking in the sky. These Germans had obviously intended on lighting up the British forward operating base on the shoreline ... but right now, Knocker White had other targets for those flares to paint crosshairs over.

After a third attempt to try and dart the heavy blade of the trench knife into the side of the case like he was spear fishing in the deathly shadows, White pitched the knife on a slightly more acute angle, creating a firmer spearing.

*The blade pierced the case.*

There was a moment of disbelief before White and Drain grew bright smirks upon their maws, and the clever soldier attempted to reel in the catch—carefully, as not to dislodge the blade from the towing weight.

The slack increased and the case began to drag ...

The snag bared the weight ...

Inch by inch, it slid across the wooden floor towards them, edging ever so closely across the spent brass casings as if it were on a conveyor line.

White explained while he concentrated. "... *we get 'em out ... we shoot it in the air above the snipers ... their own kraut fighters indiscriminately strafe them and blow them to hell ... and then we make a fucking break for it!*"

Drain nodded along impatiently.

*That plan sounded fucking good!*

The signalling kit was drawn closer and closer by the second, almost within arm's reach before *whiz-puff!* ...

*A well-placed bullet severed the shoelace.*

"*Come off it!*" White cursed after a split-second of disbelief that a sniper could even make that shot from that far. He coiled back against the doorframe, disheartened.

"You have *got* to be kidding!" Drain stated, bemused. "Nobody has worse luck than us this day!"

"*Oi, what's going on?*" Mills shouted from around the side of the house. They would have just heard the distinct bullet ricochet. "*Everyone alright?*"

"Yeah, we're good!" Drain replied.

White angrily tossed the remainder of his shoelace across the floor out of frustration, casting an eye upon his BC-41 trench knife as it remained imbedded in the small wooden crate in the middle of the kill zone. "Yeah, we're just bloody chipper!"

Peel stressed, audibly talking to himself with a declaration. His tone caught Mills' attention from beside the same corner of cover where he was cradling his pistols in either hand, longing for an opportunity to advance and engage.

"I can't stay put any longer ..."

"What the fuck are you talking about?" Mills grimaced, believing he was witnessing battlefield-mania kicking in with George Peel, watching as he climbed up from his low position behind concealment and assumed a stance that indicated he was about to make a solo run for the village. He yearned to resume his crusade for Captain Giles amidst the interval cover of the urban environment, irrelevant of the sniper scopes guarding their deadlock.

Peel cupped his hands and shouted at the wall of the house.

"*Drain?!*"

"Oi, you daft git! You can't go out there! They'll kill you!" Mills warned.

"*George?!*" Drain's voice replied from within.

"*Drain! It's up to you now if I don't make it ...*"

"*What do you mean?!*" Drain responded inside the building. His voice grew panicked. "*George don't! You will not make it! These blokes are too good 'a shot!*"

Peel shook his head. His determination was unwavering.

"I have to try."

"*George, wait! Listen to me!*"

The apprehensive voice of Knocker White boomed next.

"*Private Peel! Stay put!*" the corporal's voice thundered further, fretful that the noble private may act brash and break cover in a valiant attempt to pursue prior bestowed-upon duties—duties that were arguably paramount and worth the risk as the minutes rolled on. "*You stay put! That's an order!*"

Regardless of the wise concern, the spirited Peel's hand reached up and crossed his chest ...

Symbolically, it was as if he put a hand over his heart to further channel his faith, only instead, he was seeking enlightenment from somewhere much more in-keeping with his beliefs.

*He placed a hand upon his new bible: the silver box.*

"I have to," Peel proclaimed softly to Mills. There was an underlying determination within his tone that alluded to an unwavering earnestness to his cause, that no matter what they did, they would not be able to prevent him from endeavouring this feat for the greater good of Commando—for Operation Archery.

"*George, don't!*"

"No, no, no!" Mills stuttered, unable to physically prevent Peel from sprinting out into the open in time ...

Peel ran.

Gunshots ensued.

*As did death from above.*

*0950-hours ...*

From their positions holed-up inside the building, Knocker White and Drain heard Peel's resolute voice. He was clearly determined to make this dash, to sacrifice for the good of the mission.

*To risk it all for Commando.*

"George, don't!"

Drain was unable to physically stop his friend from exposing himself to the enemy—an enemy that Peel may still be underestimating the accuracy of.

"*No, no, no!*" they heard Mills insist—but it now too late to intervene.

Too late to stop him from running ...

Too late to stop the snipers from shooting ...

*... but not too late to use this situation to their advantage.*

With a level mind amidst the pressure, Knocker White stayed composed during the arising tension. Rather than churn and dread, he planned to act *using* Peel's sacrifice as a diversion to achieve his own goal.

As soon as he felt that Peel had begun to move, it was as if a weight had temporarily lifted, and they were no longer under the thumb of the horrid snipers.

His chewing of gum halted as his jaw tensed for a moment.

Knocker White lunged forward, fully exposing himself to the heat of sweeping sniper scopes as a multitude of long-range shots rang out in the distance at Peel in his death-defying sprint out in the open.

Like a goalie onto the ball, White's hands grappled onto the case.

Outside, Peel ran as though the devil were chasing him.

Chugging hot breaths in the cold air like a steam train, he galloped up the slope and hobbled over the waist-high garden fence that sectioned off the neighbouring property. At that moment, he had become fully exposed to the audience of snipers watching the raid from the grandstands and had undoubtedly drawn a target on his back.

Once Peel was over the fence on his unpredictable route off the pass, he shuffled and danced in a string of goosesteps for an extended moment, skidding on the ice like a Bosko skit before gaining an ounce of traction.

Gunshots boomed deeply from the rifle barrels of the snipers, all looking his way. They traced his antics in their telescopic zooms, shooting at him across the distance.

... *whiz-TUFF!*

... *whiz-whiz!*

... *whiz-TUFF!*

Pockmarks struck the snow mere inches around Peel's skimming boots as he skidded across the frost, flailing his arms around like an ice skater. Apparently, his momentary clumsiness inadvertently caused him to become an unpredictable target for the snipers to peg at range.

... *whiz!*

... *whiz!*

Bullets passed so close by his ears their velocity *cracked* through the air, making him think that he had actually been struck, but he hadn't. On various occasions, the aggressive and destructive ricochets would cause his whole body to judder and flinch in his lope, boxing him around the ears as the snipers played with their food ...

... *whiz-THWACK!*

In his daring attempt to migrate cover, the heroic George Peel took an unfortunate round to the chest. His expression suddenly drained from one of resolve and determination in the face of calamity to the realization of lifelessness.

The commando's jacket layer of padding erupted on his chest from an exacting, forceful bullet strike over his heart.

It was as if someone had driven a baseball bat into a swaying piñata. The trooper was knocked off his feet and sent backwards over a stack of wooden storage barrels which collapsed all around his now motionless body, burying him.

"*Damn it!*" Mills bellowed with a set of wide eyes.

He had just seen the trooper get tagged. To be honest, given the dire circumstances, he was surprised Peel lasted as long as he did running the gauntlet beneath all those sniper scopes. That in itself was an accomplishment.

During the amounting chaos and the diversionary incident outside, Knocker White's plunge landed him over the German case like a trapdoor spider catching prey, grappling it firm and clawing it back to the confines.

Using his embedded knife like a handle, White ripped open the box, exposing a rather odd-looking *Krieghoff* double-barrelled snub-nosed flare pistol.

His eyes glazed across the sight of the attached *Flieger-Leuchtpistole,* which was secured to the inner lid of the case via a belt strap. There were several 26.5mm phosphorous flares rolling about in the carton side, which had become dislodged from their cut-outs due to all the motion involving the case.

White grabbed the pistol, tearing it from the strap and quickly snapped it open, trying not to fumble as he inserted two fresh shells; one in either gape barrel. With a firm *chlick!* he collapsed the breach shut at the same time as he pivoted into the doorway ...

His arm outstretched, facing the rocky ridgeline of which the snipers lingered, hiding like flying rats up high.

White took the extra second to try and gauge the distance and estimate the range, windage, and probable arc of descent for firing a signalling flare in the sky to most accurately and visibly mark a target for an aerial strike—

*... whiz—CRUNCH!*

The wooden wall and doorframe around him erupted with sniper fire, near-missing his exposed position, and causing him to react immediately.

Right when the world exploded to fragments around him, Knocker White pinched his eyelids shut and retreated, peppered with hot, barbed splinters which pricked his flesh.

*... but not before completing his objective ...*

He jolted his arm upwards, pointing above the ridge and fired both flares one after the other.

*PU-PUFF!*


High above in the clear morning chill, a squadron of three yellow-nosed Messerschmitt Me-109 German fighter planes patrolled the airspace above South Vågsøy.

They were a little late for the party in the sky.

In the absence of the RAF fighters and bombers who had since completed their delivery of payloads and aerial support and were currently in the progress of heading back to England, these Luftwaffe short-range fighters had set off from the nearby airfield in Stavanger. They had missed most of the action and would soon be returning to base due to the threat of the navy in the vestfjorden, when the signalling flares caught their attention; as well as their trigger-happy crosshairs.

The method proposed was standard tactical procedure.

The flares were the ground forces' way of signalling an enemy threat on land in need of immediate aerial targeting and assault. In this case, these three Me-109 fighters perceived this to be members of the 181st Infantry Division proposing enemy Commando targets along the ridgeline ... and so, naturally, they engaged.

One by one, the yellow-nosed fighters sliced through the air in a sharp banking formation, cutting the icy wind with a harrowing pitch heard by all those within Vågsøy.

*WWWHHHIRRR ...*

The planes manoeuvred into a flightpath targeting the mark, spearheading a textbook strafing run along the cusp of the mountain ridgeline. From the air as they flew just above the hovering flare trajectory, the pilots could see the many infantry targets on the snow cap, blasting rifles down into the village.

*Their MG-131 machine guns came alive.*
*RAT-TAT-TAT-TAT-TAT-TAT-TAT-TAT-TAT!*

From their various sniper-pinned locations below, the tormented men of No.3 Commando who were accumulatively being pinged by the distant sharpshooters all saw the incoming descent of the yellow-nosed Me-109 fighters. With a whistling pitch, the planes zoomed in low across the rocky hills that surrounded the Norwegian fishing village, laying waste.

However confusing, it was a welcome strafe.

Their deadly, blinking machine guns spat hot tracers across the ridge of positioned targets situated amongst the mountainous snowcapped terrain. The barrage caused the camouflaged squadron of elite snipers to uproot from their rocky positions and displace in a hurry. Confusion as to why they were being targeted by their own planes caused great disruption.

There were probably very few wounds inflicted upon the enemy numbers, but fatalities were not the precise objective at this moment. Utilizing the time to get commandos moving from precarious positions and get hidden between the plethora of huts of the fishing village was.

The fighters rocketed by, and their barrage finally ceased ...

Not wasting a second, Knocker White peeked around the corner of the hole-riddled building entrance. The ridgeline encircling the north-west rise of South Vågsøy was concealed in dissipating fog and floating debris from the strafing run.

Presuming it was now clear to move, he led the charge.

"Let's go! Move!" he declared, finding his dangling weapon and darting out of the building and into the open as another Messerschmitt fighter roared in low overhead with its machine guns blaring at the hillside for a belated, additional attack run.

The salvo was deafening.

Rocks shattered from the thunderous assault, and a rather large boulder of a ledge collapsed in the bombardment, causing a small landslide down the slopes. Chalk-white snow coated the avalanche, pouring over the ground-level trees that skirted the fishing village.

In the forefront of that same groaning landslide, Mills launched himself from cover, running in sequence with Knocker White and Drain, who took the time to pause, deviating in his direction ...

White and Mills entered the shade of glorious fresh cover, only to turn to notice why Drain had lagged. He had strayed, approaching the corpse of the late Peel.

Munching angrily on his gum, Knocker White exclaimed a stare while Mills hunched over, temporarily breathless from the sprint.

"Oi!" Drain shouted, waving them back. "Oi!"

Mills' scrunched frown seemed to elasticize as did Knocker White's as they both came to the realization that George Peel *was still alive.*

Knocker White dropped his weapon in order to sprint nimbly back out into the wide exposed open, dashing in quick to assist Drain in propping the gasping Peel up on his shoulder.

There was a definite entry wound over Peel's chest that had torn his snow smock and singed the woollen khaki material beneath, only ... there seemed to be *no blood.*

The trooper was red in the face and writhing in pain due to the impact, but he was confused when drawing his hand back from the injury to see not a drop of blood on his palm.

"*Come on!*" Drain shouted as he struggled to carry Peel on his own.

Knocker White slid in short, immediately scooping under Peel's other arm and taking half the weight. Together, the commandos managed to hobble double-time back to safety.

Once behind concealment from any shooters and passing under Mills' guard, they collapsed, breathless and sweaty, kneeling around Peel and likely all wondering the same thing: at how the bloke was still alive after being shot through the chest by a sniper.

It was *then* Peel realized why ...

*He removed a small silver box from his breast pocket.*

There was a crumpled lead bullet tip lodged in the silver matchbox-sized trinket, which had prevented the bullet from taking his life. The two metals had collided, inadvertently absorbing the bullet's momentum perfectly without allowing penetration and barely even denting the surface.

Drain beamed a grin, his eyes lighting up once realizing what had occurred, resulting in Peel staying alive when he should have perished.

Overwatching the unveiling of his salvation, Mills shook his head in disbelief whilst he waved his handgun-wielding mittens about. "You lucky bastard!"

Knocker White straightened the man's fatigues as he clambered to his feet, still rather impoverished.

Drain slapped him across the shoulders. "Someone must be looking out for you, mate."

Peel's lids pinched shut as did his hand around the small silver box that had saved his life. He opened them again, looking straight up towards the heavens. "Thank God."

"You're close enough up here," Knocker White commented, referring to their location in Norway and towards the northmost of the hemisphere of the world globe. "He might have just heard you."

While Peel took a strange solace in that sentiment, Drain gave him the folded map—passing back the torch. The two men exchanged a modest gesture, and they continued deeper into the fray.

*HMS Oribi*
*Ulvesund Fyr, Norway*

The Oribi cruised up the connecting passage towards its objective.

The Ulvesund Fyr resembled a calm icicle river that meandered soothingly with a slight curvature, snaking its way on a north-northeasterly passage.

The massive O-class destroyer looked mighty out of place drifting up the thinning passage, passing petite fishing docks along the water's edge and adrift icicles.

In their wake, the effervesced continuance of bass like a ravaging thunderstorm grumbled. Only, the deep booming over the snowcapped yonder was not at all *thunder* ... they were *explosions*. And the bright flashing blinks were not *lightning* ... they were *fireballs*.

It was the soundtrack to the raging raid in and above South Vågsøy.

Disturbing the strange tranquillity of the Oribi moving along the pass, two potentially hostile vessels emerged ahead of its passage, coming south and likely attempting to flee the raid.

Theirs was an unavoidable collision course.

The two smaller ships sported the insignia of their allegiance, and were therefore deemed unwelcoming. They were to be shut down immediately by the behemoth Oribi.

The cannons boomed to life aboard the charging destroyers deck, hurling arcing pitches of HE salvo at her adversaries, resulting in direct hits.

The first vessel, a freighter later identified as the *Anita L.J. Russ,* was struck against her port side. The single hit was a K.O., nearly drowning the poor girl like a head being held underwater. She came to an instant halt, pushing waves as an impenetrable smoke plume gushed from the front end, sinking almost immediately.

The second ship was a smaller tug who attempted evasive manoeuvres after noticing the incoming Allied destroyer, steering starboard in a panic and throttling to run aground in a last-ditch effort to avoid utter destruction.

Identified afterwards as *the Rechtenfleth,* the tugboat took a direct hit on her port side, blowing a cavity straight through the entire ship and out the other side.

Like a through-and-through gunshot wound, the shell punched a hole through the vessel, causing the ship to unbalance and overturn within seconds. She gave out a metallic shriek as she capsized, taking on a thousand litres of water a second.

Men aboard both vessels could be seen leaping overboard, splashing down into the icy cold waters of the passage.

In the action, the HMS Oribi barely broke stride on her progression down the Ulvesund Fyr, nudging the enemy ships out of the way in her triumphant wake. A force not to be fucked with.

*South Vågsøy Village*
*Vågsøy, Norway*

*0955-hours ...*

"*... Cameramen keep in close touch with the troops as they come nearer to the Germans. They follow the commandos as they make their way along the snow-covered approach to the burning town. The incendiaries have prepared the way. With the troops are the British news reel and official cameramen, risking everything to bring you a faithful record of the raid—oh, fuck! Blast! Buggery!*"

The monotonal broadcaster Mericle was snipped short, becoming interrupted by hot rebounds from the rocks at his feet, causing him to hop about and withdraw without much grace. His cameraman captured it on film, but it would undoubtedly be edited from the final cut.

Mericle sought cover by two slumped commandos. They eyed him precariously as they witnessed *the Miracle Man* hero press reporter and journalist duck for cover like a craven deserter, but then have the bollocks to demand his cameraman not film that nonsense for the public eye.

This Troop detachment had pushed left far along the flank of the town, a stone's throw away from where Måløy Island reached the mainland. Any further west and South Vågsøy was met by rocky slopes before the snowy knolls that encompassed the land.

The commandos were set with the task of liberating the local populous from the Vågsøy parish church (the *Sør-Vågsøy kyrkje*) and eliminating the enemy location within it and the narrow livestock stables located across the yard. They had not expected German resistance from *within* the location itself, let alone situated *with* covering Vågsøy civilians.

Their doing so defied the rules of engagement to which they were supposed to adhere, but then again, this was Nazi Germany ...

Around the bullet-swept corner of nearby refuge, Captain John Frederick Giles, an already established *real-life* war hero, ducked in fast from hostile exposure in the intensity of war.

After dodging strings of enemy bullets as he switched position from the neighbouring house to a closer spot aligning with the churchyard confrontation, JFG's boxing-scarred brow peered around that same corner and fired an extended burst from his submachine gun in retaliation. He then, again, ran to an advance, outrunning a hailstorm of pot-shot rifle fire at his wake.

Chasing his every step, bullets raked the wooden walls of a hut as he came in hot, barely breaching the impediment of shelter before it became assaulted by deafening Gerry gunfire.

Situated behind nearby cover, the two commandos and Mericle had just watched as JFG charged in like a man on fire. His years of rugby football served him well for speed, stamina, and agility. Only on this field, he wasn't goosestepping an opposing prop for possession of a ball ... he was sidestepping death.

He slid in on his rump and thigh through the sleet and icy brush as slug impacts of stitching gunfire traced his movement, slamming into the snow and mud until he disappeared from their sights behind shelter.

Once safe, JFG casually upped and sought refuge beside two of his concealed commandos and began to calmly reload his weapon—the sweltering thing was chugging like a steam train chimney in this cold air.

"Boys," he greeted.

Mericle and his press camera operator were in awe of JFG.

His sheer size and courage blew their minds. Like a great many of these commandos, Giles was cut from a completely different cloth to either one of them.

The No.3 Commando captain looked as tough as he was due to his physical size after years of rugby, as well as competing and winning in the heavyweight boxing championships, the trials of which were evident upon his face; the once ruggedly handsome fellow bore a bald spot within both eyebrows due to scarring.

"What's the situation, lads?" he questioned in his raspy voice, swapping out an almost emptied drum-magazine from his Thompson and loading a fresh fifty rounds.

"Enemy stronghold up ahead, sir!" one of the men reported, referring to the church.

The other added, "Yeah, with a twist."

"*A twist?*" Giles frowned, yearning to cut the nonsense. "Why aren't we returning fire?"

"It's *full* of Weegies, sir! The entire population of this ruddy town is held up in there behind the window gunners!"

JFG inched over to the opposite edge of cover, gaining sight of the small parish church building that stood beyond a short clearing of flat land. Over a partially damaged wooden picket fence that ran around the property, the snowy flat grounds extended beyond a fifty-yard snow-clad cemetery that appeared to wrap south around the small churchyard vicinity. There was a neighbouring field to the church divided by another fence which had the backend of barn stables overlooking the stronghold—it was also occupied by the enemy, and thus they had secured an overarching angle of cover.

There were at least two or three gunners inside the lower level of the white, slanted-roof tubular-shaped church, using the sturdy windowsills for cover. They had punched out the colourful stained glass to shove the barrels of their guns through, creating arrow-slit eyelets for themselves on which to target the enemy.

At least three or four German soldiers were located within the stables across the yard. They had a firing line on Commando's southerly advance, providing a fierce dilemma from two differing enemy firebases forming an obtuse angle vector. Attacking either enemy stronghold from here would result in enfilade fire from the alternate position.

"Nobody's shooting back because there are dozens of Norwegian civilians behind the German gunners, sir," the other commando reiterated after JFG peeled back behind cover. He had received a warm reception from the direction of the church. One of the German infantrymen spotted him lurking and fired a single shot that smashed against the wooden angle with moderate accuracy.

"Dirty pricks! How certain are we that they're not just quislings hiding in there with the Gerrys?" JFG asked objectively.

Near Mericle and his cameraman cowered a handful of unarmed Norwegian civilians dressed in coats and hats. They were local residents of South Vågsøy, probably on their way to seek refuge within the church like the majority of the crowd when the raid had commenced. Their group was headed to salvation but it had got separated and they seemed to vouch for their peoples' innocence within the enemy stronghold with much fret and concern. Their loved ones were in harm's way.

Apparently, a few Germans had figured out that the church would be a logical place to stage a defence; first, as it was always the most solidly constructed building in every town and second, that as it would likely be spared bombs or shelling by the coastal aggressors, they could double-down on the pig-headedness by incorporating the use of live civilians as human shields and glorified hostages.

A Norwegian man was pleading. *Begging.*

Giles couldn't understand him, but one of the commandos present spoke some Norwegian, and did his best to accurately interpret the language.

"He says don't shoot at the church. He says his family are inside."

Giles pondered. He could deal with the strain of combat, for he had been conditioned to do so on autopilot. He could deal with the weight on his conscience regarding taking the lives of enemy soldiers during battle ... but a siege with civilians involved? The pressure quickly mounted. He cranked his neck with displeasure. "Jesus Christ!"

"He says that everybody he knows are all inside that church."

JFG wrestled with the situation for an extended moment, eyeing the ground. This was going to differ from his usual run-and-gun strategy that had been working so well for his Troop this morning. He was also aware that everything transpiring at this point in time during the raid was being documented and captured on film by the Miracle Man.

"Tell him, we're sorry, but we've got a job to do. Tell him we need to take that stronghold to complete capturing this quadrant, understand?"

"Yes, sir—"

"*Captain!*"

"*Captain Giles!*"

Two familiar British voices called as they approached from the rear of this position behind the patchy cover of fishing village buildings. JFG ceased communicating with his men in order to turn and meet the chatterboxes currently calling his name across the battlefield.

He recognized Knocker White and Mills instantly and was surprised to see them paired up with Drain, his radioman. One of the newer recruits, George Peel, was there with them, and the lot of them seemed as though they had been through the ringer to reach him. They were all men from within his Three Troop but had been vacant all morning since the partly bungled G2 landings on the shores.

The motley group arrived, reaching the last block of cover before having to make a final wide dash to reach JFG behind a shed.

Before they moved, Peel and Drain exchanged private words.

The two of them were in possession of the map that Colonel Durnford-Slater had issued them with before they left his signal post earlier and were referencing something on it and pointing out something ahead in the distance.

JFG observed, jeering in his gravelly voice. "Gentlemen! Nice of you to join the raid!"

Knocker White and Mills gaged hostility around the corner before sprinting over. They received fire from the buildings next to the churchyard, as well as the church building itself, which caught them by surprise. They avoided it thusly, ducking in low and close to their CO in this makeshift rendezvous and catching a breath.

Winston Churchill was right: *'nothing in life is so exhilarating as to be shot at without result'*. There truly was nothing quite as breathtaking as being shot at by the enemy to no prevail, however it left you just that: bloody breathless.

White slid in last with bated gasps, narrowly avoiding a pot shot of enemy fire from the church. The lot of them piled up behind the barn house in the closest neighbouring backyard of a Norwegian residence of the Vågsøy churchyard.

"Go on, then? Where the God's name have you lot been?" JFG's mention bore a slight passive-aggressiveness, throwing a finger at Drain across the way. "And *you*, radioman, are meant to be glued to my hip!" he slapped his hind with a firm, muscular slap.

"I know, sir! Sorry, sir!" the radioman replied with a shout, still winded from all the motley group's endeavours in reaching this place. He was going to sleep well tonight.

"I've needed your radio this whole time!" JFG added as he received the two extra bodies for his cause. "I haven't been able to give sit-reps or obtain new orders all morning!"

Glancing across at them, Giles absorbed their worse-for-wear wrangled postures. It was obvious the lot of them had not been lounging around off-site somewhere, and that they had seen battle. He acknowledged that, but naturally gave them an earful just the same.

"*Yes, sir! Sorry, sir!*"

"You all look like you've been through the thick of it?"

"We have, Captain!" Peel informed, stepping out from their cover. Under the watchful gaze of White, Mills, and JFG, he darted across the open to join them. He did so to better address the Three Troop commander. "Sir, in Drain's defence, you wouldn't have been sending or receiving *anything* over the radio this morning."

JFG eyed him precariously. There was something in this trooper's delivery that demanded his attention. "What do you mean, Private? Why not?"

"The shortwave bandwidth is down."

He suddenly eyed his watch, apprehensive of the time sensitivity concerning a certain matter of their raid, and everybody around him sensed his apprehension.

Peel instructed: "I've got orders from Colonel Durnford-Slater. There is a second enemy relay in this quadrant. He marked it on *this* map," JFG accepted the scrunched up, dirtied, and torn map piece from the trooper, and he examined it thoroughly whilst he spoke. "He told me to find *you*, sir, and that you would get it done. There is something blocking all our outbound signals on the island and we need to blow it before—"

"Ten-hundred-hours?" JFG took the words out of his mouth.

"Eh, yes, sir ..."

Accepting the task, JFG bobbed his head.

He was a commanding officer and obviously knew of the navy deadline at 1000-hours, and he knew that the hour was fast approaching. What he did not know until now was how dire the situation was regarding communications.

"So ... *nobody* has been in contact with the Kenya?"

"No, sir."

JFG shook his head as he grasped the gravity of the situation and felt the weight come down upon his shoulders. Looking south-west and towards the misty Vågsfjorden, he could make out the ships of the flotilla across the distance. Those aboard could undoubtedly spy the actions of Commando across the great planes, but without an official situation report, Haydon had to make a decision on whether or not to cut losses or stay the course.

This was a predicament, indeed.

For all the navy knew, G2 were all dead or dying and that the ground assault was a bust.

"This enemy relay you speak of ... I know where it is," JFG imparted to Peel, barely even needing the map after recognizing precisely where the location was rumoured. Bunching the narrow-man's uniform in his fist, he walked Peel over to the opposite edge of the cover, allowing for him to glimpse yonder and observe the churchyard. "Only problem is, it's *there* ..."

Peel inched the corner with a stern gawk upon his narrow face, spying the church building. He also saw that clambering the steeple was a cluster of black wires like climbing vines. There had to be a compact antenna on the roof somewhere, responsible for the outage ...

*That was the broadcaster jamming their radios!*

Peel reeled behind cover with a thousand thoughts roaming through his mind. "It's a church?!"

"*It is a church!*" JFG concurred with a nod. He could tell that Trooper Peel now felt the gravity of the situation. "A church *full* of Norwegian civilians. Still want to *blow it*, trooper?"

Peel could barely comprehend the situation.

*What could they do?*

*And in a hurry?*

*Rock – hard place.*

"Sir," the same Norwegian-interpreting commando implored the attention of Captain JFG, who gave the trooper his complete consideration, as did the others surrounding him. They eyed him and the scared but brave Norwegian local who was desperate to assist the British to liberate his captive townsfolk being held hostage on holy ground. "I have more ..."

JFG acknowledged the civilian with respect for his ill-fated status quo.

"... he says that the Germans who occupy this town, the permanent ones, wouldn't do this to the people. That they are mostly kind to them, that they left the church for the population to hide within. He stresses that this barbarousness is not their doing."

"Barbarousness is not uncharacteristic of a Nazi."

The soldier shrugged, siding only with the Norwegian man's sincerity. "Apparently it is for these Nazis ..."

JFG brushed past the foreign ideology this Norwegian seemed to have regarding their oppressive occupants and questioned with a frown of his scarred eyebrows. "They forcefully occupied their hands. Tell your friend, here, to *wake up*. Send him to the beach for exfil, trooper, please and fucking thank you."

The commando had no choice but to comply; ushering the Norwegian civilian off, speaking to him in his tongue to smooth things over.

"So, then, who the fuck's in the church shooting at us?"

"Quislings?" Mills interjected.

A commando nearby scoffed. "Quislings with better aim than most bloody Wehrmacht soldiers?"

JFG put his foot down. "Regardless! There are definitely some cunts in there with guns and they know how to use 'em ..."

The interpreter turned his head with a raised eyebrow. He was unsure of his own translation, but also knew that the connotation was genuine and correct. "For the record, sir, I think he means *different* Germans ..."

Confused and left scratching their heads for a moment, JFG, Mills, White, Peel, Drain, and the other two commandos paused for a moment of reflection.

"Trooper," JFG ordered dutifully, with a postponed level of respect for the civilian that seemed absent in the moment, "I don't care who he means. At this stage, he should be more worried about being shot by those supposed *different Germans.*"

"Who the devil is in that church, then ...?" Peel questioned.

*Nobody knew.*

"No idea," JFG remarked, cracking his neck in order to shift gauge and begin to formulate a plan of attack. "But what I do know, is one thing ... we're out of time."

He showed them his wristwatch.

*It was now 10:00 a.m.*

*Måløy Island*
*Vågsøy, Norway*

Assembled in the flat muddy clearing beside the toppled wireless tower on Måløy Island, the commandos of Churchill's Group 3 regrouped, awaiting their departure following the accomplishment of their objectives.

The commandos had droved almost thirty prisoners, guarding them at gunpoint, with the remainder of G3 held in low-key positions across the immediate area. Lieutenant Peace's Five Troop were located amongst the rubble and sheets of bent metal from the collapsed antenna structure, and Captain Young's Six Troop, along with Major Churchill and the tagalong American journalist, were tight against nearby vacant and partially destroyed constructs.

Men's eyes were in the sky, still watching the dissipating aerial battles between the RAF Beaufighters and perturbed Luftwaffe Messerschmitt Me-109s. The tiny yellow nosecones of the German fighters caused them to resemble the hornets of the kicked nest that was Vågsøy Island. The Blenheim and Hampden bombers had already headed home by now, while the smaller fighters stayed and fought a little longer with the German planes. This both covered the retreat of the larger crafts as well as covered the ground troops and ships from aerial attacks.

The hazy sounds of soaring aircraft across the glaring morning sky was mesmerizing to observe. The motion shimmered in the refracting light. The occasional echoic *boom* of a hit from a dogfight triumph would resonate, and from the earth, the men would watch in content as the fireball of wreckage came plummeting down; either crash into the snowy hills yonder or thrash against the icy surface of the Vågsfjorden beyond.

"You O.K.?" Hardy asked Mad Jack, taking a break from scribbling notes in his pad.

Churchill was leaning against a concrete wall beside the on-the-record journalist, observing the mainland of South Vågsøy across the water, where constant reverberations suggested that it was all happening. Unable to answer, he frustratingly listened to the call of war as it writ large by way of gunshots and explosions. The battle raged on, contained within the urban environment of the fishing village, and he was missing it.

Churchill tore his view from it. "Why wouldn't I be?"

"You just seem, I dunno, blue."

"*Blue?*"

"Yeah, about what happened before, y'know ... with that kraut hiding in the building next to that sea mine shed thing that you, y'know ... *boom.*"

Churchill watched as Hardy implied the retelling of the events using his hands in an outward motion and the grumble sound effect from his cheeks. He was referring to the lone German foe they had encountered within the final structure they had secured; the barracks, and how he had refused surrender to the point where Churchill had ordered his demise via destruction of the entire building. The whole thing *still* did not make sense to him, and Jack Churchill hated not having closure.

"Why would I care about killing some dopey bellend?" Churchill remarked defensively. "You've seen me dispatch Huns before."

"Yeah, yeah, I know," Hardy pulled up a piece of bare wall closer beside his British pal. "Y'know ... it's just like, it didn't go how you expected. You're hung up on it. Brooding beneath the surface."

Churchill eyed Hardy as he tried to articulate what he meant.

At the same time that Hardy spoke, Jack realized that he was not entirely wrong. There was some merit to his perception, that Jack was mildly fixated on an aspect of what had transpired during the drama.

"Just an observation. Pay it no mind," Hardy silenced feeling the need to change the topic and he wiped the fatigue from his face with his palm.

Moving on, Churchill returned to his distant gaze of restlessness, watching the war unfold before his eyes on the South Vågsøy main island, now also thinking about those recent events all over again. Truth was, what had happened had been a rather odd occurrence, that was for sure, leaving a few unanswered questions—such as *who* exactly it was that had defied the orders of their superior kommandant, effectively killing themselves to clash against an army of Commando. It was not *black and white* as far as warfare occurred and, in turn, triggered the instinct of such men as Jack Churchill into deep contemplation regarding the particulars of these befallen circumstances.

Something was amiss, and it set a dangerous precedent on expectations ...

"So, where the hell's this transport, huh?" Hardy questioned.

They were left waiting on Måløy for the navy to send a couple of ships for the prisoners to board and be taken to the Kenya. Once gone and G3 was no longer tasked with guarding them, their objective would either be to return to the ships for extraction or scoot across to the mainland to assist G2 with the ground assault ... strange thing was, they were yet to receive an update from command authorizing them to do so. In fact, they had overheard *zero* communications from anyone inland.

Churchill verified the time.

It ticked over to 10 a.m. on the dot as he checked his watch, and the sight of the time caused his wonder to drift absent words. Military operations rarely went according to plan, this much was scripture and well versed to any soldier in the field ... but something was unsettling about the events thus far for Archery.

Right then, filling the volume with a faint vehicular *hum* in the distance, the men on Måløy spotted from their vantage point south of the island, overlooking the fjord and the hovering warships, that several streams in the water seemed to be travelling their way.

They were the incoming transport ships.

*Finally.*

Once the POWs were hand-balled to the navy, it freed them from G3. They would be available to charge the shores after G2 and assist in decking the halls of Vågsøy Island.

The radioman, No.3 funnyman R.L. Wills, received a partially garbled transmission through his attached walkie-talkie unit from the navy. At his position near Churchill, he immediately responded and approached his CO to relay.

"Sir?"

"Leftenant."

"We just received word from the Kenya ..."

Churchill tried hard not to allow the anticipation of receiving word to possibly assist in the Vågsøy action excite him, and nonchalantly allowed for the radioman to speak. "... and?"

"Still no word from *any* of the Troops of Group 2."

*Jack's shoulders sunk.*

"Observations from the ships concluded that the ground assault is achieving success with the destruction of the factories to the north, but they're yet to give a single sit-rep ..."

Churchill probed, eager. "Do they want us to help?"

Wills sighed, feeling his major's major disappointment. "Our orders are to stay put on Måløy, sir, and await further instructions."

Churchill rubbed his eyes, masking his exasperation.

"Sounds like Brigadier Haydon wants to hear from the colonel before intervening."

"When?! It's past the deadline already!" Churchill muttered to himself, his frustrations brimming the surface. The hold on his composure seemed to slip slightly as he resembled a spoiled brat not getting his way with the war.

Wills commented. "Sorry, sir."

"Thank you, Lieutenant," Churchill dismissed, calming down.

Hardy asked after a moment. "What deadline?"

Churchill informed with a big gasp of air. "Ten-hundred-hours ..."

"What happens at 10 a.m.?"

"It's a failsafe. John—*Colonel Durnford-Slater*—is meant to have radioed in with a sit-rep prior to that time. Otherwise, the navy will assume that Operation Archery had failed, and subsequently contemplate their disembarkment of the Vågsfjorden."

Hardy grimaced. "That's preposterous!"

Churchill bent his neck. "Mountbatten's orders. The *no unnecessary risks* clause to this operation included winning at all costs. That includes knowing when to cut losses. They're not about to risk the vessels of the 17th Destroyer Flotilla for a bunch of fish oil facilities."

"Well, it's only just ten now," Hardy stated optimistically. "And it's *clearly* not a failure, I mean, look ..."

"Major, there was one more thing," Wills informed, remembering last minute and Churchill listened well. "Captain Clement's men at Holvik confronted some additional resistance at their objective. Men from an enemy unit *external* of what we were said to expect."

The news piqued Churchill's interest.

Both his and Hardy's ears pricked like attentive hounds as more details of the story unfolded—information relevant to what they had experienced on Måløy only moments ago.

"What do you mean?" Jack asked.

"Additional men. Formidable men," Wills explained, paraphrasing his learnings of Clement's encounter with just as much mysterious shrouding on the story as Haydon's men on the radio had encompassed in their exposition. "They were wankers from some SS unit, apparently."

"*SS?*"

"Aye, supposedly they gave Group One a dash for their dosh. They copped a couple of casualties 'cos of 'em, too."

"Why would the SS be all the way out here in situ of this rock?" thinking out loud, Hardy probed in the background as Churchill slowly began to step away, lost in his thoughts and contemplations of *just that.*

Leaving his American friend gasbagging conjecture with Wills, the audio dimmed for Churchill. Locked-in, he headed towards the congregation of POWs. He had just heard all that he needed to hear. This was confirmation of another German force present in Vågsøy, additional to the Wehrmacht 181st Infantry Division under the command of Lieutenant-General Woytasch, of whom their intelligence informed them they would be opposing them on the raid.

*Mad Jack had already put two and two together.*

Acting on that perception, Churchill marched with purpose towards the prisoners, gaining their concerned attention as he neared them with haste. He parted the disarmed group, seeking audience with but one member: the kommandant he had met earlier. He was the highest-ranking German officer encountered on Måløy Island.

He slammed on the brakes of his assail right before the man.

"Who are they?" Churchill demanded, unearthing the smug kommandant like a diamond in the POW rough. He became immediately flanked by armed commandos with weapons primed and at the hip. This line of questioning was certainly unorthodox, however they supported their major, keeping an eye on the others whilst he entered the den of prisoners.

The coy gleam of the absent-worded kommandant revealed nothing other than more of the same contained culpability to withholding the answer to the question.

His reticence was met with a half-cocked threat.

The crowd let out a hiss of alarm at the intimidating sight of Jack Churchill's three-foot claybeg as it became drawn from his scabbard with a metallic *shwinggg.*

It was not due to Churchill abandoning professionalism or gentlemanly qualities ... it was simply that he preferred the showman antics of which to stir the pot.

In an absence of trepidation from the kommandant, the surrounding POWs gasped in conjoined unease as the blade tip rested by his gullet, affectively levelled at his German maw.

With a firm confidence, Jack Churchill was behind its knuckleduster hilt, twisting the sword on an angle to better gaze into the ogle of the enemy combatant. His piercing blue eyes punctured through to the man's soul.

Even the British Commandos about the vicinity exchanged a few concerned glances. They were uncomfortable with the situation, but who were they to question their crazy commanding officer?

*He was called* <u>*Mad Jack*</u> *for a reason?*

"The enemy force hiding in South Vågsøy!" Churchill elaborated with a stone-cold demeanour, beginning a more thorough and direct form of interrogation. "We know they're off the reservation. We know they're SS. How many of them are there? What are their numbers?"

At last, the German kommandant inhaled to open his mouth.

He was still seemingly without distress of the situation and of a sword being waved in his face behind the gaze of a wrathful British officer.

He said simply. "... many."

Churchill and a few of the other commandos who had converged on the state of affairs, including Young, Wills, Peace, Bruce Giles, and Felix Hardy, each swapped unsteady sideways glances. That answer was just as ambiguous as it was ominous.

The kommandant added with a hint of indulgence in his tone.

"Viel glück, Major."

In the silent seconds following the confirmation of their intelligence, as well as discerning the kommandant's forewarning, a noticeable discomposure began to set in among the commandos. They grew agitated.

The sun may have risen, but a darkness swelled upon the horizon ...

They could all feel it coming like a thunderstorm.

Churchill eventually lowered his sword.

The steel blade dropped from proximity of the kommandant's face, and yet he still showed no sense of anxiety or even relief now that the pressure was off. This old Hun was eternally stoic and remained as such.

He had given them everything and nothing.

Churchill's downward glower started to rise, but it lingered ...

He was snagged on a minor detail.

His instinct insisted upon further investigation.

"*Major*," Peter Young muttered from over Churchill's shoulder, breaking the silence. The captain stepped in beside Churchill, offering him a subtle gesture of reconsideration before their Mad Major lived up to his title, attempting to gain more information from this established prisoner of war.

When Young subtly laid a hand on Churchill's sleeve for the sake of driving him clear of the kommandant, Jack pulled away with a squint and a puckered brow ...

It wasn't an objection born of disrespect.

He was on to something here.

There was an answer teetering on the edge ...

*... and Jack was about to give it a little shove.*

Hitched on something, Churchill suddenly tilted his view and banked his stance to the right, inching in towards other members of the crowd. POWs shuffled in their submissive stances, allowing for the sword-wielding loose cannon commando to pass until Churchill reached the two prostitutes. They now wore more clothing and were rapidly sobering, staring back at the British commanding officer with wide eyes of trepidation.

If Churchill had put two and two together before, then this was four and four, drawing him closer to the truth. The truth was that the two men they encountered by the sea mine building on the rear of Måløy Island had in fact not only been German soldiers, but German soldiers *posing* as quislings—the most outlandish of his brief conclusions.

His focus honed at something on one of the women's bodies, and he looked her in the face. He immediately noticed her fear at the sight of his sword, at his prior demeanour, and endeavoured an alternate approach of discord. "Ma'am, please excuse my forthcoming. You two were *with* the German's last night, were you not?"

They may not have spoken much English, but they certainly understood that question, as well as the lingering potential of brutality lurking beyond the interrogator lest they fail to respond. Now that their heads were clearing, they knew just how much trouble they were in. Shaking with regret and fear, the panda-eyed women obeyed and bobbed their heads.

"Jack?" Young tried again, more stern.

Churchill ignored him.

He removed his grip from the ringlets on his claybeg hilt and raised his palm non-threateningly towards the girls, still causing them to baulk in trepidation.

Everybody—the prisoners, the women, the British Commandos— watched as Churchill gradually trod closer ... eventually touching the right-side arm of one of the comfort women, causing her to turn slightly and reveal that the military jacket that she had borrowed from off one of the two German soldiers and quisling imposters they had serviced last night, must have belonged to one of the two men not from the 181st.

*The insignia was different.*

Churchill popped her collar up, revealing the SS symbol.

On the arm was a white band with a black logo ...

Bruce Giles, the younger brother of the legendary JFG, was astonished. Alike everybody else, he did not recognize the badge. "What is that? A star or something?" he queried in a strident whisper, completely unknowing of that unit's particular sub-emblem. "What the hell unit is that?"

Others moved through the crowd, rising on their tippy toes in order to see the unveiling of their new enemy's insignia: it was a black flower bud. Young Young was one of them. They all knew the Schutzstaffel sig runes, but the star-like icon was foreign to them.

"It's a black star."

"Nah, that's a flower, innit?" Wills remarked with a confused frown, glancing over Young's shoulder, who was just as enthralled to see the article that Churchill had just unveiled to them all.

*Surreptitiously, he recognized the symbol with a great concern ...*

Then, with an appreciative nod, Churchill allowed for the woman to return to her comfortable stance as he backed away from her—from them all, the POWs—now leading his intrigued gathering of men on a march away. All the while, Churchill spoke not a word, only aiming to seek out Wills.

"*Sir?*" Giles questioned after they all seemed to notice that Churchill recognized the unit insignia. "*What is it, Major?*"

"*Major?*"

"*What does this all mean?*" the men started to ask amongst themselves, all equally confused and with a growing anxiousness.

"Get me Brigadier Haydon on the wire at once," ignoring all their questionings regarding the unveiling of the enemy unit's insignia, Churchill ordered explicitly to his radioman, rolling up close on Wills who like the others wore concern upon his brow.

"Do you recognize the flower thing, sir?" Giles asked after a moment, and subsequent to the hushing of all the men; awaiting a response from their CO now that a few seconds had passed, and Mad Jack had found the words.

Churchill wobbled his head, uncertain. Or perhaps just in disbelief.

"That's not just any *flower*, gents," he stated as Wills handed him the walkie-talkie unit attached to his wireless radio backpack. "That's an *edelweiss.*"

A few of the commandos wordlessly exchanged a glance.

It appeared they had never heard of it.

"It means that they're *Gebirgsjäger,*" Churchill added before cupping the microphone to the hand-piece, tilting his view aslant from the others as they whispered and talked among themselves in conjecture. "*This is Major Churchill; I need to speak to Brigadier Haydon urgently ...*"

Some of the commando men had heard of the term *Gebirgsjäger* before, but the men were confused as to the exact translation of the unit into English.

From the group of mumbling, inquisitorial rubberneckers, Hank Peace suddenly piped up, quick on the translation. His fury eyebrows were cocked in curious wonder. "*Jäger* ... I'm fairly sure that means *hunter.*"

"Aye, but the *Gebirgstruppe* are *mountain troopers* or something? Right?" another man furthered, somewhat educated on foreign enemy unit designations.

"Sounds like these Gerrys are *special forces* or something ..." Giles added as his shoulders sunk. "There could be a whole fuckin' secret army over there, lying in wait. We're shagged."

"What do you mean *special forces?*" Young frowned, probing above the crowd as Giles then said something to Wills, and Wills spoke to Peace, then Peace muttered to someone else and someone else ...

The volume rose like a crescendo of Chinese whispers and rumour.

The conjecture spiralled out of control—

"*Alpine Huntsmen!*" an American accent interrupted the noisy debate with the answer to their translation. Their gaudy debating stopped at once and they each stared at the journalist as he parted the sea of Commando like Moses.

The seize of attention included Churchill, who was painstakingly waiting for Haydon on the wireless. He already had all of the answers. Hardy had been holding them back to not start any form of panic, though, the cat was out of the bag now.

Hardy now had the stage. Held everybody's upmost attention.

"It means *Alpine Huntsmen.* The edelweiss is their callsign."

In the quiet that followed, they all heard the static pitch from the radio as Haydon finally responded to Churchill.

The flock of mildly discomposed Commandos turned their heads, listening to their major while he filled Haydon in on the invaluable news of which they had just acquired.

"Sir, this is Major Churchill. I believe it to be within the best interest of the operation that you helm an executive decision, and send in the entire floating reserve, as well as Group 3 in Måløy, into South Vågsøy *immediately,* over ... Do you copy? Over!"

The faces of the commandos waited silently, watching ...

"Hullo, sir, do you copy me? Over!"

"*Major Churchill ... I heard you loud and clear, but you already know I am unable to even consider issuing that order without a verbal request from Colonel Durnford-Slater ...*"

Eyes closed, Churchill tipped his head in frustration.

He realized that the navy could not assume command of the army reserve without the commanding officer's authority, that being the absent colonel. Durnford-Slater, along with Mountbatten and Whitehall, had put this combined operation detail into progress. It was a sure plan, and they had to stick to it.

"*You are to stay put, Major. Over.*"

Churchill tried hard not unleash the panic of alarm that currently resided within the tenor of his voice, for he had no choice but to comply.

He obeyed through gritted teeth when prompted a second time for his compliance. "Yes, sir. Over."

The voice returned. "*Major Churchill?*"

"Acknowledged, sir. Churchill out."

After a full three seconds ... he handed Wills the walkie back before pacing away and observing the distant action currently unfolding on the mainland of South Vågsøy. There was still an ongoing battle within the village limits, resonating stridently.

A patiently waiting commando trooper informed from the rear:

"Major, the transports are here."

Churchill broke from his chain of contemplation. "Leftenant Peace, load them up. Ferry them out of my sight."

"On it, sir," Peace responded. His men of Five Troop were on prisoner detail and would now escort the group of POWs to the shore where a transport boat would load them up and ferry them to the Kenya.

"... *would annexation prevail* ...?" Felix Hardy muttered audibly as he scribbled within his notepad, basically scribing Jack Churchill's internal meditation.

In the quiet seconds that followed, Churchill happened to gawk upon him, and the journalist's wording lingered ...

"If we didn't know what we know now, about the Huntsmen ..." Jack actively remarked, answering the rhetorical question that the writer had scribbled on his notepaper, "... then I would have said *yes* to that."

"And what about now that you know?" Hardy then asked.

Churchill paused a moment before facing him, quoting, " *'a thousand battles, a thousand victories'* ..."

The surprisingly optimistic response called for Hardy to frown with mystification, his mouth agape and his head atilt.

Finally, Mad Jack elaborated, quoting a wise Chinaman's wisdom and using it to forge insight upon their situation. A declaration, he nodded towards Vågsøy Island.

His cleft chin uttered:

"We already *know thy self.* And now, we *know thy enemy* ..."

When the tenor of Sun Tzu's words struck a chord, Hardy paused from scratching in his notes, ceasing to record the words coming from Churchill's mouth. "Is that that *long-dead Chinese dickhead,* again?"

Churchill torqued his neck. "This war has only just begun ..."

# 9
## *Thy Enemy*

*The Ulvesund Hotel*
*South Vågsøy, Norway*

*8:48 a.m. ...*

The Greeks called it ataraxia: a state of serene calmness.

A little over an hour ago, the placidity of the tranquil Vågsøy Island could have been described as absolute contentment as it slumbered in unending repose.

For all those stationed, living, and holidaying at the South Vågsøy village, today followed a few big days of merry celebrating of the season of Christmas. Much feasting, drinking, and partying amongst the sociably coerced Norwegian locals of the small town, of whom had been so amiable of their residing Wehrmacht's recent visitors from an especial Schutzstaffel division unit known as the Gebirgsjäger.

Their unit tag: an edelweiss.

The fifty members of the elite Alpine Huntsmen of the Gebirgsjäger unit had been dispatched on leave to this quiet sector of occupied Norway for some well-earned *R&R* over the holiday period. After the festive season, they would be returned to the bestial Eastern Front for further conflicts leading into 1942.

During their stay, they were lodged in the tallest and possibly most fortified building in the village, the four-storey Ulvesund Hotel, located at the rear of the coastal community. During the daylight, they had the lay of the entire winter wonderland from this vantage point.

A sudden thunder shook the coastal village this morning.

The groan of the bass shook the glass in window frames.

Disturbed ceramic ornaments. Rattled metal cutlery in drawers.

Anyone awoken by the disembarking disturbance paused for a moment to ponder seconds before the subsequent sudden strike of lightning illuminated the dawn atmosphere of the Vågsfjorden.

Only that thunder wasn't thunder.

Nor was the lightning, lightning.

Glistening barbs of salvo screamed across the dark skies of South Vågsøy and its neighbouring locations. They were under attack from the sea. Anyone who was asleep or gently shaken by the tumultuous *booms* of the naval cannons were suddenly rattled wide awake by the seismic earthquakes that followed.

The enveloping surrounding mountainside seemed to contain the echoes of the barrage, magnifying the intensity and the shake of the shockwaves, even causing them to reverberate.

Within the top floors of the Ulvesund Hotel, most of the Alpine Huntsmen *guests* were under the safeguard of the occupying force, Generalleutnant Woytasch's 150-man garrison from the 181st Infantry Division. The unit was under the command of his subordinate, *Hauptmann Schröder*, a man who also took up permanent residency between the hotel and a local residence that he had commandeered for himself early in the German invasion of Norway. The home was located just up the connecting thoroughfare.

Down the stretching halls of the Ulvesund Hotel, the alerted Gebirgsjäger guests ripped open the doors to their rooms and took a brash step out, conversing loudly with one another in the open corridors. Their killer instincts kicked into overdrive. Within moments, most of the battle-hardened soldiers became uniformed, poised ready for action wearing their unit's unique white balaclava head piece; a ski mask-style, with twin eye holes for viewing and mouth covered. Most of the balaclava head gear remained rolled above their faces like beanie hats whilst indoors.

More artillery shelling detonated upon local German targets.

Impacts sounded quite close to the hotel, causing the men to sway inside the quaking multilevel building and dust to leak from pinches in the ceiling and skirting.

The Huntsmen were collected and calm among the residing Heer *(Army/Wehrmacht)* soldiers who were present. The Wehrmacht men were distinguishable from the Huntsmen due to their attire and armaments.

There were two Heer guards on every floor of the Ulvesund Hotel; one sentry stationed at both east and west stairwells. Although bombardment at the island had everybody alarmed, the off-duty Gebirgsjäger members were more composed than the infantrymen.

Men shouted in the halls, hugging the walls during turbulence as the very underpinnings beneath their feet trembled. As a siren sounded within South Vågsøy, alerting them of the attack, they shouted in German. Soldiers were quick to react and rush to their battle stations, running outside to man the fortified guard sites, stocking up on weaponry from an armoury located downstairs of the hotel.

Even though some Huntsmen had wound up sleeping at various residences and barracks outside the Ulvesund Hotel, the majority knew what to do when the war alarm bell rang.

They were battle-hardened veterans of combat.

This urgent circumstance felt more homely than the vacation.

The white balaclava troops converged upon their commanding officer's room on the fourth floor, and they were welcomed at the door by the battle-scarred face of their fearless *Hauptsturmführer (head storm leader* or *chief assault leader),* who was already mostly in his alpine grey uniform attire, complete with strapped leather belts and webbing upholstery loaded with combat accoutrements, prepared for a war.

In the cozy room, he rolled his white beanie over his head, then peeled it back up to show his scarred and weathered face to his men. He was flanked by his *Hauptscharführer (chief squad leader),* a man known solely by the name *Jürgen;* the second-in-command of the Gebirgsjäger.

"Wir < *'We're under attack!'* > riffen!"

The Hauptsturmführer exclaimed the obvious as he let in his finest men, all officers, seemingly *Truppenführers (Troop/Platoon Officers)* and in charge of specific units for the ground forces within the Gebirgsjäger. This included a *Sturmscharführer (assault squad leader),* who commanded the marksman detachment.

A handful of Huntsmen followed the Hauptsturmführer deeper into the open hotel room which had a broad dawn view of the dim Vågsfjorden and some of the fishing village, awaiting the orders of which he relayed with immediacy.

The Sturmscharführer stated as he put the pins in his dressage and even slid his tailored white gloves tightly over his digits. "Wir we < *'We will bear arms and help the 181st Heer to defend this rock against the aggressors.'* > verteidigen,"

Their Hauptsturmführer issued the order with rock-solid composure, and his Truppenführer obeyed with a singular nod before rolling down the beanie upon his face into a ghostly balaclava. He carried an MP40 at the ready.

"Truppenführer Kretschmann < *'Troop leader Kretschmann, you and your Huntsmen help secure the mobile headquarters. I believe Hauptmann Schröder specified that in the local church. Be sure to use the Wehrmacht's outbound wireless maestro transmitter to constantly broadcast once the enemy destroy Måløy Island. It will weaken their communications.'* > kommunikation schwächen."

"Jawohl!" with a disciplined accordance, the Truppenführer complied through his woollen facemask. He gave a brief salute before disembarking through the tight hotel doorway to perform his duty.

"Sturmscharführer Diehl < *'Squad leader Diehl take your sniper hunters north and mount the rocky slopes that angle South Vågsøy. Wait until morning before you break cover. Engage the enemy at will.'* > Belieben an."

The faceless man named *Diehl*, who wore an eyepatch over one eye over his ski mask, dared question their faithful leader. "Jawohl < *'Yes, sir. But, sir? What enemy?'* > feind?"

Their fearless chief assault leader did not dismiss the matter and addressed it thusly. He was stoic in his resolve. "Diese Salve < *'That salvo is being fired from the cannons of at least three warships located in the Vågsfjorden, and those ships are loaded with enemy infantrymen, probably British Army. Once the shelling ceases, they will storm the shores in an attempt to raid the island. This shelling is just the beginning. We shall have the element of surprise, here, gentlemen. These British dogs will be expecting mere Heer grunts: hungover, tired, and sleepy-eyed ... Not wide awake, elite Gebirgsjäger! We shall cut them in half.'* > sie halbieren."

The scarily masked, unidentifiable Huntsmen cheered in accord with their Hauptsturmführer.

"Lasst < *'Let's get to it!'* > ngen!"

"*Jawohl!*" the remaining men shouted.

On his exit, the ski-masked Truppenführer passed the captain of the 181st Wehrmacht, who was on his way in. In Woytasch's almost permanent absence from the north, he was the commander of the 150-man South Vågsøy infantry division—and right now, he seemed awfully directionless. In the presence of these influential Huntsmen, he seemingly had not even the command of his own jurisdiction due to this bombastic Hauptsturmführer.

"Hauptmann Schröder," the Hauptsturmführer greeted the small man in the door as he calmly filled his pockets with his own private military paraphernalia from his open duffle bag on the bed of his hotel room. This included his service pistol, spare ammunition, a knife, and ... *a sheathed ceremonial sword.* This German was kitting up with the whole nine yards and then some.

In a panic, Schröder bounced past several of the eager Gebirgsjäger men as they vacated the room in a stampede of white balaclava masks and metallic weaponry. "Wir < *'We're under attack, sir!'* > Herr!"

Steadily in the chaos, the Hauptsturmführer faced him.

The German leader was a renowned nihilist within the ranks of the Gebirgsjäger. Up until this point, he had no need to utilize hierarchy superiority with Schröder, however they were never certain of a combat situation on the island. It fast became clear of who was the alpha and who was the beta of this chain of command.

"Sind Ihre < *'Are your infantrymen in their positions? Do they know their defensive duties?'* > gungsaufgaben?"

"Na < *'Of course.'* > ich," Schröder replied, but not confidently.

The weather-worn and battle-scarred face of the Hauptsturmführer discerned the uncertainty in his tone, arranging the words in his head to pose a challenge.

"Haben Sie < *'Have you hailed the local Luftwaffe for air support? Have you signalled the bordering lookouts requesting mortar support? Rugsundøy? Halnoesvik?'* > oesvik?"

Schröder bore a stern defence, somewhat safeguarding his professional ability with further incompetence of armament positioning. "Halnoe < *'Halnoesvik has no mortars. It's just our reserve garrison on the outskirts,'* > trand ..."

"Hab < *'Have you signalled them of the pending invasion?'* > iert?"

"We < *'What invasion?'* > ion?"

The Hauptsturmführer's jaw clenched with a brooding frustration. "Das ist ein < *'This is a raid, Captain! You are about to be invaded, caught, captured, or killed. You, like your men, need to wake up! This rock is about to be crawling with Englishmen. Be sure to relay your orders clearly. Your men will need precise direction if they're to make it through this.'* > durchzukommen."

"Me ... meine Feld < *'My feldwebels have been charged with their orders, sir. They know the procedure. They train for this weekly.'* > woche."

"Dir zu < *'For your sake, I hope you are correct, Captain.'* > ptmann."

Schröder's eyes tightened as a defensive posture kicked in. "Ich habe einen < *'I have an accomplished kommandant on Måløy Island who will defend our forward position at all costs. I have three kriegsmarine captains preparing their ships for battle against the aggressors in the bay, and I have over one-hundred-fifty trained infantrymen scattered throughout the city behind defensive positioni—'* >

"Ich < *'I hate to break it to you, Captain, but three armed trawlers aren't going to make a dent in a British destroyer. And your men stationed at Måløy Island will barely survive the shelling.'* > überleben."

Following the Gebirgsjäger Hauptsturmführer's enlightening counterargument, Hauptmann Schröder visibly gulped. He was not prepared for war. The occupancy of Norway thus far by the Germans had been met with minimal resistance. They got to eat out of the hand, now they would need to hunt for their food—their survival. There was a huge difference which he was only now seeing for the first time, and he was gefickt.

He then watched as the charismatic, fearless Hauptsturmführer paced across the soft carpeted hotel room and stood before the landscape-framed window that overlooked the south bay and the Vågsfjorden. The large British warships to which he had referred were visible beneath the dawn sky. South Vågsøy and Måløy Island were dotted with spot fires from the artillery residue. The salvo from the ships cannons was continuing, raining down brimstone upon the German defensive structures.

Exuding a patience that he was not renowned for possessing, the Hauptsturmführer calmly invited the presence of his ineffectual subordinate. "Au < *'Look'* > ..."

After a moment's hesitation, Schröder sheepishly stepped nearer and shared an observation besides the menacing Hauptsturmführer through the same reflective glass of the view scape.

Whenever the distant cannons fired from the direction of the coast, the fog would part with the great disturbance of the air-pressure and ominous silhouettes of the British destroyers could be seen against the Vågsfjord. The sheer size and numbers of the warships within the enemy flotilla was enough to make the hairs stand on the back of the Hauptmann's neck.

Matters only seemed worse when Schröder's view was directed at Måløy—right as the island was peppered by enemy bombardment, destroying it in a series of unrelenting artillery batteries. They notably watched as entire detachments of the 181st were uplifted and dismembered, sprawling in momentary eruptions of extreme violence. Their bodies hit the powdered snow in the aftermath of shell-strikes, unmoving and lifeless before they even had a chance to defend their positions.

Schröder whimpered with a stutter after frowning with confusion, already submitting to defeat. "W ... wir si < *'We're but one garrison! We cannot repel a raid of this magnitude!'* > abwehren!"

He turned and pleaded to the Hauptsturmführer as the intrepid elite warrior leader collected his shined steel from his array of weaponry on the bed, sheathing the silver sword at his hip, prepared fully for battle. He affirmed as he approached the trembling Hauptmann ...

"Hauptmann, < 'Captain, you said it yourself: your men are a trained army with a defensive advantage, covered by local turrets and able air force assistance.' > wird,"

"Wenn Ihre < 'If your men are not retarded, then they'll do just fine against an invading force. The enemy has but one way onto land.' > das Land."

In response, Schröder uttered weakly:

"Wir < 'We should surrender...' > ergeben..."

Schröder's statement came as the Hauptsturmführer turned to leave his room and regroup with his men firmly in the throes of preparation in the busy halls of the hotel. Drawing a deadpan expression, he halted upon hearing the words uttered from the Hauptmann's mouth, immediately revolving around as if he had taken some offence.

"Entsch < 'Excuse me?' > Sie?"

"Kapitulati < 'Surrender. I ... I've already issued the order.' > erteilt."

The elaboration befell the ears of the Gebirgsjäger Hauptsturmführer, causing intensification of his clenched jaw with severe rage upon hearing the puny man's words.

Schröder elaborated further, however any further explanation fell upon deaf ears—ears deafened by pure hatred and fuming disdain at such a preposterous and cowardly clause.

"Meine männer < 'My men are going to defend the line as long as possible, but feldwebel on the ground have orders to retreat or surrender if the enemy pushes their advance. It would be suicide to hold onto this rock—it's not valuable enough.' > wertvoll genug."

The Hauptsturmführer found his zen and clarified to the feeble army captain. "Wenn < 'If it's of a value to the enemy, it's important.' > wichtig,"

"E < 'It makes no sense—why do the English even want it!' > upt!"

"Es spielt < 'It doesn't matter! Your duty here is to hold South Vågsøy ... is it not?' > nicht wahr?"

Fretfully, Hauptmann Schröder bobbed his head in agreement.

"Warum < 'Then, why don't you want to perform your duty, Captain?' > uptmann?" the Hauptsturmführer interrogated, slowly pushing Schröder up towards the glass window with his intimidating posture and questioning. "Bist < Are you a coward? > ling?"

Hauptmann Schröder shuddered his head.

His chin started to quiver, and his beady peepers grew wide as he watched the gloved hand of the Hauptsturmführer rest upon the hilt of his sword ...

Backpedalling, his rear contacted with the wall. His noggin tapped the glass window and like the snap of a finger, reality returned, and all attention distilled on the Hauptsturmführer's next few words.

Through his intimidating disfigured appearance, the fearsome Hauptsturmführer uttered with an unsettling smile that opened through a mouth surrounded by a face of *familiar* duelling scars:

"Es ist < *'It is suicide to surrender, Captain.'* > uptmann."

*South Vågsøy Village*
*Vågsøy, Norway*

*1004-hours ...*

"... *Shooting pictures was forbidden by the Nazis* ..." the monotonal voice of the reporter William Mericle pronounced before the rolling footage of his cameraman. They recorded a shot of a warning sign the Germans had mounted upon the wall near the grounds of the churchyard—the source of their radio jammer.

It read in German:

*'Achtung! Fotografieren verboten!'*

As the camera silently panned down, it focused over the deceased corpse of a German soldier, lying face-down in the snow. The reporter added in a stark tone: "... *so they shot the Nazis, and we went on shooting pictures* ..."

A few of the nearby commandos chuckled at the humour behind the report as they watched the fabled Miracle Man work his newscast magic in the heat of the battle.

Ignoring the reporter and cameraman nearby them, Trooper Peel lowered his view from checking the time. It was four minutes past their deadline ... and there was a last-ditch plan afoot by those bravest in the Troop.

Behind the same barn house shelter athwart the enemy at the churchyard, Captain John Frederick Giles' gaze was upon him as he dropped the face of his wristwatch and despairingly muttered a swear word beneath his breath whilst caressing his bruised chest.

The two made eye contact, and JFG nodded with composure.

"No time like the present, Trooper."

"Sir."

"Are you ready for this ...?"

Peel nodded firmly, but not entirely convincing his captain.

JFG inspected Sergeant Mills. He was an experienced commando and was raring to go to town with his twin American .45s charged. Outside of their double-strapped shoulder holsters and down by either side, Mills had one in each hand with the hammers cocked. Mills saw JFG's gaze of regard and responded in-kind with a singular nod of preparedness for battle.

Radioman Drain, Corporal Knocker White, and another half-dozen British Commandos present to commence this rushed final assault on the churchyard were locked and loaded, and now also preparing the use of an LMG *(light machine gun)* that had been carted forwards to the front by the new additions.

One of the troopers had just fed the Mk.II Bren machine gun with a fresh magazine into the top-mount of the receiver and racked the lever on its right side. Every trooper was secure behind cover, preventing the enemy at the church and stable from knowing their true numbers.

These brave souls of Three Troop had formulated a plan to execute: a daring and desperate resolve birthed from the mind of their courageous leader, JFG, who was also the point man for the strategy and had the most to lose if it went sideways—which was a likely probability.

But desperate times were calling for these desperate measures.

They *had* to get rid of that enemy antenna or die trying ...

The plan was simple:

JFG, Peel, and Mills were the roamers for this sting. They would be darting out and along the right flank, doubling-back into the village in favour of advancing around and blindsiding the occupied and fortified livestock stables that oversaw the churchyard flank. Once on approach from an alternating angle, preferably still holding an element of surprise, Mills and Peel would halt their advance to take fire positions for JFG, who would charge the stable building solo and run amuck.

They would perform this feat at a quick interval, not stopping for concealment or rest. All this while, back behind the village houses and sheds, the few Three Troop troopers which included a Bren gunner, Knocker White, and Drain, would provide heavy and loud suppressive fire at both the side of cattle stables and the church—aiming low, as not to accidentally put a bullet in a window and risk endangering the civilians inside. They believed that this should keep Gerry busy long enough for JFG to blindside their first target at the stables. With their defending offside down, Commando could take the church by brute force and knock out the antenna responsible for disrupting their radio waves, thus getting a signal out.

"Are you?" Peel finally replied to the confident captain. He did so quietly, just between him and Giles, to which the courageous commando emitted no immediate response.

After an extended moment, JFG gleamed at Peel grimly. The keen eye of the trooper must have captured the sliver of an instant that an ounce of fear pushed the limits of his courage's guise.

"My word, I'm ready," JFG truthfully responded with a certainty that exhumed his preparedness for success or to utterly perish. This was do or die, and JFG's very attitude scared the shit out of George Peel.

Like a child watching from the shadow of his hero, Peel watched as Giles began to step into position ahead of the others, preparing to lead the charge into the fray with his Thompson freed from its strap loop and bound with a white-knuckle grip.

"You sure you don't want me on the flank with you?" White double-checked, understanding and willing to obey whatever curveball of an action their captain required them to perform in order to overthrow this Nazi firing position at all costs.

"Negative, Corporal," Giles grunted, planting a hand upon his shoulder as he stepped past. Knocker White was truly one of his best and most competent men. "I need you here to lead the charge on the church once I take out the stable guns."

Knocker White accepted this role with a solemn nod gesture, happily masticating away on fresh bubble-gum. "Yes, sir."

JFG reiterated, facing the lot. "You lot need to press *hard* and *fast* during that window. You hear me?"

Speaking for the Troop, Knocker White concurred wholeheartedly.

"You sure you can make this run, sir?" one of the commandos beside Drain questioned as his companion loaded up spare LMG banana magazines in a stacked row beside their firing position for easy access. "Be some two-dozen krauts in there with well-oiled firing positions. You are going to have to run like the *fuckin' wind* out there ..."

"Aye, sir," another added, addressing the three men about to leap and bound from cover. "You lot better run like the devil's tryin' ta grab ya willy."

Giles, Mills, and Peel nodded confidently and in unison.

"We will make it. You lot just keep us covered, yeah?"

Reaching the boundary of concealment, the captain took a look back over his shoulder, seeing that the brave men of his Troop were all prepared—ready for war. This objective may very well be the most important thing they accomplish this raid.

The British reporter and his cameraman were present and attempting to load more film into the gun-cam with which they were having some technical difficulties. It mattered not for the men of Commando, but they would fail to capture this triumphant moment on film.

"Let's go, No.3 ..." JFG stated softly, quoting their battalion motto as well as giving the command.

Ready to lead the run, JFG prepared one last element ...

He set the countdown timer in the form of a pair of hand grenades with five-second fuses out into the churchyard. His trusted comrade Knocker White did so as well, tossing them far in over-arching trajectories so that they landed in the clearing between the barn and the church, of which, they were thrown purposely short of. Their purpose was to act as an immediate deterrent for the enemy gunners and as a start-gun for their sprint.

It worked like a charm.

A second before they exploded, they heard the distant and alarmed German cry of: "*Granateee!*"

*B-B-Boof!*

Dirt, smoke, and snow powder flung everywhere, blocking visibility for a few seconds—the same time that the flankers bolted off the mark like jack rabbits out of a frozen hell.

White racked the foregrip of his pump-action as he bellowed the command order to the others amidst cover. "*Covering fire!*"

JFG sprinted from position and out into the open, chugging like a steam train as if he had a clear run along the upskirting touch-line at the goal, and he had the ball. Only, instead of cradling an oval-shaped football in a tense grip, he swung a weighty drum-fed Thompson M1928A1 submachine gun from left to right.

Peel and Mills were on his heels, charging the line.

The three commandos were midway from the first interval of cover, sensing the heat of potential enemy weapon sights tracking their movements when behind them, the deafening pout of the Bren gun opened fire on the church shooter locations. The pounding support weapon was swept across the lower and upper side of the building, pelting against the stone architecture and causing the German shooters posted at the windows to think twice about tossing pot-shots at the runners. They mostly recoiled, squatting behind the cover of the windowsills as their shelter was painted in high-calibre ricochets.

Beside the Bren gunner, Drain stepped out from behind a shed house with his gun ablaze, crackling away with controlled bursts of sustained fire, hosing their concentrations between the church building and the horse stables on the right flank angle, keeping enemies pinned down in all directions.

Knocker White elevated from cover and charged blast after blast from his pump shotgun at the enemy positions, peppering every stone surface with a billion buckshot ball-bearings, causing stahlhelm-clad heads to recoil out of sight.

It fast became a firefight trade-off, with both British and German parties spraying quite destructively and aimlessly at one another as their own automatic barrages assaulted both vectors in an array of debris-flung chaos and clamorous torrents of gunfire.

Leaving in the wake of blaring battlefield, JFG, Peel, and Mills utilized every bullet their comrades had used for covering fire, charging parallel to the gunfight now to make as much ground as possible. The trio disappeared behind the concealment of a residence, grappling onto the edge of the house with a spare hand as they took the corner at haste, turning sharply in their sprint, and progressed on the new trajectory.

Moving up, they cleared another opening between unexplored real estate of the village, receiving little to no attention aimed in their direction. The enemy were too busy focusing on the aggressors across the yard, under the impression that was where the push would originate.

JFG rounded another bend, sacrificing a bit of speed in exchange for raising his weapon, covering their charge forth. They were now in uncharted territory. Commando had not yet ventured this far into South Vågsøy, and they were now blindly rushing into an occupied area behind the location of the narrow stable house. Not even God knew what was lurking behind some of these quiet corners, and it was an especially real possibility they could run head-first into a cluster of cocky Gerrys.

Mills and Peel were a step behind JFG, bringing about their weapons as their sprint slowed into a cautious jog. They scanned alternate paths, windowsills, and checked around corners ahead of imperilling themselves.

JFG stayed ahead and on-point the entire time with his submachine gun tucked into the fold of his firm shoulder and his scar-slit eyebrows scanning across the iron-sights.

Leading their detachment, he rounded another of the larger double-storey buildings which appeared to be a boarded-up shop in an open strip of street. They may have just entered the beginning of a commercial district within this small fishing village. There were faded Norwegian signs and market titles, even what appeared to be eroded chalkboard produce advertisements. The paved streets were eerily empty of German occupation. It was as if they had slipped between the cracks of the enemy line.

The men grouped together and slowed, hearing what was unquestionably the sound of heavy jack boots trotting around in the upstairs of the building—German infantrymen, for sure.

JFG put up his fist, halting their advance entirely. They lowered to a crouch beside a building with their eyes peeled.

"We can't push the stables with them here," Mills gauged, forward-thinking. This double-storey position could oversee any stable assault they mounted. "They'll have a firing position over us."

"Affirmative," Giles remarked, swapping his position to the other side of what must have been the closed-over back exit of the building.

Mills exchanged and moved up tight beside Peel, covering two directions at once; one handgun trained on the doorway exit of the building and the other watching their back, arms-split like a modern age wild west gunslinger.

"Sounds like two men," ears pricked, Peel informed after they heard more hurried footsteps moving from one end of the house to the other. The Germans inside would undoubtedly be fixated on all the gunfire across the churchyard cemetery and be trying to gain a firing angle.

Mills gestured to JFG that he would remain to take them out.

Giles heard his selfless proposition, nodding in agreement of the unspoken order. "Clean 'em out—but *quietly!* Give me thirty seconds to make the stables before you go loud from this position."

Mills affirmed confidently with a single bow of his head.

Trooper Peel, who was in no way of the same calibre of these two veteran commandos, could bring nothing to the table but the promise to try and keep up and hold his own. He accepted that they were talking about ending the lives of these enemy men within with silent brute-force tactics, and that was that. He reminded himself to not to linger on the fact, and that dwelling too long on such would only get him killed.

JFG turned and progressed on, keeping quiet. "On me, Private."

The last thing Peel saw of Mills was him holstering one of his pistols to be able to draw his combat knife. Resembling some sort of murderous assassin, crisscrossing the two weapons at the wrists as he sneakily receded into the building to get his hands dirty.

Peel gulped, momentarily questioning if he were anywhere near this level with these brave, deadly killers. He trembled, suddenly feeling out of place amongst this breed of men.

He was so nervous that it was like he had tunnel vision.

Colours desaturated. Sounds drowned out.

His heartbeat bounded so heavily it was like a drum inside his brain.

... however, the constant adrenaline high seemed to plateau his angst.

Peel stayed on JFG's six, remembering to watch their own rear vector whilst keeping their exposed right flank covered with the sights of his own submachine gun. The pressure was well and truly on.

Ahead, Captain Giles halted and peeped a blind corner.

Down the echoic aisle, loud and distinct gunfire from the ongoing churchyard fight ensued. After a split second, he progressed onwards, discounting it.

Peel moved on behind him, somehow still falling behind.

"Stay on my arse," Giles whispered, waiting a moment for the trooper to catch up after crossing the street and hugging cover.

Peel bobbed his tin-hat head, still trying to hold it all together. He paused for an instant when movement caught his eye from the side, and he dropped to a kneeling stance with his weighty Thompson at the ready, prepared to fire ...

It ended up simply being curtains blowing about a shattered window.

He panted, scared out of his wits, and picked himself up to keep up with Giles when he again noticed what he thought was more movement from an upstairs hole in the wall across the street and, again, Peel stiffened his advance and raised his weapon sights, finger tense on the trigger ... but it was, once again, a false alarm.

He whimpered, shivering due to the fear of enemy exposure.

Desperate for air, almost to the point of what seemed like hypoventilation, he nervously searched left to find Giles, discovering that he was now completely gone from sight.

He slowed in his pursuit, unsure of which direction to—

Suddenly, following the path of which he believed JFG to have just taken seconds ago, a wooden panel door unlatched from within and began to slowly open inwards. It was three feet ahead of him.

Quiet as a mouse, the hollow access began to pull open ...

Mostly absent noise, it had fortunately caught his attention, and Peel etched up alongside it in a perfect blind spot with his weapon raised and ready to kill ... but, in that decisive moment, two things shot through Peel's mind at the speed of light:

One, was that *it would surely not be a Norwegian, they would not be that stupid, and therefore it must be a hostile German.* The other, was that *JFG* wanted them to *stay quiet* until he was in a position to take the stables ...

... *he couldn't shoot!*

An overbearing sense of panic set in as everything unfolded quickly.

Against the wall, Peel clutched his Thompson tight, finger on the trigger. He was prepared to kill this enemy combatant if he needed to, of that much he was sure ... however, he couldn't bring himself to attempt this dispatch any other way. Sure, he had a knife, he had his fists, but there was no way he could bring himself to taking another man's life with his bare hands—not to mention the risk of failure that was involved with such primal pugilism. All in that split-second, Peel found himself in a pickle ... and then it was too late to consider anything.

A German soldier in a grey uniform and carrying a walnut-brown rifle began to emerge from the doorway, peering outwards and towards the direction JFG had just wandered with his stahlhelm-covered dome ...

*The soldier failed to check his only blind spot which was right where Peel was hiding ...*

*It was time to act!*

What must have been Peel's inner commando courage took the wheel. His palm released the handle and trigger guard of his Thompson, and he reached down blindly, unsheathing the thin F-S combat dagger trench knife from his belt.

Unlike the blade we had just seen Mills draw, Peel's was the newer type of 'commando knife' made by *Fairbairn-Sykes* that came into production when manufacturing for the heavier knuckleduster-style BC-41s became too high of a demand due to the increase of Commando recruits. The device was more of a dagger than a knife, resembling a poignard with a foil grip. Frequently described as a stiletto, the F-S was a weapon optimized for stabbing attacks.

Moving in low with it out before him like a sneaking assassin, Peel felt a surge of empowerment and confidence overcome him. He pounced forwards in one big stride, bringing his boot into the door as the operator carefully dragged it open by its rattly knob.

With a sudden *thump!* Peel kicked in the stilted lower panel, fully sighting the lone, wide-eyed German soldier of whom he had just now taken by surprise and given an ungodly fright.

Before the enemy could react, Peel thrust his dagger straight into his exposed middle with as much brute force as he could muster. The double-edged blade slid the whole way to the hilt.

*Schlish!*

Face to face, the eyes of the two soldiers met, and they each discovered that they had more in common than one might think ... only, there could be only one winner in this contest.

What was only a few seconds felt like an eternity.

Bearing a tense grimace, Peel watched as the young soldier's shocked stare seemed to dilate as he keeled, releasing hold of his weapon along with his intent, collapsing into his arms in the door. Peel instinctively caught the falling body, lowering him down, before waking to his senses and heaving him clear.

He retracted his dagger with a tug, bewildered at the sight of the blood now sticky between his fingers. The brave face he had worn during this engagement suddenly began to falter, fading into one of wavering and hesitation.

He watched as the lone German soldier clenched quietly at the stomach wound, panting hysterically as his life bled from his body within seconds. Neither one of them made much of a sound.

There were no cries of pain or fear ...

No Hollywood *Wilhelm scream* ...

No life. Just death.

*Something suddenly interacted with Peel from behind.*

On edge, Peel spun, steering his clenched bloody blade at the face of JFG. The captain had doubled-back to find his man.

"Oi—*whoa!*"

Giles's fast reflexes coiled, grabbing at Peel's wrist and deflecting the sharp point of the dagger an inch from his nose. The two exchanged an unsettled stare for an instant before Peel subdued and allowed himself to catch a breath.

Peel was amped-up and jittery, whereas Giles was in complete control.

JFG glanced into the door, spying the dispatched German soldier with the stab wound. His eyeline returned to Peel, confiding in the commando.

"Breathe."

JFG's wise words fell upon Peel's ears, resting his heartrate. The two shared a serene moment before Giles understood what it was Peel had just done. Contemplating, he simply nodded his head, warranting that he was alright and that he had done a good job by doing a bad thing. That it was *kill or be killed* and there was no two ways about it, but they had no time for such platitudes or pleasantries.

"Stay on my arse. We've got to keep moving, here," Giles grunted, needing to lead the way onwards.

Peel was absent words—even absent a mindset.

Still in the same doorway, he lingered.

A difficult view to vantage, his eyes descended back down the deceased man whom he had just stabbed to death, appalled by what he had done.

Born again of his religious beliefs, the trooper wanted nothing to do with that tainted knife anymore. He dropped the blood-lacquered Fairbairn–Sykes blade onto the floor beside the dead body and quickly vanished, chasing after his captain.

At a snail's pace, Sergeant Mills crept up the rasping timber stairs of the double-storey house which overlooked the stables and churchyard.

Though the constant barrage of gunfire being exchanged across the nearby clearing covered any instances of volume he may have emitted, he was quieter than a mouse,

The two shuffling Gerrys up top, were not.

Flustered, they shambled about on the wooden floorboards. Their hefty German boots scampered and scurried on the rug-laid decking, creaking and thudding away, projecting precise beacons of activity. Mills was able to accurately pinpoint their positions within the upstairs rooms due to their constant, anxious motion.

With a knuckleduster knife crisscrossed with his gun hand, Mills closed in, inch-by-inch, step-by-step, not daring to move at a pace that may emit any noise of his own and potentially give away the element of surprise he still currently had.

Once reaching the summit of the claustrophobic staircase, he slowed to a halt to peek towards either corner at a T-section. Shoulder pressed in tight against the inner corner, Mills extended his ranged weapon at the more distant rooms at the end of the hall. These were the same rooms he had heard the commotion coming from. With his knife before his chest prepared to stab, he glanced up the opposite end over his shoulder and halted to listen.

He was absolutely ready for anything—*thuck!*

Unexpectedly, a German soldier who he had mistakenly predicted to be in the same room as the loud trotting at the end of the hallway, rounded the opposite corner, happening to opt a venture downstairs at the same interval as he had upped them ...

*Mills had reacted thusly.*

The commando jabbed his dagger deep into the man's sternum.

The unexpecting German soldier was winded by the metal lung injection, robbing him of air—and fortunately for Mills, his voice. The impact of the BC-41 hilt against his breastbone hit with a deep thump from his diaphragm.

Stubbornly, he refused to die as fast as Mills had anticipated.

The two locked frowns. After a wave of shock flooded them both, the German dropped his heavy rifle loudly in the pursuance of latching onto Mills' left hand, which still clamped the knife buried to the hilt in the man's chest. During the tense grapple and shuffle of might, Mills brought his pistol around, aiming it square in the man's face, in heavy contemplation to squeeze the trigger and finish the struggle before it could fully kick-off—a moment's hesitation that may cost the fight to save the war.

*Mills' tense trigger finger relaxed.*

The intent to shoot the German in the face desisted and, instead, he used his handgun as a club, striking him across the dome instead with the grip bottom. There was a metallic *clunk* as the soldier dipped his stahlhelm at the last moment to protect himself from the brute of the blow.

The two pulled in tight and wrestled for an instant, twirling at a struggle.

The maimed German became reinvigorated by adrenaline, and overpowered their scrummage, thrusting Mills boisterously into the opposite wall of the narrow hallway. The impact dislodged his brimmed brodie helmet in a noisy disruption, and Mills whacked his elbow on a doorframe, causing his hand to spasm and throw his .45 handgun.

The tussle became increasingly loud.

While the struggle persisted, the two bumped against the walls like a pinball, nudging over inanimate objects in the homely environment, such as bouncing hanging tapestries from off the walls and smashing dangling picture frames.

During the wrangle, the remaining German soldier within the premises became aware of the disturbance. Breaking from overwatching a portion of the churchyard assault, he called out to the other room, undoubtedly able to hear the commotion in the hall and wondering what the hölle was going on with his kamerad ...

Fastened against the wall by the impaled kraut machine, Mills ramped up his own ferocity, fighting fire with fire. Survival mode kicked in, and his savageness escalated.

The ferocious men bared teeth and clenched white-knuckled fists.

They tore clothes and drew blood from scrunching grapples.

He released his tensed grip on the German's bloody hands which were attempting to dislodge the knife blade from his chest, and instead began sending vicious hooks into the man's ear and jaw at point-blank range, busting the chinstrap to his stahlhelm and sending it flying with a heavy descent on the hardwood floor.

The two interlocked men began to audibly grunt, even yell.

Blood leaked everywhere from the chest wound of the German, lathering both their uniforms as well as the floor, making it slippery beneath their fighting stances.

Concerned, the second soldier emerged from a bedroom with a tense look upon his face. He had not been expecting to witness what he saw inside the hall passage, and the shock hit him like a gust of wind that caused him to hesitate. Straight after the realization, he raised his karabiner rifle and began to shout threateningly in German.

He held his fire. The rifleman did not possess a clear shot at the intruding commando whilst they were still interwoven in such grappling combat.

With sneering expressions, the Brit and the German roughly revolved in the scuffle, and Mills spied out his peripheral vision that this new soldier was now targeting him with a gun, attempting to gain a clean line of sight—it even looked like he was about to take the shot regardless. Mills saw no option but to spin and forcefully trip this German soldier backwards and down the flight of stairs, taking them away from his sights.

On the edge of the stairs, Mills withdrew the blade from the man's chest with his now red, sticky fingers through the eyelets of the trench-knife. The meaty withdrawal resulted in the German losing all air from his lung like a depressurized gas leak.

He audibly hissed from both the mouth and chest.

Mills then shoved him clear with his free hand and struck him across the face with the knuckleduster hilt of the trench knife. There was a metal *ching-thump!* as the punch made contact with the man's chin bone.

Unexpectedly, the soldier managed to clutch onto Mills' fatigues, dragging him sailing with his collapse from the punch. The two went bashing down the tight confines of the staircase with a dozen crashing *thumps* and *bumps,* cascading the whole way down to the bottom flight, and out of the range of the remaining rifleman down the hall.

The lone German was beside himself.

After a three-second pause, he lowered his guard and charged down the hall to the staircase, picking up his aim again in favour of drawing a bead on Mills at the bottom of the stairs and chase him with a bul—

*Blam! Blam!*

Shooting first, Mills had landed on top of the dead German during the fall. He had split his brow in the kafuffle, which now leaked down his squinting eye that zeroed across his pistol's iron-sights.

From their crumpled position at the bottom of the claustrophobic flight, he had managed to draw his other handgun and raise it back up the staircase in time to greet the rifleman as he emerged around the corner, planting two accurate shots in his centre mass.

The bloody hits erupted in the man's chest, depleting his health to zero. The soldier sneered as he quivered, barely able to stand after absorbing the bullets to his body. He prematurely squeezed his trigger of his hip-level rifle and discharged a bullet into the stairwell wall above Mills. The 98k was loud within the close quarters, giving off an ear-splitting gunshot compared to the two from the pistol.

He slumped afoot of the stairs in the hall, dead, and Mills caught a breath on his new comfy kraut mattress.

Outside and nearby, Giles and Peel froze having heard the shots.

The few muffled gunshots had certainly come from within the double-storey house on the quieter side of the street. The two of them simultaneously assumed correctly that it had been Mills engaging the barn stable overwatch sentry.

They paused to swap a look.

The Germans who they were advancing upon in the stables would have also heard those gunshots and would possibly reposition within the stalls in order to guard their rears from a rear attack ...

"Move!" JFG rushed, picking up the pace and Peel along with him. They had to push them at the stables before they had the chance to fortify their positioning.

The two sprinted to the angle of the very next house on the backstreet before barely slowing to approach the very last corner. They both ran at full pace with their Thompsons before them, gaining time.

"Hold!" Giles called before he lowered his weapon and prepared to break the final line of concealment. As expected, there was a short interval of land and a low wire fence before the stable grounds—zero cover.

JFG looked back at Peel. "It's now or never. Cover me."

He nodded, planning to stay out at the edge of the building. He took a knee in a partially concealed position, aiming to cover the crazy captain as he charged forwards through the mud at the stables.

Off the mark, JFG charged, once again reliving his rugby days. He gained as much ground as possible while they still had an ounce of a surprise attack element.

As predicted, German gunners began showing their faces at the rear of the stables, taking a break from suppressing the onslaught of British shooters by the barn house across the churchyard. That noise was fast becoming a realized distraction to these men.

Over JFG's dashing shoulder, Peel spotted movement ahead at the stable gates, and he closed an eye to accurately target him across the simple sight of his Thompson and not hit Giles by mistake.

He fired with controlled bursts.

The side of the enemy-occupied stall ahead of JFG rapidly became a hive of activity as the men within started shouting and displacing, aware of his incoming presence. The gig was well and truly up for their surprise attack from the rear and, even though Peel did his best to suppress them over a distance, soldiers still spotted JFG as he dashed towards them.

Whilst running full-pelt, hurling like an unstoppable juggernaut, JFG raised his hands and fired at the hip with his submachine gun, stitching lines of splinters across the wooden structure from left to right and back again.

The stable doors exploded into timber shards beneath the peeking German helmets, causing them to retreat instantly. One or two of them were even tagged through the timber plank as the powerful .45 ACP rounds that the Thompson expelled chewed through the saturated lumber like it was wet cardboard.

Judging by all the movement and gunfire within, there had to be at least a half-dozen infantrymen inside the stable.

The low perimeter fence almost caught JFG by surprise, almost snagging like a tripwire. The brute compensated for it at the last second, allowing for himself to tumble in a controlled shoulder roll, revolving easily and continuing to shoot with his submachine gun whilst he regained speed.

Maw and machine gun roaring as he stampeded onwards, JFG peeled right at the last minute and slid down low against the outside of the wooden shed, becoming lacquered in sludge by the mud surrounding the location. The brunt of his full-flight impact shook the entire exterior wall and even knocked down hanging metal tools from the inside to the hay-littered floor.

The enemy soldiers inside were aware of his arrival. Panicking within, they desperately endeavoured to blind-fire through the shaky wall in an attempt to hit him.

They were almost successful in doing so.

From the inside-out, bullets ripped through the moist lumber and splattered into the sludge around the commando's feet as he quickly trundled away in a perceptive manoeuvre.

JFG dodged the enemy intensity by inches, losing his tin hat and some of his peripheral gear in the process. Once slightly further away from the impact zone of incoming projectiles, he flaunted a deadly *peek-*

*a-boo* tactic, springing up with his gun tight through a sawed port in the wall and drilled two of the soldiers within, wounding another.

The remaining Germans reacted, chasing him with their gunfire as JFG vanished and moved further along the exterior.

Below the next viewport, he popped his arms above his head and sightlessly fired with his upside-down submachine gun as he continued to move around the outside of the stable house.

In the distance, Peel continued to lay down suppressive fire, as did Mills from the vantage point above. He had taken a Karabiner rifle off one of his victims and was using it to fire upon the wooden structure from an elevated position. Both commandos covered Giles as he thrived to complete his final objective here and get rid of the German firing position all together.

Skirting the stable, JFG moved low below the cattle doors, firing his weapon at any open interval he found, feeling his weapon finally click dry. Halting in the sludge to reload the damned thing, a sweaty pair of kraut claws lunged out from the stable door above his head, encompassing his shoulders like a lasso. They belonged to an impulsive infantryman who had taken the opportunity to attempt hand-to-hand combat with the aggressor outside their fire base.

Over the wood stall, he reefed the commando up in a bearhug, about to dissolve JFG from sight and drag him into the enemy nest where he would undoubtedly be devoured and never seen or heard from again when ...

*... little did Gerry know that this commando was an ex-boxer.*

Giles briefly tried to scurry away from the stable wall as his new attacker grappled him and his empty weapon, fast realizing it was futile, for the assailant's grip was too strong. Instead, JFG anchored with his core, then used it to snag with all his might in a fold, yanking the German soldier over the edge of the stable gate. The force of the pull brought him toppling down head-over-turkey outside and into the mud along with him.

The enemy combatant was fast to his feet.

After first attempting to use it on the Brit, he surveyed the empty Thompson that JFG had let him win in contest.

*Rising to his feet, Giles smirked at his misfortune ...*

*... and he charged.*

This German was least expecting the commando to stampede at him the way he did.

Like an entrant to a rugby scrum, Giles put all his weight onto his back legs as he asserted his momentum and strength into a shoulder charge. From a low and unavoidable angle, he crash-tackled the soldier, lifting him up and carrying the infantryman almost four whole paces before slamming him down into the earth parallel to the stable wall.

Snorting hot fury like a raging bull, JFG retracted off his winded recipient, letting the winded soldier turn over and clamber to his feet in the sludge.

Now undoubtedly regretting his decision to engage this opponent in hand-to-hand combat, the German watched nervously as JFG began to bounce on the spot, light on his feet, as though he was dancing.

Giles raised his balled fists in front of his face, guard-up.

*This intimidation put a greater fear into the German.*

Raised to his feet, he hoisted his own fists, ready to throw-down.

Wasting not a moment, JFG bobbed in, circling his fists, keeping the soldier guessing as to where—*smack!*—he would get—*smack, smack!*—hit from next—*smack, smack!*

Jab after jab, hook after hook, Giles finally ended the opponent with a muddy uppercut to the chin which caused Gerry to bite his tongue and flail backwards into the side of the shed, unconscious.

*K.O.!*

JFG let his boxing stance drop in exchange for pulling a handful of hand grenades from his pouches. He cupped five grenades in his palm against his stomach as he moved, pulling the pin and tossing one into each individual partition of the stable as he jogged a circle around the exterior beneath Peel and Mills' trading fire with those within.

One after the other, there was a detonation, clearing each section of the stable.

Men screamed from within between each explosion.

With one of the blasts, a German soldier attempted to hurdle the stable door in retreat—but not in time—and the explosion discharged behind him, tossing his body rag-dolling out over the mud.

*Boom! ...*

*Boom! ...*

*Boom! ...*

*Boom! ...*

Each enemy-occupied partition within the stable house detonated, systematically eliminating the German shooters from within the firing position and now freeing up an arch of resistance for the rest of the commandos to approach the church—the next step in JFG's plan.

The giant figure of Captain Johnny Frederick Giles found his feet following the elimination of the stable position. He shouted as he drew his sidearm and led the final charge towards the church from the stable point. *"Let's go, No.3!"*

His advance was matched by the figure of Peel at his six who could not believe the level of heroical bravery he had just witnessed from JFG; taking on an entire enemy outpost on his own. But he had—and was victorious.

Same with Mills, who also heard Giles' battle cry and instantly became drunk from his hurling provocation. Energized and eager to rejoin the fight on the ground, he had since discarded the German ranged weapon and trudged past the German corpses littering the staircase, emerging outside with both pistols swinging by his sides.

Following a cavalry charge led by White and in a combined roaring might, the other dozen and a half British Commandos present within the churchyard battle upped from their firing positions and, as one, swarmed the open cemetery grounds towards the remaining enemy relay ...

... *towards vict—*

*Whiz-thwack!*

Just as Captain Giles began roaring again at the top of his lungs in a full-fledged charge at the enemy, the first of many commandos storming the position, he was suddenly shot through the head.

Headshot by an interval of sporadic enemy gunfire, JFG's body lifelessly collapsed into the open mud before Peel and Mills' advance from the rear.

In a scene that moved in slow motion, even from the view of the neighbouring assault charge, Drain, Knocker White, and the other commandos of JFG's Three Troop witnessed their fearless leader's endeavour collect a harrowing consequence as he was struck between the eyes by a random bullet fired from the rear church entrance.

Everything seemed to go unnervingly noiseless following the echoic discharge of the fatal gunshot that claimed their commanding officer's life.

Other Germans from within the stronghold fired out the windows of the church, inflicting another couple of casualties upon the wave of incoming No.3 Commandos as they rushed the churchyard. JFG was not the only to fall during the assault.

Bright tracers lazed the sky around the advancing men as they leapt the picket fences that cordoned the yard, hurdling the tombstones of the graveyard as they pushed against the defence of their onslaught. Once they were closer and had clearer shots, some of the commandos slowed to fire upon the flustered German gunners, dropping them through the shattered stained windows and creating unguarded pockets.

A dozen commandos pushed up close to the stone exterior of the church building, waving on more incoming troops as they made the mad dash across the open grounds.

*They would take this land or die trying.*

Troops browsed around angles with their weapons, searching for the enemy targets that lurked within the building, swaying their sights across the crowd of cowering Norwegian civilians within the shaded confines, hiding between church pews. They wept and whimpered, terrified out of their minds at the sound of the battlefield stampede their way.

German helmets skimmed between some of the pews within the church, followed by the rising of their weapons. They shot at the advancing commandos through the windows in desperate efforts to hold the point.

Coming in hot, a courageous commando cannon-balled through the partially destroyed stained window, landing inside and behind the hostiles who remained, spooking the soldiers.

These remaining enemy combatants were noticed at a glance to be wearing slightly differing uniforms to all the others they had encountered (so far). They were SS troops, which explained their tactics and the formidable fight, but all the same were caught completely off-guard by the balls-out tactic and were met by the end of Knocker White's shotgun as he landed on his feet amidst the raining glass.

*Boom!*

*Chit-chit—boom!*

Two SS men were cleaned up.

One of them was hit under the glenohumeral joint by the powerful blast of buckshot, shattering his shoulder blade and forcing him to contort in an unnatural way. His guts audibly sprayed on the church pew of which they hid behind, and his friend spun and stood, wearing the follow-up shot across his puffed chest. The buckshot blast sent him flailing lifelessly *over* the heavy pew, slumping with his knees bent over the edge like coat hanger hooks.

*"Stay down! Stay down!"* Knocker White shouted at the Norwegian civilians as they cowered and shrieked. He pumped shell after shell through identified foes who lurked inside, then moved onto the last remaining enemy by the altar. White targeted them next, however, upon thrusting his foregrip and abruptly clicking dry with his pump-action, he failed.

Consequently, the enemy gunmen rose from behind their covered positions to shoot back at him, and Knocker White reacted, collapsing backwards beneath their incoming fire like doing the limbo. Pinching a tight breath whilst he heaved, he performed a reverse-shoulder roll behind an up-turned pew in the nick of time.

The two remaining shooters fast became shredded by the multiple submachine guns as a half-dozen commandos arrived via the destroyed window cavities to save the day, mopping up all who remained within the holy premises with a waft of deafening gunfire.

The noise of the fight decelerated so quickly that shells could be heard tapping on the floor and rolling into crevasses.

Smoke rose, as did the souls from the departed on holy ground.

Sorrowfully passing Captain Giles' resting body in the sludge, Peel and eventually Mills pressed on and made their way into the back door of the church. They took cover on either side of the entry point—the same doorway from where JFG had met the flightpath of a bullet.

They advised that one more assailant appeared to remain inside.

This entrance was to the rear quarters and a different partition to the church building from the main area and would undoubtedly be the last stand for any enemy remaining within, however, whoever was left was now in a commando sandwich ...

The two commandos did not skip a beat. They channelled JFG's spirit, thrusting in the heavy closed-over door with force and it opened. Pushing inside with aggression, they charged their aims with their weapons blazing ...

Catching him off guard, they met a lone SS soldier—an officer— holding a Karabiner rifle. The kraut appeared to be seeking concealment from the attack inside the church—led by Knocker White and the other commandos—when Mills and Peel had busted in behind, taking him by surprise.

There was no doubt that this was the man who had shot JFG ...

It had to be. He was the last one left, and the shot had originated from this section.

Both Peel and Mills fired two shots each through the man's chest and shoulders as he spun to face them, knocking him flat on the floor where he rocked a bookstand that lined the wall. Thick, heavy, leather-bound tomes collapsed upon him, adding insult to injury as they rained down, slog after slog.

Barely of life and suffering severe shock, the wounded SS officer's gloved fingers wriggled, feeling for the handgun pouch located on his hip.

Mills advanced first, stomping on the German's forearm as the officer attempted to draw the weapon, causing him to flinch in pain and cough up blood from his fatal wounds.

They got a good look at their defeated adversary: his SS insignia upon his collars and his unit symbol stitched upon a black armband ... *a white edelweiss flower.*

"*Friendly?!*" a voice shouted outside the door.

"Friendly!" Mills responded aloud, and the wooden door creaked open. From the main area, Knocker White strolled into the rear quarters, making eye contact with the circumstances surrounding the wounded SS officer.

It was as if they both acknowledged what had to be done to just vengeance and, without a moment's hesitation, Mills' scowl glanced from

White and back downwards onto the Gerry, putting a bullet through his head ... but that was not all he deserved.

Not after further endangering these innocent Norwegians; holding them hostage against their will. That's after invading their town—their homes.

*Especially not after taking the life of John Frederick Giles.*

Smoking gun still extended in Mills' hand, he fired another round, rendering the German grotesquely unrecognizable.

White eyed Mills. Although he didn't agree with that level of mutilation, he also didn't dispute it, given the vengeful circumstances surrounding the deaths of their own. JFG was a well-renowned Commando. His loss was heavily felt.

The extra gunshot made Peel flinch, as he wasn't expecting Mills to further deface the deceased SS officer. They eventually made eye contact after Mills lowered his pistols, and while no words were spoken, they each said a thousand grievances.

The two of them watched Knocker White as he sauntered through the quarters, still panting from the running, and still reloading his gun.

Feeding shells into his Ithaca, he eyed the two men as he passed by them, pausing just out of the door and beneath the daylight, where the body of JFG could be seen in a direct line of sight in the clearing ...

In a moment of mourning, White lowered his view from the departed captain. It was a solemn loss.

"Sir," Peel remarked, pulling his attention to the opposite wall, where they all now stood before two arranged desks, full of German radio equipment and broadcast frequency units. There was power going to them, evident via the powered lights and buzz of static.

It was undoubtedly the source of their shortwave preventative.

"How do we turn it off?" Peel questioned the two veteran No.3 Commandos, of which, after his efforts today, he would certainly now be considered himself.

The response of Mills and White was synchronized.

*George Peel took cover.*

They both poised side-by-side and raised their weapons ...

... then preceded to shoot the absolute shit out of the radio wall, destroying everything in an array of sparks, fizzing components, and trashed metal housing. Electrical sparkles popped from the bullet-riddled wreckage as they walked away, leaving Peel in dismay at the sudden outburst, watching the smoke rising from the corpse of the enemy relay.

*South Vågsøy Village*
*Vågsøy, Norway*

After witnessing the deaths of two of their men to enemy snipers almost twenty minutes ago, Colonel Durnford-Slater, his adjutant Charley Head, and radioman de la Torre, had remained put. Cloaked within the shadowy recesses of the Norwegian house of which they had attempted to establish as a signal post for the land force on Vågsøy Island, they were still holed-up and due for progression.

*Little good a signals post was without radio communiqué.*

"John, please!" Head implored to his commanding officer and friend, Durnford-Slater. Grown too apprehensive about the progress and welfare of the scattered men of Group 2, Durnford-Slater had desired to establish communications with each of his Troop leaders himself. In person. This meant that they needed to leave the safety of the post and reach the units in person.

"We must look out for snipers!" Head beseeched further.

"*Lookout nothing!*" Durnford-Slater snapped with a heightened degree of stress mounting to commandeer his manner. He was, foremost, a soldier, and a proficient one at that. It would take more than fear of combat or death to suppress his impetus. He was not one for apologizing for his character, but Durnford-Slater looked to his friend with a smidgen of remorse in his tone. "Look ... we must hurry. It is already after ten-hundred! Well beyond the agreed-upon deadline! I fear Commando could be losing grip on this stranglehold."

Head and de la Torre were upstanding behind their cover now, prepared to follow their leader into the sniper scope-swept streets.

*They'd follow him into hell if they had to.*

"On your lead, sir," de la Torre commented, weapon in hand. The kid looked scared out of his wits but prepared to march in their colonel's footsteps come hell or high water. He seemed smaller without his fifty-pound wireless backpack, which was currently still on the table in the middle of the kitchen.

de la Torre's face panned onto sight of it. The unit had been so close to the action that it was spattered in Trooper Pattinson's scarlet smears from when he had been shot moments ago.

"The radio ... should we bring it? It doesn't even work."

Durnford-Slater glanced back into the room from his position by the rear door. Moments ago, he had crawled beneath cover in order to access the entrance safely from the shooters' range. Head was now on his feet alongside him, and their thought process about the radio seemed simultaneous and unanimous.

"Leave it," they both uttered concurrently.

Durnford-Slater expanded. "It's not worth your life, trooper. There have been far too many casualties on our side due to this new nuisance as it is."

de la Torre crouched down low and approached the others, and one by one they slipped out the back of the Norwegian residence-slash-shooting gallery, abandoning the wireless unit forever ...

... as they vacated the premises, fading in distance, view fell upon the lone wireless radio. The metal box was absent noise for a few seconds, as it had been since they reached Vågsøy Island, until ...

*< Static >*

There was a flutter of frequency interference over the walkie-talkie piece. It was the most action it had transmitted in ages.

*Comms were back!*

But *they* were *gone* ...

*... or were they.*

Out of focus in the doorway, the figure of de la Torre miraculously reappeared. His ears were pricked and attuned to the static noise he was convinced he had just heard from a distance.

*And there it was again!*

The static was followed by the voice of radioman Drain of Three Troop on the easterly quadrant of the island. Their presence on the radio, and anybody's presence via the shortwave bandwidth, meant that their objective of eliminating the enemy relay in the churchyard had been completed.

*"This is Three Troop, reporting in!"*

de la Torre's eyes widened, hearing the communiqués.

*"Does anybody copy?! Over."*

"Sir!" the excited de la Torre shouted, squatting in tight in the doorframe. "Colonel! You've got to hear this!"

When Durnford-Slater returned to the house, he couldn't help but notice his radioman's goofy ear-to-ear grin moments before he, himself, heard the radio talkie hash, which thankfully, de la Torre had possessed the foresight to turn and leave on the highest volume setting in case of this very reason.

"You hear it?!" he questioned excitedly as Durnford-Slater paused in the doorway, practically holding his breath he listened so hard.

*... then, he heard it fully.*

*< Static >*

*"I say again, this is Three Troop! Communications reestablished! Does anybody from Group 2 copy? Over."*

*< Static >*

*Voice filled the airwaves ...*

*"This is Four Troop, we copy!"*

*"One Troop, copy."*

*< Static >*

"Oh, my days!" de la Torre remarked as Durnford-Slater pushed past him in the constricted cover space beside the doorway. He held him back—even after a seemingly effective airstrike across the ridgeline a quarter of an hour ago, they were still awfully conscious of the high-probability that there were snipers still watching every inch of the signal post.

"Sir, we need that radio!"

"Stay back!" Durnford-Slater ordered as he inched further into the danger zone. The only life he was risking was his own. A beam of daylight through the window shined upon his skin, revealing that the German shooters, also, could see him from their higher ground.

"Sir!" de la Torre warned, watching anxiously.

Head was now behind them in the doorway, viewing intently.

Eyes the size of saucers, he watched his brave friend risk death at the mercy of the skies outside. The value outweighed the risk, even of death.

Once inching close enough, Durnford-Slater stepped out, fully exposing himself in the light streak—and in the telescopic zooms of the countless enemy snipers—to snatch the radio from the table in the centre of the room.

He immediately dropped down with it low to the floor and out of sight, seemingly without inciden—*whiz-PING!*

*A sniper shot missed him by inches!*

The well-placed bullet ricocheted from the metal case of the wireless' exterior housing, causing a spark to ignite bright before Durnford-Slater's face as he allowed for himself to collapse on the floor with it. Luckily, it was not damaged.

Holding a tense grimace from the pressure, he rummaged for the attached walkie-talkie piece and used it to communicate a response.

"This is Lieutenant-Colonel Durnford-Slater! All Troops, report in! Over."

*< Static >*

"*This is Three! Enemy HQ in the eastern quadrant secured! Communications are good. Awaiting orders! Over.*"

"*This is One Troop! Fish and herring factories in flames, moving to assist in-land assaults!*"

"*Four Troop, here! Powerplant destruction imminent!*"

Durnford-Slater formed his first smile of the day as the sit-reps were like music to his ears. He beamed as he faced Head in the doorway, bringing back up the walkie to his grin. "Roger that, men. Maintain all objectives. RVP at the hotel objective! Out!"

With the radio in his lap and his back up against a wall Durnford-Slater was sick of being where he was. He planned to immediately readdress the radio waves, turning the knobs to a differing frequency so that he could reach the navy. "This is Colonel Durnford-Slater for the HMS Kenya, over."

"*Colonel, it sure is grand to hear your voice,*" the hazy voice of Brigadier Haydon responded from out on the fjord. "*We've been wondering what in the devil had happened to you lot ...*"

"Yes, sir. Apologies for the delay! We ran into some unexpected guests upon this merry lil' northern raid, and it has unfortunately set us back an inch."

"*You can relax, Colonel. We're still here, and the ships of the Royal Navy have still got your back,*" Haydon regarded on behalf of the entire flotilla. "*What's the situation? Over.*"

Durnford-Slater's eyes met his men.

"Situation under control, sir. However, we could use some help to smooth things along ..."


*HMS Kenya*
*Vågsfjorden, Norway*

Raid life appeared easy aboard the Kenya.

A sailor carrying a silver tray strolled through the busy bridge deck of the destroyer, sidling up beside Brigadier J.C. Haydon in time to service him with a beverage once he had finished communicating with some of his seamen.

"Cheers," Haydon remarked, graciously receiving the provision. The kitchen hand offered him a small decorative pot of tea and a saucer. Haydon took to the platter, straining himself a hot tea, stirring it thus before dismissing his wait staff and facing the forward panoramic view of the island.

He took the time to take a sip before preparing to relay the communication sit-rep details and instructions from Colonel Durnford-Slater. He declared his orders loudly, so that all radiomen and seamen could hear as one. "Gentlemen, we have received word from the ground troops within South Vågsøy. Affirming as our spotters observed, the demolition objectives have been completed on relative schedule. Captain, if you could begin assistance by sending in the transport ships to the coastal FOB as before mentioned by Group 2. We can begin ferrying back the wounded and prisoners from the land."

"*Aye, sir!*"

"Open communications to Group 1?"

"*Sir?*"

"Inform Lieutenant Clement to bring his prisoners to the coastal FOB for collection, and to send a portion of his men along the north-east hills to eliminate a group of enemy snipers giving our Group 2 chaps a hard time. Advise they are hidden sporadically amidst and are heavily trained. Inform him to proceed with caution."

"*Aye, sir!*"

"Group 5, progress update?"

A headphone-wearing dispatch assistant leant over on his chair. "*Sir, Captain Birney just checked in. Group 5 is en route to their objective along the Ulvesund passage, due to reach shore with minimal deferral. They were delayed assisting the capture of stranded prisoners who had escaped the two unsuspecting merchant ships that the Oribi attacked; a tug and a freighter.*"

"Aye," Haydon nodded contently. "Someone want to get me Group 3 back on the line. I better address the persistent Mad Major myself."

A radio operator along the console board of the bridge slid out on a chair, offering Haydon a hand-piece. "*Sir, Major Churchill is already on the line for you ...*"

"Of course he is," Haydon sneered as he collected the microphone with an open hand whilst nursing his tea in the other. "Major Churchill, this is Brigadier Haydon ... I've got some good news for you, son."

Måløy Island
Vågsøy, Norway

"... *once Group 3 has finished assisting the transports load the POWs and* *sent them back towards the Kenya, Colonel Durnford-Slater requests* *your assistance in South Vågsøy. Over.*"

Waiting patiently and still on the ground at the captured Måløy Island objective, Major Jack Churchill's eyes fluttered upon hearing the words beckoning his call. The only words he truly listened to from the Brigadier's voice were the ones informing him that he was needed in South Vågsøy.

"Fine-o-fine, sir."

"*I will be committing the entire floating reserve under command of* *Captain Hooper. You are to await the arrival of Group 4's primary* *detachment, led by Lieutenant Black. They'll escort a Troop of your* *choosing into the village ...*"

*A Troop of his choosing?* Churchill thought to himself.

*He'd be heading the damn thing, himself!*

"Understood, sir. Churchill out."

"*Kenya out.*"

Churchill swiftly passed the hand-piece back to Lieutenant Wills, who juggled to catch it given the spontaneity of the throw. Wills had not expected the conversation to be over so soon, especially considering that Haydon still appeared to be talking on the other end.

"It's about *bloody* time!" Churchill remarked to himself, straight away searching for someone in the crowd of commandos and POWs. "Let's get in the bloody fight."

Wills glowered, having just heard the same communiqué as Churchill. "Eh, sir? Don't we have to wait for Group 4?"

"Negative, leftenant. I didn't hear any such a directive, did you?" Churchill questioned sardonically. He knew they both had heard Haydon state that, but it was as if Churchill was questioning Wills' loyalty: *Commando* or the *Royal Navy.*

A wave of pressure fell upon the young lieutenant, and Wills stuttered. "Eh, n-no, sir. I didn't hear that at all. What directive from *the* *Brigadier in charge of the entire flotilla of warships?*"

"Good lad," after a moment to process the man's humour, Churchill smirked and marched on, shouting out to one of his other lieutenants. "Lieutenant Peace?!"

"*Sir?*" Peace replied from down on the coast. His hands were busy processing prisoners with the navy men in the additional LCs.

"We have orders to head to the mainland to assist with the assault. Six Troop and I will be heading there now, Five Troop will remain here to transport the prisoners and await the arrival of Group 4 from the Kenya. Join us ASAP."

"*Wait—you're leaving now?*" Peace frowned, a little apprehensive. With Churchill and Six Troop leaving Måløy Island and heading over to Vågsøy Island, it halved their forces in the interim of G4's arrival.

"You'll be alright ..." Churchill regarded as he stepped away from the slope's edge. He was now pacing in the direction of the stationary Six Troop, then towards the southside of Måløy Island where there was established a narrow bridge connecting it to the mainland of South Vågsøy.

"Gentlemen, on me!" Churchill announced, barely even slowing his strides or waiting for the alignment of the two dozen men of Captain Young's Six Troop unit. Felix Hardy was amid these commandos, tagging along for the ride. "We're heading to Vågsøy to join in on the fight!"

"Major?" Young questioned, seemingly unconvinced that *that* had been Haydon's direct order. It seemed unnecessarily rushed.

"Captain Young, ready your men," Jack reiterated over his inquiry, however, the captain was incessant.

"They want us to move in without the floating reserve? Without Group 4?" Young probed furthermore, this time cocking his head in possible misperception of the relayed orders.

"Affirmative, Captain," Churchill implored, eyeing him gravely. There was a hint of desperation and assertiveness towards their new goal underlying Churchill's tone. "Ready your men, or I will."

Young Young hesitated for a moment, watching as an out-of-character Jack Churchill stormed off the mark on his own, leading the fight solo towards the mainland.

"... alright, gents, lock and load!" Young verbalized as he grudgingly took control of his section. Something was not right about this, nevertheless he had no choice but to follow the orders of his commanding officer.

Captain Young jogged up ahead to catch Churchill's compliant strides, leaving Lieutenant Bruce Giles to commandeer their direct leadership.

"... *That's it, you heard the Major ...*"

"Major Churchill," Young called as he ran ahead of the assembly of Six Troop, catching up for a discreet converse with Churchill's pace as he progressed stridently. "Hold your horses!"

Churchill's direction had them fixed on the bridge, onwards to the mainland. He could barely even wait for the others he was in such a hurry. "Double-time it, Captain. We're late for a war—"

"Sir, what's the hurry? Worried you're going to miss the fight?" Young jeered to instigate an exchange with Churchill, possibly expose the true nature of his sheer determination here—because it wasn't natural or orthodox.

Mad Jack didn't slow.

Didn't stop.

Young continued: "I didn't realize you were in such a hurry today to get yourself shot at! ... Wait, oi, c'mon, sir, this is idiotic!" Young outburst, causing Churchill to slacken his pace, even halting in his advance. "For someone preaching the mandate of *no-unnecessary-risks* to me earlier, this is a pretty big bloody unnecessary risk, don't you reckon?!"

Churchill's tense expression rehabilitated.

*Young* did *have a point.*

An obvious moment of reflection passed, and Churchill exhaled.

Young cued. "There is more to this ... isn't there?"

Churchill tensed his jaw as he strode on with him in tandem.

Keeping in pace, they marched on, still ahead of the other men.

"Give me the God's honest, here, Jack ..." Young enquired with a genuine interest and concern. His withdrawal of a formal title showed that he was speaking not to his superior officer, a *major*, but his friend, *Jack Churchill*. He conversed in a lower tone as the rest of Six Troop began to catch up and overtake them. "I needn't remind you that this order to march on without the reserves is absolute *bollocks* and that Six Troop will follow my order to withhold if need be."

Churchill's sterling stare sought his, spying for his bluff.

Either he wasn't in the right mind frame, or this time, Young didn't have one. He was fast becoming a big man and was wearing big boy pants, finally befitting his rank. He was champing at the bit for more responsibility, and somehow thought questioning his superior's motives was a way of obtaining that. He may have been wrong, and two lefts didn't make a right—but three did. Particularly considering the mandates he questioned were from his CO speaking out of line and, unbeknownst to Young, Churchill was acting insubordinately, himself.

Young pushed further. "Yeah, sure, you're the *big bad Group 3 CO*, but do you really want me to get Haydon on the wire and get *him* to pull rank?"

Churchill held his rally to deliver him an evil eye.

Young had him at a standstill.

"What do *you know* that we don't?"

Jack expounded particularly, conceding and divulging his admissible knowledge. "These *Gebirgsjäger* bellends—the *Alpine Huntsmen*—they're a group of expert *hunter-killers* born out of the deepest, darkest recesses of the Schutzstaffel cesspool. Our Troops on the mainland aren't expecting an attack of that calibre or competence, and they're going to need our help."

"You heard the same communiqué as I did from the colonel? Everybody checked-in, Jack! Even with these unlikely entanglements, the raid is going to plan!"

"*So far,*" Churchill muttered. "Trust me, they're going to need our help! I know of these guys ... the Huntsmen are elite!"

"Hang on, last time I checked, so are *Commando!*" Young responded bluntly—and truthfully, again stopping Churchill in his wayward tracks. "And we're stronger *together—you* just gave me an ear-full on *charging in half-cocked,* remember?!"

Six Troop caught up, passing the quarrelling officers on the single-lane bridge into mainland Vågsøy. They paid no mind to their topic of conversation.

"*Keep going up ahead, men! Regroup on the far side!*" Churchill remarked, steering the two dozen men on. He and Young remained a moment longer while they passed. Their discussion was not yet over.

"Look, Young, I need you to trust me, here. It's a long story, but I have fought this cruel contender before ..." Churchill finally admitted, suddenly correcting himself and beginning to elaborate.

"*What?*—How?—*When?*"

"Well, not *them* but, *their leader* ... and, lad ... I *lost!*"

Young frowned as he listened, genuinely concerned and intrigued.

As far as recent history would have it, Mad Jack Churchill never lost a fight ...

Young Young stood, perplexed. Processing.

"Did you hear me? *I lost!*" Jack clarified, searching his mind for the words best to describe what they were in for. Churchill breathed in. "If *he's* here ... then I fear we might lose again."

Young's taut expression seemed to relax as a smile formed upon his maw and he glanced out into the distance.

Churchill angered upon noticing his exceptionally out-of-place expression of humour. He had been serious in his description and reasoning behind his angst at getting his men over to join the fight against the Alpine Huntsmen.

"Pardon me, but is something in what I told you humorous?"

"No, no! Of course not!"

Young's face returned to view, and he loosened his smile.

The two soldiers progressed on.

"That's all you had to say, Jack ..." Young stated discreetly between them. "*Revenge,*" he eyed him in stride, "You want *revenge.* This is about getting *payback.*"

Churchill compromised. "Well, *yes,* I suppose ..."

The two lastly continued after Six Troop, bringing up the rear with pace, they had now all crossed from Måløy Island and onto the mainland of South Vågsøy.

Young questioned as they trundled, fixated on war. "This *enemy leader* of yours, he got a name?"

Churchill bobbed discouragingly ... "Actually, yes. *Enemy.*"


*The Ulvesund Hotel*
*South Vågsøy, Norway*


At the present hour, the view over South Vågsøy from the Ulvesund Hotel was a morbid one for the occupying Axis forces.

It was essentially a front-row seat to their own defeat.

From the fourth floor, they had watched as the invading British forces systematically struck the coast and Måløy Island, pushed through the urban environment on South Vågsøy, and were now ploughing through multiple defensive positions further inland. To the west, the barracks at Holvik had been destroyed, and the fish factories and kerosene and coal oil manufacturing factories located by the docks had been set ablaze. The power station appeared to be under attack as they observed further chaos unfold ...

*The island was now an array of disarray.*

Smoke pillars climbed into the morning sky, echoing the Allied victory upon this land. It would all be over soon.

A battle-kitted man stood against the glass, leaning forwards.

The reflection of his scarred face was low as he watched the fires burn. His eyes glimmered as he watched his hope for conquest turn to ashes ...

"*Mein Herr ...*" a voice summoned from the rear of his hotel room and his glum expression stirred. He viewed his attender in the mirror of the window, like him, he was kitted in white and balaclava-clad. It was fellow Huntsman Hauptscharführer Jürgen.

He could immediately tell that whatever news was to be communicated was not positive.

"Was ist los, Jürgen?"

His man reported. "Der ausge< *'The outbound wireless maestro transmitter at the church has been destroyed. The mobile headquarters ... has fallen.'* > gefallen."

Turning away from his man at hearing the news, the Gebirgsjäger Hauptsturmführer's expression fell flat, though his exhumed sigh was perceptible. He knew the outcome before Jürgen announced it ...

"Truppenführer < *'Troop leader Kretschmann was killed in the action.'* > getötet."

"Da < *'Pity. He was a good man'* > Mann ..." the Hauptsturmführer said unto himself in a sorrowful tone.

"Unsere < *'Our snipers along the north ridge have experienced resistance from the north-west direction. Diehl reports they are unprepared for close-quarters combat, so I have issued a retreat to the hotel for formation.'* > rückgezogen."

"Kom < *'The English are coming from behind us as well?'* > hinten?"

"So < *'It seems that way, sir.'* > Herr."

Visibly confounded, the Hauptsturmführer conceded with a nod, accepting of this fate. He was far from giving up the fight and acknowledging defeat.

"Wissen < *'Do we yet know if the Captain aboard the Foehn managed to destroy his Enigma code machine before he foolishly ran aground?'* > lief?"

"No  < *'Not yet, sir. Our early estimates suggest that he failed to do so,'* > getan hat," Jürgen reluctantly relayed.

An apparent possessor of a short fuse, the Hauptsturmführer did well to contain his rage.

He did the thing where he tensed his jaw until it was about to pop ...

He asked the next question fearing the answer regarding the competency of the useless Schröder. "Hat Hauptmann < *'Did Captain Schröder get word to his 181st kinsmen in the warehouse district, ordering them to destroy their encoder before the enemy can take their ground?'* > einnehmen kann?"

Jürgen waited for the Hauptsturmführer to make eye contact from across the room, prompting a response. He merely shook his head with remorse.

The Gebirgsjäger CO glared across his shoulder at the subordinate for an extended moment before returning his gleam across the spectacle of real-time decay throughout South Vågsøy.

"W  < *'Where is Schröder, now?'* > jetzt?"

Jürgen swallowed, hiding his hesitation. "Wir glauben < *'We believe he's either downstairs with his remaining infantrymen ... or he has retreated back to his quarters across the street, awaiting a personal surrender to the British.'* > gewartet."

The Hauptsturmführer scoffed beneath his breath at Schröder's pathetic nature. They were aware of his local residence in South Vågsøy, located down the thoroughfare and across the street from the Ulvesund Hotel.

"Br  < *'Bring him to me ...'* > mir ..."

The all too recognizable mug of the duelling-scarred Gebirgsjäger Hauptsturmführer finally twirled, showing his fluency, and putting a name to the face ...

*Gebirgsjäger Hauptsturmführer* <u>*Friedrich Feind*</u>.

The familiar character muttered his favourite motto in his best English: "*It is zuicide to zurrender.*"

# 10

## *The Foehn Effect*

*HMS Oribi*
*Ulvesund Fyr, Norway*

For the past hour, the men of Captain Birney's Group 5 had been missing out on almost as much raid action as the floating reserve of Hooper's Group 4—and they hadn't left the starting line yet.

Authorized by Brigadier Haydon aboard the Kenya moments ago, their cruise aboard the Oribi had been given the *go ahead* to continue upstream along the Ulvesund Fyr passage and towards their boundary objective.

Birney sounded the order to his fifty men, which included the likes of Second Manchester Regiment veteran and *Merry Man of Mad Jack* alum, Sergeant George MacWilly MacWilliam. The one-eyed carrot-top Scotsman was acting as Birney's second-in-command for their detachment north of the coast. Their mounted LCs would soon disembark from the destroyer and beach along the northern coastal route, cutting off any potential reinforcements called in by the enemy.

In the narrowing fyr, which was essentially a river passage bleeding off the main Vågsfjorden and continuing along the northern coast, the massive O-class destroyer seemed out of place during her gradual travels.

Reaching the edge of a restriction of passage, the Oribi slowed.

The clock struck 1020-hours and the two landing crafts filled with roughly twenty-five commandos per piece separated from their decelerating mothership. Resembling fired torpedoes, land-bound, the motorized ships traversed across the water like skimming stones. They sped fast onto the quiet northerly shores, where the troops dismounted, weapons drawn and guarded.

The Commandos proceeded up the wet coastal rocks and trudged through the piled snow to a nearby road. Fanning out, the assorted troopers were able to determine that no vehicles had toured these far rustic roads this morning. If there were any reinforcements coming to aid the 181st at South Vågsøy, they were certainly yet to come. They had perfect timing to establish a perimeter defence, safeguarding the operation.

"This'll do," Birney regarded to his Group.

Like clockwork, the men established a boundary, with bipods and rifle sights facing north, using variations in the terrain to cloak their presence and establish overarching angles of defence.

Sergeant MacWilly ran in, planting down his trusty Lewis machine gun over an embedded rock. He folded out the bipod, checking the charging handle that reciprocated forth at a spring, aligning a round into the receiver. The ratcheting teeth of the horizontal-mounted disc magazine cycled like a revolver, cycling the round into place.

Bullet in the chamber, MacWilly was sure to rattle the bullet in his head, involuntarily feeling the need to waddle his head for a moment before settling behind the mounted weapon—his lone eye across the flipped-up rear battle sights.

The eyepatch-wearing commando had planted her rough on the rocks, racking the mechanism. He was prepared for war should it come knocking on this day of days ...

*By his watchful eye, nobody was making it* in *or* out *of South Vågsøy.*


*HMS Kenya*
*Vågsfjorden, Norway*

In the confines of the lower deck, along with his men of G4, Captain Hooper visualized Brigadier Haydon giving the order. He could imagine him standing amidst the Kenya command bridge, nursing his Earl Grey teacup and saucer like a proper contrite knob.

Geared up, locked and loaded, together men of the Group 4 floating reserve were eagerly awaiting the order to assist in the raid ...

*... an order they just received.*

*Haydon had committed the reserve!*

Out of an impatient frustration, Hooper slammed the telephone piece back onto its cradle on the wall with a *clack* that resounded the inner bell.

"About bloomin' time!" he testified, turning to face his second in command Lieutenant Graeme Black. The man with the permanent scalded look and blonde imperial moustache suddenly shifted a smile, positively over the moon with the idea of finally charging into battle.

Without a word audibly spoken between Hooper and Black, the Group 4 lieutenant hiked his banana-mag top-fed Mk.II Bren LMG up over his shoulder and spun to address the class like a schoolteacher giving a seminar in a lecture hall.

"Mount up!" he grunted in a bellowing tone. "We're going to fuckin' war!"

The No.2 Commandos of the unit each raised a fist in toast to the order. It was the pre-battle cry chant.

The armed men each knew their places. Knew the drill.

War faces on, they turned and filed into assorted formations, funnelling through the narrow corridors of the Kenya where the morning light irradiated them. They next mounted the many ladders along the sides of the ship, which distributed them straight into the bellies of the waiting landing crafts.

From here, they would be spearheading an assault into South Vågsøy, bringing up the rear of Durnford-Slater's Group 2 assault on the mainland fishing village, revitalizing the charge with better numbers and energy.

Graeme Black sat foremost the first LC, clasping his machine gun and frothing at the mouth like a rabid dog, hungry for war.

His brow was tensed. His lips were pursed with conviction.

Only, anyone that knew him prior to his involvement with No.2 recognized that he valued not the art of foreplay in battle. Commando enabled this warfighter with the means of which to distribute his deliverance.

*At last, it was time to fuck shit up.*

*Warehouse District*
*South Vågsøy, Norway*

Captain Forrester's Four Troop commandos arrived along the coastal side of the north-east flank, reaching what appeared to be a small-scale warehouse district located behind the South Vågsøy power station.

Since their landing this morning—with everybody else, respectively—they had battled their way through a northeastern portion of the fishing village township, pursuing the retreating enemy forces out into a snowy clearing in front of a series of large, double-storey processing warehouses beyond a wire fence.

Two of the three big warehouse structures were slightly smaller in length and a shade of natural bark in appearance, with the larger, centralized warehouse painted a carmine red, long-since weather-worn and distressed to more of a coral shade.

Two straggling German soldiers were suddenly gunned down as they attempted to leap a fence into the enclosed district, having been chased by the lethal British commando troopers in fierce pursuit.

Lieutenant Dennis O'Flaherty and a rifleman were on-point in the leg race, ahead of the Troop, and were the gunners responsible for issuing the gunshots at the two Germans as they reached the end of the urban cover. A dozen troopers from Four Troop promptly arrived, all halting at the edge of urban concealment before the open stretch of land before the warehouses.

More enemy were visible through the icy cross wind in the distance, falling back into the same compact warehouse district. The 181st infantry numbers seemed to be dwindling, either being killed or forced to surrender as their defences were outflanked or overrun by Commando. Whatever numbers they had left in the entire town seemed to be falling back towards the rear of South Vågsøy—the location of the Ulvesund Hotel: the most fortified landmark and the suspected main enemy stronghold.

Gunfire crackled from the distant targets.

The Commandos held cover. Boldly returned gunfire.

During this new small arms barrage exchange, O'Flaherty turned to see that a few of the allied Norwegian soldiers from the NOR.I.C.1 had managed to rally within the same portion of cover that they had, along the opposite end.

"What we got, men?!" the moustachioed Algy Forrester enquired as he pressed his shoulder into the block of cover, finding the time to reload his many hanging weapons. The action had been so intense and full throttle within the village he had been shooting from all his weaponry, of which this captain carried an assortment for every occasion. After feeding more 16-gauge shells into his starving Ithaca 37 shotgun, he immediately let it dangle from its khaki strap in order to cycle to his Thompson submachine gun, ripping the empty stick magazine and loading a fresh twenty rounds.

"They've fallen back into those warehouses!" O'Flaherty reported, approaching his commanding officer along with a reliable rifleman named Sherington. "Sherry and I just watched what must be the remainder of this whole quadrant vanish into *those* three structures!"

Suddenly, a bass-filled *boom* resounded, and the commandos from Four all rubbernecked further north-west along the coast, beyond the warehouse district, and towards the power station. They watched from their angle in South Vågsøy as the entire place was destroyed by demolition charges—the work of Captain Bradley's One Troop.

One after the other, large power transformers were blown up by placed explosives. Bradley would have hit the docks, the factories, and now the power station on their way to rendezvous with the rest of Group 2. The transformers gave out a god-awful sizzle that sent a torquing crackle through the morning air as the bombs went off, releasing a pent-up store of electricity into the sky in jittery flickers. It resembled a lightning storm, only upside-down, and earthward-originating.

"*Ha-ha!*" Forrester hooted sinisterly from underneath his broom of facial hair. "That's Bradley's boys! *Get up 'em, lads!*" he cheered through the hole in his face. It was like his mouth had one great big eyebrow of its own.

Observing his commanding officer keenly, the more reticent Dennis O'Flaherty never fully understood the need for applause and celebrations during combat. He realized that although encouragement was important and that some men rode the high that battle naturally provided due to surging adrenaline, he couldn't fully understand the need for such loud ovation. It distracted from the mission at hand.

O'Flaherty eyed Forrester with a deadpan gleam until he finished, noticing that Norwegian Kaptein Martin Linge was still attached to Forrester's hip. He relayed the cheer to his armed Norwegian cohorts, seemingly having a great time in amongst it, and why wouldn't they. They had the most invested in this; this was their land, and they were getting it back. Ridding home of the vile and malevolent German forces like digging out ticks.

Caring little for the revelries and eager to get back to the killing, O'Flaherty put forth a proposal. "Suggest we advance upon the warehouses before Gerry gets too settled, sir."

As he voiced his suggestion, Linge eavesdropped the tactic, ardent to assist. He treaded nearer to O'Flaherty, bobbing along merrily with the idea of attacking the warehouse district immediately.

Forrester denoted approval. "One team centre, one team on a flank. Use the cover of the village to manoeuvre closer."

The men all about Four Troop began to ready themselves for an advance, splitting into sections. Linge commanded his lot, relaying the orders from the British captain.

"Lieutenant!" Forrester abruptly remarked, placing a hand upon his O'Flaherty's shoulder.

O'Flaherty felt a sudden warmth wash over him, not unlike a gust of enchantment. He may have been a reserved type, but this was the moment of governance he had been waiting for. Longing for.

"Sir?"

"Take charge. Lead the flank."

O'Flaherty beamed. "Yes, sir!"

By his side, his friend, Sherington, who was aware of O'Flaherty's desire for authoritative commission during this operation, was equally as excited by Forrester issuing them with the responsibility of this mandate.

"Let's put 'em in the ice, lads!" Forrester shouted, signalling Four Troop to purpose.

*South Vågsøy Village*
*Vågsøy, Norway*

The soles of their Grafters black leather combat boots finally touched down upon the shores of Vågsøy Island.

Moving as one, Six Troop of Group 3 rounded the bend after crossing the wooden bridge adjoining Måløy Island to the village of South Vågsøy, charging along a coastal path with zeal and impetus, bounding rocks and trudging sleet, stomping through piles of snow and frozen brush in the direction of the Commando FOB and the fishing village—the source of ongoing gunfire and explosions booming in the enclosing distance.

Led by point man Lieutenant Giles and his Thompson, Captain Young's Troop applied the brakes to their journey when, through the fog hovering above the shoreline rocks, they discerned the spot fires of a recent ship wreckage.

It was a curious sight: a ship out of water, beached on land.

The rushing commandos decelerated upon the discovery, cautious to progress at haste. They communicated; raised their weapons at guard, tracing their aims aboard the fresh target to properly secure the situation.

She fast became identified as one of the German armed trawlers that the navy had encountered an hour ago and shredded to steel streamers. This one was labelled *Foehn*. The smoking ship had run aground against the coast, hull damaged and smoking hot from the furious naval battle in the Vågsfjorden.

She was littered with bodies.

Both dead ... and *still alive*.

"Sir!" Young proclaimed after Giles issued a caution to halt, and the men each found a stance amongst the knee-high rock dunes with their wits about them.

Young held for orders from his CO and, promptly, the aslant green beret-wearing Major Jack Churchill appeared, having not been far from the Troop formation of two-dozen No.3 Commandos.

Before much of a further reconnoitre of the situation could be conducted, the educated commandos made hostile identification of the bodies as the stranded kriegsmarine sailors.

Both forces reacted concurrently, and gunfire ensued.

From an indomitable high ground vantage, the encompassing Commandos were already holding a tight aim on the vessel and its stranded occupants when they became aware of their presence. With alacrity, the tattered kriegsmarines descended the sides of the vessel like rats fleeing a sinking ship. Surrender may have once been an immediate option, however, apparently it was never an option on the table for these stalwart sailors.

The Germans were uncoordinated and somewhat adrift having just washed ashore in their obliterated ship, having been destructively blown apart by the cannons of the Kenya and the Onslow—a British destroyer that was also enclosing dangerously close to land from behind them in the Vågsfjord, visible through the morning fog.

After the Foehn had become immobilized by the Kenya's long-range guns, the besieged vessel was then speckled by the superior firepower of British machine guns from elevated positionings aboard the Onslow, finishing off any resistance and chasing her aground. The British browbeat now hovered behind the wreckage, holding and likely pending the dispatch of a scout party of combat sailors to investigate the wreckage.

Churchill's commandos had beat the navy to it.

In this new contact, there were at least four immediate casualties made to the enemy numbers. They were the brave souls with Schmeisser submachine guns, heroically endeavouring to safeguard the shipwreck, assisting any of their fellow boche survivors within the wreckage to escape.

There existed a brief intermission after all the sudden shooting, where a few of the commando troops rapidly descended the rocks onto the coast in the furtherance of taking captive any prisoners.

Last boche standing, an armed enemy assailant attempted to escort another man—possibly the ship's skipper—as they ran the length of the damaged hulk back out to the waterlogged end, aiming to reach the aft that was still partially submerged in the icy fjord. The man at the front seemed to be cradling a package beneath his arm, like a rugby player charging the try line.

Commandos shouted at the impulsive movement before the final gunman held up and opened-up with a blaring crackle from his weapon, hip-firing in a sweeping pattern to cover whatever their last-ditch efforts were.

His machine gun swept left and right, hosing at the array of commandos between the pebbles of the foggy coast. The suppressive spray soaked over the troops in the rocks, causing them to recoil between fizzing sparks of ricochets.

It was fast realized that it was more a diversion of covering fire than an intent to maim. The commandos responded in-kind.

While the skipper made a dash for the end of the ship and away from the land, his deputy was cursorily annihilated by the tight stitchworks of at least three guns, blown into a blood-soaked recoil, and tumbling overboard. His demise saw a crimson-dyed splash in the crystal-clear water, lapping against the steel wreckage.

Troopers isolated and took shots at the final running man with the satchel bag, missing at a distance with their close-quarters submachine guns until a belated silent projectile finally tagged him in the back like a barb to a dartboard, dropping him face-first onto the deck; a signature arrow shaft protruding vertically.

Ceasing fire, Captain Young and a couple of nearby troopers looked past their weapon-drawn shoulders to see Jack Churchill lower his archer's poise with his six-foot longbow.

Young remarked his admiration with a nod gesture.

For him and a few other commandos, this was their first ever time witnessing Churchill's infamous *bow and arrow* action. In all honesty, they had never expected to ever see it in action during real warfare.

*Turns out, it was not a gimmick ...*

They were noticeably impressed.

"*Good shot, sir!*" a man stated, flabbergasted.

"*Well done, sir!*" other men made comment.

Churchill bowed unenthusiastically.

It was all in good sport.

*It was nothing but a thing.*

"Show off," Hardy lastly grunted, wobbling his head. Churchill heard his remark and cast him a sideways glance whilst wearing his winning grin. Without retort, he simply cast a wink at the American, soaking up the various commendations.

A fast-reloading Bruce Giles led a squad of men down close to the lapping ice water where the steel ship wreckage berthed against the pebbly Norwegian shoreline. Oil had spilt out into the clear aqua, clouding it with a murky swirl that stained everything with inky black.

They held their weapons trained on the few unarmed kriegmarines who had survived, sailors and deckhands. They complied with the surrender orders on the land, stepping out before the exposed belly of the beached vessel. They yielded to Commando; hands held high.

"That's the bloody Foehn!" Young accounted, recognizing the trawler from the detailed briefings. There was a significance underlying his tone that suggested a certain value regarding their discovery. "They must have tried to run aground!"

Churchill exclaimed derisively, eyeballing the shipwreck.

"*Tried?* I'd say they very well succeeded."

"Why wouldn't they scuttle the ship out in the fjord?" Young expanded furthermore. "Perhaps there was sensitive intel onboard—"

Before Churchill could contemplate, there resounded a sharp screech and crash within their vicinity, causing all heads to turn and gaze straight towards a row of thin sheds and boathouses that lined the edge of the coast. It was easily within walking distance from the trawler wreckage.

The incoming pitch of shredding tyres accompanied a civilian transport vehicle as it unexpectedly exploded from within one of the closed wooden barn doors of one of the sheds, apparently taking a shortcut down the slope. The car was occupied by two bold sailors, presumably originating from the same ranks of the Foehn in search for transport.

Evidently aware of the arrival of the commandos and the submission of their seafaring kamerads by the beach, the occupants of the fleeing truck were aggressive and brusquely hostile. What ensued was a valiant attempt at a last-ditch effort at triumph from blunder.

Out of the passenger-side door came automatic gunfire, levelled at the rear side of the commandos along the coast whilst these Helden attempted their death-defying intervention along the icy embankment.

Achieving nothing but a deadly response, the side of the rusty grey truck befell an immediate counterstrike from the commandos. In the form of explosive pinwheels of sparks against the metal exterior, the troopers engaged the speeding target. Their combined retaliatory gunfire impacted against the coarse surfaces of the truck, tracing its raucous exodus as the vehicle peeled in a pivot, racing away from the shoreline surprise.

Almost instantly, they capped the German gunner who lifelessly hung aslant from the window port, now less his rapid firing maschinenpistole that clattered discarded against the rocks.

Twisting at the hip in his pose, Churchill was fast on the draw, pinching the head of one of his special explosive arrows devised by QM Slinger Martin; one with a red fletching.

The expert archer found the nocking-point against the bowstring ...

*Yellow-feathered arrows were timed explosives.*
*Red indicated impact detonation.*

Outlining the passage of the speeding vehicle like an inspired hunter-killer of wild game, Churchill loosed the weighted red-tipped, front-heavy projectile with a generous lead at the trajectory path of the charging vehicle as it banked, exploding his specialized impact detonation arrow within a foot of the raggedy vehicle's rear end.

The feat resembled a bolt of lightning, striking the earth mere inches behind the car's travelling path, and discharging with an ear-splitting *crack!* of a strike and throw of powerful force.

The impact detonation arrows were packed with almost 100-grams of *Baratol* (70% equal explosive power of a Mills Bomb grenade). With a flash of light and a brunt of shock, the gravel beneath the rear of the fast-moving vehicle violently detonated, tossing the already unbalanced, speeding car hurtling over onto its roof and blowing off a rear tyre. The vehicle performed a forward flip where it scraped against the earth in a skirt of hot sparks and an unpleasant grind, sliding to a rocky stop, eventuating to a standstill.

Twisted metal and smouldering debris rained down all around the upturned automobile, and in the following moments, a fireball erupted from within the bonnet of the vehicle, turning it into a cremation of the Germans remaining inside.

Within the minutes that followed, the commandos noticed that from the Onslow hovering in the Vågsfjord, a small short-range motorized ship had become launched and was charging towards the coast. Aboard it were five armed sailors in a special antiflash naval battle armament, sent out to secure the wreckage for intelligence.

"*Oi!*"

"*Movement!*"

Snapping all attention firmly back to the Foehn, attention honed in on the last remaining interval of movement aboard the wreckage; the already skewered man with the package aboard the aft end of the vessel. Jack had already arrowed him on his way to the rear end of the boat, but somehow, the persistent skipper prevailed.

Beneath the many shouts and sights of the coastal commandos, the skipper shuffled face down on the Foehn, attempting to shove a satchel bag-looking package towards the edge of the boat; likely intelligence for scuttle.

Guns went off.

Impacts from the well-trained rifle shots impacted against the framework of the ship beside his crawl. The wooden deck splintered in his face, however, he endured, unwavering in his conviction to complete the task at hand—

He made it to the edge ...

With his last breath and as more gunfire assaulted his prone sides, exploding his underarms and finally defeating him, the sailor shoved the package overboard, sending it into the shallows of the Vågsfjorden ...

... all the while, a squinting Jack Churchill trained the sights of his hocked longbow over the target; tracing the clambering sailor as the hail of gunfire raked over him, killing him, and outlining the probable course of the package within his midst as it dropped from the aft.

*Sch-TOFF ...*

The bodkin-tipped arrow launched ahead of the target's trajectory.

As the satchel bag dropped, an arrow pinned it to the side of the vessel approximately six feet from the waterline, staking it in place like a magician's trick shot.

With the navy men inbound to escort the prisoners back to the Kenya, Churchill ordered Six Troop onwards and further along the coast towards the simmering firefight enduring in South Vågsøy.

*It was time for war.*

*Vågsfjorden*
*Vågsøy, Norway*

Less than five minutes later, four minutes after the single naval vessel from the Onslow had arrived to secure the prisoners Churchill's G3 Troop had left from the Foehn, and three minutes after the collapse of the power station, two Higgins LCs reached the vicinity.

Speeding without caution, the small ships tore ripples across the calm reflective surface of the ice-cold fjord like a pair of Black Skimmer birds catching jumping trawl.

Unlike the lone boat on the shoreline, these landing crafts weren't loaded with mere armed sailors to secure surrendered prisoners. These ones were loaded with killer commandos, Hooper's Group 4 and the majority of the floating reserve compiled of No.2 Commandos, fronted by the tempestuous Lieutenant Graeme Black.

The LCs made a beeline from the Kenya to the island landmasses.

The flat back end of the secured Måløy Island was the proposed landing zone as per their game plan. There, it was intended for G4 to dismount and assist the remaining men of G3 inland as a combined force.

Their ships would then be used to ferry back more of the captured prisoners.

However, the battle-hungry lieutenant had another idea in mind ...

"*What's that?*" the beret-clad, flowing imperial moustachioed Lieutenant Black questioned aloud in the open-air vessel to his CO with whom he shared an LC. He combined the enquiry with a pointing gesture, aiming his finger further up the coast and to the pillar of fresh smoke at an amphibious-style wreckage. There was a single navy LC there, securing the shipwreck survivors.

Standing taller beside the navy coxswain and stoker piloting the ship, Hooper opined for an extended moment before responding. His eyes squinted as he observed, bringing up a pair of shaky eyeglasses, noticing that other short-range vessels from the Onslow had everything under control.

Finding it difficult to focus his vision on their turbulent voyage, he managed to read the scraped tag of the trawler's hull through his binocular's zoom:

*The Foehn.*

"*Looks like the navy's got it wrapped up!*" Hooper concluded.

"*Wanna pull in up there instead?*" Black asked—more, requested.

Instinctually, the expert soldier's suspicions were leading him to believe there was more afoot there than met a passing-by eye amidst warfare. Black understood Churchill's men on Måløy were waiting to transport their prisoners back to the ships, but surely this took precedence—as did his lust for combat. This whole macho endeavour was a race as such between him and Mad Jack.

The two had history. This was a contest of sorts.

When they issued the list of commendations after the action, his endgame was to find himself on a podium taller than Churchill.

Persuasively, Black shouted over the wind of the air current, acting the devil on Hooper's shoulder, directing his operational directive to further assist his own agenda. "*They can drop us off and then circle back around to Måløy to get the prisoners!*"

"*And of the Group 3 men?*"

They were supposed to be accompanying them into the village.

"*Fuck 'em! They can sort 'emselves out, surely?!*" Black scowled, not desiring to have to hold the hand of these distant relative No.3 Commando brethren.

Hooper was reluctant to opt against Haydon's wishes, but the hell with it. They were army men about to be on land and in the thick of it.

That meant that, to an extent, the naval jurisdiction of command desisted shortly. This was a field call.

*Hooper gestured a nod.*

Black agreed, adjusting his grip on the Bren gun's forward carry handle and addressing the men for the change of plans while Hooper instructed the driver to follow the Onslow LC's passage, headed into land further up the icy embankment.

Perhaps presumptuous and overly cocksure to the point of arrogant, the No.2 Commandos of Group 4, by hand of Black, devised a strategy regarding a victory for Operation Archery—one with them vastly upon the pedestal.

The two landing crafts started to arrive at the modified location by the run-aground shipwreck, surprising the royal navy guardsmen who were organizing to ferry the few prisoners from the Foehn.

It was ascertained that the ship was one of the few German armed trawlers that the warships had encountered earlier on in the raid, and subsequently pulverized. The smoking ruins still steamed hot from the ferocious naval battle.

There was evidence of a secondary defeat. The dead bodies of several German seamen and kriegsmarine sailors who looked as though they had put up a fight were strewn about the wreckage site. Somewhere down amongst the ice and protruding rocks of the swell, some others bobbed about face down in their own crimson pigment, lapping against the stony shoreline.

Their LCs pulled up gently, grinding their armoured bellies against the rocks so that their drawbridge panels could engage.

The tin hat-wearing men packed aboard dismounted onto dry land quickly, orderly, and in militaristic fashion, with their guns elevated and attentions taut of their surroundings.

There was already an amassed group of surrendered prisoners on the slope, seated with their hands on their heads and surrounded by armed operatives from the Onslow. The royal navy sailors, dressed in noticeably different uniforms than the commandos, ogled Hooper's out-of-place arrival as they disembarked. Their faces were mostly disguised beneath their standard issue anti-flash gear, which was basically like wearing a fire-retardant bedsheet over their heads like a ghost. They had baggy gloves to match, cradling the hideous side-mounted magazine-fed *wired coat hanger*-style hollow stock Sten submachine guns.

"*Sirs* ..." one of them acknowledged with a salute from beneath his brimmed helmet mounted upon his antiflash gear.

"Gentlemen," Hooper gestured with a returned salute before strolling nearer their contained situation guarding the Foehn prisoners. He needed to tear his eyes from the amount of utter carnage done to the beached vessel, not to mention the exploded car just up the slope that still burned afire. "What's happened here, then?"

Black stepped in for a closer look, surveying the aftermath.

The damage dealt here was awesome, and he could not help but stare. His focus climbed the side of the trawler in the background, scanning about the ship wreckage as though he was hunting for clues; for souls to claim, treasures to trove, seeking that praise and commendation to surpass Churchill.

Black scanned across the many departed carcasses of the kriegsmarine sailors, both on the ground around the ship and on her bow, and his panning stare snagged on something: a face-down boche atop of the hull. There was presently two navy men with Stens assessing the destruction from above, both with slightly befuddled expressions about a particular dispatch ...

*There was an arrow protruding from the sailor's back.*

The feathered fletching of the medieval projectile were even more out of place than this ship was being on land.

Unlike them, Black seemed unsurprised by the finding.

His lips pursed and he huffed, turned his head back to Hooper and the navy men with whom he conversed, intercepting any response to the question mark that his CO had left regarding what had happened here.

"*Mad Jack* happened here."

"*Sir,*" a voice sternly reported, belonging to one of the two sailors on top of the trawler near Churchill's ostentatious victim. He was on his knee, peering over the bulbous edge of the ship's exterior in the interest of further observing something hanging from the hull ...

*A satchel bag strung up on an arrow.*

The navy coxswain and stoker piloting the remaining LC repositioned themselves, coming about the partially submerged aft end of the Foehn, gliding in beneath the protruding arrow and dangling satchel bag, reaching up to pluck it like a ripened fruit.

They all watched on as they couriered the valise-looking bag of luggage to an intermediary soldier who was ashore, who then passed it onto the royal navy sailor who appeared to be in-charge standing before Captain Hooper and Lieutenant Black.

"Let me have that, sailor!" Hooper exclaimed, pulling rank. The commando snatched the case from the sailors and spun it around, placing it down low on a flat rock in order to open her up and examine the contents.

Black took a step closer, peeking over their shoulders.

The case latches popped, and Hooper lifted the hood, presenting a clutter of disorganized folders with printed paperwork, stamped with German text.

He pulled one out, recognizing it almost instantly.

His eyes glazed upon the treasure, scoffing, "It's a *codebook* ..."

Black could see that beneath all the documents there were typing machine components, and even fresh ribbons and gears.

*This was an Enigma cypher machine.*

The codebooks could potentially contain a wealth of signs, countersigns, codewords, and possibly even all the radio callsigns of perhaps every German vessel in northern Europe. This was an *enormous* intelligence boon for the raiding party, and possibly the most valuable prize to be claimed this entire battle.

"Better get Haydon on the line," Black remarked in the wordlessness and absence of his CO, who was currently entranced at the finding. "Tell him we may have just struck gold ..."

Hooper pulled himself back from the alluring brink of enchantment, tripping up in his mind at the sentiment that G3 had possessed this intelligence, and left it behind for somebody else to claim.

"But ... why didn't Churchill want it?" he questioned. In and of itself for Operation Archery, the find he was presently holding in his hands was worth a medal.

Black's attention drifted, allured towards the sound of ongoing gunfire in the distance. He remarked, "Jack was never one for trinkets and trophies ..."

*He was for war.*

Eager to move out, Black was of that same like mind.

*South Vågsøy (coastline – Commando FOB)*
*Vågsøy, Norway*

A fortuitous convergence occurred along the coast outside of the ground forces' mobile headquarters. Although the Commando FOB was mostly an ammunitions depot for runners to restock the Troops at the front, it was also a mobile triage for the wounded. All round, it was a hive of activity.

Sorry Corry was the chief corpsman present, treating the many gunshot and shrapnel wounds as commandos were brought in from the advance in South Vågsøy. Although some injuries were more serious than others, the overall minimal casualties the British had sustained hinted them being quite blessed this day of days.

The injured Lieutenant Arthur Komrower and the burned portion of Two Troop who had not been absorbed by Forrester's Four Troop after their unfortunate mishap during the commencement of the operation were still present in and around the perimeter of the FOB. Many of the men were still receiving medical attention after the friendly fire disaster at the dawn of the raid, which resulted in a number of severe burns by a phosphorous shelling. Since then, those who were able were doing their part, assisting with the other injured soldiers being brought into the mobile triage from the front.

The navy were ferrying the stabilized wounded back and forth on stretchers to the transport ships that would arrive along the shoreline from the Kenya or Onslow. They also helped a detachment keep under guard the growing numbers of escorted captured enemy soldiers and quislings from the raid on the village. A large collective of POWs were situated with their backs against a rocky alcove, staring down the barrels of at least six machine guns, waiting until the next row of prisoner transport vessels arrived to taxi them to the warships.

At last, reaching the FOB from Måløy, Jack Churchill's two-dozen Six Troop commandos arrived at the established position. They took inventory of the ammo stock, taking what they needed to fill their empty magazine pouches and grenade pockets, and even positively charged some of the wounded boys with some appreciative remarks and joking jousts. Captain Young and Lieutenant Giles were amongst the ranks, as was radioman Wills and American tagalong journalist Hardy.

At almost the same time that Churchill's men arrived from along the coast and direction of Måløy Island, a detachment of familiar commandos from JFG's Three Troop entered the FOB from the western quadrant of South Vågsøy. They looked beaten, muddy, and bloodied, and were seemingly now led by Corporal Knocker White and Joe Mills. Troopers Peel and Drain were amongst the cluster. Bushed and blue, the lot looked as though they had sustained some losses after a heavy feud with the enemy. In their wake was British Pathé reporter William Mericle and his cameraman. The two of them may have seemed out of place amidst the strut of the battle-worn commandos, but they were unreservedly performing their duties, filming and providing commentary as they watched the undertaking unfold. They watched now as a group of POWs were processed and escorted along the coast.

Mericle's commentary could be overheard:

"... *Those who surrendered were sent back under armed escort to be taken care of aboard our ships lying offshore. A ferry service of barges takes them across. Local quislings made to do something charitable for once in their miserable lives and are made to carry the wounded* ..."

"Want to go say *hullo* to your mate, Felix?" Churchill bantered to his American friend, who simply gave a fake smile for an instant upon laying eyes on his rival, the Miracle Man. An avid enjoyer of displeasing his friend for a laugh, Churchill grinned upon witnessing Hardy's non-verbal response.

"Sir," Knocker White greeted, stepping near and allowing for his trailing men to slump onto rocky seats or turned over empty ammunition crates. Some even just took a knee in the meanwhile.

"Knocker," Churchill responded, generously taking his hand and not the least bit surprised to find that even in the chaos of battle, the corporal still managed to find time to chew bubble-gum.

He could immediately tell his friend had been through the ringer. He had seen that look before, in France, back during the Second Manchester days.

Churchill noticed that his rate of mastication was slower than usual. "You winning?"

White bowed grimly but could not shake a lingering thousand-yard stare. It was of sorrow, not fatigue. "Inland resistance was heavier than we expected. The lads have taken some tolls ..."

Before he had the chance to fully explain, the lot of them were made aware of yet another group's arrival upon this contrasting rendezvous point.

Colonel Durnford-Slater's detail unexpectedly towed in from another angle of the village—or, at least, who was left of it. There was the six-foot-tall Lieutenant Head and the spotless skin of de la Torre's now blood-spattered cheeks, all of which looked as though they had seen better days and had all encountered the same unforeseen and upsetting enemy sniper presence about South Vågsøy.

Jack hailed, raising his longbow as a signal. "John!"

Durnford-Slater saw the icon and gravitated to Churchill.

Drafting closer, he glanced about the crowd with his concaved brow, noticing the assemblage of familiar faces, manoeuvring amongst several wounded men on aligned stretchers.

He loved Commando.

It pained him to see some of his men this way; bleeding for the cause—his cause, or, what felt like it was once his. Now, the blood of a great many men bled just as green.

Of every brave commando he encountered in this FOB, Durnford-Slater gave them all humble handshakes, respectful pats on the arm or leg, informing them of his presence and of his gratification of their service. He had all the time in the world for his men—even when he did not.

The two commanding officers met.

They were the only ones in green berets.

"Jack! Thank God Group 3 is here. We haven't got much time to waste," Durnford-Slater regarded, aggressively shaking Churchill's hand, and then the hands of Young Young, Knocker White, and then issuing Mills and Giles respectful nods across the range in the background. His eyes wandered beyond their group and into the backdrop. "... where's the rest of the floating reserve?"

Churchill clenched his jaw.

Durnford-Slater didn't require a response.

He knew his man too well.

"You didn't wait for them, did you?"

Jack stood tall, assuring, "I'm sure they'll be along any minute."

Durnford-Slater scanned past their shoulders, searching for Hooper or for Black, but was sure he could not see anyone from G4. In fact, in his hurry to join the fight, Churchill had only brought half of G3 to this rendezvous point. His dissatisfaction was short-lived, however, as he knew at the heart of it all, he could settle happily for Mad Jack and his Merry Men.

"Figured time was *not* of the essence."

"You'll do," Durnford-Slater remarked to Churchill humorously.

Komrower limped over to their gathering from the beach. He was leaning on a crutch due to his severe scorching across his leg. Burns were also up his arm, torso, neck, and side of his face near his eye. The wounds had been properly seen to by Corry, wrapped tight in field dressings and white bandages, and morphine had been administered. A bit of time had passed since the injury had been sustained, and although the stinging sensation had gone, there was an onset of stiffness and immobility from the inflammation.

"Arty," Churchill carefully embraced his hand in a shake, checking out the well-being of his friend. "You look like a tattered turd, lad."

Komrower chuckled in laugh-or-cry sarcasm.

"Yeah, well that's what happens when a Hampden takes a hot, runny shit on your head, eh?"

"We saw," Churchill uttered, sorrowfully. "Lost a few good men."

Komrower bobbed his head. "I got lucky. Linge saved me ..."

"Marty?!" Jack splendidly remarked. Although Churchill loved Linge, he was aware of the existing rivalry and Komrower's detest of the men of the NOR.I.C.1, due to historic reasons. This likely changed things dramatically for his outlook.

Durnford-Slater asked seriously, assisting in stabilizing his officer with his arm on his shoulder. It was the first time he had seen Komrower since effectively benching him at the FOB. "How are you doing, Arty?"

"It looks worse than it feels," Komrower explained. "Keen to get back out in the fight, Colonel ... if you'll have me."

Durnford-Slater cocked his head and responded to the captain. "Arthur, I need someone here to guard the FOB. You're best fitted for that duty with your... restriction—"

"Where's Giles ...?" interrupted Churchill, realizing after looking around the vicinity for some of the other distinguished 'all-star' commandos of the service who were absent.

His question was met by silence as it befell the enquiry from the many blank faces of Three Troop.

Finally, Knocker White reported with a glum expression that developed from his blank stare out into the distance of the misty fjord. "He ... didn't make it."

The news shook the unknowing No.3 Commandos.

Churchill's sterling stare gazed across all their faces, especially noting George Peel's expression at the back. He was born with narrow facial features, but the young lad seemed especially long-faced in the wake of this loss. Even Sergeant Mills, who was generally a carefree hothead, seemed distraught by the death of the hero commando ... and then, suddenly, as though they had almost forgotten about the blood-relation, their view fell upon Bruce Giles ...

*Johnny Giles' younger brother.*

Churchill's brow sunk.

In the silent revelation, Peter Young extended an arm, grappling Bruce Giles' suddenly wavering stance with support as an invisible wind gushed against his form. The news of his brother's death fell upon Giles like an anvil, but he withstood the welling and raised his chin, even though it clearly began to quiver as he tried to hold back all emotion.

Everyone went briskly quiet in respect.

For context, Knocker White added to both Durnford-Slater and Churchill, and the others surrounding the moment. "... we took out an enemy relay that was blocking our outgoing radio communications. Captain Giles, he ... he's the reason the whole of G2 got their comms back. He led the charge. Held nothing back."

"A most unfortunate loss," Durnford-Slater declared with an undertone of sentimentality. "We've lost many brave men on these shores this morning."

Churchill bobbed in accord.

Durnford-Slater affirmed. "Sacrifices to the cause."

"Dillon?" Churchill asked quietly and Durnford-Slater shook his head bearing the ounce of sorrowfulness he was allowed to show at this point as the boss. Dildo Dillon had sadly perished during the sniper wave.

Head said from the flank. "He was hit by those phantom snipers."

"Alpine Huntsmen," well-versed in their unexpected additional adversary, Churchill informed him and all those present. "The sharp shooters on the ridge, that's their M.O. Their element is derived from a mountain ranger unit within the SS. Their unit is called the Gebirgsjäger. It's that same additional resistance that Lieutenant Clement reported in Holvik, and what we also encountered on Måløy Island."

"A monkey in the wrench," Durnford-Slater clarified.

"A pain in the arse," Churchill simplified further.

"They're a real ace up the sleeve for the 181st defences," Young added, dispassionately forward-thinking.

"I'm willing to bet that you guys came upon something similar at the churchyard?" Churchill gandered. "Extra gunmen, maybe utilizing differing tactics to the usual Wehrmacht avenue?"

Knocker White, Mills, and Peel nodded in accord.

They had encountered stiffer than usual confrontation at the enemy HQ, and he had noted that the last men they took down within the church had bared SS uniforms with a previously unrecognized unit's insignia: *an edelweiss.*

When Churchill spoke about the enemy group, elaborating with his proficient knowledge of their forces, he could feel Peter Young's attentive stare upon his words, observing him purposely withholding word of his own personal vendetta against the suspected leader of the Gebirgsjäger.

If Young had been a disloyal, ladder-climbing type, he could have spent this ammunition now to knock the legs out from his direct superior and elevate himself into the higher ranks of Commando. This was testimony not only to his allegiance to Jack Churchill, but to the honour of No.3 Commando.

Churchill's sterling stare focused on Durnford-Slater. "We must proceed the rest of the way with a heightened caution. From what I understand, these guys are extremely well trained and formidable, even to Commando."

"Understood, Jack."

Durnford-Slater was not unaware of the blood family present and was therefore, not without sentiment, but he was trained to stay on track where the others momentarily derailed.

"Who has been left in command of Three Troop?"

"Eh, no-one specific," White remarked, tensing his jaw on his squished chewy. "We lost all our superior officers taking the church ..."

Durnford-Slater stated sternly from beneath his lampshade moustache, making his admiration apparent in the process. "Corporal, you mean to tell me that you lost all your Troop leaders, and still completed your objective?"

Knocker White raised his squalid face. "Eh, yes, sir. I had a detachment of men remain at the churchyard where we have safely isolated the majority of the town's population. We've also got a group of captured prisoners there that need processing ..."

"Arthur, can your Troop spare any officers?" Durnford-Slater began to ask his knights around the table.

Komrower shook his head with regret. "I sent all my boys off with Algy. They'd somewhere along the north-east flank by now, probably near the warehouses."

*An ignored voice in the background: "Sir—"*

"What about you, Jack? Can you spare someone to command in JFG's absence?"

"*Colonel, sir!*" the small voice interrupted again, this time with a tone that demanded attention. It was Bruce Giles. "With respect ... I'll take over Three Troop."

Durnford-Slater exchanged a discreet gleam with Churchill—one which Mad Jack did not seem to oppose.

*One Giles for another.*

"Lieutenant ... are you sure you're up to it?"

Giles nodded, already past it. "Orders, Colonel?"

Churchill's eyes flowed from JFG's dutiful younger brother and back to Durnford-Slater, almost unable to contain the proud contentment he held for this kid. He began to word in his mind a prospective manifesto regarding such.

Durnford-Slater took his time and spoke clearly.

"Very well. Return to the church and adopt the men. Make sure the locals are safe and return with the prisoners. Prepare them for transport back to the Kenya. I'll signal the ferry ships for you now."

"Very good, sir," Giles affirmed. He exchanged a look with Churchill and Young, his now previous COs, before continuing with the new duty of filling his big brother's even bigger shoes.

Churchill conversed with his radioman, Wills, who he no longer required and could spare due to their Group amalgamation. "Leftenant?"

"Sir?"

"Go with them."

"Yes, sir."

Churchill added, referencing a prior context of the funny man. "Remember, if you manage to speak with your mate Hitler again, ask him about the General Franz Halder thing, will you?"

"Yes, sir. A wasted opportunity of being the holder of France."

Jack nodded. It was a joke, but he seriously wanted to pose the question.

Giles selected to also take with him Private Peel, who knew the way to the church, and who would support him—both mentally and emotionally—for the remainder of this day ... if not further beyond, as this friendship would undoubtedly endure afterwards.

"Excuse me?! Sir?!" Peel called, halting their en route advance oddly. It was in earshot of all of the officers on the beach, who watched the exchange.

Stride prematurely broken, Bruce Giles paused silently, turning to face him. His eyeline lowered, watching as George Peel held out his fingerless gloved right hand in offer of an honourable handshake, and then looked him in the face to notice a sliver of emotion welling behind his eyes. Peel had obviously fought alongside his brother—perhaps to the end. They had formed a bond during battle—an unbreakable one.

Peel muttered, unwavering in the confidence of his gesture, "I just wanted to shake the hand of the brother of the bravest man I have ever met ..."

He hadn't fully known it, but Peel had been with JFG during his final foray into the fray, and been present when he had made the ultimate sacrifice. In a way, he had gotten to know his brother better than he could.

A second after, Giles took it. Firmly.

His chin furrowed.

The two pulled each other into a shoulder-to-shoulder embrace, allowing temporarily for emotions to escape.

Overcome with sentiment, Churchill regarded his reflections aloud now that he was only standing before Durnford-Slater, Young Young, Knocker White, Mills, and Komrower.

"That kid ... he just got hit harder than any casualty present on this rock, and he's vowed to keep moving forward. Let that be a testament to us all."

Tranquillity silenced the air for an extended moment.

After a brief silence, Captain Young raised a question as an icebreaker. It was inferring that the entire No.3 band was back together for the rest of the Archery tour, '42.

"What's next for us, then, Major? Colonel?"

Durnford-Slater bobbed his head, exhuming preparedness.

They were now one big unit, restocked and ready to leap back into the fray ...

"*Sir,*" a radioman rushed in from the FOB offered intelligence to Komrower, and thusly Durnford-Slater, Churchill, and every other high-ranking superior who was present. He carried news as he did his walkie-talkie piece to his radio backpack. "*Captain Forrester has just requested assistance in the warehouse district. He said the remainder of the enemy have pooled there ...*"

The warehouse district was the final stop before the hotel.

Durnford-Slater understood the broadcast, and shared an accord with those surrounding him, still awaiting his response ...

He said singly: "Reload."

# 11
## *Necessary Risks*

Crisscrossing the countless corners of the spliced streets through the winter warzone, the second wave of British Commando reinforcements stormed the front. They progressed shy of the view of the notable snipers, aware of the likelihood of their positioning upon the distant ridgeline, and journeyed through the war-torn village of South Vågsøy.

They regarded the handiwork left in the wake of Four Troop's warpath; spot fires, smoking rubble, spent cartridges, and dead Germans, who now rested peacefully in the spattered snow.

Captain Young and Knocker White took point for Durnford-Slater's newly embroiled entourage of commandos as the combined Group chased the frontline—which wasn't difficult to track. They simply followed the sound of warfare.

Guns locked and loaded; a weapon was present in every trooper's hand. Berets, beanies, or brodies were clad, donned upon scowling and dutiful expressions, bearing the weight of a war on their shoulders.

These were ready for anything on their warpath.

Unstoppable. Unkillable.

*Lieutenant-Colonel John Durnford-Slater ...*

*Major Jack Churchill ...*

And *the Merry Men:*

*Captain Young, Lieutenant Head, Corporal Knocker White, Sergeant Mills, de la Torre.* Tagalong American and British reporters *Felix Hardy* and *William Mericle* were in amongst the rest of the other two dozen commandos compiled from the motley sources of Two, Three, and Six Troop.

"*... Reinforcements have landed as we set about the destruction of the garrison ...*" the Miracle Man commentated into the microphone of his portable dictation machine as the entourage of commandos advanced. Hardy was in front of Mericle and his cameraman—thankfully, so that they did not see the American newspaper journalist roll his eyes at the running commentary. Pencil and notepad in hand, jotting detail, he was admittedly just jealous of the tech Mericle afforded ...

They met little resistance on their way west through the battle-stricken wintertime village, catching up with a detachment of men belonging to Captain Forrester's cumbersome Four Troop upon the northeastern flank of South Vågsøy. Also with them would have been Martin Linge's men of the NOR.I.C.1, however Four's unit numbers had been expanded upon when it had absorbed the men from Three Troop. It had therefore made the biggest impact on its vector, leaving enemy positions in flame and ruin in their charging onslaught through the quadrant.

Forrester and Linge's combined brute force had pushed hard through the town, easily winning any urban or street combat, and were now situated somewhere along the outskirts overlooking the spacious warehouse district.

On-point for this modest foray, the baby-faced Young Young looked around each corner of the eerily quiet battle zone. The men traipsed in the echoic footsteps of Four Troop's advance, observing fresh suggestions of warfare that littered every corner, evident here via a burned-out emplacement. The snow-blanketed floor was embossed in boot treads and muddy abrasions, even coloured with crimson blemishes from dripping wounds.

They were hot on the tail of Algy Forrester's Four Troop.

Forever monotonal, Mericle narrated the scene as they advanced quietly past dead Germans in the streets and burnt houses. "... *Germans begin defending from house to house, which means we have to engage them in the most deadly form of warfare: street fighting. Barricading themselves in houses, many Germans are burned to death ...*"

They could hear the pounding bass of gunfire further north and through the village and see towering smoke plumes from what appeared to be the remnants of the recently destroyed power station beyond that. It was a beacon for their direction towards the action.

"This way ..." Young commented past his shoulder and to his following of almost thirty commandos, which included their CO and second-in-command, Durnford-Slater and Churchill, respectively.

The beret-clad dome of Jack Churchill bowed, allowing for this own second-in-charge taking the lead and relaying his order. He had Knocker White with his pump-action and Mills with his duel pistols moving up at his flanks, and the colonel amongst some of the other commandos from Six Troop at their six.

Suddenly, a sniper shot cut off their advance.

A well-placed bullet pierced into the snowy street an inch before Young's barrel chest, causing the trooper to recoil behind cover as the resonance of the shot boomed through these momentarily quiet streets.

The standstill reeled Churchill in his stream.

Longbow looped about his shoulder and Thompson in hand, Jack moved up, and the two re-peeked the edge of the corner, spotting the gunner in the second-storey attic window of what appeared to be an abandoned Norwegian home with an advantageous position guarding this open thoroughfare. He had himself a valuable position above the street, firing again and again from his semi-automatic Mauser rifle, punching pockmarks into the snow before their cover, pinning their advance.

Young exchanged a glance with Churchill.

"Your call, Captain," Churchill regarded between them, implying that he was entrusting the next call of action to his subordinate. He used a respectful teaching voice, prepared to take charge in this action but waiting to see the capability of Young Young. It seemed how Young was moving forth with Churchill's hunger for vengeance and personal vendetta close to his chest, it was only fair for him to finally allow for the ambitious Troop leader to take charge—possibly earn a Distinguished Conduct Medal of sorts.

Still acceptant of the challenge, Young conveyed thoroughly his sit-rep. "Single shooter ... fifty-metres north ... second window, left ..."

He next glanced back at Jack, momentarily tentative on how to progress at this juncture. He had said his piece earlier to Churchill, making it clear he desired control. This was Churchill's way of letting him take charge, and he knew it. He was behind the wheel.

This urban environment was a shooting gallery for these dug-in defenders. They had to do something to eradicate this shooter, for running past and leaving him could simply put another man in jeopardy from another position.

*Bam!*

Cutting off his chain of thought, another, new shooter announced his presence. He had a slight angle on them from an alternate position.

"*Sniper!*" a voice shouted aft their commando cavalcade.

Shots suddenly erupted from another location, somewhere behind their position. It was as if they had somehow inadvertently manoeuvred their progressive advance into a pocket of remaining enemy that Four Troop had somehow moved past, thus leaving behind stragglers who were now apparently coming out of the woodwork.

Young had to think fast. Act faster.

Churchill's stare intensified in the sudden onset of chaos.

He could see Young fret, optimizing his calculations to retaliate against the fabled Alpine Huntsmen rather than regular Wehrmacht strays, of which these likely were, for they would need to tailor a response towards either enemy appropriately. Churchill stated to Young, in reference to the shooters potentially being the dreaded Huntsmen. "This isn't them ..."

"How do you know?" Young questioned as he pressed his shoulder tight into cover as the intensity of war increased all around them.

Churchill flicked him a glint. "... because we're not dead."

"Shooters behind, Jack!" Durnford-Slater commented above the increasing noise in the tight confines of this back street, trundling around Mills and White to address the point men. The environment was ripe for an ambuscade. "We've got to move—"

"*Sir! Enemy close!*" a panicked voice shouted as loud, automatic gunfire exploded from within their queue of troopers in the street that had snaked its way in a column between houses.

"*Ambush!*" another Brit shouted as commandos everywhere dropped down lower and tensed, putting their backs to a wall or against one another, weapons raised and defensive.

In the moments to follow, the men were hit from multiple elevated enemy positions by standard 181st infantry, judging by their lack of overall coordination and marksmanship.

Nonetheless, the ambush still bore them fruit.

Two Six Troop commandos were hit by a shooter with a submachine gun lying prone on a low rooftop that had an inclining angle on their column. He sprayed over the edge with his automatic, striking the two unexpecting troopers from above across their shoulders, causing them to collapse and drop their guns as they writhed in an overbearing agony.

A handful of other commando troopers were fast to react, shooting back at the gunner and annihilating him through the wooden awning he occupied. The entire panel collapsed in a released curtain of cached snow and broken wood. They traced his collapse with the many spurts and chatter of their own automatic submachine guns, drilling the tumbling corpse after the German landed in amongst the rubble, killing him dead.

"*Move! Move!*" Knocker White bellowed as the timber cabin beside his locale vented to splintered cavities, chasing his movements behind Mills' displacement in the open. The two darted across the open to seek refuge as all of the commandos displaced.

Around the vicinity, the Commando troops split up to survive. To survive this ambush, they would have to engage in a deathmatch of skirmishes through the snowy and steamy village streets.

Another German shooter in a window who had allowed for these targets to advance into their kill zone finally began to fire, striking radioman de la Torre in the middle of the back, thrusting the young trooper into a grimacing face-plant in the sludge between their scampering boots as they fled.

Amidst the chaotic displacement, Durnford-Slater witnessed his loyal radioman's collapse, and he immediately searched for the origin of the gunfire. He paused for a half-second in order to draw a scowling gleam of determination upon the shooter's location. Dropping to a knee, he then clamped his wrist and unloaded the entire seven-shot clip of his pistol blindly through the sliver of a gap between two closed-over wooden shutters. Even the bullets that hit the shutters still penetrated through the timber, impacting against the flesh of the enemy infantryman within with meaty brunts.

Durnford-Slater watched through the smoke of his empty, slide-locked handgun as the perforated culprit seemed to bounce from a wall behind the window, stumbling forwards and through the hinged shutters. Collapsing out the port, he plunged to the snow outside.

"*Trooper!*" Durnford-Slater shouted amidst the disordered bedlam of the ambush as volleys of fire strafed his flanks and peppered the walls of the surrounding housing. He bravely reached down to assist de la Torre, and it then became evident that the trooper had sustained the shot via the wireless receiver backpack. The radio was smouldering, popping with combusting electrics, emitting effervescent electric smoke. It was damaged beyond repair but had inadvertently saved this commando's life.

The ever-sardonic Lieutenant Head appeared covering Durnford-Slater as he helped up de la Torre. "Sir! Let's get you—and me—out of the line of fire, yeah?!"

As this happened, the guarding Head suddenly copped a bullet to the bicep, and he reeled with clenched teeth. The shock of the surging pain caused him to fall to a knee, almost dropping his weapon.

"*Charley!*" Durnford-Slater shouted, freeing his clutch on the raised de la Torre to collect his old friend and leftenant, catching his collapse into the snow. The lot of them were a combined mess out in the open of the back-alley sludge. They were in a bad position.

de la Torre was fast to slip off his destroyed radio pack and collect his sleet-covered weapon from the sludge, immediately loosing rounds at the shooter who targeted them, desperate to lay cover, however, they seemed to be getting shot at from all angles.

Persevering the chaos, the trio upped and sought refuge ...

German aggressors opened up with automatic fire from a ground-level house at the end of the street. The barrage caused a tangent of covering Six Troop soldiers to duck and displace as the area about their stance became unrelentingly assaulted. It also caused Hardy, Mericle, and the camera operator to scurry for shelter as the world around their televised bubble became an actual warzone.

Hardy was quicker to react, shoving them both through an aslant doorway that led into an honest Norwegian home, and he shuffled in behind them through the maelstrom, avoiding death by inches.

They stumbled in through the door like loaded drunks.

Hardy was fast to contain their retreat by closing over the rickety timber door, enveloping them in shade and immediately quietening the chaos.

"*Fuck! Cunt!*" Mericle cursed profanely, finding his breath in the mayhem. He grappled with his cameraman. "*Christ on a bike!*"

Hardy gazed at the man: the intimidating, intrepid, and infamously high-profiled, well-respected connoisseur columnist from Pathé, notoriously nicknamed *the Miracle Man* ... for the first time, seeing his boundless cowardice. The man was a phoney.

Felix Hardy always saw himself as half the journalist reporter that William Mericle was. He used to idolize his professionalism ... now, he despised his timidity and this false persona that he wore so egotistically— an act that could get others killed through his craven inaction. He was nothing more than a spineless correspondent, well away from his sedentary position. This forthcomingness towards becoming the world's greatest war correspondent was a certain façade.

Hardy was the real combat journalist here, and he suddenly felt empowered.

"*How are we not fucking dead?!*" Mericle shouted.

Hardy calmly retorted in the deafening silence that followed in their ringing ears. "Day's young, *Miracle Man*."

"*They're shooting from everywhere!*" a panicked voice commentated.

Young exclaimed through the cacophony of surrounding gunfire.

"*These fuckers were waiting for us! We're fish in a barrel!*"

In the tight urban streets, Young shouted above the anarchy as he and Churchill reared against a shaky wall below a sloped awning with their guards up. Commandos on either side of their flank happened to get tagged by fire, resulting in them falling to the ground, hurling clouds of powdered snow.

Like many other of the commandos dreadfully seeking refuge within the houses on the streets for cover, Churchill and Young reacted fast as they felt enemy lines of fire draw a bead on their position. Not unlike falling dominoes, closing in on them from either side, they felt the heat of it: of iron-sights aim, lining them up like a spotlight in the darkness.

Nowhere to run.

Nowhere to hide.

They both pushed off the wall of their cover as it became assaulted by a hailstorm of gunfire, and both men took a galloping charge towards the boarded window of a residence across the tight street. They tucked their legs after a running leap, cannonball-smashing through the closed-over window and disappearing inside with conjoined shatters of breaking glass and tumbling wood splinters.

Outside and still on the street, Durnford-Slater and de la Torre reversed through a held-open doorway, carting with them the wounded Head, right as Knocker White appeared with a few other courageous commandos.

He covered their retreat with his ruinous shotgun, trading fire with some of the ambushing German grunts as another pair of enemy rooftop shooters appeared above.

They were quickly pegged by the British after they gunned down another commando trooper in the open street who was running for the door, and they both collapsed to the slanted rooftops, shaking the icicles from its edging before sliding off and onto the ground below with an almighty crunch.

Knocker White traced their demise with his gun, blasting another shell into the cloud of powder fogging their collapse before towing inside behind the others.

Once inside the unoccupied premises, Durnford-Slater, Head, and de la Torre were welcomed by Mills as he returned from running the internal perimeter.

"It's clear," he reported, kicking over a wooden table in the middle of the room for more protection. He then questioned upon seeing Head's messy arm injury. "Purple heart, sir?"

"I bloody wish!" Head retorted through a grimace as Durnford-Slater shoved him into a blanket-lined cushion chair within the residence, thrusting clear a knee-high tea table, sending someone's long forgotten cold beverage splashing to the floor and breaking the ceramic.

"Flesh wound! Strap it tight!" Durnford-Slater stated as he stepped back, observing the first aid as de la Torre moved in with a prepared bandage roll, wrapping Head's blood-soaked arm tight. Now clear of his cumbersome radio backpack, it appeared he had been devalued to field medic.

While de la Torre applied the field dressing, the caring colonel sidled beside his trooper, assessing the scorch marks left to his shoulder and spine from the exploded radio pack.

"Trooper, you good?"

"Good, sir!" de la Torre admitted modestly. "Helps to keep me warm in the cold!"

Mills declared once Knocker White returned after closing the door. They were all still in panic. "Pricks are shootin' from everywhere!"

"Crafty buggers," White concurred, reloading. "Orders sir?"

"Hold the ground," Durnford-Slater said sternly. "They're stragglers left behind from Forrester's flank. Their heads are barely above water, lads. This is our ground now and they're on borrowed time. We must clear this avenue for passage."

"*Sir.*"

"*Yes, sir.*"

The men spread out, holding their position in the house.

Knocker White stepped in low to a front window, breaking the frosted glass with the butt of his shotgun before protruding the barrel and firing off a blast towards an enemy-inhabited position, and Mills did the same out a back window with an extended handgun, pelting a blindsided shooter with a hit to the back and jostling him over into the snow.

Another two stahlhelm soldiers emerged with rifles, charging around the corner to obtain a flank on commandos in the street. Mills fired a round into their chests, folding them both over and into a collapse in the mud and sleet.

After a few winning strikes, Mills' window was assaulted in a different kind of way ...

*A stick grenade.*

The weighty potato masher clipped the edge of the broken glass above his hand, tumbling in and falling to the rug-lain wooden floor with a weighty *thump.*

Mills looked down, scanning for it in the confines, identifying the M24 stielhandgranate as it rolled. Smoke emitted from its wooden-handle end cap, signifying the countdown fuse.

"*Fuck!*" he shouted. "*Grenade!*"

Knocker White reeled inwards from his position shooting out the opposite window. His eyes were wide upon realizing the existence of the explosive, helpless to do anything in time. The same thing with Durnford-Slater, de la Torre, and Head. They stooped in low behind the up-turned table, hoping it was enough for salvation from the device.

Acting quick, Mills dropped to his hip in a controlled collapse and swept up the stielhandgranate. In the same scoop manoeuvre, he accurately flicked it straight out the same window hole with enough force to hopefully send it clear—

*Bhoom!*

In a blinding flash and brunt of orange fire, the timed explosive detonated mere feet from the outer wall of the building.

The window glass shattered. The wooden slats of the wall dislodged.

Part of the rickety wall collapsed inwards from the force of the blast, bringing down a portion of the roof that sealed the opening almost as fast as it had become exposed.

Dust and smoke enveloped everything in the aftermath.


*... boom.*

A *distant explosion.*

On-point as the unit moved through the snowy streets of lower South Vågsøy, observing the aftermath of the Commando battle zone and the wake of war, the attentive Lieutenant Graeme Black's ears pricked like a bloodhound on the hunt ... they were hot on the trail of the elusive Six Troop and No.3 Commando who had recently left the FOB—and not waited for them.

His tracker senses honed in on the direction of the action, sourcing it out from the numerous other bursts of gunfire and random detonations in the surrounding distances.

This one was fresh, close.

This one ... *was Jack.*

"There!" he asserted, holding their tactical progression in the pursuit of G3. He turned and looked back to his CO, Captain Hooper, who corresponded to the clue with a nodding gesture, signalling for his blonde moustache point man to carry on and lead the way.

Clutching the folded bipod like a forward grip, Black led the way from behind the folded-leaf rear and canted foresight of his Bren gun.


Although the volume of the surrounding ambush was appearing to subside, gunshots still resounded in intervals about the vicinity.

By usher of Hardy, Mericle and his cameraman had sought refuge in a modest little home in amongst the bedlam, remaining concealed and quiet while the battle raged on around their establishment, letting Commando take the fight while they hung back.

In the shade of the indoors, Hardy inched over to one of the slat windows, peeking through the curtain out into the light and viewing some of the outdoor commotion.

"Are you insane! Get away from there!" the cringing Mericle exclaimed from his corner in the shadows, huddling down low beside a mattress on a bedframe, tucked in tight beside his equally as frightened cameraman.

Leering in his position, Hardy cast them an appalled gleam.

"Relax, we're safe in here," he stated, observing the situation and making a calculated guess on Commando's scenario resulting positive, considering the clamour was fading. He could make out more green berets out in the open than hostiles. Commando was persevering through the crossfire. The threat may have still existed, but these stray Germans had nothing and were clambering on the threads at the end of their rope even mounting this ambush. Commando would win this poxy arm-wrestle, it was a matter of time.

Suddenly, as if an intrusion to prove Hardy wrong was on cue, a disturbance in a connecting room at the rear of the small house caught all three of the men's attention. It sounded like a window lifting and an element of weighted furniture shifting across floorboards. It sounded specifically like someone climbing in through a budged crawlspace.

Hardy's coy expression seemed to drop, mimicking one more in-line with Mericle's own of dread and concern.

Their heads turned and followed their sideways glances towards the back rooms of the property.

*Could it have been a commando ...?*

*Perhaps seeking refuge from the fight in the streets outside ...?*

Before the issue would be fully contemplated, the suspenseful question answered itself, and two instinctive enemy infantrymen saw themselves inside from the cold of the winter wars of Vågsøy and the heat of the firefight. Snow on their shoulders from rolling around in the ice and displacing, the two riflemen saw themselves in, sweeping the area with their big rifles to secure the main area. Becoming quiet and communicating in German whispers, they next entered the bedroom from behind the sights of their guns. The room was ... *empty?*

Hardy, Mericle, and the cameraman were nowhere to be seen.

The two brute soldiers advanced into the room, perhaps sure they had heard somebody within. Eventually content with it being empty, they leant in close and peeked through the window in order to gain a vantage point on some of the British Commandos running about the street.

As one soldier did, his view panned into one of the blind spots: a backroom ...

... where, just out of his sight, were three war correspondents lurking in a petrified silence, praying he wouldn't check.

"*Shhh*," Hardy regarded in a hiss, bringing his finger across his lips. Almost terrified out of his wit, he carefully and quietly withdrew his sidearm from his holster. He knew not much of militaristic tendency, but he knew right from wrong. Enemy from friend. *Kill or be killed.*

Thankfully for them, Hardy had been in the peril of warfare before. Usually bringing up the rear behind the unkillable Jack Churchill, perhaps now it was time to cut the cord. Maybe now it was time to prove to himself that he could, too, become somewhat of a warfighter.

Hardy reached for the cocked Colt M1911A1 in his hip holster.

His fingers touched the cold steel as he slowly drew the weapon up by his face, channelling his best Bogart whilst silently extending his arm towards the door, predicting the unwanted company at any second ...

*If Gerry showed his head, he was prepared to blow it off.*

The German infantrymen in the next room continued about their business. Their guards were still mostly up, moving from window to window, searching for hostile targets in the streets to unleash their fury upon. It was evident they believed this room to be clear.

Whilst one situated himself along a window frame, observing some of the action in the street and waiting for an opportunity and a clean shot, the other decided to venture further indoors. With his rifle clutched diagonally before him, he strode towards the bedroom within which Hardy and Mericle were hidden ... and he halted just shy of the doorframe.

Like a sixth sense had tickled the hairs on the back of his neck, the clearly experienced stahlhelm-clad soldier reeled his progression before entering the room. He angled his weapon, sweeping inwards as he progressed with caution ...

... straight into the mouth of Hardy's gun barrel around the corner.

The head of the enemy soldier entered the room, facing forwards.

Without moving, his peripherals clicked left after passing the doorframe; the barrel of a pistol was levelled against his earhole ...

Hardy pulled the trigger.

*Nothing.*

Hardy attempted to squeeze the trigger again, this time harder, and again to no avail. The trigger mechanism just wouldn't budge, as if it were stuck or locked.

He frowned, confused.

And then remembered ...

*The safety lock.*

The German had temporarily frozen after the scare, realizing that he had just walked into the crosshairs of a killer ... only, the shooter had whiffed.

*His would-be executioner had fucked up.*

Perhaps it was the fright of the realization, but the German's movements were lagging. However, the Wehrmacht rifleman finally snapped to, bringing his two-handed weapon around within the tight confines, swiping Hardy's gun from existence.

The barrel of Karabiner rifle conviction now faced the trio as they huddled against the inner wall like limp penises.

*Combined, their eyes grew wide with trepidation.*

After their impromptu entry through a window, now inside the mild quietness of a furnished Norwegian home, Churchill and Young found themselves pit against more of the enemy, lying-in-wait and within close confines.

Already occupying the civilian residence were a group of quislings armed with rifles and mismatched gear, in assistance of two Wehrmacht soldiers in stahlhelms.

*They had literally crashed their party.*

Before he even had a chance to shake the glass out the folds of his fatigues, Young was forcefully disarmed by multiple off-side attackers. Yanked from the floor and placed in an arm-lock by a pair of Nazi-supporting Norwegian civilians, he was fast stripped of his hanging Thompson. They cut the khaki sling with a short, two-inch carpenter's blade.

In a fit of squirms and grunts, the quislings held him up, exposing him vulnerably so that a foremost stocky German soldier could step forth with an unquenchable thirst for violence. Emitting overflowing confidence amidst the armed quislings, the Soldat handed off his Karabiner rifle, cracking his gloved knuckles in the furtherance of ramming his fists into Young's stomach. Without hesitation, he did so again and again before issuing a fierce right hook that sent him flailing from the quislings' grasp and into a tabletop, smashing ceramic ornaments.

Lying in the ruins of the window-barge entrance, Churchill quickly became aware of this new ensnarement. He pushed up swiftly from the debris with his submachine gun still within his grasp, quickly using it to send a blaringly loud burst through the chest of a quisling aggressor wielding an improvised bludgeon in his direction. The muzzle flash lit up the dark confines of the room.

From the string of sudden gunfire, the squealing quisling was blown in a somersault, thrown out the front door of the residence. The door came off its busted hinges, allowing for a lateral bloom to diffuse this dark fight scene with some natural light.

While Young battled with his attackers in the background, Churchill spun in time to see another proper German soldier emerge from the recesses of a dim corner with a raised rifle and shoot at him. It was a bad shot and would have missed his body, however it struck the submachine gun out of his clutches with a spark and strident *prang!*

Blindsiding him in his disarmed stance, a quisling charged in and shoulder-barged Mad Jack with all of his might before he had a chance to react. The two toppled like a rugby tackle, wrestling on the floor—Churchill's eyes widened as he caught a close-up view of the offender. The man was sickly and possessed a mighty snotty nose. He was unsure of what to be threatened by more: the act of aggression on his life or having one of those dangling slugs touch him in some way.

*These two had really wandered into the hornet's nest with this foray.*

This collaring attack on Churchill granted the gun-wielding soldier the time necessary to bolt his rifle for another shot, right as, in the backdrop, Young Young slung his seizing quisling over his shoulder like a potato sack. The man's flung, ferocious tumble knocked the legs out from the rifleman just as he shot again at Jack—*bam!*

The shot hit the ceiling as the soldier's boots knocked under him, crumpling like a bowling pin struck by a strike. The blown hole in the roof rained thatch sticks and insulation from above, shining another ray of blinding light into the confines.

In amongst the dozens of thuds and crashes of the close-quarters combat and audible soundtrack of grunting men like a fast-paced tennis match, the restrained Churchill managed to fold his attacker's arm back and roll across his crumpled aggressor's body on the ground, pinning him, and able to cleanly draw his revolver, extend it, and fire it. A high-powered bullet cracked into the German rifleman's stahlhelm, whipping back his head with a streamer of blood, and sending him anchoring in revert like a sack of shit.

Still scrumming with a quisling at his waist like he was a Greco-Roman wrestler, Churchill's extended pistol arm pivoted right and behind Young's scrumming position, firing a round into one of his multiple quislings right as, abruptly, his arm became subdued by his troublesome assailant who had wriggled free. The man's anchor of an arm sprung up like a jack-in-the-box, swiping the sidearm from Jack's grasp, and the revolver fumbled across the debris-littered floor.

Churchill shifted his balance holding the bloke, restraining his flailing claw with a firm hold, about to issue a headbutt into the quisling—but opting against for fear of touching those drooping tentacles of snot hanging from his face. Instead, he managed to contend with the fellow, attempting to inflict some painful strain in their firm grapple and the man grunted.

Bloody-teethed and frantic, Young reeled his fists in a dire defence as two more quislings and the same brawling German soldier opposed and outnumbered him. The two Norwegians parted in order for the remaining uniformed Gerry to mount pivotal, now drawing a ten-inch Karabiner bayonet from his hip and gripping it in a stabbing-motion beneath a sinister gaze.

In turn, Young drew his shorter BC-41 combat knife and eloped the knuckleduster eyelets, prepared for battle ... and the two clashed in a knife fight.

Meanwhile, Mad Jack wrestled with his attacker across the carpet-laid floor of the debris-littered residence. Gaining an ounce of momentum in their energetic tumble, they trundled up and over a table, breaking a chair on the way down and adding to the mess. Churchill watched as the tall, snotty-nosed quisling picked up a solid table leg to use as a club—complete with protruding carpenter's nails at one end for maximum affect. During the interval, Jack took the opportunity to quickly unloop his cumbersome longbow from around his shoulder, even if only to use it as a mêlée during this segment of hand-to-hand combat, in which the British Commandos were deadly trained ... the quislings, however, not so much.

The quisling attacked Churchill with a snotty snarl that lacquered his teeth and chin, lunging with the raised improvised spiked club. With ease, Jack parried it clear with his longbow as a bow staff, gliding the high limb in and hooking it beneath the man's wrist before then sweeping his legs out from beneath his charging posture with the low end, bringing the man down like a house of cards among the jagged debris. Churchill then drove the heel of his boot hard into the man's exposed gut.

An additional uniformed Wehrmacht infantryman with a Schmeisser flanked by an armed quisling emerged from outside through the bright light of the open doorway, appearing like seemingly unending reinforcements to the brawl.

Churchill's head twisted at the neck, distinguishing their entry.

He welcomed them by dropping to an anchored knee on his fallen foe, driving the full weight of his body into his chest, whilst aptly drawling an arrow from over his shoulder quiver and slotting a peg through the arriving stahlhelm soldier's throat, pinning him to the wall by the entrance like a pinned butterfly.

*Sch-toff–THUCK!*

The infantryman gargled crimson past stained teeth, desperately reaching at the wooden barb through his neck with his spare hand, barely able to even draw breath.

Involuntarily, the soldier's cradled automatic went off.

As the arrow through his bloody neckline caused more gore to spurt in pressurized trickles, his dead man's grip tensed, and the trigger squeezed. The uncontrolled recoil caused the gun to climb into the ceiling. Shots from the discharged weapon thundered away like a dropped garden hose, causing it to rain down smoking fragments from the thatch above all their heads.

Squirting red blood everywhere like a leaking watermain, the soldier kicked at his feet whilst he held the trigger, fast draining of life. His boots slipped in the slime of his own leaking gore, but the arrow embedded firmly into the wooden wall held him in place like he was on the end of a noose.

The quisling who had entered with him was stunned for a moment, snagged on the sight of the dying German. He turned around in time to face the Commando archer with a face full of dread and, before he even had the chance to think about continuing the attack, Churchill launched another strung arrow from the draw through the man's chest with a bassy *thuck!* The arrow passed through him and disappeared, causing him to glance down and pad his sternum for an instant before he noticed blood. The shock flooded his nervous system and he concaved, dying in the puddle of the dying German's blood.

Shuffling about involuntarily due to the snotty nosed quisling held forcefully beneath his knee, Churchill drew a third arrow right as his pinned adversary struggled beneath his knee. Rather than use the strung shaft as ammunition in his longbow, Jack's wrist twirled his grip on the war arrow like a drummer with a drumstick, then used it to stab the man through the breastbone, through his heart, issuing the final blow. The quisling died almost instantly, blowing a snot bubble with his final breath— Jack vacated quickly lest it pop on him.

Across the room, Young wrestled arm in arm with his formidable German soldier, rolling across walls and into furniture. The razor-sharp points of each other's blades were aimed at one another like aggressive cobras, hocked back and ready to strike like a pair of scorpions locked into a duel. With each push and shove, the two interlocked men cut one another with the blades of their pointy instruments whilst grimacing, growling like ravaged animals.

The two remaining quislings who watched in awe at the fight noticed that Churchill had proved victorious across the house, and they chose to advance upon him simultaneously. One of them went for the rifle on the ground while the other launched at the soldier with a stick, like an untamed, untrained wild dog.

Churchill tilted his view and quickly rearranged his dagger-arrow from a hold down by the bodkin-tip to the fletch, but failing to nock the feathered rear before this new attacker came in like a stumbling juggernaut, tripping on debris and swinging wildly with his armament, and missing every mark imaginable just as widely.

With composure under pressure, Jack parried the man's obvious right-shoulder swipe with his longbow reach, and revolved low around the fellow, sweeping his stumbling feet with his boot as he erected to stand. He landed with a loud, painful collapse amidst the wreckages of the home.

In that same second, a gun went off, merely missing Churchill and hitting the wall yonder. Now in a crouching stance, Churchill paused for a split-second, glimpsing at the gunman: the remaining quisling trembling with the rifle. The inexperienced shooter blinked perplexed about the weapon, fast attempting to cycle the bolt-action on the walnut-brown Karabiner-98k rifle in an untrained stance.

Jack aptly nocked his bloody arrow, drawing the bowstring at almost full draw without the care to check for elbow clearing. In doing so, the bend of his arm cocked at his rear and directly impacted into the partially incapacitated quisling's face as he lurched up from the floor, striking him fucking hard! It was an impromptu yet deadly combo by Churchill.

*Whack!*

As if it were choreographed, he then loosed the arrow.

*Sch-TOFF!*

The arrow sprang inside the elongated living quarters of the gloomy Norwegian residence, propelling a line straight through the rifle-fumbling quisling.

The second before Churchill loosed, the wide-eyed quisling's panicked shout could be heard as he released hold of the gun with one hand and raised an open palm of submission. "N< *'No, I surrender!'*> meg!"

The arrow penetrated his open appendage, pinning his hand to his chest.

The velocity from the charging javelin uplifted and impaled the surrendering quisling to a wall behind, immediately lacquered in dripping red ooze. Ran-through and pig-stuck, the man hung stunned for a second before his lungs drained of air. Losing consciousness within seconds, his head folded over, dropping the weapon as his life left his body.

Inspecting his trusty longbow for damage after needing to resort to using it in mêlée combat, Jack Churchill stood and watched as Young finally overpowered his knife-wielding attacker by headbutting the brawny boche, which astonished the kraut infantryman into a daze.

That one was *the Liverpool kiss—Brits were the only military to teach that in CQC training!*

Young then crimped the man's slackened wrist, causing him to drop hold of his bayonet, before forcing him clear and then punching him across the skull with the brass handle of his brandished trench knife.

With a metallic *clonk!* that was thick enough to taste, *brass* met *bone.*

Cranked regressively at the neck and at an unnatural angle, the meat-headed enemy's boots kicked out from beneath him as if someone had pulled the carpet.

The kraut was down and out from that hit—possibly even lifeless.

Bloody and breathless, Young caught sight of Churchill across their destructed room space, and the two exchanged a victorious nod of accomplishment.

Like precognition ...

Like a sixth sense ...

... Churchill's attention snapped sideways and through the door, entertaining an inapposite interference in the background which had caught his attention during the kerfuffle within his vicinity and close quarters chaos.

*It was a silhouette in a stahlhelm through the fog of war.*

He drew another war arrow and swiftly fired true.

The bodkin tip projectile travelled out through the door, crossing the street, before smashing through the salt-fogged glass window with tinkle tone, and impaling another enemy target there within.

The German soldier with the rifle pointed at Hardy and Mericle was Churchill's outlying target. An arrowhead penetrated him from behind, suddenly exploding out from his chest and surprising them all—especially him, who after a moment's pause, fell forwards and dropped his gun.

Hardy, Mericle, and his shutterbug watched with a stare of perplexion. The threatening soldier who held them dead to rights with a

Karabiner rifle had just been killed from behind, seemingly of divine intervention.

They were stunned, noticing the lone protruding arrow shaft erected from between his shoulder blades.

The other, outstanding German rifleman within their residence had heard the smash of the glass break and the whistle of an arrow flight, and now witnessed the passage of the slung projectile that had claimed the life of his kamerad.

The foe drastically displaced, shoving his shoulder below the window frame, taking cover from this miraculous archer across the road. He shouted and cussed in German, panicking, sweating.

Although Mad Jack had no shot on this remaining roamer, the situation had bought Hardy the seconds he needed to collect himself and to remember the ample degree of crash course training given to him by Churchill aboard the Kenya at 4 a.m. this morning.

Against the bedroom corner before Mericle and his cameraman, Hardy dipped to collect the disarmed gun. Down low, he tipped the pistol sideways in his grasp to better inspect the mechanisms.

While Mericle and his cameraman stared in awe at the dead body that had dropped right before their wide eyes, paying note to the feathered end of the arrow, Hardy finally clicked off the safety of the Colt pistol.

Realizing the dire circumstances, he acted on the remaining enemy.

He took a big casual step out across the dead body in the doorway, fully exposed and gaining a clear view of the remaining soldier still within the Norwegian home. He raised the pistol behind a squinting eye ...

The two locked stares.

In the same second that he acquired his target, the fast-becoming inundated soldier who sought sanctuary from the apparent, wildly out-of-era British bowman, noticed the hesitant assailant with a handgun.

*Reacting rigidly, he pointed his rif—*

The loud shooting caused Hardy to shut his eyes closed and flinch.

*Bam ... bam ... bam!*

Three shots.

Two hits.

One kill.

Tense and taut for an elongated moment, the grimacing German soldier resembling a renaissance sculpture with running red ink, finally dropped dead.

Still alive, Hardy opened his eyes from behind the smoking gun, witnessing the soldier he had just killed hit the floor.

Mericle peered out, observing the aftermath in complete awe.

It takes a special kind of soldier to run *towards* gunshots.

To run *towards* pending doom ...

*Towards war* ...

It took *commandos.*

In charge and set to purpose on their flanking manoeuvre, Lieutenant Dennis O'Flaherty's detachment of helmeted men from Four Troop rounded the corners of several wooden houses in the icy urban environment, throwing caution to the wind. From behind the sights of their assorted weaponry as they progressed, these commandos may as well be invincible.

Slowing their pace now they were fanning out upon the outskirts of this urban ambush in their backtrack, O'Flaherty's men were quick to establish overarching angles of crossfire upon the numerous German targets who seemed to be advancing on a detached group of friendly Brits somewhere within the vicinity of the village.

They opened fire immediately, dispatching blindsided enemy units from their exposed perspectives. The German infantrymen were caught mostly off-guard, spun around by bullets to face their enemy advancement only within the final seconds of their lives.

Of O'Flaherty's men, which included his pal, Sherington, all took a knee as they arrived in the peripherals of the shootout, catching the Germans out as they whaled on a group of Commando.

They pelted enemy targets both on ground level and up on the roofs in elevated positions. These perverse predators were firing down at cornered prey who had been progressing in the streets. The oppressed belligerents here were fellow commandos from G2, and it was time to tip the scales of this battle.

From a stern stance, their wave was like a firing squad, wiping out the array of positioned 181st Wehrmacht infantrymen, laying them out in a line of blitzing discharge and widespread, continuous automatic fire.

Obliterated, the oppressors made short work of the enemy.

Once the deafening rattle of gunfire and screams had subsided, Colonel Durnford-Slater emerged in the silence, from within one of the houses in the impending kill-box of the foiled German ambuscade. He and the wounded Lieutenant Head, clutching a bloody mitt at his left bicep, stepped out into the street following Knocker White and his smoking shotgun as he scanned the rooftops above one final time before the friendly forces met out in the cleared open.

"Lieutenant O'Flaherty?" Durnford-Slater acknowledged their redeemer. Their assistance helped turn the tide from worst to bad.

"Colonel, sir. Are you guys okay?" O'Flaherty responded with a modest nod, escorted by his men with raised weapons who helped secure the perimeter. He spoke with satiric tone. "I see you found the few Gerrys we missed ...?"

"That we did," Durnford-Slater agreed, skimming some of the deceased 181st in the street. This lot would have been quite the nuisance if they hadn't shown up. "Cheers for the assistance."

They both turned their heads as, from across the street, they discerned the bloody and frayed Young and Churchill as they made an entrance from the shade of a Norwegian house, stepping over the body of an amputee German who laid in the sleet. Churchill was now carrying his longbow out before him and Young seemed as though he had copped a few good hits to the melon in a victorious bout of fisticuffs.

"Dennis," fixing the tilt of his beret, Churchill acknowledged the rendezvousing newcomers after a quick pause and scan of the aftermath of the ambush outside.

O'Flaherty turned his head with a grin. "Major."

The two enclosed steps and prepared an embrace, but not before an exchange of bullshit ...

"You fellows lost or something? Battle is that way."

"We are on a flanking mission, sir. Heard the commotion."

Jack remarked with a playful grin. "A mission? What hairy sod thought it was a good idea to put you in charge?"

"It really is nice of you and Group Three to finally join us Group Two chaps on the mainland," O'Flaherty retorted extraneously, hitting Mad Jack where he knew it would hurt the most. "You've been missing all the action."

Churchill extended a hand to meet O'Flaherty's welcoming gesture, and the two shook hands firmly, allowing time for Jack's witty response. "Hopefully you left some for me, then?"

Durnford-Slater then seemed to put them back on track:

"Lieutenant, where is Captain Forrester and the rest of Four Troop?"

O'Flaherty repaid his attention to their overall CO to report. "We pursued the majority of the enemy resistance through this town. As we predicted, they retreated north-east towards the hotel, but a rather large detachment stopped in the warehouse district."

"Another stronghold! Blast!" Durnford-Slater cursed, checking the time to mentally prepare for another delay.

O'Flaherty continued. "They look to have intent, perhaps guarding something. Captain Forrester and Kaptein Linge are holding an offensive position just south of a clearing on the other side of this block, which is where the warehouses are located. I've been charged with a flanking mission to hit the warehouses from the west side while the others draw the fire of the front machine guns."

"Roger that," Durnford-Slater commented, then eyeing his number two. "Jack, take Six Troop and support Lieutenant O'Flaherty, I'll take the rest south and rendezvous with Forrester. We'll coordinate an attack on the warehouses once you're in position, and then we'll envelope the hotel together."

"Fine-o-fine."

"*Let's go No.3!*" Durnford-Slater shouted, steering his men in one direction while Churchill took his followers on an alternative approach towards their next objective.


*Smash! Smash!*

The shots of the nearly invisible snipers upon the distant ridgeline barely missed Commando Graeme Black as he drove his men inland. He whipped his head and torso back behind cover, cursing in harsh exhale.

"*Son of a cunt!*"

A third and even fourth belated ricochet pelted into the quayside stone wall of which Group 4 were currently spread out behind, seeking cover from an exposed clearing in South Vågsøy that left them subjected to the formidable cliffside snipers. It was taking them forever to catch up to the war.

Thankfully, the snipers were yet to claim a victim of their Group.

Their first shots whiffed by inches, alerting this lagging band of commando reinforcements of the open range. It was the same disconcerting feeling one had after discovering they had walked several paces into a minefield—only, with bullets. They had all promptly dispersed as a subsequent wave of deadly sniper rifle fire zeroed over their formation, taking accurate potshots.

Black squirmed behind low cover, examining their route.

"I think this might be why the Colonel took his men directly through the town," a trooper by the name of George Herbert remarked to Lieutenant Black.

"The town is a deathtrap!" Black regarded, and with good reason. The urban fighting through those tight urban streets was the perfect recipe for an ambush, much alike what sounded to be happening not one-hundred metres north-east from here. With Hooper's approval, Black was thus attempting to take G4 through a route that avoided as much potential combat as possible.

*T'was Mountbatten's motto: no unnecessary risks ...*

"Rather save my ammo for the frontline, lad," Black justified to which Herbert and his flanker understood and nodded.

"*Sir.*"

"*Yes, sir.*"

In the musing moments to follow, Captain Hooper emerged from the line and assessed their stalemate situation.

"Should we double-back?" he posed to Black, whose operational experience he trusted more than he trusted his own decisiveness today.

Graeme Black took a second to brush his blonde imperial moustache with his gloved hand whilst he considered their options. Making a constant string of short-burst dashes forwards and between cover could progress them through with minimal casualties, however, it would be painstakingly slow compared to how quickly he wished to reach G2 and the frontline. Not to mention that these Alpine Huntsmen sharpshooters were apparently top-shelf elitists at a range. It seemed that if given even half a chance, they would take someone's head off, and that was unacceptable just to win a race with Jack Churchill to the frontline.

In a playbook being conducted under the premise of *no unnecessary risks*, it seemed no matter what, up every avenue awaited a necessary risk. There were no shortcuts.

Black sighed.

It seemed that even doubling-back to find a safer alternative, probably bringing up the rear behind Durnford-Slater's throng, could be their only other viable option.

"All I know is we can't just bloody sit here," Black responded with a grimace, turning to inch his eyeline above the stone wall and spy the faraway ridgeline housing a small army of ranged snipers.

There was but one unconsidered alternate proceeding, a Hail Mary to their predicament, and a prayer vowed right now by the British Army's most unreligious compatriot.

"Come on, Clement ... where are ya, ya cunt?"

*Ridgeline above South Vågsøy*
*Vågsøy, Norway*

It had taken Lieutenant Clement and his small detachment of Group 1 men some time to scale the snowcapped ridgeline that encircled some of South Vågsøy. They had approached it from a south-westerly coordinate, arriving from their completed objective in the small outskirt village of Holvik to the far south-west.

As ordered by Haydon, their detail had the new objective of blindsiding the enemy marksmen force located erratically throughout these rocky peaks. They were to hunt the Huntsmen.

They may not have been able to eradicate them entirely, but a bit of noise to make them shift their focus should have been enough to remove their sniper scopes from off the commandos down in the village long enough for them to complete their main raid objectives unhindered. They needed to distract and divert, prod the ant's nest, and then eventually retreat for disembarkation once the job had been completed.

This crew of a dozen G1 commandos quietly traversed the snowy rocks, homing in on the elevated ridgeline that overlooked South Vågsøy. The bolt-action gunshots from the snipers pinged like beacons, aiding them in closing the distance on their unsuspecting elusive enemies.

They approached completely unnoticed ...

Clement signalled his Group to hold once they were closer, now able to discern the back end of the summit of the low ridge where the snipers appeared to be perched. Able to identify where each marksman was located due to their rifle's intermittent fire, the gunshots were significantly louder now.

Clement used their own separated advantageous positions against them, coordinating his men in groups of twos and threes, advancing in the plodding snow like winter predators from the Huntsmen's blind spots. They were aligned with guns at the ready, evenly spaced, like a marching death squad on the trail.

Suddenly, their trudging advance halted as Clement and his rim spotted a group of snipers ...

They were low in the snow, leaning on smaller capped rocks. Almost invisible, due to their camouflage white fatigues, natural leather webbing and white balaclavas, hiding their attributes. They moved as minimally as possible.

It was the thunderclaps of their gunshots that echoed out across the far distance that gave them away, alerting Group 1 of another target as they progre—

*Thud-thud-thud ...*

One misplaced boot heel broke a shelf of snow, sending a hidden soccer-ball sized rock tumbling down the slight slope.

It was as barely audible in amongst the overall volume of the sniper shooting high in the echoic elevation of the hillside, however, the swift movement of the rock gained the attention of one of the balaclava-clad Alpine Huntsmen who was apparently exceedingly competent.

His wool-covered head lifted over his telescope cap, and he pivoted in his stance, analysing the space behind them in the snowcapped rocks—immediately spotting the mousy force of interrupting Commando, sidling their position from the six.

At first, his eyes remained calm through his ski-mask ...

*... then, he sounded the alarm with a big inhale and sh—Blam!*

His white wool balaclava exploded red from a savage headshot delivered from one of the commandos.

It was the sprinting gun sounding off ...

*Now came the contest.*

The commandos unloaded their guns at what few targets they had thus far identified, clapping away with automatic submachine guns into the rocks and snow, tossing grenades throughout the ridge.

*Trees exploded.*

*Piles of snow slid from surfaces.*

*Rocks shattered with smoke and sparks.*

White snow splattered red like tossed ink whenever a combatant was tagged on either side, and the hillside suddenly erupted with static intervals of deafening close-quarters combat and the shockwaves of flung fragmentation grenades.

Needless to say that, in any case, the fully automatic force of the No.3 Commando Thompson submachine guns predominantly outgunned and outmanoeuvred the long-ranged, slow-cycling bolt-action rifles of the Alpine Huntsmen at such close range.

A Huntsman crouched low from his position amongst the rocks, falling victim to the overbearing British advance. The man was struck multiple times across the chest and arms, twirling on the spot and tossing his rifle just as his closest marksman reacted. The next white masked assailant twisted low and fired blindly at the commandos with a revealed handgun, moving and fast seeking cover from the onslaught by leapfrogging over a small boulder—but instead, he became swatted from the air by an alternate submachine gunner.

The man's corpse was assaulted almost half a dozen times in mid-air, launching him out over the open air of the sheer rockface that he brimmed. Surrounded by droplets from his own fatal wounds, the body of the sniper free-fell off the edge, plummeting motionlessly down into a rocky grave where he splashed quite grotesquely.

After several of the Huntsman soldiers became dispatched, outflanked by the aggressive assault tactics of the commandos, a particular sharpshooter managed to outplay them, and creep behind some dead tree trunks that were still erect in the snow. He gained an advantageous position upon a defilade, and he plugged two brodie-wearing Englishmen with his secondary weapon; a slung MP40 submachine gun with a collapsed buttstock. The troopers' chests brutally burst with crimson carnage after they assisted in hosing down several of the enemy, each trading lives.

A nearby commando who had been preparing a hand grenade during the assault spotted the balaclava gunner, and instead selected him as the target for the arch. The bomb he held was a No.69—an impact detonating grenade with a smaller destructive radius than the No.36M Mills Bomb, however, once armed, it exploded when it made contact with a source.

He pegged the small ball grenade at the tree the German gunner hid behind, and the explosive made contact directly behind the trunk, exploding like an instantaneous firework. The petrified wood of the dry tree cracked in half with a bone-torquing detonation of sharp splinters, both big and small, and the top half collapsed instantly within the hill-scape battle zone.

The German on the other side reacted the same way one would being hit by a speeding car—he was launched, back bending in an unnatural way and sent flailing down the countryside, parting from his weapon and likely, his life.

A lone enemy sniper recoiled after returning fire, fast suppressed by some other commandos. He sunk down low behind a hip-level boulder, taking the time to calmly cycle the bolt on his scoped Karabiner and count his breaths as he realized his kamerads' numbers were quickly dwindling. With good reason, he was starting to feel the walls close in around him. Both his flanks were coated in deceased Huntsmen and blood-spattered snow, and his remaining bullets in his slow rifle were as numbered as the seconds left of his life.

After pacing his actions and accepting the suppressive automatic barrage on the opposite side of his big rock, the balaclava sniper engaged his core and bent like a venomous snake around the curve, leading tight with his rifle sights. He fired again, pulling the hair string trigger of his 98k and dropping another pushing commando with a harsh shoulder wound that dropped him to the snow like an anchor.

He recoiled, under more intense fire, bolted his rifle.

From the side, Clement saw this Huntsman perform his skilful manoeuvre, almost dropping another advancing commando. No matter what they did, they could not properly advance on this adversary while he was in such a defendable position.

"Grenade!" he instructed his offsider, who obliged with an overarm impact grenade in his bastioned direction. The impact grenade soared through the air at an arch and hit with a *BHOM!* just behind the cover of the sniper's boulder, dislodging the rock from its setting, rolling down the hill, and causing the man to become buried under it. The sniper's bones were instantly crushed, and he was squashed like a bug as the rock rolled over him, tumbling off the edge of the cliff and causing a minor avalanche that was visible to all within South Vågsøy.

A few shooters remained and fought while an innumerable amount of the Huntsmen seemed to quickly disperse, descaling the slopes and disappearing from sight. One of which came closer to Clement and his flankers than expected, and they came under direct fire, with Clement catching an arm wound and recoiling to the deep, soft snow of a natural crevasse while his men returned the salvo, eliminating the last of the men.

Clement's view fell elsewhere. Through some brittle foliage, he could spy a sole remaining Huntsman killer lurking with a bayonet around the gorge of a rock formation ...

He snuck up behind two of his men who were taking cover; the hunter proceeding not unlike a pouncing jungle cat, about to attack the men with his bayonet fang while they were unexpecting.

From a ground angle and grimacing in pain from his wound, Clement fast drew his weapon and fired, slaying the balaclava-masked foe within inches of the enemy claiming another life.

They had certainly bit off more than they could chew engaging these elite adversaries, but their tactic worked. Of the few they managed to dispatch, the rest took to the slope decline, disappearing over the posterior ridgeline and into the misty whiteout of the snowy abyss.


Meanwhile, Captain Young and Lieutenant O'Flaherty led an apprised flank attack of their own. It was now compiled partly of Six Troop and a portion of Four Troop.

Naturally, Jack Churchill felt out of place not leading from the front of their arrowhead formation into this pending battle—as well as not leading, at all. Young was at the wheel.

Approximately three-dozen of the British Commandos manoeuvred through the last portion of Norwegian township in the centre of South Vågsøy. They moved from house to house, progressing slowly in case of another enemy ambush lying in wait. Unsurprisingly, they countered an encore of enemy resistance, dug deep into the remnants of the Norwegian residency like maggots in a rotting carcass.

They spotted the movement of a shooter in a tall house and called it out a split-second before the German's gun sounded off in their direction, missing the multiple targets in the white-out street by mere metres.

The commandos scattered, ramming through doorways and behind building corners for cover before peeking around the edges and returning fire at the enemy's elevated position upon a double-storey window ledge. He was shot dead by several extended bursts of submachine gun fire, settling him within the vacant premises.

Suddenly, a sergeant from O'Flaherty's unit copped three shots to the back by another enemy gunman who had let them pass below in the streets.

Everybody spun and engaged the remaining shooter as the man recoiled after claiming a casualty.

Young took up the charge, dashing low in front of Churchill as men everywhere took cover. O'Flaherty met Young's position and the two of them fired several more shots into the darkness that lurked inside the angular position, seemingly missing the enemy rifleman loitering within. Due to extremely effective weatherproofing, the layer of the house had been reinforced with sheet metal. It was nigh bulletproof and would prove a more difficult hindrance to dispatch before they could progress.

"Little prick!" O'Flaherty cursed as he reared into cover after expelling what remained of his weapon's capacity, hurriedly snapping clear his empty Thompson stick-magazine and preparing another from his kit. When he did, he noticed that the front door was open to the cottage. There was an eerie silence that skulked within the dark and abandoned home.

Depending on how well emplaced this lot of enemy combatants were, they would have to breach and eliminate them before they could advance towards the warehouses and their flanking objective. Otherwise, they left themselves vulnerable to attack from behind.

"I'll lead!" O'Flaherty took point, raising his Thompson and nuzzling the muzzle of the weapon between the crack of the open door—

"Wait!" Young exclaimed. An idea had sprung to mind after he had laid his eyes on a series of gasoline canisters located beneath the timber frame of the steps leading to the front door. They were only partially concealed beneath a weather tarp.

He smirked, patting O'Flaherty tenderly on the shoulder.

"We'll smoke him out."

O'Flaherty nodded beneath his shaky, strapless helmet.

*No unnecessary risks.*

The sound of Clement's surprise attack on the rear of the pesky snipers along the ridgeline was audible as distant crackles and fizzes from the pit of South Vågsøy.

Down on the ground, a smile formed beneath Black's blonde imperial moustache as the attentions of both himself and his G4 men panned and tilted towards the surrounding mountains, able to witness the flashes accompanying the distant echoes.

The battle freed them of their stalemate, allowing for them to raise anchor and move onwards with their objective to seek out the frontline without fear of engagement from the ranged shooters in the grandstands of the field.

"Thank fuck for that," he remarked, leading the charge with his big Bren gun out before him in case of trouble. They had spotted some passing figures in the streets: displacing enemy, identifying them by their lengthy greatcoats and attire silhouettes. This urban wonderland was still very much a skirmish of war, and not even God knew what could have been lurking around each corner.

Leading the onslaught, Black took his men from house to house. They pursued the siren song of pronounced gunshots close-by in town, cluing them in to their correct course chasing G3 and G2 respectively.

Black and his Troop shuttled door to door.

On their progressive, guarded journey, they discovered only vacant homes and frightened civilians cowering in their cellars and behind their furniture. But soon after, they found remnants of battle ...

Bright red bloodstains on the white snow soon lead them to deceased German soldiers and, eventually, a pair of maimed and seemingly trapped men from No.3 behind a wall.

Black moved in low, signalling for a few of his men to flank forwards and then the rest to stack-up behind his poise behind himself in cover.

"Lads," he regarded, gaining their attention.

One of the men called at the friendlies, gesturing to stay put and low with caution. "Sir! Stragglers in the house across the thoroughfare," he warned. "They've got a shooter in a window with a line on us here. We're pinned down!"

"Fret not," Black remarked, acknowledging their predicament like some sort of compelling lord and saviour. Whether they entrusted his conceited concern or were simply delighted to have support, the two commandos motioned compliance.

Black inched the edge of his cover.

Across a street and a wider than normal clearing he spotted the house that they claimed housed a talented shooter. The windows seemed motionless upon his short-lived focus and in the seconds to follow, Black noticed a triplet of displacing Germans making a dash from left to right, moving parallel to their passage.

Salivating for combat, his urge for action overcame his conscious tactical mindset of caution and Black inched the corner to raise his Bren gun steady, immediately thumping out a controlled string of fire at the strafing targets through the fog two hundred yards away.

After a few non-contact volleys, the running men in coats and stahlhelms adversely reacted; two of them copping hits across their torsos and collapsing to the icy street. The third, a man with a Schmeisser submachine gun, halted stern and boldly returned fire at Black. He swept from the hip with his gun on full-automatic, hitting nothing with his panicked retaliation.

Black's next burst was targeted.

He fired with a kick of his powerful support rifle, slapping a triplet of brutal impacts across the soldier's chest and head, causing him to perform a reverse-barrel roll into a still collapse in the snow when, abruptly, Black was issued a salvo of savage automatic gunfire from an unseen location.

In a fluster, the wall on either side of his positioned rifle erupted with dazzling flints of blinding ricochets, causing him to immediately clench-up and react, albeit, not fast enough to avoid injury.

Of the onslaught of surprise gunfire at his position, his left forearm was hit three times by biting bullets, exploding his thick arm sleeve to frayed dismay and breaking his wristwatch. His LMG was collected with a spark and a distinct metallic impact, and the entire event caused him to drop the weapon over the ledge of his cover in order to sink safely behind, embracing his stiff maimed limb.

"Bastard!" Black swore as one of his flanking commandos behind cover saw to his bloody, torn-up forearm. Another inched the wall, firing blindly in retort at the window shooter for an instant before dropping behind cover.

"Sir! You're wounded!" Herbert asserted, immediately exchanging his weapon for a bandage from his own medical supplies. With an ounce of trepidation underlining his tone of voice, he called towards the rear of their line. "Medic! Can we please get a medic up here!"

A cleanshaven sergeant by the name of *Bill Challington* inched forwards and low behind cover, cradling a Tommy gun. He oversaw Black's wounds and also gained a quick scope of the enemy in the house nearby.

"Don't bother, trooper," Challington dismissed Herbert, knowing Graeme Black too well. It would take more than a trice of bullet wounds to the forearm to stop this man's warpath. He was bred a little differently to most. "How do you want to play it, sir?"

"Strap me up!" Black grunted, holding his limb extended and bearing his tea-stained teeth below his handlebar moustache. Herbert obliged, applying a field dressing over his sleeve. "Tighter, goddammit!"

Black next ripped a 9mm Browning Hi-Power from his chest holster, using his wrist to rack the slide before tensely holding it up beside his face, ready for action. He glanced down the line, spying his couple of commandos in tow with machine guns.

"Lads!" he gained their attention and with it, direction. "I reckon a two-inch group at one hundred yards isn't too bad!"

The gunners nodded, preparing their guns for combat and slightly repositioning for action.

Once ready, they gestured with a nod.

Black sternly eyed Challington and Herbert. "Want to come for a cheeky flank, lads?"

"Do I ever," Challington enthusiastically replied while Herbert remained much more reserved, yet prepared to do whatever he must.

"Covering fire when you're ready!" Black issued the order after Herbert tied off the sloppy bandage and collected his weapon. The three of them readied for a dash across the open, past the two pinned No.3 boys, and into another row of houses. From there, they intended to push a blind edge on the shooter's position.

With not a moment to waste during this war, the machine gunners heaved and hoisted their rifles onto the ledge of cover, immediately sounding off with volatility, correcting their aim towards the window shooter after their initial volleys of suppressive gunfire. Their intentions here were not to kill the shooter, per se, although the result would have coincided with Black's endgame. It was merely just to suppress the gunner for the latter of the manoeuvre.

As the clamorous concurrent Bren gunfire drowned out all other sound, Black, Herbert, and Challington made a mad dash from point A to point B, quickly bursting in through the doorway of a smaller cottage.

Black was on-point with his handgun and bandaged arm cradled, the three were welcomed warmly by a brightly decorated Christmas tree and a yuletide holiday display. They paused for an odd moment before continuing with caution, pressing through the vacant house and into the next, then the next, before the retaliatory gunfire from the window shooter could be discerned from the suppressive Bren guns.

They carefully inched out behind the edge of the building, peeking the edge to spy the barrel of the enemy's weapon, which appeared to be a Madsen light machine gun, probably confiscated from the Norwegians by the Germans. It was identifiable by the grooves in the barrel extension making it almost like a German MG34, just lacking the same oomph.

Like a carnival shooting duck gallery, while Black traced the machine gun-protruding windowsill, another threat popped into sight in his peripherals: in the open doorway to the occupied target house, a secondary enemy combatant sighted their flank status.

Perhaps guarding the machine gunner's locale, this rifleman reacted accordingly, immediately aligning Black's position with his Karabiner rifle and preparing to fire.

Black's outstretched arm raised and shot first.

*Bam, bam, bam, bam, bam ...*

He unloaded over half of his high-capacity magazine through the slat space, unknowing if he dispatched the shooter or if it simply caused him to reel out of harm's way. Either way, their jig was up and the enemy occupying the house now knew they were being skirted.

"*Grenade!*" Black barked to his side after expelling a few more suppressive rounds through the doorway and tucking his pistol into his belt.

Herbert readied a hand grenade at his periphery behind cover.

After priming the timed Mills variant, he upper-hand flung it to Black, who caught it, and then swiftly flung the device through the door with a softballer's accuracy.

"*Again!*" he called.

Herbert primed another before the first had even detonated, tossing it in an easily catchable arc like a round of hot potato.

When he did so, the same German rifleman unexpectedly returned to the doorway—even in wake of the thrown grenade which had just passed this goalie's guard—and lined Black up in his presently unarmed state.

Before he could squeeze his trigger, Challington's submachine gun sounded off from nearby, stitching a tight line across the man's core. He grimaced in a strained spasm before keeling over to the floor, out of sight.

Black caught the cooking grenade in the air, and this time stepped out three feet farther to peg it straight through the machine gunner's window with extreme prejudice and accuracy. It would have bounced off the ceiling and landed with a *thud* next to him.

One after the other, the grenades detonated within the household, blasting outwards and shaking timber slats loose, blowing smoke from every structural orifice.

Undoubtedly killing all occupying opponents within, the result emancipated their hindered development, enabling their progress towards the frontline ...

*They were about to catch up to the war.*

# 12

# *Red Warehouse*

*Vågsfjorden*
*Vågsøy, Norway*

While the battle raged on Vågsøy Island, the remaining sentry ships of the 17th Destroyer Flotilla remained a vigilant guard in the wide-open, crystal-clear Vågsfjorden.

Guarding the westerly wing of the reflective surface of the bay, the **HMS** Chiddingfold and **HMS** Offa encountered another enemy-steered armed trawler, foolishly attempting to either creep up on their position for an engagement—or possibly sneak away from the fight altogether.

*Either way secured them death at the hand of the Royal Navy.*

The deafeningly loud cannons of the destroyers boomed to life across the serene aquatic plane, shelling the absolute shit out of the drifting trawler, later identified as the *Anhalt*, who nearly made it midway out of the mouth of the Vågsfjorden.

The Anhalt fired only after she was noticed by the floating British armada, leading to further speculation that she was trying to slip out the back of the incursion.

The warships would have sent rescue vessels out to perform their duties if it seemed necessary ... *it did not.*

Of the shells that quickly crippled the tiny armed trawler, two of the hits were responsible for disabling her, however a third shell had provoked something combustible aboard her inner bowels. Whatever accelerant that ignited within caused a bright contrast of fiery orange against the cold blues and crystal whites of the brisk, northern atmosphere.

Forthwith, the disabled trawler exploded loudly into a million pieces upon the cold fjord surface, sinking almost immediately after letting out a painful, metallic groan like a mechanical whale song.

Shortly after, the Onslow engaged against a particular pesky squadron of German Messerschmitt Me-109 fighters who had successfully shot down several Bristol Blenheim bombers.

The RAF fighters had met fiery demises in full view of the floating ships in the Vågsfjorden, and it pissed them off watching powerlessly from below.

From their extended range, the Onslow decided to take on the nimble, zigzagging ships in the wide skyline, attempting to wreak some havoc in retaliation.

They weren't overly successful with their flashy anti-air guns; however, an operator, who had been toying with the ancient 4-inch cannon retrofitted onto the destroyer's main deck for shits 'n gigs prior to Archery, decided to loose a shell at the cluster of floating specks in the sky.

The lucky bugger hit one.

The Me-109 within the formation of fighters was instantly disintegrated as it travelled in flight.

The event was like shooting a buzzing fly with a shotgun.

It just ... ceased to exist.

Unbeknownst to them as a complete fluke, a one-off, and complete and utter stroke of luck, it became needless to say that the other enemy fighters fucked right off after witnessing that takedown from the fjord.

They bugged-out of the engagement entirely.


*Warehouse District*
*South Vågsøy, Norway*

After journeying through the war-ravaged village of South Vågsøy, collecting their dregs left in the backwash of Four Troop's warpath, Knocker White and Mills took point for Durnford-Slater's afresh Commando clique as they finally caught up to the frontline. They were approaching the new warehouse stand-off, notable by the simple fact that the gunshots were getting louder ...

They came up behind Four Troop's position.

Once discovering the clearing and Forrester's detail positioned along the final boundary of concealment before the wide-open clearing and the warehouse district beyond the fence line, they allowed for their colonel to take point.

"Algy!" Durnford-Slater recognized the Four Troop leader tucked away with a few of his troopers and Norwegian counterpart, Martin Linge. As it were now, Linge's boys of the NOR.I.C.1 made up one half of the force present.

With an exhausted groan, Forrester upped from his crouched position, trading his grasp on his many weapons in order to officially welcome Durnford-Slater to the front with a salutary embrace.

His maw beamed below his enormous broom moustache that took up fifty percent of the real estate on Forrester's face, looking superimposed. He proclaimed beneath a dipped brodie. "Colonel!"

Durnford-Slater wasted no time getting on the same page as his Troop captain as the two of them folded into Forrester's position overlooking the clearing and the warehouses yonder. "We ran into Lieutenant O'Flaherty on our way in. Thought we might lend a hand."

Knocker White, Mills, Charley Head, de la Torre, as well as the dozen more British Commandos from the following fanned out and restocked the frontline with their presence, restocking their numbers. They were around eighty troopers strong now, all about to press the final enemy position before what would be the grand finale showdown at the Ulvesund Hotel: the six-level multi-storey location, the lurching height of which was now visible to the ground-level eyeline, resting just at the rear diagonal to the warehouse district.

It was the next—final—stop on this route.

On all routes.

Durnford-Slater continued, "I ordered Major Churchill and Six Troop to tag along with your boys on the flanking mission. They should be reaching the position at any moment. What are your plans?"

"Well, as you can see," Forrester informed, passing Durnford-Slater a pair of binoculars he had been using to scout out the warehouses in the distance. "The Germans have machine gun emplacements on each corner of the district fence line. That red warehouse in the middle seems to be their primary stronghold, as they have mounted another MG up in the guard tower. You see it?"

Durnford-Slater scanned the wind-blown, frosted horizon through the telescopic lenses for a moment before replying. What Forrester had conveyed appeared to be one-hundred percent accurate, and there seemed to be a heightened enemy focus on defence surrounding the red warehouse. "I see it."

"We're going to give them *the Houdini* ..." Forrester explained his plan of attack: a title for the plan he had made up on the spot. Once obtaining Durnford-Slater's interest and attention, he elaborated further.

"They already know we're here. We are going to create a thick smoke-screen from our hold, blanketing visibility across the range. Gerry will think we are going to advance momentarily, but we shan't push an inch. Prior to the smokescreen, my men are going to assume targets and open a partial blind fire through the thick veil, engaging the enemy and giving the illusion that we're still about to advance their positions ... but again, we shan't. By then, Linge's men will have followed O'Flaherty's—and Churchill's, if he's tagging along—flanking position back into town and around the side, of which they're about to set upon now. We'll all attack them from the sides while their guns are still watching the front."

Durnford-Slater finally lowered the binoculars and gave a nod of approval. The logic in this plan was sound.

"Sir, we can see Lieutenant O'Flaherty's troops along the flank. They're in position," a trooper from Forrester's Troop informed with convenient timing.

Forrester acted.

"Deploy smoke!" he ordered with a shout to his surrounding commandos while he, himself, equipped two smoke grenades from the hanging tabs of his webbing, passing one of the canisters to Durnford-Slater. "Care to lob?"

Durnford-Slater torqued his head, keen to partake. "Yes."

Within the next few seconds, Forrester and his men about the forward position pulled the pins on their smoke bomb canisters and tossed them as far as they could towards the fence line that surrounded the warehouse premises.

The smoke grenades hissed and kicked up an asthmatic fit, discharging billowing piles of thick, cloudy smoulder, eventually forming an impenetrable synthetic fog that limited visibility. It blocked range visibility for the enemy, and would no doubt catch their attention, feigning advance.

"Open fire!" methodically, Forrester then ordered, and from various locations along their firing positions, riflemen and gunners alike sporadically let loose intervals of fire through the rising cloud, assaulting the distant warehouses and the enemies situated about the proximity. If the smoke alone had not caught their attention, then the incoming salvo would certainly catch the scruff of their necks and face them forwards.

They were conservative with their gunfire, spacing out their bursts and timing the onslaught with the objective of time elongation rather than accuracy or casualty infliction.

After men expelled whole magazines or clips, as commanded, they upped from their position and displaced into a file headed to link with the flank led by Martin Linge, where they would pile in and join the blindside assault ...

The remaining Wehrmacht infantrymen were well deluded.

In the panic of the withdrawal during the squandering defence of the invasion, they became convinced of a frontal attack on the warehouse district by these assailing British Commandos. They devised a counter-attack by sweeping returning fire blindingly into the growing smoke at the south end of the clearing and the seeming origin of the offensive push—and blind to their defences on the west perimeter of the warehouses, where Captain Young and Lieutenant O'Flaherty led a swift flanking mission, overshadowed by helicopter parent Major Mad Jack Churchill.

While the enemy fired downrange at Forrester's smoky distraction, he and his motley band of Six and Four Troop commandos rushed from an enfilade strike on the fortified position.

The slicing of a wire fence barely slowed their balls-out gallop across the ice-swept open space. They were almost within cover of the real estate within the warehouse district before the partial Gerry even caught on to their blindsiding parade.

As per his appeal to Major Churchill, Captain Young remained on-point for this portion of the operation and in command of Six Troop.

On their daring approach to the vicinity, he was skirted by men with Tommy guns set to *full-auto* and spraying at the hip. They pushed forth, hammering the opposition stronghold where the enemy challenged to thwart their charge with defensive discharges.

Behind their rush, fresh through the slashed gauze perimeter fence, Jack Churchill was poised in a position that oversaw the attack but allowed for other commandos to pass beneath his wing and pour into the fray. Where others carried clunking weaponry, he still insisted upon his six-foot longbow.

After spotting an exposed German figure silhouetting against the white of the sky on the roof of the nearest warehouse, he paused for an instance among the charging commandos to nock, charge, and loose an arrow. The target was at barely 250-feet with zero windage—an easy mark.

With a silent *schoof* amidst all the gunfire, the silently sailing arrow impaled the soldier with a *thook!* dropping him.

The kraut hunched over, coiling from the thin wooden barb lodged through his middle, protruding between some ribs and jabbing through some organs. Giving in to shock, he keeled into a tumbling roll down the angled slope of the warehouse roofing, dropping along with his discarded weapon and eventually falling all the way down to the ground in a freefall that seemed like forever before the *thump.*

On Young's right, O'Flaherty, Sherington, and a dozen commando shoved forwards in tight formation towards the building, their own guns crackling both high and low, avoiding closely impacting fire by mostly unseen defenders. The group of them reached the outer walls of the tall warehouses for cover. They each took a breath to break empty mags from their weapons and recharge with fresh ones in this moment of warfare hiatus while the world around them became a thunderous torrent of exchanging gunfire.

Behind them parallel to the building side, Young was fast on the reload of his submachine gun just in time to glance up and stitch a line of holes through the torso of a loitering rifleman above their position in an exterior guard tower. After being shot, he collapsed painfully down the ladder rungs, thus sighting Young a ground-level side entrance into the warehouse just as a smartly turned-out German grenadier stepped into view ...

The partially visible man cranked back the under-arm throw arc of a primed stick grenade, aiming right at them along the outside of the warehouse—however, Young Young was too fast for that bollocks. He swerved his hip fire down and to his left in time to sketch a line of bullets across the cranked doorway, dropping the grenadier along with his cooking timed hand grenade ... *BOOF!*

The doorway exploded in a pocket of air and scalding fire, bringing down half an exterior wall panel and throwing charcoal and debris for tens of feet outwards.

Partially concealing himself as he slid into cover, Young squatted behind a stack of snow-covered wooden crates and obscured his face with his smoking machine gun as the cloud of incoming force blew across him and his men along the line.

Blanketed in ash and seared splinters, they were alive.

*They had gained the flanking position.*

"Jack!" the avowing voice of Durnford-Slater called from the rear of the fence line as some reinforcing commandos from Forrester's Troop arrived within the urban outer wing.

Churchill's beret-mounted brow spun to observe the incoming commandos.

From between the residences of the back end of the village, they flocked through the gaps in the cut fence and charged into the assault, fuelling the force of this blindsiding flank led by Captain Young.

Of the amassed group, there appeared to be an abundance of commandos continuing straight and headed north, seemingly to journey along with another objective—the last objective: *the hotel.*

Durnford-Slater, Head, de la Torre, and Forrester appeared in view, standing amidst Kaptein Linge's NOR.I.C.1 soldiers and a large detachment of Four Troop. They must have at least left a small tangent of men behind the smoke to sustain the illusion of an invading force for the enemy within the warehouses.

Their discord unravelled in the foreground of sporadic gunfire and war action in the respective warehouse vicinities.

"Group 4 is here to assist!" Durnford-Slater shouted, referring to the overflow of even *more* fresh commandos into the fray ...

Churchill witnessed that filtering between the humble houses of the Norwegian village to the south, Captain Hooper's G4 floating reserve had finally arrived on South Vågsøy from the Kenya. This was a significant ground force commanded by Hooper, with half of that lead by the talented and formidable and fanatical Lieutenant Graeme Black to reinforce Four Troop.

These Commando numbers had just been rejuvenated and reloaded to a total strength greater than it had been when G2 had initially hit the shores.

Churchill smirked upon seeing the fresh commando numbers charge the hold, assaulting the warehouse positions with precision and tact. Their numbers swarmed in dutiful advance, following through the barrier and towards the warehouses. They passed Churchill at the fence line, and Jack spotted the arrival of some of the newer No.2 Commando recruits, such as Herbert and Challington, and of course their leader, Black.

"Nice of you to join us at last, leftenant!" Churchill could not help but jest with his former aux-ops compatriot.

"Yeah, we got the invitation. Did you lot forget how to use your radios over here, or what?"

"A minor inconvenience, old boy."

Black disconcertingly eyed both Churchill and then Durnford-Slater as he passed the two high-ranking commandos, charging the fight with his men. Favouring his left bandaged arm, he looked as though he had already seen an ounce of war on the way through the village, likely catching more straggling Germans or quislings hiding within the houses. "By the way, thanks for waiting for us at the coast. We cleaned up the scraps you left on the way in!"

"Didn't want you to miss out," Jack quipped quick.

"Yeah, well, one of them broke my bloody watch with a bullet, didn't they!?"

"Blood-y-hell, lieutenant," Durnford-Slater spied the conversation piece. The broken watch was part of multiple bullet wounds along Black's field-dressed arm, bloodied from combat in the streets. The bandages looked substandard, bleeding through. "Do you need a medic?"

"Huh?!" He scoffed, shrugging it off. "And miss out on even *more* action? I'll be right, Colonel, cheers."

Churchill jeered, blowing past it. "Yes, well, we figured we better leave some Gerry for you. Didn't want to have all the fun."

"Aye!" Black responded to Churchill with a grin and a playful slap on the arm before ducking up through the fence and charging on into the haze of war between the warehouses. The man appeared in his element.

Durnford-Slater gained the attention of his man again, eager to move on with the final objective along with Captain Forrester's men. "Jack!"

Before following suit with the flock of Commando into the warehouse district, Churchill pulled nearer, detecting the desire for discretion in Durnford-Slater's manner. "Sir?"

"Have your men get the warehouse district under control, A-SAP! We've received word that Clement's men have pushed the enemy sniper teams from the north-west ridge, forcing them to displace the slope. Some have entered the city. My guess is that they will congregate with the remaining 181st Wehrmacht numbers at the hotel, bolstering their last stand ..."

Churchill's attention was focused.

"Yes, sir."

"We don't want that!"

"No, sir."

Those shooters along the ridge positively belonged to Friedrich Feind's Huntsmen group, and were the ones he was after. So far, all their G2, G3, and now G4 forces had encountered on ground level were primarily from the 181st Infantry. If there were any Gebirgsjäger left alive, and if their commander was present in Vågsøy, they would be at the hotel. The Ulvesund Hotel would indeed be their *Alamo*.

Churchill had informed the colonel about the existence and aptitude of this unforeseen enemy assist to the 181st at Vågsøy, but not told him about his prior history with the leader of the Gebirgsjäger, hence his enthusiasm to assist in the capture of the final point.

Notwithstanding, John Durnford-Slater knew Jack Churchill.

He knew him all too well, in fact, and considering how rocky their operational rapport had been on the road prior to Operation Archery, Churchill saw fit to not add further turbulence to their voyage together— especially now that they were so close to the final destination, therefore he stood down his eagerness to be at the front for now ...

Stood down his private search and destroy mission ...

*His personal vendetta ...*

After a brief thousand-yard gleam into the possibilities of vengeance that may be, Churchill's attention returned to Durnford-Slater as he continued to verbalize his proposed strategy.

"Now that the enemy overwatch is gone from the ridge, we can move into open positions around the hotel more freely and surround it. Algy and I are going to take his portion of Four Troop and the Norwegians and head directly north before the retreating enemy get too dug-in at the hotel."

"Very good, sir."

"As we speak, Captain Bradley has One Troop on approach to the hotel from the east and Captain Hooper has his section here to help you with the warehouse district from the coast. Once you're secure, get Lieutenant Black to move up north and reinforce our assail."

Churchill frowned. "You don't want us to help at the hotel?"

"You'll have your hands full capturing this," Durnford-Slater decreed with a sense of fulfilment, gesturing to the warehouses. "Stay here, secure the warehouses properly, procure any intelligence, and process the prisoners."

*This directive meant he was not to engage the hotel ...*

*Denied the possibility of confronting Feind ...*

Heartbroken, Jack bowed. "... yes, sir!"

Durnford-Slater disengaged their discourse. "Good luck."

Silently, Churchill watched as the detachment headed onwards and into the last disunion of South Vågsøy, located just north of the warehouse district. This housed some of the tallest structures on the island, more specifically, the Ulvesund Hotel: the final enemy stronghold and final objective of Archery.

*Victory was within their grasp.*

Subsequently, he saw Linge in their colossal Commando crowd, headed north. The famous Norwegian leader took a second to make his way down to the fence line in order to offer Churchill a respectful handclasp in passing. This had been the first time the two esteemed comrades had seen each other since before the raid.

"Juck!"

"Marty!" Churchill grabbed him firm and shook tight. "How fares your men?"

"They are good," he responded. His Norwegian section had been glued to the hip of Forrester all morning and were supporting Four Troop in the fight. They had worked well together, covering a lot of ground as a team, suppressing and overwhelming many enemy positions.

Churchill accredited his ongoing service.

"Thanks for the assist, earlier ..."

"Thank you for the raid," Linge snickered. After all, the British were technically backing Linge and his Norwegian Independent Company's fife into occupied Norway. This was his land they were fighting for, and he could not retake it without help from his adoptive big brothers in Britain. The whole fight was a win-win situation.

They departed.

"Be careful."

"You too, Juck."

"Oh, and look after Algy, would you?" Churchill hollered after the Norwegian as Linge drifted away with the flow. "Sometimes he can't see properly over his moustache!"

With a grin, Linge nodded with deep eye contact, and the two separated their converse.

Churchill also noted the jaw-flexing Knocker White's presence in the mass that Durnford-Slater drafted to take the hotel.

The once-Second Chester brethren looked bushed, covered in grime smears, and his uniform in tatters compared to most of the other commandos. He swapped hands with his battle-worn Ithaca pump-action shotgun in the interest of casting his friend, Mad Jack, a respectful and wordless salute gesture, which Churchill proudly returned in-kind with a sincere bow.

He would have wished him good luck, and Knocker, Jack.

The look they gave exchanged a thousand words.

This, the final chapter in this raid ...

After a brief assault engagement, the commando battering ram thrust against the German infantry's defences, penetrating their flank of their defence. Before Gerry even knew it, many of the British guns were in below the enemy's fortifications, preparing to ransack their strongholds.

Taking point, Captain Young peeked around the south corner of the first warehouse. He was abruptly met by the stiff resistance of the displaced turret guns of several German infantrymen who were now aware of Commando's enfilade manoeuvre from the west and had relocated thusly.

From the front of the warehouses, where the enemy remained scattered and in assumed positions near forward-facing sandbag barricades, a volley of mounted machine gun fire cleft past his face as he recoiled from the edge, dodging death by inches. The metal frame and wooden sheet board beside his stance became battered by the fusillade of deafening machine gun fire, causing him to recoil further.

They were denied entry from the front.

Under the cover of the machine gun, enemy infantrymen outside the warehouses displaced their deteriorating defences, falling back within the actual warehouses; predominantly, they seemed to favour the *middle* warehouse of the three; the red warehouse.

"Shit!" his heartrate through the roof, Young took a breath after pulling his back against the exterior wall of cover, showered in sparks. He was amongst supportive commandos, stacked behind his point, presently immobilized from advancing around the corner and subsequently gaining safe access into the first warehouse via the open entry. The German defences at the front were too steep, and now they knew where to look.

"Rear entries?" he turned and questioned the others who had moved up this far to scout the location, notably Lieutenant O'Flaherty, who was in command of his half of the commando Troop.

O'Flaherty passed on the question as a trooper came jogging from the length of the warehouse outer wall, already shaking his brimmed tin hat. It was apparently the same on the other end. The commandos had been met by machine gun fortifications around both ends of the warehouse. The troop reported as such. "Denied access, sir!"

"Blast! We *need* to get in!"

"Sir, what about the hole?"

Young followed his momentum back to the small side access doorway. It was the same entranceway where they had shot an enemy grenadier moments ago while on approach. The explosive had detonated within the walkway, bringing down half the inner scaffolding and supports, impeding the option of a viable entrance into the rest of the warehouse.

"Maybe—"

"Captain Young!" the lower-ranking, hotheaded Lieutenant Black emerged, running in close with an abundance of fresh G4 reserve commandos. They were fully stocked with ammo and energy and were keen to make waves.

"Lieutenant!" Young Young replied, glad to see him and he felt the support of such a renowned soldier, however, it would likely not be without altercation. Black was a control freak, and would likely try and steal the reins from him. Young also saw that Major Churchill had also crossed the clearing with a few of Black's G4 reserve, but hung back ...

Mad Jack—usually the man on-point—was merely observing Captain Young at this juncture. Not only was this a sign of confidence for his captain, a charge of responsibility and show of leadership, but a clear indicator that Churchill's focus was being split in two directions: his duty for Commando and his revenge crusade.

An ulterior motive at bay, if the possibility to delegate command of this wing should arise in order to allow him to forward his attention onto the hotel, then Churchill would exact that commission without hesitation.

Two seconds in and Black asserted his dominance.

"Well?! What are we waiting for, gents?!"

"Enemy remains about two-dozen strong. They're holed-up in these three warehouses—predominantly the red one in the middle," Young reported, jousting his head to motion that it was the next warehouse over. "They've got both corners of this one guarded with machine guns and they're not letting us pass."

"Let us have a look, then!" full of zeal and with an apparent death wish, Black inched over past Young and aligned his shoulder with the edge of the south corner. After a lungful of psych, he quickly glanced around the brink ... gained a mental photograph of the enemy emplacements ... and fast retreated as a barrage of gunfire poured down upon him, missing him by milliseconds.

He took a quick exhale before exchanging a glance with Young and raising his eyebrows. "Yep! Two MGs, one still facing front, the other on our flank. They're covering their men's displacement inside. They've got that shit wrapped tighter than a nun's knickers that's for sure!"

Young nodded. "Agreed."

The impulsive Black did his best to contain any condescension in his tone of voice. "They're going to get more and more dug in the longer we stand here tugging our bollocks, Captain."

The reality hit Young with force.

Audio from this battle was fading as their push subsided.

"I am aware ..."

"Suggest we breach or *something*."

He was well aware that delays in orders could be calamitous to Commando. Every second they wasted deciding a plan of attack, the enemy used towards bolstering their defences, making their job of eradication and eviction that much more difficult and dangerous.

Within eavesdropping range of their immediate position, Churchill oversaw the entire debacle from a safer location beside a rusty shipping container. Churchill's focus on the present warehouse raid conquest seemed to be distracted; his attention constantly gravitating north, towards the district of South Vågsøy.

In the direction where Durnford-Slater, Forrester, and Linge had progressed moments ago, Jack spied the high-standing Ulvesund Hotel.

... within that structure lurked his arch nemesis ...

... and he would miss the fight—

"*I am aware, Lieutenant!*"

The sneering exclamation by Young at Black seemed to lure Churchill's attention back to the present and away from the overarching vendetta that called to him from the distance.

It was clearly Black's overzealotry to want to leap into the flames of the fire that caused these flames to stoke. He was a race car stuck at a red, revving and salivating for more war, and his eagerness was causing him to overstep and start leaning on the newly promoted captain.

Jack knew this predicament all too well—a beast that he had learned to tame.

"Captain!" Churchill called from the rear, gaining Young's attention. He tilted his view upwards. "Suggest we think *vertically*."

Young and Black both stepped out from cover, looking up. There was a wainscoting of partially broken glass panels, possibly part of the warehouse sky lighting.

"Grenades?" Young questioned to both O'Flaherty and Black by either side, who both swapped a look with first each other, and then to Herbert and his partner, Challington.

They all swapped another look of agreement.

The commandos concurred.

"*Agreed.*"

"Yes, sir!"

While Black looked to his men and relayed the orders, Young took a second to glance towards Churchill, casting him a sly wink for giving him the idea.

Within a few seconds, they timed an attack with Black's G4 men who were all geared with Mills Bombs and other various grenades. Their hands were cold, and their fingers fumbled as they felt for their pins and spoons to prime the timed explosives.

They inched back for distance, establishing a delivery line with sights set on the glass windows that ran across the heights of the warehouse building.

"Ready?" O'Flaherty asked wielding his Thompson and aiming high, as did a few of his Six Troop wingmen between the others who were all spaced out and holding throwable timed explosives. Young stood with his own gun out before his wiggling stance.

"*Ready!*" Black nodded along with Herbert, Challington, and several other equipped commandos whom each had fists full of primed hand grenades.

Young gave the command, and they brushed their combined fire across the glass, shooting out the remaining panels that shielded the roofing of the warehouse. They hammered every piece and broke every window frame within a few loud seconds of side-to-side sweeping with their automatics and then ceased fire.

The follow-up was the other men then lofting their grenades.

They threw about two or three each between five men, lobbing one after the other of the timed Mills Bombs in over-arm tosses. The commandos accurately arced their throws to land within the margins of the warehouse, causing them to land sporadically within the space.

From within, multiple German men panickingly shouted.

"*Granate!*"

"*Granateee!*"

The timed bombs then began to detonate within the warehouse, exploding out walls and coughing a humongous cloud outwards and over the top of the few enemy positions located about the sandbag barricades out the front, which included the machine gun nest that was covering the angle.

"I'll get the MG!" over the concurrent explosions within, Black shouted in deliberation whilst he arranged his Bren gun, on the move before Young even had a chance to process his plan.

Young's head turned, observing the enthusiastic Commando take off the mark ahead of some others, sprinting the length of the warehouse with no intentions to halt once he rounded the choke point.

"Oi, wait!" Young bellowed over the chaos of the charge.

The forceful puff from the grenade detonations inside of the warehouse caused a cloud of smoke and debris to cough out of the gaping entrance, pluming over the emplacements and causing the operators to stoop and splutter.

Just as the German gunner on the machine gun became momentarily debilitated, a flock of commandos swooped tight around the edge, aggressively pushing forth and thrashing his position with intervals of gunfire. Graeme Black was on-point, leading the blind charge in an all-or-nothing, leap-without-looking manner, rounding the corner with his Bren gun charged and instantly firing.

Combined with the other brave souls following his caution-to-the-wind approach, they killed the stahlhelm-donning soldiers dead, eliminating the emplacement on their way into the smoky and shook warehouse.

*Volatile gunfire ensued within the smoke ...*

The first warehouse was cleared.

*The Ulvesund Hotel*
*South Vågsøy, Norway*

In the meantime, the village streets in the rear district of South Vågsøy had become chaotic.

The British were converging on the final precinct still occupied by the Germans. All the enemy who remained on Vågsøy Island frantically retreated to the Ulvesund Hotel, taking up positions within proximity of the surrounding blockades.

These dwindling numbers were a mix of Wehrmacht infantrymen and quislings alike, although most of the loyal locals who supported Generalleutnant Woytasch's occupation of Vågsøy Island had all since surrendered or gone seemingly—and conveniently within this eleventh hour—extinct of their required collaborations, shedding themselves of Nazi memorabilia and quickly abandoning any swastika insignia. Like chameleons camouflaging into the foliage of war, they were for now concealed among the civilian populous, postponing judgement for another day.

Upon a top-down view of the vicinity left to conquer by the raiding forces, the view of Vågsøy resembled a sentient torrent through the clefts of the city streets. From the east, the south, and the west, around every danger-swept corner, armies of British Commandos rushed in like a raging wildfire, surrounding the final quadrant.

The last streets neighbouring the hotel were compiled of double- and single-storey Norwegian residences built upon former businesses. The four-storey hotel stood focal behind them, and the last stand for the antagonistic Axis.

From the crooks of the street corners and from between the buildings, desperate and intimidated German soldiers fled their posts as the bullets from the guns of the British nibbled at their heels, removing the enemy's hold on the skirmishes of prior avenues.

Their backs were against the wall once they hit their final defensive hold at the hotel; a last stand, as ordered by their neoteric superior—a man who outranked their 181st commander: the dreaded *Hauptsturmführer Feind* of the *Schutzstaffel Gebirgsjäger*.

His orders had countermanded their Wehrmacht charge, Hauptmann Schröder, who had issued a hold and retreat moments after the raid on Vågsøy Island had commenced. His order to surrender was issued as a secondary initiative—one that was also countermanded by Feind, who insisted that surrender to the British was not an option.

It was a firm resolve, and hope was fleeting.


Down on the icy streets within the German position, amongst the plethora of ongoing warfare commotions, a different type of activity occurred. One of venal flight ...

A black tub car came revving into existence from a nearby parking garage. The shiny Volkswagen had previously been sheltered from any naval salvo targeting prior to the raid and existed without a scratch.

The vehicle belonged to Generalleutnant Kurt Woytasch's own private chaperone whenever he was present in Vågsøy. Right now, though, apprised of the knowledge of the speedy vehicle's stowed presence, the fearful Hauptmann Schröder and one of his trusted 181st subordinates had another use in mind.

They planned on using the car to run from the town on the northerly road which led out of South Vågsøy and the neighbouring townships in the municipality of the island, yonder Rødberg.

As the sizzling conflict crackled and singed about the cusp of the immediate area, burning the edges of the map towards their position in the middle, the tub car skidded to a hold on the street a half-block from the Ulvesund. This was the acquired private residence of Schröder during his campaign on Vågsøy Island.

The house was once a civilian residence. The occupants had either offered their establishment to the German order or, equally as likely, the aggressors had evicted the previous owners onto the cold streets.

The young 181st driver was shaken within the car by the skid and sudden brake. Desperate to depart the village, he tapped twice on the horn to signal his valued passenger of his hasty arrival.

Anxiously, he peered out of the passenger's side window at the front door to the residence and waited for his superior to quickly jump in with whatever luggage he could carry.

Struggling to carry three big bags of suitcase luggage and probable loot within his two weakling appendages, Schröder emerged from the vacated property in a panic. He juggled the baggage whilst attempting to shut the door to his live-in home. The sound of close gunfire from up the road caused him to duck and quiver in his strides, scared out of his wits.

The walls were truly closing in now.

He quickly reached the idling car and tilted his view to shout through the glass window. "Öffne < 'Open the trunk!' > rraum!"

The panicked occupant obeyed, releasing the lev—SMASH!

After an unfocused figure appeared outside the car, the driver's side window shattered inwards due to a forceful blunt impact. The shatter was not from a bullet ricochet, but instead from the vehement influence of a leather-gloved fist.

Glass exploded inwards. The arms of the attacker rudely reached in, grappling with the driver. The act resembled some form abduction or carjacking.

Kicking and screaming, the driver was yanked through the broken window of the locked door, torn completely out from the vehicle. Whimpering and concussed once his head hit the road, he submissively laid in the street at the mercy of his captor.

At that same moment, Schröder was rounding the tub car, wearing a look of confusion. His scared eyes grew even wider with horror when he realized who it was ...

*It was Hauptscharführer Jürgen.*

Right-hand henchman to the Gebirgsjäger Hauptsturmführer.

He was flanked by two other faceless Gebirgsjäger goons, clad in drawn white balaclavas to hide their characteristics and emanate a sense of intimidation—it worked too fucking well, even on their own people.

One of the two ski-mask larkies with submachine guns stepped in swiftly to drive a boot into the deserting driver's gut, punishing him. He then swooped in low anchor, striking him across the exposed head with the receiver of his folded-stock MP40. It further subdued the fearful infantryman, splitting his brow. They weren't going anywhere.

"Hauptmann < 'Hauptmann Schröder ... Hauptsturmführer Feind *would like to see you'* > schen ..." the Gebirgsjäger foot soldier requested as he made eventual eye contact with Schröder.

Jürgen and the other Huntsmen seemed unbothered by the state of warfare currently enveloping around the precinct, surrounding Schröder's attempted exodus out on the street. They clearly had a sub-objective here to collect the deserting Schröder, and their mission for their Hauptsturmführer superseded everything—even an advancing war and impending doom.

Caught in the act of betrayal, Schröder dropped his bags from beneath his arms as the goliath grasp of Jürgen reached out and harnessed his jacket collars, coiling him in close to his gritted teeth for an elongated grimace. The seven-foot German henchman then dragged the absconding captain back towards the hotel for trial, judgement, and possible execution by Gebirgsjäger Hauptsturmführer Feind.

The men mounted the street back across the icy road towards the Ulvesund, and stray rounds from the impending firefight whizzed and snapped past their position. Some of the emerging British soldiers could see them from afar and had let loose a few rounds in their direction without avail.

Fearless and bold, Jürgen merely strode on with the Hauptmann within his grasp. He drew his hanging machine gun with his spare hand and fired down range at the British targets as commandos became visible brimming the many corners of cover.

*Hannibal was at the gates.*

After expending a few extended bursts at the enemy, Jürgen and Schröder reached the hotel and disappeared inside as the tide of war became a flood surrounding the final occupied real estate left on the island.

Intervals of exchanging gunfire grew loud as the British Commandos pushed to the boulevard corners edging the open thoroughfare exposure before the final enemy location at the Ulvesund Hotel.

The four-storey-tall building towered over them as they encircled it at ground level. The men became suddenly aware of the height advantage this gave the enemy holed up within and predicted defensive fire from all windows on all elevated levels. This defensive fusillade was in conjunction with the multiple machine gun emplacements established at ground level, by the foyer entrance. The position would be a hard nut to crack.

Leader of the Allied march, Captain Algy Forrester, shouted the order to hold and maintain as he and his commandos of Four Troop reached the outer limits of cover before the last objective. Advanced men everywhere fanned out to a collective capture of the vicinity, remaining secure behind cover, and establishing a perimeter. Their actions were much alike the wriggling of fingertips formulating a chokehold around the enemy's jugular.

His men were quick to obey his command, dropping to a knee and stacking behind concealment, cautiously peeping from cover to lay eyes upon the hotel from behind the offensive stances of the iron-sights of their many loaded weapons. There were enemy positions visible all about the stronghold: the heavy-kitted machine gun barricades at ground level and upon the elevated level eaves and awning that sheltered the lobby entrance, as well as countless sharpshooters positioned throughout the windows on the second, third, and fourth stories.

Multitudes of gunfire were promptly exchanged.

The building was jam-packed with German defenders. It would not be long before they had shooters on the roof of the building to shoot down at their street positions.

As per the advice of Colonel Durnford-Slater, who was nearby Captain Forrester's point, they had decided to hold the line surrounding the hotel and wait for greater numbers before attempting to assault the stronghold. They knew that reserve numbers from Hooper's group, Churchill's group, and Bradley's group would eventually be filing lines behind their boundaries, and that that would be the correct tactic to make a push on the final objective from all sides concomitantly.

The commando troopers fired upon any clear targets if they had the line of sight. They drained the ammunition of the enemy sentries by glancing above cover and distracting the shooters, all the while wearing the enemy ordinance thin and their numbers and morale even thinner.

"Soon, Gerry'll have no choice but to surrender or die!" over the sporadic gunfire remarked Head, who was nursing a tied-off bullet wound to the upper arm. His friend and CO, Durnford-Slater, nodded in accord from his position in tight beside cover while they observed this juncture.

Forrester seemed to be displeased with their current standing. He shook his head, muttering from the hole beneath his broom moustache.

Durnford-Slater was aware of his disconcerted body language.

"Captain?"

"Colonel ... I believe we should seize the opportunity and wage an assault," Forrester commented after much deliberation, assessing the entire situation in his mind's eye. "The Huns are on the back foot. They're still rushing to man positions and coordinate defences. We should strike them *now*, before the ticks get any more dug-in than they are ..."

Durnford-Slater allowed the suggestion to process for a moment.

He looked to his confidant, Charley Head, and then back to Forrester. The option wasn't completely off the table; however it would require an entire participation from all sections within the command.

"What does Kaptein Linge think?" he asked.

Forrester grunted, confused. "Sorry?"

"Algy, the Norwegians presently make up fifty percent of the manpower we currently have here at this objective ..." Durnford-Slater communicated somewhat cryptically to the Four Troop commander. By his tactical intellect, Durnford-Slater foresaw Linge's reluctance to follow

Forrester into the meatgrinder that was a full-frontal assault into multiple machine gun nests. "If you're going to happen upon a suicide mission for your men, perhaps talk it over with the Kaptein, first? You don't want them leaving you and yours in the cold out there."

Durnford-Slater's logic was sound.

What Forrester proposed was attainable, but they would have to go all-in. They would have to drive one hell of an uppercut to knock out this towering enemy. In order to do so effectively, they would require all fingers of that fist enclosed and in unison to deliver the punch.

Forrester awkwardly twisted to search out Linge in the crowd of commandos and soldiers cramped behind the cover of the thoroughfare clearing.

Linge was present and had heard his name in conversation.

Forrester waved him over.

"Kaptein, are your men prepared to make a final assault?"

"When?" Linge responded, confounded.

"Now."

"*Now?!*" enclosed by Norwegian men within the ranks of the NOR.I.C.1, Linge exclaimed with his Nordic-accented voice. Although the Germans were still in the process of retreating, they still had daunting fortifications already established at the hotel and along the street. "But, Captain ... we need more men! We will barely make it over the road!"

Although he could see the Norwegian's point, frustration got the better of him for an instant. Forrester sighed as he bowed to the dissent surrounding him, opting now to wait for reinforcements before plotting their assault against the Germans ... that was until a man named Arthur Komrower rocked up to the fray.

Commandos within the vicinity all cast an eye as a squad of a half-dozen extra No.3 Commandos from Two Troop arrived on scene, piling up behind cover. Komrower was injured and mummified in bandages from his time spent at the forward operating base along the coast, where he had missed out on most of the raid this morning.

Forrester was astonished. "Arty?"

Komrower bowed. "Algy."

Durnford-Slater squinted upon the arrival of the figure. Komrower had disobeyed his direct order to remain behind, but he was also glad to have him fighting with them at the frontline.

"Lieutenant Komrower."

"Colonel," Komrower greeted as he hobbled in closer. An explanation for his desertion at the FOB was not respectively provided nor requested by either superior upon his arrival to the front.

Forrester turned to Durnford-Slater who was beside him behind cover, wanting to obtain direction on his mood following the arrival of Komrower's small posse in addition to the aforementioned plan to immediately assault the hotel. As he did, he saw beyond the lieutenant-colonel, witnessing the battle-worn summoning of Knocker White and Joe Mills, and he realized this present batch of Commando had all the capable numbers necessary to accomplish almost anything.

"No unnecessary risks, Captain," was Durnford-Slater's final response to his contemplation, however there was something in his tone as he delivered the operation's motto: a decree bequeathed not by him, but by those at Whitehall prior to the operation.

It was in that moment that Forrester settled, accepting the pronouncement to hold position. He huffed out his nostrils, blustering the bristles of his moustache.

A random trooper's voice called from the west and their heads all turned. *"Sirs! We've got an incoming force from the north! Approximately two-dozen enemy numbers falling back towards the hotel from the ridge! Maybe more."*

*"Two dozen men?"*

The trooper emphasized. *"Affirmative. Maybe more, sir."*

"Blimey, that's a whole other unit!" Forrester regarded as he did the maths. That would be in addition to what the Germans already had in the hotel as well as whatever dribs and drabs fell back into the streets.

"From the ridge you say?" Durnford-Slater questioned, referring to the north hills that book-ended the city of South Vågsøy. He frowned as the intelligence fell upon his ears, but more so to the follow-up detail within the information, which was what caught those who had already clashed against this opposition's attention.

"Yes, sir!" the troop recalled. "Men wearing white masks ..."

The lieutenant-colonel's and his brow loosened.

*Two dozen Gebirgsjäger was the equivalent to a small army ...*

"The sniper army!" gloomily deemed Head, casting a sharp gleam onto Durnford-Slater. "They'll be retreating from the ridgeline and back into the city ... They're going to try and make it to the hotel; to reinforce their last stand!"

Durnford-Slater sternly bobbed his head as the realization of what has happened came to pass. "Clement's men must have proper shaken their tree. They've pushed down from the north!"

"Yes, sir! It appears that way!" the trooper agreed in accord.

*Chit-chit!*

The loud pumping of the shotgun asserted Knocker White into their conversation as the corporal, remaining low and behind cover, moved in closer to within the officer's crowd. Spitting stale chewy out to the side, he brought with him in tandem the equally as battle-worn Sergeant Mills.

For an extended moment, the huddling officers seemed to cast them an extended warrant of their presence ...

"Yes, Corporal?" Forrester queried with an underlying scepticism.

"Just wondering what our orders are for dealing with these wankers, sir?" White replied, displaying both insubordination and obedience that made Durnford-Slater's quiet radioman de la Torre uneasy. "These are the guys that got JFG ..."

Rather new to the planning schemes, Komrower pitched an idea from outside the box, like Jack did often, and Durnford-Slater recognized the ever-courageous tone that spoke gospels of their pedigree in black-ops years ago. "We should be heading them off. We could prevent them reaching the hotel and strengthening their defences ... maybe even take them out entirely!"

"We don't yet have the numbers to split our offensive perimeter," electing a momentary mindset of a democracy, Forrester reasoned, gleaming ever so slightly towards Durnford-Slater's shared *on-paper* opinion. "We should hold here, and keep Gerry pinned at the hotel until the reinforcements reach us. We'll make our next move when we have the numbers to do so."

"What?" Knocker White resented. "But those Huntsmen will reach the hotel!"

"Corporal."

"It'll become ten-times harder to take! We'll lose ten-times as many men!"

"*Corporal!*" Forrester raised his voice. "They are your orders. Time is short."

White hissed beneath his breath, frustrated. "All the more reason to *move! Now!*"

"Our orders ..." Durnford-Slater announced loudly and above all others during their irritated discussion to break the choleric resilience. "... are to take the hotel!"

There was something in his tenor that implied exhilaration; an eagerness to stride forwards in the face of danger, rather than play it by the textbook and await reinforcements, which was what any commanding officer should have been instilling within the minds of his men—such as Mountbatten's *no-unnecessary-risks.*

Forrester swapped a look with the other highest-ranking officers, Komrower, even Head.

"But, sir ... it's an unnecessary risk."

"*But* nothing," Durnford-Slater appended as he arranged his weapon and brushed the sleet from his squat. His body language suggested that he was through with *playing it safe*. "This entire operation is a *necessary* risk. Charley, Corporal White, Sergeant Mills, you're with me ..." he ordered to his surrounding men. "Algy, Arty, Kaptein Linge, take everyone else present and, if before the reinforcements arrive you see a window of opportunity to advance upon that hotel ... take it with *everything* you've got. Gentlemen, the windows ... they're all quickly closing. This is about to become an absolute shit-fight of a stalemate."

"*Sir!*"

"*Yes-sir!*"

"Sir," Forrester upped and hounded to Durnford-Slater's fife as he led his march towards the north perimeter. "W-where are *you* going?"

"We're going to head off the Huntsmen reserve ... and hopefully buy you lot some time to crash the gates!"

"*Just the four of you?!*"

"It's all we've got," Durnford-Slater cast him an over-shoulder gleam. "At the very least, we'll slow them down long enough for you lot to take the Ulvesund."

Forrester held an extended blank stare.

"Good luck," Durnford-Slater nodded, continuing. His eyes twitched onto de la Torre, his loyal radioman, who had been glued to his hip all morning. It was now time for their umbilical cord to sever, and for him to join the battle as a regular warfighter, swapping his radio for a rifle.

With a trace of lingering admiration, Forrester watched them leave with his head bobbing ...

This was happening.

All or nothing.

*This was the end.*


"Don't you think we should be *hanging back?*" wise advisor Charley Head denoted softly as they faded in audible range of the others. He was forever a conscience on Durnford-Slater's shoulder. "Y'know, *watch the frontline from the rear, leading from the back,* that sort of thing ...?"

Durnford-Slater cast him a cock-eyed gleam as they began to jog, picking up the pace along this long-winded flanking manoeuvre, circumventing the Ulvesund Hotel block.

"Where it's safe?"

"Exactly."

"And miss out on all the fun?"

Head tilted his expression in retort.

It was like he didn't know his old friend at all.

"You've been hanging around Mad Jack for far too long, John."

"Algy knows he must attack the hotel before the enemy gets any more fortified than they already are—definitely before any more of those additional Huntsmen arrive to reinforce them. We're going to earn for them that time."

Head knit his brow. "So ... why not just order Algy to attack?"

Durnford-Slater wanted not to have to point out to his direct subordinate that he desired to not be responsible for giving such a brash and treacherous command. He was incapable of giving such an order; an instruction that would result in the certain death of many commandos. It may have been sacrilege, but he loved them too much for that. Besides, on the white paper of an after-action report that would undoubtedly critique the decisions made on the field, the jobs of those at Whitehall hunting for somebody to blame regarding the loss of life for Operation Archery would be made far too easy if they could see that by simply waiting for further numbers to arrive, the results would have varied.

"In that situation, for the soldiers of any army it would be suicide to assault a position so heavily guarded by any enemy."

"Okay, so the question still remains, why order them at all ...? And why the *fuck* are we doing this, then?" Head questioned as they jogged into the fray, circumnavigating the perimeter of the hotel in order to head-off the Huntsmen reserve. He grimaced—the running made the bullet wound to his arm hurt.

"That's a trick question," Knocker White commented in Durnford-Slater's absence of a rejoinder, having been eavesdropping their conversation from the rear of their four-man pack. He was holding a packet of bubble-gum to his face and using his teeth to remove a single strip from the package.

Head eyed him, waiting for some type of punchline from this subaltern commando.

"He didn't give the order because he doesn't need to!"

Seemingly the only one still yet to get it, Head switched his glance back onto Durnford-Slater.

"We're not soldiers, for good soldiers follow blind orders ..."

Head scowled. "If we're not good soldiers then what are we?"

"Better."

*They were commandos.*

"Wir sind < *'We are soldiers! Not Commandos!'* > mandos!" the frightened, worse-for-wear Hauptmann Schröder exclaimed while he pled his argument at the hands of the unforgiving Gebirgsjäger Hauptsturmführer, Friedrich Feind. Since seen last, Schröder had now a bloodied nose, scruffy hair minus his officer's cap, and a torn uniform collar all from being mistreated under Jürgen's custody.

His voice trembled.

They were back in Feind's hotel room: his would-be war room.

Schröder's trusted subordinate was also present in the room with them. With a freshly smashed face, he had been tossed in and onto the carpet by the other two white balaclava-wearing guards who stood behind Jürgen in the doorway to the base of operations for the Gebirgsjäger.

The fourth-floor hotel room beheld an intact window with a view of the current chokehold the British army had on their building below.

Viewing this battle, Feind twisted in an imperious pose to face his insubordinates from the diminishing 181st Infantry Division. In a way, he was holding Schröder responsible for this losing battle.

His stance was immediately followed by a swift advance across the carpet. The air was quiet for a moment following Schröder's frightened counterstatement. Nothing but the ambience of close ground-level gunfire and the occasional exchanged hand grenade detonation reverberated through the calm indoors setting.

"*Kommandos?*" Feind finally questioned, his stern strides braking an inch from his nose, causing the scared Wehrmacht captain to whimper in fear of death. Feind was hung up on Schröder's use of the term rather than the connotations regarding his contention. He obviously valued the case of Schröder's interrupted desertion, freshly hung-up on this circumstance, however it did not waiver in his disappointment over the 181st faltering insolvency towards defending South Vågsøy.

Feind shared a gleam with loyal man, Jürgen, who had since been keeping his Hauptsturmführer up to date with the cause of the raid. Jürgen was as surprised as Feind was.

*It explained a lot.*

The German war machine had heard much about these troublesome British specialists known as *Commandos*. Due to their advanced training and skillsets, these unique troopers differed from regular types of soldiers and battlefield specialists in that they primarily operated in covert combat, frontline reconnaissance, and amphibious raiding. If one commando was worth ten G.I. soldiers, a trade-off conversion could place the Gebirgsjäger within their ranks as formidable foe.

Jürgen input from his position holding Hauptmann Schröder vertical. It all suddenly made sense: their tactics in advancing assaults, outmanoeuvring their snipers, their unprecedented abilities and accuracy during combat in the streets, and how they took the church stronghold so easily ...

"Das wü < *'That would explain the rate of their progress.'* > rklären."

"Di < *'The Wehrmacht are paper-people compared to them.'* > leute," casting a fast look down at the cowering subordinate of Schröder as he lay bleeding on the carpet, Feind stated.

That was said with both humble respect for thy enemy, as well as unwarranted exaggeration. The fact that they were British Commandos was why they had been so successful at combat in their advance against the easily defendable island.

"Mein Herr," a younger Truppenführer of the Gebirgsjäger entered the thin hotel doorway behind Jürgen and the balaclava-clad guards. He was breathless and slightly alarmed. "Die Briten < *'The British are surrounding the hotel! They've flooded the streets!'* > überflutet!"

Feind calmly accepted the intelligence. "Schicken < *'Send all of our available shooters to the roof to assist in defence of the building. The navy wont risk artillery with their foot soldiers so close on the ground. Tell them to conserve ammunition, to inflict casualties on higher-ranking personnel only. Sever their leadership. Seal off the stairwells! Nobody gains access to our floor, not even the useless 181st ... Alpine Huntsmen only!'* > alpine Jäger!"

"Aber < *'But, sir, what if the Heer try to fall back?'* > zuziehen?"

Feind exclaimed harshly. "Töte sie! < *'Kill them! Use their corpses to block the stairwells! Go now!'* > Geh jetzt!"

"Ja, Mein Herr," the Huntsman replied with a salute before running back into the hallway of the hotel, barking orders to other men within the Gebirgsjäger to perform the said tasks.

Feind eyed Jürgen behind the captive Hauptmann Schröder, who was still held standing in the walkway by the colossal kraut. "Sie < *'They are more useful in death than in defence.'* > verteidigung."

His insult against the 181st Infantry Division caused Jürgen to hold a humorous smirk.

The Truppenführer respectfully nodded with compliance before disappearing with guards down both hallways of the fourth-storey level.

Getting back on track, Feind paced with his gloved hands behind his back.

As Feind next spoke, Schröder took his words in a tone not unlike a trial hearing. *This* was his Reichskriegsgericht. His court-martial. Next, a likely execution. "Wo waren wir < *'Now, where were we ...? We've talked about your incompetency, Hauptmann Schröder. Your inability to lead an infantry division, as well as strategize and conduct an arduous defence against an invading enemy force from an easily defendable location ...'* > und durchzuführen."

"Wenn dies < *'If this were to be conducted in Berlin, you would be trialled for war crimes by the Richter in Roter Robe.'* > Gericht gestellt."

Feind halted in his stride to glance over his shoulder at Schröder, witnessing the fear and utter trepidation he had cast upon the man.

"Aber ... wir sind nicht in Berlin," Feind concluded matter-of-factly. His tone momentarily enlightened Schröder's sombre mood. "Das ist < *'But ... we aren't in Berlin. This is war. We are to be, here, either captured or killed by the enemy, and therefore there is no time for your trial to be held properly ... Only the punishment ... and that punishment is death.'* > der Tod."

Schröder and his subordinate both suddenly—and prematurely—stopped breathing.

Through whimpers and tears and panicking short breaths of dread, they suddenly became even more afraid before their withdrawn submission at the hands of Jürgen, before the armament of the balaclava guards.

Feind stated in a calming tone as he strode out before them on the soft carpet. "Keine < *'Fret not, Captain, you've gotten off lightly. I did not mention your weakness. Your cowardice. Your desire to desert the battle ... Did you honestly think you could just drive out of town?'* > Stadt fahren?"

Jürgen held a smile at Feind's art of torment.

This was clearly not the first time this lot had mongered compatriots into capitulation. Perhaps not his first time planning out executions, either.

"Haupt ... Hauptsturmführer," Schröder stuttered, wheezing in his trepidation. "Ich < *'I was not deserting ...'* > ssen ..."

Feind's stoic expression fell even flatter. "Bock < *'Bullshit.'* > st."

"Ic < *'I was merely driving around to the hotel garages'* > ren ..."

"Bockmist!" Feind shouted again before deciding to humour Schröder's excuses. "Wa < *'Then what was in the garage?'* > age?"

Schröder seemed reluctant to tell.

Perhaps there was truth in his lies.

"Wa < *'What did you see?'* > hen?"

He hesitated with his words before finally placating with a cringe.

"*P... Pan ... Pan ...*"

Feind formed a smile across his duelling-scared mug.

*This confirmed his suspicions.*

His mouth itched a leer.

Smugly, he eyed Jürgen.

His expression falling flat, he approached Schröder to speak up close, belittling him further and in a sombre tone that made him almost foam at the mouth. "Die ganze < *'This whole time, Captain ... you mean to tell me that the men of the 181st Infantry Division ... were in possession of an armoured beast? And you did not think this would be a relevant form of defence of the island?'* > sein würde?"

Schröder winced under Jürgen's firm hold while Feind stared into his soul. He stuttered, unable to contain his tears.

"Es hat < *'It has ... minimal fuel ... minimal munitions'* > unition ..."

Feind soothed him like a scared child. "*Shhh.*"

After a moment, Feind considered the details and chartered a new course for himself. For Schröder, however ... his destiny had already been preordained by the heartless Hauptsturmführer.

"Erinnerst < *'Do you remember what I said about surrender, Captain?'* > Hauptmann?" Feind questioned the impassive Schröder as he stood idle and glassy eyed. After a moment, he followed up the question with a glare of raised eyebrows that caught his attention. "Hmm?"

Schröder gulped his phlegmy throat.

"Das < *'That it was ... suicide'* > mord ..."

"*Zuicide,* ja."

Feind retrieved something from the furniture in the room. It was a small PP pistol. In front of the Hauptmann, Feind racked the slide and then ejected the clip, offering in his open palm the single shot-loaded handgun to the captive German in order to take his own life. Such was ritual for his insolence and incompetence.

Schröder shuddered his head in a shake, sobbing inconsolably.

"Du hast < *'You surrendered. This was your decision.'* > cidung."

Feind's dark eyes were demonic in their stare of resolve.

His beam moved from Schröder and onto his subordinate who was still lying on the carpet, nursing the wound to the side of his head. The offer of the handgun gravitated towards him, which he also fearfully declined. Neither man was ready to die.

All the while in their silence, the sound of warfare boomed in the streets below, surrounding the hotel. It was a constant reminder of their predicament at the hands of the British.

Hauptsturmführer Feind abruptly bellowed stridently, further frightening the captive men. "Die Engländer < *'The English are everywhere! Do you not remember?! You let them into your land! Remember?!'* > Merken?!"

Feind's scornful gaze beamed from Schröder and to his subordinate on the floor. "Hier! < *'Here! Let me show you!'* > zeigen!"

Before Schröder's incapacitated eyes, he watched as Feind lunged down and violently grappled with his infantryman. With volatile strength and potency, he ripped him up, audibly tearing his uniform. Wrestling with a firm hold, he tossed him across the hotel room, sending him staggering into the wall below the panoramic glass window that overlooked the battle on street level.

Feind was fast behind the flailing soldier, quick to harness him with a tense grapple, hoist against the glass window and pressing painfully, smearing the blood from his headwound.

The view of close warfare was intimidating.

From their position, they could *see* the enemy forces down below, clear as day. They could watch their movements and formation. Even perform a headcount if so desired.

The point of view was not without a sense of exposure.

The same feeling of exposure one felt when their head peeked from cover during battle—probably because, to a sharpshooter, they were just that.

*Exposed.*

"Leg deine < *'Put your arms up! Like you surrender!'* > ergeben!"

The scared soldier did so, pressing his sweaty palms up against the transparent glass. He started to sob uncontrollably.

"Sie < *'Do you see them?!'* > sie?!" Feind shouted from behind his head.

After a second, the fearless Hauptsturmführer took a brash step in withdrawal, drawing his sword from his hip with a scraping *shwing!* He pressed the tip against the 181st captive's spine as he remained against the glass, smearing skin oil and sweat across the once sparkling clean display.

"Gut. < *'Good. Because they probably see you, too.'* > sehen."

From all the way down below on the streets, shots punched thick holes through the plate glass with loud *smashes*. A trajectory angular from street-level, the lead projectiles penetrated the glass and hit the ceiling above them.

*Whiz-smash!*
*Whiz-smash! Smash!*
*Smash-THIC!*
*THIC!*

The pinned soldier was finally hit through the glass pane.

Bullets punctured his torso again and again.

Feind raised his blade and reeled back a step from the display.

The soldier's body convulsed two, three times before his surrendering stance pulled away from the scape, and he collapsed, cupping the many wounds to his abdomen.

Falling to his knees, the spider-webbed window shattered loudly behind him, raining inwards from the updraft of cold air and sprinkling across the carpet like icing sugar across a red velvet cake.

The air was now windy within the hotel room.

The sound of the gunfight that raged down below was now much louder. These final hours were all extremely real.

Fearlessly, Feind stepped forward, towards the opening, driving his boot with force into the kneeling soldier, kicking him out of the opening without any hesitation or resistance. Perhaps regarded as a mercy kill, it was the end of him.

In the open air ambiance and wind of the hotel room, the sword-wielding Friedrich Feind took self-confident strides back towards the remaining catatonic captive, Hauptmann Schröder. Although even the hostage knew that his time had come, Feind stretched out the next execution all the while longer—a final form of torture.

Schröder whimpered. "Du ... < *'Y ... you killed him!'* > tötet!"

Feind corrected: "Ich habe < *'I did not kill him. They say that the lives of the men you kill in this life, wait to serve you for eternity in the afterlife ... I have enough slaves.'* > Sklaven."

While the words of pure evil and wickedness settled in with the captive Wehrmacht Hauptmann, Feind addressed his right-hand man, Jürgen. "Bei unserem < *'Our last stand here will be about inflicting the maximum sum of casualties to the British. Find out if he's telling the truth about the tank.'* > Panzer sagt."

Jürgen beamed evilly.

He released his hold on the stupefied Schröder, allowing for the man to stand on his own. Confused, Schröder clutched at the sore spot on his collar and neck, caressing them thus while he glanced wide-eyed at his killer.

Jürgen observed silently. Calmly.

In the blink of an eye, Feind dashed forth and thrust his sword six inches through the centre of Schröder's abdomen, causing the cowardly captain to gasp in pain and clutch at the razor-sharp blade for an instant before Feind subtracted it with a moist, metallic removal.

*SLISH ... sshhluck.*

Weakened, Schröder subsided to the floor, clutching at the wound and writhing in sudden agony from the location of the incision as his own warm blood began to leak into his cupped hands as he failed to apply adequate pressure.

Feind left him maimed.

"Wirf seinen < *'Toss his body down the stairs. He can be to the first of many to clog the passageways'* > Durchgänge verstopft ..." he said, revealing an entity of his defensive dastardly plans to defend the hotel against the British marauders.

*Warehouse District*
*South Vågsøy, Norway*

Inside of the first contained warehouse, the defending infantrymen who were not killed by the broadsides of the grenade eruptions were swiftly stricken by gunfire as the commandos advanced on the position with brute force, taking the upmost advantage of the concussed state of those within.

In precise assault formations that they had practised a hundred times prior to the raid, the No.3 Commando troopers rounded the angles and pushed inside the fortified premises, stacking behind and flanking each other's coordinated movements as they advanced through the smoky and well-shaken interior.

With surgical precision and extreme prejudice towards any existing threat, they either shot dead or detained with ruinous influence all those who remained alive inside.

Most of the German soldiers who survived the bursts of grenade salvo were concussed and consequently incapacitated, but there were a few within the shadows who had endured the onslaught, opting still to put up a fight. They defended their positions until their last breaths.

"*Hande Hoch! Hande Hoch!*" the English shouted in German so that the enemy could understand as their khaki numbers poured inside, shaking the sights of their weapons at multiple targets, fingers firm on the triggers but exercising discipline.

Young and Black led the frontal advance through the open double doors of the warehouse, shouting and directing the business ends of their guns at anyone who bore arms or possessed anything reminiscent of lethal intent. If they seemed hostile, they cut them down with a brunt to the chest and moved on.

Through the single door at the back, O'Flaherty brought up the rear with a detachment of men. They had to shoot two enemy riflemen who had survived the grenade blasts by hiding behind several stacked pallets of de-icing salt, including another who was hiding near the rafters up above, filling him with hot lead through the grated floor he was perched over.

The two teams met in the middle like two tides in a green beret swirl, and within seconds, they had taken the warehouse.

Longbow in hand, arrow nocked against the bowstring and prepared to draw, Churchill entered after the initial assault team. His guard was cautionary, but his stern gaze was unparalleled.

Young performed a brief headcount as he met with O'Flaherty in the midpoint of the messy warehouse floor. They had rounded up four shell-shocked prisoners and killed nearly twice that by either grenade detonation or gunfire.

"Good thing we rushed them before they finished setting *that* up," O'Flaherty remarked, gesturing up above on the railing where there was a makeshift sheet metal barricade with a mounted heavy machine gun partially deployed above it. Fortunately, the enemy had not had the time to completely install the weapon so that it was operational, otherwise taking the position through the front could have been a bloodbath on their side.

"I'll take my guys outside and secure the area between the buildings," O'Flaherty detailed, leading with trooper Sherington.

Young immediately reaffirmed. "Dennis, hold at the next warehouse and wait for me and the lads, alright? You don't want to walk into one of *those* things set-up!"

Young gestured to the same machine gun in the same manner that O'Flaherty had done only moments ago.

Dennis O'Flaherty dipped his brodie helmet with the defective chinstrap in concurrence, then he, Sherington, and his few other Four Troop galivants moved on to secure the potentially hostile space between warehouses.

Nearby, Churchill kicked over a shrapnel-pelted corpse and examined the uniform tag of a few other deceased bodies. He was quietly cataloguing the enemy's unit insignia in hopes to discover the men from the Gebirgsjäger ... unfortunately, they were merely all Wehrmacht.

These guys weren't his fight—he was in the wrong part of the raid to encounter any of Feind's Huntsmen.

Young strode nearer to report, noticing that Churchill was searching for his own personal enemy amongst the dead: a vendetta that he was a privy to. He serenely interrupted by his acknowledgement to the fact. "Jack, this isn't all of them. The remainder must be next door in the red warehouse ..."

Churchill peeled his eyes from off the littering deceased across the dusty and bloody-clotted warehouse floor. He nodded in concurrence.

"I sent O'Flaherty around to secure the area between the buildings and gain a foothold for the next breach," Young informed as he tilted at the neck and examined the interior design of the warehouse they occupied, sourcing it for intel on the next building for any sort of possible advantage as they seemed to be of similar if not identical design, apart from colour.

Churchill filled Young in on the plans as he knew them. "Colonel Durnford-Slater has taken Captain Forrester's section and headed north towards the Ulvesund Hotel. I am going to meet them there once we have secured the warehouses."

"Sure."

Churchill hooked in discreetly, hinting at his desperation. "I need to see this raid to be over and done with ..."

Young nodded respectfully of Churchill's circumstances.

*Of his yearned vengeance.*

"We should breach the next warehouse A.S.A.F.P.," Black remarked brashly, inserting himself into their conversation. Coincidentally to Churchill's cause, he was too hyped up to wait.

Black was flanked by a few of his gung-ho G4 boys, Herbert and Challington. They seemed anxious to rack up some more kills on the tally since he and his group had missed out on the action of the initial invasion of the raid. "This one was easy. We should punch on."

"Hold on," Young halted with a palm raised. "We've got to play this smart."

"*Smart?*" Black frowned, scolding this young superior with a glance up and down. Quite personally, he was surprised Churchill was not taking point of the unit and was allowing his subordinate to helm the reins while he sat shotgun.

"No unnecessary risks, Lieutenant," Young thumped into his No.4 Commando inferior Mountbatten's motto for Operation Archery. "Remember?"

Churchill could not help but let out a single snigger.

He knew Black. Knew how negatively he received that comment.

Young was only regurgitating precisely what and how he had said the words to him barely two hours ago on Måløy Island. What was even funnier was that Black's reactions were identical to Young's from that very same moment an hour ago.

"*Excuse me?*" Black scrunched his face.

Young informed with a certainty. "We got lucky with this ... These Germans were shell-shocked and barely established, and with hardly as many troopers as what Four Troop saw retreating from the town. Our spotters saw a dozen more men than this bank into the red warehouse. It'll be much worse next door."

"*We're commandos!*" Black reasoned firmly. Herbert and Challington concurred in accord of his words, seemingly loyal to the end to their fervent commander. "We flash like lightning! These stupid krauts won't even see it comin'."

Young glanced at Churchill, noticing that his major was awaiting to hear his decision on how to proceed with the men, as well as how he dealt with the peer pressure from Graeme Black. That, or he was just enjoying the show watching his subordinate speak his own contextual words.

"Look," Young devised in reference to the next warehouse, "the interior is made of wood, not metal ... it just has metal sheeting on the outside ..."

"Yeah, *so?*" Black squabbled with an itchy trigger finger.

"*So,* it'll burn ..." Young considered, stepping over and further demonstrating the wooden structure to the interior of the warehouse. "We burn them out."

"*Sir!*" jogging inside and short of breath, a flustered voice interrupted the officers. "Lieutenant O'Flaherty is leadin' a push inside!"

"*What?!*" Young glared.

The trooper appended. "He says it looked clear!—"

"No! Tell him to hold! Immediately!" Young shouted, shoving men out of the way in the pursuance of intervening personally.

"We told him to wait, sir, but he said he had an opportunity! Sir, the side door was unlocked an' everythin'!"

"*Trooper!*" Churchill's voice thundered. The atmosphere filled with a sudden urgency. "Run! Tell Lieutenant O'Flaherty to wait for orders!"

Jack's voice boomed sternly as Young sprinted off the mark, bolting in person out of their warehouse and around the bend to the neighbouring red warehouse ...

Churchill watched the courageous commando sprint into action. "Young!"

Fast behind him was Black instructing Herbert, Challington, and another dozen No.2 Commando loyalists from G4 to instead follow *his* lead in what would probably be a full-fledged assault on the red warehouse *with* or *without* Captain Young's command.

Too much youngblood, the entire mission unravelled in a heartbeat.

"Bollocks!" Churchill remarked with haste, picking up the pace in order to catch up to the ensuing mayhem ...

*The Ulvesund Hotel*
*South Vågsøy, Norway*

On the outside ground level of the hotel and the enemy's final stronghold, the men of Four Troop scattered thin along the perimeter that encircled the position.

From the many tessellating window panels and overhanging eaves of the Ulvesund Hotel, German shooters fired down on British targets as they held the edges of the buildings at street level. Any frontal advances from their stances along the southern side would be met by the barrels of numerous desperate enemy offences, tucked thoroughly behind barriers.

Positioned front and centre amongst them, Captain Forrester and his men spotted and fired upon two infantrymen who they had been tussling with since they arrived. They had finally gained the upper hand on their position when one of Linge's **NOR.I.C.1** men struck a gunner with a lucky clip to the collar bone, becoming exposed after recoiling another aggressive shot. The poor cunt wore three gunshot wounds from three different directions before he hit the concrete.

His partner was now vulnerable to flanking from either side and they did so, pushing on him and flushing the position with close-quarters Thompson action and blinking muzzle flashes.

Commandos then assumed the newly gained position, closer to the hotel than ever, however the troublesome window snipers above fast became a nuisance.

Suddenly, a trooper nearby their location got hit in the chest.

With a dash of dark red droplets, he dropped to the bleached white snow with a crunch. He was fast dragged behind cover by his pals, though they all watched with dread as the young commando bled out within a minute from the fatal wound. It was yet another tragic casualty of war on their side.

They had come to a minor standstill at this juncture.

Determined to regain the momentum for their assault, Forrester beheld the men at his flanks. He was surrounded by brave and battle-proficient commandos—troopers that did more damage standing up than sitting down.

*At last, he understood what Durnford-Slater meant ...*

He hailed to one of his nearest leaders after a moment of realization and reflection. "Sergeant! Ready your men for a charge."

"*Sir!*"

"*Yes, sir!*"

"Captain?" the accented Kaptein Linge queried having just witnessed that particular harrowing order be given. "We are ... advancing?"

Forrester denoted decisively. "Kaptein Linge ... we are."

Linge stared impassively, tiling his view like a trance.

"We have to!"

"... where are the reinforcements?"

"Kaptein ... the longer we wait here, the tougher it's going to get to *evict* these Gerry guests from the hotel. Do you understand?"

"... we will lose many men pressing this objective," Linge stated after a pause and consideration. This was not an avenue that he would likely take if in charge.

"We will lose more in resistance the longer we wait, and the more time we give Gerry up there to get dug in deeper. We need to attack *now* while the window of opportunity is still open ... do you understand?"

"I ..." Linge's focus wandered. The direction was not lost in translation, but perhaps in ideology. He was only just learning to think like a Commando.

"Martin, I need you to understand, and for your men to follow ... this *has* to happen ..." Forrester keenly eyed Linge. This was not a threat to intimidate, or an ultimatum demanded of the Norwegian combatant. He merely needed to have the willing support of Linge.

Given the moment, Linge finally saw the value in the risk, and he lastly nodded—a firm nod, one of resolve.

"Good. Tell your men to prepare! We'll move on my command within the minute," Forrester stated before pushing up from the snow and moving along his line of Four Troop commandos.

"Okay, okay," Linge repeated. It was sold on him, now he had to sell it to his men within the timeframe. He went off to discuss the direction in Norwegian to his people, talking quickly.

"Reload with freshly topped mags, gentlemen!" Forrester shouted amidst his commandos. "This is it! If you have smoke grenades, have them front and centre to blanket our attack!"

Men down the defensive line relayed the order.

Commandos who were not equipped with fully loaded guns took this instance to reload. There was zero to no cover between the last row of houses and the hotel to seek refuge. Once initiated, their assault would be comprehensive, start to finish—and the finish line was the hotel outer walls, itself.

If they died, they failed. If they failed, they would die ...

Total commitment.

Forrester took a fast headcount of his Troop and an inventory of his men's ordinance. He had a formidable unit at his disposal, even more so when he factored in the NOR.I.C.1 contingency. It would be tough and not without loss, but they could pull this off.

He took a moment to pull the used drum magazine from his submachine gun and swap it out for a fresh fifty rounds. Forrester then glanced up above his unstinting womb broom, seeing commandos feed shells into shotguns, stick-magazines into Thompsons, and even a few men charging their pistol sidearms at the ready, with the understanding that if their primaries ran dry out there, there was no time to stop and replenish ammo. As per their training, it was always quicker to switch to a secondary than stop to reload.

In Linge's group, the Norwegians loaded their Automatgevär rifles and assorted surplus British weaponry, such as the Lee-Enfield and rattling Sten guns.

Men primed grenades and prepared them at the ready, all the while watching and waiting with their eyes upon their fearless Four Troop captain and his unwavering determination towards charging his men to victory.

There was an eerie silence during the wait.

The Germans had since ceased their shooting at them as they halted their offensive brunts, in favour to prepare for an attack—and it would not be long before the enemy sensed a calm before a storm.

"Smoke!" Forrester called, pulling the cap on his own No.76.

Others who were ready did the same all down the line. With a look cast both left and right, it appeared that through a daisy-chain configuration, Four Troop had a line-of-sight manacle of visual communication.

The men were all prepared and ready for launch, waiting for their closest neighbours behind protection to relay the command from their moustachioed captain.

As the awareness of the quiet seemed to overcome everybody on either side of the fight, Forrester brought forth his attention and lobbed his grenade over his barricade and into the open street space beyond ...

*This was it ...*

*The beginning of the end, regardless of the outcome.*

Other commandos all along the circular perimeter did the same, lofting their smoke grenades overhead and into the open thoroughfare between their offensive perimeter and the Ulvesund Hotel. Some of the metal discharges tinkered across the gravel or splashed in muddy sleet puddles, others landed with a thump in thick mounds of snow.

Like a consistent string of pyrotechnics, the hurled No.76 smoke grenades detonated in a line, popping into smouldering clouds of sizzling white phosphorous, emitting a haze of visibility-impeding smoke to cover their daunting advance.

It was then, almost as a gag, Forrester decided to utilize something No.3 Commando had performed only in practice back home, on the Largs training grounds ...

After a deeply drawn breath, Forrester bared his teeth to bellow at the top of his lungs: "*COMMANDOOOO!*"

Bravely exposed, he led the bound out from behind his concealment as the smokescreen in the streets wafted, climbing high into the thoroughfare, keeping everything from their assault a surreptitious visual— all except for the overwhelming *battle cry* that resounded behind the wall of white by the British Commandos involved in the charge.

*Warehouse District*
*South Vågsøy, Norway*

Ever since the fiery Lieutenant O'Flaherty impulsively assumed the directive to breach the side entrance of the red warehouse, several commandos had congregated along the broadside of the outer wall. They were poised with their guns at the ready, unwilling to follow the roguish endeavour and awaiting orders.

Once outside, Young could see that O'Flaherty and two other commandos at his clips had processed entry of the dark and mysterious, hostile environment—the curious red warehouse—via the side door. Assuming they were weapons hot and overconfident, empowered by the success of the prior warehouse raid, they had at least entered tactfully; weapons up and fingers on the triggers. A valiant sentiment, but one disregarding orders all the same.

Captain Young came in a hurry.

He didn't shout. Didn't command.

He ran at full pelt towards the gathering at the open side access door, deducing that the point of entry had been where his men entered the presumptuous kill-box. Assuming they were weapons hot and overconfident, still empowered by the success of the prior warehouse raid.

"*Did they go in?!*" Young interrogated a guarding commando among those stacked up and awaiting orders on the outside. Before they even had a chance to respond, Young impatiently repeated the question with fire in his breath. "*Did they go in?!*"

Hesitant to respond, a commando bobbed his brodie-helmeted head—

Muffled gunfire erupted rashly from within the red warehouse ...

Men shouted inside the echoic interior.

"*Dennis!*" Young called. His concern heightened from the sudden overdose of adrenaline. He pushed in tight beside the open doorway with his Thompson clutched rigidly, seeking refuge from the abrupt loudness within. His voice echoed. "*Dennis?!*"

Retaliatory gunfire sounded off and Young peered around the corner, becoming somewhat veiled in silence. The sporadic muzzle eruptions had been from just inside the doorway, pelting bursts upwards and towards shooters located upstairs and on the second level by the internal wood rafters.

The interior was dark and abyssal.

Blinding muzzle flashes within the confines of the warehouse strobed like a lightning storm in the pitch black of night. The reverberations from within the inside of the metal tomb were deafeningly echoic. The otherwise blissful serenity of a dark and quiet space was now nightmare fuel.

The red warehouse was the biggest of the few located in the district. It was also the one with the most places to hide within, and the most fortifiable.

It went quiet ...

*Too quiet.*

Submachine gun first, Young inched inwards, entering what he knew to be a kill-box. In the darkness, he spotted both O'Flaherty and Sherington as they hobbled in retreat from what must have been an extremely short-lived gunfight upon their foolish entry. Whether they had won or lost was at first indeterminable, though judging by the aftermath, even if they had won ... it was a Pyrrhic victory.

The two commando men limped weirdly and staggered; O'Flaherty even firing a few more rounds up and towards the lurking enemy in an elevated position before his weapon clicked dry.

He followed after the shambling Sherington, shuffling at the shoes, having been shot in the leg and foot. In fact, half of his combat footwear was completely missing, and smoke resonated from the gaping hole in his boot. Toeless and with a tense gritting of his teeth, he hobbled towards the light of the open doorway, and the brightness unveiled the look of fear and anguish on his ghostly pale face that was full of shock and regret.

Sherington passed by the stumped Young, who covered his retreat with poise, and was met by two commandos who reached in and pulled him from harm's way, yanking him back out to safety. They assisted him in exiting the shooting range while O'Flaherty seemingly brought up the rear of their irrational infiltration from the dark.

After Young made way for Sherington, he took a better glance inside the gloomy warehouse, scanning the creepy interior with his weapon. He watched O'Flaherty sauntering backwards, hobbling and generally acting strange. The overenthusiastic lieutenant was still pointing his smoking Thompson up at the ceiling after expelling what was left in his magazine at the rafters, having created nothing more than a bright firework display of sparks against the metal. His finger was clutching the trigger even though his gun was empty.

"*Dennis!*" Young hissed from the light of the door. He was close enough to reach out and tow the lad in now, but something was just *off* about the whole situation ... about O'Flaherty's movements ... about his actions ...

His weapon was out of ammunition, yet he squeezed the trigger, causing the empty weapon's receiver to emit a *click-click-click* rattle.

It was in that sliver of a moment, something surreal transpired for Young Young.

Although they held distaste for the Germans, this one Wehrmacht infantryman guarding the side entrance had obviously been a gentleman fighter. He had hit these men in (arguably) a just defence, denying them entry into the stronghold, but not abhorrently killing them for the sake of taking their lives. He saw fit not to outright slaughter these fanatical British aggressors in their gallant push. They had been tagged, and that was enough.

The enemy combatant let them live and stagger away ...

... and he let Young live, also.

The light finally illuminated O'Flaherty's front, and Young would have been lying if he said that the gore that he witnessed did not shock him to the very core.

Dennis O'Flaherty had been shot in the face—possibly more than once.

A bullet had hit him through the eye and seemingly exited out of the roof of his mouth, splitting his lip and chin to the raw bone shimmer. Another bullet—or possibly the same travelling ballistic—had also damaged his neck and shoulder, causing blood to drip profusely from an open wound, coating his snow coverall and saturating his khaki uniform beneath. From the incision pumped a sticky crimson bloodletting, sapping down his uniform as if he was carrying a punctured water flagon on his shoulder.

"*Christ in Heaven!*" Young cursed, allowing for his weapon to drop to its shoulder strap in order to collect his blinded lieutenant with both guiding hands. He quickly escorted O'Flaherty out through the doorway and, as he did, Young cast another quick gleam inside the mysterious warehouse space, realizing for the first time just how exposed they all were

*... he saw multiple German gunmen watching them from above,* weapons poised and tracing his exit.

These men had just ... *let them go.*

*It sent a shiver down his spine.*

He dared not look back.

Once outside in the bright morning light and safe from the hidden defenders inside, Young eyed Graeme Black as he and trooper Herbert jogged near in a fuss. They had been advocates of a frontal assault into the unknown environment since even before O'Flaherty's escapade.

*They now witnessed first-hand how that wasn't such a great idea ...*

Young eyed them as he passed, escorting the spectacle of the tattered and blood-soaked O'Flaherty to sanctuary.

"Get the petrol cans from the other warehouse," he ordered, and this time, they would listen due to his serious attitude and the grave tenor in his voice. "Splash the walls and set them alight. Set up our Bren guns at the front and side exits. We'll turn the heat on ... those lurking inside can *surrender* or *die ...*"

"Yes, sir!" Herbert replied before disappearing.

After Young allowed for the wounded O'Flaherty to be taken by some of the other men and escorted back towards the forward operating base for medical attention, he found a discreet moment he could share with just Black, and in reference to a prior debate.

"Just for the record, lieutenant, *that ...* that was an unnecessary risk."

With Captain Young's leadership abilities proven, the directive of his plan soon came to fruition regarding the taking of the red warehouse.

The enemy still within the structure soon surrendered before the array of Bren machine guns, quick to vacate their flaming Alamo with their hands held high, and their eyes wide open in respect of their capture and not damnation.

Assuming the role of the wise advisor, Major Jack Churchill observed the due process and together, his men of G3 Six Troop, Black's men of G4, and the few remnants of Four Troop, watched the precinct burn in a waft of climbing smokestacks into the morning sky ... the same skyline that retained to the north, the Ulvesund Hotel, and their final objective for the Combined Operations and Commando ... *but not for Jack Churchill.*

Strangely, Churchill's observations amidst the simmering down conclusion of the red warehouse objective seemed to fall onto his subordinate, and Young acknowledged his major with a subtle and respective nod ...

This was an indication of many things, such as his understanding of how command constructed, the respect of his duties performed ... as well as the acknowledgement of that *other* factor of Churchill's crusade: a vendetta, still in the wind.

*It was time for him to go.*

# 13

## The Ulvesund Assail

*The Ulvesund Hotel*
*South Vågsøy, Norway*

"*Cooommaanndoooo!*"

Like a live concert crowd, like a rampaging riot, the commando troopers collectively rumbled with an earthquake of bass in their tenor and collective combat boot charge.

*A boast of machismo.*

*A tidal wave of courageous gallants.*

Commandos roared as they charged the smoke cloud, storming the fiery gates of Hell. They fired their machine guns and rifles as they emerged from the opposite end of the hazy veil, sprinting the open grounds of the bare thoroughfare like a wild stampede, trundling towards the last enemy stronghold.

Within a few seconds, all the established machine gun emplacements ignited along the German defensive at the gates and lobby of the Ulvesund Hotel. They riotously clapped to life, drowning out the mighty battle cry of the surging Commando tidal wave; waves thrashed against the rocks.

The clamorous, electrostatic buzzes of the stationary Maschinengewehr-34 turrets drowned out most other noises during the onslaught, rendering things such as shouting and lesser small arms fire almost inaudible. The bright white and continuous blinking from the elongated muzzle flashes of the machine guns fizzled unendingly, sweeping from side-to-side on their mounted bipod fixtures, drawing lines across the snow-covered streets, sufficiently turning men into red mist.

Although the sights of the remaining Wehrmacht shooters were mostly spraying blind through the cloud of smoke, those deadly volleys were still not without fruition. Even before they cleared the smoke, the strides of commandos faltered at the fate of a bullet, collapsing face-first into the abrasive street plane.

The German defenders poking the various overhanging eaves of the building became rapidly panicked by the daring attack, but they managed to inflict casualties among the charging commando line.

Barely visible through the same hissing smoke-screen that protected their advance, British troopers became deleted from sight by the carnage projected their way by the German defence. Limbs were shot off by the devastating velocity of the German machine guns. Whole heads were removed if in the path of the sweeping high-power, high-rate-of-fire volleys as they brushed from left to right like a painter streamlining a coat, almost as if they had walked into some sort of magical cutting laser from an *E. E. Smith* fiction.

Rounds that overshot the charging commandos made fiendish matter-warping *vhoop! vhoop!* sounds as the projectiles shot like barbs through the air at a subsonic velocity. Some of the bullets had phosphorus tips loaded, and the sketching of their tracer trajectories beamed golden through the air.

The chests of men were torn and spattered red, struck by the stray rounds of auspicious shooters as they pelted pot-shots down into the rising smoke, softening the onslaught of crusading commandos before they even had a visual.

One of the first figures through the smoke was Algy Forrester, heaving his Tommy gun at his chest while he ran, unleashing a fully automatic barrage at the defending barricades.

His shaky automatic spread hammered the frontal sandbags below the rival shooters in the lower windows, causing them to actively burst and pop with parades of tossed sand and sizzling smoulder. Like hosing a garden, Forrester changed targets in an instant, waving his aim downwards and to the right, spraying gunfire at the machine gun emplacement by the foyer entrance. Bullets chomped at the Germans behind a machine gun mount as the operator struggled to alternate the angle of the turret for the sake of blitzing the numerous incoming threats arriving close on his flank.

This was an overpowering invasion, and the heat was on.

The dark MG34 before the front doors of the hotel became hot and rattled with deafening strikes of offensive small arms fire, erupting in a vivid display of sparks and fumes as both the operator and belt-feeder were struck from Forrester's sustained fire on his approach through the smoke-screen. Either deceased or mortally wounded, the gunners dropped out of sight behind the barrier, right as a man on Forrester's left flank exited the smoke with a prepped impact grenade. It was the icing for the cake.

Leaping out of the smoke and through the air, a trooper over-arm tossed the *all-ways* impact fuse No.69 grenade directly at the emplacement, and with outstanding accuracy.

The small circular bomb passed just over the sandbags, detonating with force outwards from behind the emplacement, toppling frontwards the stacked sandbag barricades and hurling the deceased gunners' lifeless bodies across the muddy floor like bails and stumps after being bowled.

With a flash and crack, the impact grenade not only eliminated the front machine gun emplacement but gained them access to a straight shot at the lobby entrance to the Ulvesund Hotel by blowing the reinforced doors ajar.

A split second later and the commando by Forrester's side who had tossed the faithful grenade and was presently juggling his hold on his weapon, was struck through the breastplate by an above window shooter. A neighbouring elevated sniper then took a shot at Forrester, missing him by inches as the inspirational captain raised his weapon to hose across the side of the surface rendered building. From side to side, he swept a suppressive pattern, covering other commandos at his rear as they leapt through the smoke cloud and into the fray behind him, following in his wake.

Shouting like mad men, the remaining commandos of Four Troop gained valuable ground, pushing against the German defence and clustering taut behind newfound elements of concealment. They were now a stone's throw from the hotel lobby entrance.

Soldiers from both sides now traded shots within close and dangerous suppressed positions, ducking down low and blind firing past the edges of tight cover.

There were combatants killed in action on each side, both out in the street and in the lobby bottleneck of the hotel, as Germans desperately attempted to gain a footing on the seized premises.

Stahlhelm-strapped bodies dropped from the eaves above, freefalling and landing with plumes of debris in the snowy streets beneath the flood of commandos.

Martin Linge verged nearby Forrester's frontal lead, charging in with his many men of the NOR.I.C.1, shooting at German targets at the westerly machine gun emplacement that had a line on them.

Many of his courageous men fell casualty to an alternate machine gun nest, failing even to cross the thoroughfare once they exited the smoke-screen.

Linge and a few of his men were fast to react to the gun's affront, halting in their advance in the open street and in a pinch, returning fire at the gunner.

In what felt like an eternity of locked exchanging gunfire, Linge became buried by collapsing men on either side of his kneeling stance as the machine gun cut left and right all about him, somehow missing him by inches with each curving arc.

The forces traded punch for punch with the protected machine gun before the German gunner finally copped a strike to the head, causing his metal stahlhelm to part from his bald scalp as his face exploded. At the same time as the metallic *clang* of his helmet's removal, his finger released from the trigger and the smoke-chugging machine gun ceased its blaring bombardment.

Linge's scrunched face rose behind his smoking submachine gun. He had no time to collect himself. His brow loosened, and he shouted to his remaining men about his vector, rallying them to push forwards from their intermittent charge.

They worked together, converging on the unmanned machine gun position as a German runner attempted to make a dash out to the emplacement to resume firing. They shot him down in the open whilst they moved, overrunning the position and then using it for partial shelter from the many window shooters up above.

Commandos bolted through waves of incoming fire that zipped past them like flashes of golden lightning to painstakingly dive behind cover. In desperate exchanges of gunfire, men slid across the icy street in the open mayhem, shooting back at stationary targets to somehow hail victorious.

Once exiting the cover of the smoke-screen, a British gunner near the eastern corner of the push dove low out of a sprint burst, skating on his chest on some ice like he was at a try-line. The quick-witted trooper slid a dozen feet on his stomach across the flat managing to deploy his Bren machine gun on its forwards mount in the process. Skidding low, he returned fire at the final machine gun nest that triangulated the hotel, located above the lobby entrance on the reinforced awning. Improvised access to the nest by the Germans was made by a first-floor window.

The Bren thumped away at the emplacement, causing the gunner to stoop for shelter and cease fire with the MG34 long enough for a bunch of commandos to charge the open thoroughfare, fast tossing some of their impact grenades up at the many open windows above. They gained close access to the hotel, exchanging fire on an upwards angle with the remaining window shooters that dared to fire down on their advanced positions.

Gaining ground from the front entrance to the Ulvesund, Forrester protected his surrounding men's advance with his submachine gun until the circular extended drum-mag clicked dry. The group of commandos prematurely cut in low behind the concealment of a burning truck carcass in the small outdoor valley parking section.

German infantrymen peeped around the corners of the lobby entrance, firing back at the British where they could, but their long-range bolt-action rifles were no match for the automatic Thompson submachine guns and powerful Ithaca pump-action shotguns that almost every British Commando wielded.

There was no time for him to reload.

They had to secure that entrance.

"*Cover me!*" Forrester shouted.

Instead of replenishing ammunition into his sizzling hot gun, he placed it down on the floor and obtained two impact grenades from his webbing, one for each hand. He popped their caps and exposed himself from cover by several cautious steps, sighting the open and seemingly unguarded mouth of the hotel lobby now closer than ever—close enough to taste victory.

Above him and the entrance, the breezeway awning that housed a machine gun nest was still intermittently active. Before the enemy managed to accurately target his motion, the highlight of Forrester's sights honed in on the mark: the wood-reinforced stilts that elevated the awning.

One after the other, equally as ambidextrously coordinated with his left overarm as his dominant right, Forrester lobbed the plum-sized impact grenades at the lobby zone located barely thirty paces away, and he dove clear.

With bright flashes of white and red, the two HE grenades detonated a split-second apart, instantly turning the erect hardwood to splinters as the beams fractured under the weight of the metal canopy.

A pair of opportunistic Wehrmacht submachine gunners who had unfortunately decided it to be an advantageous moment to attempt to break out from within the lobby, rushing those British soldiers who had gained ground close to the entrance, were incidentally met by the same blasts. The grenades exploded not six-feet above their position as they poured into the open foyer, chattering their guns from the hip with a pair of automatic Schmeissers.

The two were launched from their stances, thrown towards Forrester and his few wingmen as they ducked below shelter following the tossing of the hand grenades.

They dropped low and behind the sightline just as one of the flailing bodies of the ragged and scorched soldiers slammed into the top of their ensconced cover, skimming over the surface and rag-dolling out into the thoroughfare beyond their position.

The other one slammed into the side of the hotel, breaking every bone in his lifeless body before pooling to a steaming lump of Wehrmacht meat with a stahlhelm on top.

*South Vågsøy Village (Northern District)*
*Vågsøy, Norway*

Comprised of Charley Head, Knocker White, and Joe Mills, Colonel Durnford-Slater led his four-man team on a northerly approach around the Ulvesund perimeter. This residential sector held nothing of value to the raid, and was therefore uncharted territory for Commando. Even the Germans had no interest, and therefore there were no defence emplacements or guard posts set up. It was eerily vacant.

In their circumventing trek past numerous antiquated cottages, the group heard the increased volume of the gunfire and explosions of a battle at the hotel resonating in their distant wake. It echoed thunderously through their quieter sector.

In the quietude of the vector, their ears pricked. They halted momentarily behind Durnford-Slater in order to glimpse back towards the direction of the hotel and the position they had just vacated.

"Forrester must have attacked," Charley Head commentated after a held breath, listening. "Crazy fool."

"Good luck to them," Durnford-Slater solemnly regarded, continuing with his handgun gripped firmly out before his core.

"*Sir! Sir!*" Knocker White suddenly called out. There was an urgency in his voice that caught Durnford-Slater's immediate attention, and the group promptly lowered their stances or sought shelter. White then added with a whisper of importance, hissing through the balled chewy between his front teeth. "*Incoming ... Up ahead ...*"

The lot of them were concealed along the last few small houses to the north that remained between the hotel block and the edge of the rocky slopes. These were the same mountainous slopes where the Huntsmen snipers would be relocating from their elevated positions on top of the ridge overlooking districts of South Vågsøy: the same locale where they had inflicted the most casualties to Durnford-Slater's G2 an hour ago.

Spaced out behind random intervals of concealment in the street, Head, White, Durnford-Slater, and Mills suddenly necessitated their need to be at the ready; weapons up and staying quiet.

They barely had a plan beyond Durnford-Slater suggesting only a moment ago that they should try and determine down which avenue the Huntsmen snipers would be travelling and stage an ambush. Their overall goal was to delay their arrival at the Ulvesund, replenishing the numbers defending and further thwarting Forrester's efforts. However, the reality was, the very success of them taking the Ulvesund Hotel hinged on their ability to deny this lot entry to the fray ...

In the tense silence, Colonel Durnford-Slater became paired with Mills across a gap between quaint, snow-clad cottages. Across the way, he gave Head and Knocker White a particular nod which signified that *this* was now the ambush spot.

Engaging in operative silence, they returned the gesture.

With his submachine gun up by his shoulder, Head cynically muttered into Knocker White's ear, "we're going to die ..." as they crept further to the edge of the hiding spot, preparing to spring their attack.

Opposite them, the other two did the same, with Durnford-Slater signalling something to Mills, who promptly nodded. The adept Commando then raised his duel M1911A1 pistols by his head and snuck out low, disappearing behind the opposite side of the shed on some sort of discreet flanking mission.

As the suspense increased exponentially by the second, Durnford-Slater carefully inched half his face around a corner. He was vulgarly surprised to find almost two-dozen white balaclava Huntsmen soldiers frantically making their way between the houses. Faces hidden by portentous ski-masks, they were a faceless kill squad, and moved with militaristic exactness and coordination in their formation. They carried scoped precision rifles with customized camouflage patterns that matched their pale jumpsuits and leather-strapped attire. They were, for the most part, on guard and checking each corner and passage between the buildings as they moved in rough formation throughout the town.

Undoubtedly, they could hear the battle currently underway at the hotel, and it caused urgency. The noise pinged its location in South Vågsøy like ringing a dinner bell. However, their haste to reach the destination in the shortest amount of time was about to become their disadvantage.

After obtaining sight of the killer krauts, Durnford-Slater retracted behind cover, eyeing Knocker across the way.

He reciprocated the signal gesture... *then engaged.*

Like a flash of lightning, Durnford-Slater wrapped the corner, extended his arm and eye over the edge of the wall, and squeezed off his handgun at the incoming string of Huntsmen.

Visceral red impacts exploded across their snow-white camouflage attires in a violently stark colour contrast. Hastily, the firm-firing fusillade dropped two of the charging enemy and maimed a third before he quickly receded to reload, dodging all retaliatory fire.

From his neighbouring side, Knocker White probed his shotgun around the other edge and opened intervals of blasting shotgun fire. He bent at a squat, lunging out wide with his leg to unload shell after shell with his pump-action at the crew, dropping more hostile targets and maiming several others with buckshot ball bearings.

For a brief moment, the Huntsmen became the fish in the barrel. *How the tables had turned.*

Another two Gebirgsjäger thrashed heavily to the snow, blown off their feet by the pump-action's 16-gauge potency. White seemed to possibly clip another two soldiers with buckshot before snapping back behind cover with the energy of a rubber band, narrowly escaping the severance of his head from a quick-scope sniper down the street as the Huntsmen scattered their formation to seek refuge from the surprise ensnarement.

From the opposite side of the cottage, Head strode out and into the fight while White replenished his shotgun, discharging with his best controlled bursts with his injured forearm cradling the forwards grip of the submachine gun. Every ounce of recoil sustained causing the lad to wince and grimace, flexing his damaged bicep, but he persevered through the pain.

Head jagged his machine gun sprigs left and right at the displacing enemy in the street as their column dispersed, sweeping from side to side and back again before recoiling from the heat of their overbearing, avenging gunfire. He may have dropped one, but predominantly just made them scatter.

The exterior sides of the wooden cottage walls became quickly torn to shreds nearby them and the snow exploded with fizzing pockmarks at their feet from the exchanged fire by the Huntsmen as they held their ground.

With a fresh clip inserted, Durnford-Slater closed his pistol's drawn slide with the thumb release and immediately leaned back around the angle with the sights of his weapon, squeezing off a few more rounds at a cowering target before deciding it was too hot to further exhaust this ambush point.

"*Displace!*" he bellowed over the bedlam.

Knocker's hands fumbled about, fast to load cylindrical shells into the feeding tube of his weapon before racking the forward grip. He gave a nod of concurrence and prepared to move along the opposite side of their building, while Head simply raised his arms by his side, shouting over the gunfire and ricochets. "*Displace where? We're stuck here!*"

"*We need to make four men feel like an army!*" Durnford-Slater retorted in reference to their objective holding back an outnumbering force from moving on their position. This would be accomplished by the few men constantly changing their positions yet still maintaining a hold of their defensive contour.

Knocker White quickly approached the opposite end to their building in time to hear the distinguishable sound of trotting combat boots in sludgy snow; the enemy endeavouring to straightaway flank their position, and they were already within close proximity.

He was fast to react, poking the barrel of his weapon around the edge of the building and, before even sighting a target, squeezing the trigger in a pre-fire fashion. A fast-running Huntsman who was moving up on them from the parallel met the shotgun blast at close-range: a fist-sized hole punched through his chest meat and ribcage bone from the velocity of the muzzle blast, and he slumped dead in his tracks, snagging like a dog on a leash.

Knocker White racked the pump and dragged his arms out of range of the tumbling corpse as the Huntsman's dead body flounced past his position in a lifeless huff in powdered snow. He then quickly fired again, wounding another incoming soldier who was lining him up with a rifle. Another two soldiers were situated beyond, and their overpowering gunfire caused White to react by allowing himself to collapse with his weapon's recoil to his rear, where he managed to expel another ground level shot that clipped both distant men in their exposed limbs at the same time.

The two maimed Huntsmen recovered quickly, dragging themselves behind concealment, becoming backed up by more numbers from a little further behind who had their sights set down range, so Knocker White acted fast to get out of dodge. Covering his own return to refuge, he pumped the shotgun and blindly fired again and again as he rolled in a reverse-shoulder roll back onto his feet now frosted in snow. Cheating death, he dove clear of the incoming wave of fatal ballistics that turned his vacant position to shredded snow moulds and clouding steam from hot lead.

"Come on, sir!" Knocker White breathlessly remarked as he collected Head in a whirlwind, about to follow in Durnford-Slater's footsteps and arc on a north-easterly vector along the line.

"Eh, balls!" Head exclaimed pulling up his heavy Thompson and preparing to bolt across the open street to displace location. They had to keep dancing in this skirmish to stay alive.

White inched the corner and pegged a timed hand grenade down the far end of the street, followed by three rounds from his secondary weapon before the two of them darted out of view and the blast covered their interchange from any possible shooters.

They ran as the explosive detonated, covering their obvious excursion across the danger zone.

*The Ulvesund Hotel*
*South Vågsøy, Norway*

After the costly yet effective frontal Ulvesund assail, those who remained of the enduring Four Troop were now dwindling within the diminishing percentile. They may have reached the objective, encircling close around the outer walls of the hotel, but it was at great sacrifice.

Under the unrelenting gunfire from the multitude of dug-in defenders, the Commandos at the perimeter enclosed upon the hotel grounds, gaining a firmer foothold against the final German stronghold—a precarious position that could just as easily be lost as it was so boldly gained.

Out in the thoroughfare fray, one of three pinned troopers peeked out from the scarce cover of a snowcapped vehicle, and was abruptly taken out by a window shooter high above on an overhanging eave of the structure. The trooper was dropped brutally by a tidy headshot that drew a line through the top of his woollen beanie-covered scalp. It caused the nearby men to huddle closer behind their shared concealment, daring not to hunt for the responsible shooter in fear of becoming the next victim.

From nearby and against the shelter of the hotel building itself, Captain Forrester witnessed this helpless portion of his brave Four Troop commandos become casualties to the cause, and it only further instigated his resolve. They had clearly tried to make the distance during the advance, but had fallen short, likely due to the firm enemy defence.

"Sir, we're stuck!" a desperate commando voice shouted behind Forrester, splitting his concern. There was a group of almost ten of them cluttered up within a small pocket of shelter from the elevated riflemen on a perilous eave. They had collapsed the awning of the lobby, which had caused the infantrymen within to close-over the large double doors and fall further back into the hotel entrance interior, effectively bottlenecking their defence. It would be a struggle to push through the funnel.

"Sir!" the voice shouted again. It belonged to somebody Forrester didn't directly recognize from within his Troop roster. He may have been one of Komrower's Two Troop.

Forrester had heard the young trooper and understood his concerned rationale but was yet to respond solely because he was still weighing up options to advance.

"We should pull back! Wait for reinforcements!"

"Settle down, trooper!" Forrester grunted, still more determined than ever to maintain the raid's momentum. They had the ball and were headed for the endzone. Truth was, they were in too deep now to retreat. "We fall back now, we die! Who is your CO?"

"He was killed during the charge, sir."

Forrester's eyes scoured the numbers of the few men he had with him at the hotel. There was not a single officer capable of leading a charge, other than himself.

Suddenly, Forrester's vision focused on a few men cornered near the other thrown westerly machine gun emplacement. It was men from the NOR.I.C.1—of Martin Linge's command to be precise. He and a few of his Norwegian soldiers had almost made it to the hotel position, pinned in the thoroughfare.

"*Kaptein Linge!*" Forrester bellowed loudly, immediately somehow gaining Linge's attention in the noisy expanse. Linge was pinned down and low behind the sandbag barricades of a former machine gun nest and cast a helpless gaze.

Stuck low behind cover, he had a handful of soldiers with him, all equally as restrained behind the limited cover due to the countless elevated shooters viewing their position from the eaves and windows.

Forrester bellowed over the war volume, waving them over with an overhead gesture. "*Kaptein! Move up!*"

Powerless to act, Linge showed his palm in retort, signifying his inability to reposition at this juncture. As he did so, further proving his point, a shooter from high up on the building saw the motion of Linge's exposed hand and fired, missing the targeted limb by an inch, resulting in a rebound on the icy street below, causing them all to flinch.

"Shit!" Forrester cursed amidst himself, now even lower on options.

They needed to breach the lobby as soon as possible, thus pulling the attentions of the advantageous defenders from this *exterior* guard and into the *interior* in an attempt to hold.

*They had to get in there!*

While they were stalling outside, Forrester could envision the enemy inside, fortifying the defences and establishing even better strategies within. They would be lurking in any and every ensconced nook and cranny inside that foyer with advantageous covering positions, creating an air-tight fissure. Every second they waited out here to impose, many more British lives would be lost attempting to overthrow the position.

*They needed to progress!*

"Alright, lads, we're it!" Forrester remarked, turning to face the few men within his vicinity. There may have been many more in pockets around the circumference of the hotel foundation, but he had not the time to rally a force. There were nine of them in total, himself included. "It's up to us. We must finish what we have started!"

The men all cast him a gleam.

They each felt the surge of adrenaline.

Forrester's voice affirmed: "It's do or die ..."

There was a collective gulp of the men's throats.

The captain handed his weapon with his final drum-magazine to a nearby trooper, who had currently been carrying a slow bolt-action Lee-Enfield. He gladly accepted the upgrade, and in exchange, Forrester plucked the large No.73 hand percussion grenade the trooper had hanging from his shoulder belt. A rare anti-tank ordinance amongst the troops, the weighty cylindrical item was eleven inches in length, often referred to by the troops as a *Thermos Bomb* due to the resemblance to the drinking flask.

"I'm going to move up close, crack the door ..." Forrester deemed, handling the anti-tank grenade in his midst while he spoke. "... and then toss this little devil inside ..."

The soldiers huddled around nodded intently.

The No.73 was designed to punch a hole in the side of a tank or an armoured vehicle ... a device of such potent yield would blow a cavity in the side of a building, certainly killing everyone in the adjacent compartment. The catch for this improvisation tactic was that the Thermos Bomb was an impact detonator once thrown—a weighted tape remained held in the soldier's hand once thrown, like a yo-yo (but without the second yo), and unravelled, eventually plucking the safety pin that was attached to the same type of *all-ways* fuse as the No.69 grenade. The idea was for the operator to sneak up close to a tank route or stationary target and toss the unit clear from behind concealment ... however, there was no cover left by the lobby entrance for Forrester. He would be rolling the dice in a gamble with his life to see if he survived the dive clear in time ... lest be shredded by shrapnel, if not blown apart by the force of the explosive.

*It was a bet he was willing to wager if it meant winning this war.*

"You lot move up with me and provide cover. Stay clear of the bomb blast once I reach the doorway."

"But sir, those Thermos Bombs blow big ... there's no—"

Forrester snapped. "Don't you worry about me!"

"Yes, sir."

"Once this thing goes off, we push up and breach in with everything we've got. Anything still alive in there will be momentarily concussed if not in pieces. Kill anything that looks like it has a pulse, men ... Even if it's dead, kill it again!"

"*Yes, sir!*"

"*Yes, sir!*"

The men were petrified ... but competent.

Forrester offered one last parting sentiment.

"We're commandos, lads. We've already won."

With the vigour of *The Flight of the Valkyries*, Forrester moved out low with the weighty Thermos in hand, flanked a few steps behind and on either side by a handful of armed commandos with their weapons up and fingers on the triggers.

They slowed and fanned out as he arrived near the ominous lobby entrance, almost immediately attracting fire from the defending enemy above at a window peek—a gunman who became silenced promptly by one of the pack with a quick elevation draw.

Treading lightly through the carnage and debris already so far littering the battlefield, Forrester approached the shot-to-shit thick doors of the hotel lobby. The environment smelt like charred wood and gunpowder.

The troopers at his six were hesitant to progress any further.

This wasn't necessarily due to their hesitance at peering into an enemy clusterfuck lurking within the shadows, but because they knew that once Forrester lofted that highly explosive device, they would literally have the item's two seconds of free-fall to get clear.

Once up close and remaining tense, Forrester scanned back at the men in order to give them the head-nod signal that he was about to initiate the radical manoeuvre.

He carefully wound the tape several feet in his spare hand ...

*... pulling ... and pull—click!*

The pin at the end of the tape plucked from the device.

*The enabled Thermos Bomb was now armed ...*

If anything touched the tip of that volatile device, it would explode.

The iron-sights of the men's weapons were trained on the door. If somebody attempted to open it to shoot Forrester, they would surely have them pegged with good odds—

*Bam!*

An unexpected above shot suddenly claimed the life of one of the flanking commandos, and one of the good guys dropped from a wound to the neck.

The supporting men scattered in their positions. During this tactical taciturn manoeuvre, they had become inadvertently exposed by several vantage points above in their flanking formation. There was another pesky overhang that offered a line of sight on the entrance from above, and a German shooter had a prime position to camp it out.

Two of the men nearby Forrester's fife twirled and brought about their weapons, firing back at the shooter whilst the others adapted their positioning as much as they could muster ...

... all the while of the setback, they took their eyes off the prize.

Carrying the bomb like an unstable hot potato in one hand, Forrester reached out to feel the door handle with the oth—

*The door opened away from him.*

Algy Forrester's eyes grew wide as the door handle pulled away from his grasp, and the barrel of a kraut rifle thrust out into the daylight out from the dark hollows within.

*Blam!*

A single gunshot struck him in the sternum, winding him like a gut-punch. The Four Troop captain flinched an arm up in defence, but it was too late and futile against a bullet. The shot was centre mass, and he was done for.

... the door closed back over as the stunned and shaky Forrester instinctively revolved about to walk it off, struggling to catch a breath in his winded state as a wave of shock overcame him. He appeared momentarily disorientated.

... whilst cradling the valuable Thermos Bomb against his chest, he buckled at the knees and dropped down to his palm, holding himself up in an attempt to catch a gasp. However, it was like there was a hole in his boat and no matter what he did, he was sinking fast.

... he dropped his hold of the heavy grenade, managing to place it safely upright beneath him, where he sheltered like a human canopy above it for what would be his final moments as a stream of blood leaked out from his mouth.

The troopers nearby scattered.

Their extreme exodus was from both the shooters above and the foiled plans as they unfolded right before their eyes.

Shaking in a struggle for strength to remain upright, Forrester's life seemingly left his body at an exponential rate. The hero soldier would imminently keel over in the doorway to the Ulvesund Hotel ...

*... and collapse on top of the live grenade!*

The troopers shouted as they bolted in every direction.

*"Christ! Fall back!"*

*"Move! Move! Fuckin' mo—!"*

In his dying breath, Forrester's heavy eyes gleamed under him and at the armed Thermos Bomb; at the sensitive trigger of the impact-detonation head that he was about to collapse on.

Beneath his legendary facial brush ... *he gave a blood-soaked smile.*

*He dropped.*

*BHOOM!*

The No.73 highly explosive anti-tank grenade detonated from under the body of Captain Algy Forrester. In a blinding, powerful blast of white light, a cloud of hellish orange fire ignited and plumed horizontally, consuming everything like the belch from a hell gate.

The hero commando's body was immediately cremated, discharging outwards like disintegrating ashes along with the bright blast of the explosive. The brief cloud of crimson mist was visible only for a split second amidst the fiery display of the explosion and shockwave.

The surrounding debris and entire entrance of the hotel building was immediately affected, blasting inwards from the detonation and killing a cluster of defending Wehrmacht infantrymen within the flash radius of the blast. Half of the exterior wall caved in along with the impact, which in turn brought down some of the first-level flooring with a fog of thick black soot and dust, further feeding the already growing cloud of heat.

The commandos outside managed to get clear of the blast, leaping at the last second following Forrester's demise in the doorway. Two of the men were uplifted from the shockwave, sent sailing through the air and into safety almost against their will. They lost their guns and helmets.

The explosion rocked the entire area like an artillery barrage—a bang easily five-times louder and more ferocious than a typical Mills Bomb.


*Bhoom ...*

The sound of a massive detonation downstairs quaked the entire building. The seismic tremor rattled the stilts of the walls, even cracked concrete housing within the structure, dislodging some of the wooden beams that formed interior walls, exposing inner workings.

Every German soldier occupying the building reached out to brace for stability as streaks of dust sprinkled from the ceilings of each floor, hinting at a possible instability.

"Mein Herr," Hauptscharführer Jürgen announced as he entered his commanding officer's hotel room in a huff. The ambience of the surrounding conflict battle raged on below and around the base of the Ulvesund Hotel. It had been for a hot minute, and grew exponentially.

With a calm resolve that was beginning to show damage, Friedrich Feind pivoted his attention from the fractured window that overlooked the raid outside. He acknowledged his man's return, hopeful of welcoming positive news to follow regarding their new objective ...

Instead of asking for the outcome, Feind self-confessed their harsh reality about the counter-assault. "Wir < *'We're losing grip'* > Halt ..."

Jürgen was hesitant to respond to the observation—which was more of a statement—and was evidently withholding an important update which he was eager to relay to his discontented superior.

"... wir haben < *'we have found the tank.'* > nden."

*Friedrich Feind grinned.*

An evil smile transformed the landscape of his weathered and duelling scar-indented face as he bared his pearly whites.

"Anschl < *'Apparently the crew were caught in the first artillery attack and mostly killed, the rest scattered out into the ground force.'* > ruppe."

"E < *'It will not matter, Jürgen, excellent work.'* > Arbeit."

"Si < *'You can drive, Mein Herr?'* > führer?"

"Pac < *'Pack your things, Jürgen. It is time to go.'* > gehen."

From a nearby dresser in the converted hotel room, Gebirgsjäger Chief Squad Leader Jürgen collected an additional maschinenpistole with a folded buttstock, looping the strap around his neck. He pinched the pin on the receiver, cradling both weapons and leered, gesturing that he was now *packed.*

Sword on his hip, pistol in his pocket, Feind gestured that he was also ready to vacate, collecting his only carry bag. The two exited the room into the hallway. They would seek to discreetly evacuate the Ulvesund mid-contest; the deserted and solitary tank was their ticket out of the fray.

"Mein Herr," the oath made comment as they passed multiple other Alpine Huntsmen, men dutifully waiting stations in the hotel hall. As loyal as they were, they were all oblivious to their CO's soon-to-be abandonment of the station.

Jürgen spoke mindfully to Feind, outside of the earshot of any other soldiers in-keeping with their hidden exodus. "Die Bri < *'The British have cast a net over South Vågsøy. How will we evade them?'* > ausweichen?"

Before the staircase access, Feind halted and faced his comrade. "Ein Panzer < *'A tank will cut through a net.'* > durchschneiden."

*South Vågsøy Village (Northern District)*
*South Vågsøy, Norway*

Biding his time during the initial stages of their ambush against the Huntsman reserve retreating into the village, Sergeant Joe Mills flanked two rows of houses over, where the action hadn't yet kicked off.

Resonating gunfire in his recent wake, his wits were about him.

A pistol in each hand, tracing every corner with his free-flowing iron-sights, Mills was prepared for an imminent skirmish. The rogue commando nimbly progressed through the small residential cabins on the analogous strip to the Huntsmen snipers encountering a Commando ambush.

Consumed in battle and oblivious to his flank, these enemy Huntsmen were presently engaged with Durnford-Slater, White, and Head's ensnarement between their retreat from the slopes and the hotel.

Unscripted, Mills planned to surprise some shooters by attacking them on the enfilade sweep. As the shooting resounded nearby, Mills roamed along the edge of a small, snow-buried shed until he found an angle of exposure that cut their defilade. He spied a group of Huntsmen as they sought refuge from the ambush, continuing to pour gunfire onto the down range targets.

The volatility of this surprise ambush was causing the falling-back enemy to adjust and displace, attempting a flanking manoeuvre ...

*This would be where they would encounter Mills.*

Since they knew the goal of the Huntsmen was to make it to the hotel A.S.A.P., they would be less likely to stall and attempt any type of entrenchment. They would strive for immediate progression via a fringe.

Waiting for an opportune moment on which to strike, Mills peered around the corner, watching them receive gunfire from the others. He saw them pitch a plan to flank the other side of the street ...

*Like clockwork.*

Pistols by his head and silent as an assassin, Mills let a bunch of the balaclava boche pass by his position for a few seconds before following them, casually stepping around the bend. There were a half-dozen of them—probably more than he should attempt to handle solo ... *but fuck it.*

A few paces out from concealment and behind the patrolling men, Mills halted and raised his guns outstretched. "*Oi, cunts!*" he shouted, gaining their immediate attention before letting loose shot after shot into the bodies of the unprepared German soldiers.

He dropped three and wounded another two before a remaining able soldier managed to spin and target him. Mills gave out a roar of fury as he emptied his handguns at the remaining foes, maintaining recoil and viciousness upon the targets. Once clicking dry with both guns, he decided on the latter of fight or flight as a hailstorm came his way from the remaining fighter.

The surviving shooter returned fire, just barely missing the dual-wielding commando as he trod fast from his exposed position, ducking around cover.

His back against the wall, volleys of fuming lead pelted the weather shielding tin in strident, scraping noise. Mills ejected both empty clips simultaneously and prepared to obtain fresh mags just as a whole other faceless figure appeared at his side, catching him off guard.

It was an unaccounted for balaclava-clad Huntsman who had sidled up to him, raising his scoped Karabiner rifle like a lance and using it to swipe both of the guns from his paws in one quick Mordhau before buttstroking Mills in the head with the solid wood of the buttstock.

Brow split and face aching, Mills folded over to the snow where he leaked blood profusely in a bright contrast against the pure white powder beneath.

Lightning-fast in his recovery, Mills upped, twirled, and fought.

The two grappled over ownership of the rifle between them, locking eyes and baring teeth as they flexed their tense grasp over possession of the armament.

This was a fight to the death.

The ambush had become a skirmish.

After the initial ensnarement that drew the attention of the greater enemy numbers, and then giving the order to displace, Durnford-Slater had peeled off from the others and from the waylaying stage of gunfire. This improvised ambuscade, successful in its objective to prevent the Gebirgsjäger reserve troops adding to the resistance in the Ulvesund Hotel and therefore allowing Four Troop to mount a conceivable assail, had now all boiled down to a sticky and frantic deathmatch.

Encounters and conflicts steered his path through the streets.

In the fog of this war and the wind-swept street corners of this simpler district, the vigilant lieutenant-colonel skirmished the maze-like Norwegian residentials with his lone pistol out before him like a lantern in the darkness.

Motion, again, fell before him and he instantly paused his pace, identified his target, and plugged two slugs in the chest of another woollen-faced Huntsman.

The shots planted him ass-first in a snowy collapse, and Durnford-Slater progressed up to him, confirming the kill.

Surrounded by a fog that hid any progress further than twenty paces, identical-looking residences, and echoic sounds of surrounding conflict, Durnford-Slater twirled around upon hearing more movement pass by a space. He squatted low to make himself a smaller target, cradled his wrist and narrowed his sights.

Another eluding enemy soldier entered his vicinity, and the chief commando released a quick double-tap at his centre mass.

*Blam, blam!*

The German buckled and dropped, stifled of life.

Overdosing on the epinephrine of the moment, Durnford-Slater's squinting stare fought back the onset of asphyxiating tunnel vision. He concentrated to hear noises over the pounding of his own heartbeat that resounded gaudily within his own head.

He and his men were outnumbered, outgunned, and quite frankly, feasibly out-skilled or at least evenly matched in this skirmish, however the Commando colonel took solace in knowledge of the fact that this very delay of the enemy reaching the hotel was, alone, evidence of their mission's success.

In the intensity, the world around him was spiralling.

He caught glimpses of movement darting between houses and down narrow street passages. A few times he raised his gun in order to potentially engage the enemy, electing rather to reserve his ammunition for a fight he knew he could win. His trigger discipline was punctual in that regard.

In all the rotary guarding, surrounded by the thunderous sounds of close combat drowning out his every thought, Durnford-Slater felt turned-around and adrift. He had become temporarily lost in his direction.

"... *Colonel* ...?"

A tiny voice bellowed between the echoes of blurting gunfire in the neighbouring streets. Durnford-Slater was not sure that he had even heard it, or if it was an onomatopoeic haze of drama playing tricks on his ears.

There it was again:

"... *Colonel* ...?"

"Charley?!" Durnford-Slater responded; sure he recognized the tenor of the vocalist this time to be Lieutenant Head.

*There was more shouting he could not interpret.*

"Lieutenant, where are you?—"

Sudden close movement caught his attention, and Durnford-Slater welcomed another charging balaclava-wearing guest as he came drifting around a snowy street corner. He was the first of a trio.

Durnford-Slater halted firm and dropped the first and second soldiers with what was left of his handgun's capacity, recognizing that he had just spent his entire clip in the exchange and the slide was locked back.

With teeth clenched in full-clutch fury, Durnford-Slater's hands were like lightning as he dropped the empty mag, swiped another from his belt and slotted it into the hollow grip beneath his palm. His thumb clasped the slide lock, and the weapon promptly discharged at the remaining third entrant into the field right as the Huntsman let off a shot from his large sniper rifle.

It missed the crouching Durnford-Slater, who inadvertently ducked the shot, striking a wooden exterior wall over his left shoulder with a discharge of splinters.

The German flaked into a disordered slide in the sleet from the shot to his ribs. The man wasn't dead, evident by his sudden bodily scurry in the snow, attempting to regain grasp of his rifle. Reacting quickly, Durnford-Slater elevated confidently, delivering another three bullets into his body for assurance of his demise, settling the last German amongst his fallen kamerads.

With a huff, Durnford-Slater fast prepared another—final—seven-shot magazine in his spare hand for a prompt reload whilst he continued to search the streets for his commandos.

They had perchance succeeded in delaying access of the reserve enemy troops to the Ulvesund Hotel, therefore making it possible for Forrester and his men of Four Troop to assail the enemy stronghold ... but now, the coordination of this makeshift ambush had decayed into combat-chocked confrontation.

With dwindling ammunition, this skirmish for survival had their numbers almost up.

"Colonel?!" Lieutenant Head called out again as he and Knocker White navigated the warren of snowy houses, off on a tangent of their own. The two had been wandering the hollow Norwegian streets for several minutes now, without any contact of any kind, lost and seemingly abandoned of objective. Even the enemy had become scarce.

"*Shh!*" White hissed as he watched their back with his shotgun drawn. He remained on guard where his lieutenant had noticeably wavered.

"Corporal, the enemy has surely passed us!"

"Keep it down! They could be around the next corner!"

"We have to find John! We're lost out here!"

"With all due respect, sir, you're going to find more than the Colonel if you keep shouting out—"

"*Shh!*" Head hushed White with his fist up above his shoulder. He had heard something dead ahead in the fog and his eyes were wide open and glaring.

Suddenly, a group of Alpine Huntsmen soldiers entered the vicinity from between dwellings. A glass house window nearby smashed as members from the Gebirgsjäger who had kicked in a door for shelter managed a vantage point on the two commandos out in the street.

They were hesitant to fire since losing their CO in the urban skirmish, but not unwilling.

As soon as the enemy were identified as such, Head and White both engaged thusly, exchanging volleys with the armed soldiers as they strafed to a side, anchoring towards a close nook for shelter.

Savage gunfire ensued.

Head managed to drop one of the gunners in their scurried strafe.

Once they hid in cover, White heard further smashing of glass through the barrage of small arms shooting, and his attention honed in on the source directly across them in the street, spotting the emergence of a hostile weapon from the premises in the form of a gun barrel pointed their way.

He immediately craned his shotgun around and pelted the window socket, cycling the foregrip and firing again and again into the hole, shredding the mounted timber frame to splinters as well as slaughtering anyone within.

"Fuckers!" Head shouted as his smoking submachine gun ran out of bullets again, and he twirled around a corner to desperately attempt a reload, inadvertently barging into Knocker White in the process who was already seeking shelter.

Searching his pouches for ammo to reload, Head panicked. He thought he still had at least one stick-mag left, but apparently not. "Oh, fuck. I'm out!"

White glanced at him with wide eyes.

*Their luck was running out—fast.*

Head discarded the empty submachine gun with a puff in the snow, and he retrieved a handgun from his belt, charging the slide.

Feeling as though they had overstayed this position, they had to move. White picked up the offensive pace with his shotgun around the corner's edge, keeping the enemy at bay as they pushed forwards.

*Boom! Chit-chit, boom!*

Stacked in formation, Head brought up his six.

Spying movement through a sideward window, the lieutenant quickly coiled—*blam!* Head's gun discharged, delivering a brilliant headshot through the glass and silencing the foe who had them almost dead to rights.

They pressed forth, shotgun-first and keeping the creeping Huntsmen at bay, however ... *the walls were closing in.*

*Boom! Chit-chit, boom! Chit-chit ... click!*

"*Shit!*" White exclaimed, fast recoiling the edge to reload.

He quickly rummaged through the depleting ammunition bag on his hip for some extra shells, frantic to feed them into the hungry tube of the shotgun whilst Head tag-teamed the point, rotating forth and firing a few sporadic pistol shots at the holed-up Huntsmen ahead.

As good as they were, they were running out of good fortune ...

A flicker of movement captured his attention whilst White was busy reloading—it was through a frosted window directly across them inside of one of the abandoned houses. Judging by the thumping of heavy boots that accompanied the movement inside, it was more enemy attempting to flank them.

In a flurry, White racked and raised his weapon after only inserting a few shells and put a shot through each glass window of the occupied house, causing anyone who resided within to think twice about peeking them. He, too, was running low on ammo, and they were in an easily overpowered position and an even easier spot for an enemy to land a ...

Right as he thought it, an enemy potato masher thudded into the snow between their feet.

"Oh, *fuck!*" Head exclaimed beholding the sight between his legs, fast pushing off in order to run for his life.

White did the same, but with an ounce more gallantry: the corporal reached down and snatched the handle of the stielhandgranate, lobbing it in their mad dash like a throwing-axe back at the Huntsman across the way. In the manic seconds, the Germans saw the return of the timed explosive and retreated in panic.

Both Knocker White and Charley Head took three or four fast paces in clearance before the explosive detonated at their backs.

The fuse hit zero in mid-air between them and the enemy, shoving both parties apart with the brunt of the shockwave blast, peppering everything with shrapnel in a three-hundred-and-sixty-degree radius.

The blast blew the ice off every frozen surface.

The explosive intensity hit the two fleeing commandos across their backs. They cranked at the necks, tossing their weapons out their sides before subsiding into face-first slides in a blanket of snow as a haze of grey smoke buried them ... *potentially forever.*

In a street nearby, Sergeant Mills was in his own fisticuff nightmare.

He had reacted after taking the blow from the Huntsman's buttstock to the head, lunging forth and grappling with the elite soldier over the rifle. They still tensely tussled.

The two scuffled about in frenzy with their combat boots sliding in the snow, interlocking their limbs like wrestlers in vain attempts to falter each other's balance. Harsh blows were struck before the overpowering Huntsman flipped the Commando from off the rifle, utilizing some sort of advanced hand-to-hand combat exercise that took Mills by surprise.

He used Mills' own body weight against him to fling him clear like deadweight. The commando had not been expecting that and thus fell victim.

Dazed and concussed after landing on his back and pounding his cranium, Mills' cross-eyed stare fastened to an upside-down view of the Huntsmen staring down the sights at him, about to deliver the kill shot.

Right as this happened, another handful of balaclava-wearing Huntsman emerged by his flanks, all with weapons trained and all with looks of hunters on their expressionless faces.

This was it.

This was the end.

*He closed his eyes.*


*The Ulvesund Hotel*
*South Vågsøy, Norway*


Back at the Ulvesund assail, Norwegian officer Kaptein Linge and his few surviving men of the NOR.I.C.1 remained scattered in situations of scarce concealment, having gained ground in the late Forrester's triumphant disruption of the enemy position.

Although calling his gallant attempt a success was debatable from an armchair standpoint, it was unquestionably a critical blow and a potentially unrecoverable position for the enemy forces.

NOR.I.C.1 men and remaining men from No.3 Commando Four Troop, respectively, were stranded in pinioned positions between the last row of Norwegian real estate that they had formerly been using as cover from the hotel, and the four-storey Ulvesund, itself.

They could not move forward. Could not fall backwards.

*Their gallant charge was robbed of all momentum ...*

*Their grip, although tight, was starting to slip ...*

Linge and his men had just watched the heroic attempt by the Four Troop captain at storming the fortified lobby of the hotel. The action had ended unsuccessfully, claiming more commando casualties from No.3, inclusive of Algy Forrester, who had fallen on his own grenade.

After the few commandos who had made it all the way up to the breach were denied entry by the stiff resistance by the internal Wehrmacht defenders, their morale had suffered an even harder blow than their severed leadership.

This vital attack was stalling.

With every moment that passed, the combined operation risked being shoved back afoot by the Germans, for what would be the first time today. The very success of Operation Archery now hinged on Commando's ability to conquer this final position ...

Someone had to take charge and do something, and fast.

With his back against the concealment of the sandbag barricades of a once-German machine gun nest, seated amongst his handful of remaining NOR.I.C.1 men, Linge questioned amid his folk: "Who's in charge now? Who is next in-charge?"

There were a few swapped looks and glances about before a nearby Englishman from the No.3 piped up to the foreign ally. "Eh, I believe you are, sir ..."

Linge's attention fell flat upon this commando after hearing his words.

*The spotlight was now upon Martin Linge to manage the frontline of the entire raid.*

"All other officers are ... *gone.*"

"You're in-charge now, Captain!"

*Tunnel vision set in upon the Norwegian Kaptein.*

"*Sir?! Captain?!*"

"*Sir?! What are we going to do?!*"

At the partially destroyed entrance to the Ulvesund Hotel, movement began to stir through the smoke and ruins as the German infantrymen holding the defensive line started to probe for prospects in the wreckage ...

*They sought an opportunity to advance their fortifications ...*

The British stranglehold on the enemy was slackening.

The Wehrmacht was coming up for air ... and it would ensure failure of the entire raid.

"*Sir!*" a British Commando who was ducking down low behind shelter questioned Linge with a worried crinkle in his brow. He was one of the half-dozen—mostly Norwegian Independent Companymen—taking cover behind the northern machine gun nest, along with Kaptein Linge himself. "*What are we going to do.?!*"

With a heavy frown, Linge finally announced after careful consideration. "We must retreat!"

It was like he had given in to this solution, playing the odds of logic rather than the spirit of the unit. His decision made his men of the NOR.I.C.1 contented, but the lone commando troop, who by proxy vouched for the opinions of his men, forlorn.

He reiterated while everybody around him was still attentive. "We must retreat and regroup with the others to launch a secondary attack!"

Martin Linge was no amateur leader, and his years prior to the NOR.I.C.1 in the Royal Norwegian Army had introduced him to the stress of warfare and the pressure of leadership under fire. Linge's hesitation was simply an artefact of transition combined with the possible expectations of the majority of the men now under his command being *commandos* instead of regular *soldiers.* He did not think like one of them—it was not in his training—however ... it was *possibly* within his nature.

Linge *wanted* to progress.

He *wanted* to follow in Forrester's footsteps.

He was, after all, an *honorary commando*, as his friend *Juck Churchill* had said during their pre-raid drinks. And he had meant it.

A Norwegian soldier next to him nodded in agreement to Linge's decision to fall back, and immediately began to prepare himself and the other NOR.I.C.1 men for a full-scale abandonment towards better cover—all the while, the few British Commandos were hesitant in their willingness to retire.

One of the Commandos glanced out over the battlefield, glazing over those lost in the struggle, sharing a similar moment with Linge, himself. It would all be for naught if they retreated.

"What about the others, sir?" he questioned the Kaptein.

Linge was engaged in a thousand-yard stare.

Tactically—mathematically—they would lose less men in a retreat than they would to continue Forrester's push. He snapped back to reality, acknowledging the commando and continuing his extensive observation over the scenario. There were men all around the circumference of the Ulvesund Hotel, held up in all sorts of ensconced nooks and concealment. Not all of them would be able to retreat safely, if at all, let alone even distribute the order in time for an opportune combined reaction.

*Advance or retreat ...* right now, it mattered not. Either one would result in more loss of their numbers, and probably both equally end with defeat.

His decision weighed heavily upon his mind.

Linge could barely see through the brain fog, through the overbearing tension. For all he knew, the men would not make it ten paces in retreat—albeit, that was five paces more than what they would make if they continued to advance.

Around them behind the small concealment of the overthrown machine gun nest, the Norwegian men stripped from their extra bags of ammunition and carry-ons to be able to run more nimbly, and dance to avoid the gunfire from the countless shooters above. They would have to literally run the gauntlet to survive this retreat to safety.

Linge watched them dismantle their gear and disrobe their heavier attire for the sprint. It was then, he saw that the reality of the situation had started to settle into the minds of even his NOR.I.C.1 men as they had the realization that this could be the end.

"I think we're too late to do anything ..." the British Commando amongst their stranded crowd made comment as he assessed the direction of the hotel by boldly peeking beyond a safeguard.

Linge followed his stare, spying for himself the 181st infantrymen from within the Ulvesund as they started to emerge from their holes, weapons out and courage up.

*They were still fighting.*

*Unrelenting.*

*... this was a harsh loss.*

Then ... there was a sound ...

A deep, bass-filled hum poured through the air ...

It was followed by a penetrating pitch ...

A trenchant skirl cut through the volume, filling every inch of the air around the vicinity of South Vågsøy. The stupefying tone caused all the

Allied men within the Combined Operations present to pause and hold a breath while they listened ...

While they absorbed the sensation ...

Felt the familiarity ...

*Scottish Bagpipes.*

It took only a few seconds of play to fill the air with the deep tone before the song type of the tenor became recognizable for *all* the British Commandos: *Reveille.*

The familiar militaristic tune through the Scottish instrument boomed through the streets and across the land throughout South Vågsøy, audible to all those in hardship and combat. It washed over them like a wave from a gentle rejuvenating current, full of warmth and, most importantly, conviction.

*At the Ulvesund Hotel ...*

The sound collected the many ears of the stranded No.3 Commandos amidst the outer perimeter of the Ulvesund Hotel, such as Lieutenant Komrower in his deteriorating perimeter stronghold.

It reached those who had pushed up in the assail, like Kaptein Linge, and those who had been within proximity of the late Captain Forrester, now adrift crouching behind cover by the building or trapped treacherously behind trivial shelter across the thoroughfare.

It filled the chests of the men with an undying hope ...

Reignited their hearts with everlong courage ...

Refuelled their quintessence with a confident certitude ...

A warmth washed over them, comforting them.

Tears swelled in the eyes of those straining.

Trapped men everywhere who may have considered their predicament a sure defeat, brought their right hand up and laid it across their breast, over their heart. They became reinvigorated from it; recharged from it. The Scottish bagpipes were a much-needed boost of morale, resuscitating them all. This was a fight song to see them through; to charge them into battle.

Commandos everywhere heeded intently, recognizing the harmonious accord, and it imparted them with valour and virtue. The sound reminded of the reason they were here fighting, as well as the reason they needed to win.

*In the northern streets ...*

Knocker White's face raised first from the ice.

He thought he heard a resonance of familiar sound but wasn't sure.

Sore all over due to the grenade blast wave, the commando corporal wakened more cognizant and glanced askew to his right.

Attention dulled and vision ablur, he stirred awake the sleeping Lieutenant Head who, after sharing the brunt of that same explosive charge, looked equally as deserving of a full body cast.

"Charley! Oi, Charley!" he harassed the dozing commando, shoving Head alive from his apparent concussion.

"*Bloody Nora ...*" Head murmured with a grimace as he stretched his neck and painfully revolved his torso. There were streaks of blood now leaking out his ears, and he quickly padded them with his fingers to visually assess the damage.

White rotated around in the snow with a widening watch, searching for any remaining enemy that may still be within their vicinity. Through the dissipating smoke lingering in the ruinous aftermath of the environment, he could see that the same stielhandgranate had also killed two more of their own Huntsmen soldiers.

There was, however, evidence of more movement about the area.

They were still well within a hostile zone.

"Come on! We have to move!" Knocker White stressed in a grimace as he pushed up from the snow, hobbling sorely to collect his discarded weapon before becoming attentive to the sound of the distant bagpipes' pitch ...

It was the same Scottish serenade that had awoken him from his unconscious slumber, barely recognizable through the constant ringing in his head from the close-range explosion they had just survived.

Head found his gun and rose to his knees in the cold slush, scanning about the aftermath. After lying in the slush, he was drenched through to the sack. "They all dead?—"

"Shh!" White hissed holding up a hand. He was listening to the skirl of the distant bagpipes with a confused expression upon his maw. It was as if he was second guessing what he was hearing, unsure if it were true or not.

While his ears pricked, his eyes surveyed the walls of the buildings, eventually scanning the white skies for a possible fighter plane or bomber that may have been accountable of emitting the pitching sound.

It was unusual to see White pause his chewing of gum, but he did so for a moment of concentration. "You hear that?"

"... hear what?" Head glared, wiping snow and grime from his face. "The ringing?"

"The pitch ..."

"Yeah, the ringing? Don't worry, I'm fucking deaf after that, too—"

"No, *shhh!*"

The men both held their breath for a second and listened, absorbing the atmosphere for an extended moment as they both locked eyes, coming to the same realization.

*That sound was of bagpipes.*

"That!" White exclaimed as Head nodded his head, hearing it too.

"I hear it, alright! I feel like I'm back at bloody base!"

"Yeah, and it's time to wake up!"

"Only one bloody clown would be playing that right now, eh?"

Knocker White knew and couldn't agree more with who was playing.

*Elsewhere in the northern streets...*

In his seemingly endless wander, Durnford-Slater glanced down another narrow alleyway from behind his pistol sights. He was still trying to navigate his way out of harm's way whilst searching for his commandos, eliminating enemy Huntsmen whenever he encountered them throughout this Norwegian residential maze. Still displaced and lost, the lack of direction could be his undoing ...

Whilst moving cautiously through the northern district, the sound of aloof bagpipes warmed the atmosphere around him—like it did for the whole snowy town, for that matter.

It was a beacon for the hero commando.

Durnford-Slater lowered his guard and pivoted in his advance, all of a sudden becoming certain of the direction he should have been headed.

Beneath his lampshade moustache, his maw curled in one corner as the realization sunk in. There was only one bloody fool who would be making that racket during the middle of a war.

He muttered: "Jack ..."

*Nearby in the northern streets ...*

The masked Gebirgsjäger sniper who had the drop on the downed and disarmed commando lined up the sights on his target: Sergeant Mills.

Dead beat and bloodied, Mills watched helplessly as his opponent prepared to execute him. After their brief bout of hand-to-hand combat, in which he was defeated, the soldier now stood over him with the advantage along with two other Alpine Huntsmen. The group of balaclava boche surrounded the sombre setting of his aspirant execution.

It was the first time Mills had seen these formidable members of the intimidating Gebirgsjäger up close, donning their particular battle attire; leather strapping atop of winter-themed camouflage. The symbol of the edelweiss was prominent on their SS uniform beneath the smocks and webbing.

Staring down the barrels of multiple weapons, Mills let close his eyes in favour of calmly welcoming the bullet that would finally end his life.

"*Letzte worte Engländer?*"

A pair of sinister giggles followed the German's question, which Mills aversely ignored. The tone of the words spoken resembled something akin to *any last words.*

The Huntsman then manoeuvred his spare hand up and engaged the bolt-action lever of the Karabiner rifle, cycling the chamber with fresh brass to shoot and kill this enemy of the Third Reich.

*... the purr and skirl of the bagpipes filled the air ...*

The sound flooded the vicinity around the men.

They were puzzled.

Through the eye holes in their ski masks, they blinked about in confusion.

The sound touched Mills' ears.

He recognized the origin—and the likely composer, which would have been none other than Mad Jack Churchill on his doodlesack somewhere nearby.

Although the Englishman recognized the sound of the instrument, the two German observers and standing executioner did not. The expressionless Huntsmen took a stay of execution for a split-second to look about themselves. They questioned the foreign sound that they were hearing; that assaulted their ears. Fearing an airstrike, one of them even searched the skies, adjusting his mask to search through the cut eyelets as he tilted his neck.

Pending his execution, Mill's eyes reopened, being issued the sight of his momentarily distracted executioner. Although he maintained his stance with the rifle, his balaclava-wrapped mug was raised and his attention had drifted elsewhere.

The commando acted without even thinking.

Mills energetically lunged out and grabbed onto the length of the 98k bolt-action with both hands, shifting the dark circle of the barrel from his face. In that same instance, the Huntsman's attention returned and the weapon discharged with a deafening blast.

The snow exploded beside Mills' head, and the two re-engaged in a tussle for the rifle, although this time, Mills was at a vast disadvantage due to surrounding numbers.

"Nein!" the soldier shouted, using all his might to wrench the weapon away from the Englishman, resulting in Mills using the Gerry's own prior tactics against him.

The Huntsman reeled up the weapon like a fishing rod.

The prize catch on the end: one British Commando fighting for his fucking life.

Mills allowed himself to be hoisted from the ground in a stream of snow and mud, and he immediately followed through from the launch by driving a closed fist into the centre of the white balaclava target zone ...

... only, his punch packed a little extra *wallop* than usual, thanks to the brass housing of a BC-41 trench knife that was now attached via his knuckles.

*Chunk!*

The brass knuckleduster of the BC-41 collided against a face beneath the wool, breaking bone. Mills had struck the German sniper so hard that the troop was either knocked-out cold or instantly dead.

The Huntsman's hands released a hold of the rifle, and, like a bulkhead, the troop anchored down into the snow with his lights out.

Mills was now upstanding and in possession of the rifle.

The other two Alpine Huntsmen finally realized precisely what the hölle was going on. They were still slow to react due to the disorientation of the piercing sound that confused their ears.

Sergeant Mills wasted no seconds.

He flicked the knife at one of the men, impaling him through the shoulder and causing him to drop his gun, sinking against a close wall. He then fast brought around his confiscated German rifle and cycled the bolt, delivering a perfectly aimed bullet between the cut eyeholes of the remaining soldier with an ear-splitting blast from the powerful sniper rifle. The bullet blew out the back of his skull through his balaclava like a dropped meat pie with generous tomato sauce topping, oozing warm, chunky innards.

In the blink of an eye, the Huntsman's brain painted the white wall of the house behind him, and he dropped dead in the snow.

Mills cycled the bolt, realizing he had no more rounds to finish the remaining soldier with the knife in his cadaver, so he instead switched his hold on the weapon to use the butt-stock end like a cricket bat against the man's head.

In the run-up, he even tapped it against the ground twice before assuming the pose to sweep vertically with the weapon, like an upper cut.

*Crack!*

This once prospective witness to his execution now bore a head like a deflated soccer ball. The full force of the rifle swung at him, smashing him in the face so hard it bulged an eye from displaced brain matter.

Breathless, he let drop the bloody rifle to better search for his two pistols in the snow. He was eager to continue with the skirmish beneath the sound of the bagpipe's song.

*He was back in the fight.*

*In the Ulvesund Hotel ...*

Using the echoey emergency staircase which was located within the Ulvesund Hotel north-west wing, Feind and Jürgen both suddenly halted their shuffling over the creaky timber steps. The sporadic gunfire and bass-filled grenade blasts from outside were distant echoes from within these hollow confines; however, it was the purr of the bass hum and the pitch of the bagpipes skirl that seemed to pierce the walls not unlike a ghost. It stopped them in their tracks.

The howl of the tune filled the air, even within their confined recess, and it caused the two Gebirgsjäger officers to exchange a glance.

After a second's pause, Jürgen turned on the staircase and faced up to his Hauptsturmführer. There was a sudden surge in his tone as the Hauptscharführer panicked.

"Das < *'The English! It's an airstrike!'* > Luftangriff!"

"Nein," Feind replied with a sense of calm about him as he brought his scarred face about his comrade, more certain than he had ever been about anything thus far in this raid defence.

"Es < *'It's him. He is here ...'* > hier ..."

# 14
## *Reveille*

*The Ulvesund Hotel*
*South Vågsøy, Norway*

From his concealed position behind the Ulvesund enemy stronghold, the extremely battle-worn Arthur Komrower became upstanding to the unexpected musical summons. He cast a stark stare towards the source.

Like many presently beaten-down and dusted No.3 Commandos, the bandaged and sutured lieutenant, who had just watched the foiled assault upon the hotel and the deterioration of subsequent offensive endeavours, became uplifted by the ambiance of the bagpipes' tune.

*The Reveille.*

It edified all commandos to keep fighting.

To hold on. To see it through.

Simultaneously, the curious German soldiers whose successful defence of the assail offered a valuable chance at repositioning, reacted uneasily upon hearing the strange, foreign, and outlandish Scottish pitch sail through the airwaves ...

They momentarily halted in their duties to exchange a few ambiguous contemplations. Some gazes were of confusion, others beheld a certain humorous quality at the obscurity.

Mostly ... *it seemed to repel them.*

After rearing their ugly stahlhelms from the defendable recesses in a bid to reclaim the land gained by the British, the Wehrmacht warriors recoiled back within their dark holes in fear of another attack.

And finally, returning the air to a clear and eerily tranquil, the bagpipe tune seemed to conclude in a resonating absence of reverberation. The volume of warfare that had once filled the atmosphere was suddenly gone, leaving a hollow vacancy.

Behind Komrower's hobbling position across the open thoroughfare from the hotel, and in wake of the reveille, a stampede of incoming combat boots trampled through the snow, pouring around each corner of housing like a flood. At least three to four dozen more men of Group 4 stormed the front and replenished the numbers.

*Reinforcements had arrived.*

Fresh commandos dipped their helmets to the burned and bandaged Komrower as they arrived, quickly passing the officer along with a detachment of men, who were fast to establish themselves along the outer perimeter before the ominous and tall hotel stronghold.

"Lieutenant!" an authoritative voice called, distracting Komrower from the exhilaration of watching their numbers grow all along the southern lines.

He turned to greet Captain Hooper of G4.

At last, the captain had made his way from the forward operating base along the shore and caught up with the rest of his Group in the warehouse district. Lieutenant Black's detail of men presumably remained to finish up at the warehouses, thusly moving the remainder of the reserve to the Ulvesund Hotel objective.

"Captain!" Komrower acknowledged with a gratified tenor underlining his voice. "Aren't we bloody glad to see you lot!"

He started to bring him up to speed about the hotel roof shooters blocking their advance when Hooper, who had been in contact with Captain Bradley of One Troop via radio wire, cut him off and affirmed him not to worry in the slightest ...

That Captain Bradley had a surprise in store.

*That it was one big enough to end the fight for Vågsøy Island.*


Jack Churchill finally removed the blow-stick from his lips ...

Observing across the distant perimeter of the hotel warzone, he saw that those commando groups who were trapped about the base of the Ulvesund and across the wide thoroughfare had become enriched and refuelled by the reveille. It was as if a metaphoric sun had re-emerged between the clouds above, shining down light upon them in the darkest moment of the raid.

"*Major Churchill?*" an Irish voice interrupted his triumphant glower over the battlefield. Churchill's head turned to acknowledge the man while pushing his doodlesack holster about on his webbing for comfort.

He bore witness to Captain Bradley's One Troop as they enclosed from their demolition objectives along the eastern coast. One Troop had been a distant combatant the entire raid thus far, however it now seemed that all roads led to the Ulvesund Hotel: the final objective. All units were converging.

Bradley was flanked by the distinguished Sergeant Ramsey and twenty other commandos in a sporadic formation, including a few from the No.6 demo detach, whom Churchill noted were carrying something not technically on the armoury register: *a 3-inch mortar cannon.*

The component was a compact variant, possibly improvised/customized by the gun monkeys in Bradley's outfit. This particular portable artillery unit was perhaps a relic of his previous experience in the artillery service.

"Set 'err up o'err therr, lads," Bradley instructed his men before enclosing his full attention to Churchill. The tall and rather wild-looking northern Irishman beamed a grin as he savagely took Churchill's arm off at the elbow with a handshake. "Mad Jack, 'ow arre ya?"

Churchill regarded with a lark. "Better now you're here, you crazy bastard."

"Ya still lewkin' for'er foit, eh?" Bradley remarked with a heavy accent. And in reference to his death wish: "Yoo fooken mad coont."

"Always."

"Well, a'parently ta lad's 'ave a wee pest problem at tha hotel. We'rre 'bou'ta shell tha fecken shite out'ta tha roof, mate. If ya wanna rush in for'er brawl, it'd soon be time ta do it."

Churchill tipped his beret-clad dome with concurrence.

"Fine-o-fine with me, my lad. Raze it to the ground for all I care," Jack insisted, casting a gleam towards the hotel that hid a certain concern for the well-being of his festering vendetta; a particular *Hauptsturmführer* of the *Gebirgsjäger Alpine Huntsmen ...*

"*Mills?*"

Still standing over the enemy he killed in the heat of the action, the bloody face of the vivacious Joe Mills glanced up. He twirled upon hearing a series of incoming footsteps enclosing on his position in the deathly fog of the Norwegian streets.

He recognized the voice calling him from the incoming.

Thankfully, they were friendlies, as it didn't look like the sergeant could go another round in the ring.

Dispassionately, he reloaded his two handguns and replied to their call, wincing to shout over bruised ribs. "Over here."

Arriving at a jog were Knocker White and Charley Head, both sapped and clammy from all the fighting.

"Bloody hell," Head remarked upon witnessing all the dead bodies located in the circumference of the bloody-faced and muddied Mills. They were almost elegantly positioned like fallen petals from a bud. "Been having fun, Sergeant?"

"Rough neighbourhood," Mills threw away.

"You seen the Colonel anywhere?" White enquired, letting drop to the snow his almost empty Ithaca shotgun, trading it for one of the deceased German's weapons. The fallen Huntsman had a Schmeisser strapped to his shoulder as a back-up for his sniper rifle. White discovered several spare magazines in his pouches and transferred them into his own dressage for easy access.

"Negative," Mills replied, latching forward both slides on his pistols with his thumb and index finger, respectively. He was now prepared again, with a gun in each hand. "We separated."

White and Head were speechless.

They shook their heads, beginning to dread the worst for their fearless leader when, suddenly, a whistle blow in the wind caught their attention from the end of the connecting street ... there was a man standing there, tall and weathered:

*It was Lieutenant-Colonel John Durnford-Slater.*

An ounce of hope became restored in that moment.

From the distance, he waved the cluster of his bravest commandos towards him, not willing to miss a beat. *"Let's go No.3!"*

Bolstering what strength they had left, the three men upped and approached their colonel at the end of a street which widened onto a clearing that led them all back to the Ulvesund Hotel. All they had to do was follow the sound to where the bagpipes had resonated, and it would bring them back to the war.

During the skirmish and fighting that followed their improvised—albeit effective—ambush of the Huntsmen reserve, they had ended up back near the hotel.

Durnford-Slater waited for them to reach him, and he silently gestured down a strip.

"That's the hotel!" Head remarked, finally realizing their locale.

The men started sauntering down the block as one, closing their expanse but still remaining at a safe distance.

From their northern position, they could see the rear side of the four-storey building where there was a couple of closed garage doors and a bolted rear access door. There were the silhouettes of multiple shooters arrayed throughout almost all the windows from the upper storeys, and the roof was crawling with protracted rifle barrels.

"Forrester's assault must have failed ..." Knocker White alluded at a whim. They could make out the flanks of a few stranded commandos stuck behind cover midway between the houses and the hotel, and almost twice as many still lining the street. There were a lot of commando bodies across the thoroughfare, signifying that casualties had been greatly sustained during the onslaught—though, it was not a certainty of failure.

Head gestured towards the building.

The side they could access from here seemed uncontested.

"We could get to those back doors ..."

"Not while those kraut snipers are watching out you won't," Mills informed with his vision scaling the side of the hotel, scouting laterally.

Durnford-Slater was uncharacteristically tactfully quiet during their conjoined observations and impromptu reconnaissance of the hotel. In fact, when White eventually realized this and sought his colonel's consideration, he found Durnford-Slater not even looking in the direction of the hotel at all ...

Instead, his sights were fixated on something down another connecting street; what seemed like nothing more than a Weegie house with a car parked outside of it. Whatever the detail, something had captured his interest.

White queried. "Sir?"

Durnford-Slater faced him briefly, then implied a desire to investigate further. "Lieutenant, Corporal, wait here. Don't engage the hotel unless there is another attempt made by the reinforcements. If there is a whole bunch of noise, then you have my permission to assist. Mills, you're with me."

"Yes, sir," Mills obeyed, gluing himself to Durnford-Slater's hip.

Knocker White followed the colonel's orders blindly whilst Head lingered in question. "Where are you lot going, then?"

Durnford-Slater's stare intensified.

He was fixated on a house down and across the street, the one beyond the parked black Volkswagen which had a busted driver's side window. This detail may have majorly attracted his attention, however, it was the swastika flag erected from the bonnet that partially confirmed his suspicions. Something about it sparked the colonel's curiosity.

"Just going to question the neighbours ..." Durnford-Slater stated cryptically before leading the way, discreetly bounding from cover to cover as not to attract any unwanted attention from the hotel snipers.

Among the mass piling of One Troop men with whom he had just been reunited, Churchill unexpectedly recognized a face amidst their ranks:

A.J. Cork.

*The two had a history.*

Seemingly, Cork had already noticed Churchill and had thusly shied away into the crowd of commandos.

The two men had not seen each other since the events of Operation Claymore six months ago, where Cork had been demoted and moved out of No.3, narrowly surviving a dishonourable discharge for his actions involving attempting to sabotage, immure, and get rid of Churchill. He had slipped the noose, though was forever regarded as a hushed black sheep of Commando.

In the aftermath of Claymore, Churchill had become aware that he had since turned a new leaf after falling on his own sword, although that failed to prepare him for what he would feel whilst laying eyes upon the trooper again—especially in that uniform, wearing that flash.

It would once again appear that fate had crossed their paths.

Bradley's voice commanded: "Sergeant Ramsey, brung your lads along a nurtherly approoch vector und assust assembly ov tha mortar to strike tha hotel gable."

"Yes, sir!" Ramsey complied. He was leading the small group of troopers inclusive of Cork. They deviated from their hold and started to pass Churchill, where Jack interrupted their route to accost the begrudged familiar face.

"Cork?!" Churchill declared, singling him out before all the other No.6 men of whom he had since befriended. This demo detachment were his new family.

Cork hesitated upon hearing the call, allowing for Churchill to recognize him fully in the crowd of commandos.

"I'll admit, you're not the enemy I expected to find out here ..."

Ramsey overheard the remark and remained to bear witness to this outface between the two Allied Englishmen. This was coherent to the past few instances Cork had encountered with men from No.3, and the men of No.6 were starting to detect a rather dark history of bad blood between him and the unit.

"Why does everyone seem to hate you, A.J.?" Ramsey intuitively commented, finally fed up trying to vouch for the man—let alone in opposition to a major. He left it at that, pressing on with their mission.

After a short distraction from his duty, the visible ashamed sergeant appeared eager to move on with the job—the same way he had moved on with his life following his regrettable events in the Lofoten Islands; where his pro-LayForce superiors had apparently left him out to dry after unofficially affirming his wrongful actions prior to the fact. Cork dismissively yet respectfully declared: "Excuse me, Major. I have orders."

"You're pushing the hotel?" Churchill questioned, sincerely interested. Seizing an opportunity to advance upon the hotel was his very next goal. He could potentially hijack command of this section—and quite frankly, the more the merrier for them, especially someone as highly regarded as Major Jack Churchill.

Cork halted again, noticeably uncomfortable in this conversation ...

Barely able to look Mad Jack in the eye, he was so crippled with guilt. He perhaps was unsure how to process such contact with a man who had every right to be his greatest adversary.

Churchill picked up on his shy antipathy.

"Relax, Sergeant. I am not going to fight you. I want to fight *them* ..." Jack smoothed—albeit he was well within his rights to conduct the former and it appeared nobody would defend Cork's welfare.

Cork snickered through the coyness, still obviously uncomfortable.

"Eh, demolitions ... sir"

"*Demo?*" Churchill's brow inverted, denoting that One Troop had just come from striking the herring oil factories and that No.6 demo would have lit the fuses. "What target is next?"

"The hotel garages," Cork jerked his jaw forwards. "There is apparently a tank hidden away somewhere. If it's there, they want it destroyed before the Germans can use it."

Churchill scoffed, sharing a beam with the lingering Sergeant Ramsey, who apparently equally considered that implausible. "Surely if the Huns possessed such an armoured beast, they would have used it during their defence of the island?"

"That's what I said," Ramsey input. "It's likely false or old intelligence from the submarine's original recon of the island. Probably saw a trailer or a truck with the top half up and thought it was a Panzer tank ... it happens."

Churchill harmonized and gave a modest nod.

"Fine-o-fine. Rather err on the side of caution, I suppose."

"'ere we go!" Captain Bradley informed with a loud announcement, and the men of One Troop seemed to all prepare for action like a bunch of amped sprinters in a race, just waiting for the gun to sound.

On his command, his men were all moving on the hotel ...

*Churchill included.*

Soon after, the portable three-inch Stokes-type, A-typical, muzzle-loaded, drop-fired mortar tube became set up. The men pointed the muzzle almost vertically from their position behind the concealment of a single-storey building located directly across the thoroughfare from the Ulvesund Hotel.

This would be an acute angle of elevation to target, and Sergeant Ramsey had instructed One Troop to fire at absolute minimum range.

They prepared the first round by the wide-open mouth of the mortar. Tail-first, the commandos primed and then situated the ten-pound bomb shell an inch into the feeding tube before momentarily halting. The assisting operator held with his hands up, planning to cover his ears.

After casting a look from the ready mortar crew, Ramsey questioned to his superior. "Sir?"

Overseeing, Captain Bradley simply nodded with a stiff-upper lip glare across the errant street and at the hotel of which they targeted.

"Let 'em 'ave et!" the Irishman grimly deemed.

Beneath his wobbly tin hat, Ramsey's face returned at a gleam to his men and he relayed the order. "Fire!"

The situated trooper let drop the weighted mortar round into the cylindrical tube and he hastily anchored to one side, shielding his head and ears. With a suction-like *thook!* the dropped round struck against the anvil, detonating the primer between the propelling fins of the shell within the cannon. The round emitted a metallic *donk!* and was sent sky-high above South Vågsøy at a minimal angle of ascent before a whistling descent traced it onto her target.

A pitching shrill screeched as the cartridge plummeted back to earth from the icy heavens above the snowy island, impacting the flat roof of the Ulvesund Hotel.

Although unintentional, the mortar shell threaded the eye of the needle on its inclination, slotting straight down an open brick chimney passage, surpassing the surface of the roof altogether. The round detonated several metres down between the second and third floor in the centre of the structure, causing many casualties to the enemy within and setting the place afire.

With a raucous eruption, the mid-levels of the hotel burst outwards with the shock of the explosive force—*magnified,* due to the compacted explosive within the 81mm shell detonating within a confined space.

Inner walls were devastated and load-bearing stilts folded.

Enemy riflemen stationed by the windows were shoved outside by the brash vigour of air, freefalling to their deaths in a hailstorm of falling broken glass and debris.

The sound of panicked shouts within were heard thereafter.

Not allowing for the Germans to catch a breath, another round was fed to the three-inch mortar. The tactic was a regular ace in the hole for Commando in this battle.

*Thook—DONK!*

After heading skywards, the incoming shell whistled in her descending trajectory before splashing in a loud and hot wave of orange fire against the flat roof of the Ulvesund Hotel feet from the chimney, warping the tin construct and decimating several of the Alpine Huntsmen snipers nested upon the outpost in a fiery splash of force.

While the Ulvesund Hotel defenders became mostly debilitated by the incoming mortar shells targeting the roof, commandos from multiple different situations on the ground took the chance to excel.

*The war was back on.*

*South of the Ulvesund exterior ...*

From a south-easterly approach vector, Captain Hooper gave the command to launch his pooling numbers of combined forces of the G4 reserve. This included those who still remained from Forrester's Four Troop and even loyal remnants of the NOR.I.C.1 still along the perimeter.

The worse for wear Lieutenant Arty Komrower was among them.

The brave veteran No.3 Commando tossed down his assisting crutch in order join in a limping, war-hungry charge accompanying almost four-dozen Commandos.

*"Commando!"* the booming thunder of roaring cheers amalgamated as the stampede of their combat boots rumbled towards the hotel, weapons crackling, striking the stahlhelms from many mantles.


*East of the Ulvesund exterior ...*

Within five seconds of Hooper giving the attack order from the southerly defensive line, Bradley orchestrated his command in the east and unleashed his smaller assault group from One Troop into the charge. Clear of cover, these additional commandos mounted the danger of the cause and leapt into the fray.

They did this as Ramsey and his mortar team let off another round, burrowing a hole in the hotel roof with the artillery. Their continuous shelling would cause the structure to further collapse, crushing all enemy within who did not vacate.

From demolitions, Cork and Dowling were among the few of the assault team, charging forth in the volume of war with might and valour, along with a tagalong ...

... amidst the charge, was Major Churchill, longbow in hand.

As he passed the perimeter line, he cast their CO a glance, capturing Bradley's gaze of perplexity as to why such a high-ranking officer would be charging into the scrimmage like a dispensable grunt. Jack simply gave him a nod from his green beret-covered dome.

"*Captain.*"

Bradley knew better than to question the eccentricities of Mad Jack Churchill. After acknowledging his presence amongst his men, he also accepted the fact that the crazy commando was about to perform the charge with his signature stick and string at the ready.

Bradley responded in-kind with a respectful nod of his own.

"*Major.*"

*North of the Ulvesund exterior ...*

Watching this foray finale unfold without much operational context due to their separate tangent following Colonel Durnford-Slater, Lieutenant Charley Head and commando Corporal Knocker White witnessed the mortar strike upon the Ulvesund from afar.

The artillery fire had been a direct blow against the stronghold, eliminating almost all the sniper defence atop of the building, as well as disrupting the shots from the riflemen located throughout the building's many windows.

"Good god," Head exclaimed as they felt the bass from each sequential mortar round erupting.

Succeeding the unrelenting artillery strikes, their attentions lowered as they heard in the distance the heroic bellow:

"*... commandoooo ...*"

The battle cry resounded throughout the district. So loud, it even overwhelmed the electric clapping of concurrent submachine guns and pouting rifle fire across the thoroughfare.

Breaking cover, Knocker White inched forwards, gawking past Head's cowering position as they lurked behind concealment. "They're making a final push! We should go!" he implored, press-checking the gunmetal grey receiver of his newfound German maschinenpistole. He could tell, again, by his reluctance to leap into the fray that Head was hesitant to fight.

Between confident chomps of his gum, White cast him a gleam, observing his lieutenant's submission to his wound. Head's grimace upon moving his gun-shot limb was an actual frailty and it showed.

He may not have had much to offer in this fight ...

"Stay here," White instructed, possibly exceeding his rank to take charge rather than wait for his superior's command at this juncture. He was tired of needing to constantly sell his senior into action, so instead he sold him into acceptance of his own adventure. "Wait for the Colonel to tell him that I've have gone ahead."

Oddly, Head accepted these terms with a wordless nod.

*That probably sounded good, because he could stay put ...*

He called out as Knocker White stepped off, offering a genuine token. "Oi Knocker ... good luck!"

Holding for a second, Knocker White bowed politely before sprinting directly towards the Ulvesund.

*Already at the Ulvesund Hotel ...*

From their pinned position behind an overthrown enemy machine gun nest, Kaptein Linge and his trapped men were well apprised of the next advance. Once the mortars had struck the roof, caving in some of the top floors of the hotel, it offered the men the opportunity to escape their predicaments and push forward.

Under Linge's command, a dozen NOR.I.C.1 troopers and the remnant commandos of Forrester's initial assail at the Ulvesund bounded together, thrashing forth. They bounded over bullet-riddled obstacles in the thoroughfare in order to advance upon the enemy stronghold, taking the position once and for all.

Gunfire ensued from both sides as persistent enemy shooters fired down upon the men as they charged.

Seconds after Martin Linge's influential injunction, the twentyfold multiplicity of reserve commandos came charging in from the rear perimeter defence, quaking the battlefront brandishing their thundery battle cry.

*"Commando!"*

They pushed up in swarms of white smocks over khaki clothes and brodie helmets, slicing enemy positions in half with their powerful, combined discharges.

Hobbling painfully across the thoroughfare warzone as gunfire raked the icy cobblestone by his feet, Komrower narrowly avoided death from a shooter above. He banked harshly left and dropped into a controlled collapse behind a snow-buried civilian vehicle. The rusty metal beneath the white layering was assaulted by several brunts of enemy fire after he disappeared behind it.

Limited in his abilities, the incapacitated commando drew a sidearm and inched close to the edge of concealment, popping off potshots towards the many remaining guns in the hotel windows whilst his brethren progressed with the assault, flocking around him.

Valiantly, he did all he could, but could go on no further.

Gaining a foothold after surviving the onslaught, Martin Linge and his few courageous comrades finally reached the outer walls of the hotel.

From here, they had a line on the smoking, debris-repressed entrance way that Algy Forrester sacrificed his life to blow open.

Inching the edges of the structure, they could spot German soldiers skulking within the smoke-filled crevasse of the ground floor lobby. Men in leather-bound grey uniforms and stahlhelm-donned heads were visible scurrying about, securing positions amidst the rubble of the buckled entrance. They lurked behind numerous fortified barricades, fighting till their last breath.

On his approach, Linge fast discerned the enemy movements.

Linge raised his gun to his armpit and fired upon the entrance-way defenders. His string caned multiple soldiers, mowing them down and causing several others to duck for cover, opting to fall farther back within the hotel confines. This ultimately lowered the German defences and opened an angle for their enemy's advance.

"*Move up!*" Linge shouted with confidence, assuming command at this interval. A mix of his Norwegian men and British Commandos fanned out beside him and covered his flanks. They boldly shifted their perspectives at the entrance, gaining more of a fire-line into the Ulvesund Hotel.

They had a foot well and truly in the door now.

Schmeisser cradled firmly before him and swaying with every pace, Knocker White sprinted in from the urban outskirts.

Before any of the German shooters were even aware of his northerly advent across the thoroughfare, the No.3 Commando was already beneath their snoozy rifle sights.

Energetically leaping over a small fence and tucking in tight against the building exterior of the quieter northern side, Knocker White prepared a tight hold on his submachine gun to absorb the recoil.

Still catching his breath, he traced around the next corner with his gun, discovering a discreet back door entrance into the building. Further along in the opposite direction, was a series of bolted metal garage doors, which seemed locked up tight by the besieged Nazi fortifiers. He elected to head counterclockwise around the exterior, bringing him east and towards the action of the reserve troop assail upon the hotel.

During his progression, White spotted a couple of straggler troops behind a turned-over trailer, pinned down by upstairs shooters. He saw them notice his incursion into the raid with a sudden reaction, and signalled them with a friendly open palm. Opting to assist these commandos, he quickly strafed out from his angular cover and whipped his MP40 at an eleven o'clock angle upwards, aiming at the second-storey window. Step by step, he crept further out to gain an angle of view; all the while, his sights remained trained on the windowsill, waiting for the perfect oppor—

*Baaaaang!*

The German displayed himself and White's weapon discharged, spraying at the ardent gunman. His volley hammered the white wooden window frame and wall with an assault of speckled gunfire, dotting lines across it until a notable *ding* could be heard. That was the unmistakable sound of the metal stahlhelm upon the Gerry's dome being punctured like a tin can.

The shooter's weapon dropped sailing out of the window port, shattering into the ice-covered road with an audible metallic scatter amidst all of the surrounding gunfire.

*He wouldn't be giving the lads any more trouble.*

White twisted at the core, called upon the two liberated friendlies.

"*Come on! Go, go, go!*" he directed, still anchored on the spot with his weapon pointed upwards, scanning for any other protruding targets until they elapsed his mark, reaching concealment like a finish line, and he followed suit.

"You lads good?" White joined them, taking the time to offer them a greeting motion. As he had seen his commanding officer role models do countless times before, namely Jack Churchill, the time for pleasantries during a time of war could be made if done so promptly.

However incongruous of a gesture, the men embraced White with a handshake each, and it was then discovered that one of the stragglers was none-other than Eric de la Torre, someone recognizable from No.3.

"*Yes, sir!*"

"*Thank you, sir!*" the breathless subalterns remarked, obliging and beholden of the help.

With an askew brow, White questioned. "Eric?"

"Sergeant White," he responded, unsure if the busy corporal would recognize him during all this raid chaos.

"My friends call me *Knocker.*"

de la Torre formed a smile. "Sir."

They took the time to catch a breath and steady their wits, and White noticed that the other trooper who had an injured hand wrapped in a bloody field dressing was attempting to handle an Ithaca shotgun: the same weapon he had optioned to carry when they had kitted up aboard the Prince Charles at dusk this morning.

Realizing that the pump-action required two hands to function, White looked out for the subaltern, casually stepping in close and slotting his MP40 strap over the trooper's neck and positioning it tact, swapping it out for the man's cumbersome weapon. He exchanged the appropriate ammunition, commenting that you could do more damage to the enemy trying to handle that with one paw than a two-handed shotgun.

The commando thanked White and the three of them continued towards the front entrance of the stronghold ... the bottleneck of the contest ... *their pending doom* ...

Whilst they marched on, Knocker White press-checked the breach of the familiar shotgun. He spied the scarlet sleeve of a 16-gauge shell resting in the chamber breach, racking the foregrip and pinching her tight.

The fact that he had wreaked a lot of havoc with this type of weapon thus far during Operation Archery instilled the confidence in him to do so again.

*It was time to inflict some more damage.*

Incoming with the eastern assault team, comprised of half the members from Bradley's One Troop, Major Churchill acted as a superintendent.

He may have been the highest-ranking officer present, but he was not giving the orders. In fact, Churchill was not even *'there'* in a manner of speaking. As far as his superiors knew, he was still with his men of G3 in the warehouse district, sifting through the charcoaled ruins for intelligence and processing captured prisoners of war ... on paper, he was *anywhere* but chasing his own personal vendetta against the enemy.

Mad Jack moved amidst a handful of commandos compiled from the No.3 and No.6 demo as they jogged across the hazardous thoroughfare, covered by the atmosphere of mortar shelling and exchanging small arms contest.

They charged the defensive blindside, contouring east while the attention of what remained of the enemy shooters focused on the heavier numbers approaching from the south.

However, their journey was not without incident.

Crossing the thoroughfare, they weaved between parked civilian vehicles, a horse carriage, and numerous other obstacles when suddenly they fell under fire from an elevated enemy position at the hotel.

Aggressive small arms discharge befell them. Between their combat boots as they ran, the supercharged projectiles effected the cobblestone street with stone-chipping impacts, exhausts of powdered snow, and bright flinting sparks.

While most of the troopers focused on their passage, manoeuvring through the obstacles or even seeking brief refuge behind concealment, one trooper in a tin hat between Churchill and Cork tarried to raise his weapon and return fire. A valiant attempt.

The deafening typewriter-esque chatter from his machine gun chomped away at the enemy position, brushing across the tall face of the hotel surface and unfortunately failing to suppress numerous shooters at once.

Churchill's neck cranked as he, too, paused in their exhilarating advance to watch his comrade's achievement here in supporting his troops to cross the street more securely—but in the blink of an eye, before he had even expelled a half-dozen rounds from his automatic, the soldier was shot through the chest.

Like a full-stop to a sentence, he collapsed in the street.

The weapon's thunderous flourishing ceased instantly.

Churchill altered his view with the squinting stare of an eagle's eye, immediately locating the culprit: third floor, middle window. There may have been multiple active shooters at this juncture, but judging by the way this rifleman cycled his rifle before an overconfident and expressionless gawk, he was the one responsible for delivering the kill shot on the commando.

With his longbow already equipped, Churchill's posture stiffened.

He smoothly drew an arrow from his shoulder quiver and anchored an archer's pose, drawing the bowstring as he raised his arms onto the elevated target at an easy distance—and loosed.

From the safety of his perched position high above the battlefield, the German rifleman chambered fresh brass, collectedly about to resume his sights on another target when *THOCK!* the razor-sharp head of a bodkin-tipped war arrow struck him under the eye, penetrating his head so all that remained was the feathered end. The force cranked his neck with a grotesque crack, and threw his body backwards into the hotel room by the might of the kinetic energy transfer.

Beside his archer's stance in the trekking chaos, Cork's view retracted. Having just witnessed Jack Churchill snipe the shooter on the third floor with a bow and arrow, he was bewildered.

He couldn't help but cast him a respectful head signal, which Churchill returned before the two caught up with the others, arriving at the stronghold exterior.

Around the façade of the Ulvesund Hotel, Linge and his troops continued to engage the enemy at the front entrance. They applied pressure, and more and more reinforcements ran the gauntlet of the remaining defensive sentinel fire, reaching the hotel in their wake.

From behind their chattering weapons, Linge commanded a group to progress on the position and push inside. Using their firearms like a wrench, they would pry open the ingress to the enemy's stronghold, eventually overthrowing their adversaries once and for all.

Led personally by Kaptein Linge, a group of men fringed on the blown-open foyer. With their guns clutched white-knuckled, they traced the edges of the opening as they marched inwards, tracking closer and closer to the brink before—*Bam! Bam! Bam!*

*A series of blaring gunfire erupted.*

*Baaaaaaaaaaang!*

Firearms exchanged unrelenting barrages.

Defences discharged from within the darkened space.

The confines blinked and flashed, strobing like a lights show.

*Bam!*

*Bam, bam!*

Vivid as fireworks in the dim of night, muzzle-flashes twinkled at haphazard intervals from multiple static locations throughout the shadowy lobby entrance, claiming the life of one of Linge's dearest comrades from the NOR.I.C.1.

After a hash of retaliatory fire, the Allies quickly strafed for shelter.

A couple of German soldiers realized this and clutched at an opportunity to wipe their aggressors out. They acted fast and struck hard like cornered snakes from the recesses of a pit.

With unrelenting MP40s clapping away, they chased the rearward retreat of the raiders to their concealment, eliminating another Norwegian soldier and a British Commando before Linge and one other man collided with each other in the resounding pandemonium, falling against a wall of the building as it lit up with scalding ricochets.

The audacious German soldiers challenged even them as they pulled back, seemingly hungry to inflict casualties, and broke out even further into the harsh daylight of the street battle where their onslaught finally ended. They were shot dead by several commando guns inches before either one of them could pull the trigger on Linge, saving him.

Breathless, his eventful and high-profile life would have certainly flashed before his eyes. Catching a breath and eager to try the advance again, Linge shouted after quickly reacquiring a hold of his weapon.

He and another man sprayed covering fire through the entrance space, keeping the Germans within at bay whilst waving a few more British soldiers over, bringing them across the thoroughfare and close in behind him at the hotel, increasing their stacked numbers for the ambitious assault into the building.

This was a fucking meat-grinder of a position to take, but it had to be done. And in the absence of the late Captain Forrester, the inability of Lieutenant Komrower, and unavailable leadership by Captain Hooper due to him remaining to command his reserve from the perimeter, these remnants of No.3 Commando were lucky to have the likes of Martin Linge there to guide their brave souls into the fray ...

"*Move up! Move up!*" his accented voice shouted, now bloodied from a ricochet across his nose.

"*Sir!*"

"*Sir!*"

"*Yes, sir!*"

Brave British Commandos joined the leagues of Linge's fife by the debris-littered entrance. Men moved up through the thoroughfare, preparing for the combined assault from the opposite side of the entrance. They were willing to follow their new honorary commando into the jaws of death and proud to do so.

*It was time to end this battle!*

Linge cast a gleam about his motley army of followers.

They were standing his flank, ready his mark.

Within the multitude of surrounding commandos, he swapped a glance with one particular member of Churchill's men who he had met on numerous occasions: Corporal Knocker White. He had surprisingly caught up to the battle and rejoined their ranks at the hotel from a westerly encirclement. His timing could not have been better, for shit was about to get real.

Out of place, de la Torre covered White's flank with a rifle rather than a radio. He was doing his best and doing a fine damn job.

"*Sir!*" a soldier regarded upon seeing the popular unit corporal.

"*Corporal, sir!*"

"Lads," White regarded, making eye contact with Linge. "Kaptein Linge!" he announced over the top of the noise and fuss, calling his attention. "On your command, sir."

"Yes, sir. *On my mark, men!*" Linge shouted after a few volleys of extended covering bursts subsided, and he and a few other commandos shoved clear from concealment, ready to charge forth.

Grenades were plucked from webbing and a constructed coordination saw them thrown into the entrance way. They detonated, concussing or killing almost all of the stubborn defenders inside.

*The commandos wasted no time.*

They rushed in, guns blazing.

Ferocious extended bursts of exchanging gunfire ensued.

And suddenly ...

Amongst the warfare ...

*Martin Linge was killed.*

From right beside his stance, blood spatter from the impacts across his friend's body sprayed across Knocker White's face and eye, causing him to blink profusely and misjudge his footing. *It was Linge's blood.*

The deafening onslaught of exchanging gunfire dilated as a whining high-frequency pitch overcame all audio. Things seemed to move slowly, depicting all aspects of violence and bloodshed in the gunfight.

Through crimson-smudged vision, White further floundered his footing for an instance, collapsing to a knee in the chaos. He watched from a sideline as a couple of commando troopers leapt through the action dust, overtaking him, as well becoming hit in the initial breach and falling victim to the cause, collapsing into the doorway. Linge had unfortunately been one of them.

Although the Norwegian captain was quickly dragged out of the battlefield by surrounding men as the deafening audio of the gunfight continued within, it was clear that their leader was dead.

*Could they even continue without a leader ...?*

Sound suddenly restored. The volume narrowed.

"*Hold the line!*" the bloody-faced White shouted, angered by the sight of his comrades shot and killed. He racked his shotgun and took charge—and point, moving into the doorframe and letting off round after round along with another couple of brave commandos. He shouted heroically overtop of the ear-splitting noise, through the gore, the onslaught of violence, and the recurring loss of life. An element of gained ground was *everything* to the cause.

The firefight exchange was gruesome and grisly.

More commandos charged the entry. Some were wounded, some even killed as they forcefully thrust their way through the enemy's durable defences, eventually maiming or killing all of those who withstood the assail in the hotel foyer in an absolute bloodbath.

de la Torre acted gallantly, pushing his way through incoming fire and giving some back with his Thompson. He shook his fire as he moved in on White's tail, teeth clenched and grimacing in the face of fear.

After expelling all his shots from his primary pump-action, Knocker White did not retreat or recoil. Standing tall in the countenance of hazard as the remaining Germans persisted to shoot from around cover, peeking out from their many concealed nooks, he drew his sidearm and continued to fire down range, pressing forward at all costs.

One by one, the remaining defenders were bested by the commandos in a series of crackling firearms and tactful manoeuvres.

White plugged one of the final German soldiers with a grouping of shots to his chest and, suddenly, the immediate interior of the Ulvesund Hotel became eerily quiet, absent the clamour of popping gunfire.

"*Move! Move!*" White bellowed, seizing command. He took a moment to wipe the blood from his eye. "Secure the foyer!"

Commandos fast advanced, swarming around him with ambitious strides, piling into the darkened interior and assuming stances around the upturned rubble within. They checked tucked corners and inched the edges of connecting halls and stairwells, engaging the depleting enemy chokepoints and securing the sector.

It was now time to take what was left of the building.

*The enemy foothold had fallen!*

The plunge had brought them to their knees.

*It was time to deliver the final blow ...*

Victory was *finally* within reach.

With an abrupt *crunch!* and shower of splinters, Durnford-Slater drove his combat boot into the wood door of the suspicious residence, kicking it in with force. He noted a second prior to the breach that the copper door handle was sticky with fresh blood smears.

Now wide open, he slowly entered from behind his raised and cocked handgun, scanning the shady, silent interior. There was something rival haunting this dwelling. Something relevant. He demanded answers.

On his six, Mills followed him in, pistols out and tracking the first room on the left, which appeared to be some sort of vacant guest bedroom stacked with superfluous possessions, inclusive of dismounted picture frames, books, and albums—quite possibly a hint that whoever currently resided within these walls was not the original owner. An eviction as such was not uncommon by the German occupiers of the lands.

In their cautious entry progression, Mills split from Durnford-Slater's lead and moved down a thin connecting hall, scanning above the sights of his pistols and towards what appeared to be a well-lit windowed kitchenette—

"Mills!"

The glorified gunslinger bent his elbows and spun, quickly trotting back and into the first space on the right where Durnford-Slater had wandered. It was a wide-open, homely living space, decked with a soft carpeted floor and fine timber furniture. The room had a stone-set fireplace and soft cushions, and was clearly the residence of one of the more well-off citizens of South Vågsøy. It suddenly all made sense as to why the Germans would want to commandeer the residence for their own residing billet during the island's occupation, and also incriminated whoever had occupied it by force as being high-up in the hierarchy of Generalleutnant Woytasch's 181st Infantry Division.

Standing in the centre of the carpet over a bloodstained two-seater couch was Durnford-Slater, actively training his weapon's sights at a hostile figure who must have been lounging upon it.

Entering the room, Mills noticed the dark crimson smears staining the carpet and handprints across the back of the furniture. Somebody who was heavily wounded had recently limped their way into this house, knocking shit over and lacquering everything with their leaking burgundy fluids.

Mills rounded the lounge and took view of what it was Durnford-Slater had found: a fatally wounded German officer beholding the rank of captain. This man was clearly one of the higher-ranking enemy combatants present in South Vågsøy, if not *the most* highest-ranking in Woytasch's absence.

The Hauptmann was barely clinging to life.

His grey uniform was covered in blood from an obvious gut-wound, which he clenched his sticky paws over. His gaunt face was clammy, drained of colour.

Upon noticing the English soldiers enclose upon him, the barely conscious German officer let drop the sole item in his possession with a metallic *thu-thump* against the carpet. It was his sidearm, a small Walther PPK. Whether it was due to him losing grip in his dying state or an act of surrender was anybody's guess.

"Don't you move," Durnford-Slater commanded sternly.

"You move, you die," Mills affirmed as he strafed the lounge, securing their peripherals from within the room; one gun on the German, the other leading his way. Satisfied with his partial check of the connecting room, which appeared to be access to the same brightly lit kitchenette that he had sighted earlier, he returned to the living room to oversee his colonel's interview of the captured officer. He held his wits about him and his guns by his hips like a skier about to off-piste.

Softly, from behind his gun, Durnford-Slater questioned the dying German. "Are you alone here?"

Neither one of them knew it in that moment, but this event was basically a parley. A congress. A meet between the two most high-ranking belligerents of the clashing warfighter armies.

The German was barely cognizant and bleeding out fast.

In late response, the Hauptmann softly blinked a nod.

After a cautionary moment, Durnford-Slater interrogated the officer some more. He gestured, referring to the insignia on his uniform collars. "You're a *captain* ...? What is your position here in South Vågsøy ...? Who is your CO ...?"

"Chap's sprung a proper leak, Colonel ..." Mills observed in the hiatus of any response from the prisoner. "Did we clip him, you reckon?"

In the absence of the Hauptmann's response to the questions, Durnford-Slater partly inspected his gut grievance from a distance. He bled profusely, though it seemed unlike a gunshot—it was more of a maim or a stab-wound laceration. If this soldier had been shot by one of the commandos, he would have easily died in the street, unable to crawl away to die in a hole such as this. Something about this circumstance was peculiar, and his beheld silence only incriminated this wayward Hauptmann more of further enigmas.

"*Schröder*. Is that your name?" Durnford-Slater asked, tilting his head. He was able to read it from his uniform.

The answer to his question was evident by the way Schröder's eyes tweaked upon hearing his name be spoken. It appeared to wake him up an ounce, restoring a slight bit of reality to the dazed German.

Durnford-Slater flipped the safety on his pistol with a disengaging *click*, lowering the weapon completely so that Schröder felt more at ease. He would try diplomacy over threat with the next sequence of inquiries.

"What happened to you, Hauptmann Schröder?" he asked calmly, concerningly almost, eager to gain the man's trust enough for some light to shine. "Was it shrapnel? Crossfire?"

Schröder's expression of disinterest retained.

With barely the energy to breathe, he undeniably had no interest in assisting these enemies of the Führer with their questionnaire.

"My men have surrounded the hotel. It's only a matter of time before they seize complete control and with it, the entirety of South Vågsøy," Durnford-Slater probed. "Your men will die. You should order them to surrender."

Schröder huffed and wheezed at the question.

*Perhaps surrender was out of the question?* There seemed to exist an underlining irony that sparked an element of humour for the Hauptmann.

Durnford-Slater disregarded it as noncompliance all the same.

"How many of your men are left inside of the hotel?"

Schröder eyed him and tried to talk.

"*N ... n ... not ...*"

Durnford-Slater crouched on the carpet, coming closer so that he could hear the dying man's whispers. "Sorry?"

"Sir," Mills guarded, not liking the idea of his CO that close to an enemy combatant. In these tense circumstances, anything could happen—and happen quickly.

Durnford-Slater cast him an assured glint, and Mills kept his distance for the time being.

Just to be sure, Durnford-Slater reached down with his free hand and collected Schröder's discarded service weapon. It felt loaded and in condition zero.

Suddenly, they discerned the sound of furniture budging—shifting, bumping—on rugged-laid floorboards upstairs, within the same house. It was scarcely audible over the many reverberations of distant gunshots and explosions of the war down the street, but discernible, nonetheless.

It caught Mills' acute attention. After instinctually cranking his neck up and towards the ceiling, his eyes followed the direction of the movement, squinting into the darkened residence where there was a narrow internal staircase leading up to the second floor.

"Ask him again if we're alone in here?" Mills requested calmly before reacting with trepidation. Growing incisively more agitated, he intentionally bumped the occupied lounge sofa with his hip, shaking the Hauptmann and riling him up. "Oi, cockhead, are we alone in the house?"

"Sergeant ..." Durnford-Slater replied respectfully, feeling as though he was almost getting somewhere with Schröder about the hotel before Mills' aggravation stoked the settling embers.

Finally, Durnford-Slater could understand the fading Nazi's words in retort to his previous question about the hotel occupation.

"*Not ... my ... men ...*"

"The *Huntsmen,* yes?" Durnford-Slater stated. "The *Alpine Huntsmen,* that's who you've got left in the hotel?"

"*N ... n ... nein,*" Schröder pronounced, adding with a bloodstained grimace. "*In ... the h ...*"

"In the hotel?"

"*In ... the house!*"

*Both Durnford-Slater and Mills' faces dropped flat.*

As if right on cue, there was an unexpected creak on the wooden staircase that neighboured the living room. The attentions of both Mills and Durnford-Slater snapped at the sound in time to witness a balaclava-clad killer and his equally as ghost-faced comrade tiptoeing down the final steps of the Hauptmann's billet. Their sidearms were drawn, perhaps attempting to gain a sneaky line of sight on them in the lounge room in the interest of gaining guaranteed kill-shots.

"*Fuck!*" Mills reacted instantly to the presence of the creeping masked Huntsmen standing in the connecting space. Having just descended the stairs, they had glimpsed into the living room and pointed their weapons with a killer's intent a split-second before the two Commandos became spooked.

An orchestra of deafening gunfire suddenly filled the confines of the home.

Arms up and immediately blasting, Mills blitzed low with both his guns as fast as he could in their direction, firing wildly.

Durnford-Slater reacted too, and also with a gun in each hand—both his M1911A1 and the Hauptmann's tiny PPK—sidestepping in the opposite direction from Mills' strafing reaction.

Their reaction was followed immediately by several shots fired by the Huntsmen duo by the staircase, missing the two commandos as they parted like the Red Sea. The log wall in the backdrop erupted in pockmarks. Ceramic ornaments fractured and splinters shattered from the detonating furniture within the once-comfortable living room.

Bullets chasing their parting ways, the two commandos plunged in their respective evasive manoeuvres from the gunmen, narrowly escaping death.

Mills collapsed behind the concealment of another chunky timber chair in the living room, trailed by a line of destructive gunfire. His retaliatory fire peppered the enemy locale with hot .45 ACP lead, shaking their resolve. The papered wall behind the Huntsmen became shredded and pocked. The timber handrail guarding the staircase exploded from countless bullet impacts, bursting to flinging kindling and a smoke vapour that filled the space along with floating debris.

The closest gunman on the stairs rushed in lowly advance, attempting to duck incoming fire whilst he covered himself. He promptly received several hits to the chest by both Mills and Durnford-Slater's combined pistol fire, blowing him over. His white snow camouflaged fatigues convulsed with sprays of red, and he spun to a collapse during the hailstorm of gunfire, collecting several more hits posthumously on his way down.

Durnford-Slater was closest to the hallway and with more of an angle on the remaining Huntsman, who managed to evade their combined counterstrike. The ski-masked kraut retreated up the stairs, shooting blindly in his wake as he hiked multiple steps at a time.

Durnford-Slater's evasive strafe ended with a slide on his shoulder.

He shot all six rounds out of the small calibre Walther, effortlessly letting it fall out of his left hand and then cupping his right, resulting in a tighter grouping from his heavier Colt at the man's fleeing feet as they disappeared up the stairs.

On the last shot of the clip, a perceivable *thwack!* resounded, followed by a cry of pain from the Huntsman after his left shinbone took a hit before it could tuck out of sight.

An upstairs collapse was audible when the man hit the floor above, likely now relatively incapacitated. He cried in brief agony, muffled through the wool of his balaclava.

Covered in fluff from the lounge cushion's insulation which now lingered in the air of the room, Mills climbed up to a knee with his two guns still trained on the stairway access whereas Durnford-Slater crawled to find better shelter, as well as find more bullets for his empty gun.

"I hit him once!" he informed in a stressful shout, quickly managing a fresh clip and rack of the slide. Ears ringing in the silence, he upped and knelt beside Mills' guarded posture.

The eyes of the two commandos suddenly fell upon Schröder, who was somehow still alive even after being the piggy-in-the-middle of a close-quarters gunfire exchange and not inadvertently shot through the back of the couch cushions.

Through the veil of white duck feathers following the perforation of several comfy pillows that lined the furniture, Durnford-Slater evidently still hungered for intelligence. "Try and catch this bastard alive!"

He didn't see it, but Mills cast him a sideways glance that expelled disapproval.

*Fuck that.*

If Mills gained a clear shot, *he'd bloody take it.*

"Oi, you up there!" rearranging his stance, Durnford-Slater bellowed through the smoke and floating debris. Both he and Mills watched an angle of the staircase. "Surrender now and throw your gun down the stairs! Walk down slowly with your hands up!"

Mills smirked and whiffed a remark. "Yeah, right."

"You never know ..." Durnford-Slater tilted his frown.

Interrupting them was the distinct sound of a weighty, solid object systematically thumping down the timber stairs of the flight after being dropped by the wounded remaining Huntsman.

The two men swapped a look.

A little surprised himself, Durnford-Slater shrugged. "See."

Mills frowned.

*That was a little too easy ...*

He did not even think that the German would even understand English, let alone give up. Such an elite and pretentious unit member complying with the wishes of an enemy combatant let alone surrendering was the last thing he actually expected to happen.

... and it was then they realized.

*It was none of those things.*

The stares of both Durnford-Slater and Mills locked onto the rolling egg-like object as it made its way down the stairs after being discarded by the enemy.

It was no gun ...

*It was a bomb.*

A *M39 Eihandgranate* fragmentation hand grenade to be exact.

"*Oh shit!—*"

"*Move!*"

Almost falling over each other, the two barely made it out of dodge before the timed explosive detonated indoors, caving in half the ceiling above with a collapse of dust, smoke, and fractured timber support beams.

Furniture in the lounge room was directly hit by the blast.

Wooden cabinets were thrown by the fragmentation blast, smashing against the wall and shattering into pieces. The lounge sofa that the wounded Hauptmann Schröder occupied toppled into the sea of upturned debris, turfing the unfortunate occupant callously onto the carpeted floor.

Mills and Durnford-Slater both narrowly survived the blast by throwing themselves into the attached kitchenette area. They slid rough against the back wall, protected by a whole other wall lining and a floor-to-ceiling solid timber cabinet, loaded with cutlery and ceramic plate wear. All of it broke and shattered out onto the tiled floor as the cupboard tilted forwards from the grenade's might, towering over them. Coincidently, the solid furniture acted as shelter from the caving-in wreckage of the floor above as the entire section collapsed—ironically dropping the now even worse for wear culprit spilling out before them in the kitchen in a cloud of scatter.

Through the thick dust, Mills was up first, firing with his handgun a couple of times into the murky surroundings. The shots were sporadic and random, more covering them from a possible unseen assault than at a specific target.

They fast realized that the remaining threat was now on their level, possibly with a few broken limbs to accompany the gunshot to his leg.

"Mills!" Durnford-Slater shouted holding back splutter as he breathed through the debris, becoming upstanding in the haze. The two of them trained their sights on the remaining dazed Huntsman as he clumsily climbed to a limp, blinking profusely through the fog. He appeared concussed from the fall.

He waved his empty hands out before him, holding them above his head at the sight of the weapons. "Nein, nein!"

Still catching a breath, Durnford-Slater cradled his gun at his hip as they encircled the soldier. They had won this ... but Sergeant Mills' blood was up from the fight that had nearly claimed their lives.

*Or perhaps he was just fed up with being shot at today?*

*Maybe he just liked killing Nazis?*

From behind his two raised handguns and a dusty pout, Mills responded with a degree of sinister tone: "*Ja, ja!*" and shot him with a bullet from each pistol, killing him dead.

The unarmed Huntsman crumpled to the wreckage-covered floor.

"*Sergeant!*" Durnford-Slater exclaimed in offence, pushing Mills' gun-arms down, albeit too late to save the defenceless soldier. Incensed, he waved a hand at the mess. "You shouldn't have done that!"

"Fuck him!" Mills cursed with a headshake before adding respectfully to his superior. "*Sir.*"

This guy really hated Nazis.

*But who could blame him.*

Embarked upon a fleeing exit of the hotel warzone, Friedrich Feind rode the slipstream of his right-hand Hauptscharführer as if he ushered an entourage of one through the chaotic halls and passageways.

The VIP Gebirgsjäger Hauptsturmführer followed his steadfast German muscle, Alpine Huntsman Jürgen, as the brute approached another corner of the noisy Ulvesund Hotel.

The kingdom ... *was crumbling.*

Although the fearless Feind was a firm believer in what he preached— that it was *suicide to surrender*—his absconding from the present situation was not solely a strategy of self-preservation. Rather, the antagonist had something much more diabolical in mind, and it required taking a step back in order to stride forward.

The gunshots were a lot louder as they had reached the staircase joining the first level to the ground floor. The fight was inside the building on this level now, and the Wehrmacht defenders were backing up and clogging the thin, dark hotel halls like constipation.

The two opted for an alternate route that circumvented passing by the foyer entrance and connecting halls. There was a door, just up ahead at a corner, that led into the maintenance corridor—a back way.

They pushed on. Jürgen led their flee from behind the hold on one of his two MP40 maschinenpistoles.

The displacing duo downed the dim, claustrophobic hallway, passing several shuffling soldiers in their retreats and reaching the closed-over maintenance door labelled *'vedlikehold',* before spotting unidentifiable movement at the far end. Their halting saw two additional Wehrmacht infantrymen fall back after receiving a volley of fire from the invading commando enemy as they pushed in their assault through the foyer.

One of the men collapsed, screaming from hot, scalding gunshots to the back of his legs, crippling him. The other ran on, panting and scared out of his wits, firing several more times behind his retreat. Coming in close in the shadowy hall, he noticed the Alpine Huntsmen officers, and quickly beckoned with them for help beneath his sweaty brow and tilting stahlhelm.

Feind scolded with a death stare, certain perplexion underlining his tone. The sentiment appalled him.

"Wa... < *'Why are you falling back?!'* > ...rück?!"

The soldier was already terrified.

"He... < *'Sir, the British are advancing. There are no defenders left in the foyer!'* > ...er!"

Feind lent out from behind Jürgen. "Bleiben Sie dran!"

The soldier shook his head. The request was not feasible.

"Zurü... < *'Push back! Engage! Until your last breath!'* > ...temzug!" Feind hissed with a venomous ferocity.

Again, the soldier either trembled or shook his head. His gestured response was lost in the overbearing emotions of warfare.

After another moment of noncompliance, Feind again utilized the Gebirgsjäger's understanding of Russian battlefront tactics.

"Kä... < *'Fight or die.'* > ...irb!" he stated simply.

He leaned out with his pistol and shot a round through the cheekbone of the wounded soldier on the floor, finishing his unsettled squirming. He was no longer of use, and therefore nothing more than expendable waste in the eyes of the nihilist Hauptsturmführer. His death provided more use in relaying a message than his suffering incapacitation.

The execution shook the remaining soldier. More so when Feind then raised the pistol towards him, insinuating that he was next unless he performed the crucial task of prolonging their defensive line.

The soldier indicated agreement, affirming compliance.

He raised his weapon in his quaking hands and returned to the hallway where the raiding British Commandos lingered somewhere around the edge.

The soldier would be nothing more than a momentary distraction.

A sacrifice.

He inched up to the corner—*immediately shot dead.*

Jürgen and Feind progressed in his wake, entering through the doorway off the narrow hall which took them down a quiet service corridor, leading towards the back of the building and towards their destination. They locked the door behind them.

Shortly thereafter, manoeuvring around the fallen Wehrmacht soldier in the hallway, the same area was overtaken by English soldiers in Brodie helmets who methodically secured the zone, passageway by passageway.


Due to the adrenaline in their system, the men of Commando were able to maintain their focus and determination, which assisted them in overcoming the impulse to take flight given their current circumstances.

Beneath the harsh light of day, nearing the northern rear entrance and garage doors, the men of One Troop appeared proper bushed and rosy cheeked. They had just traipsed the live battlefield, coming in beside the hotel building.

Visually, the tin hat-wearing troopers were burdened with the constant dutiful fraught and the broiling pressure of warfare, gritting their teeth and squinting ... then, in amongst, was the pencil-thin moustache and sterling stare of the beret-wearing Mad Jack Churchill, composed, gleeful, even.

"Rear entrance here, Sergeant!" a trooper remarked after an observation, and the group advanced on the chained up single door located just shy of the neighbouring metal roller doors: garages housing their conceivably fictive demolitions objective.

"You and the others see about gaining access," Cork replied, to which he was met by a quick comply by a competent man. Contrasting the majority of their Troop detachment, Cork and the other sapper from No.6 demo continued past the rear entrance, allowing for the commandos to breach. Cork and Dowling began to test the security of the chained metal roller doors for a way inside. Their objective was still to locate the 181st's *supposed* tank depot and destroy it—*if* it even existed. This late on, it was extremely doubtful—perhaps luckily for Commando.

Churchill, a maverick out of duty and in attendance at the Ulvesund assail harbouring his own personal agenda, and only chaperoning One Troop's advance to hopefully wander into a poetical upshot by happenstance, simply watched Cork's commandos toil. With his bow and arrow down guard, he shadowed these men at work.

A troop pulled a pair of hefty bolt-cutters from the sack webbing of his mate, quickly hustling up to the door and shimmying the clipper tips in against the metal chains that the Germans had used to tie the exit shut. This happened right as shouting could be heard within.

After the snip, the commando dropped the bolt-cutters as gunfire abruptly imploded from inside the building, hammering through the wooden door by the anxious and desperate defenders positioned within. The Germans pre-emptively shot through the closed entry at the raiding commando troopers, causing them to retract and recoil. Some of the men even fired back through the door, aimlessly spraying the ligneous surface with automatic gunfire in attempt at settling the enemy inside. This was going to be another chokepoint resulting in a momentary deadlock.

A lot of shouting and shooting ensued, and Churchill grew somewhat tiresome of the incurring stalemate, deciding to leave this lot and pursue after Cork and Dowling towards the neighbouring garage doors ...

Dowling gave one of the roller doors a wiggle from its bottom.

It was bolted shut and locked up tight, like every other door on this northern sector.

"Look," Cork said as he kept watch with his Thompson. Holding their heads just right, he discovered that their eyelines could peek through the gap around the exterior housing of the roller door's metal frame, gaining insight to what was stored in the darkness beyond, albeit at an acute angle. The dusty and echoic garage space seemed empty, and was only confirmed as such after Cork pulled a portable *Everready* flashlight from his webbing and funnelled his beam within the grimy, reticent interior.

Six-foot longbow in hand, Churchill caught up to this demolitions search party, wondering if they would have more luck at gaining entrance to this enemy stronghold. In their wake, he shared their intrigue through the gap after they picked up and moved along to the second garage door out of the three, total, located around ten paces apart.

Churchill's crystal-blue stare spied through the slit.

There was nothing but stale darkness lurking within. Nothing but the bounding reverberation of the gunfire from the enemy which echoed down the connecting halls, even sighting the occasional flickering of a muzzle flash against the inner walls—

*And then, suddenly, a flutter of soundless movement.*

Churchill's stare barely caught the interchange.

In a twitch, his head shifted view on the oblique angle in order to track the cavorting silhouettes and slithering illuminations in the inky blackness.

Whatever it was within the recess moved deep within the garage space, bounding in shuffles across the open area and into the next interconnected garage chamber via a connecting doorway. They made little sound, but Jack was sure he had seen *something* within, and the sight resonated ominously with him.

Unlatching his hunter's gaze from within the garage, Churchill glanced to his right, seeing that Cork and Dowling had progressed farther along the exterior, and were already checking out the next compartment with the flashlight. They had no idea that they were potentially being stalked by a force within the connecting garages.

"*Clear! Just a car in there,*" he heard Dowling's mumbly voice state through his underbite as Cork shuffled on, towards the third and final door ...

Churchill's mouth opened and inhaled.

*He was about to speak ...*

*About to warn them ...*

As he prepared to announce what he saw—what he *thought* he saw—he was strangely hung up with hesitation. What he couldn't understand was *why?*

It could not have been out of fear of facing Feind.

*Surely not.*

Could it have simply been the apprehension of the situation, overall?

Of the heaviness of the circumstance; the burden. After all these years carrying the weight from a fight in 1939 that had left physical and mental scars. Jack Churchill was anxious about finally having the opportunity to see Friedrich Feind in the flesh—and not a hallucination incited by his ghostly haunt and often misleading exposition of wisdom, Sloan MacLeòid.

In that moment of complexity, Churchill felt a hot flush.

A warmth overcame him, fogging up his brainwaves.

Pushing on and pulling out of a nosedive, wrestling the clammy urge to vomit, Churchill focused his sterling stare. Upon advancing in their wake, his intent view crept upwards, and he spied through the second garage gap, over what appeared to be a black shiny vehicle ...

... and at the two men within the dark confines wearing the recognizable attire not awfully dissimilar to the Wehrmacht infantrymen, however *the arm patch* symbol bore the edelweiss representing the Alpine Huntsmen.

The reluctance of reaction was not only that Jack had spotted Huntsmen within the garages and it had shocked him ... but because he had spotted *the Huntsman.*

*His Huntsman.*

*His enemy.*

*Feind.*

For the first time since Oslo, Churchill laid eyes on that boche bellend, and it flared his fury. All the long-since-buried, deep-seated anguish and bitterness he held for the man suddenly rose to the surface and boiled in the pan. His heartbeat became pronounced, and Jack had to force himself to remember to breathe.

This was not some vision trickery cast upon his mind by his forever present deceased mentor nor was it a delusion caused by battle fatigue ... this was fate.

Churchill warped back to reality and hollered, quickly moving to catch up with the demo duo on a mission. He called out again as he attempted to retain view of the enemy men through the second sliver. "Sergeant Cork!"

Reluctant to oblige Churchill in that instant, Cork gesturally responded. He and Dowling cast a concerned stare allowing for the eccentric Mad Major tagalong to their objective to elaborate, suddenly mindful that they may have missed something in the previous garage spaces.

Jack's head twitched.

His gaze searched vigorously.

*He had lost sight of the men inside—*

Cork questioned. "Sir?—" *SHHHCT!*

Out of nowhere, nearly running Cork through the middle as he strode warily past the second garage roller doorframe to reach Churchill for a proper conversation, a four-foot-long, double-edged silver blade slit through the vertical edging.

It looked like a sword ...

*One guess as to who the welder.*

The coarse scraping sound of the steel as it stabbed out towards him, missing Cork by an inch, caused him to halt in his progress and glare with absolute foreboding.

Unsuccessful, the blind blade retracted as quick as it had appeared.

*Schlish.*

Silence ...

Cork's wide eyes raised and viewed Churchill.

*What the fuck?*

There lingered an extended moment of absolute confusion between the men, and even Dowling braced his shoulder tight into the wall, keeping his guard for attack.

"Move!" Churchill fast shouted as he lunged out, grabbing at Cork and reefing him clear—*just in time*—as the penetrating sword blade returned with the same degree of prejudice, protruding a different hole and stabbing at them through one of many gaps.

*SHHHCT!*

The blade struck meat, gashing Cork in the ribs.

The grimacing trooper whimpered, and Churchill reacted instantly by driving his combat boot into the protracted blade in attempt to seize or snap it.

Tugging beneath his tension, the blade retracted, only to immediately return in another sliver of edging space, missing them both by an inch as they shuffled clear.

Outthinking the manoeuvre a second before it happened, Churchill's eyeline wormed upwards, spying a lateral gap that ran the length of the roller door.

Churchill dropped at the knees, pulling Cork down with him as the sword revisited with a vengeance through the horizontal line, swishing like a visionless executioner at their decapatable locale, missing their ducking heads by inches.

The soldiers watched the sword blade swish above their location and then retract before they tactically rolled clear. Upstanding from the ground, they reeled away from the wall and out of reach of whatever savage, faceless monster seemed to lurk within the shadows of the garage.

This torturous sequence crescendoed high enough for Churchill.

Knowing now without a doubt who lurked within, Mad Jack shouted: "*Feind!*"

His perplexed stare widened with certainty. There was a sudden rage empowering his body language as the two happened to lock eyes through the centimetre-thick gap.

Illuminated by the daylight through the thin chasm, the duelling-scarred mug of Friedrich Feind froze, staring back at the shadowy figure outside the garage door. Subconsciously, Feind had been searching for this particular man after learning that it was the No.3 Commando force at South Vågsøy for the raid—a force he happened to know Jack Churchill was a part of—and now he had, also, found his adversary.

"*Churchill!*" the German stated, housing a notable sinister smile and a laugh to follow. He appeared unafraid. "*Herr Churchill ... iz that really you out there?*"

Jack lunged forward and grabbed at the door, giving it a rattle.

Baring his teeth with wrath, he was anxious to get inside.

"*Haz you come for a rematch, English-man?*" Feind taunted. "*I hope you brought your zword thiz time, eh?!*"

Before Churchill could so much as reach for the claybeg on his left hip, abrupt gunfire exploded in sparks at his position, emitting from *behind* the metal roller door. The shooting caused him to wince and retreat alongside the solid concrete wall for safety.

Out in the open, Cork and Dowling did the same on the opposite sides with their weapons and guards up.

Feind's flunky, Hauptscharführer Jürgen, had broken the exchange of the nemeses with his machine gun on fully automatic, spraying at the shadowy figure beyond the glimmer of light from his angle inside.

There was a hissing conversation within the garage and the two men quickly shuffled about within the grimy and now smoky garage recess, completely disappearing by the time Churchill pivoted into view. He had now drawn an arrow on his longbow, ready to put the pointed the tip of his arrowhead through the slip with hostile intent, searching for a target through the tricky angle ... but they were already gone from sight.

With an exhale of despair, Churchill collapsed the draw.

"Sir?!" Cork called with his weapon raised, nursing his side. The gash was superficial, maybe an inch deep. He and Dowling had just witnessed the whole interaction. "You know that bloke in there?"

Holding his nocked arrow, Jack withdrew from the gap.

He leant against the wall to address both Cork and Dowling.

"Long story, lads."

"Who the bloody hell was that?!" Cork exclaimed, still exceptionally confused and ticked off after being poked in the fat.

"*That* was the enemy I expected to find," Churchill unerringly informed and with an austere scowl.

*Their war had just begun.*

Behind them several paces, Johnnie Dowling stepped afoot and peered through the final third garage gap, finally gaining some intelligence of what may have lingered within ...

... what he saw made his eyes widen and his mouth even wider.

his lips murmured the words:

"*Shag me sideways.*"

Back at Hauptmann Schröder's billeted residence in South Vågsøy, the outlying battle currently underway at the Ulvesund seemed to be simmering down. Hopefully, for victorious reasons.

An ancillary objective of sorts, Durnford-Slater and Mills endured their indoor turmoil, left grime-covered and spluttering lung loads of dust from the partial collapse of the top floor due to a grenade blast. A shred of natural light now shone within the vapour, illuminating the indoor environment with a searchlight-like glow.

In closing their tangent, these two Commandos, who had narrowly survived a surprise ambush within the premises, noted that the intensity of the raid on the thoroughfare seemed to be gradually tapering off in volume.

This meant that either Commando had failed to assail the Ulvesund or that they had succeeded, and what remained of the conflict was now encapsulated within the building structure ...

*It was always going to be the latter.*

"Sir, this Gerry is giving us nothing we don't already know!" Mills stated, antsy about their positioning away from the fight. "We should let this bastard die in peace."

Ignoring Mills' discomposure, Durnford-Slater squatted low before the bleeding Schröder as he lay dying, partially buried on the debris-littered floor. "Come on, Captain ... How many men are left? What are my boys up against?"

Schröder shook his head, retracting his trust.

Although he had been dishonoured and betrayed by one of his own, he wanted not to help these *Englisch*, and he wore his spitefulness on his shoulder along with his other insignia.

Growing impatient, Durnford-Slater suddenly shouted at his face.

"*How many?!*"

Flinching at the sudden aggression from the—until just now—calm and collected Commando colonel, Schröder pinched his lids tightly closed. The involuntary reaction caused him to bear his bloodstained teeth with a clench, writhing with pain from his excruciating gut wound.

Mustering a whisper, he pronounced with what could very well have been one of his final breaths of air. "*Y ... you will nev ... never get in ... too well fortified ...*"

He would be lying to himself if Durnford-Slater said that Schröder's obstinate scepticism of No.3 Commando's ability didn't piss him off, especially considering that this quadrant of South Vågsøy was the final hour of the raid. They had practically already won.

"Oh, really, chap?" Mills taunted, stepping on loose rubble to appear beside his diplomatic colonel as he grew tired of this interview, fully accepting whatever the browbeat with itchy trigger fingers had to offer.

Durnford-Slater became upstanding beside Mills, looking down upon the German captive as he wallowed in his slow demise upon the debris-littered floor.

Mills hissed in continuance, "Because, if you aren't deaf, you'd hear that we have a *mortar!* Eh, Captain *Cockhead?* Fucking *artillery!*"

"Oi, that's enough," regaining his morals, Durnford-Slater ultimately severed the lingering animosity, trying his best to keep it civil. After all, this man was technically a prisoner of war and was to be respected as such.

Regardless, the hotheaded Mills continued, "It's going to bring the whole bloody roof in on your *dumb kopf!*"

"*Sergeant Mills!*" Durnford-Slater spouted disciplinarily, wanting not for his excited man to rouse the incapacitated enemy any further than what they had already. It was time for them to do the gentlemanly thing and assist this fallen combatant to the fullest extent. He needed a medic.

Mills added as he finally adhered to Durnford-Slater's gesture to renounce, strutting across uneven wreckage. "We have a bloody *mortar!*"

Schröder hissed like a deflating balloon. "*We ... we ...*"

With a brooding stare, Durnford-Slater watched Mills move away from the situation before returning his view onto Schröder, listening intently to what the dying man had to utter.

His words were loud enough for them both to hear ...

... and they *shivered.*

"*... we have a tank.*"

Their expressions fell flat.

*The tank threat may be real.*

# 15
## *Archenemy*

*1944, September*
*Sachsenhausen Concentration Camp*
*Oranienburg, Germany*

Beneath the overcast Oranienburg skies, reluctant storyteller Churchill told his fable to his dutiful journalist friend who recorded every detail with the scratching of his pencil on page. "... and, so, this is it. We're approaching the end of another episode in the saga, Felix. One you should be familiar with, considering you were there ..."

Hardy tipped his head, "One I'd be a little better versed in if you hadn't benched me with Captain Young at the warehouses," he replied with a residing resentment to the fact. He stopped his scratching sketch mid-stroke on his bunched notepad—that was becoming a manuscript inscribing the life saga of Jack Churchill—and instead decided to run a tangent. "Humour me—refresh my memory, huh? It's been a long couple of years."

"Fair enough."

"This guy, *Feind* ..."

While they occupied a piece of fence in the compound, Churchill's eyes defocused hearing the name. He was still leaning on the wire frame hammock, seemingly testing the tolerance of the surrounding guard sentries, whilst Hardy had dropped to a comfortable squat in the mud, glancing up from the grime with his pale features due to incarceration.

"... he's the same prick from Oslo, right? You had the pleasure of meeting him before the war?"

"The *displeasure*. Correct."

"Did you know he was on Vågsøy Island all along?"

Jack shook his head firmly. "No. I knew he was a head honcho of the Alpine Huntsmen, who ended up being the bellends holidaying on the island, and throwing a spanner in the works of the raid. I discovered that fact by accident when I tracked down his details to send him the letter earlier that year."

Hardy bobbed along, familiar with that course in Churchill's previous volume. "I bet you regret extending that olive branch?"

Recalling that pang of conscience, Churchill dipped his head. "At the time, after meeting Ros, I was trying on a fresh demeanour. A less venomous view on war."

"How'd that work out?"

"It didn't suit me."

Hardy acknowledged that fact as Churchill continued.

"Their presence on Vågsøy was too much of a coincidence to not bear such fruit for the constant fortuity happenchance of my haphazard life."

Immediately inscribed that literary gold, Hardy scratched away.

"Nonetheless, although they're a pair of good-looking broads, *Lady Luck* and *Dame Fortune* are not without a sense of humour."

Hardy nodded off-beat, glancing up. "You know, it's amazing ..."

"What is?"

"This. Your life, Jack."

Churchill adjusted his comfort. "You say that like you're scribing my obituary, not my biography."

Hardy articulated, wrapping his wrist in the air with his trusty pencil stub. "No, I just mean, your tale ... it comes full circle in regard to *you and Feind* and so forth."

Jack cracked his neck, unentertained by that portion of his life: a never-ending rivalry.

"Yes, quite a regular *Claudius* and *Hamlet*."

"I would have gone more with *Tom* and *Jerry*."

Churchill gawked at Hardy and his lack of literary intellect, especially regarding the works of *William Shakespeare* and thus preferring children's animated shorts for reference. He took a jab. "You would."

It became evident that Hardy may have been playing, given his grin.

He could barely hide the smirk after riling Mad Jack up and wearing his retort.

Churchill beamed playfully as he looked away. "Dickhead."

Upstanding and with a groan from the ache in his troublesome leg, Hardy realigned his position on the papers, flicking through the small bind of crumpled dogears. "Would you say that the world is not big enough for the two of you?"

Churchill chortled singly out of irony.

"The *war* is not big enough for the two of us."

1941, December 27
The Ulvesund Hotel
South Vågsøy, Norway

After the fifth and final shell had been deposited onto the roof of the Ulvesund Hotel by Captain Bradley's relentless mortar team, Sergeant Ramsey gave the order to cease fire.

From their position on the easterly perimeter of the district, overlooking a portion of the hotel assault, they viewed the damage they had dealt to the building structure. A thick pillar of smoke stacked out of the cracked, drooping roof. The top floor had all but caved-in, causing the load-bearing stilts of the lower levels to strain, pending an entire internal collapse of the structure.

Ramsey upped from his post by the established three-inch mortar and stood beside his CO, observing their good work. The two of them watched on as Hooper's reserve troops swarmed the thoroughfare and stacked up around the hotel grounds, bolstering the Commando numbers already present surrounding the stronghold. These numerous Troops of countless commandos were each a finger of grip choking around the throat of the Ulvesund Hotel, and the firm stranglehold was keeling her to her knees.

The vicinity was now completely within the domination of Commando, it was just a matter of time.

Ash fell from the sky like snowflakes.

Floating embers lit the haze like fireflies.

Flames crackled from the fourth-floor inferno that was now trickling off the westerly side of the building, dropping denominations of hot debris as portions of the outer edifice crumpled in stacks.

After enduring an equally gruelling exchange of gunfire in the foyer, Knocker White, Eric de la Torre, and the assorted commandos within the Ulvesund pushed into the few connecting rooms of the hotel, in the process of clearing all ground-level rooms and partitions.

The stairwells, however, were a whole other animal ...

The remaining 181st defenders had fallen back, rearing up the narrow staircases and locking them down too tight for Commando to break through ... *and as it turned out, they didn't have to.*

In one of the tight halls guarded by Brits, White stepped over a blood-spattered body, approaching one of the last hotel rooms on the ground floor. There was a lot of noise and a lot of shouting within the echoic, chaotic halls, inclusive of the odd gunshot. In the background of his incursion, other commandos secured some of the neighbouring rooms along the restricted hallway, flooding the connecting corridors with their presence. On this level, they had either killed or captured any remaining enemy men on this floor, taking a lot of prisoners at gunpoint.

"Knock, knock!" White yelled with his shotgun at the ready, driving his combat boot into the flat beside the doorknob and kicking the locked door open with a splinter-speckled, strident slam. His gun led the charge inside.

Collaborating with another armed commando in a woollen beanie and a submachine gun, they breached the small guest room. This resulting in them shooting dead a hiding hostile clutching a Karabiner in a hailstorm of crackling gunfire; a lone casualty on the enemy's side.

Lurking within, the remaining Hun collected a shotgun blast to the chest after a coinciding stitch of fire drew a line across his vicinity, and he crumpled gloriously onto an upturned mattress in the wreckage-littered space, bouncing on the springs in a spill of red on linen. However, he wasn't alone in the room ...

With nowhere else to retreat, the remaining German soldiers in the small connecting room had become cornered in awkwardly cramped positions, and—unlike their now deceased friend—were seemingly more aware of their defeat than ever, and they yielded.

Profusely shouting surrender, the three soldiers tossed their heavy bolt-action weapons onto the carpet with metallic clunks, raising their hands and shouting submission for the Commandos.

Within seconds, they allowed the British to forcefully herd them into a prisoner conga line in the hall that escorted the capitulated troops out into the thoroughfare under armed arrest. There had to be around a dozen in total.

"Room service, lads!" Knocker White shouted as they processed the last of the surrendered 181st Infantry Division soldiers from this level. "Here to turn your pillows and fold your sheets! Go on, get!" he cussed bashfully, roughing one of the Germans across the shoulders to hurry them out of the hotel.

de la Torre came running past the POWs, addressing White with haste. "Corporal! Our guys can't get past the stairwells heading up! Captain Bradley's mortar team have brought down the top level! The whole building is unstable!"

Knocker White immediately fathomed the stakes.

He placed a firm hand on the trooper's shoulder. "No unnecessary risks! Get everybody to fall back to safety! I reckon we've won this stretch.

If the Gerrys upstairs want to surrender, they can do so ... if not, they can be buried alive for all I care."

"Yes, sir."

Suddenly, a structural groan reverberated. A tremor through the walls was felt, and dust and insulation sprung leaks from the ceilings above their brodie helmets and wool beanies. Everybody within the hotel heard and felt that shift in stability.

"Time to go?!" de la Torre asked almost humorously.

"*Yep! Go now!*" White bellowed, returning his view to the trooper. He directed him with his grasp as more constant grains of dust began to leak from the ceiling like the sand drizzling from an hourglass—their time was running out.

"*Yes, sir! Evac!*" de la Torre double-timed his movements, shouting at a few other Commandos in front of them. "*Come on! Evac!*"

In a connecting, neighbouring passageway, White did the same, finding it appropriate to rally the men in the same way his superiors did—especially considering he was now acting commander.

*It was checkout time.*

"*Let's go, No.3!*"

"... shag me sideways ..." Johnnie Dowling had just breathed to himself.

The No.6 demo trooper's eyes were wide as phonograph records upon recognizing the flattened, sky-grey, steel-bolted, reinforced edges of an *armoured tank* lurking within the shady confines of the third garage partition, located almost 100 feet down from the rear exit of the Ulvesund Hotel and where a detachment of Commando were holding.

Befalling a stunting of shock, the commando sapper took a step back from the gap, tipping his head to the left to eye both Major Churchill and Sergeant Cork. The two were still near the middle garage roller door, rattled after their prior engagement from the mysterious sword-wielding adversary lurking within.

Cork questioned Churchill as they sought refuge. "How do you know a Nazi, Major? How the bloody hell did he know your name?"

Churchill shrugged disarmingly.

There wasn't really an answer he desired—or had the time—to give, so he deflected like always with humour. "Oh, *him?* We're old friends, lad. We go way back."

*Cork was more confused.*

"*Oi! Bring the charges up! Quick!*" Dowling called out to them, locking them back in on the task. There was an astonishment present in his tone of voice from discovering something residing within the depths of that last garage door. Appropriately so, the evidence of urgency was what ripped both Churchill and Cork from their present predicament while Dowling added: "*I found the tank! It's in 'ere! Quick!*"

Both Churchill and Cork ogled, jogging towards him.

Before they could say a word in question to that information, a beefy mechanical noise thundered from within the confines of the garage, drawing Dowling's attention back towards the steel lining of the closed roller door inches before his face. He spied through the opening, sighting motion; a man in a leather coat mounting the iron vehicle, upping the exterior and pulling what appeared to be a top hatch shut.

Suddenly, the *Krupp* four-cylinder air-cooled gasoline engine to the *Panzer I Ausf. A* light tank stated its presence and authority, throttling to life. The engine choke quaked the cold earth beneath all their boots outside the building, even rattling the metal garage door.

Rearing up, Dowling glanced upwards at the roller door as the whole thing jangled from the powerful bass of the engine's rev in the confines, and he suddenly felt ridiculously small and hilariously outgunned ...

Thirty feet down the stretch of the building outside, Churchill and Cork both heard the ignition of the mechanized armour roar alive, and they grew immediately concerned and distressed.

"Johnnie ... *run!*" Cork exclaimed in a panic as his pace faded.

"*Trooper! Move!*" Churchill called as hesitation blocked both their mental and physical progress.

Dowling's dopey eyes grew wide as to why ...

... *then he woke the fuck up,* and quickly dove clear!

After his nimble little retreat from the chained garage, the entire metal roller door became suddenly shredded, bursting outwards due to a thunderous and continuous discharge by the Panzer tank's main armament of twin 7.92mm MG13 machine guns, firing concurrently. The mounted turret swept back and forth.

Outside, the men shielded their faces, blocking their ears.

The mini cannons were earsplittingly loud.

The hydraulics of the rotating turret buzzed, and the guns swayed left and right, laterally perforating the sheet metal door as though it were mere tinfoil, stitching golf ball-sized holes through the alloy.

The sky-grey, snow-camouflaged vehicle that was hidden within the garage immediately skipped forwards in acceleration, shoving itself through the torn and frayed metal like an animal giving birth.

The steel beast scraped through the roller door like it was an aluminium curtain. In a pitch not dissimilar to nails on a chalkboard, the

Panzer scratched vociferously out onto the thoroughfare, gaining all sorts of attention by the invading Commandos.

Trooper Dowling dove clear in the nick of time.

He landed chest first in the snow, fumbling his gear in his rouse as the squeaky cave-bed serpent punched out through the garage door and slithered into daylight exposure.

The clanking steel tank tracks that encircled six wheels on either side of the armoured automobile cranked through the lower half of the metal roller door remnants, dissolving Dowling's dropped weapon to a crumpled hunk of iron after it passed over it.

Churchill and Cork skidded on the snow-thawed strip as the Panzer exploded loudly out onto the street, slewing in its own accelerative speed. Whoever was driving the vehicle was clearly amateuristic. The weighty Panzer seemed to stall upon braking, hopping forth in shallow, jerking gallops, and the craft was slow on the turn as whoever was steering discovered the heavy track alignment levers.

The Commandos utilized the occupants' confusion and momentary acclimatization of the navigation controls to their advantage, attempting to gain some ground.

"*Get out of here, Cork!*" Churchill shouted over the roaring drone of the tank as it idled in the street before them, grinding gears and skating on the ice during gas-applied scuds. In the distance beyond the Panzer's path, they could see Dowling climbing to his feet in a scurry, with no option left but to now run for his life. He did so successfully.

While Churchill barked orders in the face of this new threat, Cork turned to him and watched as the Mad Major stashed away into his shoulder quiver his already drawn bodkin-tipped arrow, extracting a different projectile: one with red fletching and an enlarged tip.

As the occupants within the mobile armour again attempted to turn the tracks, the Panzer consistently kangaroo-hopped in the street, slowly arcing itself around like hands on a clock. Whilst they worked the navigations, the separated top turret suddenly buzzed to life, as whoever was in the gunner's seat became more acquainted with their mechanics.

Jack Churchill showed no fear as he laid eyes on this metal menace.

He took a step past Cork and nocked his special impact-detonated explosive arrow, fast to draw and loose the HE missile at the tank before it got too situated.

He hadn't been offered many circumstances thus far during Operation Archery in which to best utilize the customized explosive projectiles that commando quartermaster Slinger Martin had issued him with prior to the mission.

*There was certainly no time like the present.*

The heavier arrow flung at the tank—a direct hit.

The small-yield explosive arrow impact-detonated against the side panelling above the right-side tracks, blowing with a vivid flash and loud bang, however it failed to penetrate or even damage the inch-thick armour plating of the beast. The tank barely quivered on its robust quarter-elliptical leaf spring suspension from the impact. At best, the damage tally consisted of the grey paintwork being slightly scorched on one side.

Churchill's nostrils flared. "Bollocks."

In the aftermath of his valiant attempt, the Panzer began to stabilize further. The hydraulics in the turret continued to hum with activity, slowly searching in a two-dimensioned panoramic fashion. Whoever was inside—namely Feind and a Huntsman cohort—had been left with nothing but ringing ears and maybe a headache after that futile Jack attack.

"*Jack!*" Cork stated afterwards. Calling him by his name and not rank resituated their prior associations and predispositions, and made Churchill pay more attention during the chaos. "*It's your turn to get out of here!*"

Longbow down by his side, Churchill twisted to face him.

Cork had retrieved from his demolitions bag three bound bricks of Composition-C plastique explosive and, in a hurry, packed it full of detonators after discarding the empty carry bag. The thing looked like a porcupine the way he had hurriedly rammed the sticks into the block. He was already trotting towards the tank in an urgent commencement of offensive manoeuvring, setting the charge whilst trying to avoid the sights of the buzzing turret as it panned their way ...

This was likely a one-way voyage and Cork seemed to know it.

That thing had no fuse and a gigantic blast radius.

Churchill called after him. "*Sergeant!*"

Jack suddenly paused—*his gaze up and wide.*

The tank's turning may have been sluggish ... but the rotating turret was quite smooth. It bowed clockwise, ahead of its body, searching for a target.

Sweat glistened below the silk brim of Churchill's taut green beret as he realized his standing position before the danger, practically staring down the barrels of the twin MG13 high-calibre machine guns.

Late to realize this, he fast decided to flee in a frantic dash away from the turret's panning course, outrunning the incoming barrels as it pivoted, about to breathe utter decimation ...

In the gunner's position within the tight, shadowy confines of the Panzer, Friedrich Feind irately roared. "*D___ < 'Turn around!' > ___!*"

The desperation of his vendetta towards this particular Englishman now beginning to rear its head, shining through the cracks of his regulation attitude.

Within the bleak, musty interior of the Panzer tank, Jürgen utilized his preceding experience within the *Panzerkommision* prior to his recruitment into the Gebirgsjäger. He had served in the *4th Panzer Division* during the initial invasion of *Poland*, earning him a merit for his duties during *the Battle of Mokra.*

Control was achievable as the Panzer I was designed to operate with only two crewmen: a gunner and a driver. He was at the helm, spying through a rectangular viewport, whilst Feind fumbled his way behind the triggers of the turret, spying through the limited circular portals, incessantly pulling at levers in an overzealous attempt at controlling the hydraulics—let alone the guns.

However, Jürgen's frown of concern was not for his dismay at their operational ability rather than their purpose here. It seemed as though Feind was only interested in chasing one target, yet there were men running everywhere in the streets.

He questioned loudly over the blaring engines, tipping his face over his shoulder and away from the forward viewport momentarily. "W__ < '*What about inflicting casualties?*' > ___fern?!"

Feind eyed him with a wicked rage.

"I__ < '*I want him* _dead! Understand?!*' > ___ch?!"

Despondent, Jürgen rotated around at the controls.

He emitted a loud sigh; one he needed not hide for it was inaudible over the deafening drone of the armoured vehicle's blaring engine.

*Regardless, he obeyed his CO.*

The vehicle gradually panned, lethargically tracking the lone British Commando in the middle of an otherwise active warzone.

Beneath his duelling-scarred brows, Feind's all-consuming brown ogle focused through the viewport; his stare illuminated by the glow of natural light through the targeting port in the turret as their tank pivoted, better facilitating his panoramic pan.

He saw a target: a lone evading Brit in a green beret.

Jack Churchill: *his target.*

Feind's serpentine leer brightened, and he hissed loudly with a devilish tendency, frothing at the mouth like a psychopath.

"*Da bist du ja, English-man!*"

*BOMBOMBOMBOMBOMBOMBOMBOMBOM!*

The turret guns lit up in a brutal broadside.

Scampering in evasion, Churchill was barely in the crosshairs when the guns engaged. Impetuously, the deafening twin MGs spewed red-hot glistening phosphorous tracers at a phenomenal rate of fire, chasing Mad Jack's path and obliterating everything in his aftermath as he darted.

The machine guns drew a lateral line across the back wall of the Ulvesund Hotel as, longbow in hand, Jack Churchill rushed past the metal garage doors. He disappeared within the open third one, sliding into a nook where the tank could no longer obtain a visual. The machine guns focused on where it had last seen him, catching up within a second and absolutely annihilating the physical environment in the hope of catching the target with a stray, perforating round (or a dozen). Glowing golden tracer rounds bounced in jagged rebounds as they skipped off the concrete walls within the garage, melting everything.

In an array of tiny sparks and boisterous retaliatory fire, a bunch of distant commandos engaged the Panzer with an assortment of small arms fire. They aimed for the view ports.

The sound of pelting bullets on the many steel surfaces caused the light tank to have to alternate its fire. The hum of the hydraulics panned the cannon turrets, where it sighted numerous afar commando troopers as they peeked multiple instances of concealment in the thoroughfare.

The tank paused for a second before roaring to life with a dragon's breath from its twin machine guns.

*BOMBOMBOMBOMBOMBOM!*

The machine guns roared in the echoic streets with six-foot muzzle flashes, discharging sizzling lightning barbs down range at the few *Davids* who boldly engaged the *Goliath.*

Hiding down alongside the light tank, A.J. Cork found himself inadvertently behind cover from Allied shooting as he skirted to the slow-moving tank body. He clenched his teeth, eardrums bursting, as the turret spun above his very positioning, sounding off at full auto. Huge 7.92mm bullet casings expelled from the chute of the Panzer, piling loudly on the street by his position.

He tried not to let the volume of the noise distract him from completing the task at hand. As the tank tracks cranked to life and began to chase the multiple commandos down the southern strip of the South Vågsøy, Cork went all-in with whatever he had set up with the plastique explosive. He had to pull the cord now, or risk this being a vital task left incomplete forever—either one resulted in an equal chance of death.

He started to panic, trundling alongside the tank's monstrous clattering tracks as his hands operated at the side. Once successfully planting the charge to the armour, he next applied the timer located on the device; an analogous knob, like an alarm clock.

*His fingers delicately pinched the knob, turning it ...*

He attempted to set it to something realistic for his exodus, but not too long to allow for the miscreant's violent expedition against a sea of soft target Commando when suddenly ... the humour-loving fate *stepped* in.

*The tank track ran over a step in his misplaced footing.*

In the shuffle of mobility, either Cork mis-stepped whilst strafing alongside the large tracks or the driver had somehow anchored the tank to turn sharply inwards against his parallel. The result was a bone-crunching squash and Sergeant Cork becoming suddenly jammed beneath the rolling tank tracks, snagged like a stick in the mud.

Half of his foot became paste. He roared in agony, unable to pull his appendage free beneath the five-tonne weight of the Panzer as it coasted.

While the tank tracks rolled in motion, they held Cork's limb pinned beneath the grind while the vehicle kept rolling—and taking the planted brick of armed Composition-C explosive ahead with it, quickly drifting out of his reach as if it were caught in a current.

... Cork had started to twist the timer knob.

... he had been interrupted arming the dial.

*The device was set for somewhere between _one_ and _ten_ seconds ...*

Where, precisely, in the countdown, Cork was unsure ...

Twisting the analogue timer had been where his fingers had scrambled, and lost control of the device in the motion due to his foot being run over.

The thought of this urgency took Cork's mind off the agonizing pain, and he broke out of his entranced state. His foot may have been reduced to a flapjack filled with blood, torn skin, and crushed bone within his boot, however, he could survive this—as long as the tank let him go in time.

Cork's stare broadened beneath his sweaty brow, his face chasing the surface of the slow passing tank, searching for the bomb and trying to read the timer countdown, unable to read. He dropped to a knee, grappling at his own leather boot, attempting to untie the laces and potentially *pluck* what was left of his foot free from the vice.

"*No, no, no, come on!*" he cried in panic, unable to free himself.

Eventually collapsing to his back in the snow, he drew an F-S commando dagger from his belt. Hunching forward in a regulation sit-up, he used the knife's tapered double-edged blade to sever the laces from his Grafters combat boot.

Realizing the machine gun turret was no longer trained on his position in the garage, Churchill shook the veil of debris from the onslaught and inched over to the edge of the chewed concrete wall, peeking around the corner to sleuth the situation in the street.

He noticed Cork's sticky predicament by the tank, realizing what had happened to the sergeant concerning his encumberment. The story read like a tragic opera, about to reach a climax.

At the same serene moment of irremediable tribulation and hopelessness, Cork witnessed Jack Churchill's observation of him; read the heroic eagerness bred in him to want to intervene ... however, Cork held up a palm to arrest his attempt at being a saviour. It was then Churchill fully noticed the lit bomb already mounted to the vehicle ...

The fuse countdown was unknown, but it was certainly seconds, not minutes. This ship had already sailed, and it was time for farewell.

Churchill accepted Cork's gesture.

*He could do nothing but watch the torment.*

Although it was bound to happen at any moment, every nanosecond that passed was a curious blessing, and offered with it a sliver of hope for salvation.

Seemingly on borrowed time, the rolling tank track finally cycled over Cork's foot at the same moment he managed to slit open his bootlaces, revealing the horrible sight of shredded meat and crushed bone housed within a flattened, sloppy sock.

Observing this happenstance, Churchill spied the direction of the tank guns once more before breaking cover, attempting to assist him where he could.

Cork yanked what was left of his squashed appendage from the indentation left by the tank track and started to hobble away ...

He got three shuffled paces clear of the tank before—

*bo-BHOOM!*

The Composition-C detonated, much earlier than desired.

*Far too early.*

The charge detonated—big.

*Far too fucking big.*

The repercussion from the plastique explosive lit up the white, cold environment with a hot orange glow and a brutal tremor of thrown, agile force.

Halting his persistent steps from the garage in order to escort the wounded sergeant to safety, the shockwave sent Churchill flying back into the darkened recess.

The resulting explosion pounded the poor commando Cork, launching him like a rocket. Airborne, amassing multiple pieces of razor-sharp, simmering-hot shrapnel wounds through his posterior-side, the man flopped to the slush and sleet nearby, deceased.

With a short slide on the icy ground, the smoked, crumpled, burnt, *and redeemed,* body of A.J. Cork finally rested.

Departed of life, he died a hero.

The explosive charge Cork detonated caused irreparable damage to the Panzer tank. The topside rotating turret and right-side mobility tracks of the armoured vehicle were destroyed, abolishing the wheel gears and disabling the vehicle in the street.

The Panzer I *Ausf.* was now an incapacitated, smouldering wreck, in situ of a torn, twisted exterior housing and groaning, clunking mechanics.

Having clambered to his feet, repositioning his green beret upon his dome, the soot-covered Jack Churchill emerged from the recesses of the Ulvesund garage. His squinting stare scoured the flaming wreckage.

Propped against the doorframe of the garage, coughing and wheezing through the thick smoke as it wafted, Mad Jack made the time to straighten his pencil moustache with two fingers to make sure it remained neat after the knockaround.

At a glance to his flank, it was obvious that Cork was not getting up. Lying face down, the vindicated commando lay dead in the street.

Nevertheless, the impromptu saboteur bid was not without success.

The plastique explosive had not only immobilized the crawling Panzer, but also appeared to have disintegrated a chunk of the light tank's armour plating. In the absence of the blown-away portion, the interior of the armoured vehicle was now moderately visible from the outside.

Things appeared internally damaged, resulting in an abundance of hurling smoke and hissing fumes leaking from the blown-open and ruptured hydraulics.

Through the clearing vapour, Churchill spied the maimed steel beast as it revved its engine, attempting to revive after barely surviving the eruption. The vehicle crunched forwards, emitting a loud pop and sizzle from the ruined machinery—a mechanical death rattle, of sorts.

The thing keeled.

The top hatch of the Panzer hurled open, and a red-faced, oxygen-starved occupant exploded into the fresh air and daylight.

It was Feind.

His exit resembled a cooked lobster emerging from the steam of the boiling pot.

Whoever had been assisting him in driving the Panzer tank must have perished from the external blast, for there was no sign of them emerging out of the exhuming steel carcass.

Finalizing his splutter, Friedrich Feind almost vomited over the edge of the canopy, sucking air like a vacuum, managing to guzzle a lung of clean air to rejuvenate his asphyxiated condition.

His bloodshot eyes promptly discovered the green beret-clad Churchill as he emerged from the garage, and the two locked eyes.

After an extended moment of inertia, Churchill suddenly snapped into action, sauntering forth and into the exposed street. In his steps, he raised his longbow, attaching an arrow to the bowstring and wound back his taut arm to formulate an archer's stance.

He basically had him at gunpoint.

Undaunted, Feind stared him down.

A few seconds passed before they conversed.

"Herr Churchill. Vhat a zmall vorld in vhich ve live ..."

Perhaps contemplating going for the kill pre-emptive of any further inharmoniousness, Churchill retained his tight draw over his archenemy whilst he conducted his retort. "Too small for the both of us, Feind ..."

Feind took a moment to clamber out from the turret hatch and slide gracefully on his rear against the slope of the armour. Descending past the damaged portion of the tank, the fire crackling away like a calm log fire, his boots reached ground level.

Now face-to-face with his archenemy, Feind appeared submissive towards Churchill, which Jack knew was against his mould—he'd more likely commit suicide than surrender.

With his draw anchored firm, Churchill cautiously advanced at Feind, drawing a bead with the razor-sharp head of a bodkin-tip arrow upon the formidable Gebirgsjäger Hauptsturmführer. He could loose the arrow and kill him in a split-second if he wished.

"Did you get my letter in the post?" Churchill casually asked, most indecorously given the situation.

The question appeared to confuse Feind.

"Vhat *letter?*"

Churchill blinked about himself in that moment.

Although it could have been a ploy by Feind to throw him off, it was equally as likely that he had never received the mail.

During his recovery out of hospital earlier in the year, Churchill had spent a lot of time thinking and reminiscing his earlier life prior to meeting the love of his life and re-evaluating himself. In one of those moments, Jack had tracked down and located a mailing address for Friedrich Feind and posted him a letter proposing a conditional clemency of his juvenile actions in 1939, where he had attacked the accomplished German Olympian and nobleman over an adolescent infatuation with a woman. The actions had led to a duel with swords at an airport, which resulted in Churchill being arrested. This had subconsciously sparked a rage-fuelled hatred against any adversary he encountered, envisioning them as Feind from this moment in time.

Unbeknownst to Feind, he had been Churchill's fixation of vengeance for ages. It was a private obsession.

Jack Churchill's mentality upon discovering the love of Rosamund Denny, and becoming a changed man, was born of an inconsequential attempt to mend that bridge from afar. The letter to Feind offering forgiveness—*among other things, such as meeting up for tea and bickies after the war*—was an attempted Hail Mary post into a forevermore googolplex of unlikelihood, as warned by the subsidiary civilian company located in France who forwarded letters to German recipients at a cost and without guarantee.

As it turned out, the mail never found the desired recipient and, in a way, Churchill was grateful. He had sent that note in a transitional stage of his life—a *honeymoon period*. Seeing life through rose-coloured blinders, he now regretted ever acting so coquettish and myopic towards right and wrong.

A few seconds absent words passed between the two adversaries.

Without Churchill even demanding for him to disarm, Feind nonthreateningly extracted his sidearm from his hip holster and let it fall to the ground. He then notably maintained a gleam over Churchill, with special consideration to the fact that Jack was armed with a blade at the hip, as he was. A precarious comparison.

He held his arms out, gloved palms open.

All that remained on Feind's armament was a sheathed rapier at his hip. Churchill focused upon the sword hilt for an instant, noticing that Feind seemed not about to remove it like he had his handgun. That he, instead, considered it an appendage; that he may have even wanted to use it against him in sporting nature ...

... like a duel.

... *like a rematch.*

Maintaining the weight of the wrench with his strong forearms, Churchill finally collapsed the cranked bowstring, lowering the longbow after disengaging the draw.

Halfway neutralizing his stance, Feind decrypted Churchill's body language, growing a sinister smirk on his maw. It was a signal of acceptance of such—or at the very least, consideration.

In a ruckus of encompassing volume around the incapacitated tank site, Sergeant Ramsey and a dozen commando troopers from One Troop with metallic-clunking machine guns flooded the surrounding area. Establishing a secured perimeter of the warzone, they observed with cautioned eyes beneath wobbly tin hats.

The fanning troopers trained their weapons about the hotel and at the captured Gebirgsjäger Hauptsturmführer: leader of the Alpine Huntsmen. This north-easterly vicinity of the thoroughfare, out the back of the Ulvesund Hotel, was calming now that the mortaring had ceased and the exchanging gunfire from the building had seemingly subsided.

This war was won.

Commandos positioned everywhere throughout the street, approaching the flaming Panzer carcass and enveloping Churchill and Feind's idle confrontation.

From the hotel, Knocker White emerged through the crowd of commandos, supporting the situation of his friend Jack Churchill. de la Torre was there also, sporting the endorsement of one of his favourite commandos—as did most.

Everyone postured perplexed as to what was happening in this altercation. Procedure suggested that this prisoner was to be apprehended, stripped for intelligence and weapons, and then taken into custody, however, it seemed such a protocol was not on the agenda. But then again, Jack Churchill was rarely one to follow the rulebook.

"Sir?" White announced after flocking in with some other men from the victorious hotel raid. They had just successfully collapsed the last enemy stronghold, evacuating the structure as some more of it toppled down behind them. "We've secured the hotel and taken quite a number of prisoners. The raid is over."

Eyes locked on Feind, Churchill's ear pricked to Knocker White's sit-rep. There was something much stronger still in his focus here, and it drew attention from all those surrounding.

From the opposite side of the encircling ring of crowding commandos, the beret-clad Captain Peter Young Young emerged along with fedora-wearing Felix Hardy. Their arrival distracted Jack for a split-second, as he had not been expecting to see them again after stationing Six-Troop at the warehouses.

Now wasn't the time or place to report their findings in the remnants of the burned-down red warehouse, but they had discovered a safe within the ashes. Upon cracking the door, Six-Troop had unearthed a valid Enigma codebook. Also, in that safe, they had discovered an operation manual for a Panzer I tank that was designated to roam the South Vågsøy outpost. Entrusting the codebook with Graeme Black, Young had taken off to personally warn the Troops assailing the hotel of the intelligence regarding the Panzer tank ... considering it was now twisted metal and charcoal, it was too little, too late.

The situation by the tank was otherworldly.

*Why was everybody just standing there?*

"Jack ...?" Young questioned as he took in the surreal scene amongst the ruins of a Panzer tank. His view extended onto the partially captive German officer—who, at this juncture surrounded by Commandos, seemed colossally fucked—and then assumed that maybe, during all this mayhem and chaos and war, Mad Jack had found his fabled archenemy.

Feeling farther out of place now than he had ever done on this day of days, Hardy inched out a stride from the khaki crowd, gawking over Young's shoulder and at the unwonted situation. He said not a word and just observed from the bleachers with the other commandos.

However unorthodox, Captain Young read the room.

He took charge in the apparent authoritative absence of their major.

Furthermore ... he knew the stakes.

"Alright, lads. Let's give them some room."

A grudge match amidst a war ...

*This was happening.*

Churchill held his stare at Feind, cracking a cocky smile.

From the south strip, some of Hooper's men, along with the captain himself in his clean fatigues and charging his barely fired weapon, loomed nearer with authoritative intent.

He was No.2 Commanding, thus command resided with Young.

"Major Churchill?" Hooper announced, stopping short and eyeing the curious German captive that everybody held in some form of esteem. His reserve troop men saturated the area with an overabundance of friendly presence.

After Jack failed to promptly reply, Hooper extended an order that countermanded Young's inexplicable directive to subvert action in this circumstance. After all, the correct SOP on this situation was to take the captured combatant into custody for due process as a POW.

"Men, arrest this enemy soldier."

"*Yes, sir—*"

"No!" Churchill thundered. He withheld his lowered stance with his longbow and nocked arrow. "This one is mine."

Hooper frowned, placing a step forward.

"Jack, he's ... unarmed?"

Churchill grew a sneer. "Oh, he's *very much* armed."

Unsure what their major meant, the phrasing caused the staunch encircling commandos to pull close the wooden buttstocks into their shoulders. They aimed on the cavalier Huntsman right as, unafraid, Feind motioned, proudly drawing the sword from his hip with a brass *shhing!*

Somehow, he wasn't instantly shot dead.

The German held it down by his side in an inoffensive yet provocative gesture, heralding Churchill to come forth.

Men everywhere shouted from behind their iron-sights ...

Fingers itched at triggers ...

Bullets trembled within the barrels of the many firearms ...

"*Oi, drop it!*"

"*Put it down, ya dumb cunt!*"

Jack shouted overtop of the surging pandemonium. "Hoooold!"

Knocker White was amongst the men who raised their weapons. Trusting in his CO, he was also among the first to hesitantly lower his guard, believing in Churchill to take charge—however unconventional of a capture this detention was.

Churchill offered one last time, however, as the tension grew to breaking point ... *he secretly hoped against his compliance.*

"This is your last chance, Feind ... Surrender."

"It is zuicide to zurrender," Feind quoted.

With a joyful kink in the collar, Churchill retorted with housed contentment as his hand crossed his hip; his fingers injecting the eyelets of his brass knuckleduster hilt, and before the many observing eyes of Commando, he unsheathed his claybeg sword.

*Shhwing!*

Holding it before him, he cavalierly tipped his head.

"I was kind of hoping you would say that."

*Feind grinned.*

Nonchalant as fuck, Mad Jack Churchill tossed his six-foot takedown longbow into the crowd of surrounding Commando. Acting as his informal caddie, Knocker White sacrificed hold of his gun to be able to catch the archer's weapon in a cradle across his chest.

Feind jeered a call back to their previous bladed duel contest.

"I zee, thiz time, you remembered to bring a zword ..."

Churchill's sterling stare admired the patterning in his Damascus steel blade, the sheen of the golden hilt. His fingers were firm in the brass knuckleduster grip below the hilt, wielding the weapon, fit like a glove.

He smiled comfortably and with conviction. "Any officer who goes into action without his sword is improperly dressed."

Feind beamed. "Treffer!"

A high-noon stance, the two stood ten paces from each other, entertaining a surrounding army of onlooking British Commandos with their weapons at the ready. No matter how this was going to end for Churchill, it would result in defeat for Feind. And with *that* came a sense of certainty, regardless, Churchill's confidence soared. His skills with a sword were much more adept this day than they were in Oslo two years ago.

Adding to the raised stakes for this unsanctioned contest, it seemed that the two men had outgrown any and all traditional formal fencing etiquette. There were no *en garde* poses and very little hints towards there being any preserved grace for this tournament.

The only thing missing from this modern-day western atmosphere was a tumbleweed. It was silent. Just the crackle of simmering spot fires in the chill of gusting winter air resonating after the collective raid.

"I zee you've had a *close shave?*" Feind referenced the lateral scar indentation across Churchill's cheek. It hadn't been there last time they had met, nor had it been one that he had left during their duel.

Churchill parried. "'t'was nothing but a graze."

"Do you remember vhat happened last time you took thiz path, English-man? How thiz vill end for you ... *again?!*" the boche taunted, placidly analysing the shrillness of his silver and black rapier's edge pre-combat. "It muzt be a bad memory for you to carry all of thiz time, ja?"

Churchill's focus was sharper than any sword blade.

"My only bad memory is you."

Feind held his smile for a moment longer before his face also fell flat. Serious. He outlined the rules of the duel: rules Churchill had heard this Hun mouth before.

"Let'z keep zis zimple, ja? Firzt man to draw blood from—"

"*First man to* *kill* *the* *other* *shall be named victor*," verbally cutting him off, Churchill announced his version of the guidelines louder than Feind's, outlining *new* rules for this contest. The two locked eyes and allowed for it to sink in for everybody present: that this rematch was a fight to the death.

*After all, like Feind always said: it was suicide to surrender.*

"No longer child'z play, Herr Churchill ...?"

Jack jeered with a sarcastic titter.

"It's your motto, *Fiend.* Time to live up to it."

It may have been arbitrary and unsportsmanlike, but it was at that moment Friedrich Feind acted out of character. In a fit of what could have been mistaken as rage, the elite swordsman unexpectedly throttled an attack, emitting a sound much alike a bellowing war-cry.

He advanced in a shuffle with flash and fury—very unbefitting of an athlete duellist, and utilizing a manoeuvre exceedingly prohibited by any standards of official swordsmanship.

It was at that subliminal moment that Churchill realized that he had been remembering Feind all this time as the *anodyne athlete* ... since then, he had apparently evolved into a *killer soldier.* All bets were off regarding the upholding of chivalry, and he would have to evolve or die in order to win this contest.

Immediately on the backfoot, Churchill accepted Feind's offensive flunge *(a flying lunge),* swishing his three-foot Scottish claybeg about his figure and parrying the German's rapier with every slash and subsequent compound attack.

*Chink!*

*Ching!*

*Tang!*

*Chink!*

*Tang!*

Metal clashed painfully loud as the two modern-day soldiers engaged in medieval combat. The growing crowd of armed British Commandos watched on, even adjusting their stances behind their firearms to allow room for the contest fight.

They humoured the unlawful effrontery of etiquette.

The commando crowd cheered Churchill on, swapping hold of their firearms in the interest of clapping their hands in applause.

"*Go, Jack!*"

"*Come on, Mad Jack!*"

"*Fuckin' get him, sir!*"

Ash drifted down like snowflakes as the sharp edges of the swords smashed together recurrently. A dozen *one-two* taps saw the clapping of steel as the two men danced at their feet, each taking turns lunging and bounding, thrusting and strafing like swashbuckling buccaneers having a ball.

*Ch-chink!*

*Tang!*

The sword blades met—and held.

The two blades melded, edges grinding together tensely.

The swordsmen traced an arch in the sky before the grunting archenemies butted shoulders and pressing apart with burliness, creating an ounce of distance.

*Schhhhscwing!*

Steel fast tapped again.

Feind shoved Churchill's way again before Mad Jack synced-up with the German's dissolute pace, matched it, and raised his bet, fast to return strikes of his own from all sides and angles, both low and high.

They retraced one another's parries.

This time, Churchill drove Feind's stance backwards, almost completely against the flaming Panzer tank wreckage in the open thoroughfare before Feind shoved forth and the two morphed together.

Feind's tractable backpedal fast anchored and the two locked blades in another tense hold above their heads. The blades parted, about to clank again, only this time, with their spare arms, the men grappled at each other's sword hand. They engaged in a strained struggle which hitched at the shoulders, bracing in perched stances, like sprinters at the mark but up against a wall, tussling like grizzlies.

Baring teeth and scowling, the two interlocked glowers as sweat broke, each holding their blades apart, above their heads, before Churchill saw the opportunity open to deliver Feind something *untrained* by his German zword instructors ... something that the German had fallen for during their last clash: the Liverpool kis—

*Whack!*

Most unexpected, *Feind* headbutted *Churchill* instead ...

*Not since Oslo would he ever fall for that again.*

Recalling the unorthodox manoeuvre from their first swordfight all those years ago, Feind socked Churchill first with a Liverpool kiss, smashing him in the nose with the ridge of his forehead.

Once the blow was done, and the blow separated the two titans, Feind allowed a momentary withdrawal.

On the other end, the brunt caused the beret-domed major to disengage their clutch, recoiling dizzily in revert, nursing a bloody nose with the back of his hand.

In his shudder and brief secession, Jack's guard stayed up.

Above their angled sword tips, the two strafed in a slow clockwise-rotation. The eyes of either adversary met across the en garde, and Churchill read in Feind's stare that he had recalled that cheeky move from the previous fight. It was also then that he pegged Feind's interdisciplinary capabilities: the man knew his fencing and swordplay, but also how to study that of others, such as how he had learned from Churchill's fighting techniques and adapted to overcome them.

To fight an opponent who retained this sort of ability was every tactician's worst fear.

A big part of playing the game is knowing how to bluff.

Churchill hid his hand, pretending not to know how to study an opponent's fighting patterns like Feind evidently did, but he knew enough to understand that this made for a tremendously dangerous adversary.

Revealing a dab of blood from his nostril, Jack sniffled.

He remarked politely. "Nice move, old boy."

Steadfast, Feind glared. "My mentor taught me nothing but duelling elegance und bravura in zwordsmanship. But, ziz one I learned vrom an opponent in Oslo zome yearz ago ..."

A worthy comeback to which Churchill bowed.

Behind them and their onlooking commando soldiers, a considerable portion of the flaming Ulvesund Hotel collapsed in the background with an earth-shaking rumble. The southern section and front-half of the building fell into itself from the top. This was a succession following the collapse of the fourth and third storey, due to the mortar rounds being delivered onto it from One Troop.

After an inferno had engulfed the top floors, the constraints keeping the structure standing had been tested, eventually faltering, resulting in an avalanche of rubble, wood, and weighty stone debris. *And Germans.*

Commandos rubbernecked the fallout, scattering farther away from the crumbling wreckage, however the distraction was not enough to sway the attentions of the two contestants.

The white cloud of dust expanded following the grumbling quake of the building's disintegration, nonetheless, the persistence and commitment of Feind and Churchill was steadfast. The commotion barely caused either fighter to waver their wrathful gawks from off one another. Their next clash was imminent.

Feind took the moment to recall from their previous stint, only he updated the vectors of his derision. "You und I, Herr Churchill ... Ve now fight like old men, married and trite."

Befitting of Feind's romanticized discourse regarding their predicament, an insulted Churchill muttered in retort: "*Trite?!* Speak for yourself, Fiend."

Suddenly, Mad Jack charged with his sword as a centrefire joust ...

The metal blade lunge aimed at the middle was deflected by Feind and Churchill, in turn, struck the armoured metal surface of the defused tank in the background. Upon a fast revolution, Churchill threw a sideward kick almost rearward into Feind's kidney that spaced the two combatants apart—also saving him from the zwordsman's incoming swipe.

Without wasting a second, the two each recovered and re-engaged in contest. Their robust blades clashed again and again with much valour and might, rapier versus claybeg.

*Chink-ching!*

Churchill swiped away Feind's practical flèche attack, then parried holding a low octave stance accepting of his next vigorous mêlée.

*Ching-ching, chink-ching, ching!*

Their blades sparred as the two soldiers weaved and brandished, eventuating in assumed alternating fencing positions: Churchill holding the raised neuvieme, pointing down against Feind in a simple sixte, and they disengaged in a slow clockwise strut, one foot in front of the other.

Even though they were not technically fencing, it was hard for the two men trained to swordfight in the art to stray from technique.

Spritely off the mark, once again, they re-engaged.

*Chink, chink, chink-ching!*

Several more deflective parries and offensive ripostes challenged in a flutter of foot shuffling within hefty combat boots, and both Feind and Churchill reposed in quarte and quinte composures, awaiting the next action like a pair of disciplined swordsmen.

The two were puffed from that.

Their bloods were flowing now.

Barely catching breath, they again attacked simultaneously, clanging oscillating edges with might and dynamism, balance and technique, slashing in a series of continuous and unrelenting brash metallic clatters whilst their footing shuffled and kinked extremities danced below them.

After a surreal saga of metal clanking, the two cut-throat surfaces seemed to somehow magnetize. The blades interlocked and glided together.

Now each held with both hands, the weapons slipped all the way down to the iron hilts between the two tough stances, giving out a god-awful scraping rasp.

The two foes tensed their holds ...

Their arms trundled to a favoured side each, and they now clashed in person, bashing shoulder-to-shoulder with both hands on their intertwined sword handles, wrestling with brute force.

The men's teeth gritted as their grimy faces met closer than the reflection in a bathroom mirror.

With a downward thrust, Jack rammed into his opponent, and the two broke apart as if a tie line snapped between them. Blown apart, the two soldiers backpedalled several paces before collecting their drives and determinations.

Almost as if an actual explosion burst had been the reasoning behind their split, more architectural devastation collapsed to the ground from the remnants of the decaying Ulvesund Hotel in their surroundings. This coincided again as the two vendetta-driven titans swung their swords about the air, ready for more action.

In a world of unlikeliness, it seemed fate had rekindled their hateful agenda. It would take more than war to obstruct this outcome.

Although it was always arguably in Feind's favour, their original contest in Oslo had been interrupted by the airport authorities and local police, so, technically, nobody had won ...

... this time would be different—in more ways than one!

*Such as elegance!*

The two men lunged in at one another.

They threw their full weights ... their full motives ...

After clashing steel time and time again, Feind balled a fist and hurled Churchill a sneaky left hook that collided square against his cleft chin, causing him to wince in retort.

A byproduct to the blow, Churchill's blade slashed unusually low and slit a groove across Feind's upper thigh, officially drawing first blood of the duel.

The German exclaimed with a grimace as Churchill recoiled, enraged from the punch. Striking viciously at Feind's en garde with his claybeg in order to lower it and gain distance, he took turn with his own daring boxer's jab—this time, with a brass knuckleduster-coated fist.

*Whoosh!*

Feind somehow ducked the jab and rammed a shoulder-barge into Churchill, powerlifting him from off the ground and against the hot metal of the roasted Panzer.

Tussling, the two hit the simmering, immovable object with an impactful collision that squeezed the air out of both of their lungs. Feind lifted his head with the power of an uppercut, striking Churchill beneath the jaw, and then again with a backhand containing the hilt of his rapier. That one made a distinct sound and drew blood from Churchill's jawbone. The close-quarters bout momentarily morphed their swordfight into a prize-fighting match but, instead of boxing gloves, each man wore metal sword hilts over their fists.

As if cornered in a boxing ring, still sword in hand, Churchill raised his forearms up defensively in a cover-up, blocking the fast jabs and hooks as Feind threw his fists like a madman. The forged metal grip of his rapier hurt the most as it contacted Jack's forearm guard as he withheld, practically on the ropes against the tank's remains. This multitude of hits scratched Jack's face up to buggery and put a slit through his brow near the ridge of his nose—but worst of all, nearly cost him the firm fit of his green beret.

Breaking the punch fighting, Churchill clinched with the fighting fiend, latching onto his sword arm with his free hand to return the punching sentiment with a timely right cross—this time, with the brass-knuckle duster handgrip of his customized claybeg.

*Chink!*

A metallic impact rang-out solid as the brass collided with teeth through his lips, and Feind took the punch, neck whipping back. The Hun became immediately bloody-gobbed, recoiling in a stunted daze in where he surveyed his teeth to make sure he hadn't just lost some. The alignment of his teeth at a clench felt foreign. His lip was now nastily split down the middle, bleeding profusely down his chin.

Momentarily disorientated from the blow, the Hauptsturmführer was finally haemorrhaging, figuratively as well as literally. Not only was he bleeding, but the man was leaking trepidation from his ardent resolve: *a far deadlier maim to suffer for a man of such tenacity.*

Through a grimace, Churchill straightened his green beret. He stared Feind down, watching him backpedal for an extended instance whilst recollecting his own stance.

Feind gathered himself and found the en garde position, winding his rapier to psych himself up and mentally realign his mindset. The blade cut the air with a *whoosh-whoosh.*

Mad Jack pressed away from the steel tank and did the same, slashing the air at his sides as he trundled towards the deathly, balls-out engagement.

The two foes met in the middle with a fresh collision of steel.

Eventually making their way over from the suburban lots bordering the thoroughfare, Colonel Durnford-Slater and Sergeant Mills were late to the block party. At last, they enclosed, close enough in their jog to designate the dancing bodies in the street and it caused an askew brow above their gander.

They spotted the smouldering tank wreckage and the gathering of British Commandos surrounding the incapacitated beast, but what they saw now caused them each to frown in perplexity.

"What in the devil ...?" Durnford-Slater whispered as he slowed, squinting to focus upon what appeared to be a *street-fight* within the congregated circle.

Only ... it wasn't an argy-bargy with fists.

*The two contestants had swords.*

At his parading flank, Mills was just as without words.

The two accelerated, picking up the pace and running towards the rally in contemplation of intervening ...

Their strikes were slower. Heavier.

Amidst the calamity of their sword duel, a few of the clashing *clangs* even flinted sparks from the striking blade edges. The blade clattering ramped up, seeming louder, more furious than before. They sounded less like structural metallic *tapping* or *clinking*, and more like hard-hitting *clanking* and steel colliding.

It was time to kill, with much more force from the shoulder in these swings.

Chipping away in a footing not dissimilar to a dance routine, the two pressed Feind's way several steps before switching back towards Churchill's direction. Upon this tidal sway, Jack found himself steered dangerously towards an obstacle: the blazing Panzer tank, from a hotter angle nearer the rising flames.

It was as though he were rearing up on an open oven drawer, about to topple into the scalding heat—*yikes.*

Amidst the rash parries, the backpedalling Churchill glanced about his flanks, spotting a folded sheet of the Panzer's damaged tank tracks on the ground about knee height. Altering his reverse angle, he instead backed onto it, elevating his position whilst continuing the swordfight as though he was walking backwards upstairs.

While Feind still pushed in a relentless raddoppio fashion, not decelerating or giving an inch in his offensive impetus, he saw the opportunity to take a swipe at Churchill's feet as the elevating commando slinked onto the hood of the damaged tank in due course.

Missing by inches as Jack recessively trod clear, Feind's blade struck the armoured shell of the Panzer with a skim and a bright spark, and he immediately raised the stakes by following Churchill's gamble up the tank tracks and onto the Panzer's carcass. They were now both standing on an isle of elevation for their contest ...

Emerging from the crowd of bushed British Commandos, Durnford-Slater and Mills made their way to the front of the audience pit, gaining a ringside view of the *Churchill-versus-some-random-German* swordfight.

Needless to say, Durnford-Slater was bewildered.

Hopefully the wind wouldn't change on his frown right now, as it was ghastly.

After a prolonged stare fixated on the two men upon the fiery remains of a Panzer tank, he uttered: "... Jack?"

Upon arriving at the venue, he was twofold confused as to why there was an unrestricted affray between a high-ranking major within No.3 Commando facing-off against what appeared to be an equally as high-ranking officer from the enemy force—furthermore, why the scuffle had not been cogently subdued by the superiors within Commando, whom Durnford-Slater could see were present within the rally of raring spectators.

Instead, they were actually *accommodating* this behaviour, fully compliant in the course of conduct. How unbecoming. How unprofessional. How *Mad Jack Churchill*.

Durnford-Slater was without the words to say.

Everybody watched as the sword duel exalted onto the centre stage of the ruins of the Panzer tank, climbing to a rather unusual spectacle. Their blades tapped and clattered in the midst.

"Sir!" Captain Young from Churchill's own G3 Six-Troop became steadfast, immediately approaching Colonel Durnford-Slater upon his unexpected arrival while the two starring figures continued to duel in challenge within the foreground. Young Young halted before the appalled

Durnford-Slater, failing to instantly offer any rationale as to why this event was being permitted to happen in the first place, let alone continue after it had gotten this far.

"What the hell is this?! Stop this at once!" Durnford-Slater ordered with a raised voice that was only partially heard over the noise of the rowdy crowd supporting their Mad Major in his gentlemanly contest.

Young pleaded. "But sir!"

"No, negative! Absolutely not! This cannot be happening!"

In the crowd of Churchill supporters, which included Young, Hardy, Knocker White, de la Torre, the hobbling Komrower, and now even the visibly acquiescing Mills, Durnford-Slater's incorruptible moral fibre attempted to take charge. They felt the mood die, and the vengeance for their major soon to be, frustratingly—again—left unresolved.

"We're done here ..." Durnford-Slater declared unequivocally, preparing to take the logical necessary step in ending this procedural unrest.

"Sir ..." Young implored again, rather improperly and for some indescribable reason, obtaining the lieutenant-colonel's astonished attention. "Jack's wishes."

"Preposterous! What if he gets injured?!"

"It's personal, sir."

"What?!" with a scowl, the lost Durnford-Slater paused, delaying taking that next step towards enacting his rank and decision. Having grown to know Churchill, a man so passionate in his resolve, he knew that the decision had not been made lightly to engage in this act of vengeance and retribution. Jack had the benefit of the doubt, as he had proven himself time and time again to Durnford-Slater. That had bought him trust and with that, the chance to see his machinations out.

*In awe, they watched on ...*

Durnford-Slater stepped in closer, now in the very front row.

He watched the contest like everybody else ...

... and just like everybody else, he believed in Mad Jack.

*He offered his blessing.*

"Get him, Jack! That's an order!"

*The men cheered louder.*

Before the lively, chanting ring of mild-mannered English spectators in Brodies and beanies, Churchill allowed for Feind to rise upon the body of the Panzer, joining him. Like a loaded gun, he focused his blade of his claybeg upon him every step of the way.

Feind emerged fully before his guarded stance, rapier by his side.

It seemed the perfect time for a throwaway one-liner, a taunt, or quip remark ... but the moment went absent any prophesized narrative anecdote, and instead, the action exploded to life.

Feind lunged at Churchill, swinging just as wildly, as ferociously, as he had ever done so prior. Fuelled on adrenaline, there seemed an absence of due exhaustion.

With continually balanced footing, like that true of a swashbuckler's form, Jack dodged and parried the strokes from his Hauptsturmführer attacker whilst balancing on the uneven surfaces of the tank chassis. Unable to rear any further, he issued some back, all of which were deflected or ducked by Feind.

The contest continued enthusiastically, and each contestant trifled hard to shift only within a few paces to remain on the flat surface of the volatile tank hull.

It was then that Churchill recognized a subluminal tact ...

As they fought, Feind shuffled his feet in such a way that suggested that although he was conscious of spacing, he was also luring him; setting Jack up. As though he was attempting to stage a manoeuvre; some sort of finishing fencing trick that called for the opponent to be situated a particular way and at a certain distance.

Churchill didn't take the bait—not intentionally, at least.

Instead, he kept his wits about him and stood his ground. He held his balance with his swings, maintaining a mental note of his footing—

*Then, it happened.*

Before Jack fully realized that he had wandered into the spider's nest, he was already clung to a web.

He wholly recognized the ploy when his eyes flickered down and at Feind's incessantly tapping feet on the metal tank chassis, striving to uncover the means to his foot-play.

It was precisely that: *a distraction.*

The whole bait was a distraction.

*Fuck, this guy was smart.*

An *appel* fencing technique, as it was known in French.

And Jack had just fallen for it hook, line, and sinker.

*Hook ...*

Ensnaring Churchill's overconfidence in this moment, causing him to swing at an obvious flèche jab which was easily able to be parried wide and to the side, this subsequently beaconed an inwards swing towards Feind's exposed core.

*Line ...*

After blocking the stab, Churchill obligatorily swished his blade back in at Feind's defenceless body: an inviting strike. Too enticing to deny, the desire was too strong ... only, therein lied the baited hook and line, dangling for a nibble ...

Sinking like a stone, Feind dropped beneath Jack's incoming blade, limbo-ducking it by inches, and thus exposing Churchill's abdomen for the slice.

*Sinker ...*

It wasn't even Churchill's first time falling victim to the fencing trick known as the *passata sotto.* Introducing it to him in 1939, Friedrich Feind had pulled the same skilful manoeuvre back during their fight in Oslo.

And just like that time, the crowd gasped with anxiety:

Commandos Knocker White, Mills, Young Young, Komrower, and now, his superior officer, Durnford-Slater, respectively inhaled a breath and held it whilst viewing the apparent ploy come to fruition ...

Even Hardy observed, as did—for Mad Jack—another fateful onlooker and critical observer to his wartime life, his Highland haunt, Colonel Sloan MacLeòid. In a glimmer of blur, Churchill even saw his bonnet-wearing noggin appear in the crowd of onlookers, watching him about to get his ass kicked again.

An assembly of commandos huffed with fright as they watched their major fall for a baited trap, resulting in a timely death once Feind ultimately ran him through with his sword on the follow-through.

Only, this time around, Feind wasn't the only one who could strategize. Wasn't the only sole intelligent swordsman who would premeditate the movements and tactics of their opponent.

Churchill may have forgotten about the passata sotto at the time of the distraction, but he remembered it in a heartbeat much to a *fool-me-once* manner. He shaped up in that last split-second moment, swinging wildly over Feind's reverting collapse onto his back hand, and he countered the counter-attack and subterfuge, assuming control.

In that askew second, as Feind felt the blood rush to his head in his planned fold beneath the slashing blade, he knew to next bring his wrist about in at an angle to then penetrate Churchill's body as he loomed helplessly above his stance. As he did so, he suddenly found Jack Churchill's leg not where it was supposed to be...

... his knee had raised, blocking Feind's sword arm from physically performing a stabbing motion as planned; as practised, before.

Whilst everybody held their breath, Churchill ended the faltered manoeuvre by slamming his sword-wielding closed fist down into Feind's bowing chest, causing him to collapse midway through his finesse as though somebody had pulled the rug out from beneath his feet.

The bottom of Churchill's hilt struck him in the sternum.

Winded and defeated, he abruptly dropped to the tank's hollow shell with a heavy *thwump!*

Mad Jack twirled over his body, flourishing his blade out by his side.

He regained his footing whilst Feind spluttered, fast reacting by rolling clear and to the edge of the Panzer tank landing. The winded German now grasped at his chest where Churchill had slogged him as hard as a sledgehammer. He winced with each shallow breath, grinding his blood-stained teeth like a Great White in recoil.

Churchill tensed his stance, holding his guard.

A hint of a smirk grew upon his bushed expression, knowing that he had just won that hand at poker (when he really should have lost), pulling the last possible high card over an irrefutable pair.

Feind grimaced with anger, struggling to wince a breath.

That hit had been near-fatal, possibly even cracking some ribs. It now hurt for him to inhale, and it showed ... but the bloodied boche, the stubborn soldier, and unparalleled pain in Jack's mental butt, raised his blade, ready for more war.

This was a fight to the death, not a fight to a forfeit.

In-keeping with that arrangement, Churchill let him have it.

Jack took three big paces across the hull and met Feind for some more sword fighting. Metal clashed and blades glistened as they swung through the air.

Feind pulled off one last incredible feat: he shoved in riposte against Churchill after holding a mild defence, only to gain enough footing area to then step *up* and *onto* Churchill's belt, using him as a human springboard to launch himself away and off the tank like an anti-gravity sidekick.

Churchill did not traipse far from the launch of the kick.

He stabilized instantly as his spare hand found the turret mount located behind him, and was therefore able to watch Feind's gymnastic display as the German soldier performed an elegant glide from off the back of the tank, preparing to land flawlessly on the cobblestone ground of the thoroughfare below.

Instead of dwelling on the spectacle, Churchill saw fit to act and flung himself off the turret like an athlete from a sprinter's wedge. Jack catapulted himself forth, bounding after Feind who was still airborne, trailing towards a perfectly stuck landing back on solid ground.

*Whilst in mid-air, a slowed-down feature of the two men each sailing to earth seemed almost a sequence from a work of renaissance art.*

Churchill regarded Feind's concentration, tracing his trajectory, his speed, and balance, tracking towards a perfect landing on firm footing ...

... little did he know that as he free-fell in his competitive mindset, Mad Jack was inbound, just as on target with a stuck landing as he was.

*The acrobatic equivalent of Robin Hood splitting the bullseye.*

Albeit nowhere near as stylish or graceful as Feind's obviously well-practised form or ability, Churchill's forward-thrusting flunge carried his flight course in pursuit of Feind's landing zone.

*With all his might, he would spear him like a jouster's thrust.*

In that mid-air second, Churchill realized something about this finale: *that for men like Friedrich Feind ... there was actually a fate worse than death ...*

Instead of holding his sword in a forward stabbing motion, prepared to imminently run his nemesis through the moment they both touched down, Churchill made a balance adjustment as he glided through the air towards Feind's 10/10 stuck landing.

Complementing his arcing descent, Churchill stretched farther out with his free hand, bringing about his sword hilt with extra might and power to envelop a punch akin to *Apollo.*

Feind landed on his feet, brilliantly exercising his gymnastic ability and perfectly escaping the contest upon the tank with a degree of tongue-in-check mannerism that rivalled Jack's Errol Flynn-ish nature.

About to return to the gravity of the situation, his eyes fixated on the surprise image of the suddenly incoming Mad Jack Churchill, soaring towards him in the air like some sort of superhuman Spartacus.

*Thw-CHUNK!*

In what had developed into a flying punch with his sword handle, Churchill arrived at Feind with the full force of his aerial dive. His feet touched down in a stick, simultaneously delivering a strong right cross that travelled from his shoulder.

In the same second that his boots grounded, the bronze knuckleduster hilt of Churchill's sword slogged his target square in the head, lifting Feind off his feet in retort.

He disarmed from the force; an impact akin to being hit by a car.

The punch sent him flailing limply, a ragdoll absent consciousness, slinking onto the street, sliding like a lifeless corpse—and quite possibly just as unalive as the phrase suggested.

The rapier dropped with a metallic rattle chasing Churchill's spaced feet from the aerial delivery, where the Commando folded to a kneel in landing. His sterling sincerity observed the transference of his impact.

The goal may have been not to *kill* Feind, per se ...

... but truth be told, the guy might just be quite dead after that hit.

With a dented forehead, Hauptsturmführer Friedrich Feind's body reacted as though hit by a battering ram. Lifeless and properly victimized, his reactionless cadaver travelled through the air for almost ten feet before sinking into the icy thoroughfare, smashing down violently. His body jagged, jerking at the joins before rolling several times and resting against the boots of a pair of No.3 Commandos with their guns instinctually trained down south.

Knocker White was there with his shotgun bore.

Mills was too, with an M1911A1 pointed at either one of Feind's fluttering eyes as the deformed German fought the wanton desire to demise.

Lastly, Durnford-Slater leant past his man's shoulder and into the upwards view of the barely conscious German Hauptsturmführer captive, offering a belated denote. "I think we're done here!"

Bloody and heavily concussed on the floor, Feind fought the urge to black-out. His eyelids flickered, gazing upon the English soldiers as more of Mad Jack's Merry Men stepped in around him, leaving a space in the grouping for one specific man with a pencil moustache and a beret to overshadow his defeated state ...

The victor himself:

*Jack Churchill.*

Triumphant, he uttered a relevant parting phrase to his enemy with the same conquering throwaway tone that he had once used on him with an *Auf Wiedersehen.*

"Merry Christmas, Feind. And a Happy New War."

Fighting to hold his cranium out of the sludge below, Feind's bloodshot eyes twinkled as he finally drifted away—quite possibly into a coma he had been slogged so hard by that punch from Churchill.

"Take this pile of knackwurst into custody, lads ..." delivering justice and a fate worse than death to Friedrich Feind, Churchill ordered surrounding Englishmen, who acted immediately. "He is now a declared *prisoner of war.*"

Conceding to unconsciousness, Feind let his dented head hit the mud, out like a light. His lifeless body became collected by men in tin hats who carried him off to be detained. Like all the other surrendered

POWs, he would be funnelled aboard the many ships of the 17th Destroyer Flotilla and ferried back to the King's land along with an army of victorious British Commandos.

The transition between warzone and safe zone was breakneck.

There was no distinctive changeover from hot to cold—or at least warm in the middle of a changeover. The entire raid seemed to simply fizzle out and exist as an eerie tranquillity after the storm of conflict passed like bad weather. Now, better weather.

Returning from the fighting, a large group of Commandos approached the shoreline from the many routes out of the village of South Vågsøy, bleeding khaki through the streets. The skies above were filled with a blizzard of flailing labels because of the destroyed canning and processing plants, the paper rain resembling snowfall amidst their withdrawal from the fishing town. Their exodus left many locations ablaze, roasting in victorious golden flames, singed charcoal-black with smoke plumes climbing high into the clear day, casting enormous shadows over everything.

Along the coast by the busy Forward Operating Base on the beach, numerous short-range Higgins LCs had banked in order to begin ferrying loads of commandos and guarded prisoners aboard the monstrous navy ships that orbited the island in the Vågsfjorden bay.

Medic Sorry Corry seemed to have the entire triage running smoothly.

There were no shortages of instances for the busy commando corpsman and his team of corpsman orderlies, with approximately fifty commando casualties accounted for thus far during Operation Archery—twenty-two confirmed killed with countless wounded; upwards of fifty.

At the FOB, a few familiar troopers that had withdrawn from the battle early, either due to incapacitation or fulfilment of duties, now witnessed with a leer upon their chops as their Commando comrades returned from their in-land crusade, conquerors.

Lieutenant Hank Peace and the Five Troop men of Churchill's G3 whom he had left on Måløy Island waiting for G4 to relieve them were amongst present and accounted for, ferrying prisoners. This included radio operator R.L. Wills, who became instantly pleased to see the commanding officers who charged him to relay communications return in one piece. He was eager to inform Major Churchill that the opportunity to send a communiqué to Hitler did not arise, and therefore they will never know why the Führer failed to appoint Franz Halder as holder of France. A poetic travesty.

Bruce Giles and the men he inherited of his late brother's Three Troop were present in the amassing crowd of champion Commandos, assisting with the wounded and the processing of POWs along with the armed navy sailors from the Prince Charles and Prince Leopold carrier ships. He stood proud. Collected. Compiled ... and undoubtedly missing his big brother.

Amongst the crowd, patiently waiting transference back to the carriers in disembarkment, co-existed the narrow face of George Peel, cradling his newly found silver bible box and newfound outlook on religion, apparently recently renounced from his life. He looked up in his ponder, sighting the incoming commandos from the mainland and gesturing to them with a respectful nod.

Equally as grimy and tattered from battle, the radioman known as Drain was crouched at his flank. Wordless, he found the energy upon observing their return and stood tall in unexpressed salutation as he recognized the calibre of heroism patrolling towards them—men returning from the gates of the coldest, frozen-over hell imaginable.

Captain Bradley and Sergeant Ramsey of One Troop were contented amongst their men, including Johnnie Dowling, who had survived his own personal encounter with a Panzer tank where his mate had perished. They appeared composed in the aftermath, their hands resting upon their weapons, safeties on. These blokes may have been at ease now, but it was their mortar skills that had tipped the fight in the eleventh. The hotel would not have fallen without their direct input.

Of the motionless wounded, there were countless familiar faces ...

Trooper Curry and Dennis O'Flaherty, with his head—namely, his eye—wrapped tight in a white bandage, carried by supportive commandos under each arm. The guy would have sported an otherworldly headache hitherto undreamt of, for he had been technically shot in the head—possibly more than once—and had survived. His friend Sherington was at his side, actively informing his conscious friend of the returning commandos from South Vågsøy like a sports commentator. In this circumstance, keeping the man awake meant keeping him alive.

Transported to the FOB for further transference to the carrier ships, were numerous accumulating to the great loss of those killed-in-action *(KIA)*. Resting amongst the two dozen bodies was Captain John Frederick Giles, Martin Linge, and the remains of Captain Algy Forrester. Corporal

Owen Dillon, A.J. Cork, Holt, Pattinson, were also amidst the those departed. All courageous champions. All heroes in their own right.

It had been approximately an hour since the capture and partial destruction of the Ulvesund Hotel. Now that the fighting was over, it was time for the emotion of the ride to settle as the dust did. Although there was still a lot to do in regard to operational oversight for a lieutenant-colonel and commanding officer, Durnford-Slater still fell victim to fleeting moments of brain-drain as the adrenaline started to wear off. It had been a big morning for all the 500 Commandos rostered for the Måløy Raid, but for him especially having received very little sleep the nights prior. He beheld the most stress for the operation, and the pressure had been riding him harder than he let on.

It visibly showed on his continual thousand-yard glower as it set in amidst the waves of fatigue, shrouded behind the veil of grime and exhaustion, sleep deprivation, and the overbearing atmosphere of jubilation that triggered them all on an emotional level. He was finally slowing down.

Every man here was a hero, and it was time to see them home.

His latent wingman, Sergeant Joe Mills, was not far from his side with his fingerless-gloved hands resting on his holstered pistols, wearing a rugged tilt in his dry-blood-covered brow. Like all the others, there was a hovering contemporaneous of satisfaction present in the air.

Charley Head was next, flipping a salute from the leather brim of his stained green beret to a nearby soldier recovering at ground level. The cynical, sarcastic man had made it through, threading the eye of the needle on his first Commando crusade.

With a bubble of chewing gum in his wagging jaw, next in this arriving Commando crew was Knocker White, Ithaca shotgun winched across his shoulders, carrying his flaccid arms. To the head, he had taken a punch or five this day in hand-to-hand combat, both scary and exhilarating. No matter, it couldn't shake his resting beam—a smile that subsided like a tide between victory and the reminder of loss, such as JFG and Linge, which he had witnessed in the flesh. Like everyone present, he had lost brothers today, but he still stood ever so tall amongst Commando family.

Beside him, strut Captain Peter Young. For the first time in his service career, the Young Young no longer looked, well, *young*. He had aged on Vågsøy Island, as if he had stepped into a time vortex out of a *H.G. Wells* short, and everyone could see it. He was a different person. He left England a baby-faced though loyal commando trooper, and he had graduated to adulthood during the journey. Returning now, he was a prominent Troop leader, second to none other than their Mad Major. A decree respectfully earned in blood.

He was no longer *Young Young*. He had graduated just *Young*.

Lieutenant Arthur Komrower had seen better days. The poor fellow had been burned half to death during the early hours of the raid. But even severe burns from the phosphorous shelling had not been enough to keel the animal within. Komrower had ran the race, albeit at a slower pace, he was about to cross the finish-line, nonetheless. An irreplaceable member of No.3 Commando, and still technically in one piece thanks to one man in particular ...

In a sorrowful moment, Komrower hobbled over to the row of dead bodies. They were still laid out upon the portable stretchers they were carried on from the front. One of them, in particular, seemed to be clothed differently to the others; an exposed arm from beneath the considerately placed sheet wore a contrarily tanned sleeve.

It was Martin Linge—the man who had saved his life.

Komrower allowed for himself to collapse onto the rocks beside the body, propping up in order to respectfully reveal Linge's top half from beneath the drape. He looked to be resting peacefully in death.

Komrower watched over him for a moment.

"Rest in peace."

A man carrying a scuffed up Automatgevär rifle appeared above. He was a Norwegian soldier from the NOR.I.C.1, and likely an esteemed kamerat of Linge. "You knew him?" he asked.

Komrower shook his head modestly. "I wish I knew him ..."

After a moment of mourning silence, the two gestured courteously, and Komrower glanced upon Linge's face one last time before covering him up and saying *goodbye*. And *thank you*.

Although not a Commando—or even a soldier, for that matter— official war correspondent for the Battlefront Gazette, American journalist Felix Hardy endured amongst the troops, seeing through the fight all the way to the Ulvesund. This was unlike his competition, William Mericle, for British Pathé. He and his cameraman had hung back near the warehouses along with Six Troop and Lieutenant Black.

Sore from missing out on that final fight involving a Panzer tank, along next was Graeme Black. Shot a total of four times in the one arm, his mate Challington administered aid in the form of a fresh bandage as offered by one of Corry's orderlies who met them at the FOB. The Group 4 lieutenant's situation at the warehouses was not without fruit, as they had uncovered the Enigma codebook from a safe located within. Finding lurking intelligence, however, was not this soldier's forte. Black was a tooth and nail warfighter, through and through, and he was seething from omitting the final action—action that his direct superior, Captain Hooper, was summoned to partake, though seemingly limited in his accomplishments in the last push.

Last but not least, was the man of the hour.

The man of the saga.

*Major Mad Jack Churchill.*

There was not much left to say about him ...

He emerged with his pale hair gleaming from beneath his aslant green beret, forever-neat moustache out-brushed, longbow down in one hand, doodlesack resting beneath the other beside the claybeg sword sheathed at his hip. Always strident with a built-in swagger, a distant pipe march forever sounding between his ears, he sauntered his way onto the rocky shore, following his comrades of Commando ...

His brothers in arms.

*His Merry Men.*

Unlike always, though, Churchill seemed peaceful after this battle.

A certain satisfaction lingered in the eternal echoes of the venture; the capture of a certain elusive Hun, perhaps enough to whet his whistle like a fine spirit.

A glance along either direction of the icy coast was a sight to behold.

Numerous blazes of blistering demolition-encouraged firestorms raged on in the distance. Either due to the flammable fatty fish factories or the kerosene and coal oil manufacturing plants near the docks, much of Vågsøy Island was still afire, an inferno along the icy coastal stretch, and would remain aflame long after the departure of Commando and the Royal Navy.

Grime smeared his cheeks and the contour of his jawline, and dried blood from a nose-bash had darkened a streak through his pencil moustache. The fisticuff engagement with Feind during their swordplay saw a few small nicks across his face, notably a gash in his brow which had already stopped bleeding.

Churchill arced his beret whilst casting a far easterly gleam at the bright warm orange flames along the coast. After a pant from the reeling exhaustion, he couldn't help but emit his winning smile:

*You're welcome, Norway.*

As dismal as the outlook was that an element of their well-being was left to be rebuilt in the wake of their brief invasion and raid, at least the tyranny of Hitler's evil Axis had been ridden from these lands. An almighty blow had been delivered, all but guaranteeing their safety from further German incursions.

Through all the destruction, all the death, and the stresses of the suddenly released oppression, that fact alone would surely be enough to help Mad Jack sleep at night—help them all sleep at night.

*They had made a difference today.*

One thing for certain was that the year 1942 was looking awfully bright for those living in South Vågsøy ...

*A happy new year to all.*


Lastly, Birney's remote Group 5 men resumed their place on the HMS Oribi.

The destroyer returned along the Ulvesund Fyr passage from the north-east. Their objective of defending the land, although essential, had been frustratingly uneventful.

"Shittest-farken-fight ever!"

Uncontainable with anger, the pissed off and irritated, one-eyed Sergeant MacWilly complained amongst his group of Commando hanging on the railing of the driving warship. Their view departing Vågsøy Island, witnessing the fiery aftermath, was nearly one reminiscent of art depicting the grand wars of old, like the *Battle of Brunanburh.*

Speaking to anybody who would listen, he tugged his head over, implying his nearby Lewis gun. "*Louise* didn't even get ta sing! She loves ta sing, lads! Yoo should hear her!"

"Not for everybody," a soldier sharing his view replied between gazes of the snowy coastline in flames. The way the orange glow of the spot fires and infernos contrasted against the whitey blues of the winter zone was artistic.

The one lady who did get to sing was the fat one.

MacWilly grunted as he watched the landmass pass adrift them on the warship. "Lucky bastards had some fun down there!"

A loud detonation exploded nearby the FOB, along the beach.

It wasn't an abnormal occurrence, even after the action of the raid had finished, as there were still tankers and factories alight in bright pluming infernos along the coast. In fact, distant booms had grown to be a part of the ambiance along with the crackling of spot fires and the flailing of ash and snowing debris.

This particular non-threatening blast was merely just another munition stash belonging to the Wehrmacht and discovered by the British, thusly going up in smoke. Evacuated of any collateral damage, the depot was rid the way the No.6 demo knew best ... with a block of Composition-C.

They were lugging a brick of high explosives on each one they found in their exodus from Vågsøy, even tossing a grenade amongst the odd box of potato mashers in a few instances—whatever it took to make sure Nazi Germany could never again utilize anything left behind.

The explosion had been close to the FOB on the coast.

It rattled them all at the shoreline, shaking the tense reflexes of every Commando, and making them snap their views towards the source.

While the arriving mob of grinning Commando dispersed amongst the masses, absorbing amid those already crowded at the FOB in a sea of khaki clothes and brodie helmets, a glimmer of sparkling light caught Jack Churchill's attention. His sterling stare honed in on a small unoccupied shed, located nearby; the glint of a glass bottle lurking within ...

*Perhaps a victory drink was in order?*

The flock of swaggering Commando swarmed Durnford-Slater as he idled in his returning march, glancing sideways and becoming strangely hung-up on a sight within the charcoal remnants of a burned-out building on the shoreline. Just out of the eyesight of the FOB existed a dozen bodies, lurking motionless alongside a partially destroyed enemy defence line. There was a blunder of deceased Germans, killed in action.

After a momentary silence by the observant colonel, paying respect for the loss of life—even though these casualties were of the enemy—Durnford-Slater was stunned to then notice one of the wounded men in the snow was still alive ...

The German soldier was young, perhaps even still a teen.

Pale faced, he had been wounded during the raid, sporting gunshots to the abdomen in a stitch to his left collarbone. Perhaps mistakenly assuming he was deceased on the initial pass, or simply not caring enough to check if he had just succumbed to his wounds, the Brits had carted his corpse along with a few others to the pile of dead bodies. The soldier was still alive—however unfortunate it was to wake up from an unconscious state only to realize that you were in fact, still dying—what's worse, you're positioned amongst the dead ahead of schedule.

Durnford-Slater's gaze anchored on the sight of the wounded man, snagged and unable to break his view free. The two made direct eye contact. In fact, the young soldier seemed to have been already fixated on Durnford-Slater in the crowd of passing soldiers before he had even realized him.

Propped awkwardly in the snow, extremely close to death, the soldier raised his hand and weakly waved Durnford-Slater over. He held out his frail paw, seemingly conceding to his death and passing.

Hesitant, Durnford-Slater broke from his formation amongst his withdrawing men. His friend, Charley Head, clued onto and noticed his strange victory lap departure upon their return to the FOB, and cautiously watched at a distance as his superior sympathetically acknowledged the fading soldier.

Head's view angled as he tilted at the neck, humbly observing his colonel's compassion.

In place of a common language, the dying soldier offered his hand to shake. It was utterly surreal.

Durnford-Slater cared not for judgement. For conviction.

He respectively knelt in the soot before the soldier; a fallen belligerent—a fellow human, like him, capable of kindness, of love, and even of death—and he took his hand with nothing less than the upmost regard. He shook it; held it, and the man passed.

The sight was enough to bring a tear to an eye.

It was in that gesture that Durnford-Slater felt the boy die ...

After such turmoil, felt his life finally fade away ...

After a respectful moment, he tenderly placed the young man's limp hand gently across his chest, even adjusting his posture slightly to be more comfortable in his eternal slumber.

Head wordlessly watched him. Absorbed this.

Emitting an exhale, Durnford-Slater stood tall, watching down at the deceased foe, surprisingly suffering yet another loss that was in many ways grander than any he had endured today of his fellow Englishmen.

*This image would stay with Durnford-Slater for the rest of his life.*

Strangely reluctant, he moved on.

*"... A number of fish oil and canning factories were then blown up together with the ammunition dumps. Lumps of burning debris are flung clear over into the town. Exploding small arms ammunition adding to the turmoil as the now successful raid reaches its climax ..."*

Nearby the de-escalation of the raid, from Pathé was the popular press reporter William 'Miracle Man' Mericle, who had somehow survived tagging along with Commando. Whatever footage the well-respected connoisseur columnist and his cameraman recorded would be sent home and edited, and later broadcast across the country.

The captured footage would be instilled in the archives of history forevermore.

He finished what may very well be his outro:

*"... As we came, so we departed. With perfect timing, the assault landing crafts are ready and waiting to re-embark the commandos. It's been a hard day's work, but Vågsøy and Måløy will no longer be of any use to the Germans. Gone are its factories, radio stations, and entire German and Quisling population, thanks to the army, the navy and the air force ..."*

Mericle's broadcaster voice changed back to normal, addressing his assistant. "Did you get all that?"

While the man recording with the microphone and headphones nodded, Mericle made eye contact with the other reporter present during Operation Archery—a man he now vastly respected:

*Felix Hardy.*

Hardy observed Mericle work for a moment longer before he noticed him take the time to gesture a respectful bow of his head—something that would have been unheard of six hours ago.

Respect reciprocated; Hardy signalled with a nod of his own.

Another Higgins pulled into the stony shoreline at the established FOB.

Lieutenant Clement and the men of Group 1 dismounted the landing craft, having at last returned from their venture to take the enemy barracks at the small village of Holvik, located west of South Vågsøy and Måløy Island. They had extended their mission to flank the Alpine

Huntsmen snipers along the northerly ridgeline, saving many lives from the turkey shoot that had become South Vågsøy during the raid.

Clement sought out Jack Churchill through the crowded coastal rendezvous of victorious comportment and organized departures from the island.

Up the slope behind the FOB, Churchill had entered a small shed beside a burned-down cottage. He was solo, and Clement found his mischievous venture somewhat curious, and felt the need to investigate.

He upped the rocky incline with scraping trudges. "Major?"

Unveiling his intriguing find, Churchill rotated from the shadow recess of the shack, blowing the dust off a bottle of red wine to better read the label. "Captain. Look at this stash ... this building must have been an officer's hut from the coast defence before they burned it to the ground. Old mate was holding out on us."

"Oh?" Clement confessed genuine interest, leaning on his knee and squinting to see in the darkness of the compacted shed. He thusly expected to see Churchill more interested in the prospect of there being significant intelligence in the findings ... but no, just alcohol.

"Yes, look," Churchill held out the bottle. "*Moselle*."

Clement pouted. Bobbed his head.

Chasing a lust for early celebration, Churchill raised the bottle.

"Must say, I'm parched," he uncorked the bottle. "Care for a nip?"

Right as Churchill posed the question, it soon became apparent as to why the area up the slope was especially vacant ...

*It had been cleared for detonation.*

The demo troopers from No.6 Commando had secured and evacuated the area prior to setting charges. An extremely close detonation erased another enemy munition depot nearby, causing the wooden wall of the shed beside Churchill's position to unexpectedly burst and collapse in a tidal wave of dust. It very nearly killed him.

A cloud coughed outwards, engulfing the two commando officers as planks of wood tumbled past their position, hitting them with debris.

"*Jack!*" Clement bellowed, covering his head and almost collapsing in the rocks of the slope. A few men nearby attended with caution deep-set upon their brows. The last thing anybody needed after this operation was an accidental casualty.

Hacking and spluttering, and fast quashing the fear of his demise, Jack Churchill emerged from the settling dust in front of the concerned stares of the cowering lieutenant and various other commandos from the shore who took a few concerned steps in approach.

The Moselle bottle had shattered in his hand, and a piece of the wine bottle had gashed Jack's forehead above his right eyebrow, causing him to hold a squint. He muttered displeasingly. "Ouch."

Funnily, it was just about the worst injury he had received today.

Calmly and nonchalant, Churchill strode briskly away from the cloud following the explosion as the coastal breeze shooed it away, casually padding the injury to his forehead with his fingertips in an attempt to gauge the severity.

As it started to bleed, he realized the extent.

Corry came running through the upstanding throng of troopers, seeing to the injured Commando. He shoved past the puckered brow of Hardy. The inquisitive journalist loomed with his fedora tilted on his sweaty brow. Once he knew it concerned Mad Jack, he was no longer as apprehensive—he knew he was unkillable.

"Major Churchill!" Corry called with anxiety, jogging to assist in Churchill's strides down the hill and into the formed crowd. He administered a dress, holding the wound. "You're a bit late to get bloody wounded now!"

"Sorry, Sorry."

"What did you go and do, then, eh?"

"I haven't the foggiest," Churchill barked over his shoulder, though not out of trepidation or annoyance. He had gotten injured by this mishap, but the man still saw a domineering factor of humour in the actuality of the event. "Where was the warning, lads?!"

"*Sorry, sir!*" a nearby No.6 trooper came running, panicked and scared that he may have just blown up a senior officer.

After a moment, Churchill gawked at Sorry as he saw to his head wound, cleaning it and taking a look. "Sorry, this chap is talking to you."

The demo troop was confused at the level of sincerity he required to communicate his apology to Mad Jack. Seemingly not acknowledging his apology properly, he considered for a moment that perhaps the major was concussed? "No, sir. I meant *you*. I'm sorry."

"Oh!" Jack bobbed. "Thought you were talking to him."

Concentrating on trying to apply pressure to Churchill's head whilst he sought a bandage from his bag, Corry beamed.

The anxious trooper explained further. "We cleared the zone! We've been detonating dumps all around here ..."

Shrugging it off, Churchill filled the soldier in. "Pay it no never mind, trooper. I don't die when people purposely try to blow me up. A mishap such as this shan't result in my squander."

Sorry Corry declared to his patient. "Hold still."

"Sorry," Churchill obliged while the doc forced Churchill to sit and removed his beret to better wrap his head. The wound was clean, but the gash was deep. It needed a firm wrap. "Is it bad, Sorry?"

"You'll live." Corry offered him a glance of sincerity. "You're supposed to get injured *during* the fight, Major. Not after."

"Thanks, Sorry."

Standing nearby, Hardy scrunched his face, unaware of Sam Corry's nickname. "Why does everyone keep apologizing."

"What's going on here?" Colonel Durnford-Slater finally appeared, and the crowd of concerned Commando made a hole.

Churchill allowed for himself to explain. "Demo's blast thoughtlessly blew down a wall I happened to be leaning against, is all ..."

Feeling bad, the trooper further insisted. "*I'm so, so sorry, Major!*"

"It's fine-o-fine, lad," Jack implored, letting Corry attempt to stop the severe bleeding from his forehead.

The demo troop became whisked away, shaking his head whilst departing. The man had almost blown up the renowned Mad Jack Churchill.

With nothing left to see, the crowd slowly dispersed from around them, leaving just Churchill, Corry, Durnford-Slater, and Clement.

Jack gleamed beneath Sorry's working hands as he fixed the wound with a bandage. His tone was one of profound ponder, and perceived as being in reference to the aftermath of the raid and all they had left to ruin along Vågsøy Island. Afterall, the sight was one to behold.

"What a loss ..."

"Well," Durnford-Slater reacted, taking a quick glimpse at some of the roasting wreckage in the background. It was indeed a harrowing sight to see. "Such is war, right?"

Jack Churchill blinked, momentarily confused.

*No. He didn't mean the destruction ...*

*He meant something else ...*

"No. I meant the *Moselle* ..." he finally elaborated, homing his focus on the sight of the recently destroyed shed housing a wine cellar.

Durnford-Slater's expression loosened, and his nostrils huffed at Churchill. Unsure if it was sarcasm—it probably wasn't, considering it was Jack Churchill—he shook his head with an underlining grin. "What a loss, indeed."

'By the end of the Måløy Raid, the enemy resistance may not have been completely overcome in the street fighting, however all the major demolition jobs were accomplished by Commando. This included the power station, the wireless antenna, the coastal defences, the numerous factories and the lighthouse. One-hundred-and-fifty Germans were killed, ninety-eight soldiers from the Wehrmacht 181st Infantry Division were captured as POWs, including a handful of Quislings. On the waterfront of the fjord, the Royal Navy destroyers sank a total of nine boats, totalling in over fifteen-thousand tons of enemy-controlled shipping. They bravely shot down four Heinkel bombers of the Luftwaffe, saving the skies. Both Herdia and Stavanger airports were bombed by the RAF, limiting their response. Seventy-one Norwegians took passage back to England, seeking safe haven, whilst the remainder of the Vågsøy population chose to stay and rebuild in their newfound sovereignty.'

'After the Commando Troops present on the island composed and regrouped, aligning various rendezvous and conducting much of the transfers of non-essentials, wounded, and prisoners back to the warships, Colonel Durnford-Slater ordered the withdrawal of Commando's entirety from South Vågsøy at 01:45, declaring the raid a success. An hour later and they were gone from the Vestland county municipality, leaving their mark on the world war and, most importantly, giving Hitler a black eye.'

'There were many instances of limitless gallantry on both sides in the taking and defending of entrenched positions of both Måløy and Vågsøy Islands. Of the total seventy army casualties, twenty-two were deemed KIA, and of the eight Navy casualties, two were pronounced dead. Additionally, two RAF Beaufighters and one Blenheim were lost in the aerial fighting.'

'This was the first time all three services (air, land, and sea) were combined in support of an amphibious incursion against a fortified coast defended by the enemy. It was needless to say that much was learned by both sides.

'Germany soon after reinforced their Norwegian Atlantic line with the supplementary deployment of over thirty-thousand additional troops. Back in their motherland, conceivably, Hitler now had concerns that Norway may be 'the zone of destiny in this war' ...'


'... then again,
maybe he just didn't know Jack.'

# EPILOGUE
## The Cage

*1942, January*
*The London Cage*
*Kensington, London*

It was dark the night they transferred the raid prisoners.

The navy warships of the 17th Destroyer Flotilla banked at Scapa Flow, just off the coast of Scotland. From there, after a week at sea, the POWs were loaded into convoys of transport trucks on the mainland, where they began their due processing ahead of implantation in various concentration camps located inland.

They had just spent almost a week as captives traversing the choppy Norwegian Seas. Of the ninety-eight German prisoners taken during Commando's triumphant raid on Vågsøy and Måløy, eighteen of them were considered 'high priority' from their preliminary debriefs and were conveyed to *London* for interrogation by the *Prisoner of War Interrogation Section (PWIS)* of the Intelligence Corps; a branch of *MI19.*

Once more comprehensively cleared and thoroughly stripped of any intelligence they may consciously—and subconsciously—withhold from England, the prisoners would then be transferred to one of two established POW camps; either *Camp No.1* in *Grizedale Hall, Cumbria* or *Camp No. 2* at *Glen Mill, Oldham, Lancashire*, where they could wait out the remainder of the war in a kind of tranquil harmony. So to speak.

That fateful night of process, the eighteen men—all officers from the 181st Infantry Division, Wehrmacht—were loaded onto a separate truck and driven a different southerly route, careering them straight into the lion's den of central London. The trip from Scotland to England had taken all night, seeing them dismount the transporter at the break of dawn the following morning.

Other than general instructions given to them by the transport guards such as *stand, dismount,* and *fall in line*, one of the only other major things denoted to the group was by an orderly who welcomed them at the premises.

He stated clearly: "Welcome to the *Cage*, gentlemen."

Sleepless days followed the equally sleepless nights, off the back of a mostly restless week floating across the ocean, the German prisoners were zombified to say the least. Though, perhaps this facilitated the process; helped disarm them.

Needless to say, by the time the prisoners were processed and in line for their official debriefs and interrogations, they were almost completely mentally depleted. This was just a welcome byproduct of the progress of POW transition, it was conceivably a happy accident, as it meant half their jobs neutralizing the prisoner's psyches was already done for them by the time they took a seat across the table.

The white light globe in the room dangled from its power lead like a clock pendulum in need of winding. Due to the arresting central light source, the surroundings of the square concrete room seemed as dark and cold as it felt. Even the floor was tiled in ceramic, like a washroom, complete with drainage and in severe need of re-grouting; feasibly some sort of repurposed shower block turned into an interrogation office.

A bald, short of sight Englishman in a white shirt and black tie seated across the table questioned after the next prisoner in the line was permitted access to the room. Adjusting his spectacles, the orderly for the PWIS was keen to check this man's name off the list in his hands and get this whole process started. It was already going to be a long day.

"Name and rank, prisoner ...?"

The German POW had seen better days.

Still dressed in his tattered grey uniform, the weary prisoner was complete with sweat stains beneath the arms and around the frayed neckline, with dry blood patches in his messy hairline and underneath his grotesquely bashed-in nose—the injury sustained during the raid had been deemed priority, and aided to by medical assistance. It had been broken, and thusly reset, now bandaged. Issued a long time before the war in Vågsøy, this experienced soldier had sustained a large number of duelling scars across his jaw and cheeks—the fresh knicks were just extra mileage.

Restrained with handcuffs and escorted via armed guard, this prisoner's arse had barely found the chair before the interrogator rattled off something else to the disorientated foreigner.

"Hellooo?" the interrogator waved, gaining his dazed attention. He prompted again, eyeing the list and ready to scan for correspondence. "Name and rank, please?"

After another pause, the POW finally looked up.

"English?"

Still nothing.

The man huffed. "Send in the translator again."

"Coming," a second English voice responded from a connecting industrious-sounding room, where the door was aslant. There stood an armed guard, overseeing the entire discourse. In a pin-striped vest suit, another operator entered the room. He brought a cup of steaming tea on a saucer and a revitalized attitude.

"*Name und Rang, Soldat,*" he questioned in perfect Deutsche as he took the second seat across the table. The wooden door became pushed closed after he passed through by someone on the other side. This office seemed to be quite the busy beehive of due process.

Following the question, there was still no response by the POW.

The initial bald man in the shirt slouched, removing his wire frame glasses and chewing the end of the temple tip whilst he stared the occupant of the chair down. This seemed as though it was going to go the hard way.

In the silence, the clock on the high wall above a labelled map of the world ticked loudly. It was the first time this captive had seen a clock in over a week, and it suggested that it was 9:30 in, what he could only presume, was the morning. However, he was so disoriented, it could have very well been night. He hadn't slept in days following a concussion that likely cost him braincells.

The armed soldier standing directly behind the prisoner cleared his throat. It became apparent that maybe this sort of type rather enjoyed the mute noncompliance from foreign prisoners ... it perhaps gave them an excuse to mishandle the livestock—hence the easily rinseable surfaces ceramic room.

*The blood couldn't stain.*

This German soldier seemed no more or less reluctant to cooperate than what the PWIS operatives were used to. They had played these games numerous times before and were quite adept at gaining the information from the captives.

*And if they couldn't, then into the hole they'd go ...*

Solitary confinement was located in the basement, and it was a lot easier to deal with the reluctancy of prisoners by throwing them in there for twenty-four hours without food, water, a toilet, or any source of light. It was quite often messy, but it effortlessly yielded results.

"Listen, mate," the bald man with the glasses leant forward, changing the language back to English. He was certain that language wasn't the reasoning behind this delay in questioning, especially considering that ninety percent of German officers knew English. Rather, they had seen this type of stubborn stonewalling countless times before. He raised his brows as he spoke. "Last chance. Speak now, or forever protect your junk from the hungry rats down in the hole ..."

He slumped back in his creaky chair and, finally, the shaggy haired and worse for wear German prisoner made proper eye contact with the men for the first time.

It seemed to be that he would only speak on his own terms, as if he carried some kind of audacity.

The bald man clicked his fingers. "Hello? You with us or what? What rank were you within the 181st Infantry Division? What were your standing orders prior to December 27?"

A few seconds of further noncompliance prevailed.

"Did you personally know General Woytasch?" the other man asked, taking an alternate route with the questioning. "The general was not present on Vågsøy Island. Do you know where he is now?"

On the surface, both questions seemed to be amiss with the prisoner.

His eye even twitched at the mention of Lieutenant-General Kurt Woytasch, however, who was the tarnished Nazi officer in command of the one-hundred-and-fifty-some German infantrymen occupying South Vågsøy.

The prisoner finally spoke, cracking his stiff neck.

"I am not a part ov Woytasch's Wehrmacht ..."

*He spoke English.*

The two PWIS operatives exchanged a look and then readjusted their seating. Baldy collected the list, searching the names until at the end he found an exception amongst the prisoners.

The interrogator murmured like a simpleton. "Ah, yes, here we go."

With unexcited eyes, the prisoner watched as the two men identified who he was on paper, marrying the source to the man they had in the room.

"Well, this must be you. You're the only surviving officer not from the 181st Infantry Division."

"*Schutzstaffel,* then, huh?" the translator articulated, reaffirming that they now appreciated how exceptional this captive was. "No wonder you got a cordial invitation to sit with us in London."

Sour in a deadlock mindset, still disinterested in cooperating with his captors, the prisoner's eyes caught sight of a wet drain in the centre of the floor. There was a drop of blood on a dry patch of tile, and it resonated quite an unsettling pretence to what might happen in his basement rooms when those who favoured the Geneva Convention weren't watching.

When the prisoner went to shift his posture in the seat to face forwards, he noticed for the first time that the guard who had been escorting him thus far had scabbed over knuckles. He was either a brawler outside of his profession as a prison guard, or he rather enjoyed cleaning these tiles with a hose after he turned them a tinge of carmine-red with a combatant's blood.

The prisoner adjusted his view central.

His movements echoed in the silence.

It became apparent that he may need to play the ace he had hidden up his sleeve a lot faster than he had anticipated. Getting to the place of bargaining where he wanted to be, he may catch more flies with *honey* than *vinegar.*

He would employ the *enemy of my enemy* tactic here.

Unlike his favourite enemy, he was no archer, but this was the only good arrow left in his quiver, and he had only one good shot to take with it.

The prisoner identified himself. "Meine Herren. My name is Friedrich Feind. I am a Hauptsturmführer within the Gebirgsjäger."

Exchanging a gleam between both Englishmen as he lurched forwards and willingly into the light above the table, Feind struck a diplomatic pose and interlocked his fingers on the desktop.

"I have important and zenzitive intelligence to zhare with your nation."

The men swapped a surprising stare, remaining silent.

It wasn't every day POWs gave up the intelligence so freely.

"Excellent," one of them replied, enthralled. "Care to elaborate?"

"Not vith you, no."

The two men were taken aback. Offended, even.

"Eh ..." one of them grumbled while the other one gasped a laugh. He attempted shrugging free the discomfort. "Pretty please? Cherry on top?"

Feind held his crooked smile as he delivered a taste of his intelligence. He whet their appetites before asserting himself the type of bargaining power that may very well see his days of imprisonment much more comfortable than the majority.

"Vhat my knowledge containz incriminatez one of Hiz Majezty's finezt war heroez in conzpiring with a key member of Nazi Germany ... a highly decorated zerviceman, whom you probably all know by name ... "

Through their speechlessness and gaping mouths, Feind could tell just how much these two were aware that this intelligence was possibly well above their paygrades if it were true.

*And it was.*

Feind added, dismissing their awkward pause on the opposite end of the table. "... you can call for your zuperior now ..."

He withheld his sinister smile as he watched them squirm.

And finally, he lounged back, nice and smug.

He blinked an eye. "Go ahead. I'll vait here."

The unstoppable warpath of the unkillable **Jack Churchill**

will continue in ...

## *King, Queen, Jack, War*

*About the Author.*

*Benjamin Blackie was born in Camden, New South Wales in 1987. Growing up, he often found more comfort outside of everyday life in watching shows and movies, reading books and graphic novels, playing games, and generally exploring the vast variety of creations and art forms made by others, as well as developing and practicing his own imagination. Still does.*

*He currently resides in Sydney with his wife and daughter, and remains close with friends and family who enrich his life with love, inspiration, and encouragement every day.*

### *Acknowledgements and thanks.*

*Joe and Laura – my entrusted proofreaders. Once more, your respective feedbacks were instrumental in the creation of this production. Words cannot articulate how appreciative I am of your time and efforts donated to me, assisting in accomplishing my work. Much love to you both.*

*Combinedops.com (Mr. Slee), and those within both Tracesofwar.com and The Commando Veterans Archive community. Your collective reservoirs of knowledge on the relative topics are incomparable. What these people do to contribute to the permanency and memory of the history era is remarkable. Thanks for keeping the history of those gone and their sacrifices alive. I will endeavour to donate to the cause from the proceeds of my related work. I thank you all for the availability of your extensive resources. I appreciate all that I found.*

*Again, I'd like to thank all those who I bored to death over the years talking about my seemingly endless endeavour about Mad Jack Churchill. I hope you all enjoyed.*

www.ingramcontent.com/pod-product-compliance
Lightning Source LLC
Chambersburg PA
CBHW020822030726
47496CB00001B/45